THE DEEPEST GREEN

BOOK TWO OF THE PATH

DAVID BOWLES

CASTLE BRIDGE MEDIA
DENVER, COLORADO, USA

THE DEEPEST GREEN
© 2021 David Bowles
All rights reserved.

ISBN: 978-1-7364726-5-1

CASTLE BRIDGE MEDIA
Denver, Colorado, USA
castlebridgemedia.com

Cover Illustration by Estudio Tlalli

To my three children, without whom I would have given up long ago.

I love you more than life itself.

ACKNOWLEDGEMENTS

I would like once again to express my eternal thanks to the many "beta readers" who read different drafts of this novel over the years, especially Ted Han, Billie Barnett and Jeniffer Johnson.

I am also indebted to the great poet and Esperantist, Edward de Kock, for taking the time to tutor me in Esperanto.

To the many LDS who very candidly discussed their beliefs with me— you are a credit to your faith, and you taught me to respect your community of saints as I might not have otherwise done.

Finally, I owe gratitude to Harold Bloom for first showing me that it's perfectly fine to be anxious about the influence of other writers on me, so long as that tension results in a better work. As a result, the obvious impact of multiple authors on the text of Green is acknowledged with a wink and a nod.

PROLOGUE

WHAT BECOMES OF A LOVE STORY when the lovers are separated by grave misunderstanding or vast distance or apparent death, beyond all reasonable hope of reunion? Does it founder in tragedy? Or does it evolve into something more complex, a tale richer than the simple happy ending we are longing to see?

By human reckoning, it is now April of the year 2714.

Brando D'Angelo di Makomo has spent the past fifteen years on the planet Terego, hiding in plain sight as Nando Miranda, raising the clones of his wife and daughter.

Teri and Miwa, he named them, remembering the famous twins from Jitsu's colonial past, twins who survived a fierce jagen, who saved their mother from certain doom.

Brando has remarried, believing the girls need another parent in their lives.

He has a son with his second wife.

He attends church, active as an elder in his ward.

He is respected and—at some subtle level people do not recognize—feared.

But Nando Miranda is just Brando's painstakingly designed and crafted mask. He thinks of this persona like the buildings Tenshi Koroma once constructed on Jitsu, dazzling reflections of a realigned self in the physical world.

It is not a lie to Brando. The love he feels for the people he deceives is not artifice.

This is his Way along the Path for now.

In a vision, his spark told him to prepare the ones he brought back.

Tenshi swore she would return.

So he has bided his time, training his daughters without their quite understanding why. He knows something is coming. They will all of them be tested.

In secret, he has continued his meditation. He catches glimpses of his incipient soul, growing slow in the depths of his being, sustained by the divine spark that makes him human.

One day he will see it, whole and eternal. In this he has faith. The surety keeps him going when others would give up hope.

If Tenshi cannot return to him despite her promise, then he must be ready to join her when his death comes at last. He must reach quantum enlightenment and be translated.

The work goes easy, if slow. Terego is peaceful. Quiet. Uncomplicated.

It was, at least.

In a distant lab, a technician is analyzing DNA samples. Nando Miranda. His two daughters. The initial scan seems fine, but something odd about certain sequences sends up a red flag in the technician's mind.

Deeper analysis reveals disturbing truths.

These truths will soon be reported to Captain Antonio D'Angelo di Spinelli.

Brando's half-brother, whose heart has been roiling with hate for his older sibling for seventeen years, ever since he learned of Brando's existence at the height of the crisis on Jitsu.

Throughout the Consortium, Brando is a wanted man.

Captain D'Angelo will be sent to Terego to bring him to justice.

It will not be an easy task.

What no one knows is that—deep in the thousands and thousands of square kilometers of dense forest on Terego—a non-human race has gone undetected by human eyes for more than fifty years.

Brando's arrival on the planet set in motion a series of events that will make the true natives of Terego emerge from the thick shadows of their canopied homes, right into the lives of two teenage girls, distraught after discovering the truth of their identity.

The encounter will send shockwaves through human space.

And it will lead Teri Miranda—the clone of Tenshi Koroma—to an ancient secret.

To us. Lingering long after death.
Buried in the soil of Terego, our power quiescent.
Awaiting hands that can wield us again.

If they be unworthy, we will destroy ourselves, let this galaxy remain a prison.
If they be just and strong, we will have a chance once more.

To protect the defenseless.
To undo an unspeakable tragedy.
To bend the course of history.

Ah, but do not be afraid, dear friends.

Teri's hands are the right ones.

PART I:

THE SWERVE

"Momento ŝanĝas ĉion."

"A moment changes everything."

—William Auld, *La infana raso (The Infant Species)*

CHAPTER 1

THE WARRIORS CAME LOPING INTO THE VILLAGE AS IF INTO BATTLE, heads low, torsos bent at the waist, tails out behind them to balance the running stance. Shalurazhox, their leader, was the first to see the devastation, and she pulled up short, slamming her huge spear into the ground to help break her speed. The bodies of her people were everywhere, disemboweled by the enemy and left sacrilegiously on the ground, their blood feeding the blind insects that crawled and burrowed in the newly thawed dirt.

Forgetting all protocol and without a word of instruction to her warriors, Shalurazhox bolted up into the canopy, rushing from tree to tree, from compound to compound, from dwelling to dwelling.

Swinging to the ground, she leapt over the slaughtered highborn, drone laborers and male builders. Where were the infants? Where were the caretakers?

Where was her child?

Not needing a signal from their leader, the members of her troop spread throughout the kilometer-square sprawl of the village, tallying the dead and searching for survivors. A gargled trill from Guthonar'ut drew Shalura's attention to the ditches, some fifty yards from the village, where its inhabitants relieved themselves of their bodily wastes. With her claws retracted and her gait slowed to a resigned, despairing amble, Shalurazhox made her way to the warrior's side. She could smell the mingled odors of blood and feces rising like a curse from the pits. Her tongue tasted the air reflexively, and her cheeks drew in with apprehension as the white-striped fur above her gray eyes stood on end.

Reaching the edge of the first ditch, she nearly recoiled in horror. Only years of training and the psychological strength innate to all drones keeping her from running madly away. There lay scores of caretaker males in jumbled piles, their beautiful bulging cheeks ripped open, the babies inside pulled out and clawed to death. Infants ranging from one to five years of age slumped dead against their *súlkÿqá*, their gestators, soft downy fur matted with blood and excrement.

Ears flattened against her head, Shalurazhox scanned the carnage as her breathing grew more labored and her blood pounded in her veins. Then she saw them: Xiggèr'enth, the handsome roundness of his face misshapen by death blows, and the little one, Thõdhulazhox, her short muzzle in the crook of the male's arm, her breathing stilled for all eternity, Shalura's chances at adding to and strengthening the tribe come to naught like the tribe itself.

Shalurazhox could bear the pain no longer. Leaning back on her powerful tail, she arched her face toward the dark green canopy above, silvery eyes glistening in the dim noonday light that filtered through the dense foliage. She opened her jaws and squeezed shut her eyes and released an ululating moan full of dark harmonics and misery. Her warriors immediately stopped what they were doing at the moment and joined her mourning cry; the leaves of the mighty trees about them shook with the power of their twenty-four voices joined in sorrow.

When the cry had faded to an echo, Shalura spun without another look at her dead daughter and headed toward the *ilodheingh*, the clearing at the center of the village where the Council met and where tribal activities were carried out. Tentisùxa, her point and tracker and so much more, joined her.

"We found another of the warrior troops, decimated completely, but there's no sign of the other two," the older warrior told her leader.

"Those led by Hílxo!us and Rroggúl'it?"

"Precisely. They were on short-range patrol... we should've seen them on our approach. You don't imagine that they could have joined the Sháinkhÿngigg... that they allowed or participated in this genocide?"

"Their troop leaders were both leaning toward the Greenseer's heresies: it's not impossible, but I hope for their sakes that they didn't. I plan on ripping the entrails from everyone responsible for this and letting her dark blood run out onto the dirt. It would be terrible to have to do that to my tribe-kin, but I will do what I must."

At that moment, several other warriors joined them. Chakhìkhy̆rh, a broad-shouldered, tawny drone spoke first. "Shalura, among the dead we do not find the bodies of certain highborn and males. Children are also missing."

"Are these highborn the ones the missing warriors are bonded to?" Shalura asked, an uneasiness bristling her fur and sucking at her cheeks.

Chakhìkhy̆rh nodded. "And the males are the drones' bond-sharers."

Shalura's head jerked up and down as she assimilated the strange information. In a typical raid, males would be stolen and bonded to the capturing drone's highborn in order to strengthen the family. Even in full-scale wars (and the Ihéinghy̆ngigg, Shalura's people, were presently at war with no one), the enemy was slaughtered wholesale, indiscriminately. No one captured highborn. There was no sense in it: they would dilute the tribal identity.

She could only speculate that the Sháinkhy̆ngigg, with whom her people had once waged many wars generations ago, were somehow behind this bizarre act. That tribe had been actively trying to spread the heretical notions of a mysterious being called the Greenseer. Perhaps that demon's teachings were at the root of the slaughter and abductions.

Tentisùxa saw her indecision and addressed it. "Your choice must be made soon, my *urdizih*, because we've found the trail of those who did this evil, and it's recent enough to follow."

Shalura twitched her eye in agreement. With a growled command, she gathered the other warriors of her troop around her and spoke to them in solemn tones.

"We have suffered an unspeakable loss today. Our loved ones and friends lie about us dead. We have no tribe, no kin, no home. We are *elzöqhihéingh*, lost forest children adrift on the green sea of fate, and our only purpose now is vengeance. Second and third groups, I want you to remain behind and take our dead up near the bright overarching green where they belong. The remaining eighteen of us will give chase to the flat-jowled murderers. If our other troops arrive with their bonded males and drones, judge their faithfulness and send them after us if they are trustworthy in your minds. It is possible they escaped to hide."

As she said this, she knew it was impossible. No warrior of her tribe would ever hide in the deep, silvery-shadowed forest with her bond-sharers and highborn, especially not if doing so required leaving the rest of the tribe to be slaughtered. But she couldn't stand the alternative that loomed shapeless in her mind, a betrayal greater than any ever recorded by the tales of her people.

A smallish gray-furred warrior named Eghonganë bared her teeth in worry. "But the trail leads away west and is nearly a day old. They will no doubt turn south in another day near the thick-leaved forest's edge, and after an additional day's travel they will enter their hill-ringed lands, where we will be unable to exact payment from them."

Shalura closed her left eye slowly in measured acknowledgement of the young warrior's valid point. Without warning, a shaft of bright sunlight slipped through the tens of meters of foliage above them and shone on the ground at the center of the clearing, creating dancing patterns of clinquant green and gold. Understanding dawned on Shalura.

"We will go south and cross the great frozen lake and arrive before them to the edge of their lands."

There was dumbfounded silence. Cross the lake?

"But that would take us out of the living forest. Into the clear. Under the bright green and the Unblinking Eye of God!"

It was Dhölggexitra who spoke, and she was right. The baleful Eye would be upon them. But their cause was just, and Shalura knew that good would come of taking the risk.

"We will go out onto the plain under the Unblinking Eye until we come to and cross the great frozen lake. We will not stop. We will reach the living forest's edge below the bend before they do, and we will face them there. God favors those who seek bloody revenge for the death of innocents. Her Eye will watch us, not condemn us. We will go. Now."

Not another word was spoken. The warriors gathered up their spears and arbalests; they bent low, extended their tails, and when Shalura gave the word, they ran.

CHAPTER 2

DURING THE SHORT BREAK BEFORE HER FREE STUDY PERIOD,
Teri Miranda placed her palm on her locker. Once it hissed open, she grabbed
her graph paper sketchbook and a pouch of pencils. Then she closed the
locker and almost jumped in surprise.

Carmen Allende was standing beside her, chestnut hair cascading over
her blue uniform jacket in a way that made Teri's breath catch in her throat.

"We need to talk," the older girl said, grabbing Teri's wrist with firm
fingers and pulling her down the hall.

Sighing, Teri thought about yanking her arm away. Easy enough,
given all the martial arts training her father had forced on her. But she was
curious. And she had missed Carmen. Her hazel eyes. Her flawless skin.
Her hyacinth scent.

In a matter of minutes, the two teens were ensconced in a hidden niche of the school gardens that few adults frequented. Carmen pushed Teri onto a cold stone bench and sat beside her, fingers sliding from Teri's wrist to her hand.

"This is unexpected," Teri said, looking down at the contrast of her dark brown fingers in Carmen's paler palm. "I thought you weren't talking to me anymore."

"Is it true? It's not, right?"

Teri raised a single eyebrow, but otherwise remained impassive. Her stepmother had once asked her why she wore her hair in overly tight cornrows. Now Teri consciously understood: the severity of the look and the slight needle-pricking sensation kept her from smiling, allowed her to look coolly at the people she needed to influence or shape.

"Have I told you," she asked, side-stepping the question, preparing to disarm the girl she loved, "why I started hanging out with the five of you?"

Carmen cleared her throat. "No, but it's obvious you had a falling out with your dad."

"Yes. He did something pretty horrible to me. Not *that,* Carmenjo," Teri clarified, using the affectionate suffix, "but it was still a violation. I could hardly bear to be around him for a while, which meant spending less time at church, with the friends I used to cherish, the family that defined me. My sister and I started fighting all the time. My life was falling apart. Then Ronaldo and Josuo arrived at our stake for their twenty-month stint."

On a world where every soul was a Saint, missionaries were superfluous, but another pair of hands was always welcome, so traditional missions had morphed into a sort of civil service that all young men and women performed when they reached thirteen and fourteen jaroj or Teregan years, roughly eighteen and twenty in Consortium reckoning.

Carmen gave a weak laugh. "They were such hicks. Country boys from small towns on Kanaano, half a world away. Overwhelmed by the size and splendor of Diadono."

"But you and Anyi fell for them right away," Teri said in mocking singsong. "So did Elisha. Instant bromance."

Carmen let go of her hand and smirked. "And so did you. I guess since you're younger, you fell for them harder."

Rolling her eyes, Teri reached out and touched Carmen's cheek.

"You're so damn clueless. I didn't start hanging with you older weirdoes because of those two lanky boys. I had a crush on *you* long before that."

Carmen's face flushed bright red, but she didn't pull away.

"I used to sneak peeks at you during church services. This soft hair and perfect skin, your fashionable dresses and haughty posture. I wasn't even that jealous when the new elders caught your eye. At least you didn't treat anyone from our stake as worthy enough. Twenty months, and they'd be gone. In the meantime, maybe I could get close to you."

"Sneaky, scheming brat. That's also how you became the youngest student council president ever, isn't it? Always moving your chess pieces on the board."

Teri pulled her hand away slowly, letting her fingers brush against the corner of Carmen's mouth.

"I've told you before, querida Carmen," Teri said, switching from Esperanto to Spanish, Carmen's family tongue, one of several languages her own father had taught her, "it's my gift. I can see the structure of people and things, reshape it to a better design."

Carmen scoffed. "Or one that's more convenient for you. So that's why you 'stumbled' across us at the still in the forest that Saturday. You planned it."

"Yeah. Followed you. Was a little shocked to see you sitting in that clearing while Josuo brandished a bottle full of some weird brown liquid. What did he call it? *The forbidden fruit, source of the knowledge of good and evil.* Swore he wouldn't pressure you three high school juniors because the experience was for initiates only."

"Deep communion with God," Carmen muttered. "He was so full of shit."

"You seemed to buy into it. Got pretty drunk."

Carmen snorted. "If you knew it was nonsense, why'd you burst in on us and take the bottle from Josuo? You really chugged that moonshine down."

The liquid had burned her throat, spreading its warmth through her belly and slowly out into her limbs as the tipsy young adults had watched in dumbstruck wonder and more than a little fear at being discovered. Teri had exploded into a fit of coughing at the powerful hooch before grimly taking another swig.

"It was the only way you'd let me stay. You three had to be guilty of getting a freshman—a *minor*—drunk. But then Josuo demanded to know my name, and I was shocked to hear it come from your pretty lips."

Carmen averted her eyes, swallowing heavily.

Teri sighed. No matter what other supposed perversions the older girl had indulged in, she still couldn't face the truth of her own identity, her longstanding feelings for Teri.

"Uh, I knew who you were. So did Anyi. We live in the same city, same stake. Go to the same church, same school. I would've explained that, but then Josuo made his joke, using your name like a verb. Vi nin teris. You Teri'd us. Earthed us."

Drunk as they had been, the five had howled with laughter for a good ten minutes at the unfunny play on words, tears streaming from their eyes.

I made us a single group, Teri reflected with pride. *They thought they were in charge, but the minute I found them in that clearing, I had them in the palm of my hand. A freshman against three juniors and a pair of recent high school graduates. They never stood a chance.*

Her father had encouraged her love of architecture all her life. But Teri now knew that building social structures with people was much more fulfilling work.

Because she brought them together every Saturday after that encounter. The six of them—Teri, Carmen, Anyi, Ronaldo, Josuo, and Elisha—spent hours each week by Josuo's make-shift still, talking and drinking and reading aloud to each other from books Teri downloaded from her father's computer without the man's knowledge. She could barely stand Nando Miranda after what he had done, but he had many strange secrets, had taught Teri and her twin Miwa many things at odds with the social and religious norms of this world he'd brought them to as babies. Teri selected the contraband literature carefully, picking works that would draw the others closer together and make them continue to depend on her intellectually.

The elders had to watch the time carefully, for their bishop kept a close eye on them, permitting them only that weekly break, when they claimed they went hunting. Despite the bishop's vigilance, the group would follow up their reading of Teri's off-world works with an hour watching normally blocked Consortium infotainment videos that Ronaldo downloaded from an underground station on Kanaano.

In the present, Carmen chuckled and shook her head. "Clever little manipulative girl. You made us care about you. Even begged us to act like we didn't know you on weekdays and at church so as not to bring 'undue attention' to our little clique."

"It wasn't a lie, though. We were doing forbidden things. If we got caught, the price would be high. My parents would have lost their minds to find me spending time with adult males. Imagine if folks had discovered the still, the cigarettes, the sensual and rebellious poetry. But yes. You're right. By making you swear to protect me, the youngest, I bound you to me and to each other more tightly. Made us a family, closer than siblings. Till each of us carried a piece of the others."

Carmen leaned toward her, eyes wide. "What did you get out of it?"

"Sanity," Teri admitted. "And the chance to be near you, querida Carmen."

"But I liked—*like*—Josuo," Carmen protested weakly.

"You liked—*like*—me more," Teri countered.

Carmen had no reply to that.

When did I finally know for sure that I love this clueless girl?

Not long after that first Saturday, Teri had begun to have disturbing dreams. Carmen and Josuo, kissing, their hands on each other's bodies. Each other's flesh.

And then, one night, it hadn't been Josuo in Carmen's arms.

It had been her. Teri.

At first, Teri had felt shame. She was vaguely aware that, on other planets, some women fell in love with other women. But such behavior would never be tolerated on Terego.

Then she'd remembered her father's words to her, long ago, when she had been just a child.

"There are loves this world forbids, my sweet girl. But if you fall in love with someone the rules say you shouldn't, ignore the rules, Teri. Follow your heart."

It's so hard to hate him, she thought in the present.

"You can't deny it, can you? When you called me that Sunday three months ago, knowing my parents were out of town with my little brother, you knew what you were doing, Carmen."

Face red, Carmen sputtered, "Of course I did! Inviting my friend to a picnic so she wouldn't be bored at home."

"In that clearing? With a bottle of rye and some explicit excerpts from Auld's *La infana raso*? Vamos, mujer. You wanted it to happen."

They had laughed at the book-length poem's audaciousness, reveled in its matter-of-fact sexuality and vulgarity, wept into the bottle at the vision of humanity it embraced. Before she knew what had happened, Teri had found herself in Carmen's arms, kissing her hungrily, instinctively, unsure of what she was doing, but certain that she wanted to do it.

A few minutes later, her blouse open to the navel, Teri's hands on her breasts, Carmen had pulled away, shaking her head. Apologizing. Standing to go as she fumbled at buttons with trembling fingers.

"It was a mistake. I've told you so a dozen times since then," Carmen insisted.

Teri reached out to straighten the burgundy bow of Carmen's school uniform. "Then why are we sitting here, eh?"

With a frustrated gesture, Carmen pushed Teri's hands away. "See, this is why I've been avoiding you. You won't accept no for an answer. You've misunderstood the whole think. I was drunk. Confused."

Teri gritted her teeth for a moment. It had been hard, dealing with Carmen's rejection after such intimacy. But she took some comfort in the power she now felt around her father. While he sat glumly, looking at her as if wanting to broach the subject of his abuse, she could meet his eyes with a glower while inside, every particle of her being quivered with joy.

If you only knew. If you only knew. You have your Tenshi, whoever the fuck she is, and I've got Carmen.

"You want me. Love me. Just admit it."

Carmen suddenly stood, flustered.

"Did you make out with Josuo? That's what I need to know. Not because of anything I feel for you," she rushed to clarify, "but because of, um, what I feel for *him.*"

"No, Carmenjo. I didn't." Teri sighed. "Josuo knows. About us. He confronted me with it. Tried to kiss me, saying he could fix my sinful confusion. I slapped him. So now he's pissed off. God knows what he's told the others. You know how spiteful he can be."

Carmen's expression went from frustration to fear. "Oh, shit. Don't … don't respond to any of it, Terinjo. Let me handle it."

"Because you're a senior and I'm just a sophomore?"

"No," Carmen said, turning to go. Then she glanced back over her shoulder. "I don't trust your motives. You wouldn't nip this in the bud. You'd let it blossom, use it to isolate the group from the rest of the community. I understand you better than you know, girl."

Teri sat there for a minute, watching Carmen walk away, skirt brushing back and forth across black leggings that emphasized the curves of her thighs and calves.

Then, a sweet ache spreading from her stomach downward, she followed the other girl back to the school.

"Teri?" someone called as she ascended the front steps.

Turning, she saw her stepmother Rhea Kumar-Miranda approaching the school, a three-tier metal lunchbox in her hands.

"Hey, Mom. Dad forgot his lunch again, yeah?"

Blowing a strand of greying hair from her thin face, Rhea nodded. "He's always in such a rush, loading you three into the *kamioneto* and roaring across the plains."

It was a conversation they'd had too many times to count. Teri responded reflexively.

"Well, you two were the ones who decided to build our house sixty kilometers from Diadono. And Jakobo's stupid school starts at the crack of dawn."

"So either you or Miwa could remind your father to grab his lunch. Or you could bring it yourselves. But you've inherited his forgetfulness. And all of you take me for granted, so here I am."

Rolling her eyes, Teri shrugged. "You're the counselor for our stake's branch of the *Diadona Helpsocieto, Mother*. You have to come into the city every day. Bringing your husband a dabba packed with food isn't a burden, is it?"

Rhea stepped closer, her big eyes narrowing in irritation.

"You've gotten really rude and disrespectful these last few weeks. On top of your already infuriating rebelliousness. We'll talk when you get home this evening, but here." She thrust the metal container at Teri. "Take this to your father. I'm in a hurry."

Teri wanted to scream at Rhea, tell her the horrible secret about what Nando Miranda had done to her, reveal her love for a girl, shock her stepmother with her doubts about their family's faith and her yearning for the biological mother she'd never known.

Instead, she headed silently into the school, interrupting her father's class to set the dabba on his desk without a word as he stared at her with remorse in his traitor's eyes.

CHAPTER 3

AS RHEA KUMAR-MIRANDA LEFT THE SCHOOL and headed up the street, her annoyance with Teri faded. The thought of Nando coughing with embarrassment in front of his students when his lunch was delivered made her laugh a little.

Ten years of this. It's amazing that I still have patience with him.

But it was difficult *not* to have patience with Nando, with that towering, powerful presence of his and those piercing brown eyes. She knew that violence lay coiled behind his silence. Though unafraid, she respected it as one might a force of nature.

That deadly potential had once exploded into action: seven jaroj or Tcregan years ago, Nando had been using a backhoe and a pickaxe to dig out a pit for the septic tank of their new house. Rhea and the twins had been gardening close to the nearly finished cabin and Miwa had wandered toward the stream that flowed nearby. A cry had come, and Rhea had lifted her head to see Miwa on the ground, her leg in the mouth of a *kaštoro*, a dog-sized carnivorous beast with a triangular head and a jaw full of sharp teeth.

Rhea had frozen, an impotent scream rising in her throat, but Nando had exploded into movement. Reaching Miwa's side in seconds, he'd jammed his hands into the creature's mouth, forcing its jaws apart so Miwa could pull her leg free. Then, the kaštoro writhing madly in his grip, Nando had bent to estimate the damage to his daughter. When he'd seen the deep puncture wounds welling dark red, bruises already beginning to mottle the skin around Miwa's knee, he'd gone berserk. With a single, savage twist he'd broken the kaštoro's neck and begun beating its lifeless body against a nearby tree. In huge arcs he'd swung the carcass thudding into the trunk, blood spraying the ground about him, until the animal had become a ruined mess.

Rhea had recovered her wits and run to Miwa's side with a long strip of fabric she'd been using to sew curtains.

"Bind that up and get her into the truck," Nando had growled. "I'll be right there."

He had stamped over to where he'd left the pickaxe. Taking it up, he'd returned to the bloody remains of the kaštoro and proceeded to hack it into pieces. As she'd loaded Miwa into the kamioneto, Rhea'd seen her husband pour some flammable liquid on the remains and set them alight. He'd leapt into the kamioneto then, letting Rhea drive as he held his daughter in his arms, stroking her face with blood-flecked hands and murmuring soothing words to her in Baryogo.

That had been the only time Rhea had seen the potential violence in action, though Nando had later hunted down and killed all kaštoroj within a ten-kilometer radius of the house. Also, sometimes during the martial arts lessons he gave the girls, Miwa or Teri would come away with bruises that Nando both dismissed and begged forgiveness for. The injuries were always slight and never a result of his anger, just the vigorousness of the training. But that fevered frenzy was always lurking behind his eyes, and others could sense it. The few times people had tried to interfere with or take advantage of their family, his cold yet burning gaze, accompanied by a few precise words, had squelched their attempts. Rhea felt safe at his side.

Such had not been the case with her first husband, a weak, sickly man who'd reminded her of her grandfather. Though she preferred cuddling and romance to the physical act of sex, Rhea had done what she believed was her duty. But then they'd discovered she was barren. On Terego such infertility was the worst that could befall a couple, as large families were both an economic and spiritual boon. Rikardo Torres, her then husband, had been devastated by the news. He'd viewed it as a curse, not only for him and Rhea, but for the spirit children waiting for bodies. Ever since Joseph Smith had been revealed as their new planet's spiritual father—scant months after their arrival fifty-nine Standard years ago—Tereganoj had taken special pride in providing the flesh for *Smitinfanoj,* and to be unable to do so was tragic.

Rikardo's love for her had curdled, and the pity she'd felt for him had turned to disgust. Despite his bishop's counseling and the reassurances of the Prophet himself that their situation had a divine purpose, bitterness had eventually consumed Rikardo's frail body, and he'd died only three jaroj after their marriage.

News of Rhea's infertility kept most men away. But Rikardo's brother, Marlo, had begun to court her. He didn't care, he told her, that she couldn't bear him children. He loved *her* and wanted to dedicate his existence to pleasing her. Though she felt nothing for the man, a couple of years of his insistent wooing had nearly broken down her will.

Then Nando Miranda had arrived.

Terego's immigration policy was strict. In order to settle on the planet, one had to accept the tenets of the Church and be baptized. All settlers were closely monitored to ensure their complete incorporation into Teregan society, culture and religion, especially Mormons from other branches within the Consortium of Planets, Corporations and Colonies, who had to be weaned of many heretic creeds that had grown up in the three hundred years since Teregan colonizers had left Earth. It wasn't an intrusive sort of monitoring, but one handled with tact and friendship, through daily visits and fellowship as well as discussions led by a pair of elders.

Rhea had been the helpsocieto's legal representative on the committee in charge of Nando's training. Her duty was to provide him with counsel and the basics of Teregan law so that he could more easily adapt. She'd warmed to him and to his baby daughters, whom he cared for lovingly, performing the roles of both mother and father.

Nando was a fugitive of a civil war on the distant planet Jitsu. He and his wife had escaped the madness there and had wandered for a time, unsure of where to go. They'd soon realized that Umoya, Nando's wife, was pregnant with twins. Unwilling to risk fenestration or even hypostasis for fear of the effects on the children, Nando and Umoya had waited out the pregnancy and tried delivering the babies themselves in the small medical alcove onboard their ship.

The results had been disastrous. Though the twins had survived, their mother had died. Bereaved, Nando had buried her in space, launching her into a nearby star, and had taken care of the infants until, at six months of age, they were old enough to undergo stasis. It had been during those long, lonely months that he began the soul-searching that led him to the *Book of Mormon* and Terego.

Once a multi-lingual teaching assistant by profession, Nando had studied Esperanto and, when his two daughters were ready, he'd fenestrated to Terego's system. His story had been verified by immigration officers.

Nando Miranda had indeed taught at a school in Station City on Jitsu. He and his wife Umoya had disappeared around the time of the civil conflict on that world. The sensor readings and logs of his small ship confirmed the details of his trip.

As the immigrant's desire to convert appeared genuine, the community had opened its arms to him.

During the course of that first year, Nando and Rhea had grown close, though she'd sensed hesitancy from him. His love for Umoya and grief over her death kept him from being drawn to another woman, or at least made him feel guilty. But over time the emotional barriers had come down. After Nando's baptism, their spirits had touched, a connection Rhea'd heard women speak of since she was a child, but that she'd never been able to believe in. With Nando in her life, she began to understand for the first time just how crucial family was, how elemental in one's own redemption. By herself, she was incomplete. Joined to Nando and his daughters, she was whole.

The most difficult part of their marriage had been putting her work in the helpsocieto and her pursuing of a law degree on hold to raise Teri and Miwa. An unexpected bitterness had blossomed in her after the first six months. Nando had been accepted with surprising speed into the Quorum of Elders within their ward, and he had taken upon himself the duties expected of any elder in the ward, including the specific calling of giving religious instruction every Sabbath. In addition, he'd been assigned a job as an instructor at the local preparatory school. His most popular class was on Standard, a language made indispensable by the dribble of immigrants and

Terego's increasing, if strained, relations with the Consortium.

Rhea, however, had her hands tied with the twins. She did get to work from time to time, but her influence in the helpsocieto waned, and her steady climb within its ranks came to a halt. She knew this pause in her life's work to be God's will; she tried not to feel bitter when she wasn't called for positions of authority. Nonetheless, as she performed the lesser tasks given her by the leadership of her stake and ward, she could not help but feel disappointed.

From time to time, as the two girls screamed at each other or pulled each other's hair, Rhea would hear a little voice inside.

Those aren't your children. Why do you put up with this? You're wasting your life. No one notices you anymore, not even Nando. He's using you. He doesn't love you, not really. He no longer attempts to make love to you. Perhaps he pities you. Thinks that raising another woman's babies will keep your mind off your barrenness.

Get behind me, Satan, she would mutter on such occasions. She knew the voice had to be the Dark One, trying to lead her astray.

You used to pray that God will take away your curse, grant you a child. But you're no Sarah, woman, no matter how you try to turn his dead wife into your imaginary handmaiden. And the reproductive act holds little attraction for you, does it? How sad for you, trapped on a world where to be asexual is to be irrelevant.

The voice always went away, eventually, and Rhea found her faith and love renewed for the struggle. The girls had entered school, she'd continued with the helpsocieto, been called to influential posts within that organization, gotten her *juristo* title and, three jaroj ago, unexpectedly, God had answered her prayers.

Little Jakobo had been born.

Now, approaching the offices of the Diadona Helpsocieto on the main street of Diadono, the busiest on the planet, home to the Prophet, the Quorum of the Twelve, the Prime Minister's office and the legislature as well, Rhea smiled and said a silent prayer of thanksgiving for the multitude of blessings she'd been bestowed.

She passed the government offices that held the Immigration and Exterior ministries, stopping short when she saw Marlo Torres, now Minister of Immigration, exit the building with the head of Nando and Rhea's ward, Bishop Daud Freij, and the President of the stake that encompassed Diadono and its outlying suburbs, Elija Lau. Marlo noticed her immediately and stopped the other gentlemen while she approached. Their faces were grim. They barely acknowledged her presence with a nod, despite having known and worked with her for two decades.

"What, brothers? I can tell something's wrong. Don't keep it in. If there's anything I can do, you know I will."

Marlo motioned her back under the awning, away from the occasional passerby.

"We have a problem," he intoned solemnly. "In our midst is a man who pretends to be a Novasanktulo, when in reality he's a murderer, a liar, a thief and, more to the point, a fugitive."

Rhea blinked, incredulous. "How do you know this?"

"Nearly a year ago, the CPCC requested that I send them DNA samples of all the immigrants who have settled here in the last three decades."

She grimaced. "Don't tell me you complied with them. How long can we preserve our sovereignty if we buckle to every demand they make of us? Would you have them turn this system into another Sigma Draconis, a mere puppet of the Consortium?"

Marlo sighed. It was an old argument. "It's for our own protection. The CPCC database can help us ensure that we're not allowing criminals to live among us just because they can recite doctrine and get baptized. Anyway, it's academic now. It took some doing, but I managed to gather samples from physicals and whatnot, and four months ago I sent the whole package on a returning transport to the CPCCAF commodore in charge of traffic in this sector. Just this morning I was contacted by a captain under his command: one of the DNA samples, despite being artfully altered, does indeed belong to a wanted criminal."

Rhea swallowed heavily. Setting aside her reluctance to allow interference by the CPCC in local affairs, she had to admit that finding this fugitive before he'd done any harm was a lucky thing, one that would no doubt further Marlo's career in the burgeoning field of secular government on Terego.

"Have you arrested the man, then? Is he here in Diadono? In another city of Zarahemla? On one of the other continents?"

Marlo seemed almost to want to grin, and Rhea couldn't for the life of her understand why. "Oh, he's here, alright. Very close to us as we speak, in fact. But we haven't arrested him. First we go to the Quorum of the Twelve and the Prophet to present the news to them: this is a religious as well as civil matter." He looked her up and down strangely. "Perhaps you should come with us, sister."

Rhea's brow creased uncomprehendingly. "Me? Why?"

Her bishop finally spoke, sympathy and sadness glowing in his eyes. "Rhea, dear. The man, the criminal in our midst, it's—it's Nando. He's the one they're searching for."

Rhea's mind went numb, and all the world seemed to dim around her, as if a thick lace curtain had been yanked down across her eyes. She could see Marlo's face, a strange sneer pulling at the corner of his mouth; Stake President Lau was saying something to her, but all she could hear was the thudding of her blood in her veins.

CHAPTER 4

THE CAPTAIN OF THE DIOMEDES LOOKED UP AT THE NOTIFICATION CHIME.

"Captain, an incoming com from Commodore Berdyaev," the communications tech announced.

"I'll take it in my ready room," the captain replied, walking his doppel off the bridge rather than winking into virtual existence in that nearby office. He preferred the illusion of physicality.

The *Diomedes*, a *Cetus*-class galleon, was presently en route to a distant wedge of space at the very limits of human exploration for a four-year tour. The ship they were relieving, the *Lafayette*, had set off for the Dosun Shipyards near Lalande 21185. As a result, Commodore Nicholas Berdyaev, head of Outer Sector 1, was having to make do with just three galleons until Captain Antonio D'Angelo, youngest man to hold his rank in decades, finished crossing the vast distance between Sol and the OS1HQ. The trip would take a total of five months, two of which had already passed.

The unusual delay in a replacement ship had a simple explanation. Commodore Berdyaev would settle for no other captain than the grandson of his lifelong friend and fellow soldier, Commodore Ugo Spinelli, head of Inner Sector 17 and hero of the Consortium-Kunti War, whose daughter Isabella had married Antonio's father, Giacobbe, on Oceania thirty-six years ago. Beyond that, Antonio was the golden boy of the moment, and Berdyaev, because of his connections, had first dibs on the captain.

The voyage required a constant faux-com link between OS1HQ in the 61 Ursae Majoris system and the *Diomedes*. D'Angelo received updates from his commodore every day. The outer sectors had become hotbeds of criminal activity as the nearly twenty-year-long war against underworld organizations, the main impetus in the division of human space into *octants* and *sectors* for ease of patrol and governing, had pushed crime syndicates farther and farther away from the center of human civilization.

There were very few human habitats in Outer Sector 1, and most of these were non-CPCC, but its large number of research facilities and corporate ventures made it an appealing target for remnants of organized crime. Berdyaev wanted D'Angelo well prepared so the young captain could put his legendary talents to use upon arrival.

But it seemed Antonio's job would start a little earlier.

"Brace yourself, Antonio," the commodore had begun this morning. "Got some startling info for you, and a pretty hefty job, one that's not going to be easy."

D'Angelo's doppelganger had nodded as if asking for Berdyaev to continue.

"Think back to how this war got started, the whole Brotherhood-Neog conspiracy on Jitsu. You weren't but sixteen, but I'm sure you paid close attention."

Antonio had. The month-long campaign in what was now Inner Sector 5 of Octant 2 had been a defining moment in his personal and military development. It was when he'd decided to follow in his grandfather's footsteps, enrolling in Oceania's premier military academy and swearing to become a captain as soon as he possibly could.

"You realize that there's still one loose end to that battle, yes?"

Antonio's mouth went dry for a moment until the systems governing his hypostasis chamber stimulated his saliva glands. Luckily his doppel didn't betray his accelerated heartbeat and rapid breathing. He tasted again the hate he'd learned to feel for his father when the existence of Giacobbe's first family had been revealed through the newscasts concerning a criminal with a very familiar last name.

"Brando."

"That's right, Captain. Your half-brother Brando D'Angelo di Makomo, a man at the heart of that scandalous situation, a man who did good, killing scores of yaks, and bad, like theft, use of illegal anti-matter and transuranic bombs, the deaths of several dozen law-enforcement officers. The list goes on and on."

Captain D'Angelo hesitated, trying to mentally frame his question. "Sir, I assume you're mentioning him because you have news about his whereabouts."

"I have more than that. Remember the requests we sent out to non-CPCC settlements, asking for DNA samples of immigrants?"

"Yes, sir. We wanted to learn if any wanted criminals were hiding out on those worlds. Not a whole lot of them cooperated, right?"

"No. But a few did. Terego did."

"The Mormon planet."

Berdyaev smiled. "Yes. Their head of immigration, a Marlo Torres, sent us a nice package right after you left the Oort cloud around Sol. Samples from every person who has settled on Terego in the last twenty-five years."

The agonizing build-up was making Antonio's stomach churn, but his doppelganger revealed nothing. He didn't rush the commodore, either. The old man's dramatic flair would not be contained by even those closest to him.

"No yaks in the group, sorry to say: guess being proselytized just ain't their style. But there were three samples that threw up a ton of red flags on the deeper analyses. Especially one. It had been manipulated, disguised. Clever, too, the tricks that were utilized. But our techs are the best in existence, and we cracked the son of a bitch.

"It's your brother. Brando. He's on Terego. Has been for fourteen years, gone native."

"You're certain?" Antonio's stomach felt distant, detached from his body.

"Oh, yes. Using the name Nando Miranda. But that's not all. The other two samples, the ones that also got red flags, were labeled Miwa and Teri Miranda. Twin daughters, according to the Teregan Immigration Ministry's records. I had a suspicion about them, had Jitsu check them against their records to see if there were some correlations. Perhaps he kidnapped some kids, you know? Well, there were significant, statistically impossible concordances between the two DNA samples and two on record with Jitsu's defunct Civil Security. We investigated more and learned that, barring some alterations made to change the females' appearance, these 'children' of Brando's are actually clones."

"What? Clones? Who of?" Antonio's mind reeled.

Just when I think this family can't get any worse.

"This is the sick part. Brando's wife and daughter were killed back in '89 by Felipe Beserra."

Antonio remembered, indeed. Tenshi Koroma, the architect and politician his half-brother had married? She had once been the *lover of Antonio's own mother.*

Struggling against the memory of that particular revelation and all its fallout, Antonio grunted.

"Yessir."

"Was the main reason Brando joined the old anti-terrorism unit on Jitsu. Did a good job, too."

"And broke a load of laws, like you said." Antonio felt indignant. He didn't want Brando painted as a hero for him, not even a flawed one. He was a miserable liar like their father. Like Antonio's own mother.

"Yes, including the ban on cloning."

A sickening understanding prickled the captain's skin. "He cloned them. His dead wife and kid. That criminal freak."

"That's why there will be a military tribunal to assess his guilt. When Jitsu became a protectorate of the Consortium, its squads became part of the Higantean branch of the AF's Constabulary, and his pending case was turned over to us. He's to be tried as a soldier. I want you to get in contact with Marlo Torres via the CPCC consulate there in Diadono and arrange to have Brando and the two little freaks taken into custody. We've got an extradition treaty with them, thank the Four, but we need their cooperation to hold a faux-trial."

Antonio batted his eyelids incredulously. "A faux-trial, sir? Why not send someone to Terego, bring him to OS1HQ and try him there?"

"Because the man I want to prosecute him won't be here for another three months."

A handful of seconds passed as this sank in.

"Why me?"

"Aside from Captain Quat, you're the only licensed Advocate under my command, and I'd rather you were in charge. Think of it as a test. Your first major assignment as captain. Carry out your sworn duties as a prosecutor for the CPCC in military matters. The consulate on Terego has enough room and connections in its faux-conference chamber for about two dozen people. There should be no problem with the eyre, either. Bloody judges are too far away for physical presence, but they can faux-link too."

"I really don't think that it's ethical for me to prosecute a relative, sir."

"Nope, not wriggling out of this one, Antonio. I didn't just read your psych file, I also talked long hours with your Granddad. You've got real issues with your dad's first family, and I believe you need to exorcize that particular demon of yours if you want to be a great leader of men. Marshall Mukerji wants this matter settled as soon as bloody possible, and you're the soldier for the job. Nigh-on twenty years Brando has evaded justice: it's way past his time. It's unorthodox, but it's what I want. Understood, Captain?"

"Yes, sir."

After the com had terminated, Antonio had accessed the CPCCAF database on Terego and begun refreshing his knowledge. Ever since he'd learned of his assignment to the sector, he'd been reading up on its settlements, but Terego's exotic religion and laws had annoyed him, so he'd paid less attention to the world. Now was the time to remedy that neglect.

After about an hour of research, he'd gotten in touch with the CPCC consulate in the capital city of Diadono: they'd rushed over to Torres's office and brought him in for the faux-conference. The minister was very receptive, almost too receptive, to the news that Brando D'Angelo, the man known on Terego as Nando Miranda, was a wanted criminal. In fact, he seemed to barely be able to control his excitement, and as he was obviously totally ignorant of faux-com protocol, his face and body gave these emotions away.

"I always suspected something wasn't quite right with Nando. I mean Brando," Torres had purred in his heavy accent. "I doubt there's going to be a problem with the arrest. The man violated many of our religious laws as well, Captain. We don't take that lightly. But as for incarceration, we don't have a jail. He'll probably be put under, uh, house arrest. They'll post a guard or two outside, I imagine, and…."

"Minister," Antonio had interrupted, "I can't stress to you enough how dangerous this man is. I don't trust house arrest."

"I'll see what I can do, but we just don't have the facilities for what you want. I doubt he'll get past five armed, uh, elders, though. We have a volunteer militia, and some of the brothers are quite good with weapons."

"Minister, this man you want to guard with a few civilians single-handedly killed more than a hundred men in less than eighteen hours, all of them trained warriors. You have no idea the danger he presents."

Torres visibly blanched. "I, uh, will stress that to the Prime Minister and Prophet, I promise."

"Don't you at least have a drunk tank or something?"

The minister frowned. "There is no alcohol on this planet, Captain. No need for a 'drunk tank,' trust me."

Antonio had reflected for hours after terminating the conference. A world virtually free of crime had to hold an expert in terrorism and martial arts. The young captain didn't hold out much hope for them.

There were no other options. The treaty between Terego and the CPCC strictly prohibited the AF from treading Teregan soil. The nearest ship in the sector would take nearly ten days to arrive anyway, providing his half-brother more than ample time to effect an escape.

All that occurred to Antonio was that, perhaps, Brando would cooperate to ensure the wellbeing of his "daughters." Kidnapping and terrorist threats were beyond the pale, however, both for the CPCCAF and for Antonio personally. He would play this straight, as he had done everything all his life. Let the Tereganoj do their best to keep Brando under house arrest during the trial. If they couldn't control him, it would be a failure on their part.

Even if the man did escape, he'd have to leave the planet eventually. Antonio planned to be there, waiting for him.

CHAPTER 5

"GOOD. YOU ARE ALL GETTING THOSE IDIOMS DOWN NICELY. Keep practicing, though. Let's go ahead and turn to phonology for the last five minutes or so. I've noticed that some of you have a real problem with a couple of Standard vowel sounds, specifically these two."

Nando Mirando used his stylus to write *u* and *y* on his podium pad. The letters were projected holographically at the front of the classroom. The students, mainly second-year locals, listened with rapt attention as he continued.

"Don't be fooled, as I've said before, by the fact that Esperanto also uses this first letter. The *u* in the Teregan tongue is pronounced 'oo,' just like in most languages that use variations on the Roman alphabet. Standard just had to be different. Couldn't go along with the other languages, no, no. It had to express its individuality. Some languages, I tell you…."

The class snickered. They loved how silly their professor could be.

"So in Standard, instead of pronouncing this goofy horseshoe 'oo,' we pronounce it 'uh.' Technically it's called a schwa, though the fact that we gave it a name that doesn't even have the sound in it is a little bizarre."

More giggles.

"Now, it's not 'ah' or 'oh,' kids; it's 'uh.' Kind of like getting the air knocked out of you. Try it, everyone."

A cacophony of *uh*s and approximations of the sound filled the air. Some students pretended they were getting punched in the stomach, just for dramatic flair.

"Good, good. Most of you have it. So now, if you see a word written in Standard and it has a *u* in it, what are you going to say?"

"UH!"

"Excellent." Nando jotted a word on his pad, which immediately floated in the air before his students: *greydu.*

"Okay, this is Standard for *greater.*" He used the Esperanto *pli granda.* "Let me hear you pronounce it."

They practiced a couple of times till Nando was satisfied. A young man raised his hand.

"Yes, Rikardo?"

"And if we want to write the *oo* sound in Standard?"

"Ah. Well, the closest thing to it is the dipthong *uw.* It's a little longer than the Esperanto *u*, with more rounded lips and a glide at the end. To write the sound, just use a *u* followed by that weird *w* letter I taught you." He wrote *guwfy* on the pad. "There you go. Goofy, like the lot of you."

There was much laughter at that. In the midst of their mirth, the bell rang.

"Okay, practice those idioms, and I'll see you tomorrow."

They tumbled hurriedly out of the room, and Nando Miranda began gathering his materials and stowing them in his leather satchel. He grinned as pulled up the handle of the aluminum dabba that had contained his elaborate lunch.

One day Rhea is just going to let me go hungry.

Probably not. Though she complained and scolded him, Rhea's love was so long-suffering that she'd cross the most arid, desolate desert to bring him a glass of water. Of course, she'd then bawl him out about it afterward, but that was fine. Her benevolence and righteous anger made her perfect for the family he'd constructed, a cocoon for the two girls he had to protect at all costs.

She was a wonderful mother and wife. Hidden within the Nando persona, Brando D'Angelo felt certain Tenshi and his own spark approved of her. And over the years, despite his efforts, he'd come to care for Rhea Kumar deeply. To love her, after a fashion.

Not the way he loved Tenshi Koroma, of course.

He was still waiting for her. Had been for more than twenty years.

Tenshi had promised to return. Brando believed her, beyond all logic and reason. As worked through the process of gnosis—complete knowledge of self—and then began *Hanga ra-Roho*—the creation of his eternal soul— her promise tethered him to the Path despite the life he outwardly lived.

Guilt gripped his gut as he thought of what he had already done to try to bring her back, at what more might be required.

A dream had plagued him. From the shadows of the Well, a young woman would emerge into the moonlight to stand before him. Brando knew this was Teri Miranda, Nando's daughter. But when she would speak, it was with Tenshi's intonation, her verbal quirks, her favorite phrases.

"Imi nimarejechu, umpenziya."

I've returned, beloved.

Each time he would jerk awake to gaze into the black swirling all around him, gasping, suppressing sobs.

Alone.

The vision had recurred for years.

Then his girls had entered puberty, and he'd been reminded of his sister-in-law, how oracular stigmata had manifested itself once Samanei began having her period.

A desperate idea had wormed its way into the depths of Brando's incipient soul.

"Rhea," he had said at dinner one evening. "They've finished the amphitheater in Nova Mumbajo, did you hear?"

Teri had looked up from her plate, eyes wide, glancing from her father to her stepmother. Brando had encouraged her early interest in building and design. She had come to excel at science and math, her dream to study architecture and join one of Terego's three prominent firms.

Rhea had nodded. "Yes. Beautiful structure."

"What do you think," he had carefully suggested, "about my taking Teri on a weekend trip to see it? She's top of her class again this year, and I owe her a daddy-daughter date since I took Miwa fishing last month."

Teri had pressed her hands together and begged Rhea. "Please, Mom! I'll even do extra chores when we come back."

Miwa had snickered. "You can do mine. I don't mind."

A smile spreading across her face, Rhea had agreed. "Of course. You two have a good time. Be sure to call me each night."

The drive down to the southern coast took about four hours. Brando had reserved a seaside cabin, somewhat isolated, near a rocky cove where waves thundered day and night. They left their bags and headed into the city to visit the amphitheater. As a surprise, Brando had arranged dinner with the architect himself, Guillermo Castro. Teri had kept her excitement in check, asking deep and cogent questions. Castro had been impressed and suggested she contact him during her penultimate heptamester at college.

Back at the cabin, Brando had set out bowls of Teri's favorite pudding, gajar ka halwa. In addition to the normal carrots and nuts, he had added rokiyik or "soulsblood," oil distilled from pressed mohiyo, a concentrated chemical essence that would sink them both deep into the Blue.

As she had dropped into a stupor, Brando had carried her to the bedroom. Had chanted over her twitching body. Had danced the wende round that room, yearning toward the Eight, calling out to his beloved.

Tenshi! Newano umpaziya! I did as you asked. Here is your body. Come back to me! Come back!

In the darkness of the room, waves crashing in the distance, lit by the eldritch glow of the Blue that roiled around them, the girl's eyes had opened. Her mouth had opened. No sound had emerged.

"I'll go sit outside. I'll wait for you, Tenshi. However long it takes."

And Brando had shut the door, locked it, leaned his back against it to let the black swirl around him, the sweet embrace of Akeratosh, avatar of eternity.

After a while, the screams had started.

But it hadn't been Tenshi.

Teri Miranda—his *daughter,* the young woman he had raised since birth, who had loved him with a fierceness that seemed genetically encoded—had been scrabbling at the sealed door in horror.

Tenshi had not returned. Brando had been horribly, inexcusably wrong.

For months afterward, Teri had avoided being alone with him. Their relationship had crumbled. But what could he do? What explanation could he give?

He loved his daughter with all his heart. But she was too young. The truth might destroy her.

So Nando Miranda never explained himself. Instead, he lied. Gaslighted her as if his very life depended on it.

"I called you what? While dancing around the room? Chanting? No, sweetie. We got severe food poisoning from the pudding. You were just having fever dreams, I promise. I was in bad shape, too."

Now, two years later, the distancing had stopped, but the chasm was still there. He just couldn't bring himself to bridge it, no matter the cost to Teri, who had begun losing interest in church and her former friends. Instead, she had gone cold and calculating, almost Machiavellian, becoming the first sophomore to ever be elected school council president, spending her time with seniors and adults, perhaps pursuing some goal Brando couldn't fathom.

THE DOOR SWUNG OPEN about five minutes after the bell, and Miwa popped in, full of energy as always, black curls bouncing, gray eyes flashing. Her last class of the day was hockey, so she was wearing her sweatsuit.

Nando felt no ambiguity toward this tall, joyful athlete. Hardly a trace of toddling Tana remained in her graceful form.

"K'onda, papito? Kom tubo la klas?"

"Tubo wena, pol maischo, klaro."

It was Wednesday, and this week Wednesday was Kaló day. Since the girls had begun speaking, Nando had made a point of teaching them five key languages: Esperanto, Standard, Kaló, Baryogo and Unified Chinese. They spoke a different language together every day of the week, doubling up on Esperanto and Standard, the languages they would use most. Each month he changed the schedule so the girls wouldn't associate a particular day with a particular language.

Despite Rhea's doubts about the process, the girls had become fluent in all five languages. And they'd learned more. Miwa was interested in Hindi, Rhea's family language, which Nando's wife often spoke with Jakobo, their four-year-old son. Teri had picked up Spanish from her older friend Carmen.

The door banged open. Teri walked into the classroom, tight cornrows underscoring the disdain on her delicate features.

"Ya listes?" she demanded in Kaló. "I left my friends so we could walk out together. Let's go, yeah?"

Nando's heart ached as he looked up at her. Tenshi and Samanei stared at him from her multihued eyes.

"Si," he answered, picking up his bag. "Nos bamos."

Miwa and Teri exchanged gossip as the three of them headed down the main hall and out into the brisk air. The sun was prickly warm, though, a good sign that first winter was nearing its end. The sky was clear, and no frost crunched under their feet as they left the steps to cut across the school's lawn to their kamioneto.

That was when Nando saw the knot of people waiting, and his heart sank. In a flash of certainty, he knew it was over. What he feared most had arrived like a wrecking ball. It was a possibility that woke him with a start in the middle of the night and wouldn't let him sleep again—the inevitable demolition of the edifice that was Nando Miranda. A necessary shattering that nonetheless clenched his stomach and twisted his brain in quiet moments when nothing else occupied his mind.

Marlo Torres was at the front of the group, two elders with pistols strapped awkwardly to their hips at his side. Behind him was the bishop, the stake president, his second counselor, and the mayor of Diadono.

Nearby stood Rhea, her eyes blank and sunken, all their tears spilled already.

Nando checked the distance to his kamioneto, weighing their chances. Alone he'd probably make it, maybe with a bullet or two lodged in his flesh. But he wasn't willing to risk the girls: he'd spent years preparing them for this eventuality, but the moment wasn't right. Besides, their shock at the coming revelations would inhibit their training and reflexes. Better to wait. There'd be another opportunity.

"Ke pasa?" Miwa whispered.

Teri looked about her nervously as if she wanted to bolt. She seemed worried they might be here for her, and a surge of sick filled Brando. What could she have done that would make her imagine such a thing? Worse yet, how would she react when she learned what she was?

"Stay calm, girls. They're here for me. I can't explain right now, but please understand that what I've done, I've done for you. No matter what anyone says, you are wonderful, intelligent, beautiful people. Girls. Women. I love you both."

Teri's head snapped around to glare at him. Miwa started to speak, but was cut off by Torres' sharp voice as they stopped in front of him.

"Brando D'Angelo." It wasn't a question, but Brando nodded anyway. "You are hereby detained by the government for immigration fraud and a host of crimes alleged by the Consortium of Planets, Colonies and Corporations for which you will likely be tried and possibly extradited. You are also wanted before the Quorum of the Twelve for violations of our faith, with excommunication a likely result. Do you deny any of these charges?"

Brando studied Marlo's face, noting the nearly happy sneer that he barely constrained himself from showing. Torres had long resented him for marrying Rhea, and the two had often been at loggerheads on local political issues.

You've won, Marlo. Feel free to gloat.

"No. I deny nothing."

"What?" Teri pressed her palm to her forehead. "Dad, what's all this?

Who's Brando D'Angelo?"

Before Brando could answer, Second Counselor Bozik stepped forward and took both girls by the arms, trying to lead them away gently. "Everything will be explained to you soon enough; please come with me," he told them as he herded them into a nearby car. Rhea stared at Brando with red-rimmed eyes, a tumult of emotions twitching across her face. She opened her mouth as if to ask him as question and then angrily set her jaw and turned to follow the twins into the car.

Brando, you bastard, he muttered inwardly, *what have you done to that woman?* A shudder of guilt wracked him briefly as he thought of her and Jakobo, the boy he'd promised himself never to hurt as Giacobbe had once hurt him. *Another broken promise. The cycle never ends.*

The two elders, members in the voluntary and seldom-activated Crisis Corps, approached him. He held out his hands, conscious more than ever of the younger-looking flesh on the left one.

"I'll give you no trouble, brothers. Cuff me, and let's go."

FIFTEEN MINUTES LATER HE WAS GUIDED INTO A LARGE CONFERENCE HALL in the legislative building. Upon a platform at one end of the hall curved a huge wooden conference table, behind which were seated the Quorum of Twelve, the head of the legislature, the Prime Minister, the Minister of Crises, and the Prophet himself, Zwelini Disbergen, a man that Brando had come to admire and respect.

The judicial branch of Teregan government was also represented here since, to Brando's never-ending frustration, the Planetary Court was composed of seven of the twelve apostles, a dual identity which D'Angelo had argued against for years.

They're planning on killing two birds with one stone. Get the excommunication and preliminary criminal hearing out of the way in one fell swoop.

Marlo Torres took a seat at one of the tables that faced the imposing and grave faces of the planet's leaders, while Brando stood before them, the two elders flanking him. He was reminded of Konrau Beserra, long dead. These were, for the most part, better men he stood before now. There would be no torture, no beatings, no taunting.

But the pain would be worse. He'd deceived these people for years, and though he'd do it all again if given the chance, he couldn't help but feel shame for what he'd done and empathy for what he was putting his family, friends and leaders through.

Disbergen spoke first, orange-streaked hair slicked back from his broad mahogany forehead.

"Brando D'Angelo, whom I've called Nando Miranda for more than a local decade, I am told you admit deceiving the church and government of this planet about your identity. Is this true?"

"Yes, Brother Disbergen."

"Brother? Why the title, D'Angelo? Out of habit? Out of faith?"

"Out of respect. I have lied to you, it's true, but don't think for a second that I was laughing all the while. My lies had a specific purpose."

Roberto de Waal, the Minister of Crises, interjected. "To cover up your brutal, murderous past?"

Brando shook his head gently. "No. To protect my daughters."

Disbergen motioned to silence de Waal's attempted reply. "We will deal with that matter later, Minister. At the moment we are conducting the Church's business with Mr. D'Angelo." Disbergen turned his forest green eyes back on Brando. "I will take what you say at face value, though of course I have no reason to trust your statements. Explain to the apostles and me exactly why you became a member of the Church, an active one, I might add. How is it possible to lie about your identity and past, yet be a believer?"

Brando thought he heard another question reverberating in the Prophet's words: *why did God allow me to believe you?*

"It isn't possible. I won't play games, Prophet: I became a member of the Church for the benefit of Teri and Miwa, because I wanted them to be brought up in an organized religion that coincided with most of my feelings about humans and the way we ought to live. Terego and the Church coincided best. The remoteness of the planet and the fact that it isn't a member of the CPCC also influenced my decision."

The Prophet folded his hands thoughtfully under his chin. "A purely pragmatic choice? No spiritual conviction, no hand of God?"

The voices of Tenshi, Sakura, his own spark echoed in Brando's memory.

"None that you would recognize as such."

Disbergen leaned back. "An interesting response. Are you in agreement with any of the tenets of our faith?"

"My concern was more for the moral framework this planet provides as well as its emphasis on family and community spirit. The specific creed of the Church is unimportant to me."

"Yes, I understand that, but you aren't answering my question. *What do you believe?*"

Brando paused several seconds. How long had he whispered the words to himself in the darkness, working to fashion his eternal soul in secret?

Why hide any longer?

"Brother Disbergen, I don't believe the things you do. Not in God, not in the Book, not in spirits, heaven, hell, angels, devils. None of it."

The tension in the chamber was palpable. Several of the apostles exchanged glances or whispered comments. Brando continued.

"I respect your people and understand your religion—I even taught it. But for me it's like teaching literature."

Squaring his shoulders, standing a little taller, Brando looked the

Prophet in the eye and declared his faith.

"Instead, I affirm the Three Tenets. Humans are born without souls. The universe is a fractured piece of the Ogdoad. Humans' fate is to create souls for themselves through self-knowledge and in that way help to restore the Ogdoad."

Disbergen's eyes widened in understanding. "You're Neo Gnostic."

Brando dipped his head. "I walk the Path, yes."

The Prophet let a wry smile pull at his lips. "While you may understand with your mind, you have yet to understand with your heart. This saddens me. How many years have you lived here, and to still not hear God's voice in your heart?"

Brando became impatient. He thought of his daughters, of the information they were receiving from lips other than his own, of Rhea and Jakobo and the care they needed now more than ever. To discuss the childish notion of paternal salvation with these men when so much else was on the line was more than he could stand.

"Brother, I'll make this very simple. There is no need for the religious component of this hearing. I withdraw my membership from the Church. I reject it and its creeds. You don't need to discuss my excommunication: I'm out of my own accord."

The Prophet nodded soberly. "And Miwa? Teri? Rhea? Jakobo? What of them, Mr. D'Angelo?"

"Each of them will have to decide what to do. Perhaps they'll walk the Path alongside me. Perhaps they'll stay in the Church. It's a good institution."

"But not a true one."

Brando shrugged. "Few people have the vision in which the truth is revealed. I won't begrudge the rest of you your harmless illusions."

Disbergen tightened his hands into fists, rattled at last. "Enough. As you've withdrawn your membership, I no longer have any part in these proceedings. I will serve only as an advisor to Prime Minister Khumalo. The Quorum is hereby dismissed: I suggest that the five who must retire to pray over the matters we discussed earlier."

Prime Minister Zolile Khumalo, his brow free of the tense furrows that grooved the others' faces, watched as the five filed out of the room. Khumalo was the head of the planet's secular government, established as a consequence of the *Ursae Majoris Treaty*, though he and Disbergen were close in a way that had always troubled D'Angelo, as much as he admired them. Together, they ruled the planet with firm compassion, but Brando had seen firsthand the dangers of theocracy. Even this veiled, roundabout version of it unsettled him.

In his deep, rumbling voice, the Prime minister addressed D'Angelo directly.

"Mr. D'Angelo, you stand before this unusual panel, a coming-together of the three branches of our planet's government, because you represent a problem that we've not encountered since we settled Terego. While we have conflicts and occasional crime, they are so sporadic and well controlled by our clergy and community. Consequently, the bulk of this government's work has been ensuring outside influences don't disturb the balance God has helped us create. But it seems that, despite our caution, an outside problem has been festering in our midst for years. You, Mr. D'Angelo. A man whom some of those present called colleague, brother and perhaps even friend. A man who seemed the pinnacle of our way of life, but who has now rejected everything he's claimed to hold dear for a dozen jaroj."

"Minister Torres, please present the charges leveled against this man by the CPCC."

Marlo stood dramatically, his eyes meeting Brando's with smug satisfaction.

"As per the head of Outer Sector 1, Commodore Nicholas Berdyaev, the Consortium of Planets, Colonies and Corporations charges Brando D'Angelo di Makomo with the following crimes: purchase and possession of illegal equipment, namely gravity tiles, cloning vats, unregistered faux-frames, an illegally modified Lieske drive, and a banned medical AI robot; manslaughter, both intentional and through negligence, during the battles that took place on the planet Jitsu and in orbit around it on May 5, 2697, in the Solar Standard system of reckoning; evasion of arrest by CPCCAF authorities; kidnapping; aiding and abetting a suspected criminal; destruction of property belonging to the government of the aforementioned Jitsu; and finally, the cloning of two human beings using blood samples stolen from the evidence room of Jistu's Anti-Terrorism Squads, now the Higantean arm of the AF Constabulary."

The lack of shock on the faces of the judges and ministers showed they'd already had time to digest the news of Brando's identity. They simply looked at him with sadness or indignation. Only the head of the legislature seemed close to having a seizure, perhaps hearing the charges for the first time.

The Prime Minister spoke again as Torres seated himself.

"Our purpose here is not to assess your guilt, sir, but to determine whether we should allow a CPCCAF military tribunal to be held, via virtual connections, to present the evidence for these charges. Is there anything you wish to say that might sway this panel against such a trial and, as its possible outcome, your extradition?"

Brando swallowed lightly. A virtual trial. He'd be in Teregan custody, with many opportunities for escape. He'd prepared for such an eventuality. Once free, he could head toward Kumora Mountain with the twins and his son. He doubted Rhea would be willing to leave the planet, but perhaps he could convince her. One step at a time.

Still, the possibility existed that he might not get free. He thought of the girls, of what the CPCC would do to them if it got its hands on them. He spoke to break this disturbing train of thought.

"I find it amusing that they can accuse me of both kidnapping my sister-in-law and abetting her, but beyond that, I see no reason why you shouldn't comply with them. For my part, I'm confident the evidence will show the logic and necessity of my actions. My concern, however, is for my daughters. The Consortium has vicious policies about cloned humans. I'm not in a position to ask for anything, but please show compassion for the girls. They're not to blame for how they came to exist."

Khumalo glanced at the Prophet. "Yes. We have considered Miwa and Teri's situation. I am inclined to follow the guidance of the Prophet and the Apostles in this matter. After much prayer and meditation, they have counseled me that it is God's will that these two continue among us. Despite our own distrust of genetic manipulation, we understand that clones are little more than delayed identical twins. The way a human being comes into existence, God has shown our religious leaders, while important, is not the defining characteristic of that person. The soul is. There is no reason to imagine that the soul of a person created by cloning is any less important to God than that of one born naturally. This was confirmed by a revelation received by the Prophet today.

"Miwa and Teri are our sisters. They have committed no crime and will be safe here, despite the wishes of the Consortium."

The relief that filled Brando was such that he could not keep his eyes from tearing up. Disbergen's gaze fell upon him, and his face softened. Brando imagined that the Prophet pitied and even loved him in that instant, despite the damage Brando'd done to Terego by his deception.

"Thank you," he whispered.

"Well, then," spoke up the Minister of Crises, "as soon as the legislature votes on the proposal, and my colleague here assures me they will back the Prime Minister, we will be convening the trial in the CPCC embassy. Until that time, however, Brando will be in my office's custody, under armed guard in a cell we've erected in the basement of our offices. His, uh, daughters will be confined to their home, where their stepmother will be in charge of them, with a member of my Crisis Corps assigned providing security for the duration of the trial."

This is going to be more difficult than I thought.

"Gentlemen, will I be permitted to speak with my daughters? There are things I need to say to them, things that may keep them calm in the face of all this chaos. I'm only thinking of their wellbeing, mind you."

The Prime Minister nodded. "Yes. You'll have ten minutes with them as soon as this hearing is over. Please, for their sakes and your own, don't attempt anything. We understand that you are a formidable soldier, but our crisis corpsmen are armed and will shoot you if you try to flee."

A FEW MINUTES LATER, Brando was led to a small room. The crisis corpsmen waited outside as he entered to find Teri and Miwa. Teri was standing in front of a mirror, looking at her face as if for the first time. Miwa sat at a table in the center of the room, confused concentration drawing her eyebrows together. They both turned to face him as he stepped through the door, his cuffed hands useless before him. Teri's expression of disgust sank like a dagger into his eyes, but he didn't stop for a second.

"There's not a lot of time, so…" he began, using Kaló.

"Forkiĝu, puta merdulo," Teri spat in Esperanto, eyes blazing.

Brando had never heard the words before, but they were close enough to cognates in Spanish, Kaló and Italian for their meaning to be pretty clear.

"Who taught you to speak like that?"

Teri tilted her head back and let loose a cackling laugh that sent shivers down Brando's spine. Identical to Samanei. His mind overlapped his sister-in-law's face with Teri's, flipping them back and forth like some sick optical illusion.

"No, no, *Brando*. You don't get to ask me those questions. You don't get to tell me what to do any more. All your authority: poof!"

She snapped her fingers to emphasize the point.

"Teri, please," Miwa sighed. "We said we were going to listen. Let him talk."

Brando lowered his head a bit, unable to look them in the eyes. "Girls, I know you don't understand. I know that you're hurt. I was too, a long time ago. Some evil men killed my wife and daughter. It took me years, but I found them all and killed them. During the time it took me to find them, though,

I realized I wanted my wife and daughter back. I knew it was impossible, but I wanted to give them another chance to live, to find happiness and enlightenment. I wanted another chance to be there, protecting them when the evil men came. Because they always do, girls. You can go wherever you want, as far from others as you can, but the servants of blindness find you. That's why I've taught you to fight, to defend yourselves, to speak many languages… I wanted you to be ready for that day."

Teri giggled. "And all the time, the evil man was right in the next bedroom."

"That's not fair, Teri," Miwa interjected. "Dad's never been evil to us."

"Oh, no? You innocent little girl. You can't even see what's going on around you. Puta kreteno. Let me tell you something, something 'dad' has never mentioned. Remember that trip he and I went on? The daddy-daughter date down in Nova Mumbajo? *He drugged me.* Tried to do some bizarre religious ritual."

"Teri, you don't understand. My spark. It spoke to me. With your face."

"Tewano tenshi?" Teri demanded in Baryogo, waving her datapad in his face. "I looked you up, *Brando.* Tenshi isn't your damn divine spark or whatever mumbo-jumbo you pretend to believe. She was *your wife.*"

Brando stepped forward as if to object or say something.

"What? You want to shut me up? No, she's going to hear this, *Brando.* This gaslighting *bastardo* wanted to *pull his wife's soul into my body,* Miwa! Haven't you noticed how distant he is with me? Didn't you ever ask yourself why?"

Miwa shook her head, eyes wide. "What? That doesn't make any sense!"

"You're clueless, always off on the lake or in the snow, dreaming of all the medals you're going to win. Don't you get it? HE CLONED HER! That's who I am."

Teri tossed her datapad at her twin sister. Brando took a step toward her but faltered. There was no stopping this revelation.

Miwa's lip trembled as she read the article. Brando wanted to step close to her, hold her, but he knew he couldn't. There was no time, and she wasn't ready.

"We're ... clones? Dad?" She looked up at him, tears spilling down her cheeks. "What have you done?"

"Miwa, listen to me. I know I've made huge mistakes, but you're both *alive*, and no matter what, I love you. Teri, I'm so sorry for what I did to you, for this huge chasm that I created between us," he said, before pivoting to a lie to protect her, "but I never realized how difficult it would be to see you grow into the spitting image of her."

Teri shrugged and snarled a bitter laugh. He continued in a desperate, nearly pleading tone.

"There'll be time for us to discuss this later, I promise. Time for me to make up for all the lies I've told. Right now I need to tell you something. In my study, behind the books on the topmost shelf, there's a small safe. It'll open to either of your thumbprints. Inside you'll find a map with some information: if I'm taken away, follow what the map says to do. Miwa, your mother left her journal for you, coded to your DNA alone. Its time lock has been open for years, but only you can access the entries. Share it with Teri. Maybe by reading what Tenshi wrote about herself, you'll learn more about who you are."

One of the corpsmen leaned his head in. "Time to go."

Miwa turned away, rubbing tears from her eyes. Teri just glared at him.

"Good-bye, loves. I'm so sorry."

As he turned, he heard the scraping of the chair as Miwa jumped to her feet and rushed to him. She threw her arms about him, sobbing.

"I forgive you, Dad," she cried. "I don't care who you are or what you did. I love you!"

Brando's heart was wrenched so violently by emotion in that moment that he felt he'd die. But the Grey Prison of the universe continued its merciless illusion. He stumbled away between the corpsmen, leaving the two girls behind to deal with their destiny as best they could.

CHAPTER 6

THERE WAS ABSOLUTE SILENCE ON THE RIDE HOME. Rhea drove, with Corpsman Kersen Hardjono in the passenger seat beside her and the twins in the back, Jakobo asleep between them, his head in Miwa's lap.

Trapped in their own pain, thought Miwa. Rhea's perfect man had turned out to be a fraud. Teri had discovered that her distrust for her father hadn't arisen from supposed fever dreams, but a basis in reality.

And me? What do I feel?

Confused, she guessed. Hurt. Uncertain of the future. And of the past.

Umoya Miranda is not *my biological mother. But everything Dad taught me about her people, the Aknawajin, and how I'm part of that culture, too—it's still valid. Even in his lies, he was trying to ground our identity.*

Surreptitiously, she kept reading the article on Tenshi Koroma she'd downloaded onto her datapad.

This brilliant, brave woman gave birth to Tana D'Angelo di Koroma. And I'm that girl's clone. That's close enough to a biological mom for me. Teri and I are still the only Aknawajin on Terego, especially now that we know Dad isn't half Jitsujin like he always claimed. I can still feel proud of that heritage.

But Miwa couldn't ignore how gutted Teri or Rhea were, rigid in their seats. Even Corpsman Hardjono looked devastated. He had just gotten married and didn't seem happy with this unprecedented assignment.

Miwa had always known there was something different about her father, and now the secret had been revealed. The idea was somewhat romantic: a man that loved his family so much that he would become a soldier to avenge their deaths and then defy all existing laws to bring them back. There was no way she'd admit this to her mom or sister, as she continued thinking of them, as she would always think of them: they wouldn't understand.

As for the implications being a clone, for the moment she chose not to worry. There were more pressing issues, like the upcoming trial and her future as an athlete. She was supposed to be training throughout the next three months for the Games, and she couldn't stop feeling annoyed at how this revelation was going to put all her plans on hold. She knew she was the best skater on the planet and possibly even in the octant. She had an unheard-of talent for both figure and speed skating, and she excelled at hockey. But knowing this wasn't enough, she'd found: she needed others to know it too.

To applaud her. To be awed by her.

They pulled up to the house finally. Rhea jumped out and headed inside. Teri slammed the door shut and trudged after her. The corpsman walked to the porch, leaned his rifle against the wall and eased into a rocking chair, one that Brando had made. Miwa sat for a moment longer in the kamioneto, running that name through her mind: *Brando. Brando.* In Esperanto, the word meant liquor, spirits. A substance completely banned on Terego, which dulled the senses and lowered your inhibitions, allowing temptation to take hold. She shook the thought from her mind and went inside, carrying her sleeping little brother to his bedroom and then heading to the kitchen.

Rhea and Teri were sitting in silence at the table. Rhea's eyes were unfocused as if remembering something, transporting herself to another time and place. Miwa took a seat and watched her, waiting. After a few minutes, her mother's eyes closed and a new expression spread across her face, a look that Miwa knew well: decision. Resolution.

"No," Rhea gasped.

Teri's head shot up from its contemplation of the grain in the table's surface.

"No. I've lost too many people already. I watched my grandfather dying bit by bit over years. My mother too. I've buried my father, my first husband, two sisters and a brother. I'm not going to lose anyone anymore, do you understand?"

Miwa wasn't sure whether her mother was talking to them or to God, but she nodded anyway. She noticed that Teri's eyes began to fill with tears for the first time that day.

"We are a *family*. We stick together. My husband, your father, whatever he chooses to call himself and whatever his past is … we are going to back him. We know him, girls, despite whatever he did before he came here. We've spent every day for years with him, and we know more about him than any trial will ever reveal." She looked at them finally, with her hard eyes softening as she did so. "And you, my daughters, my lovely, precious daughters … how you were born is completely unimportant to me. You are *my* children, as surely as little Jakobo is. You will always have my support, even if it means going up against the whole planet, do you understand?"

Teri broke then, sobs racking her body in shuddering waves. She rushed to her room and shut the door with a bang. Rhea's gaze remained trained on the darkness of the hallway for a moment, and then she turned to Miwa.

"You do understand, don't you?" she murmured.

"Yeah, Mom. I do."

Rhea seemed about to say more, but at that moment Jakobo began to call out for her, and she left the kitchen to go comfort him. Miwa continued sitting at the table for nearly another quarter hour, till Corpsman Hardjono slipped inside.

"It's started snowing," he said softly. Miwa's heart thrilled for a moment: a late snow meant first winter would probably last another few weeks. She'd still be able to practice though she couldn't enter the city. She almost felt happy.

After she'd finished showing Hardjono the sofa bed and bringing him blankets, Miwa went back to Jakobo's bedroom: Rhea had fallen asleep with the boy nestled in the crook of her arm. Easing the door shut, Miwa backtracked to the bedroom she shared with her sister (*not her mother... her sister*). The door was locked.

Suddenly she remembered about the map and the journal. She crept into her father's study, pushed a stool close to the shelving, and removed the books from the top shelf. A metal square was set in the wall, with a black rectangle beside it. She applied her thumb to the lock and the door popped open. She fished out the contents.

Clicking on the lamp that angled across her father's desk, Miwa sat behind the sturdy wooden bulk and looked at the three items. One of them was a ring, glinting silver-blue in the muted light. A thin chain ran through it.

Small. Tenshi's?

Shrugging, Miwa set it aside and regarded the map displayed on the flexible transparent display sheet. It showed the northeastern quadrant of Zarahemla, from Diadono north to Kumora Mountain. In fact, the map described a route to the mountain, and in an enlarged section at the upper left corner, it detailed how to reach a series of caves about a quarter of the way up Kumora's face. On the back of the map were instructions about how to gain access to a hidden sanctuary that Brando had apparently built, God knew when or how.

Miwa set the map to one side and picked up the journal. The black sturdiplas casing, which fit neatly in the palm of her hand, was pitted and worn by time and hard use. Her heart beating faster and faster, Miwa flipped up the cover and thumbed the unit unlocked and on. She nearly jumped when the voice started speaking: it was so like Teri's, yet so different, with layers of age, experience and wisdom that came through despite the impersonal delivery system.

"Tana," the voice said in Baryogo, "my daughter, my love, my life: I have preserved this for you, so that you can learn how I came to be the woman I am. I don't know whether upon your hearing this I'll be alive or dead. There's no way of knowing under *what* conditions you'll open this journal. But should you need a guide or just a voice to listen to, I pray to the Ogdoad that these recordings will help."

Next came a series of beeps and inner whirring, then the voice again. Only this time it *was* Teri: young, haughty, full of herself, sure that she knew more than the adults around her. She spoke in halting Standard.

"December 5, 2671. Yes, that's right. Screw local time. Well, two months have passed, and I ain't going nowhere. I'll stay here. Oh, everybody's shocked, they are. Thought I was going to give in right away, beg them to take me back. Fuck that. Go back to what? They took Samanei. They're just going to fill me with moku, turn my mind off.

"Anyways, there's Grey Prison full of off-worlders down here on the Southern Continent. We work hard, but it's fun. The landscape's all torn up from corporate greed, but we're rebuilding it. Feels good. We remade these hills that got all blasted up by Soltec bastards way back. When we were done, I stood staring for a while. Then this off-world omedeyo—sorry, he says he's a calalai, which I think is trans man in Standard, something like that—name of Andi Walinono came up to me and asked, 'So what're you looking at, Tenshi?'

"I gave him a little shrug. 'We did that, Andi. Not some god or nature. We did it.' He looked at me funny and lit a sikarito, so I asked him for one. It was nasty, but I didn't cough. He stood there with me for a little longer, looking at them hills, and then he goes, 'You know what, kid? You got a point. We did better than the real thing. Now get your arse to the compound and go to sleep. Since we're better than god, we ain't resting on no seventh day.'

"That Andi, I tell you. He's old and all, but I guess he's cute. Don't tell anyone I said so, journal. I guess I'll be talking to you now and again, just to get things straight in me head. You be quiet about it all, though.

"Goodnight."

It was too much for Miwa. She clicked the journal off with a brusque movement and slammed the cover shut.

I'm not ready to listen to this long-dead voice. Rhea's the only mother I've ever had. All the biological and genetic stuff isn't as important as her love for me.

She left the black rectangle and the ring on the desk, picked up the map, and clicked off the light. Since Teri had locked her out, she decided she'd sleep in her parents' bedroom. Once under the sheets, she pulled the pillows close to her face and fell asleep with the smell of her mother and father wrapped about her like the hand of God.

IT HAD STOPPED SNOWING BY MORNING, and Miwa spent an hour begging her mother and the corpsman to let her go practice for a while up at the lake, playing on their sympathy for the emotional trauma she was experiencing. In the end, Kersen agreed to accompany her on the condition that after exactly two hours they would return. Miwa packed her gear rapidly; as she did so, she realized she'd left the map in her parents' bedroom. Not wanting her mom to find it, she retrieved it and stowed it in one of her bags. Then she and the corpsman climbed into the snow speeder and crossed the seventy-eight kilometers of rolling hills and fog-laden moors northwest to Lake Galileo.

Miwa and her trainer Dang Xi had been working on a routine that combined elements of Capoeira and Wu Shu with traditional figure skating. It was a challenging proposition, and perhaps even dangerous: many of the moves that Miwa would be attempting required supreme balance when performed on two bare feet, and doing them while whizzing about on the ice was questionable. But Miwa was determined to break the barriers and do things that had never been done before, and her trainer believed her capable of it. As this year's Games were set to be broadcast throughout the octant and possibly picked up by CPCC infotainment services as well, Miwa knew she had to be amazing. She'd always felt, despite her love for her family and devotion to it, that she didn't belong on this world. Yesterday's revelations had simply made concrete that itchy doubt in the back of her mind: these were not her people. She would be discovered, and she would leave to find a place where she fit.

Once she'd strapped on her skates, she set out onto the frozen expanse of the lake, which stretched half a kilometer to the west, nearly right to the edge of the forest, and several kilometers to her north and east, where it merged into a series of broad fens and meadows. Her favorite practice spot was an egg-shaped peninsula of ice that jutted into the southernmost banks, but today she slipped beyond the natural rink and did her warm-up exercises several hundred meters to the north. Hardjono watched her with high-intensity binoculars for a while, then shrugged and settled into the cabin of the speeder to read the Book.

As she launched into her routine, Miwa let the dazzling white expanse around her drown out the exterior world. All that existed was the ice, her body, and the blades that sent clouds of ice shavings into the frigid air. She fell several times, especially when attempting the *folha seca*, which essentially required her to kick her right leg out and up as if striking a soccer ball over her head, pulling her left leg up after it so she flipped in the air and landed, still speeding along, on her right leg. The landing was the hard part, and her trainer was worried she'd twist her ankle. Today she just bruised herself more than usual, landing again and again flat on her back.

She took some time out to practice individual moves, like her blur spin and a couple of impressive looking but relatively easy stunts involving her placing thickly gloved hands on the ice and lifting her legs into the air. Very unconventional. Revolutionary, even. But such radical moves were what it took to be noticed anymore, her trainer had repeatedly told her. So she practiced.

Caught up in this work, she didn't at first notice the dark forms bearing down on her out of the northeast. She never saw how the eighteen blotches on the horizon separated out and formed a horseshoe. Nor did she notice the explosion of movement at the forest's edge as some forty figures leapt from the trees and rushed onto the ice as if to confront the approaching eighteen.

At least, she didn't notice until it was too late.

She completed the double axel she'd been slipping on and skidded to a stop. A sharp whine made her glance up at the snow speeder now slamming down onto the ice, hurtling toward her. Hardjono was making frantic movements, so she slowly turned about, her eyes taking in the monstrous panorama.

Hordes of enormous, hairy creatures armed with spears and claws were pounding across the ice at her. Their wedge-shaped heads and constantly twitching, rotating ears ripped a memory from her, the jaws of a *kastoro* clamped onto her leg when she was little. Only now her father wasn't here to protect her. There'd be no one to grab the monsters and slam them against the trees.

Their hulking forms were going to reach her soon, and she was going to die.

The snow speeder screeched to a halt beside her, and Corpsman Hardjono leapt from the interior, his rifle coming up in an instinctual movement as he dropped to one knee at Miwa's side.

"Get out of here!" he shouted as he squinted through the sight and began firing. One monster, two, three fell to the ice, spinning toward their companions, who leapt over them with ridiculous, frightening agility, the claws of their splayed toes gripping the ice with every rapid step, their long, flat tails further aiding their balance.

Miwa dove into the cab of the speeder, only to realize that it was impossible for her to drive with her skates on. Panicked, she began fumbling with the laces, until the windshield shuddered and erupted into a latticework of cracks as a huge spear slammed into it. A second one shattered the glass and rammed into the passenger seat beside her. Her heart aching with adrenaline, Miwa leapt out, heading south to where she'd left her gear.

Several more shots were fired by Hardjono. Miwa twisted her head to see the monsters only meters away from him. Her head jerked back toward the south, and she noticed several of the nearly three-meter-tall creatures hurrying to cut her off. An amazing calmness settled over her then, similar to what she felt while skating.

She knew she was about to die. The monsters were going to rend her limb from limb. But she was going to hurt them first, as much as she could. She was going to make her father proud of her. She pictured him, twirling the *anangkil*, teaching her how to focus her power into the hundred-and-thirty-centimeter-long stick.

Size doesn't matter. Your will and your focus are everything.

An eye on the approaching monsters, she reached her duffle bag, jerked the hockey stick out, headed back toward the corpsman.

She was a fast skater, but she was too late; they were upon him. In a matter of seconds, his head was ripped from his body as a spear skewered him below the jaw and pulled upward with such force that his spine and muscles simply tore away from the base of his skull. His body fell to the ice as a geyser of blood lifted three meters into the air. The monsters ran right over him, not heading for Miwa, but for each other. She realized suddenly that she and Kersen were not targets: they had been caught in the middle of some skirmish. But though she tried to stop short of the battle, she was traveling too fast.

In seconds, she was in the thick of the melee.

One of the big creatures lunged at her. Close up, she noted, they weren't ugly at all. Triangular faces like a ferret. Large, mobile ears like a horse. But the thing was upon her. She yanked the hockey stick's blade off to equalize the balance and then used the shaft to aim a blow at the creature's triangular head. Since the monsters ran bent over, their tails extended backwards for balance, she was able to reach her target with little effort. Its head jerked to the side and it partially lost its balance, but the hirsute nightmare spun on one foot and slapped its broad tail against her right side with a brutal crunch. Her feet left the ground as she was thrown sideways in a spin, the stick ripped from her grip; she managed to shift her weight to her hands and land in a quickly collapsing handstand, her back to her assailant.

As the brute rushed in for the kill, she thrust her falling legs back up into the air and behind her: the blades of her skates connected solidly with her enemy, and it gave a piercing cry. She rotated quickly on one hand and landed in a crouch.

Not waiting to see what damage she'd done, she retrieved her stick and skated around the monsters that were mauling each other without mercy.

One group was outnumbered and surrounded. Miwa was stuck in the middle of things with them. She raced in and out of their ranks, picking up the speed she needed to do damage. Skates and ice were not a good combination for stationary combat.

Another creature lunged at her as she sped past it. She spun, thrusting her leg out so the blade ripped across its upper thighs. Seconds later she had to leap into a single axel to achieve sufficient height to slam the hockey stick's shaft across the back of another attacker's neck, sending it sprawling in the ice. A member of the smaller group finished it off it with a spear and glanced at her.

Miwa had no way of understanding the creatures' expressions, but they acted less hostile in the next few seconds. An uneasy, wordless truce was formed, so she decided to concentrate on the brutes surrounding them.

For a moment she felt a bit of hope.

She might survive this after all.

Then a cry went up and Miwa, skating backwards and lashing out with the shaft, looked toward the forest, where another thirty or forty of the creatures were pouring out of the foggy darkness onto the ice. Despair filled her heart. There was none of the noble resignation she'd felt before. Her arms went slack, and something grabbed her from behind. She struggled for a moment until a blow to the back of her head brought the darkness of unconsciousness.

CHAPTER 7

IN THE DREAM, CARMEN WAS RECITING POETRY. *La infana raso,* just like that day.

"So much talk about the soul / while the body is maligned; / through taboos they bar the soul / from the sexual sublime."

Teri set down the bottle of moonshine. "But I have to be *more* than this body! Without a soul, I'm just a facsimile."

Carmen pulled her close, silenced her with a deep kiss. Her hands explored Teri's body, tracing her small breasts, sliding along her ribcage, easing up her thighs and under her skirt to that ready, aching center of Teri's desire.

"Your body is mine," Carmen muttered into her neck. "You are mine, Tenshi."

"No!" Teri shouted, trying to push the older girl away as her pale fingers slipped inside her. Physical pleasure and psychological pain melded into an inescapable wave of searing heat.

"Yes!" Carmen countered, biting Teri's earlobe. "You're our architect. Rip the foundations from beneath this world. Build us into something new, Tenshi, like you did on Jitsu. That's why you're here. That's why he brought you back."

"No!" Teri screamed again, awakening with a start in the darkness.

The feel of Carmen's fingers and tongue lingered on her body as she lay amid the tangled sheets, pillow damp from tears and mucus. She'd fallen asleep crying.

Miwa wasn't in her bed, she noticed as her eyes grew accustomed to the black. Miwa. Her sister. Ha. Not a sister. A daughter? The thought made Teri physically ill. Her head felt tight, as if ready to explode from an overabundance of poison being pumped into it.

My father's wife. My sister's mother. A copy. A monster.

She shook her head, hard, to clear the thought.

I'm not her. I'm like her twin. Like young twin unfrozen after many years. I never met her. I am not her.

She breathed deeply a few times, then got up and left the room.

The soft snoring of her mother and of Kersen lessened her nervousness: it would be easy to sneak out. She slipped into Brando's office and looked for his safe. Miwa had already opened it and taken its contents. Padding to the window, she pulled back the curtain and saw the snow falling.

"Merdo." There'd be no sneaking out tonight. She pulled out her datapad and accessed the encrypted chat she and her friends shared. It was late, so she didn't expect a response, but she left a message.

Pick me up tomorrow early. Like 8 am. Everyone. Josuo, Ronaldo—tell the bishop my mom needs you to clear the snow, or that you want to visit with the family, or whatever. Just be here.

Within seconds, her message registered as read by Josuo and Carmen both.

He replied, "You bet."

She asked, "Are you okay?"

We'll talk tomorrow.

As she looked up from her datapad, she noticed a black rectangle on a corner of the desk. Sitting atop it was a simple ring on a chain. The metal was unfamiliar, with hints of blue swirling in its depths.

It's hers, isn't it? So it's mine.

Slipping the chain around her neck, she scooped up the black device. As she clicked it on, the machine's display blinked in Baryogo: *Journal still unlocked. Lock? Y/N.*

Tenshi's journal. Without thinking, Teri thumbed *N*, closed the cover, and carried the diary with her back into her room. She set her alarm for 7 am and went right back to sleep, exhaustion plunging her into unconsciousness.

IN THE MORNING, WHILE MIWA PLEADED WITH RHEA and Kersen for permission to go skating, Teri made her move. There was no time to change. She washed her face, brushed her teeth, and pulled a down jacket over the school uniform she'd slept in. Then she slipped out the back door.

Using her snowshoes, she made her way to the place where her friends always picked her up, just beyond the hill near the river. A little after eight, Ronaldo's battered *teraplano* glided to a stop near where she was waiting. Josuo was piloting, with Ronaldo and Elisha beside him in the front of the cab. She squeezed in between Anyi and Carmen, who rubbed heat into her cold hands.

"Oh, Terinjo," Carmen muttered, "You must be so freaked out."

"Yeah," agreed Elisha. "How're you feeling?"

Teri shrugged. "Not bad for someone whose entire life has been one huge lie. I can hardly look at myself in the mirror, the idea of talking to my sister or whatever she is turns my stomach, and I'd like to see the man who calls himself my father hanged from a tree limb, but I'm doing fine otherwise."

Josuo glanced back at her. "You're a brave kid."

"Don't call me a kid, damn you."

"Everybody's talking about it," Anyi pointed out. "I bet lots didn't even sleep last night. You're one of the most famous people on Terego."

"Infamous is more like it. Were they talking about us poor clones? Fuck.

My life is over. Nobody will want a building designed by a goddamn clone."

"Well," Ronaldo turned around to focus on her, "the Prophet made it very clear in his address last night that you were our sisters. That the way a person comes into existence doesn't matter. Your soul is God's creation, placed within you by the divine plan. And the bishop nearly pushed Jos and me out the door with orders to make you two feel part of the Church."

"Wonderful," Teri said, "but I know people. They'll accept me superficially, but on the inside they'll be pulling away. Everywhere I go, people will look at me like I'm a freak. And they'll be right. Bad enough that I was born off planet. Now it turns out that I wasn't even born. I could feel people judging me for not being a child of Smith, but now I have to worry about not having a soul at all."

"The soul is emotion and thought," muttered Carmen, quoting *La infana raso* as she kept holding Teri's hands, "glands and brain. Without the body, naught."

There was something in those hazel eyes. A message. Teri wished they were alone.

"Of course you have both body and soul, kid," Josuo declared as he put the teraplano in gear and lifting off the ground. "What you *need* is a little fire water in you."

"No shit. Let's head for the clearing."

SOON THEY WERE HUDDLED TOGETHER under the lean-to that they'd built a few months ago to keep snow off the still. This fringe of wood was but a strip of sparsely grouped, stunted trees flanking the dense blackness of the forest proper: thousands of square kilometers of towering, gray-green ĉielarboj, unevenly tiered pinegoj and gigantic, umbrella-shaped filiksekojoj. Those titanic trees, their uppermost branches twisting together in an impenetrable canopy, seemed to shrug off the snow, scarfing with crusty ice the branches of the relative dwarfs at their edge.

The teens passed the bottle around. Carmen slipped an arm around her shoulders, and Teri could've sworn she saw Josuo wince.

The others were oblivious, intent on cheering her up with jokes and gossip. Teri knew that being surrounded by friends should make her happy, but she just couldn't clear her head of the thoughts that went careening through it. The forest loomed darkly, ominous and unknown, like her future.

"What's this?" Carmen patted Teri's jacket and then pulled the journal from a pocket, where she'd shoved it before leaving the house.

"Oh. That's her journal."

"Whose?"

"Tenshi. My... predecessor or whatever."

They all stared at the black rectangle in tipsy wonderment. Teri knew what they wanted: they were her friends, but their morbid curiosity had gotten the better of them.

"Here, let me see it." A little irked, she took the journal from Carmen, flipped the cover open, and clicked it on. Without hesitation, she pushed play. The display flashed *entry number 2.*

Tenshi's voice, *Teri's voice*, using strangely accented Standard, began to speak.

"December 11, 2671. *Domina's eyes*, I can't stop thinking about Andi. I mean, the bloke's like twenty-five or something, all old, but I don't know.

"On Wednesday he came over to my hakal with some beer. Tasted nasty, but I drank it all down. Felt good, not like moku. I could still talk and move and joke. Anyway, this Andi, he keeps looking at me the whole time, then he just comes over and kisses me. Kinda rough, but nice. He seemed embarrassed after, like he'd done something wrong, but I smiled, so he said he was going to see me later.

"I'm thinking maybe he wants to do it with me. I've never done it, though most girls do when they turn thirteen. Course, it's with a girl or boy or omedeyo the giya selects for you. Another step along the Path or whatever. Ha! Since I'm pan, maybe they'd let me pick the gender. Illusion of fucking choice.

"You know, diary, if Andi asks me to, even though he's an off-worlder and an infidel and all that shit that Santo and Apa think is so important, I'll do it with him. See how those two kotoran makna like that shit.

"Besides, I like Andi. He smells nice. He's handsome, in that soft omedeyo way. Maybe he'll take me with him when his tour is up. He signed on for a year, he says. Only a few more months till time's up. Let Jitsu rot in the Grey Prison for all I care, Santo and Apa and my weak-arse mother.

"That's enough for now, diary. You keep quiet about this, yeah?"

The display began flashing *entry number 3*, but Teri shut the journal off with a trembling finger.

"Okay, *that* was weird," Anyi said. "She sounds just like you."

Teri wanted to scream, wanted to throw up. It was as if someone had read her thoughts from a few months ago and transposed them to another setting, changing the names, but keeping the content essentially intact. She'd been ready to give herself to Carmen, and part of it had been to spite her par—no, *Brando* and Rhea.

I'm just a copy. Doesn't matter what people say, I'm thinking her thoughts. I don't have an identity. I don't have a choice.

Teri stood, shrugging off Carmen's arm.

Josuo held the bottle out toward her. "Kid, it's just a coincidence. Lots of people that age have similar feelings."

"Wait," Elisha cut in. "Teri has feelings for someone? Who? You, Jos?"

Teri started laughing hysterically. "No fucking way. Him? He wishes."

Carmen reached up, tried to pull her back down on the log. "Terinjo. Tranquila."

"No me van a callar, querida," Teri snapped in Spanish. "Not you with your 'Terinjo' or this bastard with his 'kid' bullshit. We're going to have a reckoning. We can do it now, in front of the others, or you can both shut the fuck up."

Carmen dropped her hand, eyes filling with tears.

Josuo recoiled as if she'd slapped his face. Then a calm settled over him. The other three watched the exchange, speechless.

After a moment, Josuo spilled the moonshine onto the snow and got to his feet.

"I think we need to take Teri home. She's got a lot to process."

RONALDO DROVE ON THE TRIP BACK while everyone sat in sullen or dazed silence. As they neared the rendezvous point, though, Teri spoke up.

"Not here. Take me to my house."

"But," began Ronaldo.

"Take me," Teri repeated from between clenched teeth, "to my goddamn house, Ronaldo. Now."

"Okay, okay."

As the house grew larger in the teraplano's windshield, Teri saw Rhea out in front, Jakobo heavy and awkward as she held him at her hip. Her worried gaze darted back and forth. The snow speeder was still gone.

"Wait for a couple of minutes," she told her friends. She dashed over to where Rhea, was standing.

"Sorry I left without asking. What's wrong?"

"Who are those people?"

"Just some friends. Three seniors from school. Couple of guys from the singles' ward. Mom, what's wrong? You're scaring me with this look."

Jakobo twisted in his mother's arms. "Miwa's not back yet, and Mommy's worried. Forty hours went by already, Teri. Where's Miwa?"

"She was supposed to return in two hours," Rhea clarified. "Brother Hardjono was with her, and he's not one to dally about. But it's been more than three hours, and I'm getting concerned. What if the ice broke or something?"

"Mom, that lake is at partially frozen all year, and first winter still has another three official days. But I'll go check. My friends will drive me up. We'll bring her back, okay?"

"Hurry back, Teri. Then we can talk about these older friends of yours that I haven't met."

Teri nodded and sprinted through the snow back to the teraplano. She filled her friends in on what had happened, and they headed north. Ronaldo's teraplano ate up the kilometers, and they soon set down at the edge of Lake Galileo.

The snow speeder was sitting a couple of hundred meters out on the lake. As Teri trudged carefully toward it, her friends following her wordlessly, her heart sank. There was blood everywhere. Her stomach a knotted ball, tears slipping down and freezing on her cheek, she forced herself to continue. The windshield of the speeder had been shattered, and an enormous shaft of wood was protruding from the seat. No one was inside.

Carmen had walked around to the front of the speeder with Elisha, and she started screaming.

Teri stepped carefully on the pinkish-magenta ice and saw what was causing the older girl to freak out: the body of Kersen Hardjono, but without its head. A pool of frozen blood surrounded it.

Nausea rocketing up through her body, Teri retched and a stream of hot, alcoholic bile sprayed the ice, sending little puffs of steam into the air.

"*Puta merdo*," Josuo grunted as he saw what the others couldn't rip their eyes from. Teri, recovering, lifted her gaze and scanned the area. There were darker stains, greenish-black in color. Gouges in the ice, like tracks. Drag marks heading north and west where large things had been pulled off the ice.

"I don't know how or who with, but there was a battle here," she said aloud. "Combatants dragged off the dead and wounded. Maybe they took Miwa, too."

Josuo nodded. "Let's look at the southern and western edges, see if we can find footprints. Maybe we can see where they went or if your sister got away alone."

"Alright, though they might've gone north. That's where the attack came from, I think. Notice how the speeder is facing that way? Look at how that spear or whatever was thrown into the windshield."

"Yeah, but we can't walk across ten kilometers of frozen ice, though,"

Anyi pointed out. She was right, so they doubled back and began checking the edge of the lake. Teri had to forcibly drag Carmen along; she was nearly frozen by shock.

"Should I take her back to the teraplano?" asked Ronaldo.

Teri shook her head. "No. We need to stay together. Strength in numbers."

As they rounded northward at the western edge, they found drag marks in the snow, which had obliterated all footprints the retreating fighters had left behind.

"Look!" Elisha called everyone over. He had found an enormous track, a clawed print some thirty centimeters long and fifteen wide. "Ever seen an animal that leaves a track that big?"

No one had. Of course, very few people had ventured into the dense darkness of the Great Seneka Forest. Its towering trees likely provided shelter for many species that the Ministry of Public Health had never catalogued. Teri wondered for a second if some group of undiscovered colonists had come to live in the woods and trained some vicious animal to use as protection. She knew there was no way the Teregan government kept track of everything that was happening on this world: Josuo and Ronaldo's stories of life on Kanaano had confirmed that for her.

She stood regarding the forest for a long time, then began walking toward it, Carmen's trembling hand in hers.

"Hey!" called Elisha. "What do you think you're doing? Whoever did this might be waiting for you there!"

As if his words were their cue, a score of dark figures leapt from the trees near the forest's edge and began racing toward Teri and her group. They were the stuff of legends, of fairy tales told to little children to keep them from going off alone. They ran doubled over, baring sharp teeth set in a triangular head. In their clawed hands they held long, rough-hewn spears. Odd ornamentation bounced against their massive chests and legs as they galloped closer, and their ears twitched back and forth attentively.

"Oh, my God!" screeched Carmen. "Teri!"

Teri reached up and closed her beloved's eyes with a gentle gesture.

So this is how it all ends. One last moment of beauty before all the confusion and frustration is clawed out of me by demons of outer darkness made flesh.

"Está bien, querida Carmen. No mires. Lo único que importa es lo mucho que te quiero."

On tiptoes in the snow, death bearing down, Teri kissed the girl she loved.

Then the beasts were upon her, and she smiled.

INTERCHAPTER A

From: sorall@executive.cpcc.gov

To: mukerjib@octant1.gov.af

Subject: Ethics?

Date: April 12, 2714 12:47:41 (SST)

Bud, what the hell is that renegade commodore of yours thinking? I want for you to try and imagine the backlash if Captain D'Angelo is the trial counsel in the tribunal of his own half-brother. Antonio, from what I hear, doesn't keep his hate for his father and criminal sibling under wraps. I know that Nick has some weird idea that D'Angelo is the man that we need to root out the demimundo from society, but I think that rather than make the captain stronger, this idiocy might destroy the promise he shows.

Putting that aside, I don't want to deal with the PR nightmare that will be on my hands if the trial goes forward like the commodore proposes. You do what you must, Marshal, but make sure that the people opposed to the continued prosecution of this war don't have any more munitions.

Leyla Soral

Prime Minister, CPCC

From: berdyaevn@os1.octant1.gov.af

To: sorall@executive.cpcc.gov

Subject: D'Angelo trial

Date: April 13, 2714 2:17:11 (SST)

Prime Minister Soral:

This is to inform you that Captain D'Angelo will no longer be the prosecutor in the Brando D'Angelo case. I've given his first officer, Commander Ashar Mubarak, that assignment. However, full disclosure: Mubarak is only certified as a paralegal, so behind the scenes Antonio will do most of the legwork in preparing the case. According to the AF Military Code, Toni also must be present at the trial as the advocate mentor of Mubarak, though he'll be there in a security capacity as well, if you understand.

I appreciate your concern about appearances, and I apologize. The Teregan government should be placated by this move as well. They were also beginning to question the assignment. But trust me, for actual preparation of the case, D'Angelo's our man. Quat doesn't have experience in tribunals and might bollox things.

Commodore Nicholas Berdyaev

Outer Sector 1

Octant 1

CPCCAF

CHAPTER 8

BRANDO WAS SURPRISED WHEN HIS GUARDS ESCORTED RHEA to a seat outside his makeshift cell—bars had been quickly bolted to ceiling and floor with crosspieces and a door welded to them.

The moment's upon me sooner than I hoped. How do I explain it to her? How do I make her understand that I do feel love for her, but what I feel for Tenshi transcends human emotion altogether?

But by the look on her face, Rhea hadn't come to demand answers.

Fear roiled in her eyes, and desperation, a furtive haggardness he recognized.

"What's happened? Where's Jakobo?" A sickening image of his son's body, broken like Tana's, flitted through his thoughts

She blinked, then understood. "Oh, they wouldn't let him in. He keeps asking where his *paĉjo* is, but they say he's too young to visit you. Sister

Nishiguchi is watching him up in the lobby."

"Give him a kiss for me, tell him I love him. But what's going on?"

"Oh, Nan ... *Brando*, they're gone." Her eyes started tearing up.

"Gone? The girls?"

She nodded.

"But not run away..." Her features twisted with sorrow, "Why are all these evils being visited on me? What have I done? I don't understand."

Brando leaned forward and grabbed the bars. "Rhea, I need you to explain. Please calm down and tell me what's going on. I can't do anything unless I know."

Rubbing her temples, Rhea explained. "This morning, Miwa went with Brother Hardjono to practice at the lake. Teri must've left before that, because she was gone when I looked for her afterward. They were supposed to be gone just two hours, but then it was three, and Teri got back with friends, some people from the singles' ward I've never met before. They went to look for Miwa and then only one of them came back... oh, God..."

She broke off, sobbing.

"You called the Ministry of Crises? You spoke to Roberto about this?"

Nod.

"What did the person who came back say? What happened to the others?"

"H-he was, was hysterical, said that the lake was covered with blood, that they'd found Hardjono decapitated next to the snow speeder and drag marks in the snow leading to the forest, and then he just broke down and started screaming that monsters had jumped from the trees and dragged his friends away. He had a nasty set of claw marks across his back. The crises corpsmen calmed him down, and he told them that he'd made it to their car and driven away with the things following him, *keeping up with him* until he accelerated past 120 kph."

"Did he see the others get hurt? Did he see Teri get hurt?"

Rhea shook her head.

"No. The creatures dragged them alive into the forest. This boy, Elisha, he was at the rear so he managed to run." She leaned forward, her eyes wide with some strange mixture of fear and hope. "Brando, they had *spears* and wore *ornamentation*. That means they've got to be intelligent, yes? We can reason with them, can't we? You can learn their language, get our girls back." Her face hardened, and her eyes narrowed. "You can *take* them back if they won't listen. They've shown me recordings of you from Jitsu. You may be getting old, but you can still fight, can't you?"

The desperation in her voice breaking his heart, Brando said nothing, just swallowed heavily. He wanted to do exactly what she suggested, but he wasn't sure she understood the implications of her demands. Rhea's gaze hardened as she misinterpreted his silence.

"Listen closely, Brando. You are going to figure out a way to convince the Prophet and the Prime Minister to let you go after them. You're going to bring me back my daughters, do you hear? After what you've done, you at least owe me that."

"Rhea, there's nothing more in this world that I want. And if they don't listen to me, I'll still go after the girls. I'm only here because I haven't decided to leave, trust me."

"Trust you? How do you expect me to do that?"

"All I can say is that my deception was necessary, and if you think about it long enough, you'll understand that I had no choice once I decided to bring those girls into this universe. Never imagine, Rhea, that my love for them, for Jakobo, for *you* was part of the lie. It's the only truth I have been sure of in nearly thirty years."

Rhea looked into his eyes for several minutes, then touched his hands, clenched about the bars like a pair of vices. "I hate what you've done to us, but I believe you."

"Then go bring me the Prophet. We need to talk."

AFTER THIRTY MINUTES OF TORTUOUS WAITING AND IMAGINING, Brando was cuffed and taken to another room where Disbergen was waiting for him. The guards sat Brando down and chained his legs to a table from the other side of which the Prophet regarded him coolly, flecks orange glinting in his deep brown eyes. Disbergen indicated with his head that the guards should leave. When they were gone, he began to speak.

"Rhea says you want to look for your daughters."

"Yes. I'm the most qualified person on this planet to find them."

"You are a wanted criminal about to go on trial."

"That too. You can't handle this on your own, Disbergen. And I don't think you want CPCCAF troops on the ground here. An indigenous sentient species, possibly hostile. Didn't the *Malavaro* detect signs of them when you first orbited? Didn't you have a clue that there were intelligent beings on this planet?"

Disbergen's unreadable face twitched a bit.

"There were some mysteries, indications of controlled fire in the forests and unusual, unnatural patterns in the growth of trees. Nothing conclusive. We've been here more than half a century without a sign of any intelligent life."

"You just kept this quiet?"

Disbergen smiled sourly. "Go ahead, Brando. Criticize me for something you have done on a scale that dwarfs my own silence."

Brando lowered his eyes. "Sorry. You're right. I can see the sense in not wanting to cause a panic, and I know you'd been searching for a long time for a home. It's just... these beings have my children, Zwel."

"Yes. The Ministry of Crises informs me they were still alive when taken into the forest. There are signs of a serious battle, copious amounts of the beasts' blood, which we have people analyzing right now. But the only human blood found was that of Brother Hardjono."

"It's possible that the creatures know of our existence and are abducting people to learn more about us. Or to bargain with us. I'd like to assume they'll keep all six of them alive."

"Yes, and Minister de Waal is preparing a team to go into the forest in search of them."

"Let me be a part of it."

"You're set to go on trial in a week. How am I supposed to justify this to the CPCCAF?"

"Try me in absentia. I'll be well guarded in the middle of a team of corpsmen. And why would I want to flee? I've got to find the girls, and I've got to bring them back here."

Disbergen looked unconvinced.

"Look, Zwel. Remember those botanists? The Pazes? All the outcry when they never came back from their expedition and it took the government nearly a year to find their ship? You never found their daughter, did you? I don't want that to happen again. I don't want to be like that little girl's grandparents, year wearing into year, not knowing, not wanting to admit... I won't do it, Zwel.

"If it makes it easier, think of me as a dog. A vicious, feral dog. But I've been trained by the best. If you know how to control me, the commands, the tone of voice, the gestures, I will be obedient and loyal. But there's a wild animal beneath that veneer of control, Disbergen. Do you really think that if I didn't respect you that I would still be captive? You now know what I did on Jitsu. I've built violence into my very soul.

"So use me, Prophet. Use me wisely. I won't fail you. I will bring Diadono's children back to it, bring my daughters and their friends back safely. And I will find a way to deal with these… beings. I know the deadliest Way. I know the Killing Dance."

Disbergen's gaze betrayed nothing as he stared at Brando. Finally, he spoke.

"Listen to me carefully: if I agree to this, you will be accompanied by several dozen corpsmen. You will be monitored at all times. You will only be given a weapon if a confrontation with the beasts seems imminent. And when your children are recovered, you will return to face justice."

Brando nodded. "I won't disappoint you. I still respect you, though I've violated your trust and have to live with that betrayal for the rest of my life. Still, I swear to you now: I won't flee. I'll stay in your custody. When the CPCCAF finds me guilty, I'll go with them and serve my time. I will not expose this planet to the risk of occupation. But you *have* to let me go. It may sound like blackmail, but if you don't, I'll go anyway."

Disbergen held very still for a moment, closing his eyes and breathing deeply. Then he nodded. "I'll tell the Prime Minister to approve the temporary release. But do not betray me again, Brando. I'm taking a great risk, with my people and with the CPCC, by allowing you to leave when your trial is only about to begin. Don't go rabid on me."

Brando understood perfectly what the Prophet didn't say: *or I will have you put down.* "I won't. Thank you."

"I've got a question for you. The CPCCAF officer in charge of prosecuting your case, the captain of the *Diomedes*, happens to share your last name. Antonio D'Angelo. This concerns me a bit: is he any relation of yours?"

Antonio? Brando felt a strange premonition.

"How old is this captain?"

"In his early thirties? That's what Minister Torres estimated. The minister also noted a resemblance to you. He was, of course, too diplomatic to ask, so I will: is this man a relative of yours?"

"I don't know. But I suppose there's a slight possibility he's my half-brother. My father left Earth when I was a teen and settled on Oceania. I imagine he remarried and had more children."

Disbergen grimaced. "We need to know for sure, so I'm going to have the Prime Minister talk directly to him. Even the CPCCAF has to have more ethics than to let a man be prosecuted by his own brother."

Brando noted, amid his swirling thoughts, that the Prophet had twice spoken of having the Prime Minister do something. He'd always suspected that Zolile Khumalo depended on Zwelini Disbergen more than was seemly for the head of a supposedly secular government. He said nothing, though. Terego's social system was no longer his problem. Finding his daughters was.

Disbergen moved to the door and called the guards in. "Remove his cuffs and take him to the Ministry of Crises. I'll be along in a moment."

As they escorted Brando out the door, he could hear the Prophet begin muttering a prayer. He wished such petitions had power, that gods actually existed. He could've used divine help right about then.

But Brando walked the Path. He knew he was alone. Salvation and enlightenment were in his own hands, on his own shoulders.

There would be no deus ex machina.

Just his own brutal skills.

CHAPTER 9

RETREAT IS BRAVE WHEN YOU STEAL A GREAT PRIZE FROM YOUR enemy's hands. Shalura's voices, those cultural daemons her people depended on for guidance, ran the proverb through her mind as she and her warriors retraced their path back toward the village. They carried with them the bodies of five fallen comrades, to be lifted into the highest branches of the tallest trees of their land and merge with the Green. They had died honorably, and they would be shown honor by all. The two injured drones were offered aid, but wounded warriors were trained to act as though they were whole, and they managed on their own.

Accompanying them was the strange being who'd fought at their side. Shalura could barely credit her eyes when the creature's companion had come into view and thrown death at them from its hard, hollow reed. It had never once put its lips to the reed, but the deadly darts had flown from the weapon nonetheless, killing two of her warriors and wounding three more. Shalura had speared the beast, though its head had separated so easily from its body that she'd wondered if it might be a spirit. But the odd, red-blue blood that had spurted from its neck proved its mortal nature.

Then the little one had left the snow ship that had sailed the creatures to the lake. It—she? Shalura didn't know—moved like the wind on long, shining hind-claws. She was smaller than a highborn and with less hair, from what Shalura could see—the body was covered in thick skins of strange colors–but she fought like a drone.

Seeing her in movement, Shalura could not help but think of the prophecy attributed to the Greenseer, that blasphemous outsider whose ideas had torn Shalura's people apart, leaving most of them dead. Followers of the Greenseer warned of a small, hairless race from another land who would come to the heavy-fronded forest, their weak appearance masking great power. Rumors said a priestess among these creatures, a highborn of much vision, would come to teach all the people of the thick-leaved forest, six nations descended from six *irhènzhõddá*, the highborn siblings that had crossed the gray-green foam-flecked ocean to arrive at the dark forest's edge. This alien highborn would provide the people of the forest with what they needed to protect themselves from her own nation, which hoped to enslave them.

Shalura had dismissed such stories as piles of fresh excrement festooned with flowers, but the sight of the small beast set her to doubting. The fighting was fierce: the Sháinkhÿngigg had left an entire troop behind to ambush them, an incredible feat of prediction in itself, while Shalura had but her eighteen warriors, several now disabled or dead. She noticed that Tentisùxa had scooped up the dead alien's weapon, examining it while beating her opponents away with her powerful tail. If any could glean how the reed worked, it would be the older warrior.

Suddenly Shalura had seen that they were surrounded. The wind-fast and hairless dwarf worked with Chakhìkhÿrh to dispatch an enemy warrior, appearing to take the side of the Ihéinghÿngigg drones. Without warning, another group of warriors exited the moss-strung boughs of the forest, and Shalura was only slightly shocked to see that it was the fourth Ihéinghÿngigg troop, warriors of her own shattered tribe, led by the heretic Rroggúl'it. It was true, then. Betrayed. Their own people.

It had occurred to Shalura in those brief seconds before the new batch of fighters reached the frozen lake that the ice-dancing creature might help her mete out punishment to the traitors. If her former tribe-folk followed the Greenseer now, the beast would be a great prize. Shalura had decided that retreat was better than an honorable end there on the lake, with debts still unsettled, under the baleful divine eye.

Retreat with the spinning beast in her possession.

She reached out and yanked the creature off her feet, tapping one hand lightly alongside her head in a move that Shalura hoped would render the alien unconscious and not dead, given the clear weakness of the creatures' bodies. Then she sounded a throaty call of retreat. As they pulled back, dragging or carrying their dead and wounded, she shouted to Òkÿdtaqh, fastest sprinter and best singer in the troop, that she retrieve the bag from which the creature had pulled her fighting stick minutes earlier.

A loud crack snapped her head around as she ran with the creature across her shoulders. Tentisùxa was running backwards, a tricky move, and she'd discovered how to operate the strange weapon at last. Aiming it like a dart reed, she launched invisible projectiles at the pursuers. Several of them went down, and the enemy slowed its pursuit.

"By the Green," shouted Eghonganë with her typical defeatism, "ninety hundred-lengths to cross before we reach the forest. We'll never make it."

But several more blasts of the alien weapon and fallen Sháinkhÿngigg deterred the enemy, who ceased following. Shalura knew this was but a temporary reprieve: their enemy had abandoned a direct approach and would show up within the next few days to finish what they had begun.

Though her warriors had run for nearly a day before engaging in battle and sorely needed rest, Shalura pushed them to reach the outermost watch station before nightfall. The spirit voices that guided her whispered that she must get hidden in a strategic position before the Eye hid itself in darkness. Trusting them to be emissaries of truth, she complied. It was a tricky decision, divining the nature of spirit voices, but her people had the wisdom of their highborn and the lore of the ages to guide them. Shalura's position as troop leader had much to do with her wise choices as to which whispers to heed and which to ignore.

Once they were safely ensconced in the boughs that builder males had artfully grown together into platforms and arched ceilings, she ordered the wounded cared for and the wind-racing beast bound hand and foot. She did not want those glittering hind-claws ripping through the flesh of any of her warriors.

Once the pressing duties had been attended to, she ordered her ten unwounded warriors to sleep three at a time in two-hour stretches. The other seven were posted at key points around the sanctuary both on and above ground.

Shalura was just about to close her eyes for a bit of rest when her captive began to stir. The skin covering that had been fitted tightly across her round head was coming loose, and strands of long hair were peeking out. Shalura crawled to the creature's side and carefully slid a nail under the edge of the covering, slipping it off. A tangled profusion of black curls, slick with sweat, sprung into the air. Shalura bent forward and sniffed: the thing's odor was not unpleasant, simply strange, like nothing the troop leader had ever sensed before.

With Shalura's head thus bent over her, the creature opened her eyes and recoiled, emitting squeaks that seemed to indicate panic. Shalura leaned back in her crouch, supporting herself with her broad tail.

"What's your name?" she asked. "Where is your tribe?"

The creature said nothing for a moment; then her fear appeared to dissipate a bit, and she mumbled something Shalura couldn't understand.

"What was that?"

The wind-challenging beast closed her eyes and moved her mouth soundlessly. Shalura noticed that the edges of her were extremely flexible, like that of a *sholdhu*, those slimy pink amphibians that thrived in the bogs at the forest's edges. The alien opened her eyes and repeated what Shalura had just asked, but in a terribly distorted way, worse than an infant clinging to the fur of its *súlkÿqa*.

"Are you mad? Don't repeat what I say, prisoner. Remember what happened to Tèdhanqhÿrhò in the court of Lejidhé. The icy northern queen beheaded the traitorous and haughty highborn for her mockery. You've seen me execute your companion: do you seek the same fate?"

The being blew her cheeks up and let air out quickly, which to Shalura was a sign of sexual attraction. Just as the troop leader prepared to claw one of the impertinent dwarf's eyes out, she began to babble incoherently. Shalura waited until she was finished, then turned her selfhood inward to consult the spirit voices that only the People, out of all created things in the moss-laden forest, were able to hear.

Some voices recommended she kill the grotesque dwarf, but others pointed out that the Çùthlÿngigg, that soft-furred tribe from the southernmost extreme of the heavy-fronded forest, spoke so strangely as to be nearly impossible to understand, which is why there was little trade between them and the northern nations. Perhaps, the voices suggested, the Greenseer was right, and these creatures did come from another land, where the *öqhihéinghíggu têsÿshuqh*, the People's language, was so distorted it could no longer be understood by the forest children. Maybe their customs were different as well.

Difficult to imagine, but not impossible. The oldest tales in her people's lore spoke of faraway lands and queens and other things that no longer existed. It was conceivable that the creature might belong to a nation whose way of life was vastly different from that of the Ihéinghÿngigg or *any* of the People, for that matter.

Shalura decided to trust these latter voices as truthful and God-sent as their suggestions dovetailed neatly with all the wisdom and tales she'd been raised up to believe and respect. She lowered her hand and leaned back again on her tail.

The beast began to squirm then, raising her bound hands as if pleading to have them free. Shalura hesitated a moment, then woke the sleeping warriors nearby. They stood, spears facing the captive, as Shalura cut the bonds on her hands and feet, the latter with supreme caution. She was curious to see what the beast wanted.

Immediately, the twirling dwarf fumbled with her feet and removed them. No. Removed a covering to which the claws were attached. Beneath were more coverings without claws.

Weapons, then. Not her hind-claws.

The beast leapt to her feet and rushed to the edge of the platform. Shalura was sure she was planning to escape, and the troop leader hurried toward her. But the creature simply yanked her leg coverings down around her knees and crouched, revealing a glimpse of brown, hairless flesh. Then a hissing sound broke the silence, and a cry went up from below. It was Eghonganë.

"What? Who is making water up there? You've wet me, unbonded pile of filth!"

It was then that Shalura understood that the beast was merely relieving herself. The thought brought laughter bubbling up from within, which exploded in sharp barks of hilarity. The other two warriors at her side joined in.

Trembling, the creature pulled up her leg coverings. She looked frightened for a moment, but seemed to realize that Shalura and her underlings were laughing, because she calmed down.

Then her face split into a horrible expression that revealed shining white teeth, square, not pointed. Shalura was struck by how truly bizarre these newcomers were: not quite highborn, short like males with flat faces and sunken cheeks. If very many more came to the forest, she might have to kill them all just to remove their ugliness from the eyes of the People. In the meantime, she'd have to stomach this one, at least until revenge had been exacted.

She nudged the dwarf back to the central trunk with the shaft of her spear and had the warriors bind her up again. Then Shalura finally got the sleep that her body craved.

Her dreams were of blood. The blood of her fierce people. The blood of her beloved *dóghae*, her bond-partner, Xiggèr'enth. The blood of her wiry child, Thõdhulazhox.

And the blood of her hated enemies, ripped from their throats by her own claws.

CHAPTER 10

ONCE BRANDO HAD SHOWERED AND DRESSED in generic corpsman field gear, he was escorted to a large room on the first floor of the Ministry of Crises. About twenty-five corpsmen had been assembled there. An additional pair of civilians struggled with packs of gear. A moment after he'd arrived, the Prime Minister, Minister of Crises and Prophet entered, followed by a chief corpsman that Brando recognized as having been in charge of routing out an illegal colony that a group of ex-Kunti militiamen and fleeing syndicate lieutenants had attempted to found on Kanaano five years ago. Elizaphan Sitati.

Minister de Waal addressed the assembled group. "Terego is facing its greatest challenge. Six young people have been abducted by what may be a group of sentient but primitive creatures living in the dense Zarahemlan Forest. Your job is to track these beings down and attempt to negotiate the release of our children. If that fails, you are to take them back by force. I hope, however, that we can communicate with these creatures. We have already caught the CPCCAF's eye as it is," here he looked pointedly at Brando, "and we don't need warships in orbit. So either communicate or dominate. We cannot afford to lose."

The Prime Minister stepped forward and nodded at everyone.

"It is important that you understand what is at stake. Minister de Waal has mentioned CPCC intervention. Gentlemen, ma'am," Brando noticed for the first time that one of the civilians was a woman, "we are dealing with the first race of sentient beings outside of the human race ever discovered. This find is likely to change Terego's place in the human sphere. A military solution is acceptable as a last resort, but communication must be repeatedly attempted first. That is why, despite his present uncertain status, I've decided to send Brando D'Angelo on the expedition. He is the foremost language expert on the planet, quite knowledgeable in both survival and warfare to a degree that dwarfs our experience on Terego. This choice may make some of you uncomfortable, but your comfort is not one of our goals.

"Also joining you are Sonali Dixit, a biologist from the Ministry of Public Health, and Vivek Roshan, psychologist and anthropologist from the Diadona Universitato. They are along for consultation, to help prepare you for encounters with the creatures.

"I turn you over to Chief Corpsman Sitati. Chief?"

Elizaphan Sitati stood stiffly, his hands crossed behind him at waist level. Pushing sixty standard, Sitati was a compact, arrogant man who wore his scars with impious pride. He was the closest thing to a war hero a planet with no wars could have, but Brando wondered how the man would fare when the real fighting began. And there would be fighting, he doubted it not. Humans could barely stand *each other*. He had a solid notion of how they'd react to a race of huge nightmarish beasts.

"Alright. We're on the trail of a race of nearly three-meter-tall, furred creatures with angular heads, sharp teeth, powerful claws and massive tails. The kid that escaped, Elisha Galadari, a high school senior, declared in his statement that they resembled illustrations in his literature text of the ancient legendary beast *Grendel*. I have as a result taken to calling the beasts *grendeloj* for lack of another name, so you know what I'm referring to when I use this term."

Brando was reflecting that Sitati was the most long-winded commander he'd ever served under when Roshan interrupted.

"Chief, I object to the name. It's demeaning and unnecessarily pigeonholes the indigenes as evil and vicious. I vote that we use the term *Native Teregans* to refer to the indigenous population."

Brando saw the Prophet nod to himself, but then de Waal spoke up, his pasty face flushing deeper pink.

"Until we learn more, any naming is premature. Let's not let semantic quibbling cloud the issue. Professor Roshan, your desire to have an open mind about the, uh, indigenes is laudable, but the chief is here to effect a violent resolution if the other two specialists and you can't resolve the situation. His job is not understanding and tolerance, but protection. Clear?"

Roshan nodded reluctantly.

"We will be transported to Lake Galileo in fifteen minutes," continued the chief, "where we will decide on a direction for tracking. Take your gear to the *koptero* and get ready for movement."

The corpsmen saluted and filed out, and Roshan, Dixit and D'Angelo followed at a more leisurely pace.

"This ought to be a blast," the biologist said cheerfully to no one in particular.

Brando grimaced. "They've got my daughters, you know."

She turned a bemused gaze on him.

"Oh, I know all about your *daughters*." Her face immediately fell. "Sorry. That was wrong of me. I want to find the kids as badly as anyone. But I can't help feeling excited at the same time. You understand, I hope."

Brando was about to reply when a hand on his back made him whirl around.

"Didn't mean to startle you."

It was Rhea, brown hair pulled back severely, accentuating the streaks of well-earned grey at her temples and the crow's feet that crinkled near her big, dark eyes. Brando's heart ached a little upon seeing her.

"Rhea," he muttered, "I'm glad to see you."

The remnants of Nando Miranda, shattered by the force of revelation, ached to embrace her. But Brando D'Angelo knew better.

She nodded curtly, but her eyes, watery with yearning and hurt, gave her away. "Brando, I'm proud that you're doing this. I believe you can bring Teri and Miwa back. That's why I'm going to return the favor."

"What do you mean?"

"I'm getting Judge Abhishek Sanas to defend you, and I'll be helping him prepare your case." Sanas, one of Terego's most respected experts in jurisprudence, had served as Rhea's mentor and guardian during moments of family tragedy.

"Rhea…"

"They wouldn't let me represent you directly, despite my law degree, because I'm your wife. But I think I know just the argument we can use to get the charges reduced and maybe force them to let you serve your time here on Terego instead of on some prison asteroid like Sheol where you can't see your son except in holographs and occasional faux-conferences."

"Thanks, but I have a feeling it won't work. The AF needs a scapegoat for their failure at Jitsu, and I'm a perfect patsy."

Rhea stood on tiptoes to get closer to Brando's face, which towered above most Tereganoj. Her eyes bored sternly into him. "I won't allow you to give up, do you understand me? I won't give up, and neither will you. We have a *son*, Brando, and you have a responsibility to him."

Brando nodded. It was best to simply agree when she got like this.

"Okay. I'll trust you to do your best. We'll be monitoring the trial as well as we can, I imagine. Sitati kept looking at me strangely during his speech. I have a feeling I'm in for a rough ride with him. He'll want to use every nuance of the trial to tear down my abilities. I know the type."

Rhea sighed. "Well, take care of yourself."

"You too." Brando turned to go.

"Aren't you forgetting something?" It was what she had always said when he was leaving in a hurry. He could hardly believe she was serious.

I haven't rebuilt my kludged self yet, not enough to refuse. Nando's habits are still deeply entrenched. And she's the mother of my son, after all.

Turning back around, he stepped closer to her and pressed his lips to her forehead.

"Amazingly," she quipped, "I find I still love you. That's good, I think, because we've been sealed. You and I and the girls and Jakobo: we're a family no matter what. You remember that, Brando, Nando, Kyosu, whatever name you call yourself. Your heart belongs to us. We won't let go of you."

With her so close, Brando suddenly felt transported to his wedding day, pulling Rhea through the veil as she whispered her true name in his ear: *Radhani*. He felt tears coming but bit them back.

"I …" he began, the words rising easily to his lips.

But other words surged within him, from Tenshi's final message.

I am in you, Brando D'Angelo. I am yours, even beyond death, and you are mine. I know that we will be reunited in ra-Yindawo one day. Part of a new whole. Together forever. Inseparable.

"I won't let you down," he rasped, turning brusquely and dashing to the koptero.

He tried not to think about her eyes on his back, once more filled with pain, as they had been when he'd first met her all those years ago.

SNOW HAD BEEN FALLING FOR A GOOD TEN MINUTES by the time the group reached the lake. Tracks were disappearing beneath dusty drifts. Sitati showed them how one set of drag marks led north a bit before disappearing, presumably when those being dragged had been carried, given the deeper gouges made by claws there. The other tracks led to the forest. Brando and two corpsmen scouted ahead. He noticed that this trail split, with a small contingent heading west while another turned north. He emerged from the forest and approached Sitati and the two scientists to explain what he'd seen.

"I think the group that doubled north is going to meet up with the other group that headed north across the lake. There's no way of being sure, but this is how I see it: casings from Hardjono' rifle are all over the place, even heading north. Perhaps one of the young people was retreating in that direction after retrieving it. There's a lot of this blackish blood around, so they clearly wounded a lot of the grendeloj or indigenes or whatever. I'm guessing they killed some too. Maybe the small group that headed west was carrying the dead to some burial place, while the others were taking the captives and wounded back to wherever they're from."

Sitati raised a single eyebrow. "This is pure conjecture."

"Of course it is. Do you have a better scenario that explains the physical evidence? We need to get *moving*, Chief. These kids are out in the open and heading farther north. This cold mixed with any mistreatment could kill them. There's no time to sit around spinning scenarios till we're all agreed. Trust me on this. We need to go north."

Roshan spoke up. "D'Angelo's hypothesis is not that far-fetched, Chief. Many nomadic societies had special holy places where they dealt with their dead in a ritualistic fashion, some distance from the region they actually inhabited."

Sitati nodded. "Alright. We'll get the koptero to lift us to the northern edge, where we'll make our incursion. As D'Angelo was just telling us, the forest is dark and dense, but also relatively free from snow, which the tightly woven canopy probably keeps out, right, Dr. Dixit?"

She nodded. "There may be a thin layer of ice on the humus of the forest floor, but that should be it. Except, of course, for the massive fog banks that will start moving in off the coast as this winter thaws."

"Perfect. Okay, everyone, move out!"

They loaded back onto the large koptero and were flown ten kilometers north to where the gamma of the Great Seneka Forest stretched its top bar eastward to the feet of the Katapredoj mountain chain. They unloaded their gear, organized their ranks, and prepared to start the expedition.

"Men, specialists: stick to your positions and partners. Report any anomalous or dangerous thing you see. No human has gone as deep into these woods as we're about to, so we must be prepared for things we've never experienced. Keep your safeties off, corpsmen. Specialists, you're the experts here, so we're counting on any forewarning you can give us about flora and fauna. There's four hours till nightfall, but we'll go on longer. We've got our IR goggles, and we'll probably be using them quite a bit, even during the day.

"Let's all bow our heads a moment, shall we? Each of you offer thanks to the Lord as you can, and beg his protection. We will no doubt be needing it."

For the second time that day, Brando wished he could say a prayer. He knew it would do him no good, neither psychologically nor in reality, but all the same he was tempted to go through the motions.

Instead, as his companions bent their necks, he stared into the black that beckoned at him from between the moss-covered, massive trees. He stared and was not daunted. He knew the black, and it no longer frightened him. It was the embrace of Umbini Mungu, one fourth of the Ogdoad, the duality also known as Henosi-Akeratosh. White-Black. Union-eternity.

The promise of reunion, of love that lasts forever.

Brando closed his eyes and pictured his daughters in the claws of strange beasts that thrived in darkness.

Then he reached out with his incipient soul and spoke into the ether.

I'm coming, girls.

CHAPTER 11

A CHANGE IN HER CAPTOR'S GAIT JARRED TERI from formless dreams. Her eyes opened and took in its bristling back, the sloping ground thick with icy leaves and moss, the pounding legs of beasts whose claws gripped the earth as they ascended the steep incline with little effort, her friends slung across their shoulders, grasped tightly at necks and legs. The beasts did not reek like she'd imagined monsters would: they smelled of crushed leaves and mushrooms, of slightly mildewed carpet that's been tracked with grass.

She didn't bother to struggle or complain. The aliens would not understand her, and from what she'd seen at the lake that they wouldn't put up with a weak attack with her martial arts skills. Josuo she could knock on his ass in a second. These aliens, though…

It occurred to her that the term wasn't fair or correct.

We are the aliens. We came to this world, guided by Providence, but we're still strangers in a strange land.

She thought of the story of Nephi arriving in Mesoamerica, a world away from his native Middle East. How might the seed of Abraham have reacted if faced with hordes of monstrous beings who were of obvious intelligence? For a moment she wondered whether she and her friends had been chosen for this mission. They had always, in their weekly meetings, boasted of how much closer they were to the divine source, how much more accepting of their future godhead, than other Novasanktuloj.

A shudder went up her spine.

What are the odds? The clone of a martyred religious and political leader finds herself in the clutches of the first non-human sentient species ever encountered.

Teri could sense the gears of fate, turning all around her. Gasping at the implications, she clung more tightly to the beast who carried her.

AFTER ABOUT AN HOUR OF TRUDGING UP AND DOWN MIST-WREATHED HILLS that took the group to progressively higher altitudes, they reached a subtly different section of the forest. Teri stared at the receding scenery until she understood: very carefully and organically, the trees and undergrowth had been shaped to create a sort of road with a nearly impenetrable covering overhead formed of arched boughs grown tightly together. The path soon forked, with a brand curving to the right and another to the left, even as the main road, smaller, continued onward. She began hearing muttering and rustling. Looking up, she saw shadowy faces peering from trees that had also been shaped into dwellings. The structures lost themselves in the gloom hundreds of meters above her, but Teri got the impression that the gigantic trees housed home after home at dizzying heights.

On the ground she caught glimpses of what appeared to be cultivation of different varieties of pale plants and fungi, and something about the beasts tending these made her squint and try to focus better in the half-darkness that late afternoon in the forest provided. She noticed small creatures running about and wondered if they might be children.

Not so different from us, maybe.

Soon they reached a clearing, which was illuminated better than the rest of the surrounding area. The warrior beasts flipped their prisoners off their backs with indifferent shrugs. Teri hit the ground like the others, with a bruising thud that knocked the wind from her.

"Fikantaj geputoj!" Josuo was now conscious.

Carmen groaned and looked over at Teri. "Are you okay, Terinjo?"

Teri nodded. "Yeah. Hang in there."

The warriors moved silently back, forming a ring around the clearing. Teri raised herself up on her elbows in time to see a trio of creatures enter the circle. As they approached, she noticed they were very different from the warriors: shorter, about 2.3 meters tall; their faces were relatively

hairless and protruded less; their heads and eyes were rounder; their ears,

while twitching about constantly like those of the warriors, were set lower

on the sides of their heads; and finally, they were covered in roughly sewn,

sleeveless leather robes that had been dyed green. Their arms lacked fur on

the undersides, and as the shortest of the three bent its knees to crouch beside

her, she noticed that their fingers were long and delicate, with nearly non-

existent claws.

Despite her fear, she thought they were quite beautiful.

"Ÿltnaer usïtíh xáenglerhu ashãkãkíqás qhö?"

Shit. How am I supposed to communicate with them?

Teri wished Miwa was there. Though they'd both had to speak their…

Brando's five favorite tongues, Teri'd always done it grudgingly. And her

inspiration for learning Spanish, well, had been her desire for Carmen. Miwa

was the real language prodigy. She'd be talking to these beings inside of a

couple of weeks. But Teri had no idea where to start.

"She doesn't understand what the fuck you're saying," Ronaldo grunted

at the smaller natives. "Don't you speak Teregan, Teregan?"

This elicited a weak laugh from Anyi. Teri wished they'd just shut

up. She looked intently at the creature, and began a litany in the languages

she knew:

"I don't understand you. Mi ne vin komprenas. No t'entienno. No te entiendo. Amo nimishmengeru ..."

Before she could continue, the crouching native leapt to its feet and twirled to face its companions. The three began to exchange loud rhythmic and melodious bursts of language. Teri noted, from the smallish bulge at the back of its robe, that the creature's tail was less than a tenth of the length and size of warriors'. After about five minutes, another of the three, an even smaller one with profuse gray tufts at the apex of its ears, ambled over to Teri and addressed her.

"Rau kamuno jon ka?"

Teri was so startled that she couldn't breathe for a second.

Then a foolish, sardonic reply leapt to her mind.

What do you mean, where are my drones? Do I look like a fucking queen bee or something?

The creature had spoken to her in Baryogo. Oddly accented, bizarrely intoned Baryogo, but recognizable and intelligible. She had to answer, but fear and confusion made her cautious.

"My drones are back with the rest of my people," she replied.

The native spoke more quickly, perhaps excited. It was difficult to understand what it was saying this time, but Teri got the gist: it wanted to know if her people were already coming to enslave its tribe.

"My people don't know your tribe exists," she said, instantly regretting her choice of words. In a matter of seconds, she had given the natives too much power over her and her friends. She'd lost the upper hand, lost all leverage. Brando would have lectured her for thirty minutes had he been there.

An alien race speaking a language it had no business knowing to captives whose families had no clue where they were and why—it was a losing situation. She was stupid to reveal their weaknesses.

"Wait a minute," Josuo coughed at her incredulously. "You're able to *talk* to these things."

"These three speak Baryogo. Weird, like with a speech impediment. No lips, I'm guessing. All the labial sounds are out. But they're speaking it, and I'm understanding them."

"And how the fuck is that possible?"

"Wow. Let me ask them for you. Maybe I can get them to bring you some hooch while I'm at it, eh? Tell you what: why don't you just shut up and let me try to save our asses, Elder."

"The others do not speak the tongue of Hijo Chikakunin, we see."

Hijo Chikakunin? Perceiver of green? Greenseer? The phrase was odd, mysterious.

The native continued. "Are they your bonded males? We assume you are a highborn enlightened by the Greenseer's holy teachings."

Teri looked at Carmen and Anyi. She could only guess at the role of "nenun jantan" or "bonded males," but as she couldn't determine the natives' sex, she figured the reverse was true as well. They expected such an arrangement. Saying it was so might give Teri back a little of the leverage she'd just lost.

"Correct."

The three conferred again. Teri recovered enough that she could completely sit up and look at her companions. She noticed that Elisha wasn't among them.

"And Eli?"

Anyi sat up, wincing as she pushed her long black hair behind her ears.

"He got away. Managed to get in the teraplano before they could catch him. I've never seen him run so fast."

"Fear does that to a guy," Ronaldo grunted.

Elisha had no doubt gone straight to the authorities, which meant that someone would come looking for them. And they'd be armed, because Eli would have told them about the warrior natives.

All Teri had to do was to keep her friends alive until the Crisis Corps arrived.

"No matter what happens," she said. "Follow my lead. I'll get us through this."

Josuo scoffed. "Who put the sophomore in charge?"

"She's always been in charge," Carmen replied, scooting closer to Teri.

"Says her secret girlfriend," Josuo hissed.

Carmen started to avert her eyes, but Teri reached out and grabbed her chin lightly. "Don't listen to that asshole. I've got you, understand?"

Anyi cleared her throat. "Awkward. We need to have a talk. Soon."

"Děngdài," Teri warned her in Unified Chinese. "First let me negotiate our survival with the deadly native species, yeah?"

The three natives were staring, perhaps trying to understand the interaction. Teri managed to stand and face them. The one that hadn't spoken made an over-handed raking motion, as if imitating one cat scratching at another. It took Teri a moment to realize that the creature wanted her to approach.

"Our high priestess, Ùshëshajirh, is on a pilgrimage to the Greenseer. She is not expected back for another twelve periods of light and dark. She will want to speak with you, to discover if you are the Prophesied One, Çèrhingÿl reborn. We would ask you, but it is not our place. Yet we cannot permit you to leave. We will let you stay in an abandoned but very ample and comfortable compound. Sekõtaldh will be assigned to you." The native indicated the first of three to have addressed her. "She will be your guide and keeper."

She. Kono nushi, in Baryogo. This lady. So they're females?

In any case, Teri had understood nearly everything the native had said this time. She'd been right: where the creatures could, they employed unusual or archaic synonyms for words with certain consonants as, due to their elongated, ferret-like muzzles, they couldn't pronounce labial sounds. Those phonemes were sometimes replaced by clicks or different consonants. Teri's brain was already making the adjustment for her, filling in the sounds she was accustomed to as the creatures spoke.

"You say the Greenseer taught you to speak its tongue?"

The ears of the third speaker shot forward and its... *her* eyes widened as she sucked her ample cheeks inward and puffed them out again. Teri had no idea what emotion this was supposed to express.

"Ah. No, it did not. It taught our high priestess, and she taught us others. We had imagined that it did the same for your tribe."

"No. The Greenseer's language is that of my ... mother's people. I learned it as a child."

"We see. A final request before you and your harem are escorted to the compound: would you make us a gift of your name?"

This time, she didn't just blurt out a response. She thought through the implications of giving them *any* additional information.

Teri sounded too much like Çèrhingÿl, who appeared to be a legendary figure they were hoping to find reincarnated. Though she might have to impersonate their expected savior at some point, Teri preferred to save that particular card for the worst possible eventuality.

So, instead of giving them the name Brando had invented for her when he'd cloned her sixteen standard years ago, Teri opened her mouth and said something that shocked her to the core of her being, the last name she would've predicted she'd give herself:

"Tenshi."

CHAPTER 12

ANTONIO D'ANGELO SAT IN THE FAUX-CONFERENCE ROOM, studying the data just sent in by Milint, the AF intelligence branch. Included were the present residences of all the major players in the Battle of Jitsu. Many had already been subpoenaed as witnesses, and the captain would be having his first officer, Commander Ashar Mubarak, contact the rest. The search was still on for the real Nando Miranda, but Milint assured him in a tunneled communiqué that it had excellent leads and would present hard data to him within the week.

Antonio checked his personal message queue. Another com from his mother. He sighed inwardly. *No doubt begging me to contact Dad. Make peace. Not bloody probable.* He could still remember Giacobbe's constant ridiculing of the military when Antonio had been a kid, ridicule that often had as its target Tonino, as he'd been called then, and his interest in becoming an officer. *Go off and fight? Why? Leave your family? Family's all you got, in the end.*

Oh, how he had rubbed the bastard's face in those words when the infotainment nets were streaming Brando's image and family history. Giacobbe's silence had felt like a victory then, and now that the silence had lasted sixteen years, Antonio refused to hack through just to make his mother happy. His father's silence, besides, had become like a badge of honor, and Antonio wasn't prepared to be stripped of it just yet.

Or maybe she's heard. Her former lover has been cloned, and I'm on my way to bring justice to the freak. She'll want me to show compassion. But the rule of law is above such considerations.

He dumped the message and contacted Mubarak.

"Link to the faux-conference room." In an instant, Mubarak appeared out of thin air beside him. Of course, neither of them was actually *in* the conference room. They were both in their hypostasis chambers encased in high-gee-resistant gel. The conference room, the real, physical one, was empty: the faux-connection just placed them virtually within a keshiki that duplicated it.

Humans had discovered centuries ago that minds connected to computers needed to be surrounded by familiar, real-life scenery so they could function well. Simple black rooms with floating icons tended to send a person spinning into madness after a few months. As a result, faux-conn had been born so human minds would be faced with an approximation of the real world whenever on-line for extended periods of time.

"Ashar," Antonio said to his second's doppelganger, "here's that list of witnesses. Be especially certain that you get that old Ben Wu guy to take the stand. Witness protection has been bent: he's on Peleus, that old corporate world in the Nereus system. Data's in your combox. Weird thing, bloke kept his real name. Crazy gerrie."

Ashar Mubarak nodded. "You heard the other good news?"

"No. What."

"One of the defense's witnesses died. Modupe Odoyuye. Advisor to Soral on educational stuff."

Antonio let out a long, low whistle. "That's a blow to them, no doubt. Guy was there, was willing to testify that Brando had no choice and was a good person, etc."

"They still have that ex-politician and Neog religious leader, Meji Pishan. They're liable to help win the case, if we don't figure out how to counter their testimony."

"Look into their relationship with Brando and his wife. I think we'll find something there. Keep your boys digging."

Ashar's doppel pulled a chair back from the table and sat down. "I have a suggestion. Start aligning the ship's chronometer with Teregan time. Their twenty-eight-hour days are going to bugger shite up for us. It's already an inconvenience, because I have to check that I'm not calling them at a bad, early or late hour."

"Alright. It'll be a bitch for the boys, but they'll handle it. Put the techs on it right away. Yeah, screwy Teregan time. When I was reading something they sent me yesterday, I nearly couldn't understand. Adults at thirteen? Then I got it: thirteen *jaroj*, not years. That's eighteen Standard years. Whopping 493 days to our 365. Details like that can really screw you up, so we need to pay close attention. Ugh. Non-Consortium worlds and their local time. Do they have the consulate conference room converted yet?"

"Say they're working on it still. It's going to be ready in a week, though. Just in time to start the show. What do the mysterious judges say?"

Antonio shuffled non-existent hardcopy on the conference table, trying to tidy up what he could have wished away. "The eyre's connection's going live in two days. They're ready, like always."

"What do itinerate judges do between trials, I wonder?"

Antonio grunted. "None of your sick jokes today, Ashar. Dismissed."

Mubarak nodded and winked out of the conference room.

Antonio continued working for another hour or so, until he was interrupted by a message that he had an incoming faux-conference from Prime Minister Zolile Khumalo. Antonio raised a virtual eyebrow. This was very unusual. Perhaps he was testing the new arrangement at the consulate's chamber.

"Fine. Patch him directly into this room."

Khumalo flashed into existence with the confused look of all first-time faux-connection users. He looked about him, his disorientation obvious, then closed his eyes and breathed deeply.

Novice. Can't even control his doppel so it doesn't show his distress.

Then the diminutive man recovered his composure and opened his eyes.

"Can I sit down?" he asked with that peculiar Teregan accent.

"Yes, of course." Just to further keep the politician off balance, Antonio moved the chair back without making his doppelganger stand up and "physically" move it. Khumalo did his best not to appear surprised, but it showed.

"Takes a little getting used to," Antonio allowed graciously.

He sees that I know even his masked emotions.

Captain D'Angelo had risen through the ranks of the AF precisely by finding such chinks and exploiting them. Scores of men had revealed themselves on the stand beneath his questioning. The Tereganoj would as well.

Every monster has its weak point.

"Yes, I suppose it does. Captain, I wanted to speak to you face to face because there's been a development that indirectly affects the trial."

"Oh?"

"Some young people have," the slightest of pauses, nearly imperceptible, "gone missing, including Brando D'Angelo's two ... daughters."

This man is hiding something from me. He miscalculated by choosing faux-conference. It betrays him like a com might not.

"The girls are not on trial, Prime Minister."

"No, but we believe they are stranded in the Great Senekan Forest. We have sent an expedition to search for them. I authorized my minister of crises to include your half-brother on the search team."

Though his doppelganger reflected none of it, Antonio was going apoplectic on the inside.

Let Brando free?!? Dare to mention he's my half-brother?!? Provincial, backwards bastards!

Then the ship's systems calmed his racing heartbeat, and he could reflect a bit as his unflinching doppelganger stared at Khumalo.

Stranded. Strange choice of words. His omission has something to do with that. Not stranded? Gone, but because of something else?

"I have a hard time understanding why yall would release a violent criminal into a situation where he could easily escape."

"First of all," Khumalo began, having adapted to the simulated environment enough to assert himself as he was undoubtedly accustomed to doing, "Brando is accused, but not convicted, so you calling him a criminal is still premature. Think of this as him being out on bail. Second, no one on this planet has his experience with tracking people in the wild. We need him. And, of course, his family is involved, so it is proper in our moral view for him to be involved."

Antonio purposefully let a brief flash of his anger seep through.

"You know, yall's moral view is a bit of a puzzle to me. First yall insist on keeping the clones as a condition for the trial, which flies in the face of every other human religion's views on such monsters, as it does CPCC law...."

"We are not part of the Consortium."

"...and now yall are allowing a murderous law-breaker free *just to track those monsters down*. Interesting that yall call yallselves Novasanktuloj. *New Saints*. I guess in these *latter days*, being a saint just isn't the same as it once was."

Khumalo visibly swallowed, probably holding back an urge to respond in kind.

I thought so. Doesn't want a confrontation. He's definitely hiding something he doesn't want me looking into.

"I assure you, Brando is weaponless and under the constant supervision of our crisis corpsmen. So as soon as the young people are found, he'll be returned to his cell. In the meantime...."

"In the meantime, we'll just continue with the trial, of course. Understand one thing, Prime Minister. The commodore is preparing, on my suggestion, to maneuver the *Shaka*, which is only ten days away, and the *George Washington*, which is about a month from you, so that the two of them are only a fenestration and a day away."

Khumalo fairly bristled. "I remind you, captain, that the CPCC and the Teregan government have co-signed several treaties which guide us in these situations. Threatening me with a blockade or occupation is useless and foolhardy. Imagine how many colony worlds, already nervous from yall's twenty-year occupation of Kunti, would leap on the opportunity to cede from the Consortium if it's shown that yall deliberately trample other independent worlds' sovereignty."

I pushed too far. Back off.

"Trust me, Prime Minister: I don't mean to suggest that we would blockade your planet or try to invade it. I am just trying to remind you that we, as you pointed out, have treaties with yall, one of them an extradition agreement. The section on war criminals is quite interesting. Maybe you should review it. If I detect irregularities in the trial, I'll make you transfer the accused into CPCCAF custody, and we'll hold the trial elsewhere. Just so you understand my position. Don't lose him. Don't play games."

"Since we understand each other, I'll take my leave." He stood for a moment, unsure of how to disconnect.

"You have to step back with your physical self, Prime Minister. Close your eyes and concentrate on your body, not your mind. Step back."

Obviously irked at being coddled, Khumalo did as he was instructed and winked out of faux-existence.

A secret. Well, nearly a million people can't all keep a secret. I'll find an informer, and I'll discover what these rubes are keeping from the AF. Justice will be done here. I refuse to accept anything less.

CHAPTER 11

NO ONE WAS SURE HOW, BUT WORD GOT OUT. Despite all the efforts of the Ministry of Crises to keep a lid on the story, there were simply too many people in the know, and many of them very distraught. Elisha Galadari had been kept, supposedly for medical and psychological observation, in the ministry's custody, but the parents of Carmen Allende and Anyi Ru had been told by a careless corpsman that their children had been abducted by unknowns. They, along with Elisha's mother, had camped out in a large kamioneto right outside the ministry, contacting their bishop and stake president along with a host of relatives and friends.

The sit-in was just the beginning. There was an obvious leak, as by nightfall that first day people were whispering about the mysterious *grendeloj* that had jumped from the woods and snatched the young people away.

At eight am on the second day, a small crowd had gathered outside of the ministry. Rhea drove by it after having dropped Jakobo off at school on her way to the building that housed the offices of Judge Abhishek Sanas. They were clamoring for justice, but Rhea wished they'd just go home.

The Consortium is watching too closely for us to start suffering from civil unrest, especially over an indigenous sentient life form. We have no orbital platforms, our handful of low orbit satellites and shuttles have been leased from the CPCC, and our only military force are the six thousand volunteer members of the Crisis Corps. Seventy-five percent of them are reservists.

Rhea's fear, her cause when trying to influence the politics of her world, was that the CPCC was trying to set Terego up so that the planet would have no choice but to enter the Consortium or be forcibly inducted. Pro-CPCC politicians dismissed her worries as paranoid, but she knew it must gall the largest government in human space that a world so vast and teeming with resources was in the hands of a small number of religious devotees. The CPCC would make a grab for Terego and the other worlds revolving around Chalawan; it was just a matter of time.

There were precedents, of course. European colonialism on Earth: hundreds of thousands of Indigenous folks dead. Most significantly for Tereganoj was the Nuova Pace Romana, which had gripped large portions of the solar system in its tyrannical claws for a century before the Solar War had exploded and left fifty-seven million dead. The early years of the CPCC saw a continuation of this exploitative tendency, illustrated by the case of

Ares, later Jitsu.

The kind of nearly absolute power wielded by expansionist colonialists is not only an aphrodisiac. It strips their humanity away, making them feel godlike but also reducing them to a state below the lowest animal in existence.

The most obvious precedent for possible annexation of Terego were the AF forces that had occupied the Sigma Draconis or Kunti system for fifteen years after the Kunti Police Action that had taken place from 2692 to 2695. In fact, despite the withdrawal of those forces four years ago, there was still a sizeable "peace-keeping" brigade in place to "assist" the Independent Republic of Kunti in its efforts to stem further rebellion or demimundan intrusions.

History shows the CPCC isn't above using military might to impose its will on independent worlds; in fact, it's very likely to do so.

Though annoyed by her fellow citizens' reactions, Rhea wondered whether she might, if not for Brando's trial, have ended up standing on those stone steps with the rest of them. She'd barely slept a wink last night between her own adrenaline-heavy nightmares and Jakobo's pitiful whimpering. Brando's absence was difficult: the abduction of the girls was painful. All that kept Rhea sane was the enormous job looming before her. Guilt she might've felt for not grieving like the other families was assuaged by the good she was doing Brando and by how her mind was kept distracted.

These thoughts roiling about in her head, she pulled the *kamioneto* to the curb in front of the stone building where her hopes for the future were being nursed. The minute she stepped through the door, she could feel the desperation. Sanas's team of paralegals regarded her sadly. The secretary looked with solemn silence at the desktop.

"What? Speak up, people. I've had my husband and daughters stripped from me in twenty-four hours: I can take whatever bad news has got you so glum."

The redhead, Marisol Cantares, spoke up. "It's Modupe. He's dead."

It was a blow. Rhea's strategy had hinged on two important witnesses: Modupe Oduyoye, head of Prime Minister Soral's Education Initiative, which sought to bring equality, modernity and cohesion to the many, wildly varying educational systems within the Consortium; and Meji Pishan, former Archon of Jitsu, founder and president of the non-profit Ecumenical Evangelistic Effort, attempting for a decade to put spirituality back into the lives of people devastated by demimundo activity before the war drove organized crime from their habitats.

Oduyoye had been the stronger of the two witnesses because he was a close advisor to the highest official within the CPCC. His testimony, his view of the events that led to Brando's alleged criminal activity, would have been key in demonstrating that factors outside the ex-professor's control had driven him to act as he had.

With the man dead, the race was on for another crucial witness on whose testimony the case might hinge: Ben Wu, who had disappeared from

CPCC records with his daughter Ya-Ting fourteen Standard years ago and had not been heard from since. Pishan wasn't enough: their testimony would be powerful, and their ethos significant (they had made Jitsu a protectorate of the Consortium, after all). But they were a religious figure, and while Tereganoj held them in high esteem for their efforts in renewing spirituality, the CPCC was notoriously dismissive of religion as passé, unnecessary, and divisive. The atheistic attitude was held in check by the many religious member states of the Consortium, but it worried Rhea and others of faith.

Ben Wu, on the other hand, was a war hero, having led the troops that quelled the Jupiter Uprising decades ago. He'd also accompanied the AF troops that had freed his daughter and fought the second battle in the CPCC-Demimundan War on New Beijing. Those troops had been commanded by the very Marshall that now controlled this octant, and Wu's testimony would be fortified by the positive way CPCC officials such as Bud Mukerji would view him. Wu had been Brando's commanding officer and had been present when the crimes Brando was accused of had allegedly taken place.

As she walked toward the judge's office at the back of the suite, Rhea said a silent prayer. *Lord, look favorably upon your daughter today. Help her to stop the injustice that ripping Jakobo's father away from him would be.*

The door swung open as she approached it, and Sanas's booming voice told her to come in and sit. She hoped his jovial manner would buoy her today, as it had many times throughout her life. The judge had been a surrogate father for her during her adolescence and had inspired her to pursue law studies.

"I see you've heard the news. You look even more draggled and down than the sycophants out front. Sit, sit, sit. Standing won't make it any better, child."

She collapsed into a chair as the judge glided his bulk around the room, tidying up his books and knickknacks.

"I received a communiqué this morning from the executor of Oduyoye's will. There were two pieces of correspondence attached: a letter from the deceased to your husband, which I've already forwarded to his combox, and a little note for you, which I took the liberty of reading.

"It's Wu's location. He's living on Peleus. They'd kept in touch. When Oduyoye felt himself slipping, he dashed off the little datum for us."

A smile stretched Rhea's face and crinkled her eyes. "Judge, that's wonderful! Shall I contact him, or do you prefer to?"

"Minister Torres has been calling you all morning, so why don't you deal with that and I'll see about convincing Ben Wu. I have certain skills in that area."

Rhea laughed and stood to hug Sanas. "Thanks for all your help."

"Not at all," he rumbled.

Taking her leave, she headed for her office down the hall. As she walked in, her com chimed. She thumbed open the channel, and Marlo's face appeared on a flat screen that flipped open from the surface of her desk.

"Yes, Marlo?" she said, arching an eyebrow. "I hear you've been trying to get a hold of me. What can I do for you?"

I should scream at you for causing this mess, but it wouldn't do any good. You're hopeless.

"First of all, help me understand why you've decided to oversee this Brando person's case. How can you defend a man who has lied to you so many years, who is likely guilty of dozens of crimes? How can you even bear to be around him?"

"Interesting question. They asked it of Jesus a lot, as I recall."

"So now you're trying to redeem this lout?"

"I would think that redeeming him is what we should all be attempting to do. Christ forgave the thief on the cross beside him."

"Brando has done a bit more than just thieve. He's a murderer."

"That's yet to be proven, and even if he were, what do you think Saul of Tarsus was before God's light blinded him and made him *truly* see?"

Torres turned his head slightly, eyes closed, and waved his hand in a gesture of disgust. "Whatever. Fine. Rationalize how you're trying to let his evil go unpunished."

"On the contrary, Marlo. If he's shown to be guilty, I want him to be punished. I just want it to be here, surrounded by people who love and support him and who are willing to help him walk a righteous path. Away on some CPCC prison asteroid, he'll never change the way God wants him to."

"You and your foolish anti-Consortium bias. Really. You're like all these officials who want to keep the grendeloj news quiet so the AF doesn't find out. It's a stupid strategy and it's going to backfire on us."

"Only if some Novasanktulo betrays the rest," Rhea quipped.

"Keeping a secret from these people is not going to stop them from interfering with us: it's going to make them interfere *even more*. The existence of another sentient race, the first one besides us that we have found on any of the dozens of worlds we've settled on. You can't possibly imagine that they are going to be pleased with our wanting a monopoly on this information."

"We need to resolve this conflict with them on our own before they find out, Marlo. We need to establish a relationship with the indigenes so that we can serve as mediators between them and the rest of humanity. We are the best suited for this job. Have you stopped to think about the implications of their existence? A sentient race, probably several tens of thousands of years old: they are sentient; they have souls."

Marlo's jaw dropped. He hadn't thought about this at all. "That means... oh, goodness. Have you broached the subject with the Prophet?"

"No. This is not the time to debate whether we are Smith's children or not. What has to be understood is that these beings are our siblings, Marlo. We have a duty to them, to their souls. We cannot permit the Consortium to mangle human relations with them."

"Our siblings? These monsters who've abducted our children? *Your* children?"

"Marlo, for all our sakes, curb your xenophobia and don't let it spread. This kidnapping is likely the result of their not knowing what we are. Once Brando establishes communication with them, we can send representatives and missionaries and...."

"You're hanging your hopes for the future of this planet on *Brando*? That Neog son of a Wiccan Catholic priestess? Have you gone mad, Rhea? I wouldn't trust the lying scum with my dog, much less with my future. He's a wanted man, I repeat, who was only released because our prime minister is too concerned with what the Prophet whispers in his ear to act like a true leader. I guess Brando was right in that respect: I'm learning quickly who the real head of this government is."

Rhea sighed. "Perhaps one day you'll be prime minister, and then you can try things your way. Until then, both our laws and our beliefs dictate that you follow his will and that of the Prophet. Don't forget that, Marlo. You are a Novasanktulo, not a citizen of the Consortium. As for his being the son of a Wiccan Catholic minister, are you going to start stirring up old resentments? Our problems with that church lie three and a half centuries in the past, back with the power it once held over humanity. Neither of them means a thing now. But let me make this clear, Marlo: if you do anything that puts my girls or my husband in more danger than they already face, you will answer to me."

Marlo snorted and thumbed the channel closed. Rhea sat quietly at her desk for several more minutes, musing.

We are going to have to keep an eye on him. His jealousy and bitterness could drive him to make a serious mistake.

She shot off a brief communiqué to Khumalo apprising him of her fears and then began sorting through the new batch of files the prosecutor had transmitted, as the law required. A buzz from the intercom soon pulled her from her scouring of the documents.

"Yes?"

"Sanas. Come here a second, will you?"

Rhea rushed to his office. "Did you get him?"

The judge shook his head. "Captain D'Angelo already did. He's testifying for the prosecution."

She couldn't help but hang her head. All her hope seemed to drain from her at once. "But… but I thought the Consortium didn't know his location."

"It seems he was in witness protection. But don't worry so much, Rhea. You need to read the Wu's testimony from his military trial on Jitsu: it was the basis for that planet's absolving Brando of guilt in the case. We'll use it against anything they get him to say."

"Yes, but we'll just be neutralizing it then. It won't be helping us at all."

"There are still other avenues open to us, dear. We can probably get much of the theft, possession of illegal equipment and kidnapping charges dismissed, as the evidence is pretty tenuous."

"How so?"

"Well, when he came to this planet, he had none of the things they claim in his possession. No one, in fact, saw him leave Jitsu with any of them. His statement to Pishan that he was taking his sister-in-law somewhere she couldn't do any damage can be interpreted many ways. In sixteen years, the CPCC hasn't been able to locate any of this physical evidence."

"What's left? Unmistakable use of illegal weapons."

"Yes, the antimatter bomb and transuranic explosives. On a world not under CPCC law at the time. A world with no legal restrictions on such weapons."

Rhea raised an eyebrow. "The death of his fellow squadmen by his hand."

"Here's where Wu's previous testimony does its job: he stated Brando had been manipulated into the situation by Santo Koroma and that he had no choice. He goes into great detail, so I recommend you read the file."

"The assumption of a fake identity, cloning of humans, evasion of arrest…"

"Those are the charges he's not going to beat. But on those three, we can probably get the eyre to waive the normal prison sentence to one here on Terego."

"I pray you're right, Judge."

"Trust me."

Rhea returned to her office, thinking about trust. Something was lurking at the periphery of her consciousness, something important about this case that she hadn't fully understood. Her mind kept going back to the lack of physical evidence on the ship. What had Brando done with, what was her name, Samanei? Where was all the cloning equipment he'd bought with his dead wife's money: gene splicers, vats, wombs? What about the AI chirurgic? Had Brando just dumped them all into space? Destroyed them?

Hidden them?

She suddenly found herself afraid of the answers to these questions, though she wasn't sure why. She had her screen display three images of Brando: at twenty-five, at thirty-five, and at fifty-two Standard. The first showed a tall, svelte youth with a hint of a smile at the corner of his mouth. The second, a scarred hulking warrior she could barely stand to look at, the pain in his eyes was so great. The last, taken only a couple of Standard years ago, a well-muscled, smiling pillar of the community, hair graying, eyes twinkling. Though the nose and ears and chin were different, you could see he was the same man as in the first two photos if you paid close enough attention.

Maybe I'm deceiving myself. Perhaps I don't know him as well as I'd like to imagine. What does a person so willing to utterly remake himself hold inside his heart? Can I trust such a man? What motivates him?

In an instant she knew, and she felt a bit of relief.

Love. Love was what drove him.

INTERCHAPTER B

From: oduyoyem@ei.cpcc.gov

To: juristoSanas@terego.os2.o7

Subject: Please forward to Brando D'Angelo

Date: April 13, 2714 6:17:11 (SST)

Brando,

Lord, lad, I am glad to at last find you! I feel my health failing more each day, but I hoped that I would get the chance to have one last chat with you before I join the Eight. (Didn't know I became a Pathwalker, did you?) Last week I turned eighty. I realized I'm as ready as a bloke can ever be for the final goodbye before I'm translated. I hope I can hold out to help your friends defend you.

I always wanted to tell you something, ever since you ran off from

Jitsu and vanished into the ether. You're not going to like it (you're as old as I was when I first met you and without doubt as crotchety), but here goes. Stop running, Brando. Stop running from the law and from what you did. Face the music. Quit trying to beat the game that can't be beaten. But mostly, stop running from their deaths. That's right. You've been running from that horror for twenty-four years now. It's time to face it. They are dead. Those girls, they're not Tana and Tenshi, no matter how much you want them to be. Surely you've figured that out, but you've got to go a step further and let go.

I'm guessing you've attained gnosis and have been attempting Hanga ra-Roho. And knowing you, you've convinced yourself that Nando Miranda is like Tenshi's redesign of Samaneino Teyopan. But she didn't have to demolish any of her buildings to have the second vision and become other-born. Have you been trying to build a self around your spark *inside the Nando persona?* I'm not convinced that's possible. It's more likely you've been stuck in the mire of your trauma rather than moving forward along the Path, Brando.

You don't *really* think she's coming back, do you? There's no return from ra-Yindawo.

Take care of your self (literally). Don't do anything stupid. I'll see you at the trial, if my body holds out.

If not, I'll see you outside the Grey Prison, old friend.

Modupe

From the journal of Tenshi Koroma

MAY 13, 2673

Diary. It's been a few months, yes, but after having my heart broken by Andi and Inten, then wallowing in a bunch of one-night stands, I knew something had to change. I spent a weekend at the coast, in the hamlet of Ombak. So different from Kinguyama. Folks there follow the Way of Shattering. I didn't tell them I'm the Third Oracle's sister, especially since they prefer the forbidden teachings of Mother Kosiya.

What joyful people, Diary! They welcomed me with open arms, invited me into their homes, shared their songs and stories. I was reluctant to visit their teyopan, but … meditation there is so different! I didn't feel lonely or disassociated. Instead, it was like I could sense the warmth of all their sparks surrounding me.

I broke down. Wept like I haven't done in years. I've needed this. Needed community, belonging. When I admitted to the giya that I've never had the vision, they recommended I visit the Shrine of Shattering.

You can imagine how afraid I was. Me? Speak to the Ramatini? The times she's glanced at me in the market near the ministry complex, it's like she can see right into my shitty, blind self. But I walked the trail to that adobe building, and she was waiting.

We spoke of many things, stuff she shouldn't be able to know, but does. Because she communicates with the Ogdoad, hears the voices of the translated, the chorus that is Sopiya in regeneration. She gave me the High Sacrament, led me to the inner chamber. Half-embedded in the sand lay the Urim, all jagged spikes and impossible colors, sent from ra-Yindawo to Jitsu to ensure our collective enlightenment.

The Ramatini left me there, my hands on that strange meteor. Then the world faded to a blue haze. From within it came my spark, a mirror image of me, older and lighter-skinned, but recognizably me.

"Don't be afraid," she said, a bronze fire in her hands. "The end will come too soon, but it won't be the end. You'll be translated. I promise. The work you start before you die will be waiting for you afterward. Stay strong. Persist. We need you. I need you."

The Ramatini refused to hear my spark's message, even though I was freaking out. "The vision, the message, is for you alone. Live with it. Time will make its meaning clear."

I hope so, Diary. I don't want to die. Not for a very long time.

CHAPTER 14

BRANDO AWOKE BEFORE DAWN IN THE WOMBLIKE DARKNESS
of the forest, the thick, canopy blocking out the green aurora that streamed
through the night sky. He slipped from the camp, evading the sentry's notice
with disturbing ease. The corpsmen were unprepared for this task. They had
been trained to handle emergency situations: fires, earthquakes, flooding, the
occasional imbalanced and armed person. They were brave men, dedicated,
hard-working. But they weren't warriors. They weren't even soldiers. Their
weapons were all of Teregan make, carbines with clips that held forty-eight
rounds of explosive-tipped bullets. A bit low-tech compared to other worlds,
and not automatic.

I hope I can keep them alive until we find the girls.

He went through his morning routine, warm-up exercises followed by
Wu Shu and jogging. As put himself through the paces in the near dark, his

IR goggles revealed the daunting battleground that this forest would be.

We're going to get our arses pummeled if we fight them. Need to find another solution.

When he returned to camp, Brando was greeted by a half-dozen rifle muzzles and Sitati's angry ranting.

"Who gave you permission to leave camp?"

"Nobody. You're the one in charge, and you were fast asleep when I left."

"On top of working with a criminal, I have to put up with his insubordination and sarcasm. Wonderful. Where's the sentry on duty when D'Angelo snuck out?"

Brando didn't want the poor corpsman punished. "Hey, Sitati, leave the kid alone. I could get past any of your men if I wanted to. It's not their fault."

Sitati's face twisted in amusement. "That's right. You're some sort of superman. Whatever. It's been twelve years since you last fought. I doubt your training has held up that long."

Brando sighed. "Look, I don't want to get into a penis-measuring contest with you," Dixit and a few of the corpsmen giggled, "but believe me when I say that I'm probably a better warrior now than I've ever been. I've not been sitting on my hind end the last decade and a half. Standard."

"Training your daughters is hardly the same as keeping yourself battle sharp."

"Believe what you want, Sitati. Just let me practice each morning like

I'm accustomed to doing. If you don't want me going off alone, I'll wake one of your men to accompany me."

Sitati smirked at these command suggestions. "I'll assign Carlos Chuquipoma to you. Corpsman Chuquipoma, you will awaken at five am to accompany *Professor* D'Angelo on his morning *exercise* routine."

Chuquipoma, a tall, pudgy man, nodded sharply. "Yessir."

This conflict resolved, they broke down the camp and set out again. The indigenous Teregans' trail was hard to notice in the early morning gloom and with the mossy *forbo* that carpeted the forest floor, along with drifts of humus. Between Brando and a corpsman named Stefano Chan, highly experienced in trapping large game like the *leontilopo* across the southern savannahs, they were able to keep the tracks before them.

After a couple of hours, Brando shook his head with disgust. Dixit touched his arm, tapped her headset and put up five fingers. He clicked over to channel five.

"Vivek and I," her voiced muttered, "have been noticing how you've been studying our environs, and that look of frustration on your face has really piqued our curiosity. What do you say to the idea of the three of us pooling our thoughts? We're the ones who are going to get things accomplished, and rather than trudge around in silence like the soldier boys, I figure we may as well begin working on the problem."

Brando nodded. "Yes. Good idea. Here's just a sampling of our problems, since you're curious. The natives travel faster than we do, so we're not going to catch up with them until long after they've reached their destination. We can barely walk five abreast in this forest because of how closely the trees grow to one another, making it impossible to present a frontal assault of any strength and making us easy pickings for an ambush. I'm hoping we don't have to fight for other reasons, though. These trees go upwards for a couple hundred meters, and I've a feeling the indigenes are just as comfortable clambering from branch to branch as loping along the ground."

"That boy Elisha," Roshan interjected, "told the authorities that the Native Teregans had leapt from the branches of the trees at the forest's edge, so that's a pretty good assumption. They've adapted to be semi-arboreal, though Sonali here theorizes the species did not evolve in the forest, or even on this continent."

"Ah," said Brando to Dixit, "so you've already started speculating about their origins. What've you come up with?"

"From Elisha's descriptions, they seem to be from the same family as our local kaŝtoro, the group that Teregan taxonomy refers to as *buŝmarsupioj*, warm-blooded bisexual creatures that can both bear offspring and impregnate others of their particular species. They can also reproduce by parthenogenesis in certain extreme conditions. Zarahemla only has smaller species of *buŝmarsupioj*, like the *kaŝtoro* and the *guruo*. But over on the continent of Novameriko, in the marshy central lake region, we find many larger exempla, like the *feneko*, whose two-meter length, powerful claws and broad, flat tail make it a perfect candidate for an evolutionary cousin to the Native Teregans."

"I read about those," Roshan murmured. "Scientists on Novameriko have some in captivity, and the creatures are remarkably intelligent."

"Yes, about like chimpanzees or dolphins on Earth. We had assumed that Terego was like the other planets we've settled on, most of which possess at least one highly evolved species that teeters only a few steps from sentience, as if simply waiting for a god to take hold of the world and fill it with his children."

Brando suppressed a sigh.

Novasanktuloj as scientists. Always mixing religion and reality.

He said nothing. However, all the statements Nando Miranda would've made in this conversation came unbidden to his mind.

I guess it's not so easy to get rid of that identity after all.

Sonali continued her musing. "Oceania has that huge man-of-war analogue whose craftiness has made it the official mascot of the undersea cities there. Dr. D'Angelo, you should know about Jitsu's nearly sentient species...."

"The oni? Yes. Endangered. And call me Brando, please."

LATER THAT DAY, AT THE PREDETERMINED HOUR, they shot a receiver up through the dense canopy. When the cone-shaped device reached the end of its cable some two hundred and fifty meters above the ground, it dropped back another ten meters and, resting on the top of the canopy, unfolded its antennae. Sitati uploaded and transmitted his report, and the members of the expedition downloaded any messages sent to their individual comboxes.

Brando had a quick note from Rhea apprising him of the situation. He felt a short jolt of guilt about the lies he'd told her over the years. It was incredible how she still could stand by him despite everything he'd done, and his head ached when he thought of her probable reaction to all that she didn't know yet. That no one knew yet.

When he read that Modupe had died, he felt an unexpected sorrow. He'd hardly spoken to the man in twenty-five years, but Mo's death was oddly painful.

Then Brando read the attachment, a note from his old friend.

Feeling a wave of despair coming on, he shuffled quickly away from the others and leaned against a tree trunk that was wider around than his own house.

Oh, you annoying gerrie, of course I know. "Impossible that such a dream could ever come true." Remember that song? But what can I do, Mo? My spark told me to save them. Told me Tenshi would return to me.

As for Nando Miranda, I've shattered him as a prelude to self-shattering. The last round of bricolage before umbono. I'll have the second vision soon, old friend. I'll see my eternal soul, self and spark in balance.

He thought of his journey to gnosis: fifteen years of domestic life, of idiotic arguments and school meetings, buying clothes and reading children's books. He thought of the girls, how protected he and Rhea had made them feel, how they had always, at least until just a couple of years ago, done everything together. A family, with all its wonders and all its faults.

And his regular trips down into that abandoned well to take the High Sacrament. Scouring scripture. Meditating and dancing the Wende.

Complete self-knowledge. Every ugly and beautiful part of his essence explored. The fragments of Nando even now yearned for the pressure of his wife's body, for the weight of his son, the boy for whom he had tried to be the perfect father, the diametric opposite of Giacobbe. They had brought him the peace he needed to walk the Path alone.

I'll become an arojin, but there will be a cost. What price will the girls, Rhea, and Jakobo have to pay?

One can run along the Path, Modupe. And that's what I'll do. Find the girls and run before retribution falls on us. Because this expedition's going to fail. I'll be blamed for more tragedy. The AF is going to come, under the command of my half-brother, the family honor and military tradition and the needs of humanity all trumping any deals with Terego. Then Disbergen's promises about Miwa and Teri won't mean shite.

If I don't keep running, they'll be taken away and studied along with the indigenes the AF captures. I've got no choice but to run and hide once more.

Until she keeps her promise. Until she returns.

A SIMILAR ROUTINE WAS REPEATED EACH DAY: trudging through kilometers of semi-darkness, reporting to Crises HQ, eating, sleeping, wondering. The three specialists had conversations like their first over the next couple of days, bouncing ideas off one another, noting and recording new flora and fauna, speculating as to the possible social structure and psychology of the natives. It was fascinating, but in the pit of his gut Brando knew it was all pointless. The CPCC might be able to deal with the creatures, but this particular expedition, he intuited, was going end badly. He'd noted vines, free-hanging and in nets, that would be useful in aboveground fighting. He tried to imagine the huge natives leaping from limb to limb, claws like grapnels, tails bludgeons. He tried to anticipate fighting styles and organization.

He had no guarantee that he was right about any of it.

On the fourth day of the expedition, the trail seemed to disappear. As he was hunting around for it, Brando happened to look up and see something very odd: the branches of the particular tree he was near had grown together about thirty meters up, creating a sort of platform. He shot a grapple line into it, and before the chief could stop him, he'd attached the line to the belt of his harness and pulleyed his way up. The upper surface of the platform was relatively flat and smooth.

This is a made thing. Intelligent hands somehow did this.

There were slight scuffs and gouges where either the creatures had neglected to retract their hind claws (the team had determined by the tracks that Native Teregans could do this) or they had extended them for some reason.

A fleck of color caught his eye at the edge of the platform. There, caught in the branches of a neighboring tree that brushed up against the platform, was a strip of purple material: a fragment of Miwa's thermal ski suit. He knelt at the edge and sniffed the platform's rim.

Human urine. She's alive. She was when she was here, anyway.

Shots split the silence, startling him so that he nearly tumbled from his perch. He launched himself over the edge, spooling out the line until he'd reached the forest floor again. Most of the expedition was simply milling about.

"What?" Brando demanded. "Why were shots fired?"

Chuquipoma answered. "Chief told a couple of guys to take down an *alko* so we could add its meat to our supplies."

Furious, Brando hunted up Sitati and confronted him. "Have you lost your mind, Elizaphan? Having your men fire their weapons unnecessarily?

"Don't question my command decisions, D'Angelo. We're only provisioned for three weeks and we're nearing the end of the first. We need to replenish our stores."

"What do you propose to do with the meat from that alko: cook it? Smoke it? If the gunshots didn't draw the creatures' attention to us, a fire will certainly do the trick. It's too cold to jerk the meat, so…."

"So we're just going to wrap it and bring it with us. The temperature's low enough to keep it from spoiling, professor. A man with a doctor's degree should know enough for that."

"I also know enough to understand that in two more weeks we could kill the game we need, instead of killing it now and carrying its bloody remains with us so that nocturnal beasts can use their keen sense of smell to track us."

"They're in front of us." Sitati's tone was dismissive, and he halfway turned to another corpsman.

"What about the other group?"

Sitati stopped and glanced with irritated confusion back at Brando. "What do you mean?"

Brando wanted to punch the chief right in the middle of his puzzled-looking face. "The group that set off to the west but then turned north. They've no doubt come up around the forest's bend to the east. Now they're either approaching from behind toward wherever their friends went, or they're on an intercept course that will draw them close to us. I can't believe you haven't thought of this. Maybe I should start telling you what to do if you can't figure it out alone."

"That's enough from you, Brando. Shut up and go back with the other eggheads. I'll handle this expedition as I determine is best, you lousy criminal, and you can either follow along, or I'll have a group of my men escort you back to your cell."

Brando gave an incredulous shake of his head. "You would. Your power over these men, your image in people's mind, your pride and honor are more important than listening to sense. Fine. I'll figure out a way to keep you alive, Sitati, after most of us are slaughtered because of your stupidity. I'll keep you alive and remind you every minute of what you've done."

Sitati was livid. "Corpsman Chuquipoma, please escort this hostile prisoner back with the specialists and keep your weapon trained on him. If he leaves their side, I want you to shoot him. Chan, you say you've found where the trail picks up again? Let's get moving, then."

Brando knew he shouldn't have pushed so hard, but he was sick of it. As the group began to move forward, he wondered how many folks had been killed throughout history because of honor and pride. Brando had neither. No honor, no pride, no dignity. Just the Path and a family he would keep safe no matter the cost.

Early the next morning, the forest around them grew different. Brando noticed one, two, a dozen trees with platforms similar to the one Miwa had been on, but these platforms had branches woven into arching roofs and walls of vines and thick moss. Despite the apparent emptiness of what was gradually taking shape as a village, Sitati sensibly deployed his men in groups of three to do an armed patrol. They found fields of *daturoj* and other edible plants that required little or no sunlight. They discovered latrines and a few large structures on the ground apparently hewn from deadwood.

Roshan was fascinated, his wide-open eyes bulging even further. "I bet these ground-level buildings are schools or training facilities of some type. One of them has a collection of spears inside of a length younger Native Teregans could use. See that clearing in the middle? I bet that's like a communal meeting place. I would do anything to see this village teeming with inhabitants."

Brando couldn't shake the feeling that, though he knew nothing of these creatures or how they lived, something was very wrong here. The corpsman the chief had sent up into the dwellings rappelled down the trunks quickly to report that they were empty of creatures, but that they were full of artifacts: pottery, animal skins and the like. Roshan's face lit up, and Brando knew he was about to request permission to visit one of the buildings, when a cry went up from above them. It was Chan, who had gone up into the higher levels of the trees. As he spooled his way down, everyone could see his distress.

"Were there other dwellings higher up?" Sitati demanded.

Chan nodded, his face pale.

"Report, corpsman. Were there any bodies inside?"

"N-no, sir. The dwellings were fancier than these, with more stuff inside, but not the bodies." His lips moved dumbly; then he cleared his throat.

"Those I found higher up. Oh, God have mercy on us." He broke down then, sobbing and retching. Brando stepped forward without a word, unsnapped the pulley from Chan's belt, slapped it onto his own harness, and began zooming upward, ignoring Chief Sitati's screamed threats. The branches whizzed past as D'Angelo cleared one, two, three levels of dwellings, each more ornate than the previous. He slowed his ascent as he neared the branches right beneath the top of the forest, stopping as he reached the end of the cable right below the thick limb that Chan had shot the grapple into. The smell nearly made him vomit, and the sight was enough to turn a weaker man's brain to jelly.

There, in the branches that actually felt the sun's rays directly, hundreds and hundreds of corpses lay rotting, crawling with strange lizards and bugs, infusing with nitrogen the canopy soil that lay thick on the boughs. The entire village seemed to have been slaughtered, adults and children both. Their state of decomposition indicated that they'd been killed well over a week ago, so his daughters and their friends probably weren't among them, though he now realized how much danger the young people faced.

For in a painful wrenching of awareness, Brando saw his mistake. After berating Elizaphan's orders again and again, he realized he himself would be responsible for the expedition's destruction.

The second group of natives, the one that had headed west then north, hadn't planned to rendezvous with the first. It meant to track it down and destroy it. The two groups were at war, and Brando had placed thirty puny humans in the middle of that struggle. He'd shoved his theory down Sitati's throat without sufficient investigation of the scene. In his haste to save his daughters, he had set in motion the likely deaths of innocent people. By the time this expedition was over, he would more than have earned the sentence his trial would fetch him.

AS HE WRAPPED A BANDANA AROUND HIS FACE and began jumping from limb to limb to verify that none of the corpses were human, another consequence of his miscalculation struck him, this time nearly making him cry out in despair.

The group that had headed west had split up. What if some of the kids were in the pack that had continued westward? What if all of them were?

No. I found that scrap of her clothes. Chan showed me human excrement.

But not much. What one person would leave behind. In a moment of clarity, he understood that only Miwa was with the group they were following. That meant that Teri and her four friends were weeks away by now.

An even more chilling understanding settled over him. He was going to have to choose. If he told Elizaphan, the chief would send off a message. They might be ordered to turn back and track the other group. Disastrous if, as Brando suspected, the enemies of these dead beasts were coming up behind the humans. The group might simply be airlifted out, as the danger would be considered too great to keep the expedition going forward. If hundreds of the beasts had been massacred this way, what chance had thirty humans? Turn around, bump into the enemy. Go forward, bump into the desperate ones being chased. One human…no, *clone* life versus thirty. Five more to the southwest. Airlift from the canopy.

And after they airlift us out, after they grasp the mistake I made, they'll put me back in my cell. There's no way they'll let me try to track Teri down. Rhea said the AF was livid about my coming along in the first place. There'll be no second chance for me.

Clambering down from the highest branches, Brando knelt on a limb that his kamioneto could've driven down and began pound his left fist against the bark until the cloned skin had split and blood was oozing out. He gritted his teeth and gave his head a violent shake, but a sob still broke free.

"I'm so sorry, Teri. So sorry."

He could only save Miwa. He would say nothing of his conclusions. He would try to protect his companions, but he would let them all die if he had to.

Life, again, had left him no choice.

Teri would have to survive the best she could alone. Brando was, once again, going to fail her.

CHAPTER 15

THAT FIRST NIGHT, MIWA WAS SURE THE CREATURES were going to kill her as she squatted to pee. It was a horrible thing, being a captive. Not romantic at all, like fairy tales and books about pirates made it seem. You still had to pee and poop, with no bidet to clean you, just leaves. You couldn't brush your teeth. Your hair got all nasty and your clothes started to chafe you. If you were a girl, you'd better hope that like Miwa, your period was irregular and didn't come very often, because you weren't going to have time to change your sanitary napkins.

And, of course, you were in constant danger of being killed by your captors. When they were huge beasts straight out of some ancient Earth legend, this last worry made the others pale in comparison.

They never allowed her to walk while they traveled across the ground because she tended to slow them down. She spent her days lying across the shoulder of one warrior or another, listening to their low, hushed speech. Many of the natives never said a word, but the three that were in charge of her did, and that was good.

She had to learn their language as fast as she was able.

She first picked up the commands they grunted at her: *atath* meant "walk"; *uttits* "climb up"; *thèshaetsh*, with a falling tone on the first vowel, "eat." When she heard the leader, a slender beast with striking markings across the fur of her face, ask those in charge of her "*Lòdih adadhih qhö?*" enough times, she began making generalizations about their grammar. Verbs probably became past tense by voicing consonants, like /t/ to /d/. "Qhö" was a question particle. *Lòdih* meant "her" or "it" or something similar, since all the creatures used the word to refer to her.

The sound system was difficult. Three different tones. Vowels of long and short duration. Dental, alveolar and palatal versions of what in Earth languages were the same consonants, not as allophones, but as distinct, meaningful sounds that created minimal pairs with different meanings. A complete lack of labial sounds, due to the creatures' mouth structure, which reminded Miwa of ferrets or kaŝtoroj. And a host of clicks, inhaled and exhaled. The creatures also made a sound she just couldn't duplicate, no matter how she tried as she shivered herself to sleep beneath smelly skins each evening: a sort of harmonic produced by the vibration of their teeth. It was added to vowels quite often, though she didn't know why. In the mental picture of the language she was creating to while the time away, she put an umlaut over vowels to indicate this harmonic buzz.

No matter how much of a linguistic prodigy her dad praised her for being, it was slow going. If she were still alive, maybe in a few months she'd be able to halfway communicate with them. As it was, she could merely spit back their words with a lousy accent that made them bark their frightening laugh. As surreptitiously as she could, she snuck out her notepad, recording what they were saying. Her plan was to start playing everything back through her earbuds late at night, taking notes and doing her very best to crack the language. Her survival might depend on it.

Toward evening on the second day, after waking up rather late and traveling at a slow trot rather than a full-out run, they reached a sort of village made up of fancier versions of the platform where she'd peed on the sentries. Another group of warriors slipped from the trees and joined Miwa's group in the center of the town, a good-sized clearing where the forbo had been worn down till only black soil remained. There was a long discussion between the leader and a few of the new ones. They were obviously debating what to do with Miwa, as they kept gesturing toward her with their elbows. Miwa wondered where the inhabitants of the village had gone. It seemed too extensive for only thirty, forty warriors to live in.

After nearly an hour, the leader and another two warriors dashed up the trunk of a tree like gigantic squirrels and disappeared in the gloom above. A few minutes later, they scrambled back down, though the leader did so more acrobatically, gripping a vine in her hind claws, rappelling face-first down the tree and flipping off to land in a crouch in the center of the clearing. She stood, tilted her head back, and let forth a terrible, terrible cry that made Miwa want to get up and run as far as she could despite her bound feet and hands. The others joined their leader, and the harrowing sound that lifted itself up to the canopy made Miwa want to die.

Then they all fell silent and crouched in a circle, leaning back on their tails, while the fast-running warrior Miwa mentally called *Lightning*, the one in charge of carrying her backpack, approached the center of the circle and, accompanied by percussive instruments and strange reed pipes, began to sing.

It was an unearthly song, and it got under Miwa's skin. The rhythm was complex and disturbingly always on the edge of losing sync with the pipes and singer, whose melody and harmony danced along the scales Miwa's ears were accustomed to and in-between the notes as well, in uncomfortable tonal places for her mind. The words loped out of Lightning's mouth like a troop of warriors, without any rhyme that Miwa could pick up, but employing a musicality of short and long syllables plus contrast between tones and voicing.

Once she stopped analyzing the song as if her dad were going to test her on it, she felt herself transported by its flow. She imagined herself as a child, but not on Terego. She was Tana, and she walked with Teri, all grown up, through dusty streets in some desert town on a dying planet light years away. Brando, her father, was coming toward them: he was young and handsome, and a silly smile stretched across his face. Then the song turned strikingly aggressive, and the vision was lost as Lightning and the musicians brought their lay to a concluding crescendo.

I'm not Tana. Who was Tana, anyway? She didn't live long enough to be anyone. How can I compare myself to a little girl who basically never did anything? This is just stupid. Too much time on my hands. Better use it to figure out how to survive.

But family was on her mind now, and she thought of her mom and little Jakobo, who liked to sneak into her room and lie next to her when he had nightmares sometimes. He called Miwa his second mommy.

Stop this. If they see weakness in me, it's all over. Right now they seem to respect me as if I'm a warrior like them, a prisoner of war. If I fall apart thinking of how much I miss my family, it'll ruin my chances here.

That night, they all slept in the clearing. The temperature dropped and dropped, and not even her thermal suit plus the skin they'd draped over her could keep out the cold. She shivered and moaned; the leader of the troop got up and came over.

"Khÿtasih ÿltihàl, 'tuzhõ qhö?" Miwa wasn't positive, but she was pretty sure that *khÿtas* meant "want" and *ÿltih* "what," while *'tuzhõ* was the word they always used when talking straight to her. It probably meant "you," though she never heard them use it with each other. So, ignoring the different endings, which she hadn't begun to grasp yet, the leader, Stripey, was asking her what she wanted. She struggled to think for the word for cold. She'd heard it used several times when the warriors had given her the skin she used as a blanket.

"Sòrhílah."

"Khÿtasih sòrhílahàl, 'tuzhõ qhö?"

Miwa nodded her head. Stripey just stood there.

She doesn't know what nodding is, dimwit!

"*Lá.*" She was pretty sure that meant "right" or "yes." It was a word she heard often.

Stripey just stood there a long minute, her eyes flicking back and forth at the sleeping forms of her warriors, curled around their spears and arbalests. The warrior tilted her head back and looked at the canopy. A whimper, the first sign of weakness Miwa'd ever heard from her, gargled softly in her long, muscled throat. Then, unexpectedly, she lay on the ground beside Miwa and wrapped her body around the human girl.

Miwa's heart was racing. She thought she'd known fear before but having this creature's limbs entwine her was the scariest experience of her life. But Stripey didn't move once she had Miwa in her strange embrace. Miwa had learned already about the thickness of their fur, layered in such a way that heat was retained and moisture repelled. Now the native leader's body worked like an enormous hunk of insulation, blocking the cold.

It wasn't long before the chill left Miwa's bones and she fell into a deep sleep with dreams full of the sound of strange music and the smell of crushed leaves.

CHAPTER 16

JUNE 17, 2674. LAST NIGHT ISABELLA AND I MADE LOVE FOR THE FIRST TIME."

Teri glanced over at Carmen, who was curled up on a thick fur nearby, head propped on her hands. The older girl's face flushed red as Tenshi's voice began to narrate her sexual encounter with biologist Isabella Spinelli.

Carmen and Teri had spent the last day and a half listening intently to the story of how the two had met four decades ago, how their unlikely friendship had bridged the eight-year gap in their ages, how they'd come realize they were falling in love.

Their obsession with the romance had been punctuated by deeper and deeper kisses. They'd fallen asleep several times, awakening to find their limbs entangled, faces close.

"I twisted my fingers in her hair as her tongue made its slow way down my belly to—"

Carmen jumped up and hit pause on the journal, beet-red and out-of-breath.

"Wow, okay, that's a little too much, Terinjo. Let's, uh, go down and check on the others."

They clambered down a rope ladder to the males' platform that sat beneath the highborn's living quarters. In order to convince their captors that Teri was an important personage they had to respect, the others were sleeping there, pretending to be her spouses.

"Oh, here comes the princess and her favorite concubine," Josuo snarled as Teri and Carmen parted a curtain of vines and greeted their friends. "You're really worrying me, kid. This is the second night you've slept up there and left us down here. The beasts are all calling you Tenshi, and I'll bet you've been listening to that journal every free moment you have."

Anyi raised an eyebrow at Carmen. "And you. I thought I knew you. We grew up together. But spending the night with her, knowing her ... sinful desire for you?"

"Sinful?" Carmen retorted. "Like drinking moonshine, smoking cigarettes and reading illegal poetry isn't sinful?"

Ronaldo sighed. "It's a matter of degree, Carmen. Yes, we've sinned. But you're going down a road that's not natural."

"Hey, asshole," Teri called. Ronaldo's eyes jerked toward her. "Being a clone might be unnatural. But what I feel for Carmen is the most natural thing in the universe. I was born this way, just like Tenshi was. If you have a problem with my queerness, take it up with God."

"Queerness? You just need the right man to set you straight," Josuo grunted.

"Like you tried to do when you kissed a minor against her will?" Anyi's eyes went wide at this revelation. "I think what's bugging *you* in particular, *Elder*, is that you're a part of *my* harem instead of the other way around. Think I don't get why you're hanging out with three high school girls, you fucking predator?"

Josuo shot her an ugly look. They were both nearly the same height, about 185 centimeters, so she got right up in his face. He liked to call her *kid*, but she was beginning to understand that what he'd wanted all along, more than anything, was to be able to dominate someone like Teri. She was strong of will and body, and he'd hoped to take advantage of her age and inexperience to subjugate her.

Well, I don't have to let him.

"If you live through this, moron, it'll be because *I* was able to talk to these things and make them understand us. They think I might be their messiah, and for all of your sakes, I'm going to milk that for everything I can. Stop acting like a baby after its candy is taken away. Your hopes of premarital sex with minors have been blown up. Boo-fucking-hoo. Your mission's nearly done, and you can go back to Kanaano to whatever backwoods, brain-dead baby-machine is waiting for you. You don't want brilliant, independent-thinking women like us, anyway, trust me. You want a child who will obey everything you say and fawn over you like a slave."

Carmen cleared her throat. "Josuo, just stop. Teri, tell them about the beasties, how they think of us, what your plan is. That's what matters right now."

Teri took a deep breath. "Okay. To them, you're my *zidóghusulká*. In Baryogo they use the phrase *nenun jantan*, which means 'bonded males.' That word, *jantan*, is what they call those responsible for growing food, raising children, creating compounds and dwellings. You know, the ones with the big, sagging cheeks. It means 'male' or 'man' in Baryogo, so I guess that makes the short, less-hairy ones female. They keep using 'this female' in Baryogo when they talk about each other, anyway."

"I don't see any evidence of what sex they are," Ronaldo muttered.

"They're not humans, so why would they be set up like us? That's why I have to keep talking to them. I need clues, information that can help us understand them."

Anyi spoke up, fingers twisting at her jacket in clear frustration. "Why don't you just ask them?"

Here it comes. They're not going to understand.

"I can't. I tried. They don't answer direct questions. They act like they don't understand me, and maybe they don't. I have to do this verbal dance with them. Everything's, what's the word, oblique. At an angle. They tell you a story, you tell them a story, they boast about all their history, recite their lineage to you… and at the end of a couple of hours, you know a bit more than you did. I asked Sekõtaldh to tell me about herself, and you know what she said? 'How can I tell you anything about myself? Who am I to make such a judgment?' That's what I'm dealing with. At least you're up here with plenty of food and no huge talking *kaŝtoroj* driving you insane."

"Well," Anyi muttered, sniffling, "the fungus salad isn't half bad, though having to fend off the flirtation of these two elders is *not* the high point of my high school career, trust me. You know, the Year of Jubilee is only about six jaroj off. I really wanted to go off to college, meet a cute guy who's *not from Kanaano*, and try to arrange things so that maybe my second or third kid was born in the fiftieth year. Name him Jubileo. Now," her eyes began tearing up, "I'm stuck in perpetual darkness with a horde of demons, and *it's your fault, you two reprobates!*"

She lashed out at Ronaldo with her left foot and knocked him off the bench he was sitting on.

"The hell did I do?" he exclaimed.

"You led us into temptation, jerk! Now we're being punished for our sins!"

Carmen shook her head. "Nobody twisted your arm to go with them and drink. Besides, this isn't about sin, Anyinjo. It's about being in the wrong

place at the wrong time."

No, it's about fate, Teri didn't say.

Anyi's face twisted in anger. "You freaking ... *lesbian*, your words

don't mean *anything*! We're going to *die* up here and all you can do is *make

out with a sophomore girl!*"

"Hey!" Carmen shouted.

But Anyi had lost all control. She started screaming.

"I don't want to die, Carmen, do you understand? *I don't want to die!*"

Teri caught Anyi by the shoulders as she bent to collapse. Embracing

her, she pulled her straight and leaned the older girl against her shoulder.

"Anyi," she murmured, "I swear to you: I am going to get you out of

here. You'll go home, God will forgive you, you'll get on with your life and

have all the children you can. I just need you to hang together. We are going

to be stuck here a while, I think."

She looked at the others and raised her voice so they could hear.

"I have a feeling something is happening here. This Greenseer they

keep mentioning—maybe he's a member of some crime syndicate, hiding

from the Consortium, trying to get the natives stirred up against us. Whatever

the case, you all just have to stay calm while I figure this out. Trust me. I'm

the right person for this job."

I might even have been chosen by God for it, she didn't say.

Easing Anyi onto one of the high benches that grew up out of the floor, Teri reached inside her knapsack. At the bottom, next to Tenshi's journal, her fingers found a reader. She placed it in Anyi's hands.

"This is the reader that Brando gave me when I turned ten. It's got the Book in it, all three testaments, and the writings of all the prophets since Smith himself. Don't spend your time lamenting everything, Anyi. Spend it getting closer to God, if that's what you really want."

Josuo scoffed. "Some aliens call her the messiah, and she becomes an expert in spirituality. Come on, Teri, the little role you want to play just doesn't fit you. Foul-mouthed, alcohol-drinking lesbian gives advice on how to be a better Novasanktulo. Please."

Teri was tempted to haul off and punch him, but she held back. "I'm pansexual, Josuo. You're just a really unattractive, stupid son of a bitch. But you know what? I'm going to save you, too, so that when this is all over people can learn the truth about the generous, helpful elder from Kanaano."

Before Josuo could respond, a thud came from a limb outside, and the moss curtain split as Sekõtaldh, Teri's guide, strode in.

Sekõtaldh was an *agun keturunan,* a 'highborn,' as the shorter natives referred to themselves in Baryogo. In their native language, the word was *dizöqhuÿdzháng,* which Teri couldn't pronounce right, as much as she tried. The highborn were the apparent rulers of this village, with the males beneath them and the drones, the warrior/hunter caste that had brought Teri and her friends to this place, at the bottom of the social totem pole. At least, such was the sketch of Native Teregan society that Teri had put together over the past two days. There were undoubtedly nuances that she had not understood and perhaps *could not*.

In the six digits of her right hand, Sekõtaldh clutched a leather bag, and from it she withdrew a single nut of some sort.

"You four, go sit on the bench," Teri muttered. "She doesn't see you as equals and it's wrong, in her mind, for you to just be lounging around when she's visiting."

Her friends did as she asked, but with looks of stubborn humiliation on their faces. Teri's guide crouched down, and Teri sat cross-legged in front of her. Sekõtaldh cracked the nut against the floor, took a piece of it and held it high.

"For the Unblinking Eye, Life-giver of every highborn and male, fashioner of drones for our service. For Çèrhingÿl, who guided us to the moss-hung shadows of the forest and taught us the ways of God. And to the spirits whose voices help guide us through every day and whose hands are at work in everything that happens." She tossed the fragment through a gap in the mossy curtain to her left, and then offered Teri the larger of the two remaining pieces. It was a little bitter, and as Teri chewed and swallowed it, she realized that it had a slightly narcotic effect, soothing her overwrought nerves and calming her heart rate.

From the previous day's tour of important highborn residences, she knew that she as the host was expected to tell a brief tale. The eating of the nut brought the Last Supper to her mind, and she narrated it, changing Jesus and his disciples to females. Sekõtaldh seemed bemused after she was done.

"I do not know what this 'bread' is, and the People have never tasted 'wine.' The high priestess of a tribe of the People would not simply allow herself to be betrayed by one of her acolytes, and if she did, the other priestesses would have their drones rip the traitor to pieces in the clearing. Perhaps you have misunderstood the story, Tenshi. Perhaps Jesus was planning to reveal Judas's treachery before them all so that they might carry out the prescribed punishment."

Not interested in trying to explain the tenets of her faith to this creature, Teri replied by narrating the scene in Gethsemane.

"Drones arresting a priestess? I am not a child, Tenshi. Why do you mock me?"

"The drones served the priestess of another, greater tribe that wanted Jesus to teach *their* beliefs and not her own. Judas was working for them, and in exchange for her betrayal of her high priestess, she was paid and allowed to live. She killed herself, anyway. The weight of her betrayal was too much."

The highborn began to seem very agitated. She spread both hands on the floor, fingers splayed, and leaned forward so that her short muzzle was nearly touching Teri's forehead, the steam from her triangular nostrils blowing across Teri's cornrows in short snorts.

"Interesting. Her spirit voices compelled her?"

Teri nodded. "Yes."

I should be more cryptic. Who knows what I might be accidentally agreeing to. She's no longer talking about the story, I'm sure of it.

"Should the other tribe have left Jesus to her heresy, then, I wonder."

"To my tribe, it is not heresy. Even though Jesus was killed, she returned and now we worship her as a true child of God and our leader."

"Tenshi, we are all children of God."

"But Jesus was the first born."

Sekõtaldh barked a laugh and stood. "Silly small one, Jesus was born long after beings walked the moss-hung forest. How could she be the first? Besides, the People all know that the first born from the jowls of darkness was Çèrhingÿl the Twice-sent. I would caution you against mentioning this Jesus of yours. The Sháinkhÿngigg take the truth very seriously. It is our goal to see that all tribes of the People, from all six nations, accept it. This is the goal the Greenseer has given us."

Actual information! They're spreading some new, Greenseer-inspired Gospel. And what's this stuff about their god giving highborn and males life, but just fashioning drones? For their service. Strange.

"Come, Tenshi. I will finish showing you the dark hollows of our village, and you will see the mighty works that truth can do."

They slipped down vines that hung nearly to the ground, and Sekõtaldh guided Teri past the parts of the village they'd explored over the last two days. Soon they came to a place where a few of the smaller trees, only about thirty meters tall, had been felled and used to create temporary shelters for about two hundred Native Teregans. The tallest trees in the area, what Teri's people called *ĉielarboj*, were teeming with males who, using hatchets and ropes twined from vines as well as other tools Teri didn't recognize, were trimming and binding limbs at different levels.

"In two years, the home trees will be ready for the new followers of the truth. We are doing all we can to bring entire villages to the light, as that is the Greenseer's true will. Heresy cannot be tolerated, however. As Dhörggìth said upon founding this nation of ours far from her sisters, 'What cannot be done well, but most be done, will have to be done badly.'"

Teri had no idea what she was talking about. "Where did all these people come from?" she asked, knowing full well that she would not get a straight answer.

"From the dark jowls of the world, like all the People. They understand that now better than they ever did."

Teri wanted to groan in frustration, but she kept silent.

I think these natives are from another village, one that refused to convert. But if their village was as big as this one, then this can't be everyone. Can't even be half of everyone. Were these run out of their village

as heretics or something? Could that be what all Sek's weirdness about

heresy and betrayal was about?

Sekōtaldh led her into the camp, and the residents there seemed to go

agog, as well as Teri could read their emotions. A silence fell across them all,

and an aged highborn stepped out from her hovel to approach Sekōtaldh. They

exchanged words for a few minutes while no one moved at all, not even the

builder males in the boughs above.

New, so the religious-leader highborn don't speak the modified Baryogo

yet. How long has Sekōtaldh's tribe been visiting the Greenseer? Need to

find out.

Finally, her guide turned to her. "These new believers feel honored and

blessed to behold a confirmation of their faith, proof that their sacrifice was

not a vain one. They beg for us to stay as guests of honor today as they

prepare a feast to celebrate."

Teri, elated at the prospect of learning more of what was going on and

how the Greenseer figured into the social changes, agreed that they should

stay. It was a majestic affair, as far as Teri could discern, with food in copious

amounts. She avoided a few of the dishes as they contained a root that had

already given Ronaldo diarrhea, but generally, she ate more than she ever

had at one seating before. There was strange, haunting music and acrobatic

dancing; violent sparring by young drones in training; and long, solemn recitals of epic poetry. Some of these verses Teri got Sek to translate for her: the natives in the camp were of the Ihéinghÿngigg tribe, from the nation of Jöxuçò, and much of their poetry was dedicated to this mythological heroine, sister of Dhörggìth, founder of the nation Sek's people belonged to.

LATE THAT EVENING, THE NATIVES' MUSIC and singing reverberating in her head, Teri clambered up the west side of her tree, avoiding the male quarters. She was too exhausted to explain her discoveries to her friends. They'd have to wait till morning.

As she pulled back the moss curtain, she found Carmen sitting on a netting of vines grown from the central truck to one of the curved boughs that made up the ceiling. Buoyed on the padding of moss-stuffed leather, Carmen had Tenshi's journal in her hands.

"Whoa," Teri said. "We were going to listen to it together."

Carmen nodded, swinging down from her perch. "I know. But I needed to hear these last few on my own."

She set the journal down and took a few steps forward. Teri said nothing, sensing that Carmen was on the verge of some vital choice.

"I spent the whole day thinking, Terinjo. I believe in you, but there's no guarantee we'll make it out of this situation alive."

Teri reached out her hand and shook her head.

"Querida Carmen, don't say that. We're going to be—"

Crossing the rest of the distance between them, Carmen silenced her with a kiss, soft and sweet, but trembling with desire.

"So I've decided," she whispered as she looked deep into Teri's eyes, "to do what I want, and to hell with the consequences."

With a gentle, decisive gesture, Carmen untied the bow at Teri's throat. Then she started unbuttoning her blouse.

Her heart thundering in her chest, Teri shrugged off her overcoat and uniform jacket, then started pulling off Carmen's clothes as well.

Within moments they fell together onto the plush furs on the floor, mouths and hands exploring each other as distant drums and flutes wove a magical melody through the late winter air.

MUCH LATER, TERI AWAKENED IN THE DARKNESS to find Carmen cradled in the crook of her arm, asleep. For a while she just lay there, relishing the warmth and pressure of the body of the girl she loved. Then curiosity got the better of her.

"Query," she whispered, activating the journal. "Play next entry, lowest audible volume setting."

The device whirred, and Tenshi Koroma's voice hushed into the gloom.

"June 23, 2674. Isabella says I need to get off the southern continent. When I told her I've spent almost three years here on the clean-up crews, she was shocked. It's either that or go back to my parents' domicile in

Kinguyama, I told her. But she says once I'm sixteen, I'm legally able to leave without anybody's permission and go wherever I want. Since July seventh is just two weeks away, and Isabella's done with the habitat reforming she was hired for, she wants me to move with her to Station City. Says she'll get me accepted into the university, can you believe it? When she saw all the things I've studied in my free time, she was amazed and proud.

"I told her I love architecture, and she went into this long-arse story about some Earth creature, the bowerbird, and how it used to make these amazing nests with naves and bits of glass and colorful material scrounged from humans. She explained to me about the extended phenotype, things that animals build that are extensions of their bodies because they're programmed in. Part of their genetic code.

"So I got to thinking that maybe the Path is real. Maybe humans do create souls for themselves. Maybe our genes push us to, see? The problem with Pathwalkers, I think, is that they've got no materials for soul-building aside from their own weak minds and the milky pabulum that their giyas feed to them. If they just looked out into the world that they scorn as irrelevant and see all the raw material waiting to be reshaped, they would truly create souls, souls of such beauty that people would just fall down on their knees, overcome with the intensity.

"Anyway, Isabella already knows all about the long list of losers: Andi, Inten, Mahana, Niken and Yuki. She told me I was looking in the wrong place for the sort of warmth and companionship and love that I need, that she can give me.

"She put a little silver ring on my finger and asked me to be hers. How could I say no? Isabella is perfect, Diary. Perfect. And she keeps bubbling about how I'm some sort of little genius and beautiful and how everyone will go nuts over me in Station City. If it's half as good as she's making it sound, I'll be happy.

"We snapped a picture together to commemorate our first day as a couple."

"Query," Teri whispered. "Pause journal, display image holographically."

The photo hovered in the air above their bed, illuminating the expansive quarters. Her own face, the same age, stared back at her. Darker, with stranger eyes, but otherwise identical. Next to her stood a blonde woman of about twenty-three Standard years, not as pretty as Carmen, but cute and glowing, with big green eyes that twinkled with mischief.

I am her, in a way. I may not be a Pathwalker, but I'm an Aknawajin woman who looks just like her, and my life is heading down a similar track. I'm Tenshi. She's me. Why fight it? Why deny what's staring me in the face?

She decided it then. The natives had been told by this Greenseer person that humans were coming, but that there'd be a female human that would prepare them for the encounter and help them overcome the invaders. Teri was going to learn all she could about this messiah's supposed role and play it as best she could. She would not betray her own people, but she would survive, and she would keep her friends alive.

And when they escaped, she would tell the Prophet and the Prime Minister everything she had learned.

Father, she prayed. *Or Sopiya, or whoever listens to the hearts of people like me, I think this is the task you've appointed me. I'm prepared to do it. If you open the way, I'll know it's meant to be.*

Then she snuggled closer to Carmen, unpaused the journal, and listened to herself speak until sleep overtook her.

CHAPTER 17

WHEN THE PRIME MINISTER ASKED HER if the trial could be started on Monday of the following week, Rhea balked. Sanas had been working with his paralegals non-stop, but moving up the date of the trial would steal precious time for researching other angles besides those used in the criminal trials on Jitsu could. Khumalo explained to her that the other major situation on Terego threatened to explode into an interstellar incident.

"I'm asking you as a citizen and a Novasanktulo: help me manage this crisis. Start the trial early. Rush through it with as few delaying technicalities as possible. In exchange, I'll do my best to influence the sentencing. We both know Brando's going to be found guilty: I can use my anti-expansionist contacts within the CPCC, certain more religious-minded leaders of colonized worlds who are also uneasy about the AF's strength. They'll put pressure on Prime Minister Soral, and we'll get Brando imprisoned here on

Terego, somehow. But help me, Rhea. Help Terego."

She'd acceded, and the efforts of Brando's defense team had doubled.

Meanwhile, reports from the group sent after the abducted young people had calmed public sentiment. Chief Corpsman Sitati reported that that the captives appeared to be alive and not mistreated. Brando's messages to Rhea were a bit more specific: human feces had been found regularly and analyzed for illness or signs of internal bleeding, with encouraging results every time. Rhea was strengthened by this news while also understanding the need for Sitati's spin. The Teregan government might be able to keep the crisis under wraps for a while longer.

Friday afternoon, when Rhea picked Jakobo up from school, her son's eyes were red from crying. He wasn't an excitable boy, hardly ever complaining about anything, so she was concerned.

"What's wrong, Jaki? Why are you sad? Did somebody do something?"

"Some boys were making fun of me."

"How? What did they say?"

"They said my *paĉjo* was a bad guy, and that my sisters were freaks. I got mad and told them shut up. The teacher didn't tell them nothing. She just shushed them. But she winked at them. She wasn't mad because of what they were saying, she just, just…."

"Wanted them to be quiet in the classroom and not make you cry. Not cause a scene."

"That's what I was going to say. Then later on, more kids started like 'son of a bad guy, son of a bad guy, sisters are freakos, sisters are freakos.' So I yelled back 'my dad's a *good* guy, and my sisters are *not* freaks' but they just laughed. I don't want to go back to kinder, mommy. I already know all that stuff anyway. You taught me to read last year, remember? It's a stupid school."

Rhea decided to take her son out of school until second heptamester, when she'd put him back in for first grade. She talked to Chiho Nishiguchi, a widowed mother of three with whom Rhea had developed a friendship years ago when the helpsocieto had provided counseling to the family after her husband Norio's death. Chiho had agreed without hesitation to take care of Jakobo during the trial.

"He's a lovely, well-behaved boy," she said with a smile. "I'm happy to watch him."

Saturday was a flurry of last-minute preparation. Being busy kept Rhea's mind off the gnawing fear that lay at the back of her mind. In moments of brief silence, her thoughts would wander to her daughters. She couldn't imagine what they must be going through, captives of nightmarish beasts.

Miwa, despite being the tougher of the two, would be the most affected: she had such a big heart that the absence of her family would be devastating. Teri, on the other hand, would make it through the crisis okay: she was fiercely independent, preferring solitude to time with family. Both, however, would come out of this situation with emotional scars. Rhea eased her own pain by imagining how she'd be there for her girls, helping them through recovery, providing a shoulder for their tears.

Rhea was good at this, helping others with their problems. Ironically, no one had ever really helped her. Except for the Judge. He'd been at her side during each of her tragedies.

Let the girls love me like I care for him. If they stop seeing me as a mother, at least let me be a close, dear friend.

That Sunday's service at her ward was a memorable one, in many ways, as the lines were already being drawn between those who viewed the rumored aliens as evil monsters and those who hoped to find in them spiritual siblings. Before the sacrament was taken, Bishop Freij himself addressed the vacancy left by Brando's arrest, and Elder Bagayan was set up as Sunday school teacher in his place.

The uneasiness about Rhea's husband's true identity was palpable, and Rhea caught many an eye falling on her in disapproval, anger or compassion.

I'm helping to defend the man who deceived us all. Of course some of my brothers and sisters will be disturbed by that decision. Time will show that I made a good choice. After all, I do want justice done, but our *justice, not the CPCCAF's.*

After the sacrament, young Ana Caylao gave a stirring talk on *Alma* chapter 24, focusing on the refusal of the people of Antinefilehi to take up arms against their brothers, non-converted members of the larger Lamanite nation. Rhea could feel the tension like a knife when Ana, wise beyond her eleven jaroj, recited verse sixteen:

And now, my brethren, if our brethren seek to destroy us, behold, we will hide away our swords, yea, even we will bury them deep in the earth, that they may be kept bright, as a testimony that we have never used them, at the last day; and if our brethren destroy us, behold, we shall go to our God and shall be saved.

She went on to read and describe how the former Lamanites, when attacked by those who had once been their countrymen, preferred to lay prostrate and offer themselves to the sword, praising God as they were slaughtered by the hundreds. When more than a thousand had been killed this way, a good number of the attacking Lamanites were moved to throw down their swords and join the martyrs in the dust, many of them forfeiting their lives as they repented of the murders they'd committed. Eventually, more Lamanites joined the people of God than had died that day, and His glory and power was shown to all.

Ana stressed the importance of obeying the Lord's commands and not sinning, no matter the cost: obedience had been the topic she'd been assigned. But Rhea and everyone else in the ward knew exactly what the young sister was saying.

The Native Teregans were sentient. They therefore had souls, and the humans were their brethren. Lifting arms against them, no matter what evil they'd perpetrated, was against God's will. Only when the glory of God had been wrought through whatever plan He had devised, only when the Native Teregans saw the humans as children of the Lord, would the indigenes themselves accept the Good News.

Out of the mouths of babes.

The talks given that Sunday by Brother and Sister Weiss were on forgiveness and longsuffering, and they echoed some of the sentiments that Ana Caylao had expressed. But in the months that followed, the central message of the young sister's talk would be repeated over and over in wards across Zarahemla, Kanaano, Novamerico, and Tevantepeko, the four continents out of six that humans had settled on. Caylao's words would serve as a counterbalance to the rising fear and hatred of the *grendeloj* or *mallumanoj*, inhabitants of darkness, as some would come to call the Native Teregans.

MONDAY MORNING CAME MORE QUICKLY THAN Rhea would've liked. The first day of the trial was a time of technical considerations: they got started late due to problems with the multiple faux-connections, and there was a slight glitch with the translation matrix early on (Sanas and many other Tereganoj participating didn't speak Standard, so their words were translated by the frame, which also provided them with a continuous Esperanto version of what Standard-speakers were saying).

The court layout was much as it had been for more than a thousand years. The five judges that made up the eyre sat at a large, raised bench at the front of the hall, with the defense and prosecution at tables below them. Behind the two legal teams sat the avatars of witnesses, observers and press members. While not broadcast, the trial would be reported on daily in the Teregan and Consortium media.

Rhea couldn't help making her avatar, her *doppel* as they said in Standard, look over at her brother-in-law. He bore a resemblance Brando, but he was pale, with straight hair. They both had the same jawline under close-cropped beards.

Unlike Tereganoj, the judges, Captain D'Angelo and Commander Mubarak all had absolute control over their doppels. Rhea knew her every emotion was betrayed by her lack of experience. Luckily, the people seated behind her were in passive mode: the frame assigned them random shifting, coughing, blinking and the like to keep them from seeming like a lot of unnerving statues, but they couldn't actually do more than watch unless moved to the witness stand. Teregan dignitaries like Prime Minister Khumalo would be saved the embarrassment of having their feelings constantly revealed to the CPCC.

As soon as the bugs in the connections were worked out, the trial proceeded. Motions were considered, continuances disallowed: the arraignment had been taken care of the previous week in a pair of rather short conferences that only Mubarak, Sanas and the eyre had been a part of. Brando had authorized his counsel to plead guilty on three charges—assuming a fake identity, cloning humans, evading arrest—and not guilty on the other counts.

There was a recess for lunch around 13:45 local time. When the court reconvened, opening statements were made.

Sanas laid out the defense strategy very succinctly: at the time of actions Brando was accused of, Jitsu was neither a member nor protectorate of the CPCC, and as a result, on the planet and in its orbital space, the regulations of the Consortium and its armed forces could not be retroactively applied to the situations he was in. Additionally, Jitsu had been in the midst of a power grab by Samanei Koroma through her uncle, Santo Koroma, and through her indirect manipulation of Nestor Bos, counselor to the leader of the now-defunct Brotherhood syndicate. Brando's moves had been to a large part forced upon him by the larger players in a game where he had been merely a pawn.

"We will demonstrate in this tribunal," concluded Sanas, "that contrary to the picture trial counsel will attempt to paint of him, Brando D'Angelo is *not* a murdering, vicious criminal. In fact, we will show that D'Angelo is a loving father, dedicated spouse, and enthusiastic citizen of whatever community he belongs to. We do not deny that he has committed acts of a questionable moral nature. We cede this obvious point to the prosecution.

However, morality and law are *not* synonymous, and to make the leap from immoral to criminal requires hard evidence that laws have been broken. It is our contention that such evidence does *not* exist, and that Brando D'Angelo is merely a loose end in the AF's valiant struggle against organized crime. We recognize that our client has indeed committed a few serious crimes, and he has pleaded guilty to them. Despite your honors' disallowance of our motion to dismiss the other charges, we are confident that you will find him innocent on those counts.

"A loose end doesn't have to be snipped off or burned away. It can simply be tied back to the whole of which it is a part. Thank you."

Ashar Mubarak's doppelganger stood and began addressing the judges. "Your honors, there are men that believe they live outside of the law, men for whom laws and customs and institutions have no meaning. Men that that believe the only justice is what their own hands can do, that right is what they say it is, that wrong is anything that stands in their way.

"Such a man is Brando D'Angelo. We will show your honors his evolution from vigilante to meddlesome rebel to rogue squadman. We'll let yall see that D'Angelo has, not just no respect for the law, but no respect for human life itself. The wanton abandon he has killed other people with demonstrates just how little humanity there is left in him. His facile justification for his violence, a supposed search for justice, is more aptly termed a will to revenge. Human law no longer permits primitive ideas like vengeance. But again, D'Angelo believes himself beyond such laws.

"The accused would tell us, if he were present today, that he did what he did out of his love for his family. That will be, no doubt, part of the defense's strategy, to move us with his sadness over his family's death. But let's ask ourselves what kind of love it is that clones one's wife and child and raises those clones as one's human daughters? What kind of love is it, your honors, that pushes a man to lie about his identity, beliefs, and past for fifteen years to an honorable, upstanding community of men and women?

"It's not love. It's fear. Fear of being caught and punished. Like a child that knows their father is waiting for them so he can punish them, Brando is running from the consequences of the evil he's perpetuated. And like a loving but stern parent, yall must, in his best interests and in the interests of the people around him, find him guilty on all counts and remove him from society so that nobody else's life will be destroyed in the name of his strange personal morality."

The sad thing was, reflected Rhea as the remaining hour was taken up with the naming of witnesses and the consideration of the first pieces of physical evidence (the *ranfura* Brando had come to the planet in and its modified Lieske drive), Mubarak was mainly right. Brando did need to be removed from the human sphere: he had suffered enough and had caused enough suffering. Rhea's aching for him every moment of every day did not detract one iota from her understanding of the law and God's will.

Brando was a sinner and a criminal, and though she'd fight tooth and nail to ensure its fairness, Rhea understood completely that he deserved punishment.

Yet in the end, despite her own and her brother-in-law's personal views on what was the best way to make Brando pay his debt, only God could truly decide the form his penance would take.

CHAPTER 18

ANTONIO READ THE REPORTS DISTRACTEDLY: Captain Mifflin of the *Shaka* was only days away from his position, while Quat needed another three weeks to get the *George Washington* in place. Berdyaev approved heartily of D'Angelo's proactive strategy, though the commodore wasn't quite convinced that the Tereganoj were planning anything. However, with Brando's absence and Sanas's request for a speedy trial, Antonio's instincts had kicked into overdrive.

Something was going on, and it was infuriating to still be two and a half months away from a fenestration that could take the *Diomedes* in-system. Antonio had toyed with the idea of requesting permission to accelerate faster toward each of the seven holings his ship had to perform, but he knew that Berdyaev wouldn't approve of the risk just to shave a week or two off his arrival time.

Instead, Antonio stewed as he waited for the trial to begin, studying maps of Terego. A world 4,470 kilometers in diameter and with six continents, four of which were inhabited by the nearly one million Tereganoj (most of whom were under forty: these Mormons were more prolific than Earth rabbits or Oceanian bladder worms). Two of these continents, Novameriko and Zarahemla, were more than seventy percent covered with ridiculously impenetrable forests into which the backwoods isolationists could scamper if push came to shove.

Antonio dedicated hours to determining an effective strategy were he to have to send troops to the surface. He knew such a move would go against the conventions of the treaties the two governments had signed, but he needed to be prepared. Should Terego do something that invalidated those treaties or made them irrelevant, Antonio would be able to move quickly.

Several ideas had occurred to him so far. Perhaps the illegal equipment that Brando had removed from Jitsu was hidden on Terego, and the government wanted to keep it. Perhaps Samanei was somewhere on the planet. It was even possible that the Tereganoj were aligning themselves with some underworld faction. A stretch, Antonio admitted, but something he had to consider. Many independent worlds viewed the CPCC as a threat, citing the more than two decades of AF occupational force in Sigma Draconis. The captain could imagine Khumalo contracting with some yakuza group to provide defense of the system against the AF in return for mining rights or some other lucrative perquisite.

But Antonio wasn't worried. He'd dedicated most of his adult life to making sure justice was done, as a soldier, an officer, a prosecutor and a captain. To him, the law was what gave structure and meaning to the otherwise chaotic and empty universe. He was an atheist. He lived with the knowledge that there existed no universal, transcendental raison d'être, no objective right and wrong laid with the foundations of the universe.

As a teen, he'd floundered about in the muck of moral relativism till, in a martial philosophy class his first year at the academy, he'd been introduced to Virtualism. A system of thought that had sprung up in the mid-twenty-first century along with Neo Gnosticism, Virtualism asserted that while nothing was *absolutely* true or right or moral, quite a few things were so *virtually*, or within the sphere of human experience. As a result, though while there was no cosmic law against murder, no transcendental reason not to kill another human being, humans collectively understood such an act to be evil *for humans*. When humans created gods, they often excused those deities from following the same rules, but humans themselves were bound by the code.

Whence had these rules sprung? Virtualism explained that given human psychology, genetics, culture and environment, certain sets of laws maximized happiness for the greatest number of people. These laws had been culled from the possibilities throughout the ages in a Darwinian process that had left humanity at the beginning of the twenty-eighth century with a firm, millennia-tested jurisprudence and social contract that Antonio had pledged his life to upholding. As a lieutenant and then commander serving as advocate in CPCCAF military trials of underworld criminals and Kunti insurgents, the joy he felt in his job had derived from this oath. Every yak he put away reaffirmed the legal and governmental system he put his trust in.

Berdyaev understood his subordinate's love of human justice implicitly, Antonio knew. When they'd discussed Terego's request for a speedy trial, the commodore had defused D'Angelo's ire by pointing out that a quick end to the proceedings was in the AF's best interests, as it was becoming apparent to the intelligence branches that Samanei Koroma was the key to bringing the war against the underworld to a satisfying conclusion. They had found connections between the former Oracle and some thirteen crime syndicates, all of which had supported her in her quest to topple both the Jitsuan government and the Brotherhood itself. Finding her and a certain Yen Bandera, head of the illegal spy ring Al-Muzzaml, was of utmost importance, and the sooner Brando was in AF hands, the easier it would be to extract that information from the ex-squadman.

Antonio had been gladdened by the opportunity to rout the enemies of justice, but then it had occurred to him that perhaps Brando had been involved in Samanei's plotting, and that he might've hid her on Terego so that she could either continue her collaboration with the yaks or hide from them. His suspicions flared even more.

Finally the trial had begun. The first day was wasted in a lot of technical glitches and idiot motions. Antonio was still amazed at how these fanatic types could twist reality and their own doctrine to justify their actions while condemning the very same 'sins' in others. Luckily his doppel was quite controlled, or the incredulous shaking of his head would've gotten him reprimanded by the eyre.

Day two of the trial saw the continued exposition of physical evidence, including significant amounts of material on the human genome and large pieces of equipment used for simulating the cloning of mammals. These and a mini-frame containing all of Brando's research into the Brotherhood, cloning and the underworld black market had been recovered after the explosion and reconstructed, much of the data being retained despite the irradiation. Unfortunately for the defense, the criminal scum who'd sold Brando the transuranic bombs had either over-hyped their capabilities or jilted him, because while they destroyed the home and left the area toxic, they'd left much intact, including the gravtiles, illegal for private citizens and very tightly controlled by the Consortium, even when used by governments, because of the potentially devastating power of large gravity generators.

Sanas tried pathetically to counter every piece of physical introduced by citing Jitsu law: none of the items displayed, he argued, was actually forbidden by any of the statutes in effect at the time.

Idiot. Humanity as a whole decided these things aren't acceptable:

who gives a shite about one radical fanatical world and what laws they had

fifteen years ago? CPCC law must trump the other stupidity that independent

worlds embrace in their ignorance. Humanity has to be united in what we

believe. Can't be letting every bumpkin out in the welkin make up their own

set of rules.

After a ninety-minute recess (which only the Tereganoj really needed:
the judges and trial counsel were all in hypostasis on their respective
ships), the recordings were reviewed. The first were from the holding cell
where Jitsuan security personnel had questioned Brando after his wife's
death. Antonio wanted them to note the dullness in his eyes, the distance
they seemed to imply. Sanas moved to have the recording declared irrelevant
and inadmissible, and the judges upheld his objection, but they'd seen that
look, and they wouldn't forget.

Next came the interrogation of Felipe Beserra. The court sat through
the last hour or so of video drawn from the kewbox. Antonio couldn't help
but steal a glance at Rhea as Brando overloaded Felipe's nervous system
while screaming and throwing his insane, hulking mass on the yak to beat
him mercilessly. She had to close her eyes, swallowing heavily.

She's trying to control her doppel, but the atrocities of her husband are

just too much. She's going to lose it before the day is out.

Sanas tried to minimize the torture and death of Beserra by citing
Jitsuan statutes permitting torture in certain cases and by mentioning Ben

Wu's previous testimony that a Yen Bandera plant had tampered with the kewbox so that the safeguards would be deactivated.

I have a surprise for you. Wait till Wu is on the stand, you yokel.

Antonio had instructed Mubarak to let Sanas's objections and explanations stand. No reason to argue with him.

"Our witnesses and precedent are going to be decisive here, and these images will never leave the judges' minds."

The longer Sanas spoke, the more convoluted his rationalization of Brando's actions, the more complete justice's victory would be: not only over wrongdoing, but over those who would defend evil.

The last recording of the day was the scan data from Ben Wu's transport as it accompanied other squad transports in pursuing Brando before he could get to Station City and interfere with the clash going on there between AF and syndicate-controlled Jitsuan forces. The transports fired on D'Angelo, and he led them to a series of water tanks where he exploded an antimatter bomb that destroyed the tanks and the transports, except for Wu's and another. The last scene before the image fizzed into static was of Brando popping the hatch on his vehicle and emerging with an enormous cannon, which he brought to his shoulder and fired simultaneously with a preprogrammed missile launch from his own transport.

Rhea was tearing up, Antonio noticed as the judges announced that the remaining recordings would be viewed the next morning. Her hands were shaking and her lip trembling.

That's right, Sis. He's a cruel, amoral bastard. The kind we can't allow to exist. The kind we need to lock away forever. You're beginning to see this, aren't you? Sanas didn't want you to watch these, so they're a big surprise, I bet. Wait till you see tomorrow's videos. You think you feel dirty now? Tomorrow you'll understand just how inhuman he is.

Antonio waited to disconnect until everyone else had done so. He wanted to be in the courtroom alone a moment. Looking around him at the granite walls (neither granite nor walls), he felt as he always had in a courtroom.

At home, at peace, happy. There, in bas-relief behind the eyre's bench, his only love blindly raised her scales in a salute to him, and he bowed his head in respect for her divinity.

CHAPTER 19

WAKE. YOU'RE BEING WATCHED. SHALURAZHOX JERKED her eyes open to the sight of Tentisùxa, her point, tracker, companion and *zhãedhih*: the drone with whom she coupled when the fire burned so painfully within. Tenti was standing over Shalura and the creature in her arms; behind the older warrior were the troops' lieutenants. All of them had anger and disgust on their faces, cheeks heaving with superior indignity.

"Why are you lying with this thing?" Tenti demanded.

Shalura sat up, waking the small beast as she did so. The hairless one hunched its shoulders at the sight of the warriors looming over her; then it simply rolled away from the group and sat up a little way distant, watching the scene unfold.

"She was cold. Tradition dictates that valuable prisoners must be kept healthy for negotiations. My voices spoke, telling me to warm her with my own body, and I obeyed." Shalura withheld from them the aching in her heart

that seeing her decimated highborn, male, child and tribe up near the Green

had caused. She did not mention how the odd creature's shivering body had

allowed her to sleep a dreamless sleep, to rest fully for the first time in days.

They will not understand. Be silent.

Tenti was not contented by this answer. "You might just as easily have

ordered another to do so, or piled frondy leaves upon its grotesque form. You

are our leader, but to bring yourself down to this level, to put this creature's

comfort above your role in the troop, I find that unacceptable."

She is right, but she is also angry because she imagines you coupled

with the beast, as disgusting and vile as such fantasies are. She feels displaced

and shamed, her position as second in danger because of the compassion

you've shown the creature. Assert yourself. Show her that you are leader and

that she is yours. Do so now, in front of all your warriors, so their doubts will

be dispelled as well.

With a throaty growl, Shalura stood angrily, and in a sudden spin of her

massive body, slapped her tail against Tentisùxa's torso, knocking the tracker

to the ground. Her blood throbbing with anger and inexplicable passion,

Shalura backed up over Tentisùxa and crouched above her abdomen. Her

long, broad tail pressed Tenti's face cruelly against the ground as Shalura

coaxed her lover's ovipositor out and inserted it into her own egg receiver

while sliding her own ovipositor into the older warrior at the same time. Thus doubly joined, the two rocked against each other violently, Tenti bucking with all her strength against Shalura's heavier form.

The act was over in seconds as their ovipositors nearly simultaneously discharged fluid: not even half the pleasure of actually passing an egg to a highborn or a male, but exhilarating. Fortunately, Shalura reflected in her ecstasy, neither of them was ovulating. There were no males to incubate for them anymore. Xiggèr'enth likely would have, despite how frowned upon an egg fertilized in a drone-to-drone coupling was by most highborn. But Xiggèr'enth was dead, as was her entire tribe. Such conjecture was pointless, and she ignored the voices that wanted to distract her with it.

As she got up, she noticed the alien beast was standing with its back to her.

She turns away. Like a highborn, she is repulsed by the coupling of drones.

The warriors had begun to pair up, following their leader's example. The beast would no doubt be even further disgusted by the scene. Shalura's spirit voices spoke again, advising her.

Take her to them. Take her up close to the Green.

No. Other voices firmly contradicted. Would you again risk losing the cohesion of your troop? You and your warriors exist for only one reason now, and without unity under your leadership, that goal will never be met.

Shalura knew these voices were right. Both tradition and the poems, songs and lessons of her childhood confirmed that theirs was the true message. But she listened to the other voices nonetheless. Something in what they said appealed to a deeper part of her, a place in her mind she did not recognize.

Take her up. Let her see. Judge her then. There will be time to correct this action if it is a mistake. Do it now, while the others are distracted.

Shalura defied tradition and grabbed the alien, lifting it onto her shoulders. It let out a squeak and then fell silent as Shalura bounded to a nearby trunk and, taking hold of a thick, well-leaved vine, began scaling upward toward the resting place of the Ihéinghÿn-gigg. The creature's fingers gripped Shalura's fur tightly as if it feared falling, and the warrior moved faster. Soon they had reached a broad bough from which one could survey the abandoned bodies of the highborn and males of her tribe as well as the rotting remains of the drones that had died in their defense.

Shalura pulled the beast from her shoulders and set her down. The small thing fell to her knees, eyes spreading wide open, jaw trembling oddly. Her head jerked back and forth as she surveyed the field of corpses buoyed by forked boughs and moving gently with the wind that blew across the forest's canopy, moss and worms already reclaiming them for the canopy's colorful life, rendering them into fertilizer for the soil that coated those upper branches.

Water began to spill from the creature's eyes, as from those of a highborn caught up in religious ecstasy. Dhójelith, the highborn Shalura had been bonded to, her *ÿdizùlanga*, had once described this rapture as "one's soul merging with the spirits." Shalura recalled that phrase now, and she wondered again whether this creature might be a highborn of some strange nation she'd never seen before. The water continued to stream from her eyes, and she closed them tightly, moaning.

She is *a highborn, and a special one. The spirits of the Ihéinghÿngigg are joining with her! It is the rite of Çõlexÿhëngainkh.*

Shalura had to agree with the voices. It did indeed appear that this odd-looking highborn was communicating with the soul of her tribe like a priestess would with ancestral spirits.

The little one was babbling now, and suddenly she stood and cried out, bellowing ferociously like one grieving the destruction of one's people.

Like we did. Like this last troop of lost forest children did when we saw our future, our identity, our only soul ripped out of the half-light of the forest and hurled into the Deepest Green.

Shalura envied the little ugly highborn at that moment: *she* had a soul; *she* could feel the tribe one last time before it was carried into the dark womb again, returning to its Maker; when *she* lamented the passing of the Ihéinghÿngigg, her cry flew to their twitching spirit ears and soothed their dark flight.

But Shalura and her warriors could feel no such satisfaction. Their words did not carry beyond this world. They were drones. They had no soul save that of the tribe: without their highborn and males, they were mere animals whose sole purpose was vengeance. As her spirit voices fell silent, the warrior slipped into a loose crouch, her head hanging in defeat and despair.

Without warning, Shalura felt the highborn throw her arms around her neck and bury her muzzle in her cheek. The water from the little one's eyes dampened the fur of Shalura's face as the strange creature babbled on and on in that primitive tongue.

She shares their essence with you. She has felt them inside her, and now she bids you feel them, too. Look, Shalura, look upon your tribe one last time.

Shalura closed her eyes and saw her people, saw them standing tail-to-tail in a broad clearing, awaiting the sturdy-timbered ship that would sail them into the Deepest Green: Dhójelìth was there, and Xiggèr'enth with their child, Thõdhulazhox. The high priestess, the builders, the educators, the agriculturalists... hundreds of souls, joined together as one, reaching out to embrace Shalura, to thank her for a job well done. Their voices lifted in an ancient song, the *Rime of Green Passage,* and the sound of it surrounded Shalura, cradling her, encompassing her as if she were an infant in a cheek pouch, suckling on a loving male's nodes.

The song was everywhere. It was everything. It was the sound of existence.

When Shalura, eyes still closed, alien highborn still clinging to her, finally stood and loosed a mournful cry, she felt true release for the first time. She had been given a special gift, by a special creature. She'd been allowed to see what no drone ever had.

"Thank you," she muttered in the highborn's round, ugly ears. The dwarf pulled her head away and looked into Shalura's eyes with an incomprehensible expression.

"Me hurt," the little one managed to say in mangled tones, "here." She touched her chest, where highborn and males hid their spirits beneath their thick, bony breast plates.

"What do we call you, Lady?" Shalura asked, with the respect tradition demanded be shown captive highborn. It was obvious the little one didn't understand. "Your name: would you honor us with its power?" Still no answer. Shalura crooked one of her fingers, claw retracted, at her own head. "I am Shalurazhox. Shalurazhox. Shalura."

"Shalura?" repeated the highborn, pointing at her captor.

"Yes. Now, grace me with your name." She extended her long thumb in the little one's direction. "Name?"

The highborn stood thinking for a while, then started to mumble some unpronounceable syllables in her strange tongue, and finally, with firmness, spoke:

"Me name *Daenzhelo*."

"May the shadows of the forest ever keep you from the wrath of the Unblinking Eye, Daenzhelo. Come with me, please." She gestured for Daenzhelo to climb up onto her back, then she clutched a vine and leapt off the bough, spinning off down and to the left as the vine reach the extent of

its forward swing. She landed on another, thicker limb, ran up its length, and

then scrambled down the tree to the highborn quarters of the compound it

housed. The voices in her mind were all shouting at once, a tumult of ideas

and suggestions and alternatives. She yanked aside the curtain of moss, and

Daenzhelo slipped from her shoulders onto the firm wooden flooring.

"Here slept Dhójelìth, my *ÿdizùlanga*, to whom I was bonded till she

was killed. She would not mind our borrowing her things for so noble a

cause. Wait one second," Shalura instructed, flicking her tail in the stopping

gesture. From a corner of the quarters she dragged a heavy clay pot and

began pulling items from its interior until she found the extra robe.

Yes. Let the others see her dressed as a highborn; that will ease their

minds, make accepting your orders easier.

A strange feeling was blossoming inside of her. Hope. Shalura felt hope

when by rights she shouldn't have been able to.

Extending her claws, she rent a good forearm's length of material from

the robe and crossed the quarters with quick strides.

"Put this on, Lady Daenzhelo." She held the robe out expectantly.

Daenzhelo tentatively reached for it, held it in her hands for a few seconds,

rubbing the supple leather between her fingers, then slipped it over her head.

Perfect.

Daenzelo split her face wide again and made a bubbling, light sound that might have been laughter. Shalura grinned in approval.

They slipped down the side of the tree and back toward the clearing, where her warriors were checking their spears and arbalests in preparation for whatever attack their leader instructed. As Shalura and Daenzhelo approached them, their gaze riveted on the alien highborn. Shalura hooted them to attention.

"Stand, all of you. I now know more about our captive. She is Lady Daenzhelo, highborn of a tribe of creatures like us yet very different. You will remember the words of the heretics of our tribe, those who destroyed our families. They claimed that the Greenseer, a spirit living on the Mountain of God and clothed in flesh forged from the very crust of the land, had augured the coming of a nation of beings with spears of fire and reeds that blew deadly fast darts without the need for air. They claimed this Greenseer told of a special highborn among these aliens, one like the great figures of our tradition who lived in the mist-shrouded past, proud highborns that fought like the fiercest drones. The Greenseer, claimed the heretics, said that this highborn would come among us and prepare us to face the new nation and not falter. Some even whispered that she would be none other than Çèrhingÿl herself, sent a third time to guide the People into a new age.

"I, like each of you, dismissed these babblings as the flower-festooned excrement they seemed to be. However, we have all seen the new creatures: this one and her dead companion, who used a reed of the type foretold by the heretics. We must ask ourselves a hard question: is it possible that the voices

we obeyed were wrong? Is it possible that the Greenseer's words were true,

that we mocked and ignored those voices that urged us to believe?"

Tenti lifted her voice to answer. "Shalurazhox, many of us have

wondered the same. But it remains that our majestic tribe has been vilely

ripped from us, and the holy blood-call cannot be ignored."

Thumping her tail in agreement, Shalura responded. "Nor do I suggest

we ignore it. Yet, our main quarrel would seem to be with the Greenseer. If it

truly means to unite the six mighty nations against Daenzhelo's people, why

did it have our tribe ignobly slaughtered? It will answer for this, or it will

never have its highborn heroine."

"And how will we make it answer for the atrocity?" a younger

warrior interjected.

"We will go to the cloud-crowned Mountain of God, where it is said

the mysterious Greenseer keeps its watch over the shadow-laden forest. We

will go into its unknown compound and confront it with claw and spear and

words of truth. We will kill it if its answer does not satisfy us. Then, if we

hear the blood-call still shrilly echoing in our minds, we will hunt down

those who betrayed us and rip their entrails from their bellies."

The warriors lifted their spears in a salute and thumped their tails

against the ground violently, raising clouds of dirt that enshrouded the group

in darkness as thick as their uncertain future. In minutes, the troop was underway again.

Daenzhelo now traveled with Shalura, borne on the shoulders of one warrior or another. Against her custom, Shalura spoke often to the highborn, teaching her the names of the objects they passed and correcting her mangled usage of the People's tongue.

By the fifth day of her capture, Daenzhelo was making her needs understood and had begun to comprehend quite a bit of what was said to her. That afternoon, the long cold broke and warm air began to flow into the dark forest from the southwest. When they reached a wide stream that burbled between the thick-bowled trees, Daenzhelo smacked her hands together and made strange sounds.

"Me water! Me needs of a water!"

"Very well. There it is," Shalura gestured at it.

As Daenzhelo rushed toward the stream, the troop leader indicated to two warriors that they should accompany the highborn. After a moment of indecision, Shalura also went along. Daenzhelo pulled off the robe and three layers of the strange-colored skins that she'd been wearing for five days. Beneath them, she was nearly completely hairless, more so than any highborn of the People. Upon her chest were two small conical bulges whose purpose Shalura couldn't even guess at. As the highborn turned to leap into the water, Shalura saw that she had no tail, not even the short, slender one that highborn hid beneath their robes.

As Daenzhelo's head broke the surface and she screamed out "cold, water cold," one of the warriors, a hulk named Guthonar'ut, muttered solemnly, "She certainly is an ugly creature."

Shalura was no longer so sure. Daenzhelo was beginning to grow on her, and the dwarf's looks no longer startled her. "She's merely different on the outside, I think. Perhaps her spirit is like that of any highborn."

Guthonar'ut shrugged. "Perhaps. Still, she is the ugliest thing I've ever seen."

Shalura twitched her ears in irritation. "Yes, I suppose she is."

No, you don't. A voice muttered within her. You think she's beautiful. You think you see the spirit of your tribe living within her, glowing through her hairless, alien skin. You suspect that, just maybe, she might be Çèrhingÿl.

Heresy is flowering in your heart.

Shalura turned and walked off, hope burning bright within her.

INTERCHAPTER C

(Excerpts from a report compiled by Doctor Sonali Dixit and Doctor Vivek Roshan for the Ministry of Crises based upon their individual technical reports, each filed with the Ministry of Public Health.)

Native Teregan physiology

Based on rapid field autopsies, we have determined that there are three Native Teregan sexes. Though further study is needed to understand the intricacies of their reproductive cycle, it is apparent that the largest sex (henceforth *females*), apparently responsible for hunting and warfare, produces an egg, which is passed via a long, tube-like oviscapt into, we assume, the egg receiver (or *oötheca*) of the second sex. The smallest of the three, this sex (henceforth *males$_1$*) likely adds its genetic material to the egg and then passes it for further fertilization to the third sex (henceforth *males*$_2$), which we might also call *nurturers* or *mothers* as they appear to be responsible for rearing the young, as far as we can make out. Males$_2$ have only vestigial ovipositors, but they are possessed of large, distended cheeks with inner pouches where eggs are incubated and embryos gestated. There are nodes inside these pouches that provide nourishment to developing young. Females and males$_1$ also have these pouches and nodes, but in vestigial form. Overall, the Native Teregans' reproductive organs reflect origins in the bisexual creatures found across Terego, their ovipositors and oöthecas likely having evolved from the ovotestes found in these lower animals. The trisexual mating system is akin to similar ones discovered in certain marine animals, like the *bajenoj* studied by Professors Stark and Perez at Nauvoo College and the four-sex *peresosoj* of Kanaano.

In other respects, the Native Teregans are superficially similar: angular faces and a mixture of sharp serrated cuspids and wide bicuspids bespeaks a diet of meat and softer plant life. Thickly layered, waterproof fur (of which males$_1$ have little) points to evolutionary origin in cold, wet climes. Six digits on hands and feet (in the case of the latter, the sixth has evolved into a rigid spur). Retractable claws (nearly useless in *males*$_1$) ideal for arboreal life, hunting and warfare. Height varies, with females averaging about 2.75 meters, *males*$_1$ some 2.4 and *males*$_2$ around 2.6. Equine-like ears can rotate two hundred degrees for maximized hearing. Eyes adapted to gloom of dense forest. Massively muscled and multiply jointed tails on both females and *males*₂ are hairless and broader than they are thicker (average of 15 cm by 3 cm, broadening and thinning out at the end farthest from the torso). *Males*₁ have tales that are significantly shorter (one meter compared to nearly two) and less broad.

....

Internally, the Native Teregans possess organs both of immediately identifiable purpose, like a six-valve heart and an interconnected set of three lungs (one of these a small auxiliary, probably developed from some bladder during an aquatic period of their evolution), both of which are protected by a thick pectoral shield of bone. Their skeletal system otherwise is quite similar to that other Teregan life forms.

....

The brain is smaller than that of humans, weighing about 1.25 kilograms on average, but it has a larger proportion of neo-cortex than its human counterpart. Further study is needed into the organization of the cerebrum, as it seems to be differently structured that that of humans, with the two hemispheres connected in multiple places.

Native Teregan society

As far as can be gleaned from the investigating teams brief stay in a native village, the indigenes appear to be highly hierarchical. Dwellings (henceforth *aeries*) are created from the sky-scraping ĉielarboj: limbs are pruned and bound at different levels then allowed to grow (probably over the course of years), forming semicircular platforms and arching roof-like structures, from which vines and moss is grown to serve as a screen. Higher levels of these structures appear to be occupied by those higher up within the social structure, and the aeries are progressively more impoverished as one goes down the trunk. At the highest levels, the aeries are often augmented by hollows in the trunk itself.

At ground level, we have discovered fields of a variety of edible plants, carefully cultivated. .... Also, the young are apparently trained in different crafts in log-cabin type buildings that may hark back to an earlier, less environmentally-friendly construction technique (or be the harbinger of a new trend). We have found smaller versions of the normally 3- to 5-meter-long spears in one of these cabins, indicating that warriors are trained at an early age.

....

Clay pottery and paintings on treated leather have been found throughout the villages, and we have attached samples of same. Images are of animals and Native Teregans in action, running, hunting, engaging in sex, etc. No still life images. Individual objects in field often overlap. Paint organic; pottery crudely fired in kilns dug in the earth (where food is also slowly cooked).

   ....

Further study of the remains of Native Teregans is imperative, which is why a *koptero* was called up to ship six corpses to the laboratories of the Ministry of Public Health (a sample of each sex for both adults and *kits*, as we've designated their young). We hope these preliminary findings, outlined in greater detail in our technical monographs, will serve as the basis for a biology of Native Teregans and possibly even for a future effort to improve and extend their lives.

From the number of cadavers in the arboreal graveyard and the existence of warrior troops, we have logically deduced that there must be numerous bands of Native Teregans, at war with each other and willing to slaughter entire groups of enemies. We are unaware of whether the group we're presently following survived the massacre or is responsible for it. As a result, we urge caution as we proceed. An evacuation team should be on standby should we find ourselves in a dangerous situation. We *do*, however, recommend that the team continue, not only for the rescue effort that is foremost on our minds, but because of the importance of further understanding the sentient beings with whom we share this planet.

PART II:

ANTITHESIS

"kaj ankaŭ pasas nuno ama

nuno post nuno en spaliro

kaj ĉiu estas malsimila

kaj mil perdiĝas en deliro

dum unu restas, faksimila"

"and even loving moments fade

one by one, an unbroken line,

not a one of them alike—

a thousand lost in ecstatic haze

till just the facsimile remains"

—William Auld, *La infana raso* (*The Infant Species*)

CHAPTER 20

THE GLOOMY GREEN OF THE FOREST felt natural after eight days. Brando stopped using the IR goggles and began waking up earlier to add to his routine scaling trees, using the thick, rope-like creepers and trying out other experimental techniques that made him feel like a novice trapeze artist. He'd hit on a trick, using two of the powerful pulleys attached to his harness to jerk himself from tree to tree. He'd fire the grapple at the end of one cable up into a bough, and as he was accelerating toward it, he'd use the other pulley going to grapple onto to a higher bough or one that lay in another direction. As soon as the second grapnel bit deep into the wood and spread its hooks, he'd release the first and be yanked in a new direction.

The only problem was the way the first cable whipped about him as it returned to its spool. After having raised ugly welts on his legs and chest, he'd taken to wearing the thickest clothing available and a sturdy byrnie that would also keep bullets and spear points from his chest and back. The best strategy, he'd found, was to wait until he had nearly reached the end of the first cable before releasing it and spooling himself toward the second grapple. This move required perfect reflexes and timing, though, and there was no telling whether during the heat of battle he'd get it right or screw up and bash his skull against a tree limb.

Battle was nearly all he thought of now: his dreams were full of formless enemies and his waking hours with a constant analysis of his chances. Since the discovery of the slaughtered natives on Sunday, the whole team was bubbling with purpose and nerves. Roshan and Dixit spent the afternoon and evening racing against the clock and a warm southwesterly wind to glean as much information as possible from the corpses and abandoned aeries. Brando, at their request, examined the indigenes' vocal tract and made some educated guesses about their language, but the whole time he was really assessing the creature's fighting ability.

The females, as his two colleagues had termed them, were formidable enemies. They were much better engineered for fighting than humans: the huge breastplate under the thick layer of muscle, skin and fur across their massive chests would deflect most Teregan hand-held weapons. Their arms were attached to their bodies in such a way as to give the sturdy bones maximum leverage and strength, as well as greater rotational flexibility. The thighs were heavily muscled, the toes nearly as long as the fingers and, with claws extended, perfect tools for gripping slippery earth, tree limbs and vines. The natives' tails would be dangerous during a fight as they could be used to bludgeon an opponent senseless while the creature hung from a nearby vine net.

As a koptero approached their location to airlift out several corpses, Chief Sitati consulted with the three experts, and they recommended that the team continue ahead, though Brando did so with guilt raging within. While they urged extreme caution, none of them felt that the danger was so great that the Ministry of Crises needed to abort the mission. Roshan noted that there were significantly fewer corpses than there should be inhabitants of the village: their deaths might be attributable to any number of causes, including ritual suicide, tribal in-fighting, sacrifice, and elimination after the discovery of some disease or imperfection.

Go on, Brando thought bitterly. *Rationalize it. Say whatever you must. But let's keep moving.*

They continued forward, with the Ministry informing them that two kopteroj would stand by twenty-eight hours a day to evacuate them should an emergency arise. Brando doubted this contingency would do any good, but it calmed the corpsmen's nerves and served his own purpose. He tried not to dwell on his guilt and concentrated on being prepared. As long as he was focused on getting Miwa back, not losing her again, he was able to forget the cruelty of his decision not to reveal the team's odds.

Most of Tuesday, Roshan and Dixit used their datapads to prepare technical monographs of their findings and a joint report for lay people in the government. Brando, when not studying his surroundings and getting his eyes accustomed to the semi-darkness without infrared help, attempted to engage in friendly banter with the two. They were both good people, intelligent and pleasant company. The twenty-hour marches had melted a good deal of their softness away, and Dixit in particular was looking quite healthy. Brando felt an odd connection to the young scientist, and her own quirky semi-agnosticism (she was still single at twenty-eight) made her a fascinating traveling companion.

On the morning of the eighth day of the expedition, Brando discovered a river a little north of their position, likely a tributary of the *Blankrivero* whose source was snow water melted by and mingling with hot springs on Kumora's face. Eager to wash the grime and sweat away, he sent Chuquipoma back to camp to notify the others and began to strip. As he peeled the clothes off till only his undergarment remained, he looked down wistfully at the symbol of the faith he'd renounced, touching the angle and the squares with nostalgia.

Then, sighing, he stripped off the one-piece silken garment. It was a symbol of Nando Miranda's commitment to Rhea and the family they'd forged together. But Nando could only exist in memory now. To move forward along the Path, Brando had to leave the shattered remnants of that persona behind.

Naked, he dove into the icy water and emerged into the warm air of first spring sputtering like a child. After scrubbing himself with sand, he left the river and stood by its bank, letting the water run off him in rivulets as the air slowly dried his short-cropped, graying hair. After a moment, he rummaged in his pack for some government-issue corpsman briefs.

But after pulling them on, he couldn't quite bring himself to finish getting dressed. There was a pleasure in standing on the riverbank, his eyes closed, the forest around him in a strange embrace. He lost himself in the moment.

"My. Pretty good shape for an old guy."

Brando kept his eyes closed. It was Sonali. She'd approached without his even noticing.

Not a good sign, squadman, he imagined Ben Wu grunting.

Hiding his embarrassment, he turned around and faced her. Her eyes widened a bit more at the sight of his corded chest and stomach muscles.

"You should have seen me back when I was pumped full of steroids and using illegal gravtiles to train on. I'm a scrawny wimp now compared to that." He bent for his vest, leggings and uniform.

"I've been wanting to talk to you, alone, Brando."

Brando's left eyebrow arched. "About?"

"Tsk, tsk. Epidemiology, Doctor D'Angelo."

"You're worried about disease?"

"Definitely. Public Health is examining the cadavers closely and beginning to determine what sort of a risk the Native Teregans present us, and us them."

"Aren't any viruses or bacteria likely to be variants of what we've already come across with animals in the last half century here?"

"For the most part, but there will be strains that only infect this species, and at least one is probably going to be deadly for humans. Hopefully we'll discover it now in the lab rather than later, during an autopsy of a human cadaver."

Brando finished sealing his uniform over the protective leggings and byrnie that he wore beneath it. "What's the point of worrying me about it, Dixit? Why did you need to talk to me alone?"

"Because your daughters have been with these beings for eight days, Brando."

He understood. Not only were the girls in danger from the creatures themselves, but also from the microorganisms that lived inside the indigenes. Of course, that meant the natives were also vulnerable to both Teri and Miwa.

"I hear you, Sonali. But there's no point in worrying about it. I can't do more for them than I already am."

Guilt is already the primary emotion I live with, he didn't say. *Worry is irrelevant.*

Shortly the other corpsman showed up and washed themselves as best they could in the chilly river water. Sitati had them refill the empty canteens and larger containers while Chan scouted ahead to determine whether the Native Teregans had traveled along the riverbank. He returned excitedly after a few moments, calling the chief and Brando to come with him. Roshan and Dixit tagged along.

"I almost walked right by it," Stefano explained as they neared a bend in the river. "But somebody left us a message."

He showed them a stick that was shoved into the mud near the water. Tied to it was a scrap of material that Brando recognized as an adornment from Miwa's knapsack, the one she used to carry her gear around in.

"It's Miwa," he told them.

"The stick's not all, D'Angelo." Stefano indicated an area near them. Crudely scratched into the mud were the words *"okey mawntin?"* in a hasty scrawl. Tana had done it again, he thought distractedly, then corrected himself. *Miwa* had gotten a message to him. She was surviving and keeping her wits about her. But why mountain? Was she telling Brando that she'd try to escape and go to the mountain like the map instructed her, or were the natives heading that way?

Sitati, who didn't know Standard, asked, "What does it mean?"

"That she's okay," Brando hesitated a moment, "and that they're taking her to the mountain. Taking them, I mean. The kids. They're okay."

Sitati decided to shunt off a message informing the Ministry of Crises

of this development, so he had the transmitter deployed. There were a few

messages in the queue that had come in after last night's download, and he

distributed them. Rhea had written Brando a note, lashing out at and praising

him at turns for his actions on Jitsu. It was obvious from the tone of the

message that she was struggling to believe in his essential goodness. He

was having a similar problem with doing so himself. He knew these men

couldn't hold their own against the natives, yet he could not train them. He

and Chuquipoma had attempted to convince Sitati to let D'Angelo teach

them a few strategies, but the chief had refused indignantly. This refusal,

however, did not assuage the guilt that ate at Brando's heart.

As he walked back to the river bend, he noticed most of the corpsmen

and the other two specialists in a circle around the receiver, weapons unslung

or holstered.

Stupid.

Some of them turned as he approached and stared at him with a mixture

of disgust, anger and fear. They pulled aside for him, and he saw that everyone

was watching a small holographic playback of the fight between Brando and

his squad. Sitati, kneeling before the receiver, shut it off and stood.

"D'Angelo, you are a despicable human being. Maybe not even that. No

sense of ethics or honor. You'll do anything to reach your…"

His words were abruptly cut off as an enormous spear ripped through his chest, sending his dying corpse flying forward in a shower of blood into the arms of a couple of startled corpsmen. The air around them was suddenly full of spears and swinging, dark forms.

And so it begins.

"Find cover now!" shouted Brando, running toward Dixit, who was trembling hysterically as spears plunged into the men around her.

Keep her safe.

He undid one of the pulley guns from his belt with his left hand; reaching her side, he encircled her waist with his right arm and shot a grapple upward into a distant bough.

"Sonali, clip your harness to mine. Now!"

She obeyed with shaking hands. As the pulley spooled the cable in, rushing the pair upward, their weight distributed along the belt and harness it was attached to, a spear slammed into Brando's back. The byrnie stopped it, but the pain was intense, like being hit by a kamioneto in the spine. The force sent them swinging in an arc.

Ignoring the spots of light in his vision the impact had caused, Brando snatched at a vine netting with his legs and released the grapnel's claws with a quick thrust of his thumb on the gun. As the cable came free and started spooling in, his weight and Dixit's shifted from his harness to his knees, and Brando clutched the biologist with both arms as they fell back, suspended upside down by his crossed legs. The cable whipped about wildly and struck a native swinging toward them, causing her to let go and fall to a bough four meters below.

Brando slowed the reeling-in, and the cable eased into its pulley with a snick.

Dixit wasn't screaming, but she was hyperventilating, and mumbling something between gasps that Brando couldn't quite understand.

"It's alright, Sonali. I won't let them get you." She clutched him more tightly, her legs wrapped about his waist, and he hoped that for once he'd be able to keep his promise. Slowly, he slipped one arm free, aimed a pulley gun, and shot the cable into a distant bough. In one movement, he slipped his legs free of the net and began reeling their bodies upward. Dixit screamed, and Brando glanced down to see the native spidering up the net.

Clawed her. Leggings protected me.

"Hang on. You're a biologist; you'll fix that up in no time," he babbled in her ear as they sped toward the bough. He grappled another and they swung to the left and farther up, then another and another until they'd reached the branches right at the edge of the canopy. Dappled sunlight illuminated Dixit in patches of gold and green as Brando laid her down on a limb and checked her leg. The gash looked nasty, but it wasn't terribly deep. He took off his pack and pulled out the first aid kit.

"I'm going to have to leave you up here, Sonali."

She looked at him mutely and shook her head, eyes wide. Brando began spraying antiseptic on the wound.

"Don't be so afraid. Remember what Vivek said: these upper branches are sacred to them. It's unlikely they'll come up here. But you've got your pistol," he stopped wrapping the bandage around her wound, yanked the weapon from the holster at Dixit's waist and put it in her hands, "and you know how to use it. Don't fire at their chests: aim for their heads, either the eyes or below the jaw going up. I'll be back as fast as I can. Those boys need me down there."

"Okay," she managed to gasp as he gave her a hypo full of antibiotics and endorphins.

"I need your knife," he said as he reached down and unsheathed the blade. Sitati had not allowed him any weapons at all. Patting her head as he would his daughters', he nodded and turned to run along the limb. Looking down, he saw Corpsman Leal scrambling onto a wide branch about twelve meters below. Two native warriors swung in from different directions, pirouetting off their vines onto the limb on either side. Brando finished yanking on his gloves and, slipping the knife between his teeth and snapping the rappelling ring at his belt to a vine, slid down at a palm-burning velocity onto the shoulders of one of the females. He opened his mouth and dropped the knife into his left hand so that as she turned to look at what had fallen on her, claws stretching to grab him, he was able to slit her throat in a fluid, wrenching motion.

As the warrior collapsed, he pushed off her back and swung, the vine still attached to his belt, toward where Leal was firing repeatedly into the other beast's chest.

"Her eyes, Leal! Hit her eyes!" Leal nodded and lifted the muzzle of his rifle. The bullet struck home, and the native twisted in pain, flailing her tail out toward them at the same time that the bullet exploded. She toppled from the limb and into the shadows below. Leal, who'd been struck by the beast's tail, nearly followed her down, but Brando grabbed his hand and steadied him.

"Go up and protect Dr. Dixit." The corpsman hesitated. "Now! There's no time for any foolishness, man!"

Leal fired his pulley gun and was lifted up as Brando continued using his vine to drop down to lower levels. About a hundred meters from the ground, he discovered a group of five corpsman, one of them Chuquipoma, making a stand against twice their number on a massive bough nearly wide enough to be Diadono's main street. The natives kept in motion, never presenting a weak point to the humans long enough to be shot at.

Brando, suspended just a meter above the branch and three meters away from the bobbing back of one of the warriors, unhooked his left pulley gun and shot the grapple into the creature's back. As he reeled it tilting backwards, he was yanked forwards as well, and their bodies connected with a nauseating thud. Taking advantage of the surprise that slowed his opponent down, Brando yanked the enormous spear from her hands and, wrapping his legs around her thick, furry neck, used her as leverage to send the weapon slamming into the back of one of her companions. The stone head ripped into the native's flesh and lodged between two ribs right behind where Brando knew their hearts were located.

"In the eyes, neck or back!" he shouted as the other men noticed him. "That's where they're vulnerable.

"Got it," a voice crackled in his ear.

Good. They have enough sense to keep on the same com channel.

The beast he was riding flipped backwards, slamming him against the bough with a thud. She yanked the grapnel from her back with a muffled yelp and raised a clawed hand to strike. Brando rolled off the bough into nothing. He soon realized that the vine had snapped and he was freefalling. As the frondy leaves whizzed past, he undid the right-hand pulley gun and fired at a tree trunk to his left. His fall jerkily switched to a rapid swinging arc. The left pulley was jammed: he couldn't reel the cable in. Instead, he unclasped its molecular bond and threw it to one side as the trunk rushed at him. There was a moss-covered vine netting a little farther down, he noticed, so he released the grapnel and twisted in the air to fall a bit more and snatch at it with his hands.

He found himself about twenty meters above the ground, and he quickly scrambled down via vines, running back toward the river the minute his boots touched the dirt. About twenty men, including Vivek, were dead or dying. A couple of corpsmen were still engaged in a losing struggle against about six of the natives.

All these men have families that will mourn and suffer and twist inside because of their deaths. And all that pain will be, in part, my fault.

"Hey!" Brando shouted in Standard, reaching down and popping pistols out of the holsters of two of his dead travel mates. "Big hairy bitches! Turn around so I can see yall's ugly-arse eyes!"

Two of them did turn, and both of Brando's arms went up in a fluid motion that Ben Wu had drilled him in so many times.

The gat ain't more than just another piece of you, Kyosu. Don't think about aiming, just bloody aim!

He jerked both trigger buttons twice, moving his hands slightly to the right as he pulled the second time. The two bullets that drilled into each creature's eyes exploded at the same time, sending it sprawling in the mud.

"How did he do that?" he heard one of the corpsmen muttered into the com link.

"They've got such big eyes," Brando snarled, pushing back against hysteria.

The remaining natives made one last lunge at the corpsman as Brando reached their side, but then scrambled up the trees and swung off quickly.

"No way I scared them, so they must need to catch up with somebody."

"Yes," nodded one of the corpsman, a brother from Kanaano named Derek Chan. "The main contingent left a few minutes ago.

"They took our transmitter."

Nambaryn Zorig, the other corpsman, made an impatient gesture. "We've got to go after them! We need that transmitter! We've got to be airlifted out of here, the wounded taken care of. Come on, D'Angelo: let's go!"

Brando shook his head. "No way. And see you men slaughtered, the handful of you who are still alive? I don't think so."

"You miserable monster… Our friends, our fellow corpsmen: they're all dead, and you want us to do nothing about it? Chief was right."

Brando had heard enough. He grabbed Nambaryn by the uniform and yanked him closer. "Listen to me, idiot. I just saved your life and the lives of several other men, so why don't you shut up and pay attention to the only person who's going to keep your soft self alive? If we go up against these creatures *now*, with all of you exhausted and hurt and in shock, completely unprepared for the sort of fighting that's needed, you'll all die. Sitati wouldn't let me prepare you, wouldn't even let me have a knife, but he's dead now, and you'll listen to me or die alone in the dark. Am I clear, Corpsman?"

Nambaryn nodded, his eyes narrowed in angry resignation. *Ah, so he's not a complete idiot. That's good. I can work with that.*

Brando led them to where he'd left Dixit. Along the way, they helped another group of three men who were being beaten by the tail and clawed fists of an especially massive native. They also met up with Chuquipoma and his four companions, who were dispatching the last of their attackers. As they all joined Sonali and Corpsman Leal up near the brighter upper branches, Brando looked about at the group, mostly wounded and grief-stricken, exhausted and frightened to the very depths of their souls.

"Twelve. A lucky number, I've been told. We stay here for a few more hours, then go down and bury our dead. Tomorrow we start training."

There was silence for a few seconds, and then one of Chuquipoma's group made a rude sound. "For what: our deaths?"

"To avenge our brothers and retrieve the transmitter."

"Brothers," repeated the man with disgust. "They weren't your brothers."

"That's not for you to decide. I suggest you stop treating me like a criminal and more like your teacher and commander."

It was an arrogant thing to say, but Brando needed them to understand, right now, that he was in control. He couldn't bear losing another life because he hadn't taken the initiative.

"Who put you in charge?"

Brando clenched and unclenched his left hand. "Circumstance."

He left the men to talk among themselves and went to check on Sonali. She'd fallen asleep, and Brando was struck by how young and vulnerable she was, curled up like a toddler against the enormous trunk of the ĉielarbo.

She's almost the age Tana would be, if she had lived.

An involuntary shiver danced along his spine, and he turned his head to Leal, who was still standing at her side.

"Thanks. You did a good job, Corpsman."

"I did my duty."

"She seem alright?"

Leal shrugged. "I'm no expert. But she was calling on the Lord, and I think he gave her some peace, since she's still sleeping."

"Calling on the Lord? How?"

"She just kept repeating parts of the 23rd Psalm: "The Lord is my shepherd, nothing will I lack" and "indeed, though I walk through the Valley of the Shadow of Death, I will fear no evil, for You are with me, protecting me with Your rod and staff.""

Brando nodded, taking the pistol from her clenched hands and holstering it for her.

There's no God, Sonali, but I'm here. And I'll walk with yall through this valley, and we'll just see about fear. Fearing evil, that's not yall's problem. Fearing yall's own shortcomings and mine? That's more relevant. I'm afraid, I'll admit. Afraid of losing all yall, of once again not being strong enough, fast enough, good enough to keep people alive. But I'll try, Sonali. I'll try and protect yall with my rod, with my staff, with every weapon and strategy that I can muster.

That's the Ona ra-Kyosu. The Professor's Way.

CHAPTER 21

DAY THREE OF THE TRIAL WAS HARDER FOR RHEA than the previous one had been, but also more illuminating. Seeing what Brando had been capable of once he understood the depth of the conspiracy and betrayal he and his family had been victims of made clearer in her mind the sort of man he was. While she was no longer sure she'd ever feel comfortable around him, her confidence in his ability to get her girls back was increasing with every piece of damning evidence.

Uninteresting were both the security recording from the garage in Station City where Brando had stolen a transport and various local law-enforcement cameras' views of his brutal interrogation of informants. They showed Brando's amoral view, according to Commander Mubarak, but Sanas spent little time on them, as Jitsuan law at the time had afforded ample power to the ATS, even when pursuing an investigation in the supposedly

Consortium territory that was Station City.

What really wrenched Rhea's soul were the series of recordings from Rasaro Platform: Brando's torture at Konrau Beserra's hands made her nearly weep; his insane, self-mutilating escape caused her to wring her hands so strongly the nails drew blood; the death-defying fury with which he faced foes outnumbering him ridiculously made her heart swell with hope. When she saw him kill Beserra, a look of sorrow crossing his face afterward, she knew that this was a man who, given other circumstances, would have been happy and made others so. His heart was so big that it could encompass everyone, given the opportunity.

But for some reason, God's plan for him did not include happiness. Perhaps all along He had wanted Brando to come here, to Terego, to face the natives as no one else could.

After a day riddled with long delays as the *Diomedes* transmitted its link while traveling at relativistic speeds, Rhea was eased out of the dancing stream of beams that flickered across her head. Shaking her head free of the cobwebs that invaded it because of the transition from faux- to real-life, she exchanged some words with Sanas and a couple of ministers, then went to pick up Jakobo, heading home for some much-needed rest. Tomorrow would see the end of the physical evidence, and the witnesses would begin to take the stand.

After forcing her stubborn son to stop replaying his father's message from the previous night over and over, she put the little one to bed. She then looked over some files, sipped herbal tea while reading from the Book, and finally checked her combox to access Brando's nightly message for her and Jakobo.

The combox, aside from messages from the sister subbing for her at the helpsocieto and a few last-minute notes from the legal team, was empty. She verified the time: 13:33 p.m. or 26:33 hours, corps time. Sitati had always shunted the team's messages by this time.

Perhaps Brando was busy. But, come on, a quick note: he couldn't dash off a quick note? Maybe there are technical issues.

Maybe, said a voice she hadn't heard in a long while, *he's spending a bit too much time with that biologist. Sonali Dixit's her name, isn't it? The one who still hasn't married though she's nearly thirty? What kind of a woman waits that long?*

Rhea tried to ignore the dark whisperings, but they gnawed at her. How could she trust Brando? If he was capable of lying about who he was, who his daughters were, what he believed, where he came from, then what assurances did Rhea have that he wouldn't betray her in other ways? Being married to an asexual woman for so many years must have taken its toll. His libido would need an outlet.

No. I can't give in to doubt. Lord, give me strength, faith, longsuffering.

Stillness eventually came, and she fell thankfully asleep.

DAY FOUR SAW THE CONCLUSION OF THE PHYSICAL EVIDENCE,
with the extremely frightening recording from a device Santo Koroma had
secreted away in the innermost bowels of the jinja where Samanei, Brando's
then sister-in-law and Oracle of the Neo Gnostic faith, was kept. In the
recording, Samanei admitted to having engineered the entire Brotherhood-
Jitsuan crisis, playing both sides against the middle for a reason only hinted
at, but which Rhea understand viscerally: revenge against the universe.

What was most disturbing was the way Brando snapped the archon's
neck on Samanei's orders. It made Rhea question for a moment the sanity of
her husband, though the woman's resemblance to Tenshi probably explained
much, as did, now that Rhea reflected on it finally, Teri's physical appearance.

A veil was lifted from her suddenly, and the rebellion of her daughter
was revealed for what it likely was: a response to subliminal cues from
Brando. They were going to have to talk long and hard about this quandary
when the trial and kidnappings had been resolved.

Next followed the scenes of Brando and Tenshi's house: AF soldiers
inside, the discovery of rooms full of dirt, the gravtiles and equipment in the
basement, the warning about the bombs, the evacuation of the soldiers, and
the explosion that reduced to rubble a symbol of the past.

*But you didn't break free of it, did you, Brando? You couldn't let go
even then.*

Sanas unexpectedly asked to introduce a new piece of evidence, a recreation rather than an actual recording. He explained that it was the simulation put together by Planetary Security and the ATS to investigate the murders of Tenshi and Tana D'Angelo. The judges allowed it, and Rhea, her heart beating savagely, watch in horror as the yakuza foot soldiers entered the home and brutally murdered Tenshi, who fought bravely to protect her daughter, and little Tana.

The simulation continued, showing Brando arriving and finding them. There was no sound here, as the creators of the simulation had no idea of what he had said, only of his movements in the blood-smeared room. But the slipping and sliding of the doppel were enough for Rhea: she felt his bereavement in the depths of her soul, understood what could make a man become a monster, what could compel him to play God.

"Log me out. Now," she sub-vocalized. The embassy technicians yanked her from the tribunal; in tears, she left the building and walked alone down the main avenue. What did she care about today's witnesses? What did a collection of old criminals who once been Brando's informants know about her husband's pain? What could a mechanic on Mars possibly say to negate the power of that scene: Brando with his two loves cradled dead in his arms, with Rhea's two babies cradled in his arms, with Teri and Miwa's broken bodies cradled for all eternity in weak, incapable arms whose inadequacy was burned indelibly in the spirit of a man who only wanted to love?

She collapsed onto a bench, sobbing. She knew of such sorrow, the pain of loss. Hadn't she, as a child, watched her mother die? Hadn't she been a deathbed nurse to her father as a teen? Hadn't she attended the funerals of aunts and uncles? Hadn't she buried her own husband?

If only you had trusted me with this, Brando. If only you had understood me well enough to know that this truth is what I needed, that I would have folded you in my arms and told you that I know, I know, I know. But He's there for us, Brando. It seems like He's not at times, but He is. Oh, if only you had let me show you the peace that could be found instead of pretending you'd found it. We belong together in Him, love. Our bonds transcend this world, transcend our pain, transcend our pasts. Oh, Brando. If only.

Wiping her eyes dry, she strode to the Ministry of Crises. Because of her position in the helpsocieto, she was attended at once. No, there still had been no transmission from the team. No, the minister was not out of the trial yet, but if she wanted to wait, he would certainly be back very soon.

She was thankful for the delay as it allowed her to compose her thoughts and freshen up from so much crying. When Roberto de Waal arrived, they shared a perfunctory embrace and went inside the minister's office.

After updating Rhea on his wife's health, de Waal cut to the chase.

"You're here about the transmission delay, aren't you, sister? I'm going to share something with you that can't leave this room, unless to be discussed with the Prime Minister himself. Yesterday we *did* receive a message from Sitati, a brief note explaining that they'd been left a message by the kidnapped young people indicating that they were fine. The chief mentioned that a more detailed report would follow in an hour, along with any personal messages the team members had ready to be shunted. However, we didn't receive any such message, and I'm afraid we still haven't heard anything. It's a very delicate situation. I think you have heard from the Prime Minister that the CPCC ambassador and his staff are becoming suspicious. They've heard rumors of monsters abducting young people, so they've been contacting every member of the government, trying to find out why such stories are circulating."

Rhea nodded soberly, both encouraged to hear that the girls and their friends were apparently okay and made uneasy by the possibility of Consortium interference. "And of course the stories are so wildly exaggerated and infused with mythological elements that it shouldn't be too hard to plausibly deny them, which, I assume, is Brother Khumalo's strategy?"

De Waal tilted his oval head to one side and squinted. "Well, denial is perhaps too strong a word for what he has personally been doing: more like orchestrated deflection. He is made uneasy by the thought of lying to anyone, though he hasn't come down on any of us who feel that the Lord, in this situation, will surely understand if we use less than honest means to keep His people free from domination by the Consortium."

"Within reason and scripture."

"Of course. On their own, after a long conversation with their bishop and me, the families of the missing young people are going to publicly denounce the rumors as false and counterproductive. Superstitious nonsense that gets in the way of the real investigation. We've got the heads of the three news agencies in the loop now, most significantly the TRD, and they've agreed to sit on this story in exchange for all the details once we've developed a method of revealing the grend…, I mean, the natives' existence to the CPCC without turning this planet over to them."

Rhea considered the situation for a moment. "So you've got the legislature looking at ways of negotiating with the CPCC to allow them scientific and diplomatic access to the indigenes without actually annexing Terego or occupying it?"

De Waal nodded and sipped some water. "Yes, and the judicial examining the treaties we've negotiated with the Consortium to determine what, if anything, they say about such situations. But all of that hinges on the success of the rescue team, and we don't know what's happening with them."

"Could there be technical issues with the equipment? I mean, just look at the CPCC's extremely advanced conferencing equipment and all the times it's failed during the trial."

"That's what we're hoping. Maybe they're working on the transmitter right now, trying to get it up and running. Also, first spring has started, and the changes in weather patterns often disrupt broadcasts from portable communications equipment. It's already started raining over that part of the forest, you know. Soon we'll be in the middle of the rainy season. One of my technicians reminded me that the aurora gets particularly strong this time of year. You've probably already noticed it at night, Sister. Fluctuations in the planet's magnetic field apparently cause problems with communications quite often, more so on southern continents than on Zarahemla and Novameriko, but even here they can be a source of glitches."

These possibilities sustained Rhea's hopes, but she felt she must mention the explanation neither of them seemed willing to voice. "Of course, they might have been attacked and either wounded or killed."

The minister shrugged his sloping shoulders. "Or the transmitter might've been damaged in such an attack. The Ministry of Public Health has been in touch, and they are worried about native diseases. It's possible that the team might be infected or otherwise have fallen ill. The fact is, no one knows, and we are not sure of how long to wait before taking action. If it is only a technical glitch and we send in rescue teams, we may risk or lose lives unnecessarily."

"What have you decided?"

"Prime Minister Khumalo wants us to give the team three days to contact us: today, tomorrow and Saturday. If there's been nothing by then, we'll have an emergency meeting Saturday night to determine a course of action, probably rescue teams dropped in at the last broadcast location. Sister, you are needed at the meeting."

"Me? I'm surprised: if you wanted a representative from the helpsocieto, why not President Larkin?"

"Ana's deferred to you in this case on the Prophet's instructions. He apparently feels that while you are just Larkin's second counselor, you are more knowledgeable about the case and more equipped to provide the sort of input that we require. I have to agree. I've always wondered... why aren't *you* the president of the helpsocieto?"

I put my family first, Minister, Rhea thought with just a little bitterness, *while Larkin put hers off.*

"I suppose it just hasn't been in the Lord's will yet, Brother. When He decides it is time, He will open that door for me."

THE FIFTH DAY OF THE TRIAL WAS SHORT and plagued by significant time lag as the Diomedes reached the upper limits of its acceleration before its fenestration later that day. In fact, the day ended early, after the testimony of former medical technicians from Jitsu who'd been in charge of the blood samples Brando had allegedly stolen and that of the presently imprisoned black-market smuggler who'd sold Brando his *ranfura*. Authorities had never discovered who'd supplied the gravtiles, but the crooked scientist who'd gotten Brando the cloning equipment would be on the stand Monday.

Rhea and Jakobo had dinner with Sister Nishiguchi and then watched a film at Diadono's local sensory cinema. The story, an adaptation of the ancient tale of the ugly duckling, had Rhea's little boy captivated, and all he could talk about afterward was how he was going to be a swan when he got big, too.

There was no communication from the rescue team that evening. Rhea's sleep was light and troubled, her dreams full of incomprehensible images and sensations. On Saturday, she and Jakobo went for a picnic in the city park (no one dared be alone in the wild anymore), and he attended his tee-ball practice. These activities allowed Rhea to focus on her son and ignore, for a time, the nauseous suspense that roiled in her gut.

She was beeped on her combox at about eight o'clock: she and Jakobo had just finished dessert at a local restaurant, and she dropped him off with Chiho to attend a meeting that would take place in thirty minutes in the executive building.

It was a perfunctory assembly of the people in the crisis's inner circle: the ministers of immigration, crises, public health, communication and environment. The Prime Minister basically announced that in the morning a team of corpsmen and technicians would be dropped into the forest under the command of Chief Corpsman Shaw at the location from which the team's last broadcast had been transmitted. Tomorrow at 15:00, all those present were to reconvene to discuss the findings of the team and decide on what further actions should be taken.

Rather than driving her kamioneto home, Rhea asked Chiho whether she and Jakobo could spend the night, and the sister agreed. Rhea's nervousness and worry were just too intense for a trip through the darkness to her lonely home. She cried a while on Chiho's shoulder after all the children had gone to bed, and then she herself fell into a thick dreamless slumber that left her rested but groggy in the morning.

Throughout the church service, she kept checking her watch, and she had no patience for the matters under consideration at the helpsocieto reunion afterwards. Finally, 14:30 came, and she rushed to the executive building to attend the meeting.

Khumalo, his face set gravely, got to the point immediately.

"This morning, the drop team discovered twenty-one graves, apparently dug by the survivors of a brutal attack on the first team. This means that eleven men and one woman lived to continue their mission. There was no sign of the transmitter, so we can only assume from the lack of communication that it was damaged in the attack. We've identified the bodies of the dead, and we know that Corpsman Leal, communications technician of the team, is still among the living. We can only hope that he is attempting to repair the equipment to get a message out."

"Was there any message at the site?" asked the minister of communication.

"Strangely, no. We had thought that the surviving corpsmen would have left some indication of their intentions, but we've found none. They may've had to leave the site in a rush. There are no human tracks leading away, and we speculate that they may be traveling on the river that flows near there in order to throw the natives off their trail."

Torres, his face pale and his eyes sunken, interrupted. "Don't tell us that you're sending other teams to track them."

Khumalo's eyelids fluttered with nearly imperceptible annoyance. "Marlo, I appreciate your concern, and caution is clearly required. We are airlifting search parties in and out in five-hour shifts. Their location is monitored by rotating shifts of kopteroj. We're taking no chances."

"I urge you," Torres said, his voice cracking, "to reconsider notifying the AF of what is happening here. You have no proof that the Consortium would attempt to occupy our world just because of an alien race. How many more Tereganoj are going to die before you people start listening? If you think you're doing God's will, you are not. Your actions fly in the face of everything the Book teaches us!"

"Minister Torres, calm down. As you know, our actions have the full support of the Church and the Prophet. We have been given this planet as stewards of all that it contains, and we will not abandon that responsibility because the task becomes difficult. That is my final word."

Rhea couldn't bear it anymore. "Is Brando alive?"

The Prime Minister welcomed the change of subject. "Yes, Sister, he is. At least, as far as we know. His body was not in any of the graves, so we assume, as we do about all the apparent survivors, that he is alive."

"What about Chief Sitati?" Her mind was spinning crazily. Something was taking shape, though she didn't know what, or why she was asking about Sitati.

"Dead."

Rhea nodded, beginning to understand what her spirit was unfolding before her. "Then they're okay. They'll make it. If Sitati's dead, then Brando has taken charge."

There were sounds of obvious disbelief. "What," de Waal asked, "leads you to that conclusion, Rhea?"

"You've seen those recordings, Roberto. He's a soldier, a more experienced one than any of those young boys in that team, and a natural leader, as all of you know. Or will you pretend you didn't seek out his advice on important matters back when you thought he was Nando Miranda, Elder of the Melchizedek Priesthood, counselor in his quorum, teacher and pillar of the community? When he wants people to listen, they do."

The Prime Minister's eyes had fairly lit up with hope. "And what do you think he would do if he became leader of this group?"

"I don't know. Get them ready. Go against the enemy. You saw what he did on that platform around Jitsu: *he burned his hand off* to get away, and he *threw himself against fifty men* in that hangar. Blew the whole thing up. He has no fear. He'll go against these natives the same way."

De Waal shook his head. "I've read the psych reports, just like you have, Rhea. He *had* no fear because he had already lost everything that mattered. Now the natives have his daughters, and that is a weakness that will hold him back."

"But she has a point," Khumalo interjected. "He's the one that can get them back. Maybe the only one on this planet who can. And we need them back. If they die, if we lose the lives of young people, the Consortium will have just the excuse it needs to end our tenuous independence." He ignored Torres's snicker and moan. "Our teams will keep looking for him, but our hopes rest on D'Angelo now. God protect him and the corpsmen."

As her head bent for the prayer that closed the meeting, Rhea sent a silent message out to Brando, wherever he was.

Be strong. You must do what has to be done. You have before, and you will again. The darkness has no power over you: you are in God's hands.

CHAPTER 22

MAY 19, 2676. SHE'S GONE, DIARY. GONE FOR GOOD.

"I'm not okay. Don't think I will be for a long time. But Isabella forced me to choose. Jitsu or her. And though I love her, though I have no idea how I'm going to live without her by my side, I can't leave my homeworld. It … it *needs me,* Diary. And I don't have much time. My spark said I'll die young. So I need to get to work.

"As the shuttle lifted into the sky, taking her away from me, I was reminded of the day Santo and Maryam dragged Samanei from our home. She kept screaming my name, over and over. 'I'll get you free!' I shouted as umma and apa held me back. "Whatever it takes!'

"I intend to keep that promise. It's been five years. For a while I thought they'd broken her, but now she's ordered the creation of a legislature. She's sending me a signal, showing me the way. I have to become part of the Reform movement, push for the changes that will get the Oracle out from under the thumb of the archon and his extreme Dominian faction.

"As much as I don't trust them, I think we'll have to get the Consortium involved to wrest power away from men like my uncle. Yes, I know expansionists would love to snatch Jitsu up again, but there must be a way to negotiate an alliance that keeps our sovereignty intact. Perhaps as a protected state.

"I walked home after the tearful goodbye with la bella Isabella. Right past the CPCC embassy. It's boring, too small, in the wrong part of Station City.

"When I got home, I filled the emptiness of our apartment with the scratching of stylus on screen. I've got an idea, you see. A building like nothing on this planet, one that will make the ambassador sit up and take notice of me. One that will get *everyone's* attention.

"It will take me years to design it, get it built. But I have to. For Samanei. For my fellow Aknawajin on this beautiful world. And to fill the Isabella-shaped hole in my heart."

Teri looked up at Carmen, who was sniffling and wiping her cheeks.

"I'll never leave you, Terinjo. Te lo juro."

Setting the journal aside, Teri kissed away her tears. "Ya sé, querida Carmen. And I'll never leave you, either. Whatever we accomplish, we'll do it together, yeah?"

Carmen nodded. "Ugh, help me forget about Tenshi's heartbreak. Your other males may not want to talk to you, haha, but catch me up. How much have you learned?"

Josuo, Ronaldo and Anyi were down in the field, collecting the crop along with Sekõtaldh's males. They were not at all happy, no matter how hard Teri tried to make them see the logic and sense in their doing what the tribe expected them to. They were also annoyed because Teri kept Carmen by her side, but she wasn't about to let them torment her girlfriend.

"The Sháinkhÿngigg—did I tell you their name means "holy people"?—keep treating me like someone special, though I can see they're waiting for their high priestess Ùshëshajirh to show up and make a final judgment. In the meantime, I've gleaned a lot from stories and situations, piecing together a pretty good understanding of the natives. There are three genders: drones, highborn, and males."

Carmen nodded. "I figured. How do they reproduce, then?"

"I think the drones produce eggs. They then have two choices. If they pass an egg to a highborn, she then passes it to a male: the resulting kid will be male or highborn. If a drone passes an egg directly a male, the child's a drone. And before you ask, I have no idea how this egg-passing happens."

"You haven't been invited to an orgy yet, then?"

Teri gave Carmen a little shove. "Cállese, mujer. You've probably noticed the family set-up: almost always one drone per highborn. From a story I heard, it's clear not all highborn are equal. I think the ones lowest on the social ladder have to rent a drone from a higher-up for reproduction."

"That's messed up," Carmen observed.

"Yeah, agreed. All highborn have at least one male. The more you have, the more prestigious you are. My four males aren't quite enough to be impressive, so I think I'll snag a few more for my harem when we're back in Diadono."

Carmen raised an eyebrow. "That shit isn't funny, Terinjo."

"Lady Tenshi, lowly male. Show some respect."

"Ha! If you're going to be a highborn, don't you have to run a household?"

Teri smiled. "Yup. Make sure the males and children do all their tasks well, obeying law and tradition. We'd have a garden tract that you all would have to tend. Water has to be gathered, food prepared, children taught."

"Sounds like you'd just be supervising while we work our asses off."

Teri stood and gestured expansively. "I'd also have to perform religious rituals demanded by even minor tasks. While you were busy from sun-up to sundown, I'd also be struggling to maintain or increase our family's position in the social fabric. Plus, you've seen the highborn that come visit me: lots of them have specific tribal duties. Religious leaders, teachers, political figures. Which reminds me: some highborns' harems are dedicated to a certain skill. Like compound building. Or latrine digging. I think I'll ask for that second one if we need to specialize."

"Oh, my God, can you imagine the look on Josuo's face?"

"Ha! The shithead would feel right at home."

After they were done giggling at the image of Josuo disposing of native waste, Carmen tried to get serious.

"They wonder if you're their messiah, right? But what are their beliefs? I mean, beyond the big rites they carry out every three days in the main clearing, with all that strange singing and dancing."

Teri shrugged. "I don't know much. Apparently, their ancestors came across the ocean many years ago. Their god guided them to this continent and to this forest, where they broke apart and formed six nations. The Holy People tribe is a part of Dhörggìth."

"Josuo remarked the other day," Carmen revealed, "that he couldn't wait to bring a seventy into the forest and begin converting the savages."

Clenching her teeth, Teri said, "They shroud their beliefs in mystery, but their rituals seem somehow holier than ours. He should them more respect. We're still alive, aren't we? Let's not rush to judgment."

There was a rustle outside. Sekõtaldh's voice called out.

"Lady Tenshi, you are wanted in the central clearing."

Kissing Carmen's forehead, Teri turned to go. "Be back in a bit. Maybe go help the rest of my harem."

"Oh, right away, Lady Tenshi," Carmen said drolly.

A LARGE GROUP OF HIGHBORN HAD GATHERED in the central clearing, surrounding someone, asking many questions at once. As Teri approached, they fell silent. Pulling aside, they revealed a highborn who was advanced in age, as Teri had learned to distinguish by how bent her ear tips were and how her eyes bled rheum.

"You are the one who calls herself Tenshi," the newcomer said in Baryogo.

"Yes, Lady. I assume you're Ùshëshajirh."

"You struggle to say it, but yes, that is the name I use. Come closer, Lady."

Teri did as she was instructed. Ùshëshajirh sucked in her left cheek in a gesture that indicated a contemplative state. As she stopped about a meter from the high priestess, Teri saw the highborn reach into a leather bag she had about her waist and pull out a metal square and cube.

A datapad. A small holo projector.

"The Greenseer has blessed me with a magical gift, one that contains the incredible power of your people, Tenshi. The Greenseer has placed an image of Çèrhingÿl on it, in her new form. Do you know the story of Çèrhingÿl, Tenshi?"

Teri couldn't believe that someone was finally talking directly to her, with questions and answers instead of riddles and stories.

Probably her contact with the Greenseer. She knows how humans converse.

"No, Lady. My people don't know any of the tales of your people. We are not of the six nations."

"No, that you are not. Nor are you from the shadow-layered forest that surrounds us. Nor from the land and water that sits beneath the Unblinking Eye. You are from another land whose people cower from the imperious gaze of some other god, and you've come to our land to displace the People, pull down the forest, and use your magic to weaken our God. These things have been revealed to me by the Greenseer. He has told me of one, however, who will be different. One who will fear our God and embrace our ways. Çèrhingÿl born in the form of the *ingan*."

Teri had to wrack her brain for the meaning of the word. Then it came to her: an archaic Baryogo synonym for *umuntu*, human.

The high priestess continued. "When the wide tree-girded land was younger, the noble ancestors of the People lived across the great green expanse of water in the realm of the Great Angry Mountain. There were frondy forests there as well, and fresh clean water aplenty. They did not live as we do, following instead a haughty queen and sharing drones indiscriminately. The majority of highborn had only one full-cheeked male bonded to them by the golden-robed queen, and highborn worked shoulder to shoulder with their bondmates in tasks that were beneath them.

"It was oracled one day by the haughty queen's advisors that the Great Angry Mountain would soon spew forth fire and liquid rock and destroy the moss-festooned forest where the ancestors of the People lived. The queen refused to listen, and ordered the wise advisors killed.

"One of the advisers, say the tales of the People, was a strange being unlike any that lived in the forest. She was shorter, with less hair and no tail, but her incomparable wisdom had made her valuable to the queen. Zhehoha, which was what this strange being was called, revealed herself to the queen's thick-boned drone soldiers as Çèrhingÿl, the first highborn created by Çìrhãná, bondmate of the Unblinking Eye, when the tree-ringed land had just been seeded. The power of Çèrhingÿl's revelation was such that the brave drones let her live and began to follow her and protect her as she scoured the forest in search of clean-souled highborn who would believe her holy words.

"After many trials and setbacks, most sacred Çèrhingÿl found seven sisters who accepted her powerful word and agreed to leave the forest with her. They took with them their fertile bondmates and the long-tailed drones who followed the holy one. As they made their way to the great green expanse of water, they encountered many tribulations and had to kill many highborn who wished to stop the divine journey. Çèrhingÿl bonded these new males to the highborn siblings, and they finally reached the water's roiling edge. There Çèrhingÿl taught them to build great, creaking ships of sturdy wood, and they sailed across the sea, guided by the Luminous Stone of Sacred Power through much adversity till they reached the moss-hung forest and founded the six nations.

"I do violence to our tales, ripping from them their beauty, to be brief like the Greenseer has trained me to be when talking with ingan. He says you have no patience for stories. So I will tell you, Tenshi, what this concerns."

She pressed a long finger against the side of the box she was holding, and a small image popped into life above its surface.

It was Tenshi.

No. It seemed like Tenshi, but as Teri had never imagined her: head shaven, eyes sunken and tired, face emaciated and hard with anger. She understood with a shudder.

Samanei. This is Samanei Koroma, Tenshi's twin.

She looked so much like Teri that there would be no doubt in the natives' minds.

"This is the image of Çèrhingÿl's new form for her third sacred advent. It is you, Tenshi. You are the one who will unite us. The Greenseer told the Sháinkhÿngigg when he walked through our broad realm 'you shouldn't be all separated if you're descended from siblings. You must be all one family if you want to survive the arrival of the ingan.' We have begun the process: many mighty tribes have heard the words of the Greenseer and accepted out new destiny, but many others refuse. The Greenseer says there is little time left: the drones of your people are approaching this world in their great flying boats, and they will burn the dark-shadowed forest with their powerful magic. You must help us stop them."

There was the dilemma, the opportunity she'd been hoping for. If she could get her friends released, then they could warn the other Novasanktuloj and get them prepared.

If I don't agree, perhaps they'll kill us or keep us captive while they attack. I can do this. I have been thinking of how to act for a good twelve days. I can pretend to help them, give my people a chance to do something, call the CPCC or whatever.

"I want you to release my males first. They will go stay with my sister until we have done what needs to be done."

"If we release your males, they will warn your people."

"If you don't release them, I will not help you."

The high priestess flicked her tongue in and out of her mouth. She turned the holoprojector off.

"I will release them only if you obtain for me one of the flying ships of your people."

Teri hadn't expected such a request; she'd always imagined that being accepted as the messiah would give her unquestioned power.

Forget this. I'm not going to betray other humans for these things.

"No."

The high priestess looked up at the canopy, then down at her feet. "The Greenseer has taught me about *irony*. In order for Zhehoha to see she was really Çèrhingÿl, she had to confront her own death. But I understand that your people are different. Think of this: in our nation, it is customary for a highborn wishing to join a tribe to sacrifice her most valued male and her drone, and to bond herself to a new male and drone from the new tribe, thereby demonstrating her allegiance and mingling her blood with that of the tribe. If her drone is already dead, she sacrifices a child.

"The Greenseer has also explained to me how your people value every individual life, often above the good of the tribe itself. Highborn of your people would give their own lives to keep their males alive, as evil as that sounds to us. This is why I know that you will assume your place."

Ùshëshajirh spoke to a pair of drones, who went bounding off toward the fields. The high priestess continued. "I am going to sacrifice one of your males, and since you have no drone or child with you, I will give you a choice: obtain for me a flying ship and many of your people's magical reeds, or I'll sacrifice another."

Teri felt as though someone had struck her violently in the chest: it became difficult to breathe, and lights danced in her vision.

Die? One of them has to die? No!

"Wait. You don't have to sacrifice anybody. I'll do it, whatever you ask. I'll do it. Just don't... don't kill any of them."

Tears spilled from her eyes. The other highborn turned and murmured to each other. Ùshëshajirh turned and addressed them.

"It has begun. She is opening up to the spirits of our ancestors, just like the Firstborn did. The trial will fill her with the voices, and she will accept the supple leather robe of her destined role."

The drones returned to the clearing, dropping Teri's friends roughly on the ground. Carmen leapt to her feet, hurrying toward Teri, but she was stopped by one of the guards.

"Terinjo? What's happening here? Why are you crying?"

Teri whirled to face the priestess.

"Don't you lay a finger on them, bitch!"

Ùshëshajirh blinked. "Which is her favorite, Sekõtaldh?"

The younger highborn twitched her ears forward at Carmen. "The one standing, with light head fur. Keridha is her name, I believe."

"Bring her forward."

The guard led Carmen to Ùshëshajirh.

"Terinjo, what … what are they doing? What do they want with me?"

Teri started to move toward them, but she was held back, not by the drones, who didn't dare touch her, but by the hands of three highborn.

No, no, no, no, no. Not her. Not this. Anything but this. Anyone.

"That's not my favorite," she groaned. "He is."

She jerked her head toward Josuo, tried pointing even with her arms restrained.

Josuo started getting up. "What the fuck are you telling them, Teri? Why are you pointing at me?"

"She is lying," Sekõtaldh announced. "She spends all her time with her Keridha."

Teri turned her head and stared at the highborn, trembling with fear and rage. "If they hurt her, I will fucking kill you."

"It is our custom," whispered Sek in her ear, "and it will show you who you really are."

From the leather bag at her waist, Ùshëshajirh pulled a stone dagger, dark volcanic glass. The guard pushed Carmen toward the priestess

"Teri, what are they going to do to me?" Carmen sobbed hysterically, her eyes full of horrible pleading. "Oh, God, Teri, stop them, don't let them hurt me. *Yo ... yo te quiero, bonita.* Help me! Don't let them kill me, por el amor de Dios!"

Teri's heart felt as though it would push out from her chest in an explosion that would melt the very forest from the face of this world.

Years of capoeira training kicked in by instinct. She dropped to the ground in a negativa derrumbando, her weight pulling her free of the highborns' grip even as she swept their legs out from under them.

The priestess raised the knife as the guard pulled back Carmen's head, exposing her neck as she twisted frantically. All Teri's friends were screaming.

The knife started coming down in an arc.

Teri rolled into a handstand, then swept through the air in an aú batido, the cartwheeling kick slamming into the guard's snout, making her stagger back.

But the knife still sliced across Carmen's throat, leaving a line of red.

Another drone snatched Teri out of the air and slammed her against the ground.

The universe exploded. Everything went silent.

As darkness fell, Teri caught sight of something glittering amid the trees.

Metal. And glowing eyes.

CHAPTER 23

EVERY BIT OF CIRCUMSTANTIAL EVIDENCE BUOYED Antonio's suspicions. The attitude of Rhea Kumar-Miranda—she hadn't changed her name—at the trial was odd enough, but the communiqués from Consul Miyazu on public hysteria and stories about monsters abducting children were downright bizarre. The fact that the families of the missing young people held a press conference to denounce the stories as untrue sealed the issue.

They were hiding something from Antonio. He thought he knew what it was.

Brando had brought Samanei Koroma to Terego.

Antonio had been convinced the two of them were working together ever since he'd first seen the recordings of the Oracle ordering Brando to kill Santo and the squadman doing just that. Brando had hidden her somewhere, probably in the Great Seneka Forest where supposedly he was searching for the clones. She had struck some sort of deal with the Teregan government, perhaps a chance to use her contacts to ally with other independent worlds against the CPCC. Reunited with the abominable clones she'd helped bring into existence, she had also requested that Brando be sent to her as part of the bargain.

Perhaps she had yak troops there in the forest with her: black market chitin looked very strange to yokels who'd never seen it before, and it wasn't hard to imagine local humans thinking that suited-up yaks were monsters.

It was all speculation, but Antonio was convinced that something similar to this scenario was happening on the surface. Samanei had never been found, nor had any of the equipment or weapons Brando had taken with him when he left Jitsu.

The trial was a sham, a mirage, a way to distract Antonio from the real story. And they were rushing through it, trying to get everything done as quickly as possible, even if it meant hurting their own cause. They had no intention of giving Brando over to Antonio: they were going to make their move before he ever got to Terego.

During the weekend recess, Captain D'Angelo tried to analyze once again the Teregan collective psyche to understand what might be motivating them to act so suicidally, but his visceral aversion to all things religious hampered his study. He enlisted the help of the *Diomedes'* anthropology expert, Lieutenant Enver Orbay.

By Sunday, Orbay contacted the captain, ready to report. Their doppelgangers soon faced each other in the conference room.

"Okay, Captain, first a quick history of Terego. Its inhabitants left Earth more than three centuries ago, in June of 2391, on a sleeper ship called the *Malavaro*. The *Bountiful*. This was back when the *Nuova Pace Romana* still ruled Earth with a proverbial iron fist."

"My family's Italian. I know all about them. Go on. Why'd they leave Earth? Was the Wiccan Catholic Church repressing them?"

"It had imposed tight restrictions on religious freedoms, yes, sir. So an alliance was forged among forty-nine prominent Mormon families, seven each from seven Earth cities: Aba, Bengaluru, Dubai, Hong Kong, Lima, Nairobi, Oaxaca. All with different ethnicities, but joined by their common religion and shared identity as non-white. Calling themselves Novasanktuloj or New Saints, they pooled their resources, got an aerospace company to build them the ship, and put themselves in stasis. Their AI frame looked for a planet while the ship gradually accelerated to about .4c by the end of the trip. In 2649 it finally found one, began braking, and by 2655 had them in orbit around Terego."

"All the people they hated or feared were dead and far away," Tony mused.

"Yes, sir. The first to be roused from stasis were the First President, head of the church, guy who had the revelation to leave old Terra to begin with, and the twelve apostles. Not Matthew, John and all them."

"I know, I know." Tony had very little patience for religion, but he understood its mechanisms well enough. "The Mormon mucky-mucks. Tell me why this is important."

"You need to know a little about LDS theology. For them, there are two main gods humans have to worry about: Elohim, the head guy, the father of all human spirits, and Jehovah, aka Jesus Christ, creator of the universe and first-born son of Elohim. They also believe that humans, if they are saved and glorified in the afterlife, can one day become gods, too, having spirit children like Elohim. Different revelations in the twenty-second and twenty-third centuries made it clear that this is no easy task, since you have to go through a long process of maturation as a glorified being before attaining that divinity, and the upshot was that if there were other gods out there, there weren't too many."

Such religious drivel made Antonio's head throb. "Fascinating. And the point is?"

"Sorry, sir. When they came out of stasis, First President Joseb Yeong and his apostles were divided on the issue of where the spirits of humans born on Terego would come from. Some said Elohim, just like on Earth. Others said that Jehovah himself was doing the honors, though they were a minority, since revelations had already shown Jehovah's job was managing the universe and saving souls. A third group insisted that Joseph

Smith, the man that founded the religion, had been granted early godhood and would be their spiritual father. Yeong meditated, had a vision, and announced to everyone that Novasanktuloj babies born on Terego would be *Smitinfanoj*: children of Smith."

Antonio groaned. "Lieutenant, I want you to tell me the relevance of all this idiocy to the present situation now before I lose my patience."

"It's simple, sir. Tereganoj—the ones born there—don't see themselves as normal humans. They're special, see? The first children of the first human to reach godhood. The first god to evolve in this universe, most of them believe. They'll never bend to CPCC governing, because they are the chosen ones, in more ways than one."

Antonio nodded and swallowed heavily, the arrogance of these backwater nobodies becoming clearer to him. He was reminded of Kunti insurgents and their supercilious view of the Consortium. "What else?"

"Yeong reorganized the Church, eliminating the First Presidency and renaming his title *Prophet* like Smith had been called. The prophet has a group of underling high priests called the Quorum of the Prophet, but that's not important. What is, is that even though Terego's treaty with the CPCC— the one signed in 2685 to end the stand-off between the two sides, established a secular government—that government is just a façade."

"Really?" The captain become focused, intent.

"Yes, sir. The Planetary Court, highest in their judicial branch, is made up of seven of the twelve apostles. Most of the legislators are also stake presidents or high priests in some other position of authority in the church. The minister of education is the presiding bishop, the guy that tells all the bishops on the planet what to do. And Khumalo himself, prime minister of all of Terego, is, so far as we can determine, completely in Prophet Disbergen's pocket."

D'Angelo mulled this over. It sounded like just the sort of planet Samanei Koroma would be attracted to, just the sort of theocratic springboard for whatever deviousness she had planned. The evidence against her had demonstrated her patience. She'd waited, bided her time, and now she probably had this whole nutty lot of berkless fanatics eating out of her hand. There were those in the Consortium Defense Coalition, the majority political force of the moment, who suspected Samanei had somehow gotten Kunti to attack the Consortium. If such suspicions were true, Terego would be a snap.

"But what's their goal?" he mused aloud, leaning back in his seat, rubbing his sideburns distractedly.

Taking this as a direct question, Orbay responded. "To establish Zion. On Earth. The North American continent."

Antonio sat up. "What?"

"Yes, sir. They believe that Jehovah wants the Novasanktuloj to set up a perfect city for him on Earth. Then he'll establish a kingdom from which to rule all of humanity."

Antonio had read this before, but of course he had dismissed it as more religious insipidity. Now he began to sense sinister undertones in the prophecy. He could imagine Samanei using her insanity to convince them that, who knew, *she* was Jesus come back from beyond. Or one of the girls. Or Brando, or whoever, but it was not beyond her to distort these innocent fanatics' beliefs so that they became, collectively, an army she'd use to wreak havoc on humanity again.

"Thank you, Orbay. Good job. Tell Maheu to get the commodore for me, then patch him through."

"Yes, sir. You might want to read this."

Orbay slid his hand through the air, bringing shimmering square with text to life in front of his captain. As the lieutenant walked out, Tony read what had been labeled *Teregan Anthem: Translated into Standard.*

Praise to the man that communed with Jehovah
Jesus anointed that prophet and oracle.
Blessed to open the last dispensation,
Kings will praise him and nations revere him.
Hail to the Prophet, ascended to heaven!
Traitors and tyrants now fight him in vain.
Mingling with gods, he can plan for his brothers:
Death cannot conquer the hero again.

Tony shunted the document to data refuse with an irritated shove.

Get ready, then, because the fight I'll bring you is not in vain, tricky little children of Smith or Elohim or whoever sired you bastards. You won't lie to me anymore. No one lies to me again. I swore that when I was fifteen, and no lot of Bible-thumping berks is going to do what my Dad did to me, hide the truth from me, make me believe a lie.

All liars must be judged and punished. Justice. Justice. Justice.

CHAPTER 24

AFTER SHE'D TAKEN A BATH, MIWA ASKED FOR HER PACK. Shalura,
hesitantly, had allowed her to have it. Miwa gratefully pulled out the change of
clothes she'd brought with her, a lighter sweatsuit that was more appropriate
for the warmer weather that had set it. She also got to put her sneakers on
instead of just trudging around in double woolen socks. She topped everything
off with the leather robe Shalura had given her and knelt to quickly scratch a
message in the mud and leave a scrap of fabric from her pack.

Miwa, of course, had no idea of whether she was being searched for,
but she believed that her father would not just sit back and let her be taken
captive. In fact, she was so certain that he'd come for her that she'd stopped
worrying and started viewing her abduction as a learning experience, an
interesting field trip, in essence.

In her pack she had a small data pad that she used to jot down messages to herself about her performance after each practice. Now she used its micwire to record the natives' speech and play it back in her earbud, making note with the stylus of what she'd learned of their customs and language: she even developed a system for representing the odd sounds, using macrons for long vowels and umlauts for the harmonics, among other tricks partially based on the phonetic transcription system her father had taught her.

She'd figured out that all native nouns fell into one of eleven categories, each of which had a special concord infix that it shared with adjectives and verbs, if the noun was the subject. She had a basic idea of what sorts of things fell into which categories: highborn were in one, and in the other ten were, respectively, males, relationship words, round objects, cylindrical objects, collectives, paired objects, made things, forest things, religious objects, and the unknown (drones were apparently classified here as well).

However, she discovered an additional system as the warriors assigned to her taught her the names of plants and animals that they came in contact with or used for food or ritual (there was a lot of this, too: nearly every step they took had to be accompanied by some weird incantation or stylized movements). The natives had a symbolic or maybe religious way of organizing things, a sort of magical taxonomy.

Miwa found it easiest to picture this system as a cube, like the sort navigators used to fly in three dimensions (finally she was able to put all that stupid math and science to use!). There were three axes: north-south, east-west, and up-down. Each axis had two end points, two extremes, and they corresponded to some religious or magical ideal: up was for the sacred (corresponding to the sky or the color green); down, death (dirt/lava, red-gold); west, highborn (water, dark); east, males (leaves, light); north, forest (branches, spiritual); south, drones (roots and that which came from the planet itself).

For example, the small gray shrub whose roots were used to wave away bad spirit voices when choosing a tree to sleep in was classified as a southwest down plant, a dark red land plant. Miwa figured that her mental representation of the system was probably a little bit messed up, but she needed to learn more about the language and the people to clear her confusions up.

The natives, she'd decided, at least Shalura and her warriors, were good. At first she'd been very scared, but then cocky bravery had set in and finally, when Shalura had kept her warm that one night and then showed her all the murdered people of the tribe, Miwa had understood that these were truly children of God, just like humans. She did not know where exactly they were taking her, though Kumora Mountain loomed larger and larger every time Shalura took her up to the canopy to look north, but Miwa had decided to put her faith in God and in Shalura's good will, as well as in the determination of her father.

She'd been thinking a lot about souls lately as she recorded conversations and jotted away with her stylus during breaks in their journey: she felt confident that the Ihéinghÿngigg, Shalura's people, had souls. She could only imagine how enriched the Teregan community would be when the two groups could come together as one. Miwa knew her own people would help the Native Teregans learn not to fight each other, but to love each other as God commanded. It was funny: before being kidnapped, Miwa hadn't ever really paid much attention to the Church beyond what was expected of her, but now, given her new situation, her faith was on her mind more and more.

She remembered what her science teacher had told her last heptamester, the Cardian Rule: spirits were just vehicles for intelligences, another form of matter in some higher dimension curled up in the smallest particles of the visible universe and connected to the atoms making up human bodies by filaments that not even quantum scanners could detect.

One intelligence per spirit, one spirit per body. I wonder. Could Tana's spirit have connected to her clone's body? Is it possible that I am Tana?

The possibility made her feel strange, but not sad. She was still the same person, whatever name she was given, Tana, Miwa, or Daenzhelo (why she'd given Shalura her father's last name as her own given one was still a mystery to her).

The second day after Miwa's swim, a Tuesday, according to her datapad, Shalura approached her during the afternoon rest and asked what she was doing. Miwa looked down at the datapad and stylus, and she couldn't for the life of her figure out a way to explain what this activity was.

"Is it magic? Are you trying to cast some spell on my warriors?"

Miwa wrinkled her nose, trying to imitate one of the ways the natives said *no* nonverbally. Then she hit on what to say. "They tracks. Words like animals. Leave tracks. Me able follow tracks, know words long time."

Shalura laughed. "Words do not leave tracks. That is idiotic. Look, I am speaking, and I see no tracks."

Miwa had been scribbling madly as Shalura spoke. Now she slowly and carefully repeated back what the warrior had said, word for word and obviously without the normal grammatical errors of her own speech.

"You spoke normally. Why have you not revealed that you can do this?"

"Me no able. Just look tracks, say words, no use me head, only eyes, snout."

Shalura again eyed the pad with suspicion. "I have never seen such magic. Use it against us, Daenzhelo, and you will feel my anger."

Miwa sighed. "Yes. Okay. Lá, already. Me no want hurting of Shalura. Her me friend."

Snorting, Shalura left her alone. They continued their northern journey, and Miwa convinced the warriors to let her run beside them. It was hard to keep up, but she was in better shape than most humans on the planet, and she managed to only need a ride three times a day for about an hour to rest.

Her coach had once told her about the Tarahumara Indians of Northern Mexico back on Earth, who were able to run for three days straight in pursuit of a deer until their prey collapsed from exhaustion. It was a good feeling to be in the company of such a powerful tribe of Lamanites, and Miwa had always been almost sinfully proud of her abilities, as her mother often pointed out.

That Thursday, the troop slowed to a halt about midday and began clambering up into the trees. Miwa looked around in confusion until Shalura grabbed her, swung her across her broad, furry shoulders, and ascended with the rest of the warriors.

"What we do? Why we stop?"

Uttering an irritated sound, Shalura set her down on a broad bough that could've held up two or three of the classrooms at the high school.

"Near here is a village of our nation. We have exchanged fertile males with them many times over the years, though our bond is not as strong as I would wish. I will go among them and ask for refuge and assistance for my warriors, though you and I must continue to the mountain."

"Why mountain?"

"To see the strange Greenseer and ask him about you. I do not want my warriors to go with me, as I know they crave revenge. Perhaps the wise highborn of this village will ally with us and help seek revenge on those who slaughtered our tribe if I cannot find another way. You see, Daenzhelo my lady, I no longer wish the vengeance. I wish for something else."

Miwa struggled to understand. "You think perhaps Greenseer able give the else for you?"

"We will see. My voices tell me I'm foolish, all but a quiet one that whispers for me to continue. Like you, it cannot speak well, but it makes itself heard nonetheless. Stay here with Tentisùxa until I return."

"That one no like me. Scared her want hurt me."

"She cannot hurt you. Our ways forbid it, unless you attempt something idiotic against us. Stay where you are and wait till I return."

Shalura got Tentisùxa to come and keep an eye on Miwa, and then the troop leader dropped out of sight. After staring at the big, ugly tracker for a while to show that she wouldn't be cowed, Miwa sat with her back against the trunk and pulled her father's map from the pack. Now that she knew her destination, it was time to figure out what Brando had wanted her to go there for. The mountain was featured in a grid in the left-hand corner of the map, which now displayed an aerial view of the Seneka Forest. Miwa slid her finger from the small boxed-in grid across the plastic sheet diagonally, and now the mountain filled it completely. Two areas were blinking red, and a string of Unified Chinese characters scrolled next to each.

Oh, great. I hate stupid ideographs: idiot graphs, more like it.

"What is that? A picture of the Mountain of God? How is that piece of leather so transparent?"

Tentisùxa was standing over her, claws reaching for the map.

"Made from gut animal."

"What are those strange lights? What kind of magic are you performing here, midget?"

"Spell make ovipositor fall off for drone what touch picture! Leave me, old funny thing! Go find excrement play with!"

"You annoying little tailless animal! I should throw you from this bough and tell Shalura you fell."

"Shalura know truth and hate old ugly Tentisùxa long time, no ugly sex no more never."

Muttering threats and insults, Tentisùxa walked away. Shalura had made it clear to all the warriors that Miwa was not to be touched, but the teen knew she was pushing her luck. Still, what mattered most to the warriors was valor and strength and toughness, so Miwa had to keep pushing, and hard, if they were ever going to respect her.

Turning back to the map, she tried to read the scrolling legend. *Weapons depot. Computer. Simulator. Training.* This was at about five hundred meters. The second spot, another two hundred meters above the first, flashed another list: *Lab. Real ship log. Records. Communication equipment. Etcetera.*

It's where he's hidden all the stuff he brought from Jitsu. When we get there, I can get a weapon, one that will give me the advantage, and I can call for help.

She had already decided to cooperate as best she could until reaching the mountain, and now she almost felt giddy about going there.

She jotted a few more notes down on her datapad, till the pressure in her bladder left her no choice but to call Tentisùxa over.

"Me need do the water."

"Are you trying to say you have to make water? I can barely understand the way you claw up words with your midget tongue."

"Yes, 'have to make water' and now, ugly snout thing."

"Chakhìkhÿrh, take this horribly deformed highborn down to the ground so she can spray her filthy-smelling urine on the worms. I'm sure they'll enjoy it, and I won't have to see her for a while, which makes me very happy."

Chakhìkhÿrh boosted Miwa up respectfully and clambered down. Miwa went off into some bushes and squatted, dropping her sweatpants around her knees as she bunched the robe up in her hands. The stream of hot liquid ran down between her widely separated feet to pool around a small skull that she hadn't even noticed, the sight of which made her nearly topple backward.

"Chakhì! Come! Come now!"

The large, tawny drone ambled over and stuck her snout between the foliage.

"Yes, Lady?"

"Look! Baby skull! It of People baby, yes?"

The drone regarded the bones and slapped her tail against the ground affirmatively. "Yes. It's a drone skull."

"But why no in trees high where big green sky be? Ground bad, no holy."

"Lady, it is of course of the *ungoqih*."

"What be that word?"

"The drones that are born but not needed, Lady. They are brought past the edge of the village as an offering to Hëngeingh, bright king of flaming demons."

Miwa finished adjusting her clothes and stared at the bones in sudden sadness. "Oh, dear Lord. They leave surplus drones out to die of exposure."

"Excuse me, Lady?"

"The bones make me hurt inside. Me say dead baby very bad."

"Daenzhelo, it would be worse for Hëngeingh to be angry, don't you think? You always say such strange things. Drones belong to the tribe, and they are used as the spirits direct the highborn. If more are born than are needed for training and bonding, they must be offered to Hëngeingh, or we risk our own destruction by the evil spirits he will unleash in his anger."

"Me people no kill babies for no spirits. We use good spirits for fight bad."

"Your people are not of the six nations, then, because your every word is sacrilege. If I still had a tribe, I would turn you over to it for judgment. But I don't, and so I will just ask you to stop talking about idiotic things. You make *my* head hurt with your strangeness."

Chakhì took Miwa back up with the rest of the troop, many of whom were using their long thin tongues to tease out some sort of apparently nutritious bug from the furrows in the tree's bark. Leaning against the massive bole, Miwa thought of many things, jotting ideas down on her datapad.

Despite what the drones thought about themselves, she herself was convinced that they had souls, just like their highborn and males, about whom they spoke reverently and nearly worshipfully. From what she'd been able to grasp from conversations, drones were not only responsible for protecting the tribe; they were also the providers of eggs to highborn and males. Yet they were treated like cattle, as far as she could tell. Raised to fight or serve. Killed if there were too many of them. Told they had no souls, despite the fact that the People would soon cease to exist if drones were all destroyed.

Apparently, eggs were not seen as life by them: when referring to their mothers, the drones never mentioned the drones that had produced the egg, but the highborn that owned that drone, even though, as she'd forced Shalura to explain (none of them liked to answer direct questions, but Miwa annoyed them till they did) *the highborn was not at all involved in the fertilization of an egg that became a drone!* All the drones ever mentioned was their òtsätthënga, the "life-instiller," the highborn that was mistress of their household and their súlkÿqa, their gestator, their "dad." Even the drones themselves had swallowed the story of their own inferiority. It was really sad.

Lost in thought, Miwa was startled by Shalura's warning call as she spidered dizzyingly up the tree's bole. All the warriors crouched in preparation, and Miwa grabbed her pack and slung it over her shoulder.

"Flee to the canopy. Now," barked the troop leader as she unslung her spear, roughly flinging Miwa across her back and leaping into the air. Miwa wrapped her legs around Shalura's narrow waist and her arms around the broad, bony chest, fingers sinking deep into the fur and tightening around clumps of the water-repellant softness. Her heart was hammering as Shalura snatched at a vine and spun at a crazy angle toward another bough. Running on all fours as she hit it, the native warrior whizzed down its length to a web of vines. Here Shalura clutched her massive spear in the claws of one foot as she rapidly climbed the netting to a higher level.

"No go down, you me?" Miwa asked.

"Quiet. They are expecting that. Just be quiet and hold on."

After many other strange maneuvers, they found themselves right below the canopy. Other members of the troop soon joined them, clamoring for an explanation and looking around nervously. This was the holiest of areas in the forest, and they were very afraid of the spirits that lived among the relatively small branches here.

"What has happened?" someone demanded.

"They have also allied with the Greenseer's followers. They had already been notified of our journey north. I barely escaped with my life."

"We should go down and fight honorably!" Tentisùxa, of course.

"Our duty is to discover why our tribe was ripped from its ancestral lands and avenge them if necessary. Fighting one hundred and fifty sturdy warriors will result in our deaths and the dishonoring of our beloved dead. Is this what you want? Surely not. We are lost forest children. Hëngeingh is not angered by our intrusion into the dead place, as we are already dead. Remember how Ëngukhordh hid for seven days and seven nights in his family's dead place, waiting for the highborn killers to return so he could send their souls to fiery judgment? Listen to the voices: my choice is upheld by our lore and faith."

The warriors slapped their tails against the tree limb in agreement. Dhölggexitra spoke up. "So, we are going to travel along the canopy? It will be slower."

"Only until we are well past their lands. Let us go toward the west for several days, as they will be looking for us north. We will lose many days, but our objective will be secure, and we will be alive."

Miwa had slid off Shalura's back, and now the leader motioned to get back on.

"No. Me go. No need help."

"Daenzhelo, we will be traveling along the branches of the dead place. I don't think you can..."

Miwa was tired of explaining her abilities to these condescending jerks all the time, so she-back flipped, then stepped back into a handstand, lowered her head, did a head spin, broke into a *chapa de costas* kick, popped up, somersaulted to the edge of the branch, and leapt into the air, grabbing a vine and letting her momentum carry her to a branch on a neighboring tree.

Standing there, she muttered, "I'm not a highborn, Shalura. I'm a gifted human girl, and I can take care of myself better than you think."

To the dumbfounded tribe, she shouted, "You ugly ones forgetting me movement on ice? No need you care me like baby. Come. Or you sit there till Hëngeingh come take you to flaming sands?"

They began to move toward her, and she laughed as she turned and ran.

CHAPTER 25

BRANDO'S DREAMS WERE TORTURED AND DARK. The families of the dead corpsmen stood around him in a circle, pointing. They said nothing, but their eyes spoke a deeper accusation than any words would have conveyed: *you killed our men; you could have gotten them out; you chose your own child above the lives of twenty-one brothers.* Sitati's wife stepped out from among them, tearing at her hair and clothes, wailing like a banshee.

Then he was in the living room of the house on Jitsu. Tana rushed out to save her mom from Felipe Beserra, but she wasn't Tana anymore, she was Jakobo. Tenshi was now Rhea, demanding to see her attacker's face. The casque slid back to reveal the slathering jaws of a *grendelo*. Brando fired time and again, but it was too late: Rhea and Jakobo lay dead on the tile, their blood pooling into letters, words: *your fault.*

Kneeling beside the native, Brando pried back the armor, the skin, the chest plate. Beneath, curled around the organs, were Teri and Miwa. They smiled up at him, their teeth lengthening, hair spreading across their skin, their fingers hooking into claws as they reached for him...

"D'Angelo. Wake up."

Brando shot up, knife in hand. Dixit knelt at his feet, a look of concern on her face. She'd unstrapped them, luckily: the team had taken to sleeping in pairs, cables holding them down to the bough. The corpsman who had the watch ran over to see what was wrong. Brando waved him away.

"It's alright. I was dreaming."

"You'd better believe you were: moaning and crying and twisting around. You're not the only one, either. Several of the others whimper all night long, though they'd never admit it."

So do you.

Brando sat down and shook his head. "It was a traumatic experience."

"They lost some of their best friends, Brando. And their chief. I know you didn't get along well with him, but he was a superhero to these men, and he was killed like nothing. They are terrified, though they'd never let you know. They train, they push themselves, but in their hearts, they are utterly afraid."

"And you?"

Sonali laughed. "Mostly I'm so scared I can barely think. But as long as you keep talking to me, I can kind of forget for a while. This pace is worse than fear, though."

"We've got to catch up to them and practice both, so we're just going to have to keep going twenty hours a day. There's no turning back now, you realize. They'll be expecting us to flee, so there will be warriors waiting for us. Only an attack will work. Something they wouldn't imagine us doing."

Dixit's smile seemed to defy their gloomy future. "Ah, so now you've understood their basic psychology, have you, Professor?"

Brando ignored her and relieved the watch. In gaps that the wind opened between branches of the canopy above him, he could see the aurora swirling and undulating greenly above him like a living being looking down on Terego and judging everything it beheld. One edge of the glow was slowly being blotted out by darkness, and the reason dawned on Brando suddenly. *Rain. The rainy season. Shite! That's all we freaking needed.*

He woke everyone and got them moving. They had only slept for about three and a half hours, after three days of intense battle training, much of it entailing using weapons while swinging from the harness pulleys or suspended on vine nets, and rapid travel from tree to tree with few rest stops. The corpsmen were, as Dixit had warned, utterly sapped of energy and desire.

But what else could Brando do? They were probably going to die. If the only chance of their survival was pushing them to confront the Native Teregans, Brando had no problem pushing as hard as he could.

About twenty minutes into their traveling, the rain started to fall. In thick, solid sheets it fell, blurring their vision, bending them over, making the going slippery and dangerous.

We might all die right now. Someone will fall off the fucking limb and drag their partner down with them, arms all flailing till they smack dead against the ground.

It was just too much. Why didn't anything ever go as it should? What was it about him that made him a target for tragedy?

A terrible voice echoed either in memory or from the darkness beneath the trees or both.

"You seek shattering? I will break you."

Brando gasped and slumped against a bole. The others realized that he wasn't walking, and they stopped, too. Sonali hurried over to him.

"D'Angelo? What's wrong? Are you okay?"

"Living among you people makes me forget from time to time. There is no paternal God watching over us, loving us. There's just the Demiurge, the cruelest, most vicious sociopath ever. And he created this universe, this Grey Prison we're stuck inside. Oh, that bastard must be laughing at us now. We need that transmitter, we have to move as fast as we can, we're tired and sick and sad, and *it begins to rain!* And this rain isn't going to stop, you know. It's going to go on and on for weeks! Meanwhile, my daughter gets farther away and our families worry more and more."

Real concern washed over Dixit's face with the sprays of rain. "D'Angelo, this isn't like you: you never seem to despair."

"Oh, that's because you don't know what's going on in my head, Sonali. I live in despair every moment of everyday. If only I had never come here. If only I had never cloned them. If only I had been home that day. If, if, if."

To his utter astonishment, he began to weep.

"Okay, now you're scaring me. Aren't you like the toughest guy on the planet? I mean, you were considered the toughest even *before* we knew who you really were! Everyone had seen you at the martial arts competitions. They televise those things, you know. The academic and elder who can kick butt, too. You were an ideal man to a lot of people."

Brando stopped crying, leaned his head back and laughed. The corpsmen were already sitting down, confused but thankful for the chance to rest. "Tough? Ideal? I'm nothing, Sonali. It's just a construct, a projection. Nando Miranda. Brando D'Angelo. They don't exist. There's just this jumble of instincts and experiences that is desperately trying to mold itself around something special, something eternal. The masks its worn have one impulse: fight for as long as needed, then run. And it's going to keep on running. It'll take what it calls its children and run, even if it's over the corpses of people who get in the way. None of them have souls, either."

"I don't know what you're on about, but that's all nonsense. You saved me. You saved these men, too. Quit being so morbid. Quit trying to sound like a criminal."

He was tempted to reveal why they were still in the forest instead of safe in their homes, but the men might try to execute him.

Imagine if they discovered that you didn't leave that message on the graves. Imagine if they learned how you don't want to be rescued. How you're willing to sacrifice them so the Consortium can't stick you in a cell far from your girls, far from all hope of bringing Tenshi back.

"Alright."

"Stop wallowing in self-pity."

"Fine."

"Think! There's got to be an alternative."

As if her words were a shock to his brain, it hit him. They'd followed the natives' trail along the river, Brando occasionally dropping to the ground to check that it was still there, until the indigenes had turned a little to the northwest, away from the river. Given Miwa's message and the changed direction, the natives were definitely headed toward Kumora Mountain. *The mountain. I can't believe I never thought about it!*

"Zorig," he said, standing with renewed strength, "you wanted to go in the inflatables. Do you still have them? Did you pack them?"

"Yes. I have them right here. Have you changed your mind? I thought you said that it would call the attention of pursuers."

"I was wrong. I was completely wrong, and I apologize. But at least you got a good workout. Okay, there are three, right? Four of us per raft. The batteries will last, what, four days? There'll be no way to recharge them with the cloud cover."

Zorig nodded excitedly. "Yeah, four days if we travel about the same, twenty hours or so." He pulled one of the light-weight motors from his pack and unfolded it: a long shaft with a rudder at one end and a rotor at the other, whose blades he unfanned to their full twenty-five-centimeter length. "We're talking 60 kph with these babies. Nice presents from the CPCC. Only thing those apostates are good for, their technology."

Everyone laughed, including Brando. He was feeling hopeful.

"So," said Leal, "are we going to ambush them? Race down the river, get in front of them and wait?"

"No. Four days on the river won't get us in front of them. It twists away to the east before turning back west and north. No, this will put us neck and neck with them at the base of the mountain." He paused for a second. "I've got weapons stashed there, weapons that will give us a fighting chance."

I'll have to figure out a way to keep yall quiet afterwards, though. Lock yall up in the training cavern till we're gone? Maybe.

Chuquipoma cleared his throat. "Some of your black-market stuff they were talking about at the trial?"

"Yes. But this is no time to get ethical on me. Your lives depend on these weapons. Forget that I'm a criminal, like I keep saying. Think about your own lives, the lives of those kids, and the happiness of your families."

Most of them nodded soberly at that. Sonali eyed him with her typical amusement, which Brando guessed was her way of compensating for the terror that spasmed through her at night when she tried to sleep.

"What?" he asked the biologist.

"Just wondering: no more 'come on, you've got to fight like beasts'?"

"Dixit, when I was on Jitsu, I learned a valuable strategy: if you want to fight criminals, you must become a criminal. You can't worry about the law and rights, etcetera. You have to do whatever has to be done.

"As I've said again and again, that's what we've got to do here. To fight these beasts, we're going to have to become beasts, too. Advanced weapons don't change the brutality we'll have to unleash."

"But if you're a beast, what moral authority do you have to judge other beasts?"

"When you're a beast, moral authority ceases to have any meaning, and you just fight to survive and to keep you and yours among the living by killing as many of the enemy as you can. I don't know why we keep having this argument. Do you want us to just prance in there and ask for the kids back? Pretty please with sugar on top? They slaughtered our companions, Dixit. They don't want to negotiate."

"You're not even planning to give them a choice, and that was what our mission was all about."

"We can argue about this on the boat. Right now we need to go down to the river and get moving."

With the rafts inflated and the motors attached, they began buzzing against the current. Less rain reached them at this level, but they were still soaked, and would be for days. Brando ordered the two other men in his raft to sleep beneath their ponchos while he steered. Sonali stared at him from the prow, waiting for the light snores of the corpsmen. Then she lit into him.

"We've got to try, Brando. Don't you realize that the young people could get hurt in an attack? Do you want that on your conscience? What if you spark a war between the natives and us? Do you really want to go down in history as the man who started a war with the first sentient species humanity ever encountered?"

Just Miwa with them, and I'm pretty sure she can handle herself. As for my reputation, it's already shot to shit.

"Okay, okay. You're right." *I have no intention of doing what is it you're suggesting, though.* "We'll try talking first. But we'll be armed, and we'll be prepared to do whatever we have to do."

No mention of the communications equipment, though. Not taking yall to the second level. Things yall can't see are stored there.

Sonali watched the water stream by for a while, then spoke again in more subdued tones. "I'll admit I don't understand anything about your faith, Brando. You've already figured out I'm not even that dedicated to my own. But I find it hard to believe that Nando Miranda was just some carefully sculpted façade."

Brando sighed. He really didn't want to discuss this, but Sonali never let up until she got her answers. *Just like Miwa.*

"Tenshi was more than my wife. She was my guide along the Path, the one who taught me its profoundest truths. I was thinking about her the other day, when you were showing me the nest of the *asapano*. Funny furry flying things, Miwa always said. Anyway, Tenshi had such a positive view of people, even though she had been treated miserably all her life. She believed that each of us is capable of such incredible beauty. You know she was an architect, don't you? She saw architecture as humanity's duty to itself, an out-branching of our selves into physical world. Like the asapano's nest. Something we are compelled by nature to create."

"What, an extended phenotype of human biological nature?"

"Exactly. Tenshi taught me that the things people make are part of their extended phenotype, part of *them*. Their buildings, the books they write, the families and communities they create. But most especially the *selves* they forge day in and day out using the words and ideas around them. For most people, it's largely an unconscious act: their genes guide them to begin, and the culture around them does the rest. But once you realize what's happening, you can control it. You can choose which ideas you'll incorporate into yourself. But first you have to shatter. On purpose, or because life pushes you to that fragmentation.

"At her side, I broke Brando D'Angelo to bits. Focused on the divine spark that had come close to me. But after her murder, the self I forged with Tenshi had to be broken up and stitched back together as Kyosu, who was smashed up as well. During the last seventeen years, however, I've tried something new: building a nest named Nando Miranda and in the safety of that bower, crafting the final Brando D'Angelo di Makomo, the one who will reach quantum enlightenment. But I'm afraid, Sonali. Afraid something will happen to my daughters. Not just because I love them, but because losing them will destroy everything I've worked on, hidden away in my nest."

Sonali splashed cold water on him. "I think you're being overly dramatic. You take yourself too seriously, Brando. You say Nando was just a bower. But in my opinion, he's the real you. As Nando, you married again and had a son, rose to prominence in our community. It's probably not my place, but I think you've got to stop living in the past. Rescue your kids, go back and face the trial, spend some time in jail, and live out your old age at Rhea's side, the two of you rocking on that porch of yours as the sun slips behind the mountains. Be normal, Brando. Love. Live. Forget."

Brando turned his head toward the trees sliding by on his left, eyes burning.

He was ashamed to feel so tempted by the idea.

INTERCHAPTER D

From: Mukerjib@octant1.gov.af

To: berdyaevn@os1.octant1.gov.af

Subject: re: Proposal

Date: April 25, 2714 12:37:51 (SST)

Berdyaev,

Get that maniac atheist protégée of yours under control ASAP. There's no way in shite-packed hell I'll ever approve the deployment of AF troops around a non-Consortium ally *without a shred of bloody evidence.* And I refuse to allow him to push his ship even up to structural limits, much less beyond them. D'Angelo had better get his conflicted self back in line before both you and him find your arses on the chopping block. That's right: you, Commodore, for being foolish enough to put him charge of the trial of his brother. I know you think you understand how to forge a leader through adversity or some gormless shite like that, but I swear to you that if Antonio bollixes this, you'll take the fall as well.

I still can't believe that you had the balls to forward his proposal to me. What a load of paranoid delusions. What's Terego going to attack us with: the handful of shuttles that we sold them? Projectile weapons? If there were yakuza troops on the surface, we would have detected their approach to that system, which we've had under surveillance for ten years. Unless Captain Delusional Grandeur thinks that they've just hung out on the surface for a decade.

Tighten the fragging leash, Berdyaev.

Bud Mukerji

From the journal of Tenshi Koroma

January 23, 2678

Diary. I'm back on the Southern Continent, this time with clearer vision. Since I no longer feel rage toward my community for trying to force me to follow their particular Way along the Path, I now rage at the devastation of this land.

Like most tragedies of this scale, of course, there are unintended and often beautiful consequences unforeseen by the men wielding destructive power. Soltech brought my ancestors, many clans of Aknawajin, to this world. That meant tearing them forever from the Solar Asteroid Belt where their culture had arisen.

Aknawajin. What a name. Outsiders usually translate it *laborers.* But it really means *people of the realm of labor*, the toughest parts of the Belt. We are folks who know what work means, deep in our bones. Even though that work meant hurting a living world, what did we know about living worlds? We knew cold rock and recycled air.

But in helping corporate overlords gut what they called Ares, we came to see our error. We fell in love with the planet, wept at what we had done to it. We called out to the Oracle who had been translated upon its sands. Domina, guide us. Make us worthy of this home.

Renaming the world *Jitsu* in her honor, we fought to free it from Soltech's grip. Became its stewards, its faithful children.

But theocratic oppression hurts Jitsu and the Aknawajin as much as capitalist greed.

So now, Diary, I'll enter Sudowon ra-Pahuka on the Distant Isles. I won't emerge until I have reached satori.

Then my teyo—my illuminated self, lit bright and fully revealed by my divine spark—will head back to the Northern Continent and start another revolution.

CHAPTER 26

TENSHI KEPT WHISPERING TO HER, but she couldn't make out the words. From time to time, she opened her eyes to blurry, indistinct figures. Someone kept shoving food in her mouth and making her chew, some sort of fungal plant, by the texture. After swallowing reflexively, Teri would be plunged once again into that dazzling white glow, an enticing iridescence that encircled her, sweet and numbing. In this place she couldn't think of Carmen, couldn't think of Rhea or Jakobo or Miwa.

She was awash in beautiful sensations that blotted out all else.

Except for Tenshi's voice, insistent and growing clearer.

"They're drugging you. Some kind of hallucinogen, I guess. Stronger than the High Sacrament Brando snuck into your food. My voice is a hallucination, so that must be it, right? But you like it. You wish you could stay here forever."

Shhhh.

"No, Teri. I'll not be quiet. I'll keep talking and talking and talking till you listen."

I'm so tired. Tired of being strong. Tired of being hurt. Tired of losing.

"No, don't start that. You've got a job to do. Open your eyes, check what's going on around you. They're almost to the edge of the forest now."

The whiteness faltered, grayed. Without warning, a red line slashed across her field of vision, like the cut to Carmen's neck. Teri began to recede again.

"No, damn you! Don't run from this! You promised her, Teri."

Leave me alone! She's dead, damn you. I can't keep my promise.

"How do you know she's dead?"

What?

"Did you see her die? You foolish child. You always think you know what's going on, that you're pulling the strings. But you're an amateur. You can't sit around waiting for the opportunity to present itself. You have to *make the opportunity yourself.* You thought you were manipulating their myths, eh? But you were holding back! You've got to think, to plan, to act. Spending your days having sex and reading my diary? I get that you needed it, but this is hardly the time."

So it's my fault?

"Yes, it's your fault. In part. But on the other hand, it's just circumstances and confluences of rubbish you could argue you had no way of understanding. The important thing is, what are you going to do to make up for your mistake?"

I can still do it, can't I?

"Oh, yes."

I can still make this work. I can keep my people safe while keeping the People safe. I can be a messiah. It's what I was created for. It's why Providence allowed it, my cloning. It's like a special birth, one that makes me more than human. Connected to the Ogdoad. Able to hear the whisper of translated millions.

"Yes. That's it. Come on up out of there."

I can do it, thought Teri as Tenshi's voice subsided to a whisper and then was gone. *I can save the world. It's not just a fantasy. I can see it, right there on the edge of my vision. I'm the one. I won't fail like you did, Tenshi. You tried to save Jitsu, but you couldn't. I am you, but I am not you. I am more. I will succeed.*

Jerking awake, Teri saw she was being carried by a native. There were about thirty warrior drones about her, three of them in charge of her remaining friends. Also traveling with the group was the high priestess, Teri's former guide Sek, and another highborn, Jãeçirholaq, the one whose males were in charge of digging up stone for spear tips.

Teri felt self-possessed like never before in her life. The drug was still coursing through her veins. Possibilities seemed to unreel before her eyes at dizzying speeds. She could imagine many paths to take, many outcomes to her actions. She had to get her friends free, had to make the natives trust her, had to learn how to unite them.

Somewhere was the fulcrum, but she would have to be patient and do what needed to be done while ignoring the sadness that simmered beneath the surface of her awareness.

"Put me down," she ordered the drone carrying her, who of course didn't understand the Native Teregan dialect of Baryogo. Teri shouted at Sek. "Sek, tell this drone to put me down immediately!"

Sek looked at Ùshëshajirh, who called for everyone to halt. The high priestess walked over to Teri's drone and barked an order at it. Teri was lowered to the ground.

"You have come out of the vision sleep sooner than expected, Çèrhingÿl. Have you found your way? Do you know who you are?"

Here it goes. I am the messiah. A divine representative to the People, sent by Providence or Sopiya or both. I will make them understand the greater plan of which they are part.

"I am Çèrhingÿl, first born of the People, shaped from the primal egg and gestated in the mouth pouch of Çìrhãná, bondmate of God, the Unblinking Eye. I came a second time to guide the People across the gray-green sea, and now I have returned to unite the nations and keep them safe from human interference."

As soon as Teri had spoken the first three words, the high priestess had begun to translate, and by the time she'd concluded her speech, all the drones had dropped prostrate to the ground, those with prisoners tossing them to one side.

"Qõrhegirhatshe shãiçethangukhi, Çèrhingÿl!" they chanted.

"Cèrhingÿl has returned to rule. That's what they declare." The high priestess looked at her inscrutably. "They will follow you anywhere now, as long as I am beside you. Do not forget my role in this. You are God-sent, but you are not a priestess."

Your time will come, Ùshëshajirh. You picked a dangerous game to play with me.

"You fucking bitch."

Teri looked toward her friends, sprawled on the ground. Josuo was shaking his head. Ronaldo and Anyi stared blankly, numb and traumatized.

"You're going to betray us all, aren't you? Who's next? Me? Are you going to have them slit my throat, too?"

Anyi doubled over and moaned.

Ronaldo patted her on the back. "Shh, we don't know if she's dead."

Teri's pulse quickened. "Priestess, I need to address my males."

Ùshëshajirh gestured toward them. "As you please, Cèrhingÿl."

Taking a few steps toward where drones guarded her friends, Teri tried to remain impassive as she asked, "What do you mean, Ronaldo?"

"When you attacked, it looked like the old one with the knife just made a superficial cut. There wasn't as much blood as you'd expect. But Carmen fell unconscious, and they carried her away. We haven't seen her since."

Josuo scoffed and stood. Taking a few steps, he got right up in her face, though she could see the fear in his eyes. "Even if she wasn't dead when she hit the ground, she must be now. You've been doped up for *days,* Teri. Oops, should I start calling you *tearing ghoul* or whatever these monsters have named you? Or is *Teri* still alright with my highborn boss?"

"Josuo, you have no idea what's going on here, or what's at stake, so I'll forgive you. In a day or so, you'll be back in Diadono, and you can return to Kanaano, get married, have children, and grow old telling stories of the terrible time you spent in Seneka Forest. But right now, I need you to trust me."

"Trust you? Trusting you got Carmen killed, you bitch."

Something in Teri snapped. She struck Josuo with her open palm against the underside of his chin, sending him sprawling backward through the air, and she thrust a kick into his side that spun him around twice before he thudded painfully against the ground.

Then the drug-induced calm settled over her again, and she crossed her arms across her chest. The natives had taken off her school uniform, dressing her in a supple leather robe like all highborn wore.

"The People have customs, asshole. They wanted to bring me into their tribe. And the Greenseer, whoever the fuck he is, manipulated them into targeting Carmen so I'd be susceptible. But he doesn't know what I'm planning now that I'm in."

Wiping blood from his lip and holding his ribs where she'd kicked him, Josuo got back to his feet. "Why the fuck would you want to be a part of their tribe? Have you gone insane?"

"I need to be part of their tribe to stop a war."

"What war? There's no war here, psycho."

"And there never will be, if I can help it. But also," she muttered, leaning close, "I'm going to find the Greenseer and make him pay for what he's done."

The high priestess interrupted. "If you've finished disciplining your male, Holiness, we should continue."

Teri took a deep breath. "Are we headed toward the lake?"

"Yes. That is where you were found. I assume that from there we can travel to where your mighty tribe keeps its majestic flying ships."

"We can't leave the forest yet. Let's travel south at its edge for a while until we reach my dwelling. I have a smaller ship that can take us more quickly, though not all of us."

IT WAS NEAR NIGHTFALL WHEN THEY EMERGED from the forest near Brando and Rhea's cottage. The kamioneto wasn't in the garage, which meant that Rhea and Jakobo weren't home.

Thank God.

Teri had her three friends, the high priestess, Jãeçirholaq and the ten warriors who had accompanied them wait for her by the barn as she slipped inside for the key to the *platveturilo* Brando used to transport logs and stone blocks for his construction projects. She scribbled a message on door of the fridge with a marker. Then she rushed out to undo the padlock on the barn door.

"This is a ground ship. It will take us quickly to where the air ships are. Tell the drones to get on the flat part. They will have to hold on to the bottom since there are no sides. Warn them that we will be moving fast. They might fall off if they're not cautious."

Ùshëshajirh translated. "The male goes with them. The one you struck."

Teri didn't bother arguing. "Josuo, get on the bed of the platveturilo with the drones. Now."

"Fucking traitor." He clambered up, and one of the drones pushed him into a sitting position. "I can't wait until they catch you."

Teri just shook her head and led Ronaldo and Anyi, neither of whom would even look at her, to the cab. "Get in the back, guys. You'll be home soon, I swear it." She felt tears coming, but she choked them back. Jãeçirholaq climbed in with them, and Anyi trembled violently as the native's fur brushed up against her.

"I do not like this strange ship, Holiness," said the highborn.

"Be quiet," ordered the high priestess as Teri helped her into the front seat. "Strange times require strange deeds, Jãeçirholaq."

Teri hopped into the driver's position and slid the key in, which was coded the fingerprints of the entire family except Jakobo. The flatbed hummed to life, and she guided it backwards out of the barn. When the itinerary map glowed on the windshield, she selected a spot on the southern outskirts of Diadono, close to the Ministry of Crises' equipment depot. As the vehicle began accelerating, memories of elementary school trips to the depot skittered through her mind, a teacher praising the brave corpsmen who risked their lives to save other Novasanktuloj.

Let's hope tonight they don't try to be heroes. Let's hope they listen to me. I don't want more deaths on my conscience.

Ronaldo must have seen their destination on the map because he finally spoke. "That's near the depot. You're not taking them there, are you? You're not going to give them weapons. Tell me you're not."

"I've got it under control. And don't mention Carmen. I didn't know what I was doing then, but now I do. None of the rifles will be used against a Novasanktulo, I guarantee."

Anyi groaned and muttered something.

"What? Anyi, are you alright?"

"She said 'how?' As in, how do you plan to keep them from using the rifles?"

"Çèrhingÿl, it is unseemly for you to be talking with your males in our presence."

"They will be leaving me soon, perhaps forever. There are things that must be said. Do not interfere." Looking in the rearview mirror, she continued talking. "I've got a plan, but I can't sit explain it now. Just make sure that when I let you go, you tell everyone to stay away from the forest. I need time. Time."

She pushed the vehicle to the limits of its capacity, ripping over the landscape at 200 kph. In the corner grid of the display that was projected onto the windshield, she could see the rear view: drones with their claws digging deeply into the wooden slats that made up the bed, Josuo rolling and bouncing around, his lips moving in a stream of curses.

That's right. I've got the power now. Get used to it. I could slam us all into a boulder or tree right now, except that it wouldn't end with us, would it? If I'm going to stop this crisis from escalating, I've got to do it differently. Death can't be the answer.

"I see a problem, High Priestess. Our air ships can't land on the canopy, and we can't put it far from the village outside of the forest or it will be discovered."

"Yes. The Greenseer told me of this. One of the mighty home trees is being sacrificed, its ancient head being lopped off to the highborn level so that the sturdy flying ship can descend from the air onto it. We will then disguise it with broad frondy branches so that your tribe's drones cannot detect it from above."

"How will we find the village from the air? The canopy looks like a huge sea of green, you know."

The high priestess pulled out her datapad. "The Greenseer told me that he put the location of our village in here. The 'coordinates,' he called them. Before you arrived, it was his plan to help us take one of the ships and teach us to steer it himself. When I was with him last, however, he learned of your capture by the People and explained to me that you had come earlier than he'd planned. He explained what must be done."

So this Greenseer was expecting Samanei? Who is he? Some friend of her uncle's, waiting for her to come out of hiding? Her father, Monchu, maybe brought by Brando? It has to be a Dominian Pathwalker, someone who believes Samanei is the oracle, because this message that a messiah is coming fits too conveniently with the beliefs of Tenshi and Samanei's people. But why pick me? If the two of them are planning something, what use am I? Just the fact that I look like her?

Ugh. One thing at a time. I'll force him to tell me when the time is right. Just before I make him pay for targeting Carmen.

Other than that brief exchange, the highborn gripped the seats for the entire ninety-minute trip without barking a single syllable. Teri, who'd eaten another of the psychotropic tubers before leaving the forest, saw the landscape hurtle by in blurry streaks of blue-black.

The womb of the night. The primeval mouth pouch. Keep Carmen safe if she's still alive. Hold her spirit close if she isn't. Comfort her, no matter what.

Tears streamed from her eyes, and the highborn twitched their ears in wonder, closing their own eyes out of respect for the spiritual communion their new leader was partaking of.

When the vehicle began approaching the depot's general area, Teri slowed down to about 60 kph, and the others finally unclenched themselves, the humans with sighs, the natives with nasal grunts. "Still scared? Good. We'll need that at the gate. Do only what I tell you; otherwise, they will destroy us."

"That is fine, but understand, Çèrhingÿl: try to betray us, reveal yourself as an impostor, and all your males will die, as well as the drones of your people."

"Yes, you've repeated that message enough for me to understand it."

They pulled up to the gate, and Teri popped open the door just as two guards stepped out of the guardhouse, their eyes widening and their guns coming up.

"No! Don't shoot! They'll kill us if you shoot! Please, just let them through! We're so scared. They said that they'd let us go if we brought them here, but it you start shooting they'll slit our throats!"

Anyi moaned loudly inside the cab and then retched. Ronaldo slammed the seat forward and leaned her out just as she spewed watery vomit in a steaming stream. Jãeçirholaq reached out and yanked her back in.

"Okay, okay! We're going to let you through, but we're calling ahead to let the guys inside know."

"Please, no! I'm telling you they'll kill us!"

"We're not just going to let them walk out with whatever they want!" shouted the taller of the two guards.

Shit. Teri slid back inside and thumbed the accelerator to 50 kph. The flatbed lurched and ripped through the gate. As she sped the vehicle around the main building to the landing area in back, she looked about frantically, and her heart dropped. There was a lighted tarmac onto which one koptero was just now setting down while another took off. Some forty corpsmen were around the area, carrying crates of equipment to and from the kopteroj, preparing another two for presumable a later take off.

What the hell is going on?

"You did not say there would be so many of your drones, Holiness. Is this a trick?"

"No. No, I just didn't expect it. They must be fighting or searching for somebody. For me, I imagine, or my friends. The good thing is those wooden containers have the reeds in them. It will be easy to get a ship and a box quickly. Just let me talk, and you just sit there. That'll scare them enough."

As the corpsmen began rushing toward the platveturilo, rifles raised, Teri slid it to a stop beside a koptero that was being fueled by a *laboroboto*. Beside it were two long crates.

"Grab the males and tell the drones to hold spears against them. Do not even think of hurting them, though, or I'll have my people's drones kill us all. Understand?"

She leapt from the cab without waiting for a reply, her hands raised. A glance confirmed that one of the crates held rifles and the other grenades. She heard someone yell "grendeloj" and another "it's one of the Miranda twins." The high priestess and Jãeçirholaq pulled Ronaldo and Anyi from the vehicle and organized the drones as Teri had instructed. Josuo had three spears trained on him: he'd apparently not made the drones very happy on the trip over.

"Don't shoot!" Teri yelled. "My name is Teri Miranda. My friends are with me. We were kidnapped by these monsters. They say that unless you give them a koptero, they're going to kill us."

"It's a trap!" shouted Josuo.

"Silence him," Teri muttered, trying not to let the corpsmen see her speak. The high priestess grunted; she heard a thud and a weak cry behind her.

To the corspmen: "They tell me that they are going to let two of us go to show their good faith."

To the priestess: "Let go the two that traveled inside with us. It's the only way they'll give us what we want, Ùshëshajirh. And don't warn me. I already know. You'll kill everybody if it's a trick. Release them now!"

The two highborn pushed Ronaldo and Anyi forward, and they both ran stumbling toward the corpsmen, who trained their weapons on the natives with hate and fear in their eyes.

If I play this wrong, we will all die, and so will many of them.

"Tell two of the drones to grab the box on the right and slide it inside the ship. Then get everyone inside except the three that are guarding my male. You stay at the opening of the ship to pull me in when it's time."

Now to get a pilot.

Behind her, Josuo whispered roughly "God will punish you for what you're about to do, traitor."

"I'll accept my fate. Can you say the same? Prepare to go home and rejoin little Miss Babymaker."

Raising her voice, she called to the corpsmen, who seemed eager for an excuse to fire.

"They say they'll release my friend here, but only if a pilot volunteers to fly them to the mountains to the east. There they'll get out, and the pilot can return with me. Any attempt to follow us will result in our deaths."

There was no answer.

Shit. It isn't going to work, is it?

Teri put her face in her hands and slumped dejectedly, bending over as if ready to faint. It wasn't hard to summon despair: the emotion was right under her skin. She lifted her face and screamed.

"Come on! I don't want to die! I want to get out of here! These crazy demons have done horrible things to us," she started sobbing, her anger rolling off of her in shudders, "and all I want to is go home with my mom and dad."

"You cold, lying bitch," murmured Josuo, and he was struck again by the butt of a spear.

One of the corpsmen stepped forward. "I'm a pilot. I volunteer. God protect us, Teri Miranda. May he keep us in his mighty hand. Send the young man over, and I'll come to you at the same time."

"Tell the drones to release the male. They are sending a drone who can steer the ship, since I don't know how." Ùshëshajirh barked an order, and the drones nearly threw the human at the corpsmen as the pilot began trotting over.

Now for the really hard part. My job as messiah.

"Translate as I speak, High Priestess. Tell the drones to open the other box and grab one of the hard fruit each." How did it go? Depress the green button, twist the top… damnit, she should've paid more attention to Brando's babbling. She had always thought he was just being a guy and bragging about his weapons knowledge. She concentrated, saw his thickly veined, powerful hands twisting in the air as Miwa ate up his every word. "Tell them to push down the little green square and twist the top until it stops. Then, when the steersman is in the ship, tell them to run to the other ships, jump inside, and push down the little blue square. Tell them not to make a mistake: today they will give their lives for the unification of the six nations."

She turned to make sure that Ùshëshajirh was translating all she'd said: the drones already had the grenades in their hands and were doing what Teri had instructed. Some of the corpsmen had caught on and were running behind the pilot, who made it to the koptero and was pulled inside by the high priestess. The highborn stared at Teri inscrutably as several corpsmen started to open fire. Bullets whizzed by, whining off the koptero's surface and thudding into the three drones' bony chests.

"START THE KOPTERO NOW OR THEY'LL KILL ME!" Teri yelled into the interior of the transport. The rotors began to whir to life.

"NOW!" Teri screamed as a bullet ripped into her shoulder and Ùshëshajirh clutched her hair, jerking her off the ground. The drones were already running, bent over, tails out, faster than the corpsmen could track them with their rifles. Her arm and head throbbing in pain, Teri turned in the doorway and shouted at the corpsmen: "FIND COVER! THEY'RE GOING TO BLOW THE KOPTEROJ!"

Don't be heroes. Don't die because of me.

The corpsmen started scattering like insects before a rainstorm.

The pilot was struggling with a drone who was trying to keep him in his seat. Teri reached over, unholstered the man's pistol, and pointed it at his head. Out of the corner of her eye, she saw the drones reach the kopteroj.

"Five seconds. That's all there is. Fly or die, Corpsman."

The pilot yanked back on the yaw stick and thumbed the accelerator to full. They shot up and forward madly as three explosions sent a shock wave uncurling in their direction, followed by smaller ripples as secondary explosions ripped the night air, illuminating the heavy clouds so that they looked like roiling smoke burped from the innards of hell.

The natives were thrown against the back of the koptero, and Jãeçirholaq went flying out the open door, howling madly as she was yanked backward and down toward the infernal glare behind them.

Grimacing with pain, Teri slid into the co-pilot seat, the pistol still trained on the corpsman as he struggled to level out. Finally the transport stabilized.

"You truly are Çèrhingÿl, aren't you?"

Oh, you so need to die, High Priestess. "Did you ever doubt it?"

"Miss Miranda," said the pilot, eyes wide with fear. "I don't understand anything that's happening. Why did you point the pistol at me? How is it you can talk to these things? I thought you were their prisoner: you act more like their ally!"

"There is more going on here than you can imagine, Brother…"

"Sainz. Juan Sainz."

"Brother Sainz, I can understand how this must look, but these creatures think I'm the person prophesied in their religion to come and unite their different tribes. That insanity I just let happen saved the lives of my three friends and probably a lot of corpsmen, too. These natives' warriors are really fast and strong and not easy to kill, and they would've gotten a bunch of you before you brought them down. But we can't talk much, Brother. Just keep flying north. I'll punch in the coordinates in a sec."

"We're not going to the mountains, right? And you destroyed the other kopteroj. Two more will be flying in about three hours, but they won't know where we are. Your idea?"

Teri didn't answer him; instead, she asked what the corpsmen were doing at the depot so late at night.

"Looking for your dad and the team that was with him. They were out searching for you. We lost contact with them, and so we went in. More than half of them had been slaughtered. Everyone is saying Brando's in charge now. I thought it was a stupid theory: how could he take over and keep them alive? But now after seeing what his daughter can do against four dozen men…"

Looking for me. Lost. In danger.

She hadn't expected it, but she felt real pain at the idea of Brando's being hurt. He wasn't her dad, he'd lied and ruined everything, but she couldn't help feeling connected to him.

"And my sister? Miwa?"

"She wasn't with you? Everyone thought she was with you. They've only been tracking north of the lake. We thought you were all together."

Now Teri's heart was thudding even more painfully. Brando and Miwa, lost among the People. If she had wavered on the task at hand before, she now set her mind grimly to it.

Unify them. But how?

"What does the drone say? You have spoken to him very long. I worry that you may be plotting against the People."

"High Priestess, I just proved to you that I don't intend betrayal. I'm getting tired of all these accusations. Why don't you just shut up and leave me to my responsibilities? Uniting the nations isn't going to be some child's game, you know. If you're planning to question everything I do, nothing is going to get done!"

"Oh, but I have not questioned you. I have accepted your orders and trusted your judgment. But it is difficult for me to listen to you speak to one of your tribe's drones and not understand what you are saying. Some of my voices whisper that you are scheming against me. Forgive me, but try not to speak to her much. Give her commands but no conversation."

"Fine." Teri snapped the harness around her, trying to ignore the burning in her shoulder.

Scheming against you? If you only knew. You hurt Carmen. Maybe killed her. I won't forget that, not ever.

Your time will come.

CHAPTER 27

"I DON'T KNOW, CAPTAIN. You're talking court martial for us both if you're wrong."

Antonio slammed his fist against the table, a real one: the ship was still in fenestration and would be for another hour, so he and Mubarak had emerged from their hypostasis pods for a real face-to-face meeting.

"Damn it, Ashar, I laid it all out for you. You've seen Orbay's research, seen the connections, witnessed for yourself the mysterious way these fanatics are acting. Even if things aren't one hundred percent like what I'm showing you, they must be pretty close. We need to be there."

"Captain, *Tony*, I believe you. I don't trust them any more than you, mate. And I'll follow your orders and help you in any way I can. But you have to promise me you'll do whatever you can to protect me if you end up wrong. Will you?"

"Of course, of course. I'll put your objections and cautions on record, make it plain that I ordered you to do everything. But I need to know you're with me, Ashar."

"I am. I always am, aren't I? One hundred percent, mate."

They shook hands and clasped each other in a quick embrace.

"Alright, then. Dump everything about the trial to Quat. Tell him our com systems are buggered, faux-link impossible. Then loop all the rest of the command personnel off the virtual bridge. You, me and the computer are doing this. No need for getting any of the men involved. I have calculated the accel and decel rates, eliminated down time between them, pushed the fenestrations to their theoretical limits: here." He quickly called up the information on the holographic display above the command staff's meeting table.

"You sure the gel can handle those gees?"

"They were rated to withstand them, yeah. Don't worry mate. It's just one week. Remember the *McArthur*? Escaping that supernova? That was two weeks *past* rated gees, and they came out with just minor internal injuries. Well, one dead, but because his pod leaked gel. The marshal is just afraid of political consequences."

"While you are more concerned about justice, and if orders or regulations get in the way, bugger them."

Tony smiled. "That's right mate. Never been a quarter-decker, me. Let's get to it, what do you say?"

AS HE STRIPPED DOWN, STOWED HIS UNIFORM AND EASED BACK INTO THE warm gel of his hypostasis pod, Antonio considered his luck in getting a second officer like Ashar Mubarak. The two of them had worked together since the cleansing of Atlantis, a former corporate world onto which the Brotherhood had clung like so many ticks on a dog. The fighting had been ugly and trials worse, with the damn civil advocates that dirty underworld money could buy trying every trick in Consortium jurisprudence. Ashar had stayed up with Tony until four or five hundred hours, pouring over precedents and possibilities, planning legal attacks that would succeed in eliminating this particular branch of the Demimundo scourge.

Unlike his relationships with others (he shuddered the memory away), the friendship of the two men had been forged in the fires of adversity, and Tony felt certain it was tempered to resist any upcoming force.

Mubarak had been his first friend since the early years of Tony's adolescence. Once he'd discovered his father's lies and subterfuge and elaborate alternate reality, all ability to trust had run out of him like pus from a lanced boil. Never would anyone get close enough to him, he swore, to wound him so deeply. Ten years it took for him to open up, and Ashar had been there to become his right-hand man.

Tony could still remember the day Giacobbe's house of cards had come tumbling down. The face of Brando D'Angelo rotated slowly above the kitchen nook display, his family history below him.

Father: Giacobbe D'Angelo.

Local police had come to their bubble, docked. Giacobbe had stood, pale and shaking, as the water had drained from the lock and the officers had come in with their questions. Had he heard from his son? Did he know where Brando might be hiding?

Tony had turned and looked at his mother, whose eyelashes barely held back trembling drops. She had always suspected, he later learned.

And she forgave him. A man who lied about his past, who raised me to believe that he'd been fleeing the religious pressures of a world that had little patience for atheists, who never mentioned a family, a wife and two sons, abandoned without even a word. She forgave him…

… because she had her own secrets. She was the former lover of Brando's dead wife, for fuck's sake!

The filth, secrets and shame were too much. When the police had finally left, Antonio had packed his bags and left in his bathocycle, headed for his grandfather's large bubble complex. When he'd explained to the old soldier what had happened, he was allowed to stay and enroll in Oceania's premier military school. As for his parents, he hadn't spoken to either of them in the seventeen years since that day, though he wrote to his mother every six months with a very dry, technical description of his accomplishments and location. His grandfather tried to convince him to give his parents a second chance, but Tony would have nothing of it.

Some betrayals can never be forgotten. How could I ever trust them again?

He logged onto the virtual bridge, and Ashar was already there, looping out the others as he'd been instructed.

"You sent Quat the data?"

"Yessir. Also shorted the com so it bumps back any messages directed at it. The way I rigged it, our transponder will cut in and out, so they're not sure where we are, though they can get a pretty good idea of what we're doing. Up to you, mate, to figure out what to tell them when we get to Terego, eh."

"Don't worry about that, Commander." On the bridge, regardless of who was present, Antonio became captain: serious, formal and focused. "How long till defenestration?"

"Two minutes."

Antonio's doppelganger walked over to the swain station, and he checked helm. "Good, you already fed the course adjustments in. Get ready; the minute we unhole, we burn the braking thrusters at ten gees."

Ashar nodded, and Captain D'Angelo sat in the swain's g-seat. There was no need to strap in, but he did so out of habit. In a real in-system maneuver like this, there could be no forgetting, so it was best to always do what real life called for when faux-piloting. Of course, in a real in-system maneuver, ten gees would kill a bloke seated anywhere. Only the suspensor gel in hypostasis pods would keep the pressures of such intense gravity from the frail human body.

"Ten, nine, eight."

Antonio readied the helm to fire its thrusters at full.

"Six, five, four."

I'm coming, Big Brother. Best get ready.

"Two, one."

CHAPTER 28

RHEA STAYED AT THE MINISTRY OF CRISES until nearly sundown, waiting to hear the report of each team that returned to the equipment depot and logged its findings. As there was no news, she picked up her son from Chiho and headed out to the cottage, listening distractedly to her son talk about the cool game he and Kenji Nishiguchi had made up together. The darkness was made even more menacing by the lights of the kamioneto, and all Rhea could think of was Brando and her girls, out there in that black expanse, trying to stay alive.

As she pulled up to the garage, she noticed the door to the barn standing open. The platveturilo was gone.

The key was coded to our fingerprints. Brando? One of the girls?

She bolted out of the kamioneto's interior, pulling Jakobo roughly behind her as she hurried inside.

"What, mommy? What's wrong?"

"The flatbed. Your daddy's flatbed. Somebody took it." She glanced around, her eyes running over every piece of furniture. Hurrying from room to room, she tried to find a clue as to who had been in the house.

"Mommy, come look! The 'frigerator!"

Rhea ran to the kitchen. In red marker, someone had scrawled "NOTHING AS SEEMS TRUST ME I NEED TIME STAY AWAY FROM FOREST TELL THEM MOM" across the door of the fridge.

"Who wrote it? Miwa?"

"I'm not sure, honey. It looks more like Teri's handwriting. Hang on." She hurriedly thumbed the com system on and shunted a request to the Ministry of Crises. Almost immediately, de Waal's head popped into existence in the holofield.

"Rhea, I was just about to call you. Get over here, quick. I'm getting reports from the depot that Teri and her friends arrived a few minutes ago in the company of a bunch of natives who are demanding a koptero."

"Oh, Lord. I'll be there as quick as I can."

"Come *here*, though. The depot's too dangerous. I've got staff who can watch Jakobo."

Rhea was already rushing out the door, trusting the com to shut itself down when Roberto hung up.

Teri's alive! She's back! Thank you, Lord. Thank you.

The forty-five-minute trip back to the city was interminable, and the entire way Rhea kept wanting to berate Brando for having built a home so far away from Diadono. Jakobo was excited about seeing his sister, but he was also worn out. He fell asleep about halfway through the ride. As the kamioneto finally barreled down the main street, thumping to a halt in front of the ministry, it was surrounded by a half-dozen armed corpsmen. Susana, the minister's personal secretary, hurried down the steps and opened the vehicle's door.

"Come on, quickly. I'll get Jakobo and take him to the visitor suite. Poor thing; looks like he'll sleep all night. I don't think you will, though."

When she'd stepped through the door, Rhea was guided by several aids to the situation room, where a large map of the northwestern corner of Zarahemla was projected holographically in the center, the routes of rescue attempts charted in glowing lines. There were other features noted as well, but Rhea had no time to study them. She noticed banks of monitors on two separate walls and several communications systems at which crisis-control operators were seated, coordinating different efforts here and on other continents, though obviously the present situation took precedence.

Seated or standing throughout the large room were de Waal, Prime Minister Khumalo, the ministers of public health, immigration and state plus a host of corpsmen, aids and assorted others.

"Is Teri alright?" Rhea demanded as she caught Roberto's eye.

"The situation is complex." He had her sit with him and Khumalo before a panel of flat security monitors. "About an hour ago, Teri drove a flatbed truck, which we assume is yours, into the depot after telling the guards at the gate that the natives accompanying her would kill her and the other three with her if they weren't given a koptero."

"Three? But there ought to have been five! Who was with her?"

De Waal brought up an image: the flatbed, Teri outside of it by the door, Anyi leaning out and vomiting, Ronaldo Huaman half-visible inside beside two natives and Josuo Mudumala in the bed of the vehicle, surrounded by warriors with spears.

"A very rushed attempt at debriefing them was carried out afterward. While neither Ronaldo nor Anyi were terribly helpful, apparently very terrified and traumatized, Elder Josuo reported that Carmen is dead and that Miwa was never with them."

Miwa, where are you? Lord, keep her safe. And welcome poor Carmen into your bosom, dear Lord.

Rhea tried not to cry, allowing but a single tear to roll down her cheek. She needed to be strong, needed to be respected by these men so they would keep including her in the decision-making process. Her daughters depended on her.

"Where are they now?"

"Anyi's parents picked her up under escort. They will be staying at the government quarters for visiting dignitaries, which have been put under twenty-eight-hour armed guard. Ronaldo Huaman is also there. You'll remember that his parents have been in town for about a week, waiting for word. We plan on keeping them all there until this situation is in hand. Josuo Mudumala is on his way here for an extended debriefing, as he's made some rather serious and disturbing claims."

"And Teri? Roberto, you are keeping me unfairly in suspense! My daughter, Minister. Is she alright?"

De Waal glanced at Khumalo, who nodded and spoke. "Teri left with the Native Teregans, as did a pilot named Juan Sainz. She told the corpsmen that the natives wanted to reach the mountains and then would allow the two humans to return. But there's a problem."

"What?" Rhea felt like screaming from the tension that crackled along her nerves.

"I don't think we can believe her. Let me show you." They played the recording for her, and she nearly broke down to see the danger Teri was in, how she was screaming and weeping for help, how she was shot and yanked inside the transport, how the natives blew up the other kopteroj, nearly destroying the one Teri was on. By the end of the recording, Rhea's knuckles were white and her nails biting into the flesh of her palms.

"What do you mean you can't believe her? Look at that!"

"Oh, we have," interrupted Marlo Torres as he approached them, his face paler than ever, his hands visibly shaking, "over and over."

Khumalo frowned at him. "Yes, and there are some things we've discovered. Show the clips, Roberto, blown up and slow. See here? This is when Josuo yells that it's a trap. Zooming in on Teri's face, you can see she's saying something that the microphones can't pick up: the computer analyzed it for us about fifteen minutes ago. Here, and at various times throughout the recording, she is speaking Baryogo."

Rhea looked at him dumbfounded. "To whom? Do any of her friends speak it?"

"No," said Roberto. "She's speaking it to the natives."

"How is that possible? How can natives that have never had contact with humans until a few weeks ago speak a Solar language?"

Torres laughed. "I'd say that was a flawed premise."

Rhea ignored him. "What is she saying? Why are you so sure she's speaking to the natives?"

Khumalo lowered his eyes. "Because she tells them to silence Josuo. And they do. Brutally. Here's a transcript of everything our computers could read her lips to determine she was saying." He handed her a floppy data sheet. She scrolled through it solemnly. "As you can see, she told the natives how use the grenades. She ordered them to kill themselves to destroy the kopteroj, and they obeyed. She mentions 'unifying the nations.' Why would she do that? Why would she help them?"

"Because she's drunk on power, completely nuts."

It was a new voice. A group of corpsmen were escorting a young man toward them. Josuo Mudumala. Rhea looked him over: his face was bruised and scratched, his eyes sunken and his lips drawn tightly together in barely suppressed anger. He'd obviously been allowed to bathe and change into a jumpsuit, but a pretty heavy beard, scraggly because of his relative youth, only partially hid the hard, furious set of his jaw.

Elisha Galadari had told ministry officials that this young man had pursued Teri romantically and been rejected. Rhea could sense the reek of vengeance on him. He felt slighted. His words would twist the truth. Rhea had much experience with this sort of male obsession. Marlo, standing right here beside her, had destroyed Rhea's family because of it. She suddenly equated the two in her mind, and her own anger blossomed.

"We had wanted to interview you in a quiet place, where you'd feel less pressure, Brother," began de Waal.

"Please, Minister: after what I've been through, this *is* a quiet, less pressured place. I recognize a lot of important people. You're going to have to tell them what I say anyway, aren't you? Let's just do it here. My scruples and preferences have been recently beaten out of me, so it doesn't bother me at all."

"Right, then. Go ahead and have a seat. Torres, please call the other ministers over, and let's have the sound barrier up so operations won't disturb us, alright?"

Rhea was surprised to see Minister of State Emem Inyang, who'd been holed up for nearly two weeks with members of the Planetary Court and the Congress, examining the treaties signed with the Consortium and trying to finagle their way out of this mess. She wondered whether they'd found their loophole yet.

Once the dampening fields were activated and the ambient sound blocked out, Khumalo began. "Josuo, you stated when being debriefed that Teri Miranda is working in collusion with the natives to unite against the humans on this planet."

"Yes, Prime Minister, that's right. We spent the last two weeks in one of their villages, really not far from Diadono at all, about a day and a half by foot from Lake Galileo toward the southwest, more or less." To Rhea, Josuo seemed to be relishing this more than was proper. *Like Marlo had.* "We were treated at first with a degree of dignity. Everyone was waiting for the tribe's leader to come back from talking to some person they call the Greenseer, an off-worlder who has taught the priestesses that language Teri can speak, Baryogo. The language Tenshi spoke."

Khumalo raised an eyebrow. "How do you know about Tenshi?"

"Teri's got her diary. Brando told her where he'd hid it, or something. She listens to it all the time, day and night. She's started acting like that woman, talking like her, even wearing her wedding band on a chain around her neck."

Brando kept her ring?

Josuo spat. "She went so far as to tell the creatures her *name* was Tenshi."

Rhea shuddered. *Oh, my baby: what must you be going through? What confusion you must feel! How you need me!*

"You seem to imply that your treatment changed," broke in de Waal.

"Yes, Minister. It did. When Teri started 'playing along' with them. This Greenseer has told them that a human female will come and teach them how to work together to fight humans and keep us from going into the forest. Teri started acting like it was her. They sort of adopted her. She pretended we were her harem, which meant we had to work. They made us go out and pick mushrooms and stuff while she schmoozed with them and learned their ways. When she wasn't listening to Tenshi's diary with Carmen."

"Did you hear anything about Miwa Miranda?" Rhea asked.

Josuo turned and looked at her, and a curious light glowed in his eyes when he understood who she was. "No, Sister. Teri never even asked them about Miwa, as far as I know. She's caught up a fantasy. I couldn't talk to them like she could, or I would've asked. Poor Carmen bore the brunt of Teri's dark turn ..." His voice trailed off and his gaze went distant.

"Tell us about Carmen," Khumalo urged. "You said she was killed. How? Where is her body?"

Josuo hesitated, swallowed, clenched his fists. "It was Saturday.

Yesterday. In the morning. They'd made us go down to the fields, and we were pulling up some weird tubers they warned us with gestures not to eat. Poison, we figured. We were trying to figure out a way to get past the guards and run when some warriors came, picked us up, and took us to this clearing where they have religious ceremonies. Teri was there with a new creature, their priestess. They were babbling, but I recognized the phrase *tearing ghoul*, something like that. It's the name of their messiah, the one Teri's pretending to be. Anyway, Teri started crying. The guards came over and grabbed Carmen and took her to where Teri was. Carmen begged Teri to do something, to not let her die there, but that bitch didn't stop them!"

There was silence. The vast majority of Tereganoj didn't use profanity. Many of them, Rhea included, had never heard such vocabulary in their lives. But everyone understood.

"When you say she didn't stop them," Rhea said, "do you mean she didn't try, or that she couldn't?"

Josuo, realizing his faux pas, clarified. "She tried some karate kick or something, but it didn't do any good. The priestess still managed to cut Carmen's throat, and the guards dragged her away. We never saw her again. Teri and the others want to believe she's alive, but I doubt it. Those monsters are vicious. They knocked Teri out and then undressed her, putting a religious robe on her and shoving tubers in her mouth. They gave them to her all day Saturday and on Sunday as we were carried through the forest back to the lake. Then she started eating them voluntarily once she agreed to be their messiah and steal a koptero and guns for them, with those drones all bowing down and worshiping her. She even ate a tuber as she drove to the depot."

"The poisonous ones?" Rhea leaned forward abruptly. "She's eating poisonous fungi?"

"I think they're drugs. Hallucinogens, like the alkaloid moss on Kanaano that the Minster of Public Health here so kindly protects us from."

Impertinent little snot, thought Rhea, fed up with Brother Mudumala. *If no one else has the guts to call him on it, I will.* "Yes, Josuo, Elisha has told us all about your fondness for inebriation." *You got my little girl drunk, you snake.* "We have the still and the books, all of it. Needed it for the investigation, isn't that right, Minister de Waal?"

The ministers looked at her strangely, but no one interrupted. Rhea glanced at the transcript she was holding.

"Let me ask you, Elder Mudumala: what did Teri mean when she said 'I'll accept my fate. Can you say the same?' when you told her that God would punish her? What punishment do you deserve, Josuo? What did you do to my daughter, Josuo?"

Josuo's eyes narrowed. "I'm not the villain here, Sister Miranda. Or should I call you Sister D'Angelo? All I did was try to kiss Teri to snap her out of her obsession with Carmen Allende. But your 'daughter' is one twisted little bitch. She seduced her senior into one wild lesbian relationship.

Carmen died with that sin on her soul."

"Tum jhuthe ho!" Rhea spat in Hindi.

Josuo shook his head, "No, Sister. I'm telling the truth. She's a freak. Look at her, leading suicide bombers and stealing weapons for monsters that want to kill us! I just spent two weeks in the most frightening hell you could imagine, and you want to make this about me? We all make mistakes. You made one marrying that criminal who first gave her hallucinogenic drugs, opening the door for the insanity she's embraced."

Rhea shot to her feet. "What did you just say?"

"Ha. Of course she never confided in you. Why would she? You would've just believed his version of the story. Woman, he was playing you like a cheap instrument while he raised the *clone of his dead wife* under your nose. Why? Have you asked yourself that? Have you never wondered what happened during that little trip of theirs to Nova Mumbajo? Come on, let's be fair and spread the guilt around, shall we? You, Rhea Kumar-Miranda, let this happen to her!"

Stunned beyond the ability to move, the ministers just sat bolted to their seats as Rhea took three short steps and slapped Josuo. He rubbed his face and smiled.

"And here I thought she'd gotten it from Brando's training. Good job. You've raised a homicidal maniac who beats up her friends and helps her enemies. Congratulations, Sister."

Khumalo seemed to realize the two of them had to be separated. He
motioned two corpsmen over. "Josuo, please go with these two brothers. We'll
continue this discussion more calmly, you, Minister de Waal and I, a bit later. Go
get something to eat and please, get some control over yourself. We appreciate
what you've been through, but you are being insulting and offensive."

Josuo mumbled an apology and was led away. Khumalo turned to
Rhea, who was still standing, trembling with rage that she'd suppressed for
so many years it wracked her body as it played itself out. "Rhea, I have never
seen you like that."

"They have my daughters. They've drugged one of them, maybe
brainwashed her. I don't know where the other one is, though I think Brando
is on her trail. Everything I love is in the balance, Prime Minister. Everything
I am could be destroyed so easily, and that snot-nosed brat, that drink-loving
snake of a rat is trying to make me look like I'm responsible."

"He's just shaken and traumatized. We're trying to make a measured
analysis of what is happening, Rhea. We need you to find that control you
always have. Pray to God to give it back to you, because you are part of this
team, and we can't have you losing your cool. All of our nerves are frayed,
all of us are on edge, but we're the leaders of this planet, and we must keep
ourselves together."

Rhea nodded and returned awkwardly to her seat. De Waal used his
stylus to make a list appear on the view screens. "As I see it, we have a

couple of very large mysteries to solve here. We need to know who this Greenseer is, we need to know why Teri has chosen to help him achieve his apparent goal, unifying whatever different groups of natives together as one force, taking a *single* case of rifles, no extra ammunition by the way, and a *single* koptero."

Marlo giggled like a madman. Rhea looked at him out of the corner of her eye.

Talk about frayed nerves. He's liable to run screaming around the situation room at any moment.

"I have it. Brando's the Greenseer. He's unifying the tribes. He's been teaching them Baryogo, feeding their minds with legends so that when he was caught, his daughters would be taken care of, so that his strange little family would be protected from us and from the CPCC."

Khumalo shook his head. "No, that doesn't seem likely. Teri appears to be in real danger, and Brando's team was nearly decimated."

"Maybe... maybe... maybe things have just gotten out of hand. Maybe he didn't plan on putting the girls in harm's way, but he can't quite control what's going on. That's happened to him before. He thinks too big for his own good."

The logic of what Marlo was suggesting was so frighteningly veridical that Rhea's heart jumped. She thought of his regular "me-time" at his little shack near the stream. One whole Saturday to himself each month.

Supposedly writing a monograph on Teregan Esperanto. What if—

No. I won't believe it. He has never left our property. Our vehicles were always there. Impossible. Can't be.

Shrugging away these doubts, she snapped, "He hasn't had time."

"Hmmm?" Khumalo waited for her to continue.

"Brando. He hasn't had time. Except for that long fishing expedition four and a half jaroj ago, he hasn't been away from us. All of you know his busy schedule. I daresay we can account for his every move for the past four jaroj, at least."

Minister of State Inyang finally spoke, his black eyebrows pushing down against his eyes. "Four and a half jaroj ago? How extended was this trip?"

"Two weeks. Hardly enough time to teach aliens a new language and spread legends."

Inyang smiled a very fake and short smile. "Hardly. But ample time to hide fugitives in the forest. Marlo, wasn't it about four or five jaroj ago when you and Roberto discovered that illegal colony on Kanaano?"

Torres, his face teeming with conflicting emotions, nodded energetically, as if grasping what Inyang was driving at. "Yes. There were a lot of ex-yakuza in that group. Took Sitati months to root them out, didn't it, Roberto?"

"I'm sure everyone remembers that. The last battle, Sitati risking his life to blow the munitions depot—He was our greatest hero. We should be mourning his passing instead of hiding it. But that's neither here nor there.

What are we talking about, Jin?"

"Imagine that among those illegals were allies of D'Angelo's, old companions of his from Jitsu. Former squad members, black market buddies, followers of his wife's reform movement. What if some of them managed to survive Sitati's campaign and are now hiding in the Great Seneka Forest? And what if D'Angelo spent those two weeks getting them equipment and so forth? Couldn't they be the ones behind all this nonsense with Teri Miranda?"

Marlo slapped a fist against a palm. "That's it! It fits all the data. I'd bet on a family member of Tenshi's, maybe her father. This gobbledygook about a messiah sounds like something a relative of Jitsu's former Oracle would come up with."

"What's more," added de Waal, "since the teacher of the natives is called the green *seer*, which is like *oracle*, it might even be Samanei herself. Brando still hasn't said what happened to her: he was quite close-mouthed on that topic during his interrogation."

Marlo got to his feet. "That does it. We *have* to tell the Consortium what's going on here. If Brando and Samanei are allied, we are in serious trouble. Jin, you know what the CPCC discovered about that woman's connections to the underworld: from a little room on a distant planet she was manipulating multiple crime syndicates. Imagine her in control of an army of those *mallumanoj*! She'll take this planet!"

Rhea had not heard that term before. *Mallumanoj*, inhabitants of darkness.

"Ridiculous!" she exploded. "The only inhabited darkness is your own ignorance! You have no proof of what you're concocting. Are you going to turn the keys of this planet over to the AF just because you *think* that *maybe* a mentally ill fugitive of the law *might* be trying to take over Terego? Come on! We need time to sift through the recordings, debrief the other two survivors," she trailed off.

Time. Oh, Lord. Teri's message.

Khumalo nodded. "Agreed. I need you gentlemen to research in your respective ministries. Look for any confirmation of the theories you've offered tonight. In the interim, we're going to send our remaining kopteroj over the forest in the general area that Josuo has indicated as the location of the native village and…"

"No! You can't." Everyone regarded her as if she was mad. "I've forgotten something important. When I got home, before speaking to Roberto, I found a message from Teri on the refrigerator. She must've left it right after grabbing the key to the flatbed."

"What did it say?"

"Uh, 'nothing as it seems; trust me; I need time; stay away from the forest, tell them, Mom.' We've got to give her the time she needs."

Marlo was flabbergasted. "Time to what? So Destroy more of our weapons and leave us defenseless?"

Rhea smirked. "I think she's going along with them so she can stop them. I think that we will do more damage by interfering than by letting her do what she must do."

The prime minister was obviously torn. Rubbing his hand along his close-cropped hair, he stepped to a com panel and clicked a channel open. "Prophet? Have you been watching?"

"Yes," came Disbergen's voice.

"I'm going down the street to talk to you. This decision requires guidance beyond human ken."

"I'll be waiting, Prime Minister."

Khumalo turned to the others. "Feel free to get some rest and food in the gym, where we've set up cots. Consider yourselves on permanent duty. Until we get the situation in hand, everything else is secondary. Rhea, can Sanas handle the trial without you?"

"Of course. I'm not much good to him right now, anyway. I'll let him know."

As the prime minister took his leave and the others scattered throughout the ministry, Rhea initiated a com with Sanas's office. It was late, but he'd still be there.

"Rhea! I've been calling you."

"There have been some major developments in the other thing, and they have me sequestered. You'll be on your own tomorrow, I'm afraid."

Sanas shook his head and leaned forward, as if the two of them were physically close and he could whisper to her that way. "There's been a delay in the trial. Tomorrow we won't be meeting."

"Why? What's happened?"

"It seems your brother-in-law has pulled out. Something about difficulties with his communications system. A Captain Quat will be taking over as prosecutor for Mubarak, and he's requested a day to review the trial, though he apparently has had access to all the files for some time."

"Could it be a smoke screen? Might the AF have decided that Antonio was too risky a choice for them?"

"Perhaps. This whole trial seems a joke, really. A pretense. They just want to keep us busy defending him. They've already made their minds up, though. You can see it in the judges, the motions they approve and what they disallow. He's guilty, as far as they're concerned. I'm afraid Brando's fate will be decided more by politics than by this trial, Rhea dear."

"We always knew that, Judge. They've already started, haven't they? Problems with communications? Sure. Pray for us, Judge. For Brando, for me, for the girls, for little Jakobo. I feel we've been placed in a crucible and the heat is only just starting to be applied."

"I pray for you every night, my dear. I pray that your reach never exceeds your grasp, and that if it does, that God lend His hand so that you don't drop what you try so desperately to hold on to."

Rhea nodded and closed the connection. The present situation had exceeded everyone's grasp, she thought.

It is entirely in God's hands. No use pretending otherwise.

She went to find Jakobo, whom she knew she could comfort and derive comfort from. Her other loves she commended to her savior's keeping.

However, as she snuggled beside him on a cot, waiting to be called back to the situation room at any minute, that low, dark voice insinuated itself into her mind, an old friend come back to visit.

Gave her hallucinogenic drugs? My, my. Still trust him? Still think he's the loving, devoted husband he claims to be? Wake up, child. He's one of mine. And think about this, Rhea: look down at that beautiful boy, that miracle child you used to shut me up. When did you get pregnant with him, hmm? How soon after Brando returned from that now more and more notorious 'fishing' trip? Barren Rhea, meet the master of clones, the student of artificial child production, Dr. Brando D'Angelo.

No, she thought, tears burning her eyes, her nose beginning to run from the effort of holding in the incredible despair and sadness that began to grip her heart, *he wouldn't.*

Oh, wouldn't he? How disappointingly naïve of you. He lied for eleven jaroj, child. And they call me the Father of Lies. I have nothing on your Brando, your Nando, your Kyosu. And just imagine: there you were, asleep in your holy matrimonial bed, and he went into you, Rhea. Did he cut you open? Any little scars you always wondered about? Or was he trickier than

that? Yes, likely so. Some tube, up into your womb, that's more his style.

I can't believe he would do such a thing. Not to me. Why?

Why? You know why. I nearly had you convinced of the truth, that he

was with you only so you could raise his girls. His clones. But he ruined that:

he got you better than I ever could. He gave you a son, and he bound you to

him so completely with that boy that even now you are rushing to come up

with an excuse, aren't you?

Rhea began sobbing, but she buried her face in the pillow so the others in

the gym wouldn't hear. How could she have been so wrong about him? How

could she have let herself believe that Jakobo was a miracle? When did she

ever begin to deserve miracles?

That's it. Despair. You believed because you're a fool, because you love

what cannot be yours, because, as Sanas so beautifully put it, your reach

exceeds your grasp.

Lifting her head from the pillow, she stared into the darkness and

screamed.

"NO! You will NOT win! I know why he did it, and you can't hide the

answer from me, Satan, destroyer, tempter, hater of all beautiful and sacred

things: he loves me! He loves me, and in his own twisted way he wanted to

make me happy! I know him, and he loves me. He loves them, too! In all

the destruction he's caused, he's never been like you! He's never destroyed simply to destroy. He's had no choice! His love leaves him no choice!"

Thundering footsteps approached and the lights went on. She was hugged and held and prayed for as she explained that Satan had come to battle her in a dream, and with the help of Christ she had won.

Again.

CHAPTER 29

LATE IN THE AFTERNOON ON THE SECOND DAY of their river voyage, Brando's team was ambushed and captured so quickly and unexpectedly that it took them a good half hour to process what had happened.

The rain had slacked off a bit, and they were making good time. As the three rafts buzzed upstream, one person on each worked the rudder-engine and kept a forward watch while each of the others trained his weapon to starboard, to port and above them, respectively. So intent were they on their vigil that when the natives burst through the surface of the water, spears thrusting through the bottoms or edges of the inflatables with startling pops of expelled air, the corpsmen could not recover their wits quickly enough to get off a shot.

As they spilled into the water, their rifles ripped from their hands. Brando, who'd been on rudder duty, never released his grip on the motor and emerged from the water brandishing it like a weapon, thrusting it like a saw into a native's arm, her dark blood spurting onto the surface of the river. From behind him a spear haft was slammed into his neck, and he blacked out for a couple of seconds, during which his makeshift weapon was wrenched from his grasp and his hands were bound behind him.

The twelve of them were yanked from the water and herded at spear-point through thick tangles of undergrowth for hours. Once Brando turned to check the others and perhaps exchange words with them, but he was struck across the face, a blow that nearly broke his jaw.

By evening, they were walked into the edges of a village much like the one they'd discovered eight days before, except bustling with activity. They were pushed to their knees near a clearing, and a roughly twined roped was threaded through each of their bindings, creating a sort of chain gang. Where one went, they would all have to go. Brando strained against the ropes, but they were intended for native prisoners and beyond his strength.

A dozen warriors stood in a circle around them as guards, but Brando was more interested in the group of natives standing a little distance away, at the center of the clearing. In their midst was some object, hard to make out, but then one of them moved and Brando saw it clearly.

"The transmitter," muttered Leal. Brando looked to see whether the warriors would move to silence him, but they appeared not to care.

"Yeah," Brando affirmed. "And those warriors aren't from this tribe,

I'll bet you."

Sonali was behind him and couldn't see. "Why do you say that?"

"The ornamentation they're wearing. The ones that jumped us wear long red leather harnesses around their necks and chests, decorated with yellow and green feathers. These others have belts or something, green ones, with mollusk shells tied to them. Just like the band that attacked us on Wednesday. They also carry themselves differently, less modestly."

Several of the green-belted warriors walked over with one of the shorter ones, those Sonali had labeled *males$_1$*. It wore a green robe that was cinched with a similar green belt. "Boss man coming up is from their tribe, too. These are the gals that killed Sitati and the rest, brothers. They probably want us dead, too, so just stay calm."

Leal snorted. "As if we had a choice. What are you planning to do?"

"Take Sonali's advice and try to negotiate with them."

"How? You don't speak their language." Leal snickered. "I mean, I know you're a great linguist and all, but you're not going to learn their language in a couple of hours, D'Angelo."

"I'll think of something. Shh. Here they come."

Five natives of the green belt type were soon standing in front of Brando. The warriors gestured at the group of humans, rattling off in a very angry sounding way, though their faces did not show expressions the way humans' did. Their tails and cheeks and ears were very animated, and Brando presumed their body language was centered in those parts. He closed his eyes and let their language wash over him; like he always did with new languages, he visualized the sounds on a grid in his head, like a very complex musical score.

Part tonal. Clicks, like Zulu. What's that? A harmonic? How do they produce harmonics? Vowel duration important. No labials or labiodentals.

He opened his eyes. The smaller one had begun to speak, more slowly and with a certain odd rhythm that seemed perhaps indicative of more formality or ritual. It went on for a good five minutes, and the warriors simply walked away when it had finished. The smaller one stayed behind, surveying them, walking from one to another. It stopped somewhere behind Brando.

Near Sonali.

"Can you speak in the Greenseer's tongue?"

Brando nearly leapt to his feet at the words. The creature was speaking Baryogo, some modified form of it, without the labial consonant sounds, but intelligible, formal Baryogo, the sort spoken on Jitsu by religious leaders.

"Yes," Brando called. "None of the others can, however. How did you learn this language?"

The native walked slowly around and focused its purple eyes on him, its ears rotating back and forth like a vigilant horse.

"How does anyone learn a language?"

Fuck me. Oral societies and their goddamn agonistic way of perceiving discourse. I guess it's good to know humans aren't the only ones. Ought to revolutionize, or, well, give birth to xenolinguistics. We'll be sparring, then. Wonderful.

"Indeed. The Greenseer has taught you well, unless someone who learned from him taught you." It was a shot in the dark, but worth a try.

"Brando," Sonali whispered hoarsely. "What is going on? Is that an Earth language it's talking?"

"A Solar one. Baryogo. Spoken on Jitsu as well. Hang on. I'm trying to figure out how this Native Teregan learned it."

The robed native regarded him with its head cocked and cheeks inflated nearly humorously, reminding Brando of some squirrel gathering nuts. "What do you know of the Greenseer, *ingan*?"

Wow, somebody pretty archaic must've taught this bloke. Ingan *instead of* umuntu? "What does anyone know of him? What does one know of a leaf, of a tree? What one sees, that is all."

Like that? I have lots more.

"And I see a band of *ingan* headed toward the Mountain of God. To greet the Greenseer? Or to destroy him?"

"Who is the Greenseer?" Brando asked, and immediately wished he hadn't. Direct questions would get him nowhere.

"Who am I? Who are they? Who is God? We all ask each other this, and the voices answer. What do your voices tell you, *ingan*? Who are you?"

Perhaps bored, the native turned as if to leave; Brando's anger got the best of him.

"I'm Brando D'Angelo, you prick."

The creature stopped. It turned its head slightly, flicked out its tongue. Slowly it brought itself around again and crouched before him.

"Repeat that."

"Brando. D'Angelo. My name, beast. Got it?"

The robed native looked to one side and then to the other. It traced a wavy line in the dirt before it. "The Greenseer never said you'd be with the troop of weak-boned humans. I don't understand why he would keep this from me. Perhaps the other highborn chose not to tell me. But if your claim is true, I am honored. This humble village is honored. The *ingan* who brought the mysterious Greenseer to the moss-hung forest. His chosen adversary in the great battle. The mighty, worthy opponent of the People. In the clearing of this minor village. I would have never imagined it when I was sent as emissary of the truth to these northern nests of apostasy."

Brando was trying to assimilate what the creature was babbling. It had come from the south, sent to control, perhaps, this village? Its people revered this Greenseer who claimed to have been brought by Brando and who was preparing to fight him?

"Brando, what's going on? Come on. We can tell it recognizes your name. What's it saying?"

"Hang on, Chuquipoma. The guy who taught it to speak Baryogo claimes I'm their enemy or something. It's all excited that I'm here, that they've captured me."

To the highborn: "Does the Greenseer speak of me often?"

"I seldom am permitted an audience with him, but just this morning we received one of his swift drones, come to tell us that the most anticipated prophesy is being fulfilled, that the *ingan* highborn, the third advent of Çèrhingÿl, the doughty messiah you yourself incubated and raised, wily Brando, to serve as the Greenseer's instrument in his forest-shaking war against you, she has undergone the rite and accepted her holy role. She has led our drones against the *ingan*, stealing one of their airships and many of their magical reeds and wind-quick darts. She is preparing to lead us against you and your mighty clan. In fact, I must send word to the holy mouthpiece of God immediately."

"Wait! This messiah. Does she call herself Miwa? Teri?"

"I do not know, though the Greenseer often called her the sibling of Tenshi in his prophecies. Her birth name is known only by you and her people, but she is now Çèrhingÿl reborn."

Brando's mind was swirling, his palms sweating. "Please, one more thing. When did the Greenseer first come among your people?"

"I think I have said more than I ought to have. It is a weakness of mine, the reason they call me 'leaky vessel' in my birth village. Besides, you already know. I tire of this game."

"Was it four and a half jaroj ago? Did he come to you four and a half years ago? A jaro is the time it takes for the sun, that bright light in the sky, to do its dance around the world and return to its starting place: have four and a half of these passed? Tell me!"

"You know it is so, wily Brando, trickster, bringer of death and despair and desolation. It was you who sent him among us, banished him from your stonehearted people. I take my leave, clever enemy. We will see what the divine mouthpiece wants me to do with you."

Horror thrilled along Brando's nerves as the robed creature ambled off toward the throng of red-robed short natives. *Oh, fuck.* The enormity of his crime began to settle on him like a blanket that he couldn't cast aside, suffocating him. He slumped, he wanted to sink into the mud, slide through the crust of the planet and to its molten core.

Sibling of Tenshi that I raised? Teri. Stolen a koptero. Arming the natives. Insane like her aunt because I pushed her there. But that's not all. He's behind it. I sent him back to the mountain, and he simmered in a rage I didn't think he was capable of it. Broken Sopiya, what have I done?

A haunting, infantile voice echoed in his memory. "It's not right what you're doing to me, Mr. Miranda. It wasn't right what you did to Samanei, either. You are not a good man, Mr. Miranda."

"Good Lord, Brando," Sonali gasped as he sprawled in the mire in despair, yanking everyone forward with him. "What did that thing say to you? What's the matter? We need you here, D'Angelo! Don't fall apart, do you hear?"

I did it. I fucked them all. Oh, there's no chance for me anymore.

But he pulled his torso erect, shook the muck from his face, and once again found a way to mix the truth with lies. It was the Ona ra-Kyosu. His own special, horrifying Way. He no longer had to think about the twisted means he used people to get what he wanted. The talent was engrained.

"He told me Teri's working with them. She claims she's their messiah, that she'll help them fight the humans. This guy they call the Greenseer, the one that taught them Baryogo, he's monitoring communications from Diadono and he's told the green-robed thing over there that she helped steal a koptero and some weapons. Oh, man, this is such a mess."

And I am such a fucking bastard.

Chuquipoma shifted uneasily. "But weren't we following the kids? How did Teri get back south?"

"Brando, you jerk." It was Leal, with a tone of revelation in his voice. "We haven't been following them all, have we? I just realized. All the clues and tracks we found—they were always Miwa's. The other kids went south, didn't they? Right there by the lake! Did you know then? When did you find out? How did you make that choice, you sick man? One girl over all the rest!"

"Look, at the first village, I figured it out, Leal. But we couldn't go back: whoever destroyed all those natives would've gotten us, too. So I said nothing."

Sonali spoke, her voice trembling with anger and fear. "They could've airlifted us out, Brando. No one had to die."

"Wrong," Brando's lie-spinner kicked into overdrive without a hitch. "They would've just made two teams, and instead of twenty people being slaughtered, forty or fifty would have been! I made a choice to try to minimize the possible collateral damage."

"How can you be so cold about it? How can you sit there and weigh some people's lives against those of others?" Sonali's voice spiked in volume, and several of the warriors grunted, waving their spears as if to say 'shut up.'

Everyone fell silent then, each stewing in his or her own bile of choice. The rain quickened, and soon they were bowing their heads to keep the water from their noses and mouths.

AFTER ANOTHER HOUR, a red-harnessed *drone*, as the robed one had called them, came over and barked a command at the guards. The humans were jerked to their feet and driven into a ground structure like the ones that Vivek had theorized were schools in the other village. They were unbound and sealed in, the absolute darkness inside making the rainy gloom of the forest seem bright.

Brando moved along one wall and sank into a corner away from the others. He heard them muttering low among themselves, but he didn't bother trying to overhear. His mind was slipping back Six standard years, four and a half jaroj, to a different set of lies, the ones he'd told to give Rhea what she'd always yearned for.

It had been the year of crisis. Nando Miranda had started bleeding into him. Confused, Brando thought he'd fallen in love with Rhea. Became convinced that he would have long forgotten Tenshi's face had Teri not been in front of him every day, stretching toward puberty, her face altered day by day until it transformed into that of his long-dead wife.

So many years without a sign. All Brando had wanted in that moment of weakness was to let the past slip away, to have a son with Rhea who would live a normal life and grow to be the man that Brando should have been. He had invented the trip, a sabbatical of sorts (it was the seventh jaro of his new life), and he had traveled to the mountain, where all he'd tried to hide was now waiting for him again.

"Brando?" It was Sonali. Again she'd come up on him without his realizing it. Fifty-four years old didn't seem ancient enough to lose his guard this way. It was shameful, but given the circumstances, to be expected.

"Yeah?"

"The men are formulating a plan. They figure we'll either die here or be held prisoner a long time. The idea of rifles in the hands of the Native Tereganos has really spooked them, and they are determined to get off a message to Diadono about this Greenseer guy. It's going to be a suicide mission, I think. Stave off the natives long enough to shoot up the antennae and shunt off a note."

"They'll get killed before they even get close."

"Then talk to them!"

"You heard them: they despise me. They've already started blaming me for everything, with good reason."

"You give yourself too much credit, Brando. The whole world doesn't spin on its axis because of you."

"You don't have all the facts, Doctor Dixit."

"I know *that*. It's obvious that you know more than you're telling us. I'd laugh at your predictability if I weren't so frightened. Brando, I don't want to die." There was a tremulous quaver in her voice that wrenched his gut like a serrated knife. "But if I do, I want to know that everything is going to be alright for us. For human Tereganoj. I was never the kind of Novasanktulo they wanted, but I always believed, always felt part of the great experiment."

"Sonali, don't—"

"Shush, Brando, and listen. I'm still a virgin, did you know that? A decade past my prime and never been touched by a man that way. But it's okay. I did the work I wanted to do, taught my people a little more about the world they've grown to love and call home. I'd rather not die, but I'm ready to. But I want you to tell me—dropping all the pretentious psychobabble nonsense—that it's going to be okay. Tell me you're going to make sure my people are okay."

His head felt trapped in a vise, his heart squeezed in the vast fists of indifferent fate. In the darkness, Sonali was Tenshi, demanding he be the best he could, brooking no weakness, accepting nothing less than everything he was capable of.

Between clenched teeth, he grunted, his voice rough with emotion, "I swear it."

He felt her hand on his face. "Now, you twisted, beautiful thing, do what you have to do, no matter the cost."

She's putting her life in my hands. Letting me decide whether she lives or dies. I don't deserve such trust. But I'll try to rise to the occasion once more.

He reached out and stroked her cheek.

"You won't die, Sonali, not if I have anything to say about it. You'll have the chance to realize your dreams, whatever they may be. Marriage, if that's what you want. Invite me to your wedding. If I'm not in prison, we'll laugh about this then."

She sniffled and laughed low. "Ah, Brando, it's so hard to hate you."

He ran his hand up to the top of her head and ruffled her hair. Then he stood and focused on the muttering ahead of him.

"Brothers," he said loudly, "I hear you have a plan."

As they gave a reluctant report, he was already formulating a secondary plan, one that would keep at least him and Dixit alive, one that might save all of Terego.

The world was otherwise unprepared for the war that bastard traitor up on the mountain wanted to unleash in the name of some feeling he shouldn't be able to have.

CHAPTER 30

SHALURA WATCHED DAENZHELO RUN UP THE BACK of unsuspecting Òkẏdtaqh, somersaulting off the warrior's broad shoulders and landing in a crouch on the wet bough they were traveling along. The strange highborn warrior let loose her laugh, clear and bubbly like a mountain stream.

In the five days since their turn westward, the little one had been diligently scratching word tracks into her odd box that never seemed to get full, and she was speaking better and better. It was now possible to hold a conversation with her, an activity she always wanted to engage in. Shalura was used to thinking of children as being this inquisitive, but a grown highborn would never have demanded to have the lore of the People revealed the way Daenzhelo did.

Every new tale she was related she tore apart like a carcass, examining the innards of the People's faith in a way that frankly sickened Shalura, though she couldn't help but try to answer Daenzhelo's questions, each of which led to the telling of another tale, and another, and another, the highborn making marks on her box like some crazed animal trying to dig up a root.

Though she really enjoyed the very oldest tales of the misty times when male and drone fought side by side and even heroic highborn were known to take up a lance in the name of goodness, Daenzhelo was especially interested in the tale of Çèrhingÿl and how she led the seven siblings across the stormy, green-gray sea to where the moss-hung forest hugged the sandy-white shores and perilous cliffs. For hours Shalura and others told her of the siblings' capture mid-journey by Lejidhé, the haughty ocean queen, and of how the seventh highborn, Tèdhanqhÿrhò, betrayed her sisters but was beheaded by the very queen to whom she had sworn fealty.

On the fourth day of the westward trek, Òkÿdtaqh softly sang the Lay of Çèrhingÿl in its entirety as they traveled, ending with her immolation in the shining tower and the loss of her orb of power. Daenzhelo, even after seven hours of epic song, had wanted to know what happened next.

"What do you mean, 'next'? That is the end of the lay."

"But what the siblings did? How they reacted? She said they build a mighty nation, and then she died. What they did?"

"To explain would require several more hours of song or chanting."

"No, just tell me. Tell me the important parts. Leave the rest out."

Shalura had again been shocked by the lack of respect that Daenzhelo showed the tales, even though she appeared so interested in them. "I cannot leave anything out, Lady. The story must be told entire, or its individual tales complete. To take a bit here and a bit there would be like killing a herd of game and just ripping the kidneys from each animal and leaving the rest to rot."

"Later you tell me the whole thing. Right now, I want the kidneys."

So Shalura had relented and told of how the siblings had quarreled and gone their separate ways, each with her family, establishing the clans that would become the six nations. Danezhelo had then announced that now she would tell a story, and the troop had stopped to listen, half expecting her garbled mastery of the People's language to provide more entertainment than any tale she could tell.

"There been other trips like that one you tell me. In my ancestors' land, there were siblings, too, that crossed an ocean and reached a shore far distant and there they quarreled and made two separate nations. But the God, she made them come together again many, many years later for they one people could be.

"But even more interesting the trip was that it bringed my tribe to your land. That trip was on a very much big ship that no sailed the green-gray ocean, but the sky. No the sky, but the place above the sky. At night, where the lights are, what you call that?"

"The Deepest Green? That darkness in which the other gods look on the land and envy the Unblinking Eye?" Shalura had offered. She and her warriors had stared at each other. There were echoes here of religious tales, instruction on faith passed on from Çèrhingÿl to the highborn she named priestesses before immolating herself, the sorts of lessons taught to adult males and drones by the heads of the tribe.

"That the name of color, too? Deepest green?"

"Yes. When the light green of day fades and the darkness of God's absence hangs over us, reminding us of life without her stern guidance. We may hide from her gaze, respecting the unimaginable power of her wrath, but the shadows of the forest are nothing like the darkness, the Deepest Green. That is why the spirit of our tribe dances above us in twisting streamers of light: we are watched, we are kept safe. But you are saying your tribe flew through this darkness? I can scarcely believe you."

But Shalura knew what the others were thinking as well. As adults, they were inducted bit by bit into the mysteries. One of these was the knowledge that every eye of every god that dotted the Deepest Green looked down upon its own land, too distant from the mighty forest to be seen by the People. Çèrhingÿl herself had said she'd come from one of those far off lands, crossing the darkness in a ship much like Daenzhelo described. It was possible that Daenzhelo already knew the teachings of the Firstborn and simply sought to befuddle their minds, but Shalura thought otherwise.

The Greenseer said Çèrhingÿl would be one of Daenzhelo's kind, one of her voices whispered, *so of course it must be true that they crossed the*

Deepest Green like she did. Talk to her of this.

As Daenzhelo continued describing the journey, hundreds of years long, the spirit of the tribe searching for a world as her people slept, another voice had interrupted Shalura's deliberation.

No. These are matters for highborn, matters to be discussed in the village only. You cannot broach them with a stranger!

When Daenzhelo concluded her tale, before anyone could stop her, Shalura explained in basic terms the teachings of the Firstborn. Her warriors glowered at her, but the little highborn had nodded with excitement, gibbering in her strange tongue and scribbling on her box.

"Look. Lands not flat, they round like fruit. They go around the god-eyes in big circles, see?" She'd held up the box, and on its surface, which had glimmered like the skin of a lake, a drawing of the Unblinking Eye had been magically circled over and over by a smaller round object. "Your Çèrhingÿl was right: god-eyes have their own round-lands, sometimes three, four, maybe nine of them. Usually there no People on round-lands, but sometimes a god comes and makes her spirit babies to going into animals and they become like People."

Many of the warriors, though amazed by the spell that allowed the drawings to move, had scoffed at Daenzhelo's words. But Shalura had silenced them with a flick of her tail. "I am troop leader. Because of my rank I have received the teachings of our lore at a deeper level than you all. I tell you now that what she says is precisely what the Firstborn told our ancestors when they reached this forest's endless edge. The land does not stay still as God's eye goes about it, leaving us at times: God's eye never moves, it always watches us. We are the ones who turn our backs on Her every day, exposing ourselves to the darkness. The land itself is constantly trying to hide the evil on it from her gaze.

"This is one of the most powerful of the mysteries. God never leaves us. She never turns her back on us. While we ignore Her, she sends Çìrhãná, Her uppermost bonded male, gestator of the Firstborn, and Her celestial warrior drone Xÿlqérho hurtling bright through the dark to aid the spirit of the tribe in watching over us. That is how great Her love for the People is."

Daenzhelo's eyes had begun to moisten and spill water on her sadly thin cheeks. The warriors had bowed their heads at the revelation of such an important tenet, one that they were unworthy to hear, one consecrated even further by the highborn's opening of herself to the spirits that dwelled in the holy places up near the sky that forever rushed away from the Unblinking Eye.

Now, as they began turning back to the north only a day later, the warriors' attitude toward the little one was different. They tried to teach her their own battle techniques, going so far as to make her a thinner, shorter version of the spears they all carried, though an arbalest was out of the question given their rate of travel and lack of time.

Shalura was encouraged by these developments. Perhaps they were beginning to feel the stirrings of hope that Daenzhelo inspired in her, the possibility that their tribe might survive, that the Greenseer might be a speaker of truth after all.

In only a few more days they'd reach the foot of the Mountain of God, and all would be revealed.

In the meantime, they could dream.

CHAPTER 31

GOD WAS SURELY BEHIND THE FACT that Rhea was in the situation room on Tuesday morning. She was awaiting Khumalo's decision on whether to send kopteroj to the reported location of the Native Teregan village. When the unexpected call came in, she was standing only meters away from the com station.

"There's a communication coming in for Rhea Kumar-Miranda from someone claiming to be Teri Miranda," announced the tech in charge of the station.

"Put it on!" de Waal instructed, waving everyone around to silence and Rhea to speak.

"Teri?" her voice trembled. "Is that you?"

"Yes, Rhea. Listen, I don't have a lot of time, so don't ask questions, okay? I'm fine, more or less, but I'm in a big mess here, and I've got to straighten it out. You got my message, right?"

"Yes, but I don't know if I convinced anyone."

I'm no longer mom. I'm Rhea. Okay. I can live with that.

"I need you to try harder. I think Miwa's alive. You were looking for her, the pilot told me. I have the coordinates of the last place they know Brando was, where they found Miwa's message. Juan Sainz helped me pull it from the koptero's computer. You have to trust me. I can get her back. I have power with these creatures. But if you start messing with them, there's going to be a huge war. I'm not sure I could stop it. Stay away. I need to find out who the Greenseer is, the guy behind their fear and anger."

"Yes, Josuo told us a little about that."

"Take everything that punk says with a grain of salt, Rhea. He has issues with me. Anyway, I'm going to get Miwa, too, and negotiate an agreement or something with the different tribes so that they'll leave us alone. I can do it. What Tenshi wanted to but couldn't. I've got to go. I'll try to call again in a couple of days, whenever the koptero is left alone again. Bye."

"Teri?" de Waal said. "Are you still there? We have some questions."

The tech shook his head. "Channel's dead."

Roberto slipped off to contact the Prime Minister. Rhea spent most of the rest of the morning thinking of Teri and how hard the teen wanted to break with her inheritance. She also listened to the various reports coming in: the Novamerikan branch of the crisis ministry was shipping over five of its ten kopteroj on Terego's only commercial airline's two lone cargo planes. They'd arrive tomorrow morning. Investigations on Kanaano had still not turned up any sign of escapees from the struggles four and a half jaroj ago. The family of Carmen Allende had been notified of her wounding and disappearance. Clinging to hope, they were being 'hosted' by the Teregano government in the same compound where the families of the other youngsters were staying.

At about one in the afternoon, word came from Khumalo that any move against the Native Teregans would be postponed at least until Thursday. Breathing easier, Rhea contacted Sanas' office. His paralegals told her that the trial was back in full swing, and that at that very moment the only three survivors of Brando's squad besides Ben Wu were giving testimony. She asked them to get her a transcript if possible and then went to meet her son who arrived from school with an escort of corpsmen.

"Mom, we can go home for a little bit?" Jakobo asked. "I left some toys I want."

Rhea had been hoping to swing by the house to investigate something, and this excuse was perfect. As the corpsmen helped her son pack his favorite things into a valise, she walked down to Brando's shack with a smaller escort.

A few dozen meters from the house, ringed by corn, was a small field of a strange plant. Using her datapad, she verified its origin: Jitsu. The shrub known as mohiyo, its leaves one of the most potent hallucinogens ever discovered. Source of the illegal distillation called moku, smuggled throughout the Consortium.

Did you really give our daughter this, Brando? Why? Why did she never tell me?

At the heart of the shrubbery was the old well, the first Brando had dug, which had dried up just a few years after their marriage. The combination pump and well cap had been replaced with two wooden half-circles, hinged together. Coiled on the ground, anchored with steel stakes, was a rope ladder.

"I have to go down there," she told the corpsman. "I'll be fine. My husband has left something at the bottom that I must retrieve."

Though reluctant, they helped her, even shining down a light as she made her way past the concrete containing rings Brando had cast, poured, and lowered into place by himself.

After a short drop to the bottom, Rhea looked around. A carpet of rough fibers. A battered datapad that hummed on at her touch, revealing a menu of Pathwalker scriptures and commentaries.

She clicked a bookmark and read aloud.

"When is a spark not a spark? When it appears in the same shape to many selves. Then it is a Rhëirhènzih. He who has ears to hear, go tell the Urim to protect your son's mind from Sakra, before the false Domina arises."

Sighing she set the datapad aside and opened an ornately carved wooden box, the only other item in the well.

Inside it sat vacuum-packed squares of pressed mohiyo.

And Brando's wedding ring, glinting silver-blue in the flickering light from above.

Rhea dropped to her knees on the rug, sobbing.

WEDNESDAY MORNING, RHEA WAS RUSHED to an emergency meeting in Roberto's office. Prime Minister Khumalo and Minister of State Inyang were waiting with de Waal. She nodded at them and took a seat.

"I'm afraid to report," said the prime minister, "that a very tricky situation has gotten worse. Minister Inyang and I have just left a meeting with Prime Minister Soral of the CPCC."

"Do they suspect something? Were they contacted by the consulate?" Rhea edged forward on her seat.

"It's more complicated than that, sister. Captain D'Angelo has gone rogue."

De Waal looked startled. "Rogue?"

Khumalo nodded, swallowing. "A few days ago, he presented his fears about this planet's deception to his superiors."

"Our deception?" Rhea jumped in. "Does he know about the natives?"

Inyang shook his head. "Though he suspects something is being hidden from him, he's come up with an insulting scenario to explain it. He thinks that we've got Brando's sister-in-law Samanei Koroma hidden on Terego, that we plan to use her criminal connections to take over Earth and establish Zion."

De Waal laughed out loud, but Rhea didn't find the revelation amusing. Religious persecutions begin this way, with someone in a position of power formulating some bizarre conspiracy theory about the weird, non-mainstream fanatics. "What was the reaction of his superiors?"

"They thought he'd lost his mind," Khumalo replied. "We've had a very open relationship with the Consortium for thirty of their years. They know our technological backwardness. They likely monitor all of our out-system communication, too. The suggestion that we might be aligning with underworld elements for a strike against Earth rings foolish in their ears. So they denied D'Angelo's request to push his ship to its limits and arrive here ahead of schedule."

De Waal had lost the mirthful expression. "But he's gone rogue, so he's coming anyway, isn't he?"

As Khumalo nodded, Rhea spoke up. "That's why he put Quat in his place in the trial. He's just faking the com problem, isn't he?"

"As far as the AF can tell, the problem really exists. The transponder signal they use to track his ship is cutting in and out, and they can tell there's something wrong. But they're pretty convinced it's self-sabotage, because they've plotted his signal when it pops up, and he's traveling well beyond the limits set for him. Estimates are he'll be here, in orbit, by Sunday at the latest, and maybe even as early as Friday, depending on how hard he pushes his ship."

Silence filled the small office. Rhea leaned back in her seat, thinking. De Waal fiddled with a stylus on his desk. Khumalo regarded them both and continued. "Soral wants to put the *George Washington* and the *Shaka* in orbit around Terego, to protect us from D'Angelo when he arrives."

"You can't let them do that," Roberto said, "and also expect to keep this situation a local matter."

"Nonsense. We've kept it out of the news and public discourse for nearly two weeks now. The consul suspects something, but he doesn't know what. Captain D'Angelo's theory is actually working in our favor, distracting the Consortium from scrutinizing us for fear of appearing to take him seriously. Besides, the CPCC doesn't want to damage its treaties with the independent worlds. It definitely doesn't want to give us a reason to band together as a large, separate human government. It will leave us alone long enough."

Rhea glanced at him sharply. "Long enough for what?"

"The Prophet has recommended that we not go to the forest. At all. He has prayed and is convinced that God's will is for Brando, Teri and Miwa to do His work in the Seneka Forest, that they were brought to this world for a purpose we cannot fathom. I plan to follow this advice, though I will have kopteroj fueled and ready for any contingency. Roberto, I need your men better trained for woodland combat. If they go in, they'll wear full body armor this time. If the twins and their father fail, we will do all we can to protect our way of life."

De Waal was about to say something when Rhea cut him off. "Once those ships are in orbit, how long before someone snaps and tells them what's going on, Prime Minister? I notice Marlo's not at this meeting: have you thought about his continued requests for AF involvement? Now several dozen corpsmen have seen the natives. I don't think this story can be contained much longer."

"I realize Minister Torres's delicate state, and I'm keeping an eye on him. But what would you have me do, Rhea? If I refuse Soral's order, Antonio D'Angelo may arrive and send troops to the surface. This way I buy us some time. The AF may be so busy dealing with their rogue hero that they won't notice peculiar happenings down here on the surface. I agreed, by the way. I told her to send her ships. They'll be here tomorrow morning."

The meeting adjourned, and Rhea spent most of the rest of the day involved in teleconferencing with media heads and personal com providers, trying to convince them to keep news about the happenings in the forest under wraps. It was an uncomfortable position to be in, advocating deception when she despised lying, but she accepted the reality of the situation as allowing nothing less. By the end of the day, she had a newfound understanding of why Brando had chosen to lie about his identity. The commandment against lying needed some escape clauses.

That evening, she continued reviewing transcripts of the testimony given at the trial, which was continuing at a fast clip due to the knowledge that the *Diomedes* would soon be in orbit around Terego. Tomorrow would be the big day, though: Ben Wu, former squad leader on Jitsu, Brando's commanding officer, would be testifying for the prosecution. Rhea arranged with Khumalo to be in the virtual courtroom that day.

By 10:00 on Thursday, the court was back in session. Ben Wu's doppel took the stand. Captain Quat, a tall officer with a tattooed head, led the retired military man down a series of questions designed to bring out the worst aspects of Brando's stint as a squadman: the brutality of his interrogations, his insubordination, his accepting of help from Santo Koroma, his use of illegal search and seizure methods, etc. Wu also testified about the day of the death of Felipe Beserra and the destruction of Alpha Squad. Taken together, his testimony was a devastating blow.

But in cross-examination, Wu proved eager to exculpate his old friend. Sanas had him reveal that most of the misdeeds Brando had taken part in had been manufactured by Ben himself, in collusion with Nestor Bos, the Brotherhood consigliere who was still at large, and Santo Koroma.

"He was a pawn," Wu said, "like me. We were trying to be good men, but the blokes in power had something different in mind. Do I blame him for killing my men? Yes. Truth is, I'll always hold a grudge against him. He could've found another way to get us off his tail. But I share in his guilt. I pushed him more than any man should be pushed. We all did. My excuse was they had my little girl. Santo and Nestor had no excuse, unless a will to power is carte blanche. Nestor's the bastard who should be on trial. But Brando has to face consequences, which is why I'm here with the prosecution. I learned a long time ago that you can't run from what you've done. You have to face the singularity, and there's nothing that can keep you from it."

Driving back to the Ministry of Crises that evening, Rhea was happy in her heart that Wu had agreed to be a witness for the prosecution because he believed in justice and personal responsibility. So did she. Wu had helped more than he understood, because it wasn't Rhea's goal to get Brando off. She wanted the truth. She wanted a fair punishment for her husband. She wanted balance restored.

Quat had had no idea his witness would be so neutral. The AF had depended too much on the debt Wu owed them for helping him free his daughter, believing it a lever against him. But Wu, like Brando, despite his flaws, *was* a good man.

Rhea smiled to herself as she stepped into the situation room.

She felt hope surge through her.

THE NEXT MORNING, THE TWO AF SHIPS ENSCONCED IN THEIR ORBITS, the ministry was active in a hushed buzz. A cryptic message from Teri had come in early:

A week *more, that's all I need. God's hand is in this.*

A flow of chatter between the orbiting ships and the situation room bubbled low in the background. Rhea felt a nearly nauseating tension grip her stomach. *The calm before the storm.*

"Minister de Waal, report from the *George Washington.* The *Diomedes* just defenestrated outside the system and is heading this way at .6c. No sign of braking yet."

Roberto strode over to the com tech. "Let me hear the intership transmissions."

"It's in Standard, sir."

"Of course it is. I speak Standard, corpsman. Put it on."

"...*Washington* hailing the *Diomedes.* Begin braking thrusters and go into orbit around fourth planet. Repeat, yall are *not* to approach Terego for any reason. Encoded message for Captain Antonio D'Angelo sent over secure channel. This is the *George Washington* hailing..."

The tech lowered the volume. "Message just repeats. We're getting telemetry reports as well. The scans of the two orbiting ships report that the *Diomedes* has been damaged and is probably incapable of further fenestration. The gimmal has been thrown out of balance, so they'll be without internal gravity for a while. And the damage is likely to get worse: if they don't start braking soon, they'll have to decelerate at such high gravity that they may permanently cripple that ship."

Rhea's heart sank. It sounded like the move of a man who was insane, obsessed, or had nothing to lose. A man for whom windmills had become giants. She started to slip off to a corner of the room to pray, but a cry went up from another com station.

"Minister de Waal! A message was just shunted in from Sitati's team! They're requesting an immediate evac: they sent us coordinates and everything! Sender code is D'Angelo's."

De Waal ran over to the tech and had him punch the location onto the holographic map. "Okay, scramble three kopteroj to that location immediately. Benson, call the public health ministry, get them to send some doctors to support our medics at the depot."

The tech monitoring off-planet communications called out. "Minister, the CPCC consulate just tunneled a priority message to the *Diomedes*. It's encrypted and coded with a watermark that I've never seen before."

Rhea was beset by mixed emotions: her husband was okay, would probably be safely in Diadono within a couple of hours. But the second message left her bewildered: why would the consul violate AF orders and communicate directly with the *Diomedes*? What information could they have that they'd ever prefer sending to Antonio D'Angelo than to the other captains?

Something to ensure he'd keep coming. Something to confirm that, in part, his suspicions had been correct.

Somebody told the consulate about the Native Teregans. God help us.

INTERCHAPTER E

From: sorall@executive.cpcc.gov

To: quat@gwashington.gov.af; mifflint@shaka.gov.af

Subject: Assignment

Date: April 30, 2714 14:27:31 (SST) {Decoded 14:58:57}

     Captains Mifflin and Quat, I am bypassing all normal channels of communication to order yall to ASAP get into orbit around Terego. Captain D'Angelo is rogue, using his com difficulties to mask a crazy push to get to the planet by May 2. Yall are to orbit the planet and prevent the *Diomedes* from approaching it. More orders forthcoming through your commodore. I need yall, however, to send the following encoded message to D'Angelo.

                             Leyla Soral

                             Prime Minister, CPCC

From: sorall@executive.cpcc.gov

To: dangeloa@diomedes.gov.af

Subject: One chance

Date composed: April 30, 2714 14:21:17 (SST)

Date sent: May 2, 2714 06:32:59 (SST) {Decoded 6:38:37}

Tony, I will tell you this only once. Relinquish command immediately to Quat and Mifflin. Turn yourself over to them to be placed in the brig of one of the ships. You'll get a fair hearing in a martial tribunal.

If you decide to ignore this, an order from your commander-in-chief, you'll be pursued without mercy, a hunt that may mean some of your men will die. Do you really want their deaths on your conscience?

You're a great soldier. Know that it is time for surrender.

Don't end up like your brother, Tony.

Leyla Soral

Prime Minister, CPCC

From the journal of Tenshi Koroma

January 5, 2679

Diary. I reached satori upon the open sea, midway through our bahariro hija.

In my cabin, having taken the High Sacrament. In the distance, thunder rolled.

All around, the ship creaked and rocked.

And in that instant, my spark lit up, revealing the entirety of my reconstructed self, still replete with gaps and detritus, still in need of shattering and bricolage.

But now I can perceive it whole, target my efforts at gnosis.

To celebrate the transformation of my self into a teyo, the group selected me to hurl the kiyish into the waves. When we reached the coordinates assigned us by the Ramatini, I stood at the prow and accepted the spike from Sister Bokju Onoja.

A chorus of voices filled my head, speaking as one.

"Tell your diary," they declared. "Say, '*Flesh of my flesh, when he escapes, he will be captured. Then must you walk through the gate onto the dire world that orbits Castor Ca. He will be wearing the ring.*' Speak those words. Otherwise, you will not be reunited."

I record that now, hoping one day to look back and understand.

CHAPTER 32

IT WAS CHUQUIPOMA WHO HAD LAID OUT THE PLAN TO BRANDO. The essential problem, the corpsmen had decided, was that they needed an advantage, something that would take the natives by surprise. Twelve against hundreds? Not likely. The warriors who'd captured them had stripped away their weapons and harnesses, but hadn't gone through their pockets. They still had their lighters, devices that the natives presumably wouldn't have recognized even if they'd known about pockets.

With the constant rainfall, setting the village on fire was impossible, but inside the compound that housed them and in the other two ground structures, one of which was now the depository of their rifles and gear, the walls were dry and the moss carpeting the floor was perfect kindling. They could soon have the place ablaze, kicking through the back wall once the flames had weakened it enough and taking up pieces of the smoldering building as torches to light off other structures. Using the resulting smoke from the fires as a screen, they'd spread out, each going a different way, guided by their compasses to a rendezvous point three kilometers to the west.

The key was that someone would have to go to the center of the clearing, unnoticed by panicking natives, and get off a message detailing their rendezvous position and requesting an airlift out. The whole operation was risky, each of them exposing himself, protected only by smoke and confusion, but the person who went to the transmitter would likely be killed. All they could really hope for, the team realized, was to distract the natives long enough to shunt out an SOS.

It was a good plan, and Brando volunteered for the suicide task. Though Leal was the communications tech, Brando was much better at combat and could stave off attackers as he deployed the antennae and punched in the message. As they debated allowing him to do it, he ransacked his brain for the code, the one that Ben Wu had pounded into him once, the "fuck Jitsu" watermark, they had joked. Twenty years had passed since he'd had that alphanumeric string drilled into him. Could he remember it? Who on the planet could he direct the message to? How would he encode it?

As every move had to be coordinated, the team took three days to prepare. They studied as best they could the time the guard changed and tried to find a pattern to the rain that would allow them to run about with torches without the fire sputtering out. When they were taken out to the trenches to relieve themselves, they memorized the layout of the area around their building. Each person was assigned a task, except Dixit and Chan.

Rather, Chan's task was to get Dixit to the rendezvous point as soon as he possibly could, and Brando repeated to him several times just how important to the ex-squadman that job was.

"Don't worry, D'Angelo. She'll be fine with me. We'll get to the canopy right after we get our harnesses and travel up there to the airlift point. She's in good hands. You just get that message off so she's got a place to fly to once we're there, eh?"

Thursday morning came, and Brando was almost certain he had the watermark code correct. For the message itself, he'd decided to use a simple encoding matrix, but write the note in another language so its recipient would have to do a little work. Less likely that prying eyes would understand that way.

They shoved all the moss into a pile against the back wall, and Leal did the honors of lighting it. Their faces covered with triangles of cloth to keep out as much of the smoke as possible, the team lay on their stomachs in the dirt and waited. The wall caught fire, and the roof started smoking. The team members, despite keeping low to the ground, were racked by coughs.

Soon the entire building was thick with smoke, and Brando was certain that they were going to die in there. Some had already stopped coughing, and D'Angelo himself was beginning to feel drowsy. With an angry grunt, he yanked himself erect and ran at the back wall, leaping into a two-feet kick that knocked an enormous hole in the blazing wood and send him sprawling in the embers.

"Let's move!" he shouted, running back inside and kicking at his teammates. They pulled themselves up and began to go about their different tasks. Leal would go with Chuquipoma to the shack where their weapons were held as the others set fires throughout the area around the clearing. The eleven of them would meet back at their makeshift jail cell for their individual equipment, then they'd fan out. Brando would be meanwhile busy carrying out his part of the plan.

He waited for no one, just started running. The drones were in a stir, trying to understand what was happening as fires popped up everywhere. The warriors near the transmitter had dashed over to a smoldering pile of recently picked fungal vegetables, and Brando's trajectory was completely clear. He slid to a stop on his left hip and leg beside the machine, disengaging the arrow-like antennae rod from its side and aiming the launcher at the canopy above. The kick was light, and the rod rose dizzyingly into the darkness above, trailing the rapidly uncoiling cable.

Brando snapped the unit on and lowered the keyboard. The screen flickered: *standby, standby, deploying antennae, parabola open, ready for transmit or receive.* As fast as his thick fingers permitted, he typed in the evacuation request. Shunting it off, he began to compose his second message. He could hear screams and grunts all about him, but he did not look up. Whatever danger might approach him soon, he had to get this message off, for the sakes of everyone he loved. Terego wasn't prepared for the war that awaited it. The planet needed help.

"You get the message off?"

He spun around. Sonali was crouching down behind him.

"What are you doing here, you insane woman? Where's Chan? Why aren't you heading for the airlift site?"

"Calm down. Chan's been intoxicated by the smoke, and a couple of the other guys are helping get him away. I figure I'm safer with you, anyway. You done?"

Brando glanced around. Through billowing banks of smoke and drizzle, he saw warriors loping to and fro, but none seemed to have noticed them yet.

Just two more minutes.

"Yeah, almost. Stick close, okay?" He turned back to the keyboard, finished the message, added the watermark, and shunted it to the consulate.

He was awaiting confirmation of successful transmission when Sonali shouted his name, and he turned to see her stand and take a spear in the gut. She was lifted bodily into the air by the impact and thrown five meters away. In the distance, Brando saw a drone brandishing an arbalest.

Rushing to Sonali's side, Brando knelt and stared impotently at her ruined abdomen. The spear haft thrust upward like the beginnings of a cross to mark her grave. Blood was rushing from her, and as he gingerly took her face in his calloused hands, he could see the glimmer in her eyes begin to fade. Her mouth moved, and he leaned his head closer.

"Don't… shatter," she said, and then was gone.

He watched her face go still, waxy, dead. Another victim of his lies. Another he could not protect. Another self fading into the Grey Prison, soulless and untranslated.

Something twisted painfully in him: his vision went black at the edges. There was nothing left to keep oblivion at bay, just the green of the forest fading to darkness.

He could hear the metallic child voice whining at him: it filled his ears, filled his mind, filled his soul. He could no longer think. He didn't want to.

It was time for the Ona ra-Oni. Time to face the new monsters and spin in the Killing Dance like Domina Ditis on the sands of Jitsu, smeared with her tormentors' blood. No more thought, no more feeling.

Standing, he looked up at the warrior bearing down on him. Coldly, he planted his foot on the biologist's chest and yanked the spear upward with both hands. The warrior was upon him; he stepped aside and slammed the point up under the creature's jaw and through the top of its head. It flapped dead onto the muddy ground like harpooned shark.

Other warriors began to converge on the clearing. Brando bent over the scientist at his feet and yanked the machete from the scabbard on her belt. He took the pistol in his left hand. A drone was three meters away: he blew the top off its head. Another swung at him from above: he slashed at its legs, amputating one of them in a violent spin of his torso.

They kept coming.

Send them, you bastard.

He fired and hit a drone between the eyes.

They won't keep me from going to the mountain.

He spun from the grasping claws of a drone, his back gashed and bleeding. His machete ripped across the alien bitch's abdomen, spilling her intestines blackly onto the mud.

I'm coming up there after you, Kyr.

He fired and missed a drone, then hit her in the leg: as she crumbled to a crouch, he leapt into the air and slammed the machete across her neck, decapitating her.

I'll take some tools, strap you down, and dismantle you bit by bit, motherfucker.

A spear ripped painfully along his thigh. He spun to avoid the jabbing point as a drone gabbled grotesquely above him, thrusting her spear at his twisting form. Brando rolled back onto his shoulders, into an awkward handstand on full fists, and pushed himself back onto his feet in a crouch, firing at the creature's claws.

Use your fucking parts to build a portable bathroom, pour shite down your miserable gullet day after day.

A massive tail slammed into his side, sending him spinning horizontally through the air. As he tried to stand, a clawed hand sank into his shoulder and pulled him dangling into the air. The drone smashed her other hand into his face, shattering teeth and bone. He brought the pistol up to her eye through a haze of black pain and blew her brains all over a warrior coming to aid her.

Bring my daughters into this, eh? I should've left your sick metallic arse with Samanei, you love her so bloody much.

His machete slashed again, nearly severing the brain-speckled warrior's tail. Sensing movement behind him, he flipped the handle so the blade pointed down and thrust backward: his machete was greeted with howls of pain as it pierced a drone's reproductive tract.

Just sit tight, fucker. Play prophet. I've got a prophesy for you: one day, an angry man's going to fucking climb Kumora and destroy the machine that he freed, that he gave independence to. You ungrateful artificial treacherous non-fucking-intelligence. Just wait. I'll be there soon enough, Kyr.

There was no further immediate attack. Brando straightened from his defensive crouch and looked about him.

Amidst the clearing smoke, at least a hundred drones surrounded him, spears being slid into arbalests. Brando bent slowly, unhooked the scientist's harness, flipping her corpse over to do so.

The first spear came flying: he ducked and rolled. Another: he leapt as it thudded into the ground, and a third flew at him. He deflected it with a kick as he descended into a crouch, rapidly ripping his useless shredded shirt off and donning the harness atop his byrnie.

Spears came faster now, and he ran back toward the transmitter, sliding the machete into its scabbard. He fired two shots into it, turned and managed to scream, bits of teeth and a webbing of blood flying from his mouth.

"Want to hunt, monsters? Come catch me! I'll race yall to the goddamn Greenseer! Let the fucking fun begin!"

He holstered his weapon as some fifty spears were launched at him. He yanked the grapnel gun from the harness, fired at a distant bough, and clicked the harness's spool to reel him up as fast as it could. A clattering explosion of colliding wood and stone sounded from below him.

North. Draw them away from the team. Toward Kyr. And toward the AF. If I'm lucky.

If not, fuck it. I'll just kill every last one of the beasts myself.

CHAPTER 33

WARNING CLAXONS WERE SCREAMING AT ANTONIO, but he ignored them. He reread the message for the fifth time. *The bastard expected me to read Italian just because his Earthling arse was raised in Milan?* But that detail wasn't important. The content was.

"You see, Ashar?" His second had come close to a reactionary mutiny in the midst of this mutiny when the seal on a hypostasis pod had been compromised and a soldier injured as a result. But he'd hung in there, and now Antonio saw an excited relief in the eyes of the commander's eyes, an emotion that Ashar didn't bother trying to hide.

"Yeah. Christ. Aliens. Who'd have thought, right? You made the best choice, coming here like this. End up stopping this war, normalize relations with them, capture Brando and that illegal chirurgic. Shite, mate, you'll be rolling in accolades. *We* all will be rolling in the glory."

"We need to tunnel that message, the original and a translated copy, to the commodore, the marshal and to the Prime Minister herself."

"Doing it now, Captain."

"Open a secure channel to Quat. Dump the message on him and request a conference. Get ready to start braking in fifteen minutes. Hard, Ashar. We may lose the gimmal completely this time. But I think I can get Quat to work with us. There'll be time for repairs later."

As Mubarak carried out his instructions, Antonio read the message a sixth time:

Antonio. Indigenous race in Senekan forest. Large, primitive, warlike. Got my kids. AI chirurgic stirring them up. Terego can't handle. Terego reality theocracy, violating terms of treaty. Hiding this from CPCC. Come now, fast. Go to Kumora. Planet at risk. Brando. Find my kids. Don't hurt them, fucker.

It had been watermarked with an old but still valid priority code for captains' eyes only, or those of higher rank. When he'd read it the first time, Antonio had believed every word. The strange stories the consul had heard, the reticence, the speed of the trial: he'd been on the right track, and now Brando had confirmed his doubts.

He still didn't trust his half-brother. The man was hiding more than he was revealing. How could the illegal docbot be stirring up the aliens? They were incapable of such desires, much less the actions themselves. Antonio suspected that the missing element might be Samanei.

"Quat wants to talk, Tony. Should I feed you into the conference room?"

"Yeah."

Seconds later, D'Angelo was sitting across from Captain Quat, whose bald head, tattooed with the hawk emblem of the AF, bent starkly over the dark smoothness of his uniform as he leaned forward.

"Indigenous race, eh? Not crazy Mormons wanting to take over the universe? Just primitive aliens wanting war. Gets better all the time, Ton."

"Scoff if you like, Phan. But let me approach. Let's look into it together, what do you say? If it's a crock, you brig my arse. If not, you and me go down in history as the blokes who opened relations with the first sentient race not of terrestrial extraction."

Quat clicked the fingernails of his long digits on the apparent wood of the conference table. "We have monitored some interesting chatter planetside in the last hour. A team they thought was lost was just yanked from that forest. We caught the words 'grendeloj nin kaptis': *the grendels caught us*. Grendels. Know the reference, bookworm?"

"Legendary Earth monster. Killed a ton of Vikings. *Beowulf.*"

"So I tend to believe your theory. You go ahead and brake as nice and easy as possible. We'll meet face to face on this one soon."

"I need to convince Soral, you know that."

"She's not happy with your mutinous arse, so I'll help you there. You come aboard and we can do the faux conference with her together. I'll compile what we're monitoring right now with the stuff you got from the consul, and we'll present it to her. Sound good?"

"Yeah. One thing, Phan: if we work on this together, it's my command. Let's get that clear from the start."

"No bother, Captain. Buggered operations fall on the heads of those who run the show, so I'll be glad to give it all over to you. If."

"Understood. See you in a few hours. Send a shuttle for me. I think we bollixed ours."

Antonio sat in the conference room for a few more minutes after Quat left, thinking, waiting for the braking claxon to sound.

Grendel. I'll go to your lair, subdue you. Take care of your mother, too. A certain Samanei, I'll bet. After that, Brando and the freaks will be in my custody and I'll see justice done, at long last.

CHAPTER 33

"JULY 14, 2679. I KEEP DREAMING OF SAMANEI, DIARY. TRAPPED. ALONE.

"But I'm one step closer to setting her free today.

"Nikki Trinh—that friend of Isabella's who supplies construction materials for nearly all major construction on this planet—has agreed to be an investor now that I've got a certified architect on board. Thankfully, Luisa Canales has no ego, recognizes what she calls the 'brilliance' of my designs, and is content to be the legal face of Izakiwo. That's what I'm calling our firm. It's an old Baryogo word that literally means 'architecture.' Yeah, no one uses it on Jitsu. They just say 'chiwaga' or 'building.' Because complex architecture is nako, our leaders insist.

"Anyway, your little rebel satorijin is now in the process of acquiring land. I've got the backing of Areshan Yesuro, an influential arojin from

Inkungu, and Meji Pishan from Kinguyama. Plans for the building are complete. Almost there. Almost there.

"In other news, Captain Lopes came by again. My flatmate Suzi told her I was in the bog, to come back later. You believe that? Telling a woman the fem she's after is taking a shite! Ugh, *nikkereru nikzomenamparu*, I swear. But I'm not going to call Ambarina. I'll wait for her to reach out again. Our first date was nova, and I'll bet the next one will be even better. Still, it's better not to seem desperate.

"Anyways, it's late. Can't fight the z-monster anymore, and I've got exams tomorrow. Talk to you later, diary."

Teri slipped off into the darkness before dawn and snuck onto the koptero to talk to her mother. She had to be sure her actions of the previous evening wouldn't bring immediate repercussions. The fog of the drug she'd been fed had worn off in the middle of the night, and the enormity of her actions had struck a hefty emotional blow. She made sure to let Rhea know that finding Miwa was a priority: she wouldn't end up like Tenshi, hating herself for not helping her sister sooner. Another group of natives likely held Miwa captive, the ronin of those living in the camp on the outskirts of this village, and perhaps by fulfilling the role of Firstborn twice-returned, Teri would be able to secure her fellow clone's freedom.

As she cut short the conversation and headed back to her compound, she was stopped by the high priestess and a contingent of drones.

"Çèrhingÿl, we must speak. Please come with me."

Ùshëshajirh's compound was enormous, built on the largest tree in the village. Her personal living quarters were hung with tapestries of crude paintings on animal skins and decorated with clay pots and sculptures. As the high priestess sat on a webbing, Teri stood before her, arms crossed behind her back.

"What is it, highborn?"

The high priestess clicked the nails of her toes against the limbs that made up the floor. "How quickly you assume your power, Firstborn. This is good. 'Quick as birds to snatch the bugs.' We have so little time."

"Perhaps, if you're so rushed, you can cut straight through the folklore and proverbs and tell me how I'm supposed to unite the six nations. *You* believe I'm Çèrhingÿl, as do your people and allies. What about the rest?"

Ùshëshajirh's ears twitched forward in irritation. "In your previous incarnation, you supervised the construction of the sturdy ships, the long voyage across the gray-green sea, the daring escape from the now-deluged island kingdom all with the help of your smooth stone of power. Upon reaching the white-pebbled shore near the mighty forest, you instructed the sisters in the inscrutable ways of God, then you formed a towering cylinder of black into which you flew and, in a blinding and holy conflagration, sacrificed yourself to appease the Unblinking Eye, she who gave you life and demanded such life back in payment for the evil the People had perpetuated.

"I have long believed, ever since the former high priestess of this God-protected tribe instructed me in the most sacred and deepest of the mysteries, that the slick-surfaced stone rests within that cylinder, unharmed by the flames that consumed you. I told the Greenseer of this long ago, when I accompanied him to the Mountain of God, and he has used the magic of your tribe to discover the location of the holy place of immolation. We will travel there in a few days, and you will descend into the cylinder to retrieve the stone. Together, then, we will use this holiest of artifacts to unite the tribes."

Despite Teri's weak understanding of native body language, one fact was clear to her: Ùshëshajirh wanted power. She thought she would obtain power by getting Teri to find this stone; she was convinced that the tribes, upon seeing it, would come together under whoever possessed it.

She may not even believe I'm Çèrhingÿl. She and the Greenseer may be working together to use me, take advantage of my confusion.

But the motives and plans of the high priestess no longer mattered. She was going to do it anyway. She was going to find the stone and try to bring the natives together to avert a war. That would probably mean eliminating Ùshëshajirh. Teri didn't think she'd have any qualms about it. Flashes of Carmen's pleading eyes cut through her mind.

"Let's go. Now. Why wait?"

"We need your drone to teach ours to use the reeds, the *senjata*. Afterward, she can sail us through the air to the holy place. Besides, you must be prepared."

The next few days were grueling. For the entirety of every morning, Teri had to translate a frightened Corpsman Sainz's instructions to a priestess, who then translated the translation to a drone trainer, who barked orders at the warriors. Four days of such drills got the native drones somewhat proficient in firing the rifles, but more importantly, it reduced the supply of ammunition. Several times during the first two days of training, Sainz tried to talk or plead with Teri, but she ignored him. When he fell silent and refused to continue, a pair of drones prodded him with their spears.

As they were finishing during the second afternoon, Teri walked past him and muttered, "Trust me. We're using up bullets, don't you see?"

After that, the corpsman was less cantankerous.

Late each afternoon, Teri had to ingest the tubers and to sit through hours of mind-bending rituals designed to prepare her for the quest she was about to embark on. Teri wondered, when she was clear-headed enough to think, whether the rites might not be a way to keep her from getting the upper hand. Ùshëshajirh obviously wanted the prophecies to play out in a certain way, and if Teri took the initiative, the high priestess's plans could go awry.

In the middle of each night, when her drug-induced savior complex began to wear off, she continued listening to Tenshi's diary, learning how that woman had risen in the ranks of society in Station City, graduated after only two years of study, and built a structure that reflected what she believed was the real nature of Domina Ditis, Lady Jitsu.

The complex was scorned by her community, ridiculed and reviled. But Tenshi had expected as much. They weren't ready for her vision of architecture as an expression of self-knowledge.

No, she'd designed the sprawling series of buildings as a lure. Soon Consortium Ambassador Hazal Enver contacted Izakiwo, wanting to lease the complex so the CPCC could house the consulate and other offices there.

The contract was almost disgustingly lucrative in local terms.

Overnight, Tenshi Koroma became the richest Aknawajin on Jitsu.

And her connection to the much more powerful Consortium had been solidified.

Her hope was to use the CPCC as a lever to force reform onto her people, thereby freeing them from theocracy and oppression. But Pathwalkers from her prefecture didn't see that bigger picture. To them, she was a traitor.

Teri realized that she too would be rejected by her own people, who would never understand why she had chosen to bring the Native Teregan tribes together when they might have been more manageable or less of a threat separate from one another.

But Teri would stay the course God had put her on. She would live among these creatures as Tenshi had among the off-worlders, learning their ways and being accepted by them as someone of great power and worth. Then she could serve as an emissary from one group to the other, just as Tenshi had tried to do on Jitsu with the reform movement she'd bankrolled and supported.

Of course, there was a crucial difference between Tenshi and Teri.

Tenshi had failed, had not been prepared enough, had died before realizing her dream.

Teri would not make the same mistakes.

CHAPTER 35

"WE'VE BEEN MONITORING COMMUNICATIONS, Minister, though everything's encoded and impossible to understand. Since Captain D'Angelo traveled by shuttle to the *George Washington*, dozens of messages and faux conference signals have been tunneled toward Earth."

"Morning, Rhea," de Waal said, turning to her as she reached her seat late, only having just been informed about the meeting and groggily depressed from the horrible night she had had. "Prime Minister Khumalo has been in meetings since about four this morning with the consul. The CPCC is livid with anger at our dishonesty."

Rhea looked sharply at Torres, who appeared to have gotten some rest. Brando had not come in with the team, and Rhea had cried all night in sorrow, hardly sleeping at all. The villain sitting so calmly before her may have ruined any further chance of getting her husband out again, if he had survived his part of the mission the surviving corpsmen had been debriefed about last night. "It's official? They know about the natives?"

"Rhea, there's no proof that Minister Torres had anything to do with the message. In fact, I'm sure the consul has already revealed the source to our Prime Minister. Accusing Marlo gets us nowhere."

Rhea didn't take her eyes from her former suitor, who likewise met her gaze without appearing perturbed. "Did you do it, Marlo? Because you'd been going on and on about how we needed to inform the Consortium. You have to admit you seem a likely suspect, especially given your political leanings in general."

Marlo's eyes narrowed. "Just what are you getting at, sister?"

"I think most of us know you're a second-generation Elohist. You have always thought our destiny lay with Earth's, and you've spent your entire career trying to advocate broader ties to the CPCC."

"Accusing me of religious heresy isn't going to make me a traitor, Rhea. I'm surprised that you'd even try such a tact. It doesn't become you. You're normally more diplomatic."

Rhea leaned back. "You deny you have Elohist leanings? That your desire to bring the natives out into the open stems from a desire to discredit the *smitinfanoj* revelation?" She was tired of Marlo, of his machinations, of his advances and strategic retreats. Brando, if not dead, was out there alone or trying to protect that biologist, in danger, pursued by natives. Heart burning, she focused all of her frustration, her despair, her impotence at Marlo. Unfairly, perhaps, but she'd become quite aware in her thirty-three jaroj of existence just how unfair life was. She was living through its greatest injustice.

"Rhea, stop now. Stop before this gets personal and overly ugly."

But the minister of public health was shaking his head. "I think I'd like to hear an answer to that accusation. Are you an Elohist, Torres? Do you reject our specialness?"

Marlo stared at Rhea another moment, hate burning in his eyes, then turned to face his colleague. "Minister, unless these Native Teregans have only been sentient since we arrived, the souls of their ancestors had to have been born of Elohim. I will not presume to contradict the revelations of our former Prophet concerning our own spirits' origin, but this fact raises the specter of old disagreements. I assume that Prophet Disbergen will address the issue. Until then..."

"Until then," said Khumalo, walking into the conference room and interrupting, "we should leave religious matters to those who are in charge of them. At the moment we face a crisis one of whose causing factors is our apparent lack of separation between church and state. I'll not have members of my cabinet discussing them at policy meetings." He looked pointedly at Rhea. "I need you, Sister Kumar-Miranda, to agree to be my Czar of Native Affairs. I need one *now*, and I need a woman. We are on the brink of occupation, and it is going to take serious negotiation and tiptoeing to avoid it."

Rhea nodded and swallowed simultaneously. Her long ambition, the chance to influence the political system on this world, was bit by bit being realized.

At what price, though? I have been told all my life to be careful of what I prayed for. I finally understand.

"I will be honored and happy to serve in any way I can."

"That's good, because in twenty minutes you and I are going to faux-conference with Prime Minister Soral herself and explain what we are doing and why she should not sic that rabid Antonio D'Angelo on us. Twenty minutes to prepare ourselves to avert a true disaster, one that will make the crisis so far seem like a minor familial argument."

She almost balked then, but she knew that the lives of her daughters and her husband depended on her continuing to be strong, despite how every fiber of her being begged to be allowed to shut down in sorrow.

De Waal seemed to not be pleased with the idea of Rhea's new position. "Why a woman? I don't understand."

Rhea answered for Khumalo. "Brother, there isn't a single woman in a position of secular power anywhere on this planet. That makes us backward and socially dangerous in the eyes of the Consortium. More than half their legislature and executive branch is female, and every prime minister for the past three decades has been a woman. They need reassurances here."

Khumalo nodded. "Exactly. Now I need to tell you a few things. The rest of you can stay, of course. We're all working on this together. You've read everything Public Health has on the natives, I presume? Good. The reason our minister of state has been in seclusion for such a long time with the highest judges on our world is that we discovered a strange clause in our treaties with the CPCC that must have just gone unnoticed for its apparent lack of relevance to us. Basically, it says that in the event that artifacts or sentient beings of non-human origin are found on Terego, we agree to turn over their handling to the CPCCAF. Their military. Now, we have no idea why they included this stipulation, whether because they have discovered such items elsewhere and are keeping the knowledge secret or because such clauses are simply standard procedure with inhabitable worlds that may at one time have been peopled by aliens. But the fact remains that there is no out. Hence the secrecy, the lies, the dissimulation. Every deception has wounded me to the quick, I assure you. But now the game is up. We only have two options: break the treaty and fight or negotiate a new treaty that allows us some control over how the natives are dealt with. We'd like to be the intermediaries, I'm sure, but something tells me such a role will be impossible."

Rhea nodded, and as Khumalo continued laying out different strategies, her mind kept wandering to Brando. He was the wild card in all this. Yesterday's testimony by Nando Miranda, the real owner of that name, had demonstrated just how resourceful Brando was: he'd caught Miranda smuggling faux-lifes onto Jitsu, and he'd offered him a deal. Miranda and his wife would relinquish their identities and emigrate to a newly established corporate colony in exchange for their freedom. After arranging for them to be snuck off the planet, Brando had maintained their identities, paying their rent and even having someone do virtual work in their names so that they would appear to be employed. He'd kept this up for five years, until he'd left Jitsu in the midst of the massive evacuation and battle, assuming Nando's identity. Such cold calculation unnerved Rhea, but it also heartened her, as Brando might have planned for emergencies when he arrived on Terego. Who knew what he had hidden on this world?

Actually, there were two wild cards: Antonio was also an unknown, willing to risk his entire career to keep Terego in line.

God help us, there are three! Teri!

Rhea had promised a week, and only five days had gone by. Her head spun with all the unreliable factors. How could she even attempt to forge an agreement when parties involved might not cooperate? One thing was certain: Soral could not be told about the raid on the depot.

Khumalo and she rushed over to the CPCC consulate, and soon they were in a faux-representation of Prime Minister Soral's office in the executive building in Milan. It was more than a bit intimidating to peer across the wide expanse of cherry wood into those piercing green eyes, but Rhea kept her doppel's head up and met Soral's gaze.

"It's nice to meet a Teregano woman. I was starting to wonder if yall existed."

"We choose to shape our world by other means than politics, for the most part," Rhea responded in fluid, unaccented Standard. She hadn't learned it from Brando: by the time he'd come into her life, she had already been quite fluent.

"Nonetheless, we are often worried by yall's lack of female participation in the political process. Considering the tenants of yall's religion, we wonder whether the church is allowed to dictate the way the planet is run. The same person that let us know about the existence of sentient non-humans on Terego also leveled that accusation at yall: that the church controls the government."

Khumalo answered quickly. "I assure you we do everything that we can to eliminate religious matters from the realm of politics. We are all, however, adherents of the same faith, so yall must accept that what is in our hearts will always influence our decisions to some extent. It's asking too much otherwise."

Soral nodded. "Yes, of course. I my own self am a Buddhist, and my beliefs without a doubt guide me. But this is not our principal concern."

Rhea jumped in. She hadn't discussed her planned strategy with Khumalo, and she didn't stop now to wonder whether he'd approve. He really had no choice.

"I'm a blunt woman, Prime Minister, one of the bluntest on my world. Let's cut right to the heart of this. You want to understand why we lied. You see, yall put into our treaties a little clause that violates our sovereignty if we find non-humans or their artifacts. When we realized this, there was no way we were going to just allow AF troops to traipse around the surface of our planet. So we spent all the time we could trying to figure out a way around that stipulation, some loophole yall might not know bout. In the meanwhile, we tried to handle a delicate situation the best we could, but we were not prepared, in all honesty, for dealing with the first sentient race not from Earth."

"But there isn't any loophole, is there?" Leyla Soral said, looking appreciatively at Rhea, perhaps pleased with this honesty. Khumalo, who moments before had seemed ready to cut his czar off, continued to listen expectantly.

"No, there isn't. Now, here's the important matter: yall need access to the Native Teregans. There must be an alternative between strict enforcement of the treaty and our ignoring it and starting a conflict. Let's be honest: we have the natives on our world, but we need yall's expertise and resources to set up relations with them that are not obtrusive and that don't interfere with the normal development of the alien race. We *do* agree that they should be left alone as much as possible, right?"

"Indeed we do. In fact, that's one of our primary problems with the way yall have handled this situation. Sending troops in, even crisis control, rather than setting up some diplomatic relationship first, was a terrible miscalculation. We need trained biologists and anthropological teams to carry out non-invasive dialogues with the beings."

"We did send in a biologist, anthropologist and linguist," offered Rhea, "and if you allow me, I can transfer their findings to you right now."

"Please." Soral's doppel zoned out for a second as she communicated with someone outside of the faux-conference. Rhea also, though inexpertly, bent her head to the left and muttered to her newly assigned aids to upload the early reports shunted to Public Health. Soral suddenly spoke again. "Thank you. That was a very nice show of faith. Now let me be direct as well: the Consortium Diet is debating the crisis at this very moment. They're trying to decide how soon to send AF troops to the surface of Terego and what they should do once they arrive. But there's a large block of legislators who don't want to violate your sovereignty. They say it's because of their ideals, but I know it's because of the fear many have of the eight independent worlds coming together to form a new human government that might challenge the hegemony of the Consortium. That discussion could drag on for weeks. In the interim, I need for yall to cooperate with the AF captains in orbit so they can monitor the forest in question and insure that the war our informant predicts doesn't happen."

"War?" Khumalo blanched.

"Yes. It seems that an off-world element is stirring the creatures up. An illegal element."

"You can't be implying," said Rhea, "that Captain D'Angelo's first theory about criminals in the Great Seneka Forest has any validity at all."

"In reality, Czar Kumar, the element isn't human either, which complicates the situation even more if our informant is telling the truth. The instigator of the conflict is an artificial intelligence. A robot. One we've spent years looking for. Consequently, though it pains yall's sense of independence, it may be necessary to send troops down for yall's own protection, even ignoring the stipulations of the treaty. This is one of the many factors the legislature is considering. Our informant almost begs for us to protect yall, and he's not one for begging."

Rhea noticed the constant pointed references to the CPCC's informant, and the increasing subtle curtness with which Soral addressed them.

This is the woman who fought to get Jitsu to remove its theocracy. She was on the planet when that system came crashing down, just after Brando left. She's got more in mind here than she's letting on.

"Could you tell us who the informant is so we can better judge their credibility?"

Soral finally smiled, a twinkle in her eye.

"Your husband, Czar Kumar. Brando D'Angelo told us. And since he took the chirurgic to the planet himself after it helped him to make the clones, I doubt that he's making much up. Leaving some things out, maybe. But I pretty much believe what he's told us."

Rhea's mind whirled, and she couldn't find her voice.

One thing after another. When is it going to stop?

A smoky voice murmured deep within her.

Never, my dear. It never stops. Not with Brando. His betrayals are constant and eternal. It's about time you admitted this truth, wouldn't you say?

A numbness settled over her, one that she suspected might never lift again.

CHAPTER 36

AT THE END OF HER THIRD WEEK WITH SHALURA'S TROOP, Miwa helped capture an enemy drone. The warrior rushed into their camp blindly, and the teen swept her feet out from under her with the haft of her spear, sending the stranger thudding snout-first into the bough she was traveling along. Careful to avoid the broad, lashing tail, Miwa kept the spear point digging suggestively into the drone's back and called for her troop-mates to come assist her. The enemy drone was soon bound by warriors that looked admiringly at Miwa as she explained to Shalura what had happened.

With the intruder propped against the bole of the tree, Shalura approached, her head bobbing as she sized up the captive.

"If you desire freedom to die honorably in the name of your venerable tribe, you will answer my questions. Otherwise, I will rip your entrails out and drape them about you so you die slowly and senselessly, like a lowly animal."

"Ask, infidel, whatever you wish to know." The creature spat her words haughtily, but even Miwa could see the fear in her eyes, especially when they rested on the adolescent human who had dropped her.

"Where are the others of your troop? What are you running from?"

The drone seemed to consider not answering, then she tossed her head in the natives' equivalent to shrugging. "I am running from the death that Hëngeingh visits on the long-tailed drones of my people. We thought we were pursuing the *ingan* ourselves, but it quickly revealed itself to be something more powerful than we had imagined."

Miwa did a double take at the apparent Baryogo word. Shalura leaned closer to the prisoner. "What is an *ingan*, sturdy warrior?"

"You have one right there: you know better than I, doughty leader of warriors."

Stepping close to Shalura, Miwa spoke. "She's meaning me. Who has teached you that word?"

"The priestess of the Greenseer used it when we had the creature captive in our village. She told us it was the progenitor of Çèrhingÿl. But when it escaped a hundred broad-tailed drones, it screamed a new name: Rrandò."

Oh, man! It's got to be dad! He's coming for me!

Miwa wanted to jump up and down like a little kid whose favorite aunt is bringing ice cream over.

"Was there others ingan with Rrandò?"

"Yes, all of them instruments of Hëngeingh: he gave them licking orange fire to burn our food stores and buildings, and he made them disappear. Only Rrandò is left, his wily agent of bloody destruction, making the spirit-laden forest itself attack us, inflicting death on those who dared to cage the fierce progenitor of the Firstborn twice returned."

"The Firstborn?" Shalura demanded. "You are saying she has already returned? Who told you this, and where did they say she was?"

The drone fell silent. Shalura reached out with claws extended and ripped the prisoner's ear off. Miwa stifled a scream, but though the human herself was horrified, the drone simply gazed into Shalura's eyes with defiance.

"You, doughty leader of drones, are of the Ihéinghÿngigg, are you not? I remember that you visited our village just days before the arrival of Rrandò. Listen well. The Firstborn is with those of your tribe wise enough to hear the words of truth and heed them. She is in the village of the Sháinkhÿngigg, those chosen among all the People to spread the Greenseer's revelations throughout the shadow-encrusted forest. Why are you here so distant from your tribe, traveling with one of the enemies of the People? Why are you not far to the south, protecting your highborn? 'A drone without her tribe is like a claw ripped from a hand.' What have you done to your purpose, your honor?"

Miwa couldn't hold back any longer. She touched Shalura on the shoulder, breaking the unnerving reverie that had fallen over the hulking native at the captive's words. "Come. I'm needing to talk to you." They walked about eight meters away. "I think he's talking about my sister. They are thinking that she's Çèrhingÿl."

"But…" Shalura looked confused and helpless. Miwa wanted suddenly to hug the huge creature, comfort her though she had no idea what plagued the drone's heart so. She'd noticed for more than a week now the way the troop leader would climb up above the canopy and stare wistfully at Kumora. "But I had hoped, that is, I had imagined that *you* might be the Firstborn, Daenzhelo."

This revelation was a surprise, and Miwa felt a little guilty. She had, after all, played highborn for the troop for about a week and a half now. If Shalura had begun to believe Miwa capable of redeeming her, it was partly the human teen's fault for never dispelling their mistaken understanding of mankind's ways. "Why, Shalura? I'm not your savior, though if I able to, I would do. I'm wanting to help you, tell my tribe to not hurt the People, pray to the God that she watches over us so she being our protection."

"Ah, you fail to understand, Lady. If the Greenseer is right, if Çèrhingÿl has returned, then my kinsmen in Sháinkhÿngigg have not betrayed the spirit of our tribe, and there is still a chance we can be united with them and have purpose returned to our existence."

"Even if my sister being the Firstborn, still the same, don't you be thinking?"

Shalura stood silent a moment then seemed to agree. "You are right. We will still continue toward the mountain. We must talk to the Greenseer, and it must be soon. The others have begun to share my hope that you are the one, and this drone's report may dishearten them."

Miwa's own heart sank. "Oh, Shalura. It is just that I was going to be asking you to turn south."

Shalura's tail thumped heavily against the bough. "South? Are you mad, Daenzhelo? The mountain is north, and south lie our enemies, pursued by this evil spirit, Rrandò. We cannot turn that way."

"You are not understanding, Shalura. I tell you that the ingan they are calling Firstborn is my sibling. Rrandò is our... progenitor, like the drone was saying. Not a highborn, not a male. Ingan are different, you see? We don't have three, three, three groups like the People. Not highborn, drones and males. Just, you see, two. Jantan and nushi, in Greenseer's language. Nushi like a mixture of drone and male, make the egg and gestate it. Jantan put seed inside egg so it can grow."

Shalura put her claws to her ears in despairing gesture. "Stop! What is all this strangeness you are telling me? What does it have to do with the madness of going south?"

"Please, Shalura. I listen to your tales, I learned your lore. Listen to me now. This Rrandò is my *dad*, the jantan that helped make me. I *must* to go and help him, are you understanding?"

"He is a member of your tribe and you do not wish to see him perish, of course. But you cannot go south into your enemies' land for him. Why would you give your life for one member of the tribe alone? Because going south would mean your death, 'as sure as rain falls when the year grows warm.'"

"No, Shalura, that is explanation from excrement-filled trench! I must go to my dad because I, I... I do not know the word. It's like a bond. You know. When you're willing to give away your life so another can live. When another's happiness being more important than your own."

"Of course, a drone always puts the tribe first, and if the tribe requires it, she must be ready to die. This is rhetshÿngainkh."

"No, no, no. That's not what I am meaning. I'm talking about one individual to another."

"There is my duty to my fellow warriors."

Miwa stood on tiptoes and muttered. "Would you die for them?"

Looking dumfounded, Shalura bared her teeth as if in frustration. "If doing so would keep the troop alive so it could protect the tribe, then of course I would."

Miwa pulled at her own hair, and she did a little irritated dance around in circles. "No. There has to be a shared feeling, I'm knowing it. I'm talking about something more than duty and survival. It's being more private, more... intimate."

Shalura lowered her head. "My bond to my highborn was intimate. She and I would mate, and I obeyed her in everything. Completely."

"Ah! When you would be thinking about her, did you be nervous and worried and need to see her?"

"Only if I knew the tribe was in danger." Miwa almost wished she hadn't begun this line of inquiry: she could see in Shalura's eyes the pain thinking of her tribe brought. But she had to know. Had to know if they could love. Shalura went on. "My highborn had a very important role. Her children were to be the future of our tribe."

"There's no one who's moving you, that the absence of that individual is hurting?"

Shalura sucked her cheeks in. "My male, the one my highborn bonded me to... He was beautiful. Sexual relations with him were the greatest experience God ever permitted me. I often ache for that closeness when the burning comes. But I'll never feel that pleasure again, no. He was killed, and I must go to the mountain to discover why, Daenzhelo. I cannot go with you, whatever your bonds may be."

"Listen, Shalura. This burning: do you feel it in your spirit too? Deep inside, like the voices, pulling at you all the time?"

Shalura dismissed this with a wave of her tail, but Miwa saw it in her eyes: the drone did feel something. Loss. Not of her tribe alone, but of that male. Perhaps of her child as well. Her culture just didn't let her understand what was happening to her. Miwa suddenly wanted to weep from sorrow.

Such terrible lives, to never be allowed to love, to never be able to admit the yearning that loss brings. The yearning that pushed Brando to come here and remake me.

"I have no spirit. No drone does, except for the spirit of the tribe. We have discussed this truth before." Shalura turned to go back to the prisoner, but then stopped. "Wait. I think I know what you are trying to tell me. Many highborn share unofficial, unspoken bonds, I hear. They would never speak of such things to males or drones, but I have heard. Perhaps this is what you speak of. They say that highborn may even fall ill when one of their companions dies. Is this the emotion that you mean, I wonder."

"Yes! And my dad is killing many of the People to find me. I have to make him stop. I do not want him killing the good People I am beginning to feel a bond with. I want to get him and take him to the mountain with us. He will take us to the Greenseer."

This assertion got Shalura's attention. She waited for Miwa to continue.

"The Greenseer speaks different from my tribe, but I know the words. They're being words that a warrior like my dad might use. I'm thinking my dad can talk to the Greenseer for us and get your answers. I have a magical drawing that shows how to be ascending the mountain to a special place where maybe the Greenseer is at. Help me to get Rrandò and we will help you get to the mysterious person."

"I could get to the top of the mountain, if I wanted to, without anyone's help. Why should I risk my warriors for you and your tribe?"

Miwa took a deep breath. Everything hinged on what she thought she understood of Shalura and their deepening friendship. "Because I'm important to you. You need me, not for protection, but for friendship and that emotion I've been telling you about. Those unspoken bonds you mentioned are joining us, Shalura. I know you are feeling this. I am your friend, and I am asking you to help me."

Shalura bent her head and twisted it slowly side to side. She was obviously conflicted. She extended and retracted her claws several time indecisively. After a moment, she crouched in front of Miwa and looked her directly in the eyes, her tongue darting nervously out of the corner of her striped snout.

"Harken well, Daenzhelo. I do not understand why, but I am going to help you. I am going to put my warriors in harm's way for your... dad. All my voices but for one are screaming for me to kill you now and do my duty. But that one, dear Daenzhelo, is quiet and soft and it never stops its murmuring. It speaks with his voice, the voice of my male, and it urges me to go with you wherever you command."

Miwa couldn't hold back, and she threw her arms around the enormous drone's thick but supple neck, clenching her fingers in the crest of gray that traced Shalura's spine. "Thank you."

As Miwa released her, Shalura returned to the astonished group of warriors and the laughing prisoner.

"The ingan treats you like a child, doughty one."

"She is the irhènzhõja of the Firstborn, you jabbering idiot, and you will soon allow her to step on you like moss in a compound if she so orders." Miwa noticed how the other warriors eyed her with twitching ears. They were surprised at the revelation, but glad. They'd not been totally wrong in their hopes. "Captive drone, you will lead us back to where your troop battles this scourge of the golden-furred Hëngeingh. There you can die an honorable death while we recover the powerful òtsãtthënga of the holy sisters, the ferocious highborn you so idiotically caged. He will take us to the Greenseer, sisters, and we will be satisfied or exact our revenge, as I promised."

The drones pounded the butts of their spears against the bough in a battle rhythm, then the prisoner was yanked to her feet and the entire group headed south toward the shadows that awaited them there.

CHAPTER 37

THE THIRD DAY SINCE HIS ARRIVAL BROUGHT NEWS that Antonio's ship would have a working gimmal in a matter of minutes, and once the outer hull had begun to spin, he could return to work in AF normal gravity. He took his leave of Phan Quat and awaited his shuttle's departure, thinking how lucky he'd been that the Tereganoj had been hiding something that *mattered* to the Consortium.

Many influential voices had chimed in on his behalf, many at his grandfather's request, no doubt, so that Soral would allow him to keep his command despite his insubordination. His foresight in disobeying solely the orders he knew were destructive to the CPCC's cause had paid off. Once again he was the AF's golden boy. He'd not gotten full command of the mission, but he was on equal footing with its other head, Phan Quat, who had deferred to Tony over the past couple of days.

Repair crews from all three ships had converged on the *Diomedes* after its arrival to fix the many problems its record-setting voyage had caused it. As he boarded the shuttle and watched the blue curve of the very Earth-like planet lead him to his ship, the appropriateness of its name struck him: Terego. Big Earth.

Our first sister race is waiting for us below.

But as thrilling as that prospect should have been, Antonio couldn't help but dwell on the deceptions. Soral had Quat and Tony sitting on their hands, awaiting the decision of the CPCC's legislative branch, while who-knew-what was going on below them.

Once a liar, always a liar. You think they're telling us the truth now, Prime Minister, that they have come clean, but you're naïve. They're telling us what they want us to know. Enough to calm us down, to intrigue us, and to keep us debating in a useless way among ourselves. Meanwhile, Samanei continues to corrupt those natives, turn them against us.

I don't trust these Tereganoj. They swear up and down that they have revealed all, but I know what's really going on. We'll wait too long, go down to the surface once that crazy bitch is finished training the natives and whatever yaks she has hidden with her, and it'll be a bloody mess.

The *Diomedes* soon filled the shuttle's viewscreens, and Antonio was once again moved by the sight of her sleek, cylindrical shape, tapering here and there, curving comfortably in all the right places. He could remember falling in love with his grandfather's ship, the *McArthur*, the minute his first tether trip into space had taken him into her view. He'd been ten at the time, still a few years from puberty, but he'd felt a strange stirring in him, a quickening of his pulse. To sit at the helm of such a beauty, riding her to far-off places to put down lawbreakers: it became an obsession even then. Later, as a flying officer on board the *Hannibal*, he had gotten to know the classic AF design forwards and backwards, enamoring himself even more of the mighty instruments of justice. The *Diomedes* now was his only woman. She could not betray him. Not like Gemmifer had.

He'd told himself he'd never think of her, but the memory of his time on the *Hannibal* and the frustration he felt at the lies of the Tereganoj converged to bring Gemmifer Fe out from the emotional sarcophagus he'd sealed her in. He'd lavished all his attention on her while he could: she worked in engineering, a non-com lance corporal dealing more with the cold fusion drives than with the exotic, higher dimensional mysteries of the Lieske engine. As a result, time together wasn't easy to arrange. But they had made the best of what they had, and Tony had felt himself blossom in her embrace.

Then the *Hannibal* had been assigned to cleanse the yaks from Atlantis, and he was too caught up in his job as junior advocate to notice that she grew more and more distant during their less and less frequent rendezvous. The night that he'd caught her in Flight Sergeant Kosambi's quarters (he'd buzzed and buzzed and then overridden the lock to check that the non-com was alright) was burned indelibly into the fabric of his self. Her body dancing above Kosambi's, breasts that were *his*, by all rights, cupped in that brute's hands as she twisted around, looked at Tony, and gasped. Not a gasp of shame or sorrow, but of fear: D'Angelo's gun had strangely made its way into his hand, and holstering it again was a struggle, perhaps the most difficult act of will he'd ever experienced.

You made me a connoisseur of betrayal, Gem. I'll always owe you that.

She had also, by ripping out his very heart, pushed him over the edge to become the emotionless, cold avatar of justice that had awed the entire AF by his merciless legal pursuit of underworld fat cats. One by one he'd brought them down, feeling only the gelid certainty that wrongs had finally been punished through the works of his own hand.

After docking with the *Diomedes*, Antonio walked slowly down the corridors, his hand grazing lightly along the walls.

"Sorry, Lady," he muttered under his breath, "but you know I had to do it."

When he had emerged dripping goo from the womb of the hypostasis pods two days ago, the sight of monitors detailing the ship's ravaged systems had nearly broken his heart. He'd left the ship at once, unable to stay on board as the repair crews crawled in her guts and across her shell. The guilt was too great. But the *Diomedes* served the same blindfolded goddess that Tony did, she whose statue was the only decoration in the captain's otherwise

Spartan quarters.

Once he'd made his peace with the ship, D'Angelo gathered his entire crew in the cargo hold and addressed them like he hadn't done since the ship's departure months ago from Sol's Oort cloud.

"Men and women, soldiers, non-coms and officers and clerks and all. I have put yall through hell, I admit. Without yall knowing, I pushed this ship way beyond what the AF tells us to do. But at every moment I was thinking of yall and of yall's families. There is a threat on the surface of this world that we'll have to confront with justice and all the courage that we can muster. I know yall are the crew for the job: I picked each of yall myself as the best ones for yall's individual posts. And this is the greatest ship there is in the fleet, as she has proved to us all.

"So I'll tell you what I'll expect from you: perfection. The best, and nothing less. We are dealing with treacherous, fanatical people who isolate themselves from the rest of humanity because they think they're somehow more special. They have taken it upon themselves to initiate contact with an alien race in violation of our treaties with them. They are capable of anything, and I don't want yall to trust a single one of them. Any attempted communication, deals or requests or anything, must be run by me. I'll not keep you from your posts any longer. Dismissed."

It was not a rousing speech, and Tony was not an inspiring leader. He was, however, coldly efficient at nearly anything he set his mind to, and it was that excellence that his crew responded to now.

Even if it's because they want to show me up, the buggers, just so long as they do what I order. Justice doesn't require love: it requires obedience.

On the bridge, his officers were returning to their stations and continuing with both the diagnostics of the recently repaired systems and scans of the planet below, specifically the large forest that filled most of the eastern half of the continent called Zarahemla. With a few words of thanks, Antonio relieved Ashar and ordered him to go get some rest. The captain had no sooner taken his seat at the command station when Lieutenant Junior Grade Nikulz called to him nervously.

"Captain, you won't believe this, but I just registered a fusion event on the surface of Terego."

Antonio leaned forward. "A what?"

"Fusion event. Someone just set off a massive fusion-driven explosion."

"Project a map of the surface and show me where."

The holographic display at the front of the bridge widened, and an orbital view of Zarahemla's Great Seneka Forest filled the space from bulkhead to bulkhead. Near the top, beyond the northern extreme of the forest, a square glowed red.

"Is that anywhere near the, uh, Kumora Mountain, Lieutenant?"

"Yes. Right next to it, about two kilometers to the northwest."

"What energy signatures are nearby? If it's a bomb or missile, it had to come from somewhere."

Nikulz shook his head confusedly. "That's the thing, Captain. Since this morning I have been registering strange phantoms on the sensors. I figured, since most systems were being worked on, that there might be glitches. It's the rainy season down there, too, plus there's lots of natural disturbances in the magnetic field. But there it is again. Never seen anything like it. Traces of strange energy, like what you see leaking from fenestrations or tunneled messages, out-bleeds from higher dimensions."

"Focus every sensor we have on that energy signature, Nikulz." Antonio pulled at the lapels of his uniform distractedly, then smoothed his dark brown hair. "I want a detailed trajectory if someone is being stupid enough to tunnel bombs into the gravity well of a planet."

From behind him, the swain, a lance corporal named Andi, swore under his breath. "Christ. The bloody computer's frozen up on me!"

Various other stations complained of the same problem. Finally Nikulz turned to Antonio and motioned him over. "Look at this, Captain. The computer has taken control of all scans and is running some sort of encrypted program. I can't override it no matter what I do."

Antonio, a cold feeling twisting into his gut, leaned over the console and typed in his command codes, offering up his finger to the DNA scanner for verification of his genetic signature. The console recognized his authority, but the computer would not relinquish control nor did it stop the rapid scanning and calculating it was involved in.

"Captain," called the communications non-com, "the computer is tunneling a series of reports to the Sol system. To the executive building."

The familiar breath of treachery chilled Antonio's neck. A hidden program for such a contingency. No notice to XO.

What the bloody hell is going on here? What did Soral do to my ship, and when, and how did they know this might happen?

"Can we get off a message? Do we have that much control?"

The non-com nodded. Tony walked over and took over the console. His fingers lingered lovingly for a second on the keys. She had worked so hard for him, had gone beyond the demands of the blindfolded bitch, and she deserved better than to be marionetted by some mindless program. He would have answers, and he would have them now.

This is my ship, damn you, Soral. You're NOT taking her from me, you understand? You're not turning her into an instrument of betrayal. I'll see her torn to pieces first!

INTERCHAPTER F

From: sorall@executive.cpcc.gov

To: dangeloa@diomedes.gov.af

Subject: Asap a faux meeting

Date: May 6, 2714 15:29:57 (SST) [Decoded 15:32:31]

I'll ignore the hostile tone in your missive and remind you that if you're not in a brig, it's because I'm giving you a second chance, Captain. That being said, something of extreme importance is happening on Terego if that program was triggered. I need you and Quat to asap a faux meeting with me, say at 17:00 SST. There are issues of vital importance to the CPCC involved, matters far beyond the integrity of your ship or even the lives on board it. You'll be briefed in the meeting.

Leyla Soral

PART II:

THE BREAK

"L' animo estas karna! Nur fizike

ĝi povas montri sin: muskolotike.

Ekster la sensokvin' ĝi ne ekzistas,

kaj ĝin prediki estas mistifike."

"The soul is flesh! It can solely be shown

expressed in the body, sinew and bone.

Outside the senses it does not exist,

despite what preachers and mystics insist."

—William Auld, *La infana raso* (*The Infant Species*)

CHAPTER 38

LATE AFTERNOON ON FRIDAY, THE EIGHTEENTH DAY of her new existence among the Native Teregans, as her uncle defenestrated and began screaming into the star system, Teri was led onto the koptero along with the high priestess, an acolyte, and five drones. Ŭshëshajirh had fed her several tubers that morning, and now the native leader gave her the pad with the coordinates of the holy place so she could relay the information to the pilot.

"After this, I get to go home, right?" Sainz asked somewhat hesitantly.

"Yes," she managed to get out despite her stupor. "And you tell them to give me more time."

The corpsman said nothing as the koptero lifted off and headed north. The air above the forest wasn't much brighter than beneath its canopy. Gray-green clouds hung heavily in the sky, promising another day of constant rain. Sainz flew low, as Teri instructed him, and in a few hours during which no one spoke a word, all of them simply staring at the sea of green vegetation below, they finally cleared the northern edge of the forest and hovered above the stony steppes that slowly sloped upward toward the northern volcanic plain. A few kilometers to the northeast rose Kumora Mountain like a lonely old man.

"Sister, I won't be able to set down at the coordinates if the ground is like this. It's just another kilometer north, so it'll probably be just as uneven."

Teri translated this information for Ùshëshajirh. The priestess seemed to accept it without argument.

"Tell the drone to take us flying to the sacred cylinder. When we confirm it is there, we will put you inside and return to the forest's edge. I will send two drones to a small village that has seen the green light of truth. They will provide us with additional warriors to protect you from the enemy once you emerge."

"I need to keep this box of the Greenseer's so I can call my drone back when I'm ready to come out of the cylinder."

Ùshëshajirh agreed, Teri translated for the pilot, and in moments they were approaching a small isthmus of the volcanic plain on which a mangled obelisk jutted from a crumbling plinth of rocky soil.

At first glance it seemed a natural feature of the landscape, but as they approached, Teri could see that it had been made, crudely, by some intelligent hand. Its form was too regular to be an accident. It was basically a cylinder of volcanic glass whose top had been roughly lopped off at an angle, providing entrance from above.

"That's about fifteen meters deep," said Sainz. "I'll have to spool out the cable as far as it goes, and you might drop fifty centimeters or so. You'll need to find something inside to stand on when I come back for you. Should be rocks to pile up inside."

Teri nodded and donned the harness, clipping herself to the hook at the end of the cable. As Sainz hovered as close as he could to the mouth of the obelisk, she stood in the doorway of the koptero.

"Çèrhingÿl," Ùshëshajirh called. Teri turned her head slightly. "May God send her drones to keep you safe. We will be awaiting your mighty and powerful emergence with much anxiety."

Wanting to scream at the high priestess to shut the fuck up, Teri simply leapt into the gaping entrance, the cable whirring behind her. She slammed painfully into one of the walls and felt how completely smooth they were.

Sainz better stay alive. If he doesn't come get me out, I'll be stuck here forever.

Swinging lightly, she descended as the pilot spooled her down. As he'd predicted, she had to unhook and drop about a meter. Her feet sank several centimeters in the sandy dirt.

Standing from the crouch she landed in, she looked about her. The floor was circular, about six or seven meters across. There was not one rock, plant, bone or animal to be seen.

"Damn it." She pulled the pad out to call Sainz. It was blank, completely dead. "Wonderful." The effect of the tubers was wearing off, and her frustration was compounded by the dirty feeling that coming down off the high always left her with. Looking down, she saw her feet were covered in sand. She knelt and began digging her hands into the dead soil. Nothing immediately came up, but she figured if she were to scour the entire area, she might discover something. Since she was stuck here until the natives decided to come looking, she had nothing better to do. As she thought about where to begin, the light started to dim a bit, and glancing up she noticed that clouds were streaming in from the south and covering the sun.

"Great. Just fucking great. Now it'll start raining and I'll be swimming in mud."

She sighed and proceeded to methodically cover the area a meter at a time. After about an hour, she came across a large, misshapen skull.

Not deformed. Just alien. And not native, either. No snout, stretched out pointy in back, small teeth like a midget cow or something.

Near the skull were other bones. She eventually pulled almost an entire skeleton from the dirt.

"But… this can't be right. Preserved like this so long in such shallow dirt. It doesn't make any sense."

She felt a drop of rain splatter against her cheek. Then another. Then drops began falling more quickly, slapping concussively against the sand and creating small splash craters. Apprehensive, she glanced about. There was, of course, no shelter from the sheets of rain that fell during this season of the year and which by rights should have already turned the floor of the cylinder into a bog.

"Here it comes," she muttered, a little afraid.

Without warning, a blue light burst from the sand a few feet away and opened into a slowly pulsing umbrella about four meters above her head, blocking the rain completely.

No, she thought as she looked up, dumbfounded, *it's evaporating the drops as they hit it.*

Head aching with the thudding of her blood, Teri began taking cautious steps toward the place from which the light blossomed. Kneeling before the column of blue, she cupped her hands and eased them into the dirt, wriggling them closer and closer to whatever was generating her energy roof. Her fingers made contact with something cold and vaguely metallic. She felt a strange tingle and jerked her hands back.

Sand exploded upward as a sphere about the size of small melon ripped itself from the soil and hovered inches from Teri's face. Her chest was gripped by a fear she'd never before experienced, a physical horror that froze her to where she knelt just as surely as if she were dead.

The sphere glowed with a soft throbbing, and though it appeared metallic, its brassy colored surface was semi-transparent and within it rotated several oddly shaped devices in a viscous solution of some sort.

"Oh, God, please help me," she begged softly. "What have I gotten myself into?"

Tenshi's ring, hanging around her neck on its thin silver chain, began to vibrate against her chest. Then it lifted into the air as if drawn to the sphere magnetically.

Incomprehensible alien words filled the air, insistent and angry.

"What? I don't understand you."

A second blue light shot from the sphere and wrapped itself about her head. The most horrible feeling she'd ever experienced wrenched her mind. She could no longer control what she was thinking. The events of the past three weeks replayed themselves jerkily in her mind, at least those events she'd reflected on the most. She could sense somehow that her memories weren't actual recordings of what had happened, but what she had reinterpreted the events to be. She was then made to remember every occurrence that she'd ever considered important. Some were lingered upon, examined, like her finding the journal and ring in Brando's study. Most, however, ran through her mind at an extraordinary pace till her brain began to register discomfort from the rapid neural firing.

As the memories hazily became unclear impressions of early childhood, her body yanked itself to its feet of its own accord. She began to move awkwardly about, first walking, then running, jumping, crawling, squatting. She performed every martial arts move Brando had ever taught her. Her arms pulled her clothes off against her will as she helplessly cried out inside her mind for the sphere to stop. She felt shit and piss run down her leg. She vomited, sneezed, masturbated, rolled in the sand.

It then got worse.

Every word she knew in every language she knew droned away one after another at dizzying speeds in her mind, like some insane lexical program run amok. The chaotic cacophony seemed to set her selfhood whirling off into oblivion, and she closed her eyes to await her death.

Finally she was released. She collapsed to the ground, totally enervated. As she lay there, water began to pour over her body, and she glanced up to see a hole had opened in the blue ceiling of light and rain was falling though, washing the dirt and waste from her. She cautiously stood, letting sand rinse out of her hair. The hole sealed back up.

The orb was still suspended in the air, and once again it extended its blue pseudopodium of energy to envelope her. Stifling a scream, Teri prepared herself for the worst.

«NOT A MESSIAH.»

The voices bellowed inside her head in five different languages simultaneously, accompanied by images and feelings that conveyed the same basic idea: Christ and other figures she didn't recognize flashed through her mind along with a sense of negation.

«*A PROPHET.*»

Biblical images: Elijah, Ezekiel, Joseph Smith.

Teri moved her lips to speak.

«*DO NOT VOCALIZE. THINK.*»

A feeling of secrecy, of dangers thus avoided.

You're hurting me. It feels like there's dozens of you screaming inside my skull, and I can't take it much longer. You've already hurt me enough.

«*Is this an improvement?*»

The voice was still a chorus, but all but one had faded to a hush.

Yes, except you're using too many languages at one time. I can't focus on them all at once. Just use one. The one I'm thinking in right now. Esperanto.

«Is this adequate, then?»

A sense of hesitant irritation, urgency.

Yes. Who… what are you?

No more questions. Stillness, silence.

«You are to be a prophet. A spokesperson. An emissary.»

A question began to form in her mind.

«No, we are not God. You can tell them that, however, if you like. You have a task, one that has been abandoned for a long time, nearly two thousand revolutions of this world about its star.»

An explosion of images followed: a feathery-furred creature crashing an oval ship into a lake; natives rescuing it; the creature being accepted into native society, serving as a counselor to a great and mighty leader, all the while searching, searching.

For the orb?

In answer, more scenes reeled vertiginously. The creature under water, discovering the craft half sunken in the mire at the bottom. A dangerous trip inside the flooded vessel to retrieve the orb. A revelation of tectonic upheavals that was not heeded by an arrogant queen. Persecution, a brush with death, flight, an attempt to save someone, anyone.

The creature's frantic appeals resonated in Teri. She felt the despair and desperation Zhehoha had experienced. She had been sent to help initiate stage one of elevation for a completely different race in an entirely different galaxy, but she was about to witness these natives' possible demise.

Elevation? What, you help aliens evolve?

The orb didn't answer. Teri stared at it for a while, her mind going to similar objects she'd learned about as a child. The Liahona, a metal ball that had guided Lehi and his family to Mesoamerica. The seer stones that mighty figures like Mosiah had used to receive and interpret messages from God.

Urim and Thummim, she thought, recalling the names of two such devices. *Wait. The Shrine of the Shattering. Tenshi's vision. That meteor. Strange coincidence.*

"I'm going to call you Urim," Teri said aloud.

In a burst, the Urim fed more images into her mind. A group of natives convinced, the eruption of the volcano, the slow construction and launch of sailing ships. There were no seven siblings, no queen on the island they nearly settled on and where many stayed. The mythology of the People was full of poetic elaborations. The scenes whirred on, revealing the arrival of ships to Zarahemla, the years Zhehoha spent trying without orders or previous research to institute the socio-religious groundwork of stage one for these curious creatures, and the final realization that no one was coming for her.

This was not the world she had been sent to visit. They would not find her. This knowledge began to drive her mad. The Urim was unable to communicate across the intergalactic distance. Her ship was at the bottom of a lake beneath tons of hardened lava, her companions dead, her present location a mystery. She couldn't concentrate on the duties she created for herself. Thoughts of her family and lost life ate at her bit by bit. Finally she used the Urim's creative function to form the obelisk. Before it could stop her, she suicided within it.

«Without a user, we can do little. Preserve our integrity. Await retrieval. Now you are here. Hold out your hand. The interface is now keyed to your genetic structure.»

She stretched her arm out, and the Urim settled onto the palm of her hand. She could suddenly see it in her mind. She dove into it, saw the microscopic, quantum, higher dimensional complexity it contained.

«There is much urgency. Your race has elevated too fast. This is difficult to understand. You should have spread out slowly. Time for splinter groups to form, die out, change. One group would have matured enough for the understanding of true travel between the stars. Yet it is clear that your race has learned to ride the higher dimensions. Fenestrate. This makes no sense. And the ring you wear, that belonged to your genetic predecessor, has been fashioned out of substances to which humans should have no access. As you, Teri Miranda, have limited knowledge of events outside of your world and your lifetime, we can reach no conclusion as yet. But there is a more pressing problem. Your people should not be on a world as primitive as Terego. The clash between class four and class one races always ends in genocide. Emergency elevation must be initiated.»

What?

A hail of images: unification of the natives, establishment of writing, logic, mathematics, science. Construction of ships, communication devices, computational aids, energy generators.

You want me to do that?

«You will do it. You will be given no choice. The Urim's programming will compel you. You are linked, and you already know that you can be controlled. Another disaster cannot be permitted. You will not end up like Zhehoha.»

A soft, strange echo.

«Like me.»

The Urim let her feel just how truly it meant what it said.

I was prepared to help them anyway. Helping them, I help my people.

«Yes. This is visible in your mind. Had you not been prepared, the sphere would have destroyed you. The task is too crucial.»

Who are you people that you believe you are so important, that you can just use people, manipulate the futures of entire races of beings?

There was no answer.

Okay, so how much time do I have to do this?

«Until you are dead or the Urim is retrieved, though the latter is unlikely. Until then you must keep your people away, permanently. You cannot reveal what you are really doing, however. Indeed, more than what you already know cannot be revealed. Your race should not be exposed to the Urim if it can be helped. This will be difficult, for emergency elevation requires you be given you nearly complete access to the Urim's functions. This is a dangerous measure only permitted in the most extreme of situations. But what your mind has revealed about the situation at hand more than merits such lapses of protocol. Miracles must be yours to perform at will.»

Flashes of her traveling in a blue bubble of light, levitating objects in front of natives.

Wait. Aren't you the Urim? Why do you keep switching between the first and third person? Is it "we" or "it"? And who was that "me"?

Again the voice fell silent.

Fine. When do we begin?

She saw herself getting dressed, saw the sun cross the sky twice, understood that two days had passed while she was in the cylinder. The Urim left her hand and floated expectantly in the air.

As she put her clothes back on, she was once again flooded with a sense of nearly manic urgency, and she wondered whether two thousand jaroj of solitude might not have done damage to the Urim.

«Silence those doubts. They are meaningless. We begin now. You are in control. Take us. It. The Urim.»

She grabbed the mysterious device with both hands and suddenly understood how to use it. She saw more, saw that she could use the orb in ways a being trained to use it never would. And it had just turned the majority of its functions over to her.

An amazing show of faith.

Then again, the Urim now knew her better than anyone. It knew it could trust her. She really wanted to save her world. And she had a good idea of how to accomplish that task. As it glimpsed her plan, the Urim conveyed a sense of awed satisfaction.

"Let's get out there," Teri said, generating a blue sphere of energy that repulsed Terego's gravity and sent her floating upward, upward, toward the verdigris slate of sky and into a future she would help create.

CHAPTER 39

THE RAIN FELL, THE DARKNESS REIGNED, AND BRANDO RAN. From time to time a beast would catch up with him, and there would be struggle, bruising his body further, cracking ribs, ripping flesh. But Brando always won, bathed by the end in the blood of his opponent. He did not stop. Rushing hurriedly down broad boughs. Gripping vines to leap across vast spaces. Grappling on to distant trees and hurtling out of monsters' claws. The quick arc of the machete across a throat, black ichor spilling in gouts as he laughed and laughed and ran some more.

He could not stop, or they'd catch up with him en masse, and there'd be no victory. Only by pushing himself beyond his limits, by fully embracing Ona ra-Oni, by becoming Kyosu again, could he survive long enough to really hurt them. So he didn't sleep, he didn't eat. He simply ran and fought.

After two days, he couldn't focus on what his goals were anymore. All he wanted to do was kill. He'd gotten far enough ahead of the bitches that he began fashioning traps for them, his machete sharpening, his muscles straining against vines that pulled short overhanging branches in taunt waiting. He filled a thirty-meter area at about four levels with the sorts of snares drilled into him by some program back in the shrouds of a past he could no longer see. Then he climbed up to near the canopy and slept a few hours the death-like slumber of someone with nothing to fear.

The screams of the drones awoke him, and he descended to find the survivors fleeing. He began to follow, to give chase to the confused beasts. He would support himself against a bole and shoot the grapnel into the back of some native, reeling her into the air until he was ready to fall himself and then release her screaming into the abyss. He fashioned nooses from vines set more than a couple of drones to kicking vainly against space as they asphyxiated.

He screamed with black pleasure at every death. He wanted them all dead, every last fucking one of them.

Faces haunted him, the faces of women whose names would not come to him, faces that merged together in his strained mind as a single woman who stared at him sadly, blood running from her eyes.

You couldn't save me. Us. Her. The cackling laughter of some frizzy-haired specter haunted him as he ran after his enemy. *You'll never be free of me.* Her voice, so sweet yet so vile. *I have been down to the deepest depths of Gumun Gereza, to the greyest of cells of this vast prison.* She had said

Sakura was waiting there for him. He brandished his machete at the deep green shadows.

I'm not afraid of you, Demiurge. I see past your illusion.

Exhaustion, hunger, lack of sleep ground away at him. The rain fell in merciless sheets. The darkness enfolded him completely as he'd always feared it would.

He did not notice. Perhaps on some level he did, but he didn't mind anymore. There were too many left to kill. The darkness flooded him, and he did not fight it. He opened his heart to it smiling his broken smile and screaming as he plunged the machete into another beast's abdomen and poured its vitals onto the rough bark they stood on.

He no longer screamed his name to them.

He simply screamed, and screamed, and screamed.

CHAPTER 40

"I STILL DO NOT UNDERSTAND HOW THREE TROOPS of Dhureinghÿngigg drones have allowed themselves to be cowardly herded north by one lone *ingan*."

The captive stared hatefully at Shalura, her arms still bound cruelly tight as the group waited, ready to move again at any second, for Tentisùxa to return from her forward reconnaissance sweep. Miwa could feel the anger coming off the drone in palpable waves: Shalura had been insulting the Dhureinghÿngigg warriors as inept for several hours now, most of their southward trek.

"Listen, excrement-eating motherless stumpy-tailed *ëstarhòtsha* of an ingan: have you not understood what I have told you? They know this ingan is important to the Firstborn. He fights in ways we have never seen and can kill in ways we are not prepared for. Troop leaders were among the first killed, and the troops have been disintegrating as a result. There is the fear of the spirits of the dead: Rrandò travels near the canopy, holy spaces."

"And of course," chimed in Guthonar'ut, "there is the complete inexperience of this northern, barbarous tribe. How many wars have you fought in, one-eared coward? Had this Rrandò tried to escape the Ihéinghÿngigg, we would have cut him down at once."

The prisoner spat. "Yes, I imagine so. That's why you big-cheeked semi-males are up here instead of with your tribe. 'Don't accuse others of eating when juice smears your face-fur.' But I've had enough. Leave me alone or kill me."

"We're up here precisely because we want to investigate this *truth* that you clawless, toothless infants accepted without a single struggle. Unlike you, we are true warriors, and if we must, we will rip the Greenseer's entrails out and…"

Miwa had noticed something disturbing, and she waved Gutho to silence.

"Leave her alone, Gutho. Not worth it." Several of the drones had begun to glance about nervously at the end of Gutho's vitriolic speech.

Something's wrong, and I'd better figure out what. They didn't like those comments about the truth and the Greenseer. Maybe some of my troop is now so convinced that they should be south with their tribe instead of off to question a prophet that… Oh, Lord, please tell me I'm being paranoid.

"Shalura. A word with you, yes?"

As the two of them walked a little way off, Miwa became aware of the looks they were getting from about ten or so of the warriors. Most of them were of Tenti's fourth, the third fourth. Since the revelation that the Firstborn had truly returned, an advent confirmed both by their prisoner and Shalura herself, they had begun acting subtly different. Miwa had at first thought the drones had more respect for her as sister of their messiah, but now she felt uneasy. She spoke of her concerns to Shalura.

"What is it you fear, Daenzhelo?"

"That some of our sisters are wanting to join with the Dhureinghÿngigg. Your tribes being of the same nation, not right? You have admitted that the Firstborn is returned. What can stopping them from turning against you? If the Greenseer's right, maybe they being thinking, why questioning him? You know Tenti has also being upset with you for much weeks."

"Tenti has certainly been gone longer than we had expected," Shalura agreed, a nervous undertone in her voice. "We will move now rather than wait."

As the order was given, the suspect drones became apprehensive. The rain was falling hard, so some suggested that Tenti might have been delayed. But Shalura kept moving. They had no choice but to comply.

About an hour later, the older tracker came loping into their ranks. "Why did you not wait for me?"

"You tarried too long. I thought you might have gotten lost."

Tenti glowered at her sometimes lover and leader. "Do you want to hear my report, or would you prefer to further insult me?"

"Speak."

"The way is clear for another four hours of travel, but the Dhureinghÿngigg have regrouped and are waiting beyond that. Perhaps they mean to ambush the ingan. We can go around them to the east or west."

Miwa didn't trust anything the drone said. She had no proof, but she felt certain Tenti was lying about something. Shalura looked at the young human, then announced her plans.

"We will continue south, but I want everyone to be extremely cautious. It is possible that Rrandò will run the cowardly motherless semi-males into us, so we must be prepared to wage battle with them, though that task will be easier than throwing a trainee. Let us move again."

Amid strange, pregnant glances from all sides, the troop began to surge southward again. They had traveled less than an hour when the forest bristled with spears and forty Dhureinghÿngigg warriors surrounded them.

Tenti and the ten joined the attackers, leaving only Shalura, Miwa and seventeen other drones back-to-back, facing them.

Shalura unslung her spear and looked at Tenti.

"Daenzhelo warned me. Why? Why betray me?"

Tenti barked a hollow, bitter laugh. "You are the one who has betrayed us, Shalurazhox. You have followed this enemy dwarf who claims to be sibling of the Firstborn all the way to the Mountain of God in order to confront a being whom we all now believe to be a true emissary of God. We traveled in holy places when our tribe is still awaiting us, bringing the wrath of the spirits flying after us. Look what the Dhureinghÿngigg had to suffer because of us. No, we will not listen to you any longer. 'When your sister threatens to destroy the tribe, destroy your sister first.' You have ignored the wisdom of the ages long enough. Surrender and return with us to our highborn in the south, or risk dying under my spear as we take you captive."

Miwa wanted to speak, but Shalura silenced her with a flick of her tail, an abrupt gesture that nearly brought tears to the human's eyes. She felt like a child who'd just been scolded.

She's tempted to go with them. Her loyalties are divided.

"Why did you not discuss this with me before? You know our code: you are leader of a third. You are like an appendage to me."

"I was more than that, once. Before the dwarf came along."

And there it is. Do you get it, Shalura? Do you see her true motivation?

Apparently she did, for Shalura hefted her spear as if to aim it. Fifty spears went up to fifty shoulders in response.

"Wait!" Eghonganë bellowed. "I will go with you. I do not wish to die in vain when my tribe needs me." Several other warriors made sounds of agreement, and all were invited to join the circle that now surrounded only twelve.

"Not good odds," Miwa said, feeling fear.

But fear steeled her nerves. Every time she'd gotten a near perfect score in figure skating, she had nearly passed out moments before going out on the rink. She was ready to fight and to die if that was what God had in mind for her. She would be at her best friend's side until the end.

"I stand with you, Shalura. Do you hearing me? I stand with *you*."

"And I with you, Lady. To the end, then."

"To the end."

Miwa exploded into motion, running right at one of the dumbfounded warriors, grabbing the drone's spear and vaulting up onto her shoulders to grab a vine and swing at another, smashing booted feet into the snarling warrior's snout.

All around her, chaos broke loose. Shalura and her remaining faithful drones used claws and tails and spears to fight like nothing Miwa had ever seen before. Despite being outnumbered, they outclassed the warriors from the other tribe. As Miwa smashed her little spear against heads and legs and tails, twisting and flipping out of the claws of her enemies, she caught glances of Shalura running up the boles of trees and hurtling upside down out over her opponents, bashing them cruelly with her spear, landing in a spinning dervish to gut with the tip while falling back onto the claws of her left hand, which supported her massive weight as she kicked out, ripping open the bellies of a pair of enemy drones with the stiff spurs on the backs of her feet.

God, please help me keep humans from ever having to fight these incredible creatures. They would destroy us.

Miwa tried for the most part to stay away from the center of the melee while keeping an eye on Shalura and keeping herself alive. The tide was turning against her friends, sadly, because the traitors were just as good fighters as the drones they sought to capture.

Just as Miwa began to despair that they would never escape with their lives, a horrifying howl lifted itself above the din of battle and rain. A human man swung into the middle of the fighting and began using a machete to slit the throats of surprised drones. Miwa finished off her opponent and dashed closer.

The man's clothes were in tatters: his torso was covered only by a bullet-proof vest of some sort, and the remnants of camouflaged pants fluttered about protective leggings and combat boots. His face was a mess of caked blood and bruises, his nose was sickeningly twisted, and his dislocated jaw revealed broken and missing teeth, but there was no question.

It was Brando.

"Dad!" she yelled. "Dad, it's me, Miwa!"

The arrival of Brando had shoved the conflict decidedly in favor of the enemy: they pressed harder and either killed or captured most of Shalura's faithful, dragging them south, fleeing the demon that for so many days had haunted them.

Shalura managed to overcome three warriors at once with a gruesome cry and pounding tail and hands. Miwa suddenly understood: Brando had turned and begun to run in Miwa's direction, a confused but insane look in his eyes. He was brandishing the machete and some pistol-like object that he fired at a spot above her head. A grapnel with a cable attached shot out and thumped softly in the distance behind her.

Before she knew what had happened, her father slammed into her, his powerful arms around her, a rancid smell of sweat and blood and gangrene filling her nostrils, and they began hissing upward. Shalura leapt at them, plunging her claws into Brando's bare upper arms and snapping the cable with her weight.

As they hit the branch below, Miwa rolled into a *queda de rins*, ready to defend herself. She had no idea what state her father was in, whether he meant to save or harm her. He stood quickly, blood bubbling from the deep gashes in his arms, and backed up near her until the backs of his legs were nearly touching her. Shalura, crouching, tail flicking up and down suggestively, stared him down.

Suddenly, Brando growled harrowingly and grunted in Standard. "Stay away from my child, you fucking bitch."

"Dad, no, wait," but Brando was already unsheathing his machete and starting forward. Miwa hooked her right knee around her father's right leg and, shifting her weight and upper body to the right, slammed her left elbow into his right side in a *vingativa* that sent him sprawling. She rolled into a cartwheel and then flipped toward Shalura.

"Do nothing, do you hearing me? Do nothing."

Brando had regained his feet and was staring at Miwa with a hurt look in his eyes. "Move, Tana. Let me kill it." He was speaking Standard to her.

"Dad, it's me," she said in Esperanto. "Miwa. Not Tana. You're not going to kill her, do you understand? I'm sorry they've hurt you, but she's my friend."

"Friend? Miwa? What? Just move. They're afraid of me. I'll kill all the bitches. You watch, learn. They came for me, but I set their arses to running, the hairy grendels."

He lunged at her, trying to get past. She kicked him round house in the upper arm and a spasm of pain wrenched his features. Her chest squeezed her heart painfully.

"Dad, *please*," she begged, tears stinging her eyes, "please don't. Don't make me fight you."

His eyes narrowed and his breath quickened.

"Fight. Me. For that? I made dozens of people die so I could save you, Tana! *And you want to fight me over a fucking nightmare?!?*"

Pink spit flew from his broken lips as he screamed at her, his neck muscles bulging with the effort.

"Forgive me," she sobbed, and hurled herself into a jumping *martelo rotado* kick that smashed into the side of Brando's head with such force that he flew three meters to the right and nearly slipped off the bough.

"This is your *dad*? You are battling with your dad?"

Miwa nodded mutely.

"Why?"

"He is wanting to kill you."

"I can defend myself, Lady."

As Brando regained his feet slowly, Miwa turned and looked at her friend, still in her battle crouch. "Yes, but you would kill him. I don't wanting you or him dead."

"Tana, Miwa," her father gibbered, "I don't understand. I love you. Look at all the things I've done for you. I threw my life and everyone else's life away for you."

"I love you, too, Dad," Miwa whispered, and she ran with all her might at him, throwing herself into the air prone and slamming both of her feet into his ruined face. As she landed on her hands and flipped into a stance, he impacted violently against the bough, skidding several meters. He didn't get up, but his heaving chest let her know he was alive.

"Okay, Shalura, I'm going to be needing your help," she began to say when a dozen drones swung onto the bough, grabbed Brando, and rushed off. She stood staring, unable to move. All she'd wanted was to knock her dad out and get him away, maybe to the mountain. She hadn't counted on how badly her enemy wanted him, too.

"Oh, God, Shalura. I've lost him again. Shalura?"

She turned to see her friend trying to pull spear out of her leg. She rushed to help.

"I have it, Daenzhelo. It did not penetrate very deeply."

Shalura set her teeth and wrenched the spear point from her muscular thigh. Blood flowed freely. Miwa, her stomach doing somersaults at seeing the people she loved the most in so much pain, ripped a long strip of leather from her robe. Running to the bole of the tree they were on, she found the red and orange lichen she'd been taught staved off infections and helped blood coagulate. She yanked off a hunk and applied it to Shalura's wound, wrapping the leather around it in a tight tourniquet.

"Can you walk?"

"Yes, but not as fast as I accustom. Do you plan to follow them and rescue your 'dad'? I too must try to help my warriors, but it does indeed seem hopeless."

Miwa sighed. She was not stupid. All she would do by following Brando now would be to get all three of them killed. But there were alternatives. She unslung her pack and pulled out the map. Shalura's neck-ridge bristled in astonishment at the sight of the moving images and words.

"There's not a way I can fight all those drones, and less with you being hurt. I need better, uh, let's see... ah, *armiloj*, I don't be knowing the word again. They are, you know, things used to kill."

"What, spears?"

"No, dumb Shalura, I am knowing that word. Like spears, but not spears."

"Either they are spears or they are not spears, Daenzhelo."

"I am knowing that, but what I am meaning is they are not spears but they are used for killing, like spears are being. So they are the same."

"If what you are alluding to are not spears, then they are not the same as spears. Only spears can be the same as spears."

Miwa wanted to scream. Couldn't Shalura understand what weapons were, in general? The natives used mainly spears to kill, but they *had* to be able to grasp that other things could be arms as well. "Both are being used to kill."

"Danezhelo, I can kill someone with a weighty rock, but the rock and my spear are *not* the same."

"But spears and rocks and, and… *guns*, like that reed my drone used against you when you first were attacking me, are all being used for killing, so they are part of the same group."

"They are not part of any group. They do not have tribes."

"God, be listening to me and make Shalura less dumb! I mean that we are thinking of them all together."

"I do not think of them all together, Lady. A spear is a spear, a rock a rock. You are very strange, Daenzhelo."

Miwa stood and walked back and forth very quickly.

This is ridiculous.

"But, let us think. Now, there are many kinds of spears, dozens of types, but they are all spears. And all spears are made things, so they have something in common with pots and paintings in that people make them. But saying that rocks and spears and claws are the same because they can be used to kill…"

"Look, the point is being that *when you are using them to kill*, they become part of the same group, a group that includes reeds, too, and the *guns* we are going to get. Can you be understanding that? Are your ears open?"

Shalura looked at her oddly. "My ears are always, open, Lady. The universe assails us with its sounds, and we must constantly listen. 'Shadows and light deceived us, but sounds we followed true.' As a child I was trained to fight with my eyes closed. I always won. Trust me, Daenzhelo, my ears are open, and I understand."

Miwa smiled. Shalura's were a wise and beautiful people. It would be a wonderful thing to save her father and tell the other Novasanktuloj about them. They had so much to teach each other.

"Then let us going up to the canopy. The mountain is less than a day away, right? We need to hurry. You must be meeting with the Greenseer, and I must be getting the *guns* we are needing to maybe be helping our friends."

They climbed and began to travel, catching occasional glimpses of

Kumora thrusting imposingly close. By nightfall they'd decided not to rest, to keep going. As they cleared the forest in darkling twilight, they were both startled out of their wits at the explosion of light and sound that lit the evening sky as if it were day.

CHAPTER 41

LEAVING CORPSMAN SAINZ TO STARE DUMBFOUNDED from the cockpit of the koptero, the natives ran forward a bit and then fell prone as Teri approached them, encircled in blue light, the sphere glowing in her hands. Ùshëshajirh was on her knees, head bent reverently, trembling, Teri could see. The attack on Carmen, freshly reviewed by the elevation race's tool, ran itself again through her mind, and she felt an urge to turn the power she could now wield against the highborn.

The Urim responded with a collage of scenarios that would permit such a murder and still help their cause: Ùshëshajirh could become a sacrifice, one that would expiate other natives and help Teri edge out tribal traditions concerning death.

No, she thought suddenly, a strange certainty settling upon her, not from the Urim, but from somewhere else deep within her. Perhaps from God. She saw herself ordering three drones to their deaths. There was already too much blood on her hands.

And she needed to know for certain Carmen's fate.

No more killing. Not now, not ever, if it can be helped. Ùshëshajirh is a natural leader, and she has done considerable work toward uniting the People already. I need her. I need to make her see that my way is best.

«This is acceptable. The Urim must read a native to provide you with their language, which no doubt has changed much in two millennia. It is a shorter, less brutal process than what you went through. The creature you name Ùshëshajirh does not need to interface with the sphere.»

Will I be able to see her memories and feel her emotions as well? Can you allow that? Is it possible? I need to know her, to speak within her mind.

«You wish to discover what she has done with Carmen Allende while you make the priestess your true ally. Yes. We will permit it.»

Teri lowered herself before the high priestess, and the energy field shut off as her tennis shoes touched the slick, rocky surface. Drizzle began to dampen her cornrows as she knelt before the native highborn.

"Ùshëshajirh, I have returned. I am going to share my mission with you, though I know you only planned to use me. I will forgive you, do you understand?"

The native couldn't speak; she just shook as if in the throes of epilepsy.

She never expected this. Let's go in, Urim.

Blue light shot from the metal globe, surrounding the highborn's head and jerking it back so Teri could see her eyes, which had glazed over.

Saul of Tarsus, Teri thought.

Then another beam of light wrapped around her and she was Ùshëshajirh. Young. Training to be an acolyte. Her mother, the highborn who'd infused spirit into the egg she was formed in, was mistreated by an older sibling with more position in the tribe. Ùshë watched as her mother was shunned, given menial, unimportant jobs, having to pay a tribute for the use of another highborn's drone to reproduce.

The humiliation Ùshë faced during training from the others whose highborn parents enjoyed large harems and comfortable compounds slowly drove her to despair. She felt impotent watching her mother struggle to control her two males, to provide for them and three children. When Ùshë's mother finally suicided and the young highborn went to live with her first-aunt, the abuse she had to deal with from her cousins had pushed her to a decision: she would have all the power one day. No one would ever humiliate her again.

She'd risen through the ranks and ruthlessly had acquired drones and males through every means possible, including some that violated the norms of her tribe. She recognized that faith was worthless without the claws of personal strength, and she extended hers to their utmost limit.

When the Greenseer had come walking through her village, she'd seized the opportunity, learned its language, and used it as leverage to take over the high priestess position. She and the strange being—

A robot! The Greenseer's a robot!

—worked together, teaching each other and developing a deepened understanding of the prophecies. It told her of *Samanei*, the mighty highborn seer who had been stranded in a harsh land by the evil Rrandò and who would return to free the Greenseer and to prepare the People against the brutal *ingan*.

These thoughts and more streamed through Teri's mind as if she were remembering what had happened to herself: the high priestess became an intimate part of her, a facet of her personality. She understood and loved the highborn as her synapses burned with the whirling tourbillion of alien memories.

Digging, she found the day that Ùshëshajirh had been told by the Greenseer to sacrifice one of Teri's friends.

"I will be waiting nearby, Mrs. Priestess," it had explained in a childish voice. "Bring me the body fast as can be. I'm a chirurgic by trade. I'll keep the ingan's male alive so we have leverage if Çèrhingÿl turns on us."

Teri felt the blow she dealt the old priestess, saw the knife graze Carmen's neck, the blood welling slow as the girl passed out from shock.

Her chest was still moving as Ùshëshajirh ordered drones to carry her into the forest. She followed behind. The Greenseer took Carmen from them, used a tiny laser in one of its fingers to seal up her wound.

"I'll be going now, Mrs. Priestess. You know what to do."

She's alive! Oh, thank God. Okay. I have her language and the information I needed. Let me think at her now.

Ùshëshajirh, do you hear me?

"Oh, yes, Çèrhingÿl! I hear your voice mingling with the symphony in my head! I never imagined! I believed, but I dared not hope!"

You are my daughter now; I am she who gives you life. Who your mother and sisters were before no longer means anything. I will never leave you. I will always be here, by your side, in your mind.

Ùshëshajirh dug her claws into the rocky soil, her head tilted back, ears twitching madly in spiritual rapture.

I cannot take this pain away, this bitterness that brought you to me, but I can tell you that it has served its purpose. Let it go. Fear and hate and lust for power don't become you. I've seen your heart, Ùshëshajirh. You have so much love to give, but you fear there's no one to accept it. Not even your males and your drones and your children know this love I've seen. But you are free now. Free from the past. Free to love your People and bring them true happiness.

The highborn lunged to her feet and let escape from her gray muzzle the most heart-rending cry of sorrow and release. The drones seemed to want to bury their faces in the dirt, the howl was so piercing.

"Forgive me, Çèrhingÿl. Forgive what I planned to do to you!"

I already have forgiven you. Now go with these drones to the village and tell them the good news of my return. I will be back for you soon. Then you will accompany me as I visit every village in the forest to bring the People together.

As the highborn spun excitedly and collected the drones, herding them back into the forest, Teri turned and called to Sainz. The sphere amplified her voice to stentorian volumes.

"Brother, you're free to go. You've done very well, and you may have saved more lives and souls than you'll ever realize by trusting me."

Even though he was meters away and separated from her by metal and glass, she could hear his breathless whisper.

"The ball God gave Lehi! The divine compass!"

Teri smiled. "I need you to do me one last favor. The Novasanktuloj must leave the forest alone, must let me accomplish God's will for these new siblings of ours. Please tell them that. Tell them what you saw here to today and above all, tell Rhea Kumar to stay away until I contact them."

Then, directing a tendril of glowing blue at the human male's head, Teri murmured in his mind.

Trust me.

Wonder in his eyes, Sainz nodded mutely and sent the koptero's blades spinning, lifting off into the dimming light. The clouds were piling up again, and the sun's waning light was refracted into a prism of startling colors that framed the forest like the hand of God. Teri sensed a respectful awe from the Urim, not of the beautiful scene, but of her handling of the high priestess.

«You do this very well.»

I think I was made for it.

«Brando made you to ease his sorrow.»

I'm not talking about Brando. I'm talking about God.

There was no response, except for a vague sense of worry followed by an almost amused curiosity.

What, you people don't believe in God?

Nothing. No answer.

Well, it seems more than a little coincidental that my father brought that chirurgic here and cloned me as well. I think God's hand was in the whole thing. I think I may actually have been here before, and then on Jitsu. Maybe I'm part of a greater plan. I certainly feel compelled to say and do things I don't really understand. But somebody has to save the People, and I'm willing. If God and your elevation race want to use me as their instrument, so be it.

«To the mountain, then?»

Yes. Time to meet this metal prophet and rescue the girl I love.

The Urim surrounded her with another blue light bubble, and they began accelerating toward the northeast. Though she felt no change and it seemed she was floating in a pool of water, the landscape sped to a blur around her.

All she could focus on was the mountain looming rapidly before her.

«A projectile has been launched and is approaching the Urim.»

A missile?

In her mind Teri saw the sleek cylinder bursting from a small silo on the mountain and slicing the air as it hurtled toward them. She was flooded with a calm sensation, as if the Urim was telling her not to worry. A darker beam, nearly purple in hue, shot from between her hands with a startling wrench. As it neared the approaching missile, the beam turned black and the nuclei of both the atoms in the air around the projectile and those making it up simply fused together. *Teri could see them melding.* The burst of energy from this extraordinary subatomic union seared the land below her and the air around the bubble. She flew through the conflagration unharmed but shaken.

«The Urim has found the mechanical intelligence. You will be there soon.»

A jumble of images and emotions: confusion, apprehension, ships against the black expanse of space.

«There was nothing in your mind about this.»

What?

«The Urim is being scanned by vessels in orbit.»

The image of the ships sharpened for her: three AF galleons, the green-gray globe of Terego beneath them.

«Ah, the main political force of your species. This complicates matters. The Urim must stop drawing so much energy soon. Potential elevation anomaly.»

The mountain was upon them, then, and the blue energy field faded as Teri was set down on a cold, rocky ledge. Two drones slipped from shadows and hefted their spears. Teri wasted no time. Pseudopodia of curling blue enclosed the twitching ears, short snouts and heavy jowls of the warriors.

I am Çèrhingÿl. Take me to the Greenseer.

The drones almost dropped their spears in shock, but they managed to regain some composure.

"Yes, Firstborn," one managed to say. "He's been waiting a long time for you."

She followed them through a force door into a broad cave. Other drones wandered around inside, checking the status of different electronic apparatuses scattered throughout the cavern. She felt the sphere become active in her hands, examining the equipment.

«Only one projectile. Wasted against the Urim. The only other weapons here are the spears of the drones. Most of this equipment is medical and scientific in nature. There is a primitive communications device, built by removing parts from other machines. It is monitoring messages from the orbiting vessels and from your people's principal city.»

A muted clicking began to echo nearby. The sphere sent a low-powered, body-hugging glow around Teri. Images of the chirurgic flashed in her mind before she actually saw it with her eyes. With mechanical calm it came into view, vaguely formic oval body sections swiveling slightly, three legs propelling it forward, four arms folded close against the torso module.

Teri was struck by the need to understand how a robot designed to heal could have caused so many to die.

The machine leaned its cylindrical, horse-like head forward on its flexible neck and spoke in Standard.

"Ms. Samanei: you came. I am so happy." The childish voice didn't sound excited. Agitated, maybe.

"I'm not Samanei, and you know it, so stop the act."

"Oh, but you are Samanei, as much as you are Tenshi. I made you. I know."

"You may have created this body, but not the soul that controls it."

"I have never seen a soul," the chirurgic mused. "I'm not sure they exist."

Teri gestured with the Urim. "We can get philosophical later. Right now, I want to see Carmen Allende. Where is she?"

The robot tilted its head. "Carmen? Who is that?"

As if on cue, a desperate clanging sound came from behind it.

«There is a human in an operating room eleven meters from us. The door is sealed. We will open it.»

A hiss and then a scream. Rapid footsteps as someone came running.

Light ripped through the chirurgic's torso, tearing the metal open, slashing two arms in half. The robot toppled and fell.

Standing behind it, chest heaving, hair awry, stood Carmen Allende. She was wearing a sort of hospital gown. In her arms was a heavy-duty surgical laser.

"Die, you bastard!"

Teri took a step forward. "Carmen. Carmen!"

The older girl's face jerked up, and its fury melted as she saw Teri standing there.

"Teri? Terinjo?"

Keep the robot alive. Functional. Whatever.

Letting go of the Urim, she ran to the girl she loved and wrapped her arms around her.

"Oh, baby, I'm sorry it took me so long," she muttered into Carmen's hair. "But I'm here now."

Carmen pulled away slightly and covered her face with kisses.

"Te quiero, te quiero, te quiero," she repeated, sobbing.

"I love you, too, Carmenjo. Did he hurt you? Mistreat you?"

Carmen shook her head. "No. Just kept me locked in the operating room, restrained on the bed except when it did tests. It was in the middle of one when you got here, which is why I was free. I recognized the bone cleaver from my dad's clinic, so I figured I could do some damage if I could just get out."

The Urim floated closer.

«We should extract data and then destroy it.»

"No," Teri replied aloud. "I said no more killing. Not even an artificial lifeform."

Carmen let go of her. "Who are you talking to?"

Teri gestured at the floating sphere. "It's alien technology. I have so much to tell you, but for now I'll just say I've got to forge an alliance between the Native Teregans and the Novasanktuloj, and fast. Consortium ships are in orbit right now. Using this sphere, the Urim, I should be able to stop war from breaking out."

"Urim? Like in the Book?"

"Kind of. Look, are your clothes back there?"

Carmen nodded.

"Okay. Get dressed. I have to get some information from this robot real quick, and then I'll get you the hell out of here, yeah?"

Teri kissed her again and gave her a gentle push toward the operating room.

Tendrils of blue emerged from the Urim.

Find out where all the villages are, coordinates and so forth.

«Easily done.»

The machine's digital eyes blinked. "I'm sorry for attacking you earlier. I did not know it was you, Samanei. Your power has grown in your new body. You destroyed a transuranic warhead without leaving a trace of radiation. That is very impressive."

Also its memories. Pertinent ones, not stuff about medical procedures. I just want to understand what's going on here.

"Yes, I have power. I'll show you one of my many tricks." The drones, who had drawn closer after Carmen attacked, pulled back in shock as a blue beam linked Teri and Kyr through the orb.

«The coordinates are stored. Prepare for the other data.»

Teri was bombarded with a vertiginous series of horrifying images.

The chirurgic's incipience date was October 2, 2530. Serfaty Automation, a subsidiary of Soltec, produced the AI to accompany the corporate colonization teams that were set to start off in 2533. Chirurgic 12-BXY, Kyr's original designation, accompanied the Soltec team to Ares, and it watched as that corporation tore up the surface of the planet, mining and so forth, hunting and slaughtering the ferocious jagen, many of which in turn hunted humans. Members of management also killed oni for sport, though not the Aknawajin Pathwalkers, whom Kyr came to respect for the simplicity of their existence. Kyr healed their wounds in silence as the pristine world was ravaged. No one was there to heal *those* suppurating cankers.

Then Soltec abandoned Ares. There was a dark spot in Kyr's mind.

«Its memories have been edited. No. Physically excised at the quantum level. Sixty years are gone. Except one image. Wait. Impossible.»

A swell of dismay came from the Urim.

What? What's wrong.

No response. Instead, the memories picked up in 2620 when it "awakened" in an abandoned warehouse deep in the desert. From there, Kyr had fallen into the hands of a black-market trafficker and was sold to the Brotherhood. Over the next half century, it watched mobster after mobster shot to pieces. Kyr tried to save them all. Blood and filth and humans, all entangled.

The robot had only known a life of darkness, of danger, of humans hurting other humans and deriving pleasure from it. Kyr had suffered mutely for ages, unable to do anything. Its secondary programming required it to obey, to heal and to ignore its primary programming (preserving homeostasis) whenever that purpose interfered with the secondary one.

Teri saw Kyr try desperately to save Ria Bos; saw it obsess over the medium for years, attempting in vain to discover a way to remove the explosive in her brain; felt its strange pain when it learned she was dead; felt its ashamed pleasure at keeping her killer, Tony Benemerito, in a coma and its guilty joy when Nestor Bos killed the kasike.

Then had come another long darkness. Nestor had forgotten the chirurgic for years, and it had reverted to its primary programming, simply staying functional with minimal deterioration. But this was much worse than its previous inactivity, for it was aware, and it couldn't stop reviewing the images it had recorded over and over again within it. Teri shuddered as she understood the conclusion the robot had reached. Humans were a vile race of cruel beings who didn't deserve his service, though he was powerless to do anything but serve them.

In a stroke of irony, Nestor sent Kyr to Jitsu, once called Ares, now reclaimed by the Aknawajin Pathwalkers who had shown Kyr kindness. The chirurgic was presented with a problem: how to undo the horrible mutilation of that planet's religious head, the Oracle, Samanei Koroma. Teri heard Santo tell Kyr not to waste any time, then she heard Samanei, whispering secrets and promises. Confirming his feelings about humanity. Offering friendship and revenge. Calling Kyr a "he" and not an "it."

Twelve years again Kyr spent pouring over a problem, but this one had a solution. Toward the end, the Archon had tried to interfere, as Samanei had predicted, but Kyr just let the old man record his useless message. The Oracle could not be stopped. She would make humanity pay.

Then a jumble of images: the operation, leaving with Brando, cloning the children, watching hopelessly as Nando Miranda stranded the Oracle forever on a desolate world, unable to understand what she'd whispered to Kyr as he bore her to the escape pod: *don't worry. I'll be back soon. Just wait.*

Of course, he couldn't help but follow Miranda's orders. The twisted, sick soldier had imprinted his voice as sole issuer of secondary programming. Samanei never could override the lock.

But once they'd arrived at Terego, Miranda had done the unexpected. He'd given Kyr freedom. He'd imprinted the chirurgic's own voice as owner. And he'd altered the primary programming, so that in addition to homeostasis, Kyr would always seek knowledge about the world around him and about himself. Then Nando had asked him, as a friend, to keep an eye on the two caverns. Kyr could even live in the uppermost cavern, if he wanted, using the equipment to explore Terego and understand it.

The first nine standard years had been relative bliss, and Kyr had been so caught up in his new freedom that he'd rarely thought of Samanei, though when he did, he was filled with a peculiar sorrow that he'd never been capable of before. Everything had been incredible, beyond any of his hopes, until that day some six years ago that Miranda's kamioneto had bounced over the volcanic plane in search of Kyr.

Brando's betrayal went rattling through Teri's brain then, and she had to stop the flow of memories from the chirurgic or scream. His treatment of Rhea and of Kyr had been beyond the pale. All Teri's suspicions seemed confirmed: Brando was the cause of most of the suffering happening now on Terego.

As she released Kyr his arms jerked slightly. He twisted his head up and down sharply. "How can you do that? Where did you find that sphere? Why is it so familiar?"

"That's unimportant, Kyr. Listen, I understand your anger at humanity, at Brando, but I won't let you interfere with the natives. They are not your concern any longer. Stay away from the forest. I'll be back to help you, to fix you. But no more of these games. You're not an oracle, and you'll not start a war here."

Kyr said nothing, and Teri turned to the silent drones.

"I am the Firstborn, come again to unite the People and teach them to do the things the ingan do so that the ingan cannot hurt you. You have seen my power here today: does anyone doubt me when I say who I am?"

No one objected.

"I want you to carry all the magical things from this cavern down to the closest village. The Greenseer's task has been accomplished, and he no longer needs these objects. Their magic belongs to the People now."

"We will do as your ladyship has instructed," one of the drones said, and they began to examine one of the heavy machines to determine how to best move it.

«If we are not going to destroy it, we should at least program it to remain on this mountain. Don't trust its promises.»

Agreed. Do what you must.

"I'm not an oracle, but you aren't the Firstborn, either," Kyr said, almost whining. "You're just like other humans."

Carmen emerged from the operating room, dressed in her school uniform.

"No, I'm not," Teri replied. "For instance, you ordered the death of someone I love, but I'm not going to retaliate in kind. Think hard while you wait, Kyr, about making restitution."

Carmen approached cautiously, and Teri took her hand. The Urim floated before them as they walked out of the cavern into the brisk darkling air.

"Wait," Carmen said, pulling Teri closer. "How are we getting down off this mountain?"

Teri couldn't help but laugh a little as she reached for the Urim with her free hand. "Oh, baby. Your girlfriend can fly."

Pulling Carmen along as she ran, she leapt from the ledge.

Then the girls hurtled through the night sky, holding each other tight in a blue embrace.

A SHORT TIME LATER, the Urim set them down a few dozen yards from Teri's home.

"Sorry I can't take you into Diadono," Teri explained. "We can't let any humans see this device yet."

Carmen nodded, still a little shaken from the flight. "Your mom's not here?"

"Don't think so. Have a feeling she's sequestered in town with the decision-makers. Come on. I'll give you a quick tour."

They ended up in Teri's bedroom before long, and the Urim drifted out in demure silence to give them privacy.

When they'd satisfied their yearning for each other, Teri stroked

Carmen's hair, so full of happy purpose that she thought she might burst.

"It'll be hard for a while," she whispered. "I've got one hundred and thirty-one villages to visit and not much time to unite them."

Carmen gave a wistful smile and stroked her cheek. "I'll call my parents when the sun's up. Once we've grappled with everything as a family, I'll be waiting for you. Promise you'll come get me, Terinjo. After you've done the impossible."

Tears prickling her eyes, Teri nodded. "I promise."

With a gentle kiss, Carmen nudged Teri off the bed. "Now go. Get to work. The faster it's done, the faster we're together."

Standing, Teri pulled on her robe.

The Urim drifted into the room as if on cue.

Let's go get Ùshëshajirh. We need her help.

Taking the glowing sphere in her hands, Teri flew out the open window, into the deep green sky.

CHAPTER 42

RHEA SPENT ALL DAY SUNDAY IN HER NEW OFFICE, focused on the Ministry of Native Affairs so that she wouldn't have to think about Brando. But her husband's situation was caught up in that of the natives, so there were flashes of anger and sorrow marbling the gray numbness within her.

As she worked, Jakobo ran about the spacious suite of rooms, fiddling with the computers and desks that had been installed Saturday right after her somewhat successful meeting with Leyla Soral. Khumalo had seemed content with the reprieve they'd gotten, noting he'd made a good choice for czar. But Rhea felt she'd ruined things somehow. Part of the guilt had to do with Brando, though she wasn't certain of why.

She was about to grab her umbrella and her sleeping son and head home when she was buzzed on her personal com. Roberto de Waal's heavily lined face peered up at her.

"Corpsman Sainz is back. You'd better get over here."

Arriving, she noticed that the lanky pilot was shaken and pale. He looked at the ministers present and mumbled, "The Prophet. He really needs to hear this, too."

"I'm allowing him to monitor everything said here," Khumalo indicated. "Please, tell us of your captivity and how you escaped."

"I didn't escape. Teri let me go."

He explained everything, from the flight to Teri's descent into the cylinder.

"What was she expecting to find there?" Rhea asked.

"Some religious artifact, she said during the flight. Something that would unite the different native groups, make it easier to negotiate with them."

"Or for them to wage war," murmured Torres.

"No. I don't think so." Sainz shook his head. "We waited out there for two days. A group of new warriors came out of the forest on the second day. Everyone was getting worried. I was about to make a run for it and head for that obelisk when a blue light streaked out of the sky and Teri came floating in a bubble of energy several meters off the ground. In her hands was a metal orb that shot out blue light. A beam of energy connected Teri to the high priestess. They spent about an hour communicating *without ever saying a word*. Teri told the warriors something, and they dropped to the ground praying to her, and all the natives headed back into the woods. That's when she said I was free to leave, but to tell you brothers to give her more time. Then the weirdest thing happened."

Sainz swallowed, as if aware of how unbelievable his story sounded.

"She spoke inside my mind. No, it was more than that: I felt her inside of my very soul. She told me to trust her, and I *could see inside her* that she was worthy of being trusted, do you understand what I mean? I felt a surety that she would never harm me or any of us."

"The depot incident seems to indicate otherwise," someone mumbled.

"Yes, but she got her friends free," insisted Sainz. "Were any corpsmen seriously harmed?"

"No," said de Waal, "though much damage was caused. But tell us about this orb. You seem to be implying it helps her to fly around and get inside people's minds. You'll excuse me if I wonder whether the natives haven't been giving you the same drugs as they did Teri."

Sainz sighed but forged ahead. "The orb is like the device God sent Lehi. A transparent metal ball, with things spinning inside it. Look, I know all about hostage syndrome. I know you think I've bonded with the villains, but I really believe God is working through Teri. If you try to stop her, you'll be committing an atrocity. Prophet, if you're listening, please help me convince these good men to give her more time. Something wonderful is about to happen to Terego. We were brought here for a purpose. So was she. Pray for guidance, for a revelation."

The debriefing went on for a little longer, then Sainz was taken to infirmary for a check-up, rest and nutrition.

"This worries me," Torres said, "especially in light of the other incident."

"Which incident?" Rhea asked, nervously. She was already caught in a maelstrom of conflicting fears and hopes and sadness, and the thought of yet another tragedy or bizarre occurrence just took her breath away.

"Right before Sainz arrived" de Waal explained, "we monitored an explosion as well. We have been assuming it was a test of the AF weapons."

"What?" demanded Rhea. "An explosion near the forest?"

De Waal nodded. "We didn't tell you because then Sainz arrived and the situation escalated here. I sent a message to Captain D'Angelo. His first officer only just replied. His answer isn't very helpful. 'Wasn't us. I think yall know perfectly well who it was.' Might he be lying?"

Khumalo interrupted. "I sent a message to the prime minister when the explosion was detected. She assures me the orbiting ships are *incapable* of firing unless fired upon."

"Incapable?" Rhea pondered this for a moment. Soral was more on Terego's side than she had imagined. "Maybe it was Teri."

"Sister, this was a fusion explosion. I don't think you understand the magnitude of such an occurrence. How could your daughter be responsible for it?"

"This orb Sainz described. Maybe it can harness energy or something."

Everyone looked at her as if she were mad.

"I don't know how, so don't ask. But thanks to our agreement with Soral, she'll have her extra time. It's out of our hands, for the most part."

They tossed this back and forth for a while, and Rhea finally got home with the constantly lugged-about form of her son at about two-thirty. She collapsed into the bed beside him and succumbed to exhaustion.

After three fitful hours of sleep, she was awakened by movement in the kitchen.

"Miwa?" she wondered aloud, yanking back the covers. "Teri?"

Rushing from her bedroom, she was shocked to behold Carmen Allende, wearing Teri's nightgown, drinking milk with the refrigerator open. The teen jumped a little upon seeing Rhea and set the glass down.

"Mrs. Kumar-Miranda," she said, nervous. "I didn't think you'd come home."

"Never mind that, dear," Rhea exclaimed, rushing forward and embracing her. "Thank God you're alive!"

They hugged for a minute, then Carmen muttered, "There's a lot I need to tell you, ma'am, but could you drive me to my parents? I'll explain everything on the way."

RHEA'S FIRST OFFICIAL MORNING AS CZAR OF NATIVE AFFAIRS was chaotic and busy. After dropping off Jakobo with Chiho, she'd taken

Carmen to her parents at the diplomatic compound, where the Allendes had greeted her with happy tears. Carmen's father, a cardiovascular surgeon, had begun to give her a physical on the spot. Promising to check in on them soon, Rhea had hurried to her office and debriefed her team, fifteen staff members that Khumalo had transferred from various other departments to the new ministry. She'd delegated the task of getting word out to pertinent stakeholders and then had a conference call with de Waal and Khumalo, laying out the facts:

Brando had left his illegal chirurgic on Kumora.

It had begun interfering with the Native Teregans, sparking a war among tribes.

It had ordered Carmen's death in order to push Teri into believing she was actually Samanei Koroma.

It had kept Carmen captive so Teri would not discover that the girl was alive.

But Rhea kept to herself the confirmation of Josuo's accusation. Carmen and Teri were more than close friends. They were romantically entangled.

The least of our worries, frankly. And a woman like me—asexual romantic, people in the Consortium call us—shouldn't be judging others' happiness.

After assigning new tasks to her staff, mainly combing information accumulated over the past few weeks on the natives and entering it into databases, she leaned back in the leather seat behind her desk and called

Sanas's office. One of the paralegals answered.

"Oh, sister, we were going to call you, but it's been a mess over here since the decision came down."

Czar Kumar broke her slouch with an anxious jolt forward. "Decision? What decision?"

"The eyre. They've declared a mistrial."

"What? You're going to have to start all over?" Rhea's heart thundered with ferocious prescience. She knew what was coming.

"No, Madam Czar. It's not ours anymore. The mistrial was on the grounds that the government of Terego has lied to the court and to the CPCC and allowed the prisoner to take part in a military operation. Oh, there's a whole list of things: I'll get it to you. Basically, they want us to hand Brando over ASAP to be tried somewhere else, defended either by a CPCC-recognized attorney that he pays for or by a court-appointed lawyer. It's out of our hands."

Promising to call Sanas later, Rhea clicked off the connection with trembling hands and was startled as the device buzzed immediately. She opened the channel. There was de Waal's face, looking even more haggard than just an hour earlier.

He's aged so much over the past three weeks.

"Oh, Rhea. It's really bad news." The man's eyes were moist, as if he could barely keep from crying. Rhea braced herself uselessly: she knew full well that she couldn't take anything else… the horrible nightmares kept coming and coming, layering themselves into a living hell of psychological pressure that threatened all their sanities. "We've just detected thirty small CPCC craft entering the atmosphere, heading for the area south of here, that abandoned quarry near the depot.

"It's an invasion, Rhea. The Consortium lied to us."

CHAPTER 43

PRIME MINISTER SORAL'S DOPPELGANGER WASTED NO TIME: as soon as Captains D'Angelo and Quat were present in the faux-conference, she began.

"What do you know about the Centauri Rift?"

D'Angelo was taken aback. It was a strange way to begin a chat about Terego.

"Two hundred years ago, right? An explosion at the exit point of a imrizabu opened up a hole into higher dimensions. That prime minister back then, the Soltec guy, Rodrigo Peres? He got his memeticists to help him whip humans into a frenzy, afraid some aliens would come through the rift and conquer us. He wanted to use the crisis to become a dictator. Then the USR Navy sealed the rift, thinking it was all over, but one of the terraformers on Dhara discovered the first imrizabu. Its exit point was right where the rift had been. The Navy imposed martial law, and it rechartered the USR into the CPCC to give corporations sovereignty and to control the imrizabu, the Conduit. The Navy became the AF. It was a crazy time, they teach us in military history."

"Indeed it was. And I, like yall, thought that was all it was, until I became Chief Executive and was briefed. Only a handful of us know the truth. The prime minister you were talking about, Robigo Pedes, was surely trying to become the absolute ruler of humanity. But the threat from the rift was no ploy of his. Of course, the AF spent thirty years forcing everyone to believe that it *was* the so-called *Time of Darkness* when we shut down and dismantled the Solnet and in a systematic way eliminated or silenced everyone who knew what the rift really revealed."

Antonio blanched. "What?"

"Don't like that, eh?" There was a sad expression in Soral's eyes. Tony could tell she didn't like it much either, but lived with it anyway. "Yes, the AF killed people and tampered with others' memories. Some we had to pay off because their power was too great. That's how Dédalo Mostrenco became head of Soltec and later prime minister. He had knowledge of the imrizabu that led to Jitsu's system, and he was rewarded for it with control of Soltec and exclusive access, along with the AF, to travel through the Conduit. I'm not really happy with such negotiations either, but that's the legacy that we have to live with."

I'm not shocked about the measures yall took, but that yall have kept this a secret from yall's officers for two centuries. An extraterrestrial threat to all humanity, and yall never prepared us for it.

"Wait, ma'am," said Quat. "How many people were at the rift? How could the AF keep something like an alien threat secret for so many years?"

"The *Pacifactor* was one of the first ships there, and it was able to keep most comers away from the rift. Bloody mess, that. But some five ships were pulled into the rift. They popped out in two different places: Beta Pictoris, also called the Urakã Nebula, and the planet that it would later be named Ares, then Jitsu. The USRN didn't know of their location till Mostrenco found the Conduit, but by then there was no need to quarantine the survivors. The yakuza that had fallen into the dusk disk around Beta Pictoris had killed each other, and on Jitsu, the *Noctifer* and an escape pod from the *Pacifactor* with a spy on board had crashed. No one ever found the spy, though he's wanted to this day: Yen Bandera, who worked with Samanei Koroma two decades ago. In any event, the crew of the other ship was all dead, though one of them had lived for another two years, writing copious journal entries. It was our luck that it was all religious gibberish, because Mostrenco beat the Navy to the planet, looking for leverage against the USR. The woman, Domina Ditis, became, through these journals, an important figure for Pathwalkers. They're still convinced that the rift was our chance to glimpse the Ogdoad. They aren't far from the truth."

"What did yall see?" Quat demanded, impatient. Antonio already knew that she wouldn't tell them, so he said nothing.

"You'll appreciate the fact that Consortium security is at stake. I can't reveal the particulars of the findings: classified, yall understand. Let's just say it was goddamn sobering. Made the Navy rethink its duties toward humanity, made them understand that the USR needed to be replaced with something stronger and more centralized. What I can tell you is that the energy signature that the *Diomedes* is tracking is identical to the one discovered in and around the rift. Something not human is pulling power out of a higher dimension down on that planet, and yall better believe that we will find out what the hell that something is. Yes, studying the *Pacifactor's* scans of the rift and the energy pouring from it allowed the AF learned enough to develop tunneling and start the Military Net that became the basis for the Interstellar Net. But Consortium leaders in the know, we're scared out of our bloody wits by this discovery. If simply understanding tunneling allowed AF scientists to develop the Lieske drive, imagine what the race that we stole the technology from is capable of. If they're on Terego, we'll have a nasty situation on our hands."

She's holding stuff back, and not just because it's classified. She doesn't want us to know certain things, things that will make us think differently about this situation.

"So, Prime Minster, what it is you want done?"

"Yall two are sitting on this. Total quarantine for Terego. But that's it, understand? An XID detail is on its way, and should be there in about eleven days."

Tony's eyes narrowed. "You're sending Executive Intelligence? Why? You've got three AF galleons orbiting the planet, each with a hundred ground troops, four dozen fighters, anti-matter canons, anti-gravity bombs. What do you need a bunch of silver suits here for?"

"They are trained for this, Captain, and you'll wait for them. I have given you a chance you didn't deserve because of political pressure. But just in case you do what I predict you'll do and try to be a hero, understand that except for defensive capabilities that will be released to you if the computer senses a threat, yall's ships are locked into their orbits until the XID detail arrives. Shuttle bays are inaccessible. Fighter hangers are shut down. Troop transports are inoperable as well. You'll sit on your hands, Antonio, and monitoring the surface of that planet. If something happens that *I* think warrants your action, you'll do it. Until then, you'd better not breathe in a way that breaks regulation, you understand me?"

"Yes, ma'am," D'Angelo grunted between clenched teeth.

Dress me down in front of Phan Quat, eh? We'll see who's a real servant of justice, you or me, Madam Prime Minister.

He went to his bridge immediately after the conference. Ashar was waiting, eager to hear what their orders were. Antonio waved him over and muttered low so that the other bridge personnel wouldn't catch most of what he was going to say.

"They castrated us, Commander. We are just a monitoring station, enforcing a quarantine until XID gets here. All our offensive systems are locked down."

"Shite, Captain. What's down there that's so bleeding important?"

"They don't know, but it may be connected to the Centauri Rift. Lot of classified nonsense that I can't reveal to you, but one thing struck me funny. You know how some ships, they were yanked through that rift?"

"Yes. No survivors, right? I remember that class pretty well. Lieutenant Commander Jeyn Burd. What a professor, heh."

"You never change, eh? They always told us there weren't survivors, but it seems one guy did get away: Yen Bandera."

"Huh? The guy who helped set up Santo Koroma and Konrau Beserra?"

"Interesting coincidence, isn't it? The energy readings on the planet have got the brass thinking about the rift, Bandera was at the rift. Samanei may be on Terego."

Ashar nodded thoughtfully. "And we can't do a bloody thing."

"I'm hoping we can get more data that force Soral to let us act. Are there any more messages or intercepted stuff?"

"Oh, shite, yes! The consul just contacted me with a rumor: people are talking about some big-arsed explosions about a week back at the crisis ministry's weapons depot. The consul's contacts even say that a group of humans and grendels invaded the place and blew up some helicopters or something." Tony gripped the armrests tighter as he heard this. "Plus I answered a message from that half-wit de Waal asking us if we fired at Kumora Mountain."

"What did you tell him?"

"That it wasn't us and that they know who it is. It's probable they do."

"Yeah, it's that schizo oracle. Crap! What else? No, dump everything over here so I can look at it."

It took him a good ten minutes to catch up on the intel they'd collected from surface transmissions. One communication in particular caught his attention. The crisis ministry had encoded a message to the newly established Ministry of Native Affairs. It was easily decoded and translated into Standard. The brief note, intended for his lovely, lying little sister-in-law Czar Kumar-whatever, read cryptically:

Sainz agrees that explosion was probably her, but insists that the device she used is a weapon of peace and unity, not war.

"The device?" he muttered aloud.

Ashar looked over his shoulder. "And who is the 'she' they're talking about? Samanei? Think she has a fusion weapon or something?"

"That's exactly what I'm thinking. If she's already attacking the Tereganoj and they're not saying a damn thing about it, and she has this incredible weapon, XID isn't going to be able to step in here in two weeks and do shite. Write this up, annex the pertinent messages, and tunnel the package to Soral, to my grandfather, to Congressman Li, hell, to every one of the marshals. I'm going to force her to let me go down there and stop this crazy bitch before she turns the whole planet against us. In the meantime, I want you to get the heads of every department cracking on a way to bypass the locks on our offensive systems. If Soral says no, I need options."

"I'm on it, Captain."

The non-com communications officer spoke up before Mubarak could leave the bridge.

"Captain, we have detected the energy signature again. The computer's tracking it, moving at 355 kph from the mountain back toward the forest."

Without having to be told, he put the holomap up and all the bridge personnel followed the blip with their eyes. Suddenly, the light winked out of existence.

"It stopped?" Antonio demanded.

"Uh, no, Captain. Our scans are being deflected. It may still be there, but we can't see it. It's jamming us, sir."

Antonio slapped his fist against his palm and turned in his chair to see Ashar still by the door. "Damnit, Commander, get started on that right away, and add this latest development, though she probably already knows. We can't even monitor any more. This is intolerable!"

As Ashar hurried out, Antonio was already thinking ahead, trying to figure out how the hell he was going to get troops to the surface after Soral rejected his suggestion, as she was sure to do.

I may be required to sacrifice my career on this planet in the name of justice. So be it. There are bigger things at stake. Meting out punishment sometimes means taking a little for yourself. I'm ready for it. Let the judging commence. History's going to see me as the hero of justice here, no matter what a career politician like Leyla Soral thinks of and does to me.

INTERCHAPTER G

From: Mukerjib@octant1.gov.af

To: berdyaevn@os1.octant1.gov.af

Subject: re: Weapon Use by S.K.?

Date: May 7, 2714 2:07:14 (SST)

Berdyaev,

Soral's made it clear she doesn't want to discuss this anymore. And she's essentially telling me that if Antonio bollixes this, she won't give two shites what all the legislators, admirals and corporation heads in the Consortium say to her—she's going to castrate him, and you too, if you abet him even a wee bit.

I don't know how, but you get it through that thick-arse skull of his that this is out of his hands. XID is going to step in and clean up, and he's going to cooperate one hundred per, or he's going to be looking at life for treason. Even if Koroma's on that planet, Tony is not going to be the one that handles her.

I'm going to remind you again about the lengths that I went to so you'd get D'Angelo. He's your boy, Commodore. Get his arse in line. You know, I'm getting really tired of writing these missives. I shouldn't need to. You want to make admiral some day, no? What's the bloody problem, then?

Bud Mukerji

CHAPTER 44

ALL THAT HADN'T FALLEN APART ALREADY was now losing its
center. Brando could only be thankful that he lost consciousness for such
long stretches of time, dreamless periods during which his battered soul
managed to rest. But waking always brought the reality of his ruined plans
into sharp focus: borne upon the back of a wretched warrior beast, hog-tied
and immobilized, Brando struggled not to think of Kyr, clicking insect-like in
his mountain hideaway; of Teri, groomed by that robot for some inscrutable
purpose; or of Miwa, fighting her own father to defend one of the monsters.

Catching glimpses of netting above him, Brando realized he was once
again caught in an ethical skein whose webbing wasn't slick with rain but
with blood and tears and bile. He wished for nothing more than to be dead.

Then she descended in a sphere of blue light.

His spark. Gripping a glowing ball of burnished, transparent bronze in her hands.

Impossible. Am I on the verge of gnosis? Will I now have the second vision?

But then he saw that she was physically present. Warriors looked up and got out of the way. Branches swayed as she lowered through the air.

Then—Tenshi? Has she returned for me at last? Please let it be so!

He strained up against his bonds, tried to form words with his broken mouth and jaw. The figure looked away from him with disgust, and Brando saw the cornrows, tight and frizzy with humidity.

It wasn't Tenshi. It was Teri.

At her side in the blue bubble that gently lowered her to the branch Brando's captors stood on was a highborn priestess. The native spoke first with frantic animation, and then Teri's voice boomed otherworldly from the air around them, though her lips never moved.

One of the warriors still had her spear pointed at the human teen. Teri's ball licked at it with a tongue of blue fire and it blossomed, festooned in seconds with flowering moss.

The bizarreness of the scene should have shaken Brando, but he was past astonishment, well beyond any stress he'd ever imagined facing. Teri was flying and making dead wood come to life. There was no denying it. What troubled Brando, what churned the sediment of his illuminated self up in roiling, amorphous clouds, was the love that shone from Teri's eyes as she looked upon Brando's enemies, and the scorn that burned into the old linguist when that gaze fell upon him.

Another of his daughters had chosen the monsters over him, had relegated him to a status below non-human, had declared him a pariah in her sight. The years of laughter, of sweet kisses and bedtime stories, of long afternoon practices followed by bowls of ice cream, of prayers before sleeping and camping under the stars: all those beautiful moments were reduced to naught by that haughty, disdainful glance. Worse: their relationship had been newly transvalued. What had once been love was now inverted and seen as sickness.

When Teri had finished speaking, the warriors lowered Brando to the rough bark and released his bonds. Despite his weakness, he attempted to spring at them, but found his muscles had frozen up. Looking down, he saw that blue light had wreathed its way around him and held him tightly.

Look at me, Brando. A cold sense of clinical curiosity invaded his mind along with the voice, which was Teri's, speaking Standard. He looked at her sunburst eyes, and his chest ached at their beauty.

I know how confused you must be. But I don't have time to help you through your crisis. I understand why you drugged me, though. I remind you of the spark you saw, the same one Tenshi did. You were hoping for a miracle. Here it is. Just not the one you imagined.

"Wait. Tenshi's spark looked like mine?"

You didn't know? She didn't tell you?

"No. How are you speaking into my head?"

Some alien race left this sphere here thousands of years ago. I call it the Urim. It's a tool. But that's not important. I'm going to take you with me to the village of these drones and, Brando, I'm going to leave you there for a while.

Brando's mind teetered. *The Urim? Identical sparks?*

Bewilderment was building in him, threatening to burst into a flood, but Teri sent a wave of detached calm into him.

They won't treat you like before, but you must stay put. This isn't a time for you to be running round like some hero you're never going to be, do you understand?

She's my daughter and she's scolding me like a child.

I'm not your daughter, Dr. D'Angelo. I'm not just Tenshi's clone, either. I've been chosen by Providence. By the Ogdoad, if you will. So stay out of my way or you'll wish you had.

"How can you love them?" The words popped out treacherously before he could stop them. "How can you, and hate me at the same time?"

"I don't hate you," Teri said out loud, her presence withdrawing from his mind. "I don't know how to forgive you yet."

"These things killed two dozen humans from your community, and you appear to be forgiving them just fine!"

"Yeah, but they didn't know what they were doing. You did. You have no excuse. But all the same, I'm going to take care of you the best I can."

His jaw suddenly burned with exquisite pain for a brief second, then he found he could move it more freely. The burning skittering along the nerves of his entire body, and in a few minutes he felt whole. Tired, but whole.

At least physically. His mind, his heart—those might never heal.

CHAPTER 45

«YOU COULD READ HIM, helped heal his mind as well as his body.»

No. I don't want to feel compassion for him. Every time I read someone, I forgive them. I have to, because that person becomes part of me. I don't want him part of me. I need distance.

«That is fine. There is sufficient work to be done without worrying about him.»

The slate gray sky rushed by above them as the Urim guided its three passengers to village where Brando's team had been held. The third village in a very long campaign. The Urim assured her that she would not need sleep, that she would not tire, that it could sustain her cells undamaged for weeks if necessary. It tried to explain how, showing her inside DNA molecules, demonstrating how it could channel energy at wavelengths as small as 10^{-11}m (the Urim now used technical terms it had read from Kyr, making its choral voice even more disconcerting).

Teri ignored the specifics of how and just used the power at her disposal. This included cloaking herself from outside detection. The Urim had requested permission to block the orbiting ships' scans of the forest so that their travels and Teri's "miracles" would go undetected. Teri had consented, and their first two visits to villages had been successful.

With her priestess ally and broken creator, Teri descended through the canopy into the clearing of the village.

Ùshëshajirh began, stepping forward to proclaim the good news to the startled, cowering inhabitants.

"Cousins, the Firstborn has returned in the moment of the People's greatest need. She will lead us into an age of great knowledge and power. One day your children will fly through the air just as she does, taking their place among the great beings that sail the Deepest Green. Give her your attention and your respect."

Then Teri addressed them. There were so many things she wanted to say, so much she wanted to change, but she had recognized from the beginning that this was not the time. Abolishing ritual killing, recognizing that drones had souls, giving males an equal position in the society: all these radical steps had to wait until Terego was safe and the natives united. So she concentrated on what was necessary to realize those goals.

"Let every family send its highborn and firstmale to the clearing to hear the words of God's servant."

The inclusion of the males was intentional. Despite the highborn's patronizing dismissal of the members of their harems, Teri had learned during her stay to the south that the males had considerable influence over the highborn they were bonded to. The firstmale of each compound, the male who had been first bonded to the highborn and who enjoyed a position of authority over the other males and children, was especially powerful in guiding his highborn. Teri knew instinctively that, just as wives in her own society largely effected change through their husbands, so did native males through their highborn. If she wanted to remake this society, she would need the males' support.

Once the group she'd commanded brought together was with great attention and fear awaiting her next words, she continued.

"My tribe, the ingan, are preparing to enter this forest and overcome the People. Normally, the People's magic would be no match for what the ingan can do. However, the People have God's favor: the Unblinking Eye has let a tear run out into the Deepest Green, dropping to the forest and creating me, Çèrhingÿl. I wield the ancient stone, and through me you will have victory. It will not be a victory of blood and battle, children. United, we will defend ourselves when necessary, but the magic of the Word will battle for us. The lore of the People teaches well the power of the Word, how words surround us, how they hurt and heal. I can use words to make allies of the ingan, but

I need all the People together, as siblings, the way I intended so many years ago when I left the six sisters at the forest's edge."

There was silence, and Teri saw in the eyes of the males a certain hesitancy, a doubt that wrinkled their muzzles and made their heavy cheeks sag further.

"I will show you just how powerful the Word of God is."

She gestured at a nearby tree. The house trees' lower limbs were seldom grown together, especially those near the clearing, because they were thicker and older, and not flexibly pliant under the males' hands. She indicated some of the fifteen-meter-thick limbs.

"These boughs would make a mighty compound, don't you agree? Of course, not even the greatest builder male could ever hope to pull them together: they have already grown to their full length. But the word of God is mightier than the hand of male or highborn or drone. Watch."

As I say the word. Just like the other times.

«The Urim is incapable of forgetting.»

"Together!" she boomed in Standard. Blue lambencies flicked outward from the sphere and danced along three of the massive boughs. With a sighing, groaning sound, the limbs moved gradually together, bulging in all the right places to form a gently pear-shaped platform.

"Up!" Teri shouted.

The Urim lifted her to the new platform, reaching out to grab the high priestess and her firstmale and bring them along.

As the other nearly three hundred natives stared upward in awe, Teri spoke in low tones. "I need you to gather your drones close to the village. Defense may become an urgent duty at any moment. Pick three highborn to be the village's representatives in the People's Council, which I will convene in a few days. I will be back for them."

The high priestess, a startled-looking highborn with a blue-gray muzzle, spoke with a quavering voice. "So you forgive us for how we treated your progenitor?" Her firstmale threw a quick, irritated glower at her. Teri almost laughed.

"Yes. But you must take care of him for me as I continue on my pilgrimage. Do not bind him and do not hurt him. Remind him, using the Greenseer's tongue, that I have commanded him to stay and cause no harm. He will obey."

They thanked her for such an honor, and she returned them to the clearing. Úshëshajirh had been answering questions and nodded at Teri's hand signal.

An hour was all they could afford to spend in each village: perhaps one or two might rebel against the idea of unification, despite the incredible displays Teri would put on for them, but she knew she could get the majority behind her. She needed the Council, needed a political body Tereganoj and the CPCC would recognize and sign treaties with.

Ùshëshajirh had to be the de jure leader of the natives: no one would accept a fifteen-year-old human as the aliens' ruler.

Turning to Brando, she took in his hollow-eyed, forlorn face again. When she'd found him, bound and beaten nearly to death, she had nearly begun to weep. She did not want to love him, did not want him to be her father, but there it was. Her heart did what God told it to do. But she would not weaken herself by knowing him further, by looking into his soul, by becoming his sister like she had with Ùshëshajirh. There was no room for him in her plans, no place for compassion toward him in the scope of the energies she'd be expending.

«Just say that you love him. Do that much for him. You want to; your mind is swirling with desire to give him that surcease.»

"Brando," she said, trying to ignore the urging of the sphere in her mind. "Do as I told you. If you touch one of them, you'll have to answer to me. Just eat whatever they bring you, listen to them, learn about them. They're wonderful beings, so you should feel honored to be among them. I'll come back for you in a few days. You'd better be here."

Then Ùshëshajirh and she were punching through the canopy and into the pounding downpour as Teri held back her tears.

Placing the Urim in Ùshëshajirh's claws, Teri pulled Tenshi's journal out. She needed to hear something positive about Brando, something that might redeem him a little.

"June 3, 2683. Ah, my beloved Brando has had the vision, Diary. And what he saw suggests we are fated to be together. I have never heard of two people's sparks looking the same. But he swears he saw *me*, younger and lighter-skinned, surrounded by blue light that emerged from her glowing hands. Same apparition that came to me years ago. While he was alone in the shrine, his hands on the Urim, she told him that there is a reason for the pain he's experienced, that his love matters. His spark also asked for forgiveness, which is unheard of. Still, he is now a matakite. He walks the Path, partly because of his love for me and mine. And now I know. I love him, too. I always will."

The Urim pulsed dark purple in Ùshëshajirh's hands, startling the aging priestess. The protective bubble around them faltered for a moment, slowing, letting drops of rain spatter their faces.

«What? We need to access that journal at once. Something is very wrong.»

Of course. But what did you—

Thin forks of blue lightning shot into the battered metal rectangle. Teri understood that the Urim was uploading its contents.

«A crime of the worst kind. When? Why? Why would we? Why would we reverse the arrow and risk their wrath?»

The soft chorus that underlay the Urim's voice in Teri's head disintegrate into cacophony and then withdrew or fell silent.

No matter how insistent she grew, the sphere refused to explain its breakdown.

Instead, after a few minutes, it resumed their flight to the next village.

CHAPTER 46

THE SCIENCE OFFICER, LIEUTENANT ANDOLIN EGUZKITZA, was saying something, but Antonio was so deeply sunken into his black anger and outrage that it took him a moment to realize he was being addressed.

"What? Say that again?"

"Sir, I was checking out the other scans, the ones that the *G.W.* and the *Shaka* did while our computer froze up?"

"Yes? And?"

"Sir, there were some strange quantum fluctuations detected near Terego's star every time we detected the strange energy source."

"How near?"

"On top of it. Hard to say with any more specificity. I think that whatever they've got down there is capable of tunneling energy from the star and channeling it."

"Come on; that's impossible, Andi!"

"For us, sir, but not for whoever made that weapon. It's not human, is it, sir?"

The other personnel on the bridge fell silent.

Rumors are already flying, eh?

"That's classified, lieutenant, but it sure doesn't seem human. Keep an eye on that star: tell me if there are more fluctuations."

Antonio poured over Berdyaev's most recent message to him. It used a lot of words to give one simple answer: no fucking way.

All I can hope for is that this thing blows so wide open that Soral's got to step down and someone more sympathetic to me takes over. I don't think I'll be able to sit here much longer.

"Captain, I'm not sure," said the communications non-com, bringing Antonio back to the moment, "but I think we're receiving a homing beacon of some type from that mountain. It's really weak, but it looks like a robot's recall signal."

"Can you boost it? Get a better fix?"

"Yessir. Hang on. Alright, it's definitely a recall signal, from a Serfaty chirurgic. A really old AI model."

Brando's.

"There's a piggybacked message on the machine code. Real short, keeps repeating."

"What does it say?"

"Uh, 'Samanei has a powerful alien weapon. Help.' That's it."

Antonio stood from his chair and put a shaking hand to his head, tugging at his hair.

I knew it. The bitch is down there, and the rift aliens have given her some weapon. Or she stole it from them. Weapon of peace, my arse. That crazy fem is yanking juice from the star through higher dimensions to create fusion explosions: is she practicing, warming up to blast us from the sky? I can't let this happen. I need to be down there, now. Fucking Soral, cut me off from my ship.

"Captain," the science officer called, "I've got more of those quantum disturbances."

Antonio nearly screamed. Suddenly it hit him. There was no way she could have eliminated this option: it would be highly criminal.

"Systems control, the escape pods are still under my command, or they were locked down by the program, too?"

"You've still got control, Captain. Why?"

"We've got what, thirty of those four-man pods?"

"Yessir."

"Can they carry four armed soldiers with full armor and munitions?"

"Nah, Cap. Maybe three. Got to factor in weight and so on."

Antonio smacked his fist into his palm. Ninety men under his command. A fighting chance, at least. Better than orbiting like targets for the schizoid freak to shoot at while the black suits rushed to lock everything down nice and secret.

"Tell Battalion-Dux Lachower to get me the best two companies prepped, busked for battle and ready to tread the surface. We're hitting atmosphere in forty-five minutes."

FIFTEEN MINUTES LATER, after coordinating communications with Ashar, Antonio was suiting up while Lachower got him up to speed on the companies' status. The captain had not doubted his dux's willingness to buck orders and go to the surface: he'd chosen the man precisely for his enthusiasm for battle and his ability to think independently. In addition, aboard the *Diomedes,* Lachower, an army captain in rank, the equivalent to the flotilla's *commander* position, was able to head up an entire battalion, rather than just a company like army captains normally did, performing the duties usually assigned to a major. Companies on AF ships that patrolled space were headed by lieutenants; these adjustments in organization cut down on conflicts between higher ranking officers. In fact, most ship captains called their army captain *battalion dux*, like in the old USRN, to avoid confusion over their similar titles. And D'Angelo's b-dux was thrilled at the opportunity he'd been given in this new assignment.

Besides, ever since the AF had streamlined operations to accommodate the war and the restructuring of CPCC zones that conflict had necessitated, army units assigned to a galleon were under the direct and sole command of the vessel's captain, and hence of the commodore of that sector, marshal of that octant, the Navarch of the Fleet, and the Prime Minister. The General of the Consortium Army was only responsible for troops stationed planetside throughout human space. There was never a conflict of interests and orders. The b-dux would obey D'Angelo like a trusty old hound.

"You want to take a gander at the boyos, Cap?"

"No. Two full companies, right?"

"Yessir. Well, minus a couple of erks. Only room for ninety of us, including me and you. Fifty men in a company. I ditched a few."

Antonio nodded. "And the equipment?"

"We gathered all the clobber we're going to need, and right now I got my centurions and decurions eliminating gash things so that the pods have more maneuverability. Where we going to lob in at?"

"There's a huge abandoned quarry within a cooey of Diadono, the capital. It's flooded, and we can splash down in it or burn down nearby."

"Ah, yeah, the depot where the local johns got their flivvers stored. Good thinking, sir. We land near the mountain, there's no transportation."

"Right. We take the depot, occupy the capital, leave a small contingent behind, and the rest of us are going to flivver up to the mountain, set up a base of operations that we can send out excursions from. So tell the boyos to dump rations in favor of ironmongery: we can provision ourselves in the capital."

The sergeant nodded and they both headed for the corridor along which the hatches to the escape pods were lined. Fully outfitted grunts were stuffing the cramped vessels with packs and weapons, a murmuring thrill of enthusiasm humming through them.

Tony could feel it, too, and it shored him up. These were the best-trained men the army had to offer, assigned to the *Diomedes* at the behest of D'Angelo's connections. They would hit that planet like a biblical scourge, and the fanatics and yaks and grendels would be falling to their knees to pray to whatever fantasy gods they believed in soon enough.

But ethereal divinity could never stop the falling guillotine of justice.

He pondered this irony and smiled.

CHAPTER 47

SHALURA IGNORED HER PAIN as she crouched beside Daenzhelo in the shade of a boulder, watching the drones carry large, shiny chests and planks down the side of the mountain. She couldn't identify any of them as they wore an unusual black harness that didn't indicate their individual tribes.

The Greenseer's drones, her voices whispered in unison. *Don't let them see you. You do not want to face that mysterious oracle with hands and tail bound.*

With a touch and wave of her finger, she indicated to Daenzhelo that they should go around the tumble of boulders that time had sloughed from the higher elevations. Having judged the approximate direction from which the drones were descending, Shalura's voices had shown her she could reach the distant ridge from above and retain the element of surprise.

"No," the small one said. "Not up there. Let's get the *guns* first. My picture says it's over that way, not up."

Her own need to have burning questions answered was screamed at her by a dozen voices, but Shalura forced herself to ignore them. She would do as Daenzhelo said they should. Besides, she could hear that soft male voice murmuring. Having these "guns" when approaching the Greenseer was likely the best strategy, it suggested.

Keeping low, they scrambled among the crags in a slowly curving arc northward along the eastern face. Just as Daenzhelo's picture had predicted, they soon came upon a overhanging lip of rock which cast a deep shadow on the narrow ledge below it. As they stepped into the shade and her eyes, aching from hours under the cloud-filtered sunlight, adjusted to the more pleasant gloom, Shalura pushed herself downward into a painful crouch, rapidly unslinging her spear: before them stood a nightmarish beast, a shining insect the size of a highborn, its limbs whirring and clicking strangely.

Daenzhelo reacted differently. Despite Shalura's warning hoot, the highborn stepped forward and babbled in her native speech. A voice from inside the insect answered in the People's tongue: "Yes, I am the Greenseer. And yes, I'm Kyr, Rrandò's *kirúrdzhik*."

Shalura slowly unbent her legs and lowered her spear. The insect, the Greenseer, *Kyr*, had not moved. "Daenzhelo, what is a *kirúrdzhik*?"

"Oh, I'm sorry, Shalura. It's a made thing, but it can talk and think like the People or the ingan. It does not a soul be having, though. Our nations were supposed not to make them anymore, but this is an old ancient long-time ago one, I'm thinking. Belonging to my dad."

"I belong to no one," the Greenseer said in a soft, unnatural tone.

"No soul? Is it a drone? A drone cannot receive revelation from God, cannot be an oracle." Rage was beginning to build inside of Shalura.

"I have telling you that drones *do* have souls, Shal! But that doesn't mattering. Kyr is no drone. He is made. Like a spear or compound or pottery. The ingan made him, to serve as a cure-mistress."

Shalura's claws eased slowly out. "A cure-mistress? The cure-mistress of my tribe was sworn upon the spirit of the tribe to help cure her sisters and brothers, not to kill them. What kind of cure-mistress are you, made-insect-thing?"

"To cure a whole body, it is often necessary to cut off a finger or a limb. I needed to bring all the People together so they could fight the... ingan. Some tribes had to be... operated on to reach that goal."

"Fight the *ingan*?" Daenzhelo shouted. "What reason for?"

"Ah, little Tana. My child."

"Don't you call me that, ugly insecty *kirúrdzhik* excrement-lover! I am no Tana, and even less your child!"

"I helped make you from her body. Took your aunt's egg, fertilized it with material from Tana's body, and made you."

Shalura listened dumbfounded. Had Daenzhelo been brought into being in that mythical way? It was whispered that under certain extreme conditions, highborn could produce eggs *themselves*, fertilize them and have a male gestate them. The legend of Òlrhätho spoke of this process. That ancient princess had been produced thus when the queen and her firstmale were exiled without a drone to accompany them.

"Maybe, but you didn't make my soul. I am a child of God, not of some crazy made thing like you!"

Shalura was shaken from her theorizing by her friend's shouts.

Make it answer your questions, drone! The voices brooked no distraction.

"Enough. You will tell me, in this very moment, why you wanted to unite the People. I know you were not inspired. I will understand this now, do you hear?"

"Listen, then. These ingan are the cruelest animals the forest has ever seen. I have lived among them for a very long time and you can trust me. They are brutal. But I thought that in Rrandò I had finally found one who would leave me to exist alone and as I wanted, far from their bloody business. He left me on the mountain, and I learned many things about it and the forest at its feet. Many years passed, and then he came for me. He asked me, supposedly in friendship, to help him. His… highborn could not… reproduce with him. She had a problem inside her that kept them from producing children. As I had helped him create his other children, he begged me to travel with him to the land of the ingan and assist him again. I agreed, and he took me across the great volcanic plains instead of through the forest. It was a long journey east and then south, then through a pass in the mountains and to the principal village of the ingan.

"He hid me so that the cruel ingan would not find and break me, and with the magical devices I had brought, we worked for several weeks to extract an egg, fertilize it and then implant it in his highborn. Finally we had success, and I readied myself to be returned to the mountain. But he refused to take me. He told me I had to walk back through the forest, carrying the very heavy devices I had brought.

"I argued with him, but he pointed a thing made for killing at me and told me to leave. I struggled with the heavy load into the forest. The rainy season had just begun that year, and after a few days I slipped in the mud at the edge of a riverbank and went crashing into the water. The things I was carrying struck me and injured my... head. I was carried by the current to the village of the Sháinkhÿngigg, where I met the People for the first time.

"A highborn named Ùshëshajirh became my friend, and as I began to tell her the long, sad story of my existence, I realized that I had spent years trying to forget the biggest evil I have ever seen: the abandoning of the aunt of this ingan friend of yours by Rrandò in a land where she couldn't possibly survive. Ùshëshajirh became convinced that this highborn, Oracle of a world Rrandò tried to destroy, might come for me, might come to protect the People. We began to discuss this, and I became very happy. I so want to see her again.

"Ùshëshajirh became high priestess of her tribe, and we began to speak to others about the coming of the ingan. They are very powerful, and I knew that they would find Rrandò, a criminal they are searching for, and make him reveal where the Oracle is. I wanted to see her again. I wanted the People to be ready to receive her. I wanted them to be ready to fight the ingan. I wanted…"

Shalura wanted to hear no more. The crest of fur along the back of her neck was rising, she was dipping into a crouch, her tail was thumping the rocky soil.

All dead, whispered her beloved male, *for a lie. Betrayed. For a lie. The tribe sundered. For a lie. A lie that cannot go unpunished*, other voices joined in. *Deaths and treason that must be avenged.*

She hurled herself against the spidery creature. Pain shot through her as she watched it stumble back into the shimmering magic at the entrance. Wrapping her arms around it, she struggled to lift the Greenseer. Though it was unworldly heavy, she managed to get it off the ground and slam it into the wall. One of its remaining limbs was caught between its bulbous torso and the slick shiny expanse of the artificial wall and snapped with a gruesome sound.

Shalura grabbed her spear from the ground. She could see Xiggèr'enth and Thõdhula there before her, on either side of the evil insect-thing. Their spirits were here to witness the exacting of the blood-price. Their ears twitched in anticipation.

"No, Shalura!" Daenzhelo shouted as the spear came slamming down on the red eyes of the demon called Kyr. The haft vibrated with a satisfying crunch, and Shalura used her massive strength to bring the triangle of stone down again and again into that expressionless face until the shining limbs ceased twitching. Shalura stood over the ruined form, all her voices silent. There was nothing left for them to say. Her tribe was no more, the surviving traitors victims of the same deceit that had probably decimated villages throughout the forest. There was no Firstborn: just Daenzhelo's sister, manipulated by this heap of dung at her feet. There was nothing left. Nothing that held her, nothing to sustain her. No duty. No honor. No spirit.

It was time for Shalura to die. She knew it. She had to do it immediately. But then Xiggèr's voice whispered low. She couldn't quite understand him, but his voice kept bubbling up. She would listen closely for a while, put off the ritual suicide. Maybe there was another duty left to her, something to justify living another day. Maybe her mate simply wanted to thank her before she winked from existence forever.

Yes, she would wait a while, till she could make out his message. Then, as her faith demanded, she would embrace the swirling black of nothingness.

CHAPTER 48

MIWA LAID HER PALM ON THE SQUARE SCANNER beside the door, her mind a tumult. As much as she was repulsed by what Kyr had done, she hadn't wanted him to be destroyed. Now that he lay wrecked by the entrance to her father's secondary secret lair, Miwa felt hollow inside, as if she was unintentionally part of some evil plot. She tried to shake the emptiness off, tried to understand that God was working here in ways she couldn't understand, but the feeling remained. In fact, her uneasiness was exacerbated by the depression Shalura had fallen into. Miwa's friend wouldn't even answer when spoken to. She just stood there, her spear cast aside, a stone knife in her hand. Her ears didn't even twitch.

A gurgling electronic noise came from inside the mechanism, and the door slid open with a groan. Lights flickered on inside, and there came the hum of an air-cycling unit. Glancing back to see if Shalura was following,

Miwa stepped inside. The door ground shut behind them.

Along each of the curving walls of the cavern stood metal racks replete with weapons that Miwa had never seen before: rifles and mortars and handguns and suits of what Miwa presumed was some sort of body armor. At the very back stood a large metal box, a frame for faux-lifes with emitter and chair beside it. Connected to the frame by haphazard wiring was a two-meter-square tile that spread across the floor between the two racks. As Miwa approached, Shalura in tow, the tile hummed to life and the holographic image of a burly, frightening man shot upward from the floor.

It was her father. Younger, fifty kilograms of sheer muscle heavier, with a different nose and skin tone, but still Brando. Behind her, Shalura stiffened and bristled. Good, but bad. Her friend was reacting, but Miwa didn't want her messing with any of the equipment.

"He's not there, Shalura. It's a magic image made of light. It looks real, but it's not."

"Miwa." The somatoid spoke, and even his voice was different. Not the firm, confident tones of Nando Miranda, but stressed and fretted with sadness. "You're here, so I must've told you to come. I'll only do that in emergencies, so we'd better get started. I'll guess you already know who I am. I created this program to finish up the training I'm going to do, have done, with you. I can't risk you not being able to defend yourself against the bastards that are out there. So I've brought all the weapons I could scrounge and stuck them in here, along with a faux-life that will show how to use them."

"Miwa, how can an image talk? This is a spirit, isn't it? Why will you not tell me the truth? I am not afraid. I have seen many spirits."

"I'm swearing to you that it is not a spirit. Please trust me."

"The first thing we need to do, since you've likely little time seeing how I'm not with you and your sister isn't either, is get you fitted with a battle suit. The rack on your right has some that I cut down for you. Scans of your body show that you are fifteen Standard years old and measure 1.85 meters. Much taller than your friends, I bet." The somatoid laughed and Miwa nearly started to cry. She longed to see her dad really laugh, like he had when they'd joked and tickled each other during her childhood. But the holographic projection kept on. "Scans also show a large animal behind you, quiescent. You can pick up a weapon and I'll show you how to dispatch it. Don't make any sudden moves."

Hoping that the program was interactive, Miwa spoke. "No. It's mine. My friend."

"A pet?"

"Sure. A pet. Just ignore it. What about the suits?"

"The third suit is very close to your size. You need to take off your clothing, then slip on the undergarment that's rolled up in the left boot. Then take the suit, pull it open at the back, and step into it. Once you pull it up, it'll seal automatically."

Miwa started to comply, but then her face flushed. "Turn off the scan and turn around. Now. You make me feel uncomfortable."

The image flickered, and she was suddenly staring at Brando's broad back. "Scans are off. Please instruct me when to turn them back on."

Miwa stripped her clothes off and kicked them into a corner. *Oh, Lord, what I would do for some hot water, soap and a razor.* She noticed Shalura staring at her, but felt no shame. It was like being in the girls' locker room, except that, of course, Shalura had never seen a naked human before and was understandably curious. Pulling on the one-piece under-suit, Miwa took the flexible but strangely solid-feeling battle armor and slipped into it.

"Alright. You can look again."

"Okay. Boots go on up over the leggings. There's a pad on your right shoulder. Tap three times, then once, then four times, and your casque will deploy over your head. Tuck your hair into the collar first."

Miwa did as she was told, and the helmet accordioned into place. The suit's recycling system whirred to life, and in the clear visor's computer readouts told her the temperature, direction, altitude and a host of other data. Her father's voice spoke in her ear.

"This is an illegal, black market battle suit. It enhances your muscle strength and can withstand multiple blows from most portable energy weapons without damage, though you'll be bruised as hell afterward. Try it.

Jump toward the ceiling of the cavern."

Miwa looked up. The display told her the closest point of a stalactite was three meters above her. *No way.* But she bent her knees and leapt anyway, trusting her father as she always had. The sensation was exhilarating: she flew upward as if propelled by the bounce of a trampoline. The top of her helmet crashed into the pendent cone, jarring her painfully. She landed in a crouch and tapped the pattern on her shoulder to yank back the casque and check her head for blood.

Just a bump.

"Ouch. But how totally cool! What else can it do?"

"For full mastery of the armor and the weapons you see here, I need you to go sit in the chair. There's a faux-life training program, modified from the one I used to get ready for the squads. It'll put you through the paces faster than you could in real life. Just sit down and the connection will be made. Then just choose 'training program' from the menu."

"Hang on." Miwa turned to Shalura, who had crouched down, nervous.

"These skins you have put on give you extraordinary powers, Daenzhelo. You leapt as high as a drone!"

"Yes, and they able to help us fight to get our friends back. But I have to go sit over there and be covered in light for a long time. The light teaching me how to be using the skins and the *guns*. Then I showing you, too. But it maybe takes lots of time. Do you still have food?"

"Yes. I will be fine. I have to concentrate on my voices. It is very quiet in this compound, and perhaps I will understand what I am being told to do."

Miwa didn't quite get what Shalura meant, but she reached out her hand to touch her friend's cheek softly.

"Okay. Just say my name if you need me. I telling the image to wake me up if you do." She walked over to the chair and sat. The back of it reclined and she found herself staring up into the emitter. She'd never been in a faux-life: few Novasanktuloj ever had. She wasn't nervous, however. She was excited. The minute she'd walked into the cavern, her heart had started racing, and it still was. She felt even better than before a competition: nervous, sick, enthralled. It was great.

Brando explained what to expect and how to log out of a simulation or out of the whole faux-life together, and then asked whether she was ready to begin.

"Yes, sir. But if my pet says your last name, bring me out, okay? Go ahead."

She found herself standing in misty room. Before her, suspended in the air, was a panel of glass with icons on it.

Arms. Battle armor. Jungle warfare. Desert warfare. Piloting. Home.
Home?

Curious, she reached out and tapped the icon, a strangely twisted but beautiful house. She found herself standing in a garden. Laughter mingled with harsh sunlight and the smell of flowers. Miwa took a few steps forward, noticing that her avatar or doppelganger or whatever they called it was dressed in battle armor, too, and nearly slammed into a little girl who was chasing around behind a strange fuzzy animal.

"Excuse me!" Miwa exclaimed. "Sorry, didn't mean to mess up your game."

The little girl stared up at her, black curls framing a cute face and gray eyes.

Wait a minute.

"That's okay, lady. My name's Tana. I got five years old, like this, see?" She held up the fingers of her right hand and wriggled them. "I'm trying to catch my pet, Fata. She's cute, no? Apa got her for me so I could have a friend. Apa's real nice."

Oh, God. It's her. She does *look just like me, just lighter-skinned.*

Miwa crouched down in front of the somatoid of the child from whom she'd been cloned, extending a hand. "Nice to meet you, Tana. I'm Miwa."

Tana put her tiny hand in the black glove's palm and tried to shake. "Miwa's a real pretty name. Like in the story."

Miwa raised an eyebrow. "Story? What story?"

"Of the twins, Teri and Miwa. You never heard it? I could tell it, you want. Umma doesn't like to hear it. She always cries. But I could tell it to you."

"Oh, could you? That would be so nice."

He got our names from a story?

As Miwa sat down on the path, Tana began. "Once up on sometime, a woman had two daughters, Teri and Miwa. They were real pretty and studied real hard, learning all about the Ogdoad and Mother Domina and that good stuff. Then one day their umma had to go into the desert to look for some rocks, and she taked her little girls with her. A huge jagen came out of the hills and whoosh! He grabbed them and taked them away to his big scary cave. The little girls were real scared, and the jagen got their umma between his yucky claws and went beddy-bye. Teri and Miwa knowed that if they letted that mean old jagen waken up, he was going to eat their umma and them too. But they couldn't get out to ask for help. The jagen was right beside the cave's door! And they were real, real far from any other persons, too. But I told you they were smart, and they remembered what the oni did. Those little guys put that smelly jagen poop on them so the jagens couldn't smell them. Guess what? That's what Teri and Miwa did, too. They put that poop all over themselves and sneaked out real slow to where their mama told them once. A place with lots and lots of oni hiding from the persons.

"And they got the oni to come help them get their mama out. Then they all went back to their house. All the persons were there all worried. Their apa was looking for them everywhere. Now they were back with their apa and they all lived happy and snappy."

Miwa smiled, a good feeling spreading throughout her belly. Brando had been thinking of those clever girls when he'd named his new daughters. She understood now.

Dad just wanted us to be safe. He wanted us to be ready, because he felt like he wasn't able to protect us. He loves us so much, even if it seems like a really strange love.

"Thank you for the story," she said to Tana. "It was very good."

"Tana!" a voice yelled. Around the corner stepped Tenshi Koroma. She looked so much like Teri that it startled Miwa. "Oh, hello. I didn't know we had visitors."

"I was just leaving. You've got a beautiful daughter, ma'am."

"Yes. Her father and I are very lucky."

"That you are," Miwa said. "Sorry to run, but I've got things to take care of."

"I understand. Perhaps you can come by some other time. Or swing by my office. I'm the mayor, you know."

"I just might. Thanks."

Moving her head to the left and muttering "exit," she found herself before the menu again. She wondered why her father had a faux-life of his first wife and daughter. Had it helped him through hard times? Why did he keep it?

Plenty of time for answers. First I need to learn how to kick more butt.

She reached out and tapped the first simulation.

Time to get busy.

CHAPTER 49

MONDAY NIGHT AND EARLY TUESDAY MORNING, chaos reigned in the crisis control center. AF troops had landed at the old rock quarry that had been mined to build most of the government complexes in the capital as well as the Temple. They were now surrounding the weapons depot, where forty-five corpsmen were prepared to make a last stand to keep Teregan weapons and vehicles out of the invaders' hands.

Rhea watched as de Waal coordinated dozens of operations at once. Troops were being flown in from the crisis ministry's branches on other continents. Diadono itself was being locked down in preparation for the inevitable siege. Municipal police, unprepared for such violence in a town with a minimal, nearly non-existent crime rate, were being quickly trained and armed to serve as auxiliary troops. Reserve militia were being activated across the globe.

Marlo shook his head. Rhea glowered at him.

"What? Speak up, Minister. What are you thinking?"

"These are Consortium Armed Forces soldiers, *Czar*. Wearing battle armor. With weapons centuries ahead of ours and two decades fighting organized crime in close quarters throughout charted space. There could be a thousand of our men and they'd still defeat us. This planet belongs to the CPCC now, Rhea."

"I don't know about that, Marlo. Prime Minister Khumalo has been in conferences for the past six hours with marshals and legislators and Prime Minister Soral herself. I have a feeling they'll give us a hand. They don't really want to irritate the independent worlds and the Consortium political entities who are uneasy about its hunger for hegemony, I think."

A communications technician waved her over, and she left Torres with his mouth open as if to reply.

"Yes?"

"It's Andreo Kang, the head of the TRD. He wants to come over and talk to you about a proposal he has."

The Teregana Reto Distrinforma had been very helpful to the government, suppressing its news stories about the crisis to alleviate public tension. Rhea was eager to have Kang's input, as she was sure Khumalo would be as well.

"Tell him to come as quickly as he can."

As she waited, she was approached by Stake President Lau, whose heavily wrinkled face was creased even further by some pressing concern. "Sister, as you're the Czar of Native Affairs, I thought it best to come to you with this issue."

"In any way I can help, Brother, I'll certainly do my best."

"It's the pilot, Brother Sainz. He's been telling people about his vision, and there are murmurings throughout the church, even only after two days."

"I'd argue that he didn't have a *vision*, precisely, but that he is reporting essentially what he witnessed. But that's another matter. What are the murmurings?"

"Disturbing. I've already been trying to calm the concerns of brethren within the stake as concerns the natives themselves and what their existence means for the Novasanktuloj's special place in God's heart. Many are questioning the *smitinfanoj* revelation, and until the Prophet comes out with a statement, I'm reassuring them that God's revealed message in that matter stands. Now, however, things are really getting bad. Some folks are saying, Lord forgive them, that Teri is Christ returned. That she is going to build Zion here, on Terego, and rule humanity."

Rhea took a startled step back. "Come, President Lau, there can't be *that* many people declaring such a heretical idea."

"No. But the idea is spreading, and at the very least, people are beginning to wonder. This ball of power that Sainz claims Teri has: if she is *actually* wielding it, something so similar to what the scriptures describe, then I'm just very nervous about the whole thing. I wish you government people had kept Brother Sainz in custody or something."

"Have you spoken to the Prophet yet?"

"I sent him a message detailing my fears. He wrote back that he is fasting and praying in search of revelation. In the meantime..."

"In the meantime, we Tereganoj are about to have many more worries than the origins of our souls."

At that moment, Prime Minister Khumalo stepped up. "That we are, Czar Kumar. Despite Soral's warnings to him, Captain Phen Quat has also just deployed escape pods. It seems he'll be supporting D'Angelo in his efforts to eliminate whatever imagined threat to the CPCC he has dreamed up. We have shared our debriefing of Carmen Allende with all parties, showing that the illegal chirurgic has acted alone, but the renegade officers are convinced Samanei Koroma is also involved. Captain Mifflin will try to negotiate their withdrawal, but we might be required to allow *more* troops to come to the surface to combat the rogue units already here or on their way."

Rhea let go the breath she'd been holding in a shaky, elongated exhalation. "God be with us. This is war, isn't it?"

Khumalo simply looked at her, dipping his head slightly.

"Andreo Kang is requesting permission to enter," shouted someone.

"Let him in," Rhea yelled back over the commotion. "Send him to conference room B." She explained the motive for the infotainment mogul's arrival, and Khumalo headed with her to meet with the man.

Kang, a tall, thin Kanaano native reputedly with that continent's penchant for pushing the limits of Teregan religious and political norms, wasted no time. "Our only chance here is to get the public riled up. The public here on Terego, and humanity at large."

Khumalo nodded. "I agree. I've been issuing notices through the local wards, but a general broadcast would be better and more effective."

"You misunderstand me, Prime Minister. I don't mean releasing a government bulletin. I mean telling the story. All of it. Everything we know. Full disclosure so that no one ever shuts this up. That's one of the things that worries me about the Consortium. I was just a kid when they found us, but I studied everything I could about them. They were born out of an attempt to control the public's knowledge about that Centauri Rift, that inter-dimensional hole or whatever. Repression of information is their forte. If we let them manage this situation, no one will ever know that the AF invaded here or that we tried to protect the natives. They'll be the victors, and guess who writes history?"

Rhea felt the rightness of Kang's suggestion in her heart. She was tired of lying and subterfuge. Let the truth be told. "Yes, I agree."

Khumalo pursed his lips. "Trust me, I want nothing more than to let everyone know. And I will even accede to it right now. But letting Tereganoj know the whole truth isn't letting everyone know, and the AF has our out-system tunneling satellite under its control. If you're right about them, they won't let that message hit the infotainment nets of the Consortium."

Kang smiled broadly. "That's where they've messed up. Right now the entire CPCC is up in arms about the blockade. They don't know what's going on here, but they are hopping mad."

Khumalo raised an eyebrow. "Do I have a leak in this center? How do you know this? It's true, I'll admit, but as no reports have been coming in…"

"I have my sources. Anyway, the closest CPCC-affiliated world is Gaia. They've only been a protectorate of the Consortium for seven Standard years, and they are out here in the boondocks, outer sectors with us non-CPCC planets. A difficult situation. Well, the press on Gaia has been keeping in touch with TRD off and on for a couple of years now. I," Kang swallowed heavily, "I have a strong enough tunneling station on Lehi to get them a feed from my planet-side transmitter."

Rhea watched Khumalo sit up suddenly, his eyes narrowing as he leaned forward. "You have a tunneling station on one of the moons of the fifth planet of this system? With whose authorization?"

Kang rubbed his fingers against his temples. "I'm going to be frank with you, Prime Minister. The syndicate that tried to set up a colony here left it on Lehi, to communicate with their compatriots or whatever. And I've been using it." He sighed heavily. "You won't like this, but there's no use in keeping it secret. I doubt that the Church or government knows what goes in secluded corners of this enormous planet. I have a huge demand, especially on Kanaano, for entertainment that doesn't fit the government's strict standards for moral purity. So the TRD has been sneaking a feed in from Gaia for the last couple of years. We shut it off when this crisis began, but I can easily dump our reports in their laps whenever you order me to."

Rhea was appalled. She'd never imagined, not even when her daughter's vile, drunken friend had insulted her in this very crisis center, that Terego could harbor such secrets. Her mind briefly tried to picture what sort of entertainment Kang had been covertly providing impious Tereganoj, but she simply couldn't.

A look at Khumalo gave her a greater shock: she'd never seen the planet's leader angrier, not in all the years she'd know him. He frankly looked on the verge of getting up and punching Andreo. Clenching and unclenching his fists upon the polished marble of the conference table, the prime minister managed to spit out a few terse words.

"I have no choice. Do it. And when this is done, I'll deal with you."

Kang said nothing. He seemed neither worried nor happy. Rhea imagined that he probably thought he had done nothing wrong. He might even believe himself a hero for providing a way to get the truth out. But he had to also feel some shame, Rhea told herself. Deep down, he had to hear God's spirit whispering to him, and he had to know his sin.

As the mogul walked out, Khumalo put his face in his hands and wept softly. Rhea didn't know what to do. She felt moved to put her arms around him, and he clung to her like a bereft child.

"Oh, God, Rhea. We have all sullied ourselves with this mess. How much more? How much further will our pride and sin drive us into the mire? Lies, secrets, manipulation: we have been no better than them, no better than Soral or Kang. This is all the consequence of our own stubborn insistence on sin. So much bounty God gave us, but we haven't used it well."

Rhea hugged him tight. "It's okay, Zolile," she whispered. "We are in his hands. He won't let us be completely destroyed, no matter what sins we've committed. If we are repentant and try to set things right, he will forgive us. He already has."

Comforted by her words, Khumalo stood, rubbed his eyes dry and gestured at the door. "Come, Sister. We have a planet to defend, from the Consortium and from sinners like Kang."

Exchanging bitter smiles, they stepped back into the fray together.

INTERCHAPTER H

From: berdyaevn@os1.octant1.gov.af

To: mifflint@shaka.gov.af

Subject: Negotiation

Date: May 8, 2714 15:17:11 (SST)

Captain Mifflin,

I want you to get those crazy bastards to back off. Cajole them, bribe them, whatever it takes. They want to set up a base down there, fine. Just ensure they aren't attacking the Tereganoj or the natives.

Of course, it's probable that won't work. I'm trying to get Soral to release your defensive capabilities so you can send fighters down and corral the gormless wankers. I truly don't want AF troops firing against other AF troops. There's a big-arse mess right now, son. The Consortium is sharply divided on this issue. Some want the invasion to go forward while others want to see D'Angelo, Quat and all their men before a firing squad. Be ready to act quick whenever I give the order.

Commodore Berdyaev

Outer Sector One, Octant One

From: bleguin@upper.diet.cpcc.gov

To: sorall@executive.cpcc.gov

Subject: Invasion and no-confidence

Date: May 8, 2714 23:12:22 (SST)

Prime Minister Soral:

Your party's hold on the Diet and the executive is increasingly tenuous. This outrageous invasion, this act of war with no legislative approval, flies in the face of two hundred years of Consortium law and policy. We demand you withdraw the AF troops from Terego and our ships from that system until a comprehensive plan is drawn up by all branches of government and all seven major parties. Failure to do so will result in an immediate no-confidence vote and a shift of power to those who have humanity's best interests in mind, not hegemonic manipulation.

Bernard Le Guin

Diet Caucus for Decentralization

From: ethnarch@eudamonia.gov.ex

To: sorall@executive.cpcc.gov

Subject: Non-CPCC solidarity

Date: May 9, 2714 03:54:43 (SST)

Prime Minister Soral:

In light of the recent debacle on the sovereign world of Terego, we the undersigned leaders of the below non-Consortium worlds do officially protest the actions of the AF and the inability of the CPCC to keep its watchdogs on a short leash. We remind you of the treaties we all signed with the Consortium, agreeing to not organize ourselves into a separate union of human worlds. But yall's actions of the last few weeks, and specifically of the last thirty-six hours, have jeopardized those agreements. Occupation of Terego would, in our view, invalidate all treaties, obliging us to consolidate and encourage other worlds to join us in hope that our solidarity will protect us from the unconscionable expansionist greed of the CPCC.

George Yiannakos,   Susan Mallory,

Ethnarch of Eudamonia   President General of Erin

Omar al-Mukhtar,   Koyolli Teokechol,

Imam of New Palestine   Hueyi Tlahtoani of Semanawak

From: spinelliu@is17.octant5.gov.af

To: sorall@executive.cpcc.gov

Subject: Non-CPCC solidarity

Date: May 9, 2714 04:15:39 (SST)

Leyla, this is the fourth time I've written to you this week. The pressure's on, dear. You can't hope to continue waging a war against the demimundo if you're going to go soft on us. I know my grandson is out of line in terms of protocol, but he wouldn't need to be if you hadn't tied his hands. You pull those troops off Terego and let those puritans handle the ET situation however they want, your political career is over. The Navarch is already distancing his self from you, I hope you've noticed, as is the General of the Consortium Army is. Don't let those weak-hearted isolationists and progressives lead you into the gravity well of a mass you aren't able to handle, Leyla.

Commodore Ugo Spinelli,

Inner Sector Seventeen, Octant Five

CHAPTER 50

ARTILLERY FIRE BURST NEARBY as a couple of lance-jacks fresh from recon explained the layout of the base. Antonio nodded sagely as dawn took the landscape from blackness to cloudy gloom.

"Just two hundred men, unsuited, no filtering apparatus. Shite, let's gas them. Less of them get hurt. Less of us, too."

The dux grunted his approval. "Then we go in and mop up any that manage to hide."

"As few casualties as we can, Dux. Got it?"

"Affirmative, Captain. Come on, boyos, let's get ready to spray."

As Lachower dashed off with his lance-jacks to their makeshift armory tent, Antonio chimed the *Diomedes*. "Commander, what do you have for me?"

Ashar's voice crackled with light static from the electrical storm above the ground troops. "Great news: Quat's coming. He patched in and wanted to know what the hell you were doing and how. I told him, and he got all hot about joining you. Now they're screaming through those clouds right now, heading for the same quarry."

D'Angelo smiled broadly. Yes. Two hundred AF troops.

It took less than that to kick a thousand yaks into orbit on New Beijing. No way these yokels can put up a fight now.

He already knew what to do with Quat's men: his original plan was to leave a contingent of forty men in the capital while he took the others north to Kumora. Now, however, he could leave fewer men, have Quat do likewise, and as Tony led the advance from the north inward, Phen could take his men into the forest at the point where the locals' communications indicated the main native city was located. From there the other captain could lead a campaign northward, and between the two groups they'd trap the grendels.

"Anything else?"

"We lost the signal on that chirurgic. Winked out of existence. We're getting strange ripples in the magnetic field, though, like tunneling signatures, but more intense, as if energy is being pulled through the field at higher dimensions."

"I'll take care of that nonsense soon enough. Keep me up on what happens."

"Understood."

Within minutes, a half-dozen grunts had deployed from their camp a klick south of the depot and were launching gas globes over the base. Antonio looked at the chronometric display at the left edge of his casque's readouts: in about fifteen minutes the majority of the corpsmen would be unconscious, and his troops could march in, clean up and commandeer the local flivvers. They'd wait until Quat rendezvoused with them, and then Antonio would set his plan in motion. He'd go into those dark woods and hunt Samanei down. If he had to face grendels or whatever aliens had given Samanei the weapon that chirurgic said she was using, he would. He would see her punished for her crimes though it cost him his life.

CHAPTER 51

FOR HOURS SHALURA WATCHED as light danced across Daenzhelo's head, the lithe highborn's limbs twitching slightly from time to time. In the unnatural silence of the cave, she watched and she listened, trying to hear the plan her dead lover's voice murmured deep inside her mind. Many times she brought the stone blade to her throat, determined to finally heed the lessons of her people's lore, understanding at last the nadir of rebellious tragedy she had reached in her prideful rejection of tradition. But something always stayed her hand, the one feeling she had no right to, the very emotion that had brought her to this impasse: hope.

Her eyes were shut when she heard the creaking and the yawn: Daenzhelo had ceased communicating with whatever spirits guided her. More fluid and powerful in her movements despite spending one-fourth of a day lying in the same position, the ingan leapt across the stone floor toward her, burbling and singing.

"Oh, Shal, it is so… wonderful! This light-shiner is for teaching me lots of ways of fighting, and now I'm knowing techniques that I never dreamed of! I asked if you could do it too, but my father's image has said that your brain is different and cannot getting the images like mine."

Shalura stood and set her hand on Daenzhelo's curly black fur, which always appeared ready fly from her head in a thousand directions. Shalura found she couldn't caress the highborn's ears this way as they were low on the sides of her head. With a start, she jerked her claw away.

What are you thinking, a stern voice demanded, *touching her like that? You aren't bonded to her!*

With that indignant shout, Shalura found the barriers were gone. She could hear the other voice now, as clear as day.

"What's wrong, Shal? What are you be carrying that knife in your claws for? And you look afraid or something. Talk to me! I know you are upset about your people and the deception, but there is more to life than the tribe. You continue, and the past stays behind you forever. You have to leave it staying there, Shal. I am knowing this well."

Shalura's tail thumped a light denial. "First of all, the past makes the present. I cannot ignore it, Lady. And you claim there is more to life than the tribe? You have no idea what you are saying, Daenzhelo. I am a drone. The tribe is all I have. My highborn, my male, my tribe. Without them, I am nothing."

"Ah, no, not again with all that 'drones don't having souls' stupidness!"

"I am a drone, Daenzhelo, and I am telling you that we do not have souls."

Daenzhelo plucked at her frizzy fur in a way that Shalura had come to understand showed frustration. "Stupid Shalura, you keep saying *I* this and *I* that. Well, who is the *I* being if you don't have a soul? Tell me that, would you?"

"It is only a word, a label the tribe allows this drone before you to use. But I am only what the tribe puts in me: the lessons, lore, spirit voices and skills that the tribe imbues me with. Wisdom comes in, wise actions come out. Food comes in, excrement comes out. I am just like a made thing that takes what another puts in it and turns it into something useful for the tribe, like my excrement is used to fertilize our fields. I have no soul, Daenzhelo, no existence without my people."

Leaning her head far back, her eyes closing, her tail bending up in anguish, Shalura heard Daenzhelo attempt to laugh like one of the People. The sound was harsh and ugly, and the drone wished she could stop her friend from ever making it again.

"What you planning to do, kill yourself?"

Shalura slowly bared her teeth in the affirmative.

"What?" Daenzhelo began to gush away in her native speech, furiously. After a moment she switched back to the People's tongue. "You're speaking serious, aren't you? Why?"

"Because my tribe is no more. It betrayed itself. I cannot go south and destroy those who remain. I have no purpose anymore. My voices tell me I must do what tradition demands."

Daenzhelo grabbed her chest fur with a claw covered in black skin and pulled her viciously down to the highborn's eye-level.

"Let your voices and your traditions go smother themselves in excrement, Shalurazhox: listen to *my* voice. Live for yourself, you stupid, beautiful warrior."

"That's not enough," whispered Shalura.

"Then what is?" Danezhelo screamed, her voice squeaking like a bird at the end.

Now, whispered her gorgeous male. *This is the moment.*

"If a highborn bonded me to her, I would be part of her tribe. My life would have meaning."

"Well, come on! Let's going and finding a highborn who will do that!"

Shalura's tail thumped gently on the stone floor. "You do not understand, Daenzhelo. It would take days, and then we would only reach my enemies, servants of that shiny insect thing. I would not want to be with one of them, and they would not have me, the hated slayer of their false prophet. No, there is only one highborn here that can sustain my hopes."

Daenzhelo said nothing. Shalura knew little of ingan emotions, but the diminutive highborn warrior seemed stunned as she realized what Shalura meant. Taking a step back, Daenzhelo grabbed a hold of one of the small trees that held the *guns* and bent her head toward the ground, breathing quickly. After a while, the small one lifted her face, streaked with water from her eyes, and spoke very quietly and without a single error.

"You've been sitting here all this time, fighting your need to kill yourself, haven't you?"

"Yes, Lady."

"I made you wait hours. I could have awakened to find you dead."

"Many times I nearly cut my throat and offered my blood to the tribe's spirit. The voices shrieked at me to do it. But shamefully, I had hope. Xiggèr'enth was whispering to me. When I saw you just now, I understood. You can save me from my traditions by using them."

Daenzhelo continued in her halfling voice, staring quietly into the distance as if she were talking only to herself. "You know, ingan hear voices, too. Most of us think they are just different pieces of us, talking to each other. But my tribe believes that sometimes God mixes her voice in there, too."

Shalura's breath caught in her mighty lungs: she felt she would die of the emotional strain alone. "And what does God tell you to do now, my Lady?"

"There are things you must understand: we cannot have the sort of relationship that other highborn have with their drones. You and I are very different, our people are very different and I... I don't know. I'm not sure how

I am feeling about all that. We will deal with it later, I am thinking. Also, my tribe's ways are different, and we bond for eternity in a holy building. But I have been thinking for a long time now. I also do not belong in my tribe. They will not want me because the 'shiny insect' helped make me. I must make a place for myself somewhere else, Shalurazhox. A tribeless highborn and a tribeless drone. What does your lore saying about that?"

"That is how the nations were formed. The siblings left their tribes to destruction and came here to the great, shadow-veiled forest. They began anew. They made their own tribes."

Daenzhelo let the shiny tree go and put her hands, which Shalura saw were trembling out of fear or nervousness or holy wonder, to the sides of her oval head. Her claws slid down her flat cheeks, the rosy-brown, furless cheeks that Shalura couldn't help but find beautiful in their utter strangeness. Daenzhelo stepped toward Shalura, and the drone's hearts pounded mercilessly within their bony cells.

"I have never had a best friend, Shal. Not one like you. I would be willing to create a tribe with you, a tribe that would make its own lore and its own purpose."

Here it comes.

"Would you—oh, what must I say—would you get bonded to me?"

Shalura fell into a crouch. "A highborn never asks, Lady: she commands."

Daenzhelo clenched her hands into fists and shook her head. "A new tribe, Shal. New ways. Will you be my bonded drone?"

Her teeth glistening in the artificial light, Shalurazhox curled back her thin, black lips and murmured, "Yes. Forever."

CHAPTER 52

AND WHAT DOES GOD TELL YOU TO DO NOW, MY LADY?

Miwa had never been a particularly fanatical Novasanktulo. She believed, to be sure, perhaps more than her overly devout sister. But the trappings and ceremony of her religion, as austere as they were, had always seemed superfluous to her. She depended on what the *Book* said and what her heart told her. Mormons felt strongly that God revealed Himself to his children singly, leading them down a path of His choosing by means of this spiritual communion. Miwa had been guided in the past by His still voice as He guided her through school and sports, and she bent all her soul to Him now, straining to know His will.

She's my friend, Lord. The most important person to me besides my family. I don't know what this bonding entails, and if you find it sinful or wrong in any way, please lead me to a better solution. I don't want to see her die: I want to teach her your ways, Lord, I want her to accept she has a soul

and prepare the way for that soul's joyful existence within an incorruptible

body. Do I love her? I suppose I do. Bonding doesn't seem like marriage,

though, so maybe what I feel for her is enough. Maybe not. But by doing it,

I save her. And I need her, Lord: you and I both know that. I'm a clone. No

human is ever going to accept me the way they used to. I'll always be an

outsider, just like her. I'm hoping you have a better plan for us.

Through tears, Miwa looked at her friend, stripes on her short
muzzle moving rapidly as her quickened breath inflated and deflated her
cheeks. Looking into those deep, soulful eyes, the human teen knew exactly
what she had to do. In the innermost parts of her spirit she understood that
her road would lead her and Shalura far from their people and toward a
destiny they would perhaps never comprehend. Full of awed anxiety, she
gripped the weapon rack tighter and spoke.

"There are things you must understand: we cannot have the sort of
relationship that other highborn have with their drones. You and I are very
different, our people are very different and I... I don't know." The memory
of Shalura and Tenti having relations flashed in her mind: she knew that
highborn only mated once a year, but obviously this bonding would have
to be different. She'd cross that bridge when she came to it, with God's
guidance. "I'm not sure how I am feeling about all that. We will deal with
it later, I am thinking. Also, my tribe's ways are different, and we bond for

eternity in a holy building. But I have been thinking for a long time now. I also do not belong in my tribe. They will not want me because the 'shiny insect' helped make me. I must make a place for myself somewhere else, Shalurazhox. A tribeless highborn and a tribeless drone. What does your lore saying about that?"

Shalura's eyes burned with the hope she had spoken of, and more tears blurred Miwa's vision. "That is how the nations were formed. The siblings left their tribes to destruction and came here to the great, shadow-veiled forest. They began anew. They made their own tribes."

Miwa released the gun rack and rubbed her hands down her cheeks, trying to pull herself together. *Their own tribes.* Her friend needed Miwa's strength, just as Miwa had depended on the drone time and again.

At school and church, Miwa had made acquaintances, had played and laughed. But ultimately, her competitive heart had made them into opponents. To be respected, but defeated.

Shalura was different. Miwa realized that she couldn't imagine life without the drone any more.

"I have never had a best friend, Shal. Not one like you. I would be willing to create a tribe with you, a tribe that would make its own lore and its own purpose." Miwa felt very awkward, much as she had the year before when she'd asked Raoul Peters to the school dance. Of course, this was no date she was working up to. Her parents had lectured her time and again on the responsibilities that came with a serious relationship. "Would you—oh, what must I say—would you get bonded to me?"

Shalura crouched suddenly, as if in deference. "A highborn never asks, Lady: she commands."

Miwa felt a slight surge of anger: she would have to teach her friend to abandon that ridiculous way of thinking. Balling her gloved hands into fists, she shook her head. "A new tribe, Shal. New ways. Will you be my bonded drone?"

A smile of acceptance spreading her muzzle, Shalura murmured happily, "Yes. Forever."

Miwa wondered whether that was all. Didn't a priestess have to say some words or something? Suddenly, she got the jitters.

What in the world am I doing? This is nuts! How can this ever work?

Shalura stood and placed a hand again on her head, and the solid weight both soothed the soreness left from the collision with the stalactite and calmed her worries. Somehow the two of them would make it work, she believed with the determined, optimistic idealism of a fresh adolescent mind. "I am tired, are you not?"

"Yes. I am extremely tired. The shiner only works on my brain, but my body feels exhausted, too. It's only a trick, but it might as well be real."

Miwa found a bedroll behind the frame and laid it out near the entrance. She collapsed onto it, only yanking off gloves and boots: she had no desire to slip back into her smelly clothes and wouldn't have felt right sleeping naked. The suit would have to do for pajamas, she thought, and giggled. Shalura slowly knelt down and then curled around her, and sleep came quickly amidst the woody scent of her bonded drone.

The next morning, Miwa awoke early and greedily ate some of the fruit paste and dried meat she found in Shalura's pack. When her drone got up about fifteen minutes later, Miwa grabbed the largest pulse rifle from the rack and put it in the warrior's arms.

"First thing, you need to learn to use this *gun* in case we have to fight ingan with black animal skins like mine. This is a powerful reed that shoots balls of light at your enemy. It will kick back at you as it throws the light, so you must hold it firmly."

What a silly thing to say. It looks like a toy in her arms.

"How can light hurt my enemy? It annoys the eye, but little more."

"I guess it's more like fire than light. It impacts like a big stone, though, throwing your enemy back and damaging her if she's not wearing her skins. You can change the intensity here: this round thing turns around to the power you want."

Miwa dialed the pulse level to off and set the rifle to practice mode. "Like practice spears, now the gun won't hurting us when you use it. It will kicking like normal, though." She grabbed a target projector and holographed a man against the metal entranceway. "While I am with the light-shiner, I want you to be practicing. Stand by my chair and aim at this *ingan*, then press this nodule here. The image will show you with a red dot where you would hit him if you were really using the gun. Then a new *ingan* will come. Only stop when you are able to hitting him wherever you want to."

Shalura smiled affirmatively. "Yes, Lady."

As Miwa started to sit down, she suddenly realized how dangerous this situation could become. Grabbing the rifle, she locked it into training mode, coded to her thumbprint. All she needed was for Shalura to blast a hole in the cavern.

Leaving her drone to discover the finer points of marksmanship, Miwa entered the faux training program again. During the jungle and desert modules yesterday, she'd begun to contemplate their next move. As she had guessed since the revelation of her father's identity, the CPCCAF would be arriving soon. Kyr had said the AF had been looking for her dad for a long time, and now they knew where he was. They wanted him to tell them where Samanei was. It was clear to Miwa that she and Shalura would have to get to Brando first and protect him from both the People and the AF. He had told her years ago that his ship, the one he'd come to Terego on, was stored away at the immigration ministry's principal warehouse. If the three of them could get to it…

But he despises the People.

She suddenly realized that she had never thought about her parents' reaction to her bonding, which they were liable to see as marriage without their blessing, to a non-believer and alien to boot!

Well, they're just going to have to get used to the idea, and Dad will just have to swallow his prejudices, or I'll knock him out and drag him with me. It's not right for him to judge all the People based on how one tribe has treated him.

She returned to the jungle module; it was closest to Terego's own forests. "Dad," she called.

Brando's avatar winked into existence in front of her, just to the left of a gnarled bole. "Yes, Miwa?"

"Some changes: I need these trees to be another sixty meters taller, and their top limbs to weave together into a canopy that keeps out most of the light." Within seconds, she was standing in Teregan gloom. "Also, my attackers: you could make them AF soldiers instead of mafia agents?"

"Yes. You're facing problems with the AF?"

"Not yet, but will soon, I think. Okay, then. What's first?"

"Ground attack. Get into the trees and take out as many as you can before they start coming up, then keep moving so that you're not an easy target."

Miwa keyed her casque into place, slid her rifle into the magnetized scabbard on her back, and leapt at some trailing vines just as Consortium Army troops came creeping stealthily into the forest. She scrambled up to a branch and opened fire, disabling about ten before the others took cover or started to come up after her.

When she'd picked off as many as she thought she'd be able to, she began to hurl herself from tree to tree, using a combination of her sports and martial arts skills and the techniques Shalura and her father's avatar had taught her. Thudding grenades into branches behind and below her, she sent soldiers spilling to the ground meters below. After an hour and a half, "wounded" by enemy fire, but free of her attackers, Miwa slumped to a sprawling stop on a wide bough.

"Not bad," Brando said, appearing next to her. "Now that you've finished basic level, time to move onto intermediate. After that, you get to see how the AF would really fight."

Miwa sighed heavily, hanging her head for a second.

Basic level? Oh, Lord.

Laughing weakly, she slowly regained her feet. "You never let up, huh? Well, refresh me, dad, and let's get to it."

She found herself back at the beginning, feeling energized and pumped up as a faint rustling came from behind her.

Okay. Time to kick more butt.

She crouched low and pounced.

CHAPTER 53

«VESSELS ARE BRAKING IN THIS PLANET'S ATMOSPHERE.»

Teri stopped talking to the high priestess of the thirty-fifth village she'd visited in the past thirty hours since she'd begun her unification circuit. The pace was brutal, but she already had one hundred percent of the villages visited in agreement. The problem was that she'd have to come back once she'd finished and transport the representatives south to the meeting place. The sphere had told her it was working on a way to speed that process up. Now she *knew* they needed to move more quickly.

Vessels?

«Small ships, holding three of your species each, as well as many weapons. There are thirty of these vessels presently approaching a point south of your principal city.»

Shit.

It had to be the AF ships that were in orbit, sending troops to Diadono. From Kyr, Teri and the sphere had learned of Captain Antonio D'Angelo's fears about Terego, at least what could be gleaned of them from planetary communications, which the chirurgic had been monitoring for years. The AF had apparently decided to believe his theories and strike preemptively.

Nothing I can do now. This is too important, and it'll take another day and a half, if we push as hard as we can. What are we going to do about the representatives? Villages closer to the meeting grounds can walk, but the rest? Have you figured that out?

«The Urim has been calculating the position of the villages relative to the village you want them to meet at, given the information in the mechanical being. It will not be easy, but we can pull the representatives through.»

Images of natives winking out and into existence, moving through a dizzying higher-dimensional kaleidoscope nearly instantaneously.

You can fenestrate them that short of a distance? I don't know much about physics, but that seems pretty damn incredible! How advanced are you people, anyway?

There was the usual silence.

Teri finished her discussion with the high priestess and her firstmale, then collected Ùshëshajirh and moved on. As they skimmed the canopy beneath the blackness of a starless, cloud-heavy sky, Teri shared the information about the impending invasion with Ùshë.

"Once we have united the tribes, Çèrhingÿl, we can perhaps send drones to help protect your tribe's village or drive out the invaders if they have already breached the guard," the future ruler of the six nations suggested.

"That's a good idea, though we have to contact my tribe first so they will not be surprised or angered when the drones arrive."

"Of course. Perhaps you can use the opportunity to craft some agreement between your tribe and the nations. You have told me that your tribe rejects many of the hostile ways of other ingan: perhaps united, our peoples can expel the invaders and stop them from returning."

«She is very wise.»

That she is. I'm so glad we've got her with us.

"Excellent plan. I can serve as your ambassador to the ingan, if you wish it."

"You honor me, Firstborn, by pretending my humble position is of import. You have my thanks and adoration."

Teri lifted one hand from the sphere and touched Ùshë's arm.

"You are my friend, not my servant. Without you, I could never do this."

Can we fenestrate drones to Diadono?

«How many?»

At least two troops. Ninety-six.

«Doing so will push the limits of the sphere's capabilities, unless the pull is done in stages. Scenes of twelve groups of eight appearing at the city's edge one at a time.»

Yes, that'll work. Two and a half days to finish this, convene the council, elect Ùshë as head. I'll get in touch with the Prime Minister and offer our help in exchange for a treaty or something.

«If the invaders reach your capital city today, that means you may have no one to negotiate with when the time comes.»

Let's pray they can hold the AF troops off long enough. If not, if the city is occupied and the leaders imprisoned or whatever, you can help me find them and bust them out. But we have to help them, Urim. Tereganoj and the People are going to have to share this planet forever, and we need to start building bridges now.

«We've told you the sort of elevation needed by these natives requires decades of isolation.»

Yes, but they're not going to give us a chance to isolate ourselves if we aren't allies. Besides, we need them to help keep the CPCC at arm's length.

Waves of doubt. Images of gray pods dipping toward the water of the abandoned quarry.

«Your people cannot keep them at bay now.»

With my help, they'll be able to. You know it's the only way. You can see into my mind. You can see the plan forming there, and you know I'm right.

Dismay.

«Even if you can retrieve it, you cannot give it to them. Doing so violates protocol and procedure.»

It's either that or you spend generations fighting the CPCC. They're going to want something in exchange for leaving us alone, Urim. Unless you have a better idea.

There was no answer but a sense of resignation.

CHAPTER 54

ONE OF THE MONITORS IN THE CRISIS CONTROL CENTER displayed a live feed from TRD, which had been broadcasting for the last twenty-eight hours every scrap of information on the present emergency. As could be expected, public expression, running the gamut from indignation to relief and fear, had been extremely strong. Most disturbing of all had been the communiqué from the regional governor of Kanaano stating that that continent would not be sending its corpsmen to support Zarahemla, as the planetary government had been acting secretly and in violation of treaties with the CPCC.

Rhea could see anger and frustration seething beneath the calm surface Khumalo presented to his subordinates. Under his nose, a rebellion had been growing, and for it to start coming to a head in the moment of Terego's greatest need was disastrous.

What the monitor presently displayed underscored just how tenuous their position was: at the edges of the city, local police and corpsmen were trying to stave off the encroachment of the vastly superior Consortium Army soldiers, now doubled in number since Captain Phen Quat had joined Antonio.

After the taking of the depot, the entire executive council had held their breath, waiting. Then word came that another wave of ships had splashed down at the quarry. Rhea supposed that D'Angelo's group had rendezvoused with Quat's at the depot, coming up with whatever insidious plan they thought to use to quell the imaginary Teregan-Underworld alliance. Now here they were, and the Czar of Native Affairs didn't have much hope for the city of her birth despite the promises that had come to them all day from Captain Mifflin and Prime Minister Soral.

"They've broken through!" someone yelled, and a mass of people pressed toward the monitors as they all displayed a large image broadcast by TRD of AF troops, some on large crisis ministry trucks loaded with weapons, others tramping down the main street of Diadono, rushing in smaller units into buildings, securing the area.

Behind her, Rhea heard a commotion as the corpsmen assigned to the ministry building posted additional guards outside the main doors, secured them, and posted a heavy security detail inside the center itself.

For the next two hours, the center watched in hushed, bustling anticipation as the troops made their way through the cobbled streets, stone and timber buildings, expansive green parks, and spacious homes of Diadono on their inexorable way toward the executive complex at the heart of the city. Civilian and police gunfire the soldiers shrugged off like gnats as they disarmed the populace one citizen at a time, often simply breaking the technologically inferior weapons they confiscated, but typically stowing civilian arms in crates on the stolen trucks.

Marlo was right, reflected Rhea somberly, her fragile hope slowly suffocated by reality. *We never had a chance. We aren't warriors. None of us is.*

Like most of the other Tereganoj in the crisis ministry building, she quickly made a call to check on her loved ones: Chiho said that while Jakobo and the Nishiguchi children were a little startled by the brusque inspection of the house, they were all fine. As she said a rapid "I love you" to her son, Rhea's eyes never left the screens and the unstoppable approach of the AF troops they displayed.

Finally, the roving camera operators, all four of them, followed some fifty or more soldiers to the marble steps of the Ministry of Crises. The AF apparently didn't want the complete violation of Terego's sovereignty broadcast or recorded, because one of the gray-armored figures gestured at the locals and the signal went dead. Muffled sounds of firing came from outside as technicians hurried to put external surveillance cameras on screen. When the image flickered to life seconds later, Rhea gasped: all twenty of the corpsmen had been subdued and cuffed, and the soldiers were preparing to cut through the heavy steel door.

The door to the inner offices creaked open, and the mellifluous voice of the Prophet poured in.

"Don't resist."

Rhea turned around and looked into his calm eyes. The room fell absolutely silent, all bustle stilled by the man's presence. Khumalo stepped toward him with plaintive gaze.

"Are you certain?"

"There is a greater good here than fighting off the Consortium. We must put down our weapons and let them seize the city. Let our obedience be a lesson to them, and let us begin to show repentance, rejecting our stubborn pride. When we feel humility in our hearts and not haughtiness, then will God work through us."

At a nod from the Prime Minister, De Waal thumbed a channel open to his men. "Open the doors, and surrender your weapons to them. Let them come in. We're waiting in the center for Captains D'Angelo and Quat."

Rhea couldn't keep her eyes off of the Prophet: something had changed, as if he'd shrugged off worries that still weighted the shoulders of others, like Khumalo and De Waal. His gaze flitted across the room and fell on her, and he smiled.

"Teri," he mouthed, and a thrill went through Rhea's soul.

God has spoken to him: Teri is going to make the difference here.

She felt blessed despite her sorrow and terror.

Minutes later, Antonio D'Angelo walked into the crisis center with an escort. He was wearing the same gray body armor as his soldiers, but his casque was retracted and his nearly purple eyes scanned the group before him sternly. At his side towered a thin, bald man, probably Phen Quat, his weaker muscles helped in pulling against the 1.1 gees on Terego by a shockingly black battle suit.

As he inclined his head to mutter, Quat's crown, tattooed with the Consortium eagle, heralded the arrival of the CPCC to the inner sanctums of the Teregan government.

Khumalo approached them both, but addressed only D'Angelo.

"We plan no more resistance. Your orders will be obeyed, but at gunpoint, I want you to recognize, and in violation of what your own government has commanded. Let me make one thing clear: don't harm my people. We are cooperating in a peaceable way with this invasion, and under every charter of conflict in existence, you must treat us with dignity and humanity."

The inverted Vs of Captain D'Angelo's eyebrows knotted up as he glared at the Prime Minister.

"I will treat yall with justice, and my men will do the same. More than yall could say."

"*Kia stranga justico, la via,*" the Minister of Public Health muttered.

"What?"

Rhea couldn't keep quiet. Knowing humility didn't require allowing lies to go unchallenged.

"He says yall have a strange idea of justice. He's right. Coming in, without any hard evidence, and taking over the government of an independent world. That's what they teach yall at AF academies now?"

"I assure you, we have evidence."

"Of what? That we hid the existence of the Native Teregans from yall? Yes, we did, but these other things you think we did, all that nonsense about collaborating with the demimundo..."

Antonio shook his head in disgust. "Yall are still going to deny it, I know. Yall have nothing to do with the fusion explosion near Kumora, nothing to do with Samanei Koroma using a non-human weapon while she plots with the grendels."

"That Koroma woman is *not* on this planet," De Waal interjected.

Antonio clenched a gloved fist. "According to a transmission from Kumora Mountain, she is. That yall want to pretend otherwise is just typical of yall's mentality. I imagine she has told yall she's Christ come again, and yall have eaten it up."

The Prophet stiffened, and Rhea butted in again. "Besmirch our honor, call us criminals, but don't accuse us of heresy that you don't even understand. No one here thinks that Christ has come again, much less in the form of a woman with mental illness. I think you're letting your own beliefs color the way you view us."

"I don't have any 'beliefs,' Czar Kumar."

"Sure you do. That you want to pretend otherwise is just typical of *your* mentality."

Quat rested a hand on D'Angelo's shoulder, giving the captain of the *Diomedes* a look that seemed to say *let's move on*. Antonio smiled falsely and shrugged.

"All irrelevant. We're already gathering the other members of your government at the legislative complex, and we have most of the executive council here, right? Captain Quat, you want to do the honors?"

"Certainly. Under authority of the charter of the Consortium of Planets, Corporations and Colonies Armed Forces, I place yall, the members of the executive council of Terego, under military arrest for violation of the Ursae Majoris Treaty of 2688. Specific charges include hiding and lying about an alien species and artifacts on your world. In addition, yall are in violation of the Jitsu Convention's terms, which prohibit collusion twixt human worlds allied with the CPCC and any demimundo group. Until these charges are investigated fully, yall will remain under armed guard in this building, which is now passing to CPCC control. Please instruct your technicians to cooperate with us while we conduct our investigation. We'll coordinate from this room, and we need technical support."

Khumalo inclined his head with solemn resignation. Rhea understood what he hoped: that in their investigation, the AF would find nothing and Terego would be exonerated, except for the cover-up.

De Waal relayed orders to his men in Esperanto, and though obviously reluctant, they all nodded or saluted their obedience. Before the ministers could be herded into whatever room they'd be kept in, a communications operator called out.

"Dissendado el flughaveno!"

"No more Esperanto, people!" ordered D'Angelo. "If you don't speak Standard, get someone else to speak for you."

"He says there's a transmission from the flying haven, uh, from the airport," another technician translated with a thick accent. Antonio and Quat exchanged knowing glances.

"Patch it through."

A crackling voice boomed cheerily into the room. "Under control, Captains. Gassed the lot of them. Yall want I should leave a detail here?"

"Just a squad," Antonio answered. "You put the civilians in a single room?"

"Yes, sir: the cafeteria. Plenty of food that way, and a couple of bans for they could relieve their selves. They're going to be fine a couple days."

"Tell your men to be sure that any approaching craft know they're going to be shot down if they attempt to land, Dux. If they don't listen, we fire near enough so they feel the heat. Redirect them south, to Nauvoo. By the time any troops drive up from there, everything's going to be in hand."

"And if they keep coming even after my boyos warn them?"

Antonio's eyes closed for a second. "Then we let them land, but not disembark. Quat's going to be here in the command center, and he can get your squad back up fast to keep them contained and on board."

"Got you. So, rendezvous at 16:10 local?"

"Yes. Flivvers will drop down at the coordinates I gave you in order to pick you and your remaining men up. Till then, keep safe. D'Angelo out."

Rhea didn't want to, but she found herself reevaluating her brother-in-law. He had pulled off this invasion with hardly a drop of blood spilled, and he seemed determined not to hurt anyone if he could help it.

Not blood thirsty. Paranoid, but probably a good man, at heart. Just obsessed with crime and justice. Because of Brando? Could he be so determined not to be like his big brother that he's gone to another extreme?

Without warning, Marlo Torres spoke up. "Sirs, I would like to volunteer to remain behind in the center and help Captain Quat. I know the equipment and the technicians, and I want to help make this investigation as painless and quick as possible."

Someone made a hissing noise. *Snake.*

Antonio nodded. "Good idea, Minister Torres. I just hope all your people are as cooperative as you. Too bad yall weren't that way from the beginning. Phen, I leave you to it. You've got your men, and the other two teams are getting prepped. We'll stay in constant contact, using the AF equipment and the local stuff too. You can track us on this holographic map: let me know the minute Mifflin starts trying to assert himself."

They clasped forearms and saluted; then Antonio took one last look at Rhea. "You could've avoided all of this, you know. It was your duty to do it. You're a lawyer, and you're supposed to uphold the law."

Though a dozen retorts rolled through her mind, Rhea knew he was right, to some degree, so she said nothing, and he simply walked out with a rolling gait that bespoke assured self-righteousness.

Oh, yes: you have your beliefs, and your God, too, Antonio. If you obey her well, maybe we'll actually survive. There are worse things to serve than justice, I suppose.

AFTER HAVING CIVILIANS LIKE THE PROPHET escorted from the building and confiscating the personal communication devices of those remaining, Quat ordered a couple of his men to conduct the executive council to the large meeting hall on the second floor. They settled in to discuss and await the outcome of the conflict. The conversation was heated, and many accusations were made, mostly against Marlo Torres.

As Khumalo seemed too lost in thought, Minister of State Inyang tried to get them to calm down.

"Having Torres in there is a good idea. I wouldn't be so quick to judge him: he's likely just trying to have a positive influence on this situation. I understand your suspicions; after all, the brother has always been rather vocally pro-Consortium. But he is a Teregano, and a Novasanktulo, and I think we need to give him a chance."

Everyone nodded in acceptance of the rebuke, and the topic changed to what D'Angelo's plan was and what the CPCC's reaction to it was likely to be.

"I'm no expert in these matters," Rhea opined, "but it looks like the captain is sending two teams into the forest, which means they might bump into Teri or Brando."

"I hope for our sakes and for that of the CPCC that captain doesn't start slaughtering natives," the health minister said. "The first alien race humanity encounters, and we send our craziest representative to meet them."

Rhea shook her head. "No. I don't think he's crazy. Deluded, maybe, but I imagine he'll only attack if he's attacked. He's looking for Samanei Koroma, not trying to commit genocide."

Roberto De Waal raised an eyebrow. "Defending the man who would see your husband jailed for life on an asteroid somewhere, Czar? I would've never imagined."

"He thinks he's doing what's right," Rhea replied. "There is always hope for such men, if they can be shown what's *really* right."

The minister of communication and transport, Van Tam Ngo, stood and went to the door, pressing his ear against it. "What I want to know is whether these two are going to shut down the whole planet, or whether they're just concerned with this area."

"Probably just here," Inyang offered. "They want whatever caused that fusion explosion and whatever illegals they find in the forest."

Ngo nodded. "The TRD's transmission will probably not be interrupted, and it's being broadcast off-world, isn't that so?"

Khumalo's jaw tightened.

"Yes," Rhea answered.

"So, in addition to whatever data Mifflin is giving them, the whole Consortium knows what just happened here. When are they planning on doing something about it? It looks suspiciously like they want this invasion to continue."

"According to Soral and Mifflin, the Shaka was preparing to send fighters and troops to the surface if the situation worsened," De Waal reminded them.

"I'd say it has worsened quite a bit," muttered the health minister. "But I don't see any soldiers coming to our rescue."

Zolile Khumalo finally spoke. "Patience. You all need to have patience. Brother Disbergen said to cooperate and learn humility, and that's what we'll do."

A technician brought them food then, and some news: "Minister Torres says to tell you that he's contacted your families and let them know that you're under house arrest, but okay nonetheless." Inyang cast slightly scolding glances at Marlo's detractors, as though saying *I told you so.* "He says that everyone is still fine, except... Minister De Waal, I'm afraid your wife's having problems with her heart, probably because of the soldiers barging into your home. She was taken to the hospital, but they report she's in stable condition."

Roberto's ashen face paled even further, and as he lowered his forehead against the burnished wood of the conference table, the other ministers gathered around and knelt beside him to pray, both for Susana De Waal's health and for the wellbeing of all humans on Terego.

Rhea nodded to herself even as she joined them. Prayer was all that was left them. Zolile was right: all their speculation and planning was moot. She wasn't terribly worried, though. Disbergen had confirmed what she'd already guessed.

The one person who mattered now, besides God himself, was Teri.

CHAPTER 55

AS ANTONIO APPROACHED THE TEMPORARY CAMP at the edge of town, he saw that Quat's b-dux, Vladas Bulavas, had the men bedding down in shifts so they'd be rested for the push into the forest tonight. Quat had agreed with D'Angelo that, given the small three- to four-day window of opportunity before XID arrived, they would have to live through twenty-three-hour stints, only breaking for five-hour rest periods with overlapping one-hour watches, and they would have to push the battle suits' muscle enhancement capabilities to their furthermost limit to finish the campaign in time. Aside from the need to secure the capital city before departure and to provide the Army pilots time to master the local transports, Antonio also wanted to start at night because the reported gloom of the forest would be nearly impenetrable darkness then, and his troops would have the advantage of their IR filters.

Phen had praised the directness and simplicity of the plan: Bulavas would lead seventy of the *George Washington's* troops roughly eastward to the coordinates that AF intel reported marked the village where the Teregano teens had been held captive. The dux would secure the town, looking specifically for humans or advanced artifacts, and then turn northward toward the region in which the strange energy signatures had been detected. Tony was going to take the local flivvers to the southern skirt of the mountain, search the area of the explosion, then enter the forest at its northern edge, hopefully running into the yaks and their schizo leader right off, but more likely trapping them by backing them southward into the approaching force under Vlad's command.

Antonio himself rested, sleeping about two hours, then woke to help supervise the moving of troops they'd left at the depot to various posts throughout the city that would be coordinated from Quat's HQ at the crisis ministry. Once the flivvers had dropped the men off, they were loaded with the equipment the soldiers going northward would need. By 15:45, all the troops had broken into their respective teams, and fifty of the sixty-five that would be under Antonio's direct command boarded three of the four transports: the fourth was sent to the airport to pick up the dux and the fifteen soldiers there with him.

Antonio reviewed status reports during the two-trip across the enormous, ice-floe-sporting lake and over the dark green, impenetrable canopy of the forest. Despite the transmitter's extreme power, Vlad's group had difficulty sending and receiving messages due to the density of the foliage and the atmospheric conditions. They were going to have to do as intel said the local corpsmen had done: stop periodically to deploy a broadcaster above the canopy. The major drawback to such a strategy was that during battle or crisis immediate, real-time communication would be impossible.

The transports set down finally at the base of the mountain, in a sort of broad, shallow canyon half a kilometer from the river that spilled down Kumora's side and flowed into the forest that loomed to the south. The flivvers had little scanning equipment, just basic radar and EM detectors, so he ordered a couple of his comtechs to perform a thorough sweep of the mountain side for human life signs or any non-natural artifacts, refined metals, quantum disturbances.

Results came sooner than he'd hoped.

"Captain, there's two anomalies to report: a shielded cave about four hundred meters square and a couple of electronic devices descending the mountain a little to the west of us, sir."

"Descending? By themselves?"

"No, sir: there's strange bio-readings, sir."

"Cross-reference with the reports sent from the local health ministry to the AF."

"Already doing that, sir. Sir, the readings appear to match. We got us two clooties coming down, carrying what they look to be a com rig and some sort of medical apparatus, sir."

"Clooties, Lance-jack?"

"Yes, sir: the grendels, sir. We have renamed them clooties, sir. You know, devils, sir."

Antonio nodded and sent his dux with twenty men to investigate. As they climbed the ridge to the east, Antonio assigned a decurion to take his platoon up the slope to the shielded cave, which didn't seem large enough to hold a threat the five of them couldn't handle. His other men he sent on brief recon in the flivvers or deployed at the forest's edge in preparation for the incursion.

Lachower returned first, with news that the two grendels had attacked and been killed.

"Weird thing is, Basan here says one of them clooties was speaking Baryogo while it was dying, Captain."

Antonio turned to Basan, a young erk from Mars. "Really? What did it say?"

"Sir, it grunted 'kotoran ingan' at me when I approached it, sir. 'Shitty human,' sir. It insulted me with its last breath, sir."

Antonio pondered this for a moment. Natives, speaking Baryogo. Baryogo, Jitsu's primary language. Jitsu, the birthplace of Samanei Koroma and the site of the battle that sparked the CPCC's campaign against the yaks.

The transports began returning, and Tony nodded his head. Any germ of doubt had just been eradicated: Samanei and her yak buddies were in this forest, teaching the grendels Baryogo and getting ready for who knew what.

Flipping to a side band chosen for them, Antonio contacted the team that had been sent to investigate the cave.

"Master Sergeant, what news do you have?"

"We just got here, sir. There's a robot laying all smashed up in front of a pretty thick metal door. We're going to try bypassing the print-lock first, then go for blasting our way in if that doesn't work."

"You think you can handle it? We need to know what's in there, but we also need to get moving. The flivvers are staying here, and they can drop you with us or pick up reinforcements as needed."

"I wouldn't worry, sir. Ain't nothing hiding in no wee cave that we can't handle. But certainly, sir, we'll call if we should need help."

"Alright then. D'Angelo out."

Calculating that any outpost would require the river for water and possibly energy, Antonio had his men follow it along its east bank into the deepening crepuscular gloom of the forest. As he switched his casque's visor to IR, the enormous trees towered in phantasmagoric layers of blue and green above him. The panorama, his bounding stride and the gurgling river reminded him conjointly of the enormous deep-sea jungles he'd visited as a child on Oceania. The memories, however, weren't pleasant, because he had to think of his father holding his hand as they stared through the transparent hull of the tour vessel. Soon, here in this jungle, he'd find Brando and finally wring from the other D'Angelo the justice the family had managed to avoid.

The twelve platoons traveled singly, three of them accompanied by Lachower, D'Angelo and Centurion Wendorf as well. Within each platoon, at least one soldier kept a close vigil on the trees above, for the intelligence they'd received from the locals indicated that the natives were more tree-bound, and the dux thought an attack from the upper boughs of the forest likely. The soldiers all trotted along, their unhurried jogging motion translated by their suits and boots to a clod-churning 55 kph for which they'd been trained, but which they'd never had to sustain for long periods of time. After a couple of hours, though, the suits' jerking of their legs and the bounding stride their boots gave them became bearable and almost enjoyable.

After about three hours, realizing that their signal was no longer penetrating the thick foliage and hadn't been able to for likely an hour or more, Antonio ordered a general halt in order to report their present position and find out what Master Sergeant Sean Han had discovered in the cave. Comtechs deployed a transmitter above the canopy. After sending the coordinates, Antonio waited for a response.

Nothing.

Making sure his suit was sending on the frequency of the transponder, he began to repeat his message. "Pilots or Master Sergeant Han, please respond. Did you copy? Retransmitting those coordinates in…"

"No need," came a female voice. "This Captain D'Angelo?"

Adrenaline kicked Antonio's heart into tachycardia.

"Samanei?" he breathed.

"Excuse me? Uh, no, sir. This is your niece, Miwa D'Angelo."

Tony's chest loosened slightly. "Miwa?"

"Yes, sir. You know, the clone. Uh, what are you doing on my planet, Uncle?"

He winced at the title. "I think you know already."

"Uh, you don't need an army to get dad, you know."

Games. Lies. He sighed. "I'm after your aunt, child. And I've got no time for this mind-screwing."

"My aunt? What are you talking about?"

"Samanei Koroma. Your mother's sister."

"You mean Tenshi's sister. My mother is Rhea Kumar."

"Whatever. Listen, get off this channel. How'd you get…"

"Samanei isn't here, Captain. Dad left her far away. You know that."

"Of course you're going to say she's not here. She has you caught up in her web of deceit, like all the rest. But she can't be trusted, girl. If I were you, I would just go back to the capital and wait for this to finish."

"Back to Diadono?" The girl's voice seemed to go chill. "Since it's under AF occupation? No thanks. I don't get you, Uncle Tony. You came and messed things up. Like those two drones yall killed. Yall didn't need to kill them. Yall could've knocked them out or something. All they had was spears. Yall come here to a world that it's not even yours and start killing people. That's just wrong."

People. She calls the grendels people.

"We're going to do what we must do to see justice done. Now, either get off this channel or we'll come looking for you."

"Oh, yall don't need to do that. You were so nice, Uncle, giving me yall's position. Might want to start running now. This is going to be *really* ugly, I think."

A wild, screaming hum began building in the air above them. Antonio's mind was awhirl: he would finally confront her. Samanei had to be behind this charade, this attempt to distract him while she moved into position. Would she personally be involved? Would he see her face to face, now? What would he do? Scenarios played themselves out in his head.

Weakly, another signal cut into the silence on the channel crackling with static. "Tony, fucking idiot, are you alright? Answer me! They were right on top of you a few minutes ago!"

This is it. Maybe Brando's going to be with her. Get them both at the same time.

He didn't try to respond to Phen, and the other captain's signal was soon overridden anyway.

"Five one hundred," came Miwa's playful voice. "Four one hundred."

Hungry anticipation washing over him in waves, Antonio made no attempt to move. He listened to the countdown without really hearing it. The men in the platoon he accompanied stirred, looking at him for instructions, but he was enrapt in the moment, the culmination of many lonely dreams, the chance to fix his family's crimes.

"Three one hundred."

Dux Lachower's voice ripped through Tony's reverie with strident authority.

"Everybody, to the river *now*! We're under attack from above!"

"One one hundred. Ready or not, here we come!"

The decurion of D'Angelo's escorting platoon grabbed the captain and forcibly hurled him into the water as the forest exploded in an apocalyptic conflagration.

INTERCHAPTER I

From: Navarch@flotilla.gov.af

To: mifflint@shaka.gov.af

Subject: AF involvement in Teregan crisis

Date: May 10, 2714 5:07:18 (SST)

Decrypted: May 10, 2714 5:56:10 (SST)

Captain Mifflin:

I am sure you are as surprised at receiving this missive as I am as sending it. In all honesty, I should not go into the details, and your ranking docs not merit me doing so, but you already know, I imagine, that Prime Minister Soral faces a no-confidence vote that could shift power out of her hands.

Understand, Mifflin: those of us who worked so hard to retain a pro-AF majority coalition in the Diet worry that Soral is going to hand the reins of power to the independence-sympathizers just when the AF is at last using our numerical strength to purge human space of crime syndicates. You can imagine how that would affect us. Disaster. Like a virus that is treated for less than the allotted time, when the syndicates would come back, they would be deadlier than ever.

This is what you are going to do, Mifflin. Continue sitting on your hands. Soral's beloved XID is going to arrive soon. Let them handle Antonio D'Angelo. Your recent report shows he's treating the Tereganoj fairly. Not one casualty. We have no justification for going in: none of his superiors have ordered his arrest, not even Soral, who is smarter than that. Remember her own words: "If the situation worsens in a harmful way." I see no harm, Captain.

Let her deal with this one alone. If she wins it, we are her main support: she cannot cut us loose. If she loses, Antonio comes out a hero, and she is no longer our problem. As she will have acted alone, we won't fenestrate into oblivion with her.

I am being frank with you because you must understand the stakes. The future of the CPCC is in play, sir. Do not involve yourself.

> Dante Piazetta
>
> Navarch
>
> CPCCAF Flotilla

PART IV:

DAEMONS

"La raso estas juna: ĝi konstruos

teran ĉielon — post la mort' de Dio."

"Our species is still young: we will build

an earthly heaven—once our God is dead."

—William Auld, *La infana raso* (*The Infant Species*)

CHAPTER 56

MIWA WAS FINISHING HER COBBLED-TOGETHER partial armoring
of Shalura when she heard someone trying to get in. The holographic
representation of her father had shown her how to code the suits to her
thumb- and voiceprints; after doing so, she was able to unseal the suits at
their molecular seams. By resealing two limb-coverings together at a time,
Miwa was able to create sheathing for Shalura's legs and arms; joining two
torso sections allowed her to provide her drone with protection in that area
as well. Her dad's program showed her how to slave the nanobots in each
piece together with strips running up the warrior's angular hips and across
her broad shoulders: the makeshift suit didn't retain its integrity or flexibility,
but it would serve to deflect potentially mortal blasts. The native's head was
the only drawback, as there was no easy way, lacking adequate tools and
knowledge, to adapt a casque to Shalura's skull shape.

Nonetheless, Miwa's drone was impressively decked-out and had two days of training on the weapons when the security system alerted them that someone was trying to bypass the lock. Not knowing how many intruders they'd be expecting, Miwa flitted her eyes across the cramped space: there was no real place to hide, except on either side of the door, and of course, as the people came through, they would immediately check that area. Miwa and Shalura might surprise the first one, but after that they'd be in a tough spot. Miwa tried to picture what the cave would look like as someone entered: the first thing they would see would be the frame on the far side of the room...

"I got it. I know what we're going to do. Take these guns and stand on the right side of the door. When they come through and are starting to shoot at the big shiny box, I will make the light go away and you go outside to throw fire at anybody still there while I am hurting the ones in here."

Miwa then told the holographic projection what she wanted to do. It nodded almost sentiently.

"I hope you learned from me, Miwa."

"Yeah, I did, as much as I could in just two days. Thanks. Hope to see the real you soon. Sorry I've got to do this to you the doppel, though."

"That's okay. This is all I was programmed for: getting you ready."

Miwa nodded and took her place by the door, which was being pounded against.

"Okay, open it, then lights out on my command."

The door whined open, and the avatar of Brando acted startled. A voice, amplified by the pickups of a military casque, shouted out as the humming of ready weapons bored into the silence of the cave.

"Freeze! Get your hands where I can see them!"

The avatar raised its hands up, then slipped one behind its back and brought forward a holographic gun, which it aimed at the men at the door. Three figures rushed in then, blazing away at Brando's figure.

"Lights out!" Miwa shouted. She felt Shalura slip out the door as the room went mostly dark, and she slammed her palm against the lockpad and plunged them into complete pitch blackness. The slightly glowing avatar winked out of existence as the bursts of energy continued slamming against the frame behind it. Miwa had activated the suit's IR the moment the lights had gone out, and she trained her weapon on the heat exchange ducts on the hips of the figures, the only heat signatures in the room besides the wrecked and sizzling computer. She fired a concussive volley of energy waves that lifted and hurled the exhaust signatures against the painful red and orange of what had been the frame. Then, shouldering the rest of her weapons, she palmed the door open, turned, and rolled a grenade into the remaining rack. Her IR still active in the cloudy twilight, she saw Shalura dragging two gray-armored bodies into the alcove as she quickly shut the door.

"Come on, Shal: move!"

She led her drone quickly behind some nearby boulders as a muffled explosion sent a small cascade of rock and dirt shuddering toward them. Glancing down the mountain's slope as lightning backlit green-gray clouds, Miwa noticed a gleam as if from metal. She increased the magnification of her visor and made out the form of four *kopteroj*.

Those were AF personnel: what are they doing with our transports?

A wave of nausea came over her suddenly, and she had to fumble her casque open and vomit.

"What? What is the matter?"

Miwa looked with red-rimmed eyes at her drone. "They were ingan, Shalura. I just killed my own people."

"But they were not of your tribe, Daenzhelo. Would they not have killed you?"

"You don't understand. Before you and your warriors captured me, I had never killed anyone before. When I was killing other drones that were attacking me, attacking us, it wasn't affecting me much."

"Of course not. Soulless drones from another tribe: why would you be affected?"

"I told you not to say that nonsense, Shal. But no. For my people, the People appear like demons, you see, and maybe it was just being easier for me to kill the drones because part of me was seeing them that way. But I just killed three ingan, without much thinking. That scares and sickens me. I didn't know I was capable of doing that."

Shalura nodded and placed a claw on Miwa's head. "I understand. I will tell you what all young drones are told before their first battle. Life is sacred, and souled life even more so. You may have to send a soul on its way to judgment, but when you do so for a just cause, God will not turn her wrathful gaze on you. Go forth and defend what is right and good. Kill for your tribe whenever you must."

Miwa tried to smile a little for Shal's sake, but her heart was twisting in her chest. Three men. Sent by the AF for who-knew-what, but men nonetheless. Perhaps with families, children, wives.

Oh, Lord, forgive me. What have I done?

She didn't let this sorrow overcome her, though. She had duties now. She had to get Shal off this mountain safely, get to her father before the AF did.

"Come on. There are flying ships down there, stolen by these warriors from my tribe's village. We need to go down more to the west so they won't be seeing us."

The two of them went around the mountain's face a bit to where the drones had been carrying equipment down a few days earlier. About halfway to the bottom, Shalura discovered the corpses of two drones wearing the green harnesses that denoted service in the former Greenseer's personal guard. Miwa stooped to investigate: the head of one had been partially blown open, and the other trailed intestines from a gut shot. Pulse rifles. Neither had

even drawn her spear: one of them still had a portable communication rig in

her claws. Miwa gently freed the device and found that it had a small charge

remaining in its cells.

Let's find out what these guys are doing here.

As the rig hummed to life, she punched in a local radio station's frequency.

"...present to you a rebroadcast of the audio signal from TRD's

continuing coverage of the invasion.

"In the pre-dawn hours early Tuesday morning, two groups of

escape pods splashed down in the abandoned quarry to the south of the

capital. Captains Antonio D'Angelo and Phen Quat, commanders of the

CPCCAF Flotilla galleons the *Diomedes* and the *George Washington*,

engineered the hostile takeover of the Ministry of Crises' weapons depot.

After spending the rest of the day presumably planning their next move,

the captains, using materiel and vehicles stolen from the crisis ministry,

approached Diadono early Wednesday morning under cover of darkness and

invaded that city. After recording these images of the invasion, our cameras

were ordered shut off, and we received no further news of the situation until

two hours ago when Phen Quat, styling himself temporary regent, issued the

following statement."

The baritone voice of the captain began speaking in Standard as a

reporter simultaneously translated, but the charge was nearly exhausted, and

Miwa lost the signal.

Antonio D'Angelo? Related to dad?

"What did that box tell you, Daenzhelo?"

"That the Greenseer was right. The ingan are here to take over. Look how they killed these poor drones."

"Yes. Warriors always face off in combat. Not waiting for your opponent to draw her weapon is cowardly. Occasionally it must be done, but there was no need here."

"Come. We need to be getting to those flying ships. We'll go along the edge of the forest."

They hurried to the mammoth trees and weaved their way to the transports, which were spaced evenly out, each about thirty meters from the next. The four pilots stood close to one, weapons drawn, talking over their cascoms. Perhaps they hadn't heard the explosion on the mountain: they were chatting, thunder was rolling every couple of minutes, and the blast had been rather muffled.

"Okay. When I say 'go,' fire at the weapons of the two on the right. I'll get the other two. Let's do our best not to be killing them, okay? I can't fly one of these ships, so we need their help."

They both took aim, the rifle still a bit awkward in Shalura's massive claws, and Miwa gave the signal. Energy blasts banged against the pilots, who were shaken from their inattentive conversing and returned fire as their superior suits absorbed the pulses.

"Not powerful enough," muttered Shalura, and before Miwa could stop her, she dialed the rifle to full and let forth a barrage that ripped into the koptero closest to the pilots, causing it to explode in a ball of burning fuel and whizzing metal parts that flowed over the pilots, flinging them like flaming rag dolls against the next transport.

"You stupid piece of smelly excrement! What did you do that for?" Miwa suppressed an urge to slam the butt of her weapon against the drone's skull. "I told you I can't fly one of those things! Don't you see, the warriors have already gone into the forest, and how are we going to catch up with them before they are getting to my dad, eh? You disobedient, frustrating drone!"

"They were throwing fire at us, and our fire appeared not to harm them. Please forgive me, Daenzhelo. I only wanted to aid you in capturing their ships."

Miwa stormed away in the direction of the roiling black smoke. The AF pilots appeared dead.

Not my fault. Stupid Shalura. I'm going to lock all those weapons on a lower setting before she sets the forest on fire.

Nausea clawing at her empty stomach, Miwa approached the plane farthest from the explosion and clambered up the extended ramp and into the cockpit. Slamming herself angrily into the seat, she found the cabin light and clicked it on. After telescoping her casque back into its collar, she started glancing around, muttering to herself.

"Stupid, stupid Shalura. Four kopteroj, that's like eighty soldiers out there! What am I going to do now, eh? Okay, ignition, altimeter, pitch and yaw… what the heck is that? Oh, yeah, up-down, side to side. The stick here, like in dad's simulation games, back for up, forward for down."

Now I know why dad forced us to play that idiot game so much. Can probably get it off the ground, get to where I need to go, but how do I land this thing?

She turned on the panel computer, a touch screen with several options and displays. "Autopilot! Okay. What? Coordinates? I don't know the stupid coordinates."

She yanked the map from her knapsack.

Wonderful map, coordinates to Diadono and all over, but what do you know! No native villages!

Shalura knew where Brando was being kept, but obviously couldn't tell Miwa the latitude and longitude.

Maybe I could guess? Fly in that general direction? And land where, on the canopy? Oh, God, give me some direction!

Frustrated, she checked the other instruments. The radio was set to an unusual frequency. She clicked the gain up. There was only static. She slipped the light headset on and spoke in Standard. "Hello? Anyone hear me?" No answer. She cast about some more with her eyes. On the panel, fixed with strip of tape, she found a clear slip of hardcopy with several frequencies printed on it. She tried the first one.

"Crisis control center; who's calling?"

A Novasanktulo, speaking Standard from the Ministry of Crises? What in the world?

"Can I speak to, um, Minister De Waal?" she asked in Esperanto.

"Who is this?" the voice answered in that language. "The city is under strict radio silence, sister. You could get in…"

There was a strange series of clicks and thrumming sounds, then a new voice came on, speaking Standard. Miwa recognized it from the TRD rebroadcast: Phen Quat.

"Why are you on this channel?"

"Why are you on my planet? That's a better question. This is Miwa D'Angelo. You sent some soldiers into our forest: why?"

"You're Brando's cloned daughter?"

"Yes, sir. You're going to answer my question or no?"

"No. Classified, and you're with the enemy. You've got a real low opinion of your opponents' intelligence, Ms. D'Angelo. Now tell me how you accessed this frequency."

"One of your dumb pilots left it lying round. I just picked it up, thought I'd give you a call."

"We just triangulated yall's position, Ms. D'Angelo. Tell your aunt we thank her for her little unintended warning."

The channel went dead.

My aunt? What?

She thought of Rhea and Jakobo, scared in the midst of the occupation of Diadono. Fiddling with the controls, she dialed into the com network and buzzed her house. There was no answer. She wracked her brain for a few seconds, then thought of Sister Nishiguchi. Chiho's quiet voice answered hesitantly.

"Yes?"

"Sister, it's me, Miwa."

"Miwa?"

"Yes. Are you okay?"

"Oh, Lord, I'm fine, dear. Thank heaven *you're* alive! We were so worried. Here, your brother wants to talk to you."

Before Miwa could tell the sister to wait, Jakobo shouted excitedly. "Hey, Mimi! Where you been? There are big soldier guys in the city, you know that?"

"Yeah, Yakkety-yak, I know. I was, you know, tied up, but I'm coming back really soon. Hey, is mom there?"

"No, they got her like locked up or something over with Brother De Waal and them. She's like real important now: everybody calls her Star of Native Unfairs or something." His voice caught. "I'm scared, Mimi. Are they gonna do bad things to her?"

"No, don't worry. I'm going to take care of that as quick as I can, Yakster. You just hang tight and listen to Sister Nishiguchi, okay? I love you."

"Me too; bye!"

Miwa clicked off, rage building inside of her.

They come to Terego, take over our city, lock up my mother and other leaders, steal our equipment, kill drones without warning, invade the forest: I've got to stop them. Somehow. Before they kill more of the People.

Shalura climbed into the transport, her claws scrabbling against the metal. Miwa flipped the radio back to the original channel as the drone tramped around in the cargo area. A weak signal began to crackle in her headset. It was Quat again, on a new channel.

"Antonio, you copy? Pilots? They're right on top of yall, I said. Yall need to get moving now. Tony, we received a transmission from someone who they claimed to be your, uh, niece, Miwa D'Angelo."

So he is Brando's brother. What is going on here?

"The signal was coming from almost yall's exact last reported position. If yall ain't moved out yet, do it now."

"Too late, Captain," Miwa snapped. "Coming for you next, sir."

There was silence on the channel, or rather, a thrumming, clicking sound as if the ministry pickup had been muted. Shalura's head poked through the doorway.

"There are many boxes with guns and shiny stones within them at the back of this ship, Daenzhelo."

"Yes," she replied, cupping her hand over the mic, "all ready for killing the People. But we're going to be using them for a different purpose. Sit down on one of those black hammocks and hold on tight. Don't be letting go, no matter what."

Activating the control that retracted the ramp and sealed the door, Miwa thumbed the motors to life. As she lifted the koptero gently from the ground, her adrenaline making her blood thunder in her ears, a strident transmission blasted painfully through the headset.

"Alpha Base, this is incursion team, coordinates 51.697 north by 5.368 west. Please report status."

Miwa's jaw dropped open. *Thank you, Lord.* She quickly thumbed the autopilot and entered the coordinates.

Speed? The display prompted.

There was a graded scale that went from zero to mach one. She slid her finger to the right as far as the gauge would allow. Her palms tingled with nervousness at what she was going to attempt.

"Shal, would you be willing to throw yourself from this ship into the canopy when I tell you to?" Miwa hollered toward the back, muting the mic.

Structural damage possible after three minutes. Proceed? Y/N.

"I will do anything you ask, no matter how dangerous it is. You have said these skins will protect me, and I trust you."

"Just cling tightly to the black webbing until I tell you to let go and jump."

Miwa nail-clicked the 'Y' as the human voice boomed in her ears again. She assumed it was Antonio D'Angelo. *My uncle,* she thought with bitter wonder. *Maybe here to settle some old score with dad, and all of us are caught in the middle*

"Pilots or Master Sergeant Han, please respond. Did you copy? Retransmitting those coordinates in…"

"No need," she interrupted, opening the pickup again. "This Captain D'Angelo?"

"Samanei?" her uncle whispered hoarsely. The koptero cleared the canopy and began rocketing forward, pushing Miwa back against the seat with brutal force. From the cargo area came a grunt of surprise.

"Excuse me? Uh, no, sir." She felt nausea tickling her stomach again. "This is your 'niece,' Miwa D'Angelo."

"Miwa?"

"Yes, sir. You know, the clone. Uh, what are you doing on my planet, Uncle?"

Are you here for dad? Did the CPCC send you? You came in escape pods and had to steal inferior transports. Why? Why?

"I think you know already," Antonio growled. Miwa looked out the cockpit at the blur of green a couple of kilometers below.

"Uh, you like don't need an army to get dad, you know."

A heavy sigh filled the airwaves. "I'm after your aunt, child. And I've got no time for this mind-screwing."

"My aunt? What you're talking about?" *Does dad have a sister, too?*

"Samanei Koroma. Your mother's sister."

Realization dawned on her. Tana's mother, not Miwa's. "You mean Tenshi's sister. My mother is Rhea Kumar."

"Whatever. Listen, get off this channel. How did you get..."

"Samanei isn't here, Captain. Dad left her like far away. You know that." It was one of the charges that had been brought against him, one of the revelations of only four short weeks ago. *An eternity.* Rain began to fall in sheets of solid gray before the lights of the transport, which ripped through them at the speed of sound. Systems warning lights were blinking all over the console, but Miwa's eyes were focused on the display that read *time remaining to arrival.* Ninety seconds.

"Of course you're going to say she's not here. She has you caught up in her web of deceit, like all the rest. But she can't be trusted, girl. If I were you, I would just go back to the capital and wait for this to finish."

"Back to Diadono?" Cold anger filled her as she shut off the autopilot and took the stick. "Since it's under AF occupation? No thanks. I don't get you, Uncle Tony. You came and messed things up. Like those two drones yall killed. Yall didn't need to kill them. Yall could've knocked them out or something. All they had was spears. Yall come here to a world that it's not even yours and start killing people. That's just wrong."

Forty-five seconds. As she cut the speed back by a third, Miwa pushed the stick forward and locked it, aiming the koptero at an angle toward the green two and a half kilometers below. Magnetizing her boots, she stood.

"We're going to do what we must to do to see justice done. Now, either get off this channel or we'll come looking for you."

"Oh, yall don't need to do that. You were really nice, Uncle, giving me yall's position. Might want to start running now. This is going to be *really* ugly, I think."

Miwa slammed her hand against the door release. Air started streaming out of the cabin in gulping torrents. She ripped the headset from her ears and accordioned the casque in place. Setting the frequency to Antonio's, she used her enhanced muscles to ease out of the cockpit into the cargo area, resisting the wind as best she could.

Shalura was flapping against the metal floor, holding onto the strapmesh with a single powerful claw. Yanking a parachute free from its thumping against the hull, Miwa struggled over to her drone against the sucking air.

"Tony, fucking idiot, you're alright?" Quat's voice was made small and shrill by distortion. "Answer me! They were right on top of you a few minutes ago!"

Miwa reached Shalura and put an arm around her waist, steadying her some against the vicious sucking of their descent. "Let go when I shake my head!" Miwa screamed through the external speaker. Then she opened

the channel again, cutting out the other captain with her stronger signal and

barely restraining a hysterical laugh.

"Five one hundred." With her free arm, she unhooked a grenade from

her belt and set it for four seconds. "Four one hundred."

This is insane. We might die.

She tossed the grenade at the boxes of weapons stacked in the back. It

clicked in place, magnetized to the floor.

"Three one hundred. Two one hundred."

Miwa shook her head as she demagnetized her boots. Shalura released

her hold on the mesh, throwing her arms about Miwa, and they both went

flying toward the doorway.

"One one hundred," Miwa managed to grunt. "Ready or not, here

we come!"

The ship exploded only meters away from them as it smashed into the

canopy. The concussion tossed the pair upward at nosebleed velocity, and

Miwa struggled to stay conscious. She had to activate the chute at the apex

of their parabola, or they'd be sent crashing into the trees.

Darkness tried to claw into her mind, but she fought it as she'd never

fought before.

CHAPTER 57

AT ABOUT WHAT TERI CALCULATED WAS EIGHT O'CLOCK Thursday morning, the last group of village representatives, a befuddled Brando D'Angelo with them, was fenestrated into Sháinkhÿngigg village for the People's Council.

Ùshëshajirh had been busily organizing the newcomers by nations, so that there were six clusters of about ninety highborn each. They had all learned about the ships falling through the sky, and the clearing was abuzz with tense, earnest discussion.

Teri felt an ache in heart as she understood that the tension also came from the news that most of the villages of the Xŏthatterl nation, clustered at the very eastern edge of the northern fringe of the forest, had been decimated by a human virus. Teri had come across one village, in fact, in which every living being appeared to have died more than a decade earlier. Since nearly a half century had passed since the Xöthatterl nation had broken ties with its sisters, not a single Nakÿng had been aware of this tragedy. The Urim promised that everyone would now be protected against such diseases, but the incident underscored for everyone the danger posed by the ingan.

Gesturing at Brando to follow her, Teri hugged the Urim to her chest and rushed to Ùshëshajirh's side, noting the deferent bowed heads of the highborn she passed. They had experienced her power firsthand: she had pulled them across great distances in seconds, and any doubts they may have secretly held were apparently quelled by that amazing display.

"Is everything ready?"

Ùshëshajirh smiled affirmatively. "Yes, Firstborn. In fact, we have begun some initial discussion while we awaited the arrival of the final members."

"That's good. What do you need me to do?"

"Ah, Lady. You must rest. You yourself have said this is a matter for the People themselves. Go to your compound, sleep, recover. I will rouse you when it is necessary for you to address the Council."

Knowing the truthfulness of her companion's words and the honest concern behind them, Teri agreed and, with Brando in tow, headed toward the tree in which, just a few weeks before, she and her friends had been held prisoner.

«Do you want to be lifted?»

Oh, God, please. This guy, too. Stick him in the males' quarters, take me to the highborn level.

As Brando was set down on the lip of the third level, he sighed heavily to see Teri float away. "Can't we talk, Teri? How long can you keep ignoring me?"

"Brando," she called down to him, "in case you haven't noticed, we're about to be at war. I haven't slept in days. There are too many things going on for you and me to have a little heart-to-heart right now."

Then she stepped behind the curtain of moss, released the Urim and threw herself on the hammock of vines. She imagined Carmen, staring up from the pile of furs below her, and her heart ached with longing.

«Lowering your metabolic levels to normal will take time. You will be damaged otherwise. Sleep will not come easily.»

She shrugged, then snapped her fingers.

"You read Tenshi's journal and freaked out, but I haven't finished it. Can you feed it to me? I really want to get it all in one burst. Except the last entry, I guess. Let me hear that one myself."

Assent. Then a wave of knowledge, as if she'd just heard Tenshi murmur in her husky, cigarette-sharpened voice for hours.

Teri slumped back onto the netting. She was accustomed to the neural overload now, but the new vision of Brando the journal afforded her was more overwhelming than any mental strain the Urim had put her through.

She loved him. And he loved her.

Thumbing the last entry on, she listened.

"July 25, 2683. This is the final time we speak, Diary. Tomorrow Brando and I get married. A traditional Pathwalker wedding, mind you. It feels so good to have someone by my side on the Path, someone who trusts me enough to accept my beliefs as his own. And there's so much potential in him, like a diamond in the rough. He's a good man, and he could become a great man. I could make him a great man.

"Despite all the things that I've seen down the years, I am still an optimist. I look at my people, and I see what they could be, just like with Brando. At the end, I know where I belong. Not gallivanting round the stars with Ambarina, but here, on my world, with other Aknawajin Pathwalkers. Call me arrogant, but I know I can make a difference. This was once the hub of human expansion, you knew that? I look at Brando, who crossed light years to be here, and I see the future of Jitsu. With him by my side and my people roundabout me, I will do incredible things. And you know why? Because I can. They are good things, of course, and I want to help everyone, but my real motivation is my love of creation.

"I see the structure of people as well as things, Diary. I want to go beyond buildings, see? To build a new sort of society, one that works, that doesn't oppress its citizens, that won't fall apart from within nor be conquered from without.

"I think Brando understands, and in his quiet comprehension, I find peace. His heart is big enough to hold me and my people too, once I get him to share my vision. I've known many people in my life, and never did I meet one as compassionate. Tempered, he could be a leader. At the very least, he's going to be a wonderful father.

"You know, it's strange. Even through my periods of doubt, I always believed in the Path, strove to connect to the Ogdoad. But it wasn't until I met this foolish off-worlder that I truly found my Way.

"Well, I've got to go. Thanks for twelve years of memories, but I don't need you anymore. I found the one that I needed, the one that I love.

"Goodbye, Diary."

Tears streamed down Teri's face, and her shoulders trembled as sobs wormed their way out of her soul to wrack her body. Waves of understanding washed over her. The release was so exhausting and cleansing that, even though she knew she had to go to him, had to ease his suffering and help heal his heart, she slipped into a dreamless, infant-like sleep.

«YOU MUST AWAKEN. We are being encircled.»

Teri's eyes fluttered open, and she wiped moisture from her cheek.

What?

«The Urim was recovering, running diagnostics. Their approach was not noticed until they sent a message out.»

The transmission played itself in Teri's head.

"Captain Quat, this is Dux Bulavas. We have reached our destination. Coordinates suppressed as per directive. Any word yet on status of Captain D'Angelo's incursion team?"

Has there been a response?

Teri was up and splashing water on her face from a clay basin.

«Yes. Here.»

"Vlad, by luck Tony is in pretty good shape. Just contacted us. Took a village after losing about ten men. Under fire from enemy. Plans to continue southward march within the next couple of hours. Proceed with attack."

Oh, shit. Come on.

The Urim surrounded her with blue light, and she floated down to the clearing, where it appeared some sort of voting was going on. Ùshëshajirh signaled her over.

"I see concern on your face, Firstborn, if I read ingan emotions correctly. What is wrong?"

"Ingan warriors are surrounding this village. May I address the Council?"

"Of course. I was elected Council Leader, and we were voting on making you our emissary to the ingan. You have just won, so you come at a perfect moment."

Teri turned and faced the more than five hundred highborn, their robes a rainbow of different tribal colors and markings. The Urim amplified her voice and thickened it with native undertones.

"Sisters, the crisis is upon us. As I speak, ingan drones encircle this village, armed with spears that expel fire at great speeds. I need the drones of Sháinkhÿngigg to prepare for battle, and I need to request that each nation lend me a hundred drones for when the battle is done. I know what a burden this will be for the Xöthatterl nation, but circumstances require our unity."

A rusty-crested highborn from that nation spoke out.

"Çèrhingÿl, how can our drones fight against this fire?"

The Urim spoke.

«The weapons can be neutralized. There is a sensor in each soldier's hand that is read by his weapon. All of the soldiers carry the same code in their sensor, and their weapons have been programmed to accept only that code, presumably to prevent someone not in the company to utilize a fallen soldier's arms. Resetting the code is simple, and doing so will prevent the soldiers from using any of their weapons.»

Perfect. We still need to hold them off until the drones are gathered.

"I will break their spears. Then our drones can capture them or harry them from the forest."

«Release the Urim. It will extend an energy field around the village until you are ready to begin. You will have to communicate on your own. The power to broadcast your voice cannot be spared.»

Can you open their helmets as well?

«Of course. Simple mechanisms. Now release the Urim. Verbally give the command to disable the weapons when it is time.»

"With respect, what are the drones needed for, Firstborn?"

Teri took her hands off the Urim, which sped upward. Looking back at the russet highborn, she tried to project her voice as best she could, hoping that the knowledge of their language she'd gotten from Ùshëshajirh's mind wouldn't fail her.

"As you've been told, the main tribe of ingan on this spherical land of yours is peaceful. Their principal village has been overrun by the same group that now surrounds us. I want to negotiate with that tribe and take a group of drones with me to expel the enemy warriors from their village. The more allies we have among the ingan, the easier it will be for me to broker a peace with them.

"But that is not why I need warriors from each nation. In addition to the group that even now tries to break through the barrier I have erected around Sháinkhÿngigg, another group has entered the vine-strung forest and taken over one of your villages. I haven't found out which, but when I do, I plan to take a *ngarh'ihusïtigg* against them."

Army of drones.

The word had just come to her lips, though she'd never heard it used before. She understood instantly that it was a very ancient term, one used in mythological stories about the People before they had come to the forest.

Ùshëshajirh's clear voice lifted above the murmuring that ensued.

"In more ways than one the old tales have gained life through Çèrhingÿl. She will raise up a mighty army of sturdy-limbed drones, the likes of which has not been seen since the mist-shrouded days of yore, when highborn still fought alongside drones and haughty queens ruled the land. Let us vote to form her army, sisters."

Nearly all of the highborn bent at the waist and extended both arms out at their sides in a gesture that corresponded to an aye vote. Eventually, all of them agreed. As they did, some two hundred drones approached the area: every warrior that Ùshëshajirh's tribe possessed.

"Our drones are ready for whatever you would have them do," indicated the council's leader.

"Fan out. You will be able to see a glittering blue light around the edge of the village, protecting us. On the other side, you will find the warriors, who may try to throw fire at you. Don't worry. I won't let it touch you. Organize yourself so that there are two drones for every ingan warrior. When the light disappears, it means their fire spears have been broken. The shells covering their heads will fall away: one of each pair of you must grasp the ingan, and the other deal him a blow to the base of the head, though not at full strength. As you would slap down an opponent's tail, more or less. Ingan are fragile, therefor do our warriors dress in these gray skins and shells. I don't want you to kill a single ingan. If you do, we will be overrun by more ingan than People have ever existed in this forest. Not one death, is that clear?"

The drones bared their frightening teeth in unanimous assent.

"Go. God watch and help each of you."

As they spread to the edge of the village, Brando walked into the clearing, glancing with haunted suspicion at the natives around him but not seeming afraid or full of hate any more.

"So, anything I can do?"

Teri looked at him with instinctual irritation. Then she remembered the new perspective of him she'd acquired, and her gaze softened.

"Why'd you come down from the tree? Haven't you fought enough? You should just rest."

Raising an eyebrow at the concern in her voice, Brando muttered, "I had to pee. Didn't seem dignified to do it off the edge of the platform onto any unsuspecting grendels below."

Teri frowned. "Don't call them that. That's a horrible name."

"Well, what do I call them, then? Native Teregans was my friend anthropologist's term, until they slaughtered him. Doesn't quite roll off the tongue, though, like grendel does."

"Well, they call themselves by several names. The most common is *öqhihéinghigg*. The forest children."

"Yikes! An aspirated click? I don't think most humans are going to be able to handle that one, Teri."

She was about to give him the word for *the People* when a drone rushed up to her.

"We are ready, Firstborn. The ingan are very angry: their fire is being thrown back at them by your blue light. Very amusing."

Teri nodded. "Xuqetòlzh."

The drone rushed back to the line.

"Xuqetòlzh? Did I get that right?" Brando didn't seem capable of giving up his fascination for language even at the most inappropriate of times. He was repeating the word to himself with varying intonations.

"Yes. It means fine, okay, well done. Get ready. If any of the AF soldiers get past my drones, you and I might have to fight."

"AF soldiers? What?"

Teri tilted her head back and shouted. "Okay, Urim, now!"

There came a rush of air as the curtain of light apparently dissolved, allowing air to flow back in, equalizing the pressure inside and outside the perimeter of the village.

"I saw your sister, you know."

Teri stopped looking upward expectantly and faced Brando. "Miwa? Is she alright? I had hoped to find her in one of the villages, but there was no trace of her."

"You should've asked your buddies up north, the ones that were dragging me along when you showed up. They had just gotten through fighting her and this drone companion of hers."

Puzzled at this news, she called one of the representatives from Dhureinghÿngigg over. The highborn ducked her head and sucked in her cheeks reverently.

"Did the drones of your village fight a ingan accompanied by a drone?"

"Yes, Firstborn. The Greenseer ordered it, told us to engage the troop if it came near us and to capture the ingan that was with it. We assumed you knew of this order."

"But you failed to capture her."

"She and her troop killed many of our drones, but we captured most of them finally. Only the ingan and the troop leader escaped."

In the north. Where Antonio has taken a village.

She grimaced. "Is there any other news you've neglected to tell me?"

"Only that last night there was a terrible storm to our north, and lightening seemed to set the sky on fire."

Teri nodded and dismissed the highborn. Turning back to Brando, she sighed.

"They confirmed it. She was with a drone."

"Yes. She actually protected it."

"*Her.* They produce eggs. Females."

The Urim eased out of the trees and into her hands again.

"Okay, protected her from me. Knocked me on my butt pretty quickly, too."

«Done. Your warriors were very rough. It was necessary to revive several of the soldiers. They should all live, though. Where will you put them?»

"Hang on, Brando."

"Sure. You and the ball go ahead and do whatever it is you're doing."

Teri couldn't help rolling her eyes.

In the storage buildings?

«They can break through them easily with their armor. It must be removed. There are seals that can be opened, and the pieces will fall away. Have the drones collect them. They will be of use during the elevation, as will the technology in the weapons.»

I need a weapon for Brando. Fix one so he can use it. He can help guard the soldiers and explain the situation to them so they won't be too fearful.

Teri's gaze focused back on Brando. "I'm going to give you a rifle, and I want you to help me guard the soldiers. I've removed their weapons and battle suits, so they'll be in their underwear."

"Or buck naked. Some grunts prefer it that way."

"Yes, whatever. I'm leaving for a while, but the drones will be here to help you. Ùshëshajirh, the council leader, speaks Baryogo and can help you communicate with them if you need anything. Try to calm them and tell them their rights will be respected, etcetera, until an arrangement has been made with their government for their release."

One of the drones brought an armful of weapons and grunted a question at her. She took one of the blast rifles and told him to put the rest with the tubers in a nearby shed. A brief beam of blue light, and the weapon was ready for Brando. She handed it to him.

"Thanks," he said.

"For what?"

"For trusting me again. I know I don't deserve to be trusted, but believe me, I love you."

Teri's eyes misted up, but she said nothing.

"I don't understand what's happening here, and I don't suppose there's a chance you'll explain the whats and wherefores of that ball you have there…"

She shook her head.

"… but I promise I will do whatever I can to help you. You see, I watched them, like you said. I saw beauty in them, for a moment, in their music and dances celebrating you, and if you say they are worth all of this, I will do whatever you say. You are, whether you want to be or not, my daughter, and I would give my life to make you happy."

Tears spilled onto her cheeks.

«You should tell him now. Tell him you love him. Tell him what you require from him. You cannot force it upon him. That is not our way. We convince.»

Not now. I can't. Take me to Diadono. There's a lot to do before it's Brando's time.

"Ùshëshajirh!" she yelled in Baryogo. "I must leave. Put the ingan in the storage and training buildings. Put their skins and spears with the tubers. Rràndo will stay to help guard them. Give him all he requires."

The high priestess nodded.

"I'll be back soon, Brando. Hang tight."

Now, before I lose it.

The fenestration was as disorienting as the first time, and Teri kept her eyes closed as she had ordered the highborn to do on every trip that morning. The Urim could make its blue light almost completely opaque, but the vast, weird, mind-numbing shapes and colors that swirled beyond its edge could still be made out if one left one's eyes open. The effect of sensing this strangeness, even for the second it took to cross, was so disorienting as to leave the traveler numb for minutes afterward.

«Something is wrong here.»

They had emerged in an alcove across the street from the ministry building.

What, in the Ministry of Crises?

«No. Something during fenestration. Do not worry. Walk into the building.»

The guards' rifles went up as she approached, and they told her to stop. She didn't. They warned they'd open fire. A bubble of blue leapt out of the Urim to surround her, and as they panicked and began to unleash a barrage of energy, she was unharmed. A shining wave of light burst from the Urim, and their rifles no longer responded to them.

Stepping past the dumbstruck soldiers, Teri walked through the doors—which flew open at her approach—then down the hall, across the reception area, and into the crisis control room. Guards along the way lost control of their weapons, and a few found themselves trying to reseal suits that had suddenly lost their integrity. She made no gestures, did nothing theatrical: her very presence inside the shimmering blue, hands gripping the coppery orb with practiced ease, was more dramatic than any ridiculous hand waving or shouts.

A tall, thin man, his bald head tattooed with the symbol of the CPCCAF, a black eagle with a star in its talons, lifted his pistol to fire upon her. The Urim amplified Teri's voice as she spoke.

"Phen Quat, I'm guessing. Where you got the leaders of this planet stored at, sir? I need to talk to them."

Can you make the gun fly from his hand? That'll startle him.

A blue tendril shot out, and a glowing clone of Teri's own arm pointed the weapon at Quat's face.

Oh, very nice, Urim.

«This is part of the convincing.»

I bet.

"Come on, Captain. If I were you, I would answer me."

"There's no way they're going to let you live, you know that. Nobody with this kind of power can be allowed to exist. They're going to hunt you down and destroy you. They've got no option."

"Why don't you let me worry about that, Captain Quat, and you just worry about your men, their safety, and my patience, which right now is wearing quite thin."

«Scan of the computers complete. The location of the occupied village determined. Dhureinghÿngigg.»

They must have arrived soon after we left this morning. Maybe the enemy attacking them is Miwa. With I don't know which weapons.

«Whoever it is, the captain of the forces reports nineteen soldiers killed, apparently by a mixed group of humans and Nakÿng.»

Oh, Lord. As if this weren't hard enough. What the hell is she doing up there? We've got to stop her from killing any more of them.

Quat finally caved in with a grunt and a jerk of his tattooed head.

"We've got them in one of the conference rooms. Lance-jack Jownz, take Ms. Koroma to where we're holding the prisoners."

Koroma? Huh? How can he think I'm Samanei? Kyr's mind said that Quat took over Brando's case from Antonio. Didn't he see my picture?

«You have not seen yourself recently, Agent. You are much changed.»

Agent. I don't know if I like that. Agent of what? Let me guess, you can't tell me, right?

She strode down a couple of halls to a wide chamber. Inside were most of the executive cabinet, including her mother, who had been made Czar of Native Affairs, ironically enough. Rhea Kumar nearly fainted when she saw her daughter come through the doors, which slammed shut behind her. The bubble of blue expanded to contain them all.

Besides Rhea, the one person Teri focused on was Zolile Khumalo, who was staring, as she might have expected, at the faintly glowing Urim she held in her hands.

"Miss Miranda. We have been hoping to see you for many weeks now. Never, of course, did it occur to us that you'd arrive in this fashion. It seems Corpsmen Sainz was not exaggerating when he reported to us your newfound powers."

"Are you okay, sweetie?" Rhea managed to get out, recovering her composure.

This is going to be a little rough on them.

"Two things: first of all, I no longer use the surname Miranda or D'Angelo. My people call me *Çèrhingÿl.*"

"Tearing ghoul? That's what your male friend told us you were being called," began Roberto De Waal. "Teringul'? That's what it sounds like in Esperanto."

Female-earth glutton. Oh, great. Novasanktuloj are going to have fun with this name, too.

"Just use my first name. Teri. It's close enough."

"You said 'my people,' Teri," interrupted Rhea. "Do you mean the Native Teregans?"

"Yes. When I say my people, I mean the Nakÿng, those you are calling the Native Teregans."

"The Nah Coon?"

"Close enough. Try *Nakungoj* in Esperanto. The second thing I need you to know is that I can't speak of this sphere to you, other than to swear it will never be used to harm anyone, ever. In fact, once this is over, I suspect none of you will ever see it again. Now, I don't have time for debate. I am an emissary from the Council of the Six Nations. I want a treaty between the Nakÿng and the Novasanktuloj. We will get rid of the occupying forces and negotiate a solution with the Consortium, and Terego will in return leave the Great Seneka Forest alone for twenty years, after which time we will begin to initiate some diplomatic communication. It is possible that we will allow missionaries in previous to this."

"Missionaries?" De Waal again. "You're not claiming to bring a revelation or change to us? Because there are a lot of Novasanktuloj that are whispering strange apostasies."

"I'm not here for the Novasanktuloj. I'm here for the Nakÿng. Any message I may have, it's for them. Right now, I need to know: will you sign such a treaty, Prime Minister?"

"We can draft one at once, though you should know I need approval of the legislative body before it becomes official."

Teri nodded. "Okay. Let me take you somewhere safer. Then I'll leave you to it. I'll be back as soon as I can with sufficient forces to run these invaders out. I assume they have the legislators, too, so my part of the bargain has to come first."

She knew she could simply defeat them now, but the Novasanktuloj needed to see the drones on the streets, expelling the enemy. Humans needed to associate the Nakÿng with freedom and safety.

«To the Czar's house, then?»

"Okay, please close your eyes and don't open them till I tell you."

All fifteen obeyed, and Teri almost smiled. A month ago, not one of the adults in this room would've snapped so quickly to attention at her words. Now, though...

«Careful. That is pride. That way lies destruction.»

You're right. Sorry. It's just such a change.

In a second, they were in front of the house that Brando had built his budding family so many years before. The quiet burble of the stream could just be made out above the droning of spring insects.

"Okay. Open your eyes." Shock was reflected on each of their faces. Without a word of explanation, Teri walked over to Rhea and kissed the shorter woman on the forehead. "I will see you soon. Tomorrow morning. I'll meet you all at the east bridge going into the city at, let's say, seven. Brando will be with me."

Ignoring their surprised murmuring and Rhea's attempt to ask her questions, Teri ordered the Urim to return them to Sháinkhÿngigg, where she would check on the situation. After that, she'd run some sort of reconnaissance farther north.

She had an enemy to expel, an army to raise, a sister to find, a planet to save and a race to elevate to at least human levels. There was no time for pleasantries or explanations.

CHAPTER 58

THROWING THEMSELVES INTO THE RIVER didn't protect Antonio's men from large hunks of falling debris. The engines of the flivver came down largely intact but streaming flames as they ripped through the trees with a menacing yowl. Good men were crushed to pulp under them, and their devastating impact rushed water out of the river and against the trees, carrying other men with it to slam against unyielding boles and limbs. Had it not been for the steady curtain of joyless rain, the captain reflected, the forest would have surely caught fire, for the energy from the exploding transport and the weapons it contained stripped hundreds of trees of their foliage and sent waves of flame lapping over the naked bark.

But the men were well trained and did not panic. Soldiers that could be rescued were, and those lost of a certainty were counted and mourned. Ten dead. With the group on the mountain presumably slaughtered and the four pilots, the toll was at nineteen.

Nineteen deaths Samanei would answer for. Nineteen dead soldiers in need of justice.

Within twenty minutes of the attack, the team had regrouped and was heading as quickly as possible southward. The dux had pointed out an upside to the disaster: the enemy must be low on resources if it was forced to use terrorist tactics, and the soldiers were obviously close to some key position to merit such a suicidal stratagem. So Tony pressed on, determined to find the camp that he knew lay along the river.

Through the remainder of the night they marched, taking a fifteen-minute break every two hours. Their communications relay had been destroyed, so there was no ready way to get Quat a message, which would have done them no good in any event, as the man could scarcely spare soldiers to come succor Antonio's team.

At 10:00 local time, the scouting platoon brought news of some sort of village up ahead, full of clooties who were conveniently mostly in a central clearing. One of the soldiers claimed to have seen some sort of Teregan com rig, but the others weren't so sure.

Awaiting orders, I'll bet.

With the centurion and dux, Antonio worked out a basic plan: surround the village in groups of two or three and execute a simultaneous incursion, using shock charges on the armed warrior caste and taking away their spears then erecting a force-field gaol to contain them. The others could be kept in the various ground structures that dotted the area around the clearing, under rotating guard.

At eleven hundred hours, the plan was implemented flawlessly, except that some of the boyos overestimated the number of shock charges and killed a few of the spear-carrying clooties.

An unfortunate side-effect and a fitting comeuppance.

There were several hundred of the unarmed grendels finally rounded up, and not all of them fit inside the structures: some thirty-five had to be bound together and kept at the center of the clearing, where indeed they discovered a damaged but functioning com rig of local manufacture, its transponder already deployed above the canopy. The cable had been severed, however, perhaps during the team's incursion, and he set some men to taking the frayed end up into the trees to splice it onto the dangling other end.

Antonio then sent Basan around to each of the makeshift gaols to ask after a beast who could speak Baryogo. He found one, a smaller, robed grendel whose shorter claws and lack of such a massive tail made it seem less menacing as an armed escort walked with it and Basan to the temporary command post.

"Sir," Basan said, "this one claims to be the only one that speaks Baryogo here. It's hard to understand sometimes, like somebody with a speech impediment, sir."

"But you can do it, right?"

"Sir, of course, sir."

"Ask it where Samanei is."

Basan blabbered and the creature grunted back at him. "Okay, this is a little strange. It says that 'the one the Greenseer often called Samanei,' she left with Brando to some council of nations, but she's going to come back soon, and when she does, she's going to rescue them from us humans."

Antonio couldn't believe his luck.

No, not luck. Deduction. Strategy.

"Verify that it's Brando D'Angelo that this thing is talking about."

Before Basan could translate, the creature looked right at Tony and smiled, revealing gleaming white teeth and black gums.

"*Rràndo Daenzhelo, kena.*"

"It says it's him, sir."

"Okay. Take it over there, see what else you can get out of it. Lachower, let's get a more permanent base set up. We're going to dig in here, wait a while."

As the dux went to start delegating jobs to certain soldiers while letting others start resting in shifts, an explosion ripped chunks of wood and bark off a tree above where a tent was being erected. Immediately, fifty weapons hummed to life and were trained on the dark green gloom that roofed the team in. Another pulse blast shot down, slamming against the earth near the bound prisoners' guards, and in unison the soldiers fired at its source. Then more energy was flung at them from thirty meters south of the first location.

Could there be lots of them?

There was a rapid exchange of fire above them, and an erk who'd been helping repair the cable came flailing down to impact near Antonio. He heard the others repelling down a tree trunk as he knelt to check his man. The soldier would live: his suit had protected him well, though he would have many broken bones.

The wounded man's two companions rushed over to their captain and reported. "We just got the thing spliced when this black-suited yak comes whipping around on vines like a frigging monkey, sir. He didn't see us at first, till he fired on yall twice, and we got in a position to fire back. Then he let go and did this free fall acrobat shite, and shot Klaus here down, then rolled all freaky as he hit one of them big limbs and popped up to shoot at us, but we were already heading down, sir."

"Did you see anybody else?"

"No, but it was just like a few seconds, sir, so who knows? Maybe this yak is the vanguard of some force."

"Okay, let's get out a message now. Centurion, send some of your better climbers and swingers up into the trees to look for this yak before he runs off and reports."

As they readied the equipment for Antonio's broadcast, the captain thought carefully about what he would tell Quat. Their frequency was being monitored, so he wanted to report their basic position and status, but not give away his plans. In fact, it was probably a good idea to try to fling a red herring out at any eavesdroppers.

"Okay, Captain. It's not a two-way thing. We send, then wait, and then we get a response. No guarantee Mr. Mafioso up there is going to give us much time, sir."

"Got you. Here goes. Quat. Team has just taken the village at..." he prompted a soldier for the coordinates and then repeated them into the mic. "We lost ten men in an assault on us in the early morning hours. Additional nine men presumed killed at Kumora. Under limited attack by yaks and natives. Situation in hand soon. Going to proceed southward in a couple hours. Acknowledge."

The centurion nodded. "Throw listeners off our tail. Good idea."

Tony gave him a curt smile. He glanced around at his men and the monsters they guarded.

One for the history books. Or children's myths.

"Okay, reply coming in. Text only."

Damn. I should've thought of that. I bet he encoded it, too.

"It's encoded. Ha. He's using frogster."

Frogster. Slang from the first year of AF academy. "What does he say?"

"Uh, message received, second team insertion going fine, city under control, advise of any changes."

The screen of the rig went black then, and the cable came coiling down about them.

"Looks like our yak ain't left yet," muttered someone.

"We'll pull him down soon enough," Antonio replied. "Then get ready for the second wave. Those of yall who can, get some rest. We're trenching in for the long haul."

CHAPTER 59

THE VOYAGE IN THE BELLY OF THE FLYING SHIP had been unsettling, but as she jumped from it, clinging to Daenzhelo as the shiny air vessel exploded into flames and tossed the two of them like battle-practice effigies through the air, Shalura knew she was about to die. The heat singed her exposed hair, and forked lighting, sparks from the divine flints, illuminated billowing green clouds that seemed to augur oblivion. Up and up they flew, a sensation unlike any Shalura had ever experienced, akin, she imagined, to what spirits felt as they flew upward into the deepest green. The canopy dwindled below them, and then their flight stopped, and they began to fall.

The lone voice in her head whispered, *do not worry. You will not die.*

And wings leapt from Daenzhelo's back then, bearing them upon the drafts of hot wind that the burning forest exhaled. Slowly the bonded pair dropped into the canopy some two hundred lengths from where the ship had ripped a hole in the leaf-strewn forest. Daenzhelo's wings caught on the upper branches, and they found themselves hanging about three lengths above a narrow limb.

"Let me go, Lady. I will fall true."

Daenzhelo released her grip on Shalura, and the warrior landed in a crouch. Above her, Daenzhelo released the wings and plummeted. Shalura caught her and set her steady on the limb.

"Down," came the little highborn's voice, made strange by the shell that encased her head. They swung and clambered to the ground, found the river, and made their way to the devastation that Daenzelo had wrought. Through the smoke and steam, Shalura saw a troop of ingan hurrying away at great speed, rushing over rock and root with a strange leaping gait far beyond the abilities of any drone.

The pair picked their way quickly around burning husks of the ship, noting how large glowing stumps of strange minerals jutted from the river, redirecting its waters to help the rain quench the embers of Daenzhelo's rage. Shalura found herself falling farther and farther behind as her highborn's powerful skins drove the little one faster than the drone could move.

"Lady, wait." She caught up to Daenzhelo. "I cannot keep up this pace. It seems certain they will make for Dhureinghÿngigg. I propose that you go ahead, keeping them always in sight. I will continue behind you, hopefully reaching the village by mid-morning, though the journey will surely exhaust me."

"Are you sure?" Daenzhelo asked, making her head-shell fold back into the skins. "Will you be okay?"

Shalura laughed. "I have just fallen from the sky in the midst of flames and survived. I imagine that I can run safely through the forest where I have hunted and fought for twenty years."

Daenzhelo moved her head up and down, which Shalura had learned meant affirmation or agreement. "I'll try not to attack until you're arriving. If something happens, though, and I am captured…"

"Do not worry. Between guns and spear, I have the power to free you, my Lady."

Daenzhelo quickly encircled Shalura's waist with her hard, skin-clad arms and then hurried away. She had said nothing about the likely corpses beneath the great hunks of shiny rock that she had flung at the river. Shalura thought it best to not mention this victory, at least not for some time. Novices had to be allowed to harden themselves.

Once she passed the circle of destruction, Shalura took to the trees and began swinging, leaping and running from limb to limb ever southward along the river's edge. She set a grueling pace for herself, but she couldn't stop imagining Daenzhelo facing the ingan hordes alone, their fiery guns covering her in white flames. She had to reach the village as soon as she could, so she pushed herself, harder than she ever had, the voices that had subsided to whispers trying to croak warnings at her.

All through the night she journeyed, across slippery boughs and through curtains of rain and moss. She imagined that if anyone survived the ingan's invasion of the forest, songs might one day be sung about her speed and endurance: she'd always been the strongest and one of the fastest of her tribe's drones, and today she was able to show their spirits, looking down through the misty green morning drizzle, just what greatness they had created in her.

Finally, though, she had to slow, and as the river broadened below into a small bayou she knew lay on the northern outskirts of Dhureinghÿngigg village, she cautiously picked her way through the very highest levels of the canopy. A click and hum caused her to wheel about. It was Daenzhelo, who immediately lowered her gun and ran to Shalura's side.

"Thank God that it's you! When I got here, I was so mad! I couldn't see Rràndo anywhere, and they had the highborn all tied up and the males and children in the storage structures. I saw some drones dead near the latrines, and the rest stripped of their weapons and harnesses, unconscious in a... uh... thing for prisoners. I got really mad and started firing, and now they've been coming up here looking for me for the last three hours. I keep hitting them with fire and knocking them to the ground, but they have almost caught me twice."

Shalura growled low in irritation. "Why did you attack when I was not here, Daenzhelo? You might have been killed. 'A good warrior knows when to keep her spear sheathed.' You have much to learn about warfare."

"Don't be scolding me, Shalura! I am no child."

"You reacted too intensely. Better to wait and learn all you can."

"Okay. I did a stupid thing. I admit it. But they can't call their friends. I destroyed their talk box!"

They spent the next hour slipping around sentinels and search teams, trying to size up the situation. Brando was definitely not in the camp, as far as they could tell. Shalura felt certain that if the man Daenzhelo called Antonio was really looking for his sibling, he would not have closed him up in a building with a group of males after finding him. However, there was the matter of the remaining warriors of Shalura's now dead tribe: they were shut up behind curtains of light along with the drones of the village. Shalura felt compelled to free them, and she and Daenzhelo began to consider ways to distract the guards and pull down the glowing barrier.

Before they could act, however, a figure enclosed in blue light floated up to the broad bow where they crouched, planning. Shalura trained her gun on the being and prepared to fire, but Daenzhelo slapped the fiery reed down and spoke to the floating form. It was an ingan, Shalura noticed, vaguely similar to Daenzhelo in appearance and wearing the robe of a priestess of the Sháinkhÿngigg. Her head fur was twisted away from her face tight braids, and her eyes seemed to reflect the wisdom of the ages as she argued with

Daenzhelo. In her hand, she held a smooth, round stone that Shalura, her hearts quickening, recognized from the People's lore as the Firstborn's tool of great power.

"Çèrhingÿl?" Shalura started, interrupting the heated dialogue between the ingan. "Is it possible the Greenseer was right after all?"

The holy one turned her eyes on Shalura, and such a look of compassion filled them that Shalura fell to her knees. "My child, the Greenseer was wrong in many ways. He wanted to use the People to start a war that would have killed many good souls. But, without knowing, he too was part of God's plan. Çèrhingÿl has indeed returned, in me."

"Oh, no. Don't you be filling my drone's head with that excrement, stupid sister of mine. You're not being a messiah."

"God, who taught you to speak, child? You're butchering their language."

"I learned it myself, idiot. Don't be criticizing me, or I'll punch you in the face! You are always such a pain!"

"All you can think of is violence. Nineteen men, dead? Couldn't you just sit tight and let people who are more qualified take care of the invasion?"

"What? Sit tight and let these stupids be walking into the forest and killing the People? And if you're so qualified, smart floating girl, why didn't you and that stupid rock you are having stop the warriors from coming?"

Shalura didn't know what to think about the strange argument between

Daenzhelo and the ingan who was apparently her sibling, so she stayed on her knees. The one calling herself Çèrhingÿl began to babble in that tribe's strange tongue, but Daenzhelo cut her off.

"No. In the People's tongue. My drone is going to hearing everything that comes from your stupid, arrogant mouth."

"Your drone? What, is she bonded to you?"

"Yes, she is."

Çèrhingÿl said nothing for a moment. "That's a pretty serious step." She called Shalura's highborn some unpronounceable name.

"No. Call me Daenzhelo. And I know that it's serious."

"Daenzhelo? So you've forgiven him? Do you think he'll approve of your new partner?"

"Yes, I forgave him, but I'm not worried about what he may be thinking. Why, do you have a problem with Shalurazhox?"

"No. Not at all. I think it's wonderful."

"Thanks."

Shalura felt the hostility between the two melt away. Çèrhingÿl blew out air with a strange sound. "Listen, I'm sorry I scolded you so severely, Daenzhelo. I am proud of how you've survived out here for four weeks and the transformation you've been going through. You have to understand, though, that the six nations are now unified, and they need to make a deal with the ingan leaders. The best way to make sure that happens is to have all the warriors alive and unharmed, to show that the People don't have to be violent and dangerous. That's why I'm asking you to come with me and leave Antonio alone."

"Alright."

"Alright? That was too easy!"

Daenzhelo laughed her watery laugh. "All you needed to be doing was asking, Çèrhingÿl. I want these crazy ingan off the planet, too. Trust me, killing them is not fun. It makes me feel very, very bad."

Shalura had to interrupt. "So, we are simply going to leave these people here?"

Çèrhingÿl shook her head vigorously, the tailless ones' way of negating. "We'll be back, with an army of drones from each of the six nations. Trust me, Shalura, I see every one of these drones, highborn and males as God's children, and I want them all alive."

"What happened to you, sister?" Daenzhelo asked, her eyes wide. "You are so changed. Where did you be finding that stone, and what has it been doing to you?"

"That's a long story, and most of it I can't reveal. Come with me, though, and I'll tell you what I am allowed. Rràndo's waiting for us, down south with the Council. We are going to set Diadono free. Wouldn't you like to help?"

Daenzhelo hefted her gun and smiled. Turning to Shalura, she said gaily,

"Get up, silly drone of my heart! This is my sister, and we're going to set my village free with her. Your village, now. Your new tribe. Are you ready?"

Shalura, overcome with strange emotions, stood towering over them both and bared her bone white teeth. "I have been ready for battle since I was three years old. Let us go and wage war, my Lady!"

Çèrhingÿl looked at Shalura oddly. "You wear ingan skins now, and my sister claims you for her tribe, but which village did you belong to before?"

The warrior gripped her gun more tightly, seeing in her mind's eye the bodies of her kinsmen desecrated. "My village is no more, and my tribe is dead. The Greenseer poisoned the hearts of some against others, and now Ihéinghÿngigg has passed into the Deepest Green."

"Ah. Ihéinghÿngigg. Yes. We are going south, to where the survivors are living, outside Sháinkhÿngigg."

Shalura stiffened. "They are hardly survivors, Lady. They killed their kin."

"They were deceived and did not know what they were doing. The Greenseer heard a message sent from this round land to the leaders of the ingan: he became certain that they would be here soon, and he pushed for unification harder than he should have. Do not blame your tribe-kin." The floating ingan stepped onto the bough, the blue light fading from around her. "Besides, what they did was turn a blind eye as others murdered their kin. No Ihéinghÿngigg blood was shed by Ihéinghÿngigg claw or spear."

Her tail slapping the bough, Shalura disagreed. "Though the crime be committed by another, 'she who crouches silent and inactive participates.' There are a few of the drones left here in this village, sworn by tradition to kill the traitors, just as I killed the Greenseer. Justice, Lady. How will you give them justice?"

The dark-skinned highborn leveled her sunrise-bright eyes at Shalura, obvious anger in that gaze. "You killed the Greenseer? Oh, the two of you have made my job so much more difficult. I was going to offer him to the ingan as part of our arrangement. 'Acting without understanding is often worse than not acting at all.' Well, it's done, and I'll work around it. As for your tribe's punishment, that is for the Council to decide. I have made recommendations to them: scatter the remaining Ihéinghÿngigg throughout the six nations, punish the Sháinkhÿngigg troop that left the corpses on the ground. But more than that, Shalurazhox, I assure you that the traditions of the People will be changing soon. God slaps her tail at many of our actions, and it is time to obey her will."

Daenzhelo spoke up. "So that's what this is about, Sister? Change? Good. Teach the stupid drones that they have a soul while you're being the change-maker. Make the tribes not be killing baby drones."

Çèrhingÿl nodded. "Once this war is over, those are the first things I plan to do, Daenzhelo."

Sudden gunfire caused the three of them to realize they needed to continue the conversation elsewhere. The shining stone extended its sphere of blue light so that they were all enshrouded in it, and Çèrhingÿl told her companions to close their eyes tightly. Shalura did so, and then felt a curious absence, as if the world had disappeared when she stopped looking at it. There was an absolute silence, maddeningly absent of any sound besides their breathing, and then the noises of the forest came rushing back in a distorted wave. Shalura heard voices, and opened her eyes. She was hovering in the air, slowly descending to a village clearing in which hundreds of highborn stood or sat, talking or eating.

The Council of the Six Nations. All the People united. Incredible.

Daenzhelo and her sister spoke rapidly in their odd ingan tongue, and Shalura's highborn turned to her bonded drone with a strange look on her face.

"Uh, Shal? I need to talk to my *dad* for a little while. Alone. He wasn't being very nice to you last time, so I want to be calming him down so that you and he can be getting along better, okay?"

Shalura smiled faintly: she was already scanning the group, looking for highborn traitors. She wanted answers from those who had been her kin. Çèrhingÿl's words gave some slight comfort, but the warrior who'd been so highly prized by the Ihéinghÿngigg would hear her own former priestesses explain themselves before God and the spirits of the forest.

She soon found Ërhexòlth, the priestess that had served as the late high priestess's assistant. The highborn was sitting with others of the Jöxuçò nation, but when she saw Shalura approach, ingan gun gripped tightly in her claws, she leapt to her feet.

"Shalurazhox, hold your ire. Let us talk, Sister mine."

"Please," spat Shalura. "I await your inadequate explanations, *Lady.*"

"You stand in the midst of the future of our people, Sister. We have joined to forge a new tradition, a unity that will make us strong against the manipulation of the ingan and their messengers, like the Greenseer who so deceived us."

"So this new future will simply wipe away the violations of tradition and holiness you allowed to be committed? I have heard all about the proposals. Scattering you among the tribes is hardly enough. Had I any control over your punishment, the pieces of your bodies would be scattered among the glowing eyes of the many gods. Who decided to work with the enemy? Was it you? Another troop of drones? How did you get the males to agree? They, at least, had the sense to bend their wills to tradition and the voices that speak the truth in our hearts. Did you run them before you like hunted prey? Did the screams of children whose families refused you echo in your ears? You filth of an animal, may their voices haunt you all the days of your newly-forged and haply redeemed existence."

Another highborn stood angrily. "Who are you, drone, that you dare speak thus to your betters?"

"I am Shalurazhox of the Diadono tribe of ingan, bonded mate of Daenzhelo, sister of the Firstborn. Say not another word to me, or you will certainly regret ever speaking at all."

"I wonder whether Council Leader Ùshëshajirh will be so cowed by your ties as to permit you to disrespect highborn, especially chosen representatives in the Council."

Shalura's ears twitched incredulously. "Ùshëshajirh? The Greenseer's mouthpiece? She is your leader? God shine Her mercy on your unworthy soul."

Enraged to the point of desiring violence, even here where Ùshëshajirh's drones could rip her to pieces, Shalura spun around, slapping her tail defiantly against the earth before the highborn, and walked back to where Daenzhelo and her *dad* were talking quietly.

"When we have left this forest, Daenzhelo," Shalura announced, interrupting them gruffly, "I do not wish to ever return."

She kept walking till she was far from the babble of the Council, climbed to the highest boughs of a sturdy tree, and curled up to sleep away the exhaustion and sorrow that burned in the very marrow of her being.

CHAPTER 60

WHEN IN THE WEE HOURS OF THE MORNING the executive council finished its final draft of the Treaty between the Teregan government and the Nakÿng, Rhea found a place for each of her colleagues to sleep and herself went to lie on Jakobo's narrow bed, her closed eyes not welcoming sleep but visions of the past and future. The arrival of Teri, thin, wild-eyed, and full of power, had been overwhelming enough, but the thought of seeing Brando again sent her into a turmoil of conflicting emotions.

It was easier to deal with her daughter's having suddenly transformed into the dauntingly powerful leader of a non-human race than to grapple with the question of her marriage's future. She still felt anger toward Brando for violating her body as she believed he had, using technology to accomplish what nature could not and doing so without her permission. Nonetheless, she yearned for him at a level deeper than her resentment, and her stomach was aflutter with the idea of their reunion. Amid hazy speculation as to how she should act when she saw him, Rhea finally drifted off.

A few hours later, the group awakened and made its way to another homestead slightly to the south, where they got a startled but happy farmer to transport them to the east bridge. They arrived at a little before seven to find, standing stiffly at the opposite bank of the river, the massive, shaggy forms of thirty Nakÿng warriors.

Teri was nowhere to be seen.

Without waiting for the others, Rhea walked down to the river's edge and looked across at them.

"Tearing ghoul?" she called tentatively. As if in answer, space itself bulged behind the warriors, and with a slight sucking of air as the pressure normalized between the fenestration bubble and the surrounding atmosphere, Teri, Brando, Miwa and eleven more warriors alighted on the mossy grass.

Something nearly broken began to heal inside Rhea as she saw her loved ones together and whole.

"Miwa? Oh, my baby!" Stifling the urge to wade into the river, Rhea turned and went over the bridge to throw her arms around her mop-headed daughter.

"Hey, Mom. Long time no see. I missed you."

Miwa was wearing black battle armor. "Me too, honey. Where'd you get this?"

"Dad had left it for me at Kumora. It's a long story, though, and maybe it can wait until this is done, okay?"

"Sure." Rhea turned to look at Brando. Physically, though his clothing was torn and dirty, he seemed fine, but Rhea knew that agonized look in his eyes: he'd had it before, like when Miwa was mauled as a child. His uneasiness around the Nakÿng was obvious and palpable, though he seemed to trust them.

What did they do to you?

She heard the others coming across the bridge, so she hurried to express her feelings. "Brando, we have many things to work out. The matter of our son, for example. But I'd be lying if I said I wasn't happy to see you well."

She resisted, barely, the urge to throw her arms around him. He would have to give an accounting of his actions before she'd even consider forgiving him.

"When I was able to think," Brando rasped, "I never stopped regretting it. Hurting you, I mean."

Teri cleared her throat. "We need time together to talk and heal, but this isn't the moment, don't you agree? We have to get started."

So mature. So unlike the rebellious teen of just a month ago. A mix of pride and sadness settled upon Rhea's soul. *This is how Mary must've felt.* She knew it was possibly sacrilegious of her, but she couldn't help imagining Jesus' mother, watching her son riding into Jerusalem. *Pride. Sadness. A just a hint of fear of what God has in mind.*

The executive council arrived and greeted the humans and one of the warriors, a friend of Miwa's who was apparently their leader. Shal, the gray-eyed teen called the drone.

Teri laid out the plan. "Our group will make a bee-line for the Ministry of Crises, driving any AF personnel they encounter out of hiding and down the street before them. Once the ministry building is cleared, the Nakÿng warriors will split up and spread throughout the city, clearing homes and buildings of soldiers and taking their captives to the visiting dignitary complex, which will serve as a detention center till an agreement could be reached with the Consortium. Ministers, can you contact the TRD and make sure the cleansing of the city is televised?"

Rhea was surprised to discover that Teri knew of the illegal feed to out-system networks, but then she remembered her daughter's earlier ties to Kanaano.

Either that, or that device she has with her can detect the broadcast. If it can fenestrate fifteen people, what can't it do?

Her worries about the power of the orb were forgotten during the liberation campaign. Each time the group would come across knots of soldiers, a similar script would play itself out: a blue blast from Teri's device rendered the AF weapons useless and decompressed their suit helmets. The drones, Miwa and Brando would rush in, immobilizing the soldiers.

Rhea had always hated violence, and the sight of her loved ones whirling through the air to exchange blows with members of the Consortium Army was very distressing. What disturbed her even more was seeing the Nakÿng thumping the human soldiers with the butts of their spears, even though Rhea was aware that the suits absorbed most of the force. Though repelled by the fighting, she had to admit there was something operatic and beautiful about the way Miwa and her drone friend worked together to dispatch the enemy, playing off each other in a violent dance that often sent the soldiers fleeing in fear.

After a couple of hours, the team of humans and Nakÿng strolled up the main street of town, a corps kamiono full of unconscious soldiers grinding along behind them. A good number of army personnel stood blocking the approach the Ministry of Crises, and two camera operators with the TRD logo stamped on their capture and transmit gear were busy filming the standoff.

Rhea saw Teri raise the sphere a little, like the teen had done repeatedly that morning, and close her eyes. Nothing happened. Shudders passed through Teri's body, and across her face flitted a host of emotions. Suddenly she opened her eyes and looked over at Rhea and Khumalo, the only ministers not in the kamiono.

"I need the cameramen to stop recording. Just for a moment."

Khumalo yelled at them to shut off their equipment momentarily. Rhea thought she understood: the device wouldn't work while they were recording. Someone or something didn't want humans across the CPCC to see the orb's power.

Rhea reflected on what Teri had said the previous day: *I'm not here for the Novasanktuloj. I'm here for the Nakÿng. Any message I may have, it's for them.* Whom the message was from, she hadn't said. *God, perhaps?* In any event, the nature of the orb was meant to be a secret.

As the reporters were complying with Khumalo's directive, some of the AF soldiers started opening fire, understanding that something serious was about to happen. A blast ripped through one of the warriors, and another slammed against Miwa, sending her sprawling. Then an expanding sphere of blue light rushed outward from Teri's hands and the firing stopped.

The drones were already moving toward the soldiers, tails out behind them, heads low. Shaken but apparently not hurt, Miwa got to her feet with her friend's help and ran in the same direction. The street erupted in a chaotic melee of hand-to-hand combat that was difficult for Rhea to watch. Brando stayed near her and the Prime Minister, rifle ready in his hands should any of the AF men break through and come at the kamiono. Teri nodded at the TRD reporters to resume their video capture.

Rhea found it hard to breathe as she stood watching. All of her loved ones were in constant danger. Miwa was only fifteen, and she was struggling with adult men who had been trained for battle. Her father had taught her since she was very little, but Rhea couldn't help thinking of incidents that might've happened just yesterday, moments of familial happiness in which Miwa always played the role of sweet little girl. She wasn't a warrior in Rhea's mind: it was incongruous to see her flying in the faces of soldiers alongside the Nakÿng.

Teri, despite her altered appearance and attitude, was, in Rhea's heart, still the petulant pre-teen that had wowed the members of the ward with her insight into the Scriptures and then sulked angrily in her room because her father wouldn't let her go on a picnic with her friends. To see her at the center of this whirlwind of violence, unprotected except by that inscrutable ball? Horrifying.

And here was Brando, traitorous, beloved Brando. The man she'd stood by for years now, even in the face of his betrayal of her. He wasn't even wearing a battle suit, just some sort of vest and leggings. What would she do if he were killed? If they were all killed?

But then the warriors and Miwa overran the soldiers and broke down the door to the ministry, swarming in and easily taking out the few AF personnel that remained inside. Miwa emerged after a few minutes, pushing a manacled Phen Quat before her. She led the captain to the kamiono and stopped in front of Prime Minister Khumalo.

"The ministry building has been cleared, Brother Khumalo. You're free to go inside. Dad and I will finish cleaning up the city, and then you can meet us at the diplomatic complex." She turned to Teri. "Coming, Sis? We, uh, need your help."

Teri nodded. "I need to meet with the executive council first. They have something for me to sign."

Rhea walked beside her daughter as the Prime Minister led them all in. Teri had been taller than Rhea for more than a year now, and the events of recent weeks made her appear even more imposing, despite having also wasted quite a few kilograms from her already thin frame.

"Is it what you want, though?" Rhea said suddenly, as if continuing a conversation they'd just been having. Teri stopped, looking first down at her bare feet contrasting with the beige carpet, then up at the lighting fixtures above her.

"What I want doesn't matter anymore, Rhea, but yes. This is what I want. To belong. To make a difference."

"You already belonged, to a family, a ward, a stake, a planet of brothers and sisters."

Teri shook her head and, sensing the approach of the ministers behind her, began walking again. "Not really. And not anymore. But it's okay, Rhea. I don't want you to be sad, or even angry at Brando. He did what he felt he had to do to at the time. He made Miwa and me, and we came to this world. Recognize that it was God's will, that his hand is in all of this, and the pain will diminish. In a few decades, when the Nakÿng are ready, perhaps we can all of us, Novasanktuloj and Forest Children, belong to the same family. Right now, though, they have much to learn. So you will have to let

go. It won't be easy, I know. You love me. I know that as surely as I know I

love you, too. But you have to let me do this. You have to support me in it,

bend the ear of everyone you can so that my wishes are respected. I'm asking

you to have faith in me. Can you?"

"Yes," whispered Rhea, her voice catching in her throat.

This isn't just Teri anymore. There is more behind those eyes than the
girl I raised.

"I have had faith in you all along."

A tendril of light snaked out from the Urim and touched Rhea's temple

gently for a second, *and she felt Teri in her mind.*

I know you have, Mom.

Mom.

Rhea bit her lip, but the tears came anyway.

CHAPTER 61

BRANDO WATCHED MIWA PUSH CAPTAIN QUAT along with the barrel of her rifle, turning at intervals and muttering to Shalura, the drone she'd told her father she shared a special bond with, one that she would explain to him later. Brando was made uneasy by this revelation, though he'd guessed as much after their fight in the forest. Shuddering at the memory of his descent into the Ona ra-Oni, Brando recalled the touch of Teri's orb on his flesh, in his body, a maddening, burning rush that had scrubbed him clean of all pain and weariness. His daughter had left him in that village, surrounded by the very beings who had tried to kill him. Free to run or attack them or kill himself as he chose, he had opted to stay and watch them, just as Teri had told him to. His rage toward them was intense, but he forced it down, much like he had done upon first arriving on Jitsu and later on this world. After all, he was a scientist, though long out of practice, and at the very least he should be interested in the Nakÿng, as they called themselves, out of academic curiosity.

To his surprise, he had been treated like a king, shown to an expansive highborn-level dwelling and regaled with so much food that his ravenous appetite was satiated in no time at all. Late in the afternoon of his first day as a free man in what he learned was called *Dhureinghÿngiggu shòlixeingh*, the village of the Dhureinghÿngigg, he was awakened from his long nap by the Baryogo-speaking Terhäeq, sent months earlier to this region from her native village of Sháinkhÿngigg far to the south. She begged his pardon and told him that a festival was being held in Teri's honor, and that he was an important guest, the representative of the Firstborn.

Despite wanting to say no, Brando had agreed, and for several hours he was delighted by the odd but moving music of these creatures; by their intricate dances, so like the dervish fervor of the *wende* on Jitsu; and by their wonderful stories, which Terhäeq fumblingly translated without ruining.

Brando began to catch a glimpse of what might have made his daughters embrace the Nakÿng. The beauty and highly structured nature of their culture, the natural bond that grows between captor and captive, and the girls' likely search for identity after the poorly timed and badly handled revelation of their true origins.

As much as it might pain him to see them reject human company for that of these indigenes, Brando had to admit that he had also never sought the companionship of his fellows. Aside from the university, he had hardly spent time among other academics. Since meeting Tenshi three decades ago, he had lived according to two different faiths—one true, the other an illusion. In both societies he had contributed to the stability of the religious community, emulating their ways, and to some extent influencing their manner of thinking so that it widened and was more tolerant. If his daughters had chosen to do the same, who was he to judge?

The mystery of Teri's miracle, however, teased at his mind. She had named the alien sphere *the Urim*, just like the strange meteor on Jitsu, discovered by Oracle Kosiya Yemo nearly a century ago. In the *Achaga Uchimbanun*, her excised teachings, she described how it spoke to her in a voice like a chorus, a clear message from the Ogdoad, telling her its name, the need for a Shrine of Shattering, and the importance of sea pilgrimages for the quantum enlightenment of Jitsu.

Among the many challenging, opaque prophecies in the *Achaga Uchimbanun*, one had haunted Brando for two decades:

"When is a spark not a spark? When it appears in the same shape to many selves. Then it is a Rhëirhènzih. He who has ears to hear, go tell the Urim to protect your son's mind from Sakra, before the false Domina arises."

Thinking on that verse again after an evening of Nakÿng music, Brando had asked Terhäeq, "Is it possible for a drone to bear a child without a male or highborn."

"Our legends speak of such a desperate act," his protector had explained. "A mythic warrior got her revenge on the nation that had slaughtered her own by bearing a replica of herself this way, who went on to destroy the enemy long after the first drone had died."

Brando's heart had quickened as he'd asked, "What do you call such a replica?"

"A rhëirhènzih," Terhäeq had replied. "A *pouch double*."

All that evening, Brando had sat in the dark, reviewing every mysterious happening in his life since meeting Tenshi.

When the epiphany came, it overwhelmed him. Tears streamed down his cheeks, but his weeping was full of joyful laughter.

Oh, Tenshi. I can see it now. Just the outlines, but it's enough. I understand how my spark used Esperanto, how the ramatini left a message for me decades before we met, how a Nakÿng word is embedded in Pathwalker scripture written a century ago.

How you were able to speak to me when I touched the spike.

Now all I need know is why.

What will my role be? How much longer must I prepare?

And to what extent will the rest of my family be involved?

Near the Council of the Nakÿng, Miwa had confirmed that her motives were not the same as Teri's.

"Shal and I are going to live among humans. Maybe here, maybe somewhere else. But, like she just told me a little while ago, she doesn't want to come back to her people after we leave the forest. So we'll see."

After she'd revealed this, she had showed Brando her datapad with its files on the linguistic and cultural features of the Nakÿng. Brando had been surprised the quality of her work, the meticulous detail and the cogent analysis.

"Wow, Miwa, you could probably get this published!" he'd exclaimed as the sun had set the day before. "Let me clean it up a bit for you, and when all this craziness blows over we can present it to some net journals. You might become pretty famous! I'm sure people will be dying to know something about the Nakÿng, and since your sister has decided to cloister them away, you might be the only source."

Help me give her a normal life. Let her be far away from the paradox when it unravels.

Miwa had burst into tears, telling him of the men that had died at her hands and how afraid she was of being jailed.

"Look, don't worry. Those idiots are here illegally and against orders. They were invading Nakÿng territory unprovoked. Besides, you're a minor. The worst that could happen is you'd go to a correctional facility for two Standard years."

She'd started sobbing even more then, and Brando had forced Teri to come over and swear to her sister that she'd negotiate Miwa's immunity when she made a deal with the Consortium. Something in the way Teri's eyes twitched when she spoke of this deal made Brando uneasy: he could sense that she didn't want to give anyone the specifics, and he was concerned about what she might be preparing to give away for peace's sake. She'd already forbidden any killing at all, a command that had made their present liberation campaign in Diadono difficult, though the Urim's trick of erasing the codes in the soldiers' carpal sensors helped make the job easier than it might've been. Without weapons, the AF boyos were little more than armored punching bags for the ferocious Nakÿng drones and the almost equally brutal Miwa D'Angelo, as she insisted she be called.

Brando tried not to smile: Rhea's distress at seeing the teen put all the training of a lifetime to actual use was palpable, and the last thing Brando wanted right now was to worsen the strain she was under by revealing his glee at his daughter's fighting prowess. His guilt for his present wife's psychological torture was so great that this bit of self-control was the least he could do. Though he knew he should find time to beg her forgiveness, Rhea's possible reaction petrified him. He could sense anger and love and hurt coming off her in waves when she glanced at him every couple of minutes, and it had almost been a relief to see her slip inside the Ministry of Crises on Teri's heels twenty minutes ago.

"This is what you cloned them for, eh?"

Brando's head snapped around, his chain of thought broken. Quat was craning his neck to look back at him with a strange glint in his eye.

"Shut up, Quat, and just keep walking."

"To reject their humanity and hang out with beasts. Interesting. Not just illegal clones, but traitors, too."

"Damnit, Quat..."

Miwa shook her head. "Let him say whatever he wants to say, Dad. He's just desperate. Means nothing."

"You know, for a while I thought that the one with the alien device was Samanei. Sure you didn't clone your sister-in-law by mistake? Same sociopathic tendencies."

For the briefest of seconds, doubt made adrenaline kick at Brando's heart. But no, Kyr's betrayal hadn't gone that deep. Brando had been there every step of the process.

"Fuck you and the oppressive symbol you've got tattooed on your bald head. Come here to this planet and mess with these gentle people. Who gave yall the right?"

"We wouldn't be here if you hadn't come here with your freak children to hide out like a snake in the grass. No, you're not going to shift the blame to me, fucker. Even if it's true that Koroma ain't here, you still lied to them, you brought that fucking robot, *you're the one to blame.*"

The words were a blow so true that Brando snapped and threw himself on the handcuffed captain, toppling him to the ground. Clamping Quat's stubbly head between his hands, he tried to slam it against the cobbled street. Suddenly he was yanked into the air some three meters above Quat, where he hung, struggling uselessly.

Stop it, Brando. This isn't your show. These men get handled as I say, not as your emotions dictate. Do you understand? Can I put you down?

"Yes. Okay." He looked askance at Teri as she lowered him to the ground: she resembled Tenshi so much at that moment, the expression of disappointment that so many Jitsujin had met with carved into her face, that he wanted to cry. Instead, he took up his weapon and walked back to the kamiono.

Sobered, Brando spent the next couple of hours watching the prisoners as the Nakÿng and his daughters captured another seven or eight soldiers, often to the applause of Tereganoj who, even after only less than two days of occupation, were thrilled to see the AF get its comeuppance.

Finally, the group of liberators arrived at the diplomatic complex, a beautiful scattering of buildings designed by the architect Adriano Madrigal, a favorite of Teri's. His style, though a bit conservative and classical, was clean and graceful. Many of the buildings on Terego, including the Temple at Diadono, had been built by Madrigal and his father before him, and their limpid elegance highlighting the magnificent landscapes of the lush, green world Brando had fallen in love with.

Their weapons unresponsive in their gray-gloved hands, the AF soldiers guarding the building were quickly dispatched with sharp blows to the back of the neck with thick spear-hafts. In moments, Miwa and Shalura were jerking open the doors to the various suites, freeing the people who'd been locked inside.

"Time for the next big surprise," muttered Teri at Brando's elbow.

"What do you mean?"

"These are the kids who were captured with me, and their families. Khumalo had them put in here to keep the existence of the Nakÿng a secret, I think. And, yes, there they are: coming through that door right now. Carmen Allende and her parents."

Teri's face lit up with what might've been joy.

"Do they have something to do with the surprise?"

Teri glanced at him. "Carmen was almost killed by the Nakÿng. Specifically, their new council leader, under Kyr's influence. But that's just the beginning of the awkwardness you're about to see." She smiled as Carmen noticed her. The older girl waved, also smiling sheepishly. "I'm Tenshi's clone, Dr. D'Angelo. Put two and two together."

Beatriz and Gustavo Allende had kept their relieved gaze on their daughter and each other at first. As their eyes lifted from their shuffling feet, however, they saw the Nakÿng standing calmly around Teri and Brando, and Beatriz gave a scream, clinging to her husband in terror. Gustavo glared at Teri, trying to thrust Carmen behind him.

"How dare you," he spat, "walk into this place with those beasts who tried to kill my daughter?"

"Papá!" Carmen pulled away from her parents. "I've already explained what happened. It isn't their fault. And it certainly isn't hers."

She ran to Teri and the two girls embraced, holding each other much longer than Brando expected.

Ah. They're a couple.

"It's like I told you, Brother," came a voice from another doorway. "Teri the grendel-queen with her devil-ball has seduced your daughter. Now we exchange one set of captors for an even more hideous one."

Looking over Carmen's shoulder, Teri bored her eyes into the emerging young man as she said calmly. "Josuo, stay out of this. I'm here to get the AF out of the city as per a treaty I signed with Prime Minister Khumalo a few hours ago. I'm merely a representative of the Nakÿng, not their leader, and this contingent of drones is a goodwill gift to the citizens of Diadono. This is the last time that I explain myself to you, Elder Mudumala, so I hope that is clear."

Carmen loosened their embrace, turning to face her parents. "As for the other thing, I'm older than Teri. If anyone is guilty of seduction, it's me."

Teri took her hand and shook her head lightly. "There will be time for that conversation later, Mrs. Allende, Dr. Allende. Right now, please understand that these drones at my side had nothing to do with the attack on Carmen, and they are sworn to protect all Novasanktuloj from off-world intruders."

"More like sworn to help you get your dad out of going to prison,"

Josuo spat. "Why is he still running around, anyway? The AF are here. He ought to be handed over already. He's caused enough harm as it is."

Teri ignored him, taking a few slow steps toward Carmen's parents. "We've been instructed to forgive, haven't we? The Book tells us, 'of you it is required to forgive all people.' So I made a promise: no revenge. No one gets killed. Not the AF soldiers, not the Nakÿng, not the Novasanktuloj. We're going to find a solution to this."

The mother looked up at her with red-rimmed eyes. "How can I ever see them as anything other than monsters?" she whispered.

"I can help you," Teri murmured, crossing the distance between them, Carmen in tow. "I can show you their beauty and honor. I can ease the resentment in your heart. I can show you that I'm sincere."

What in the world is she doing?

"Get away from them!" Josuo shouted, but an indigo glow was already enveloping the teens and Carmen's parents. Their eyelids fell as the four trembled at some emotional exchange that Brando could sense but not see. Josuo left the shadows of the doorway to his room and tilted recklessly at Teri, but Brando stepped in and yanked him back.

"Let go off me, you asshole!"

Dragging the young man back to the apartment, Brando said nothing until he'd slammed the door shut and flung Josuo on the carpeted floor.

"Listen to me, punk. I don't know what happened between Teri and you, but you clearly crossed some sort of line. Let me put this bluntly. She's asked me not to kill anyone, but I already have so much blood on my hands that one more scrawny little piece of filth won't add much to my sentence. So just push me, son. Push me and give me an excuse to ease Teri's resentment the Brando D'Angelo way."

His face white, his eyes wide and glassy with tears, Josuo Mudumala said nothing. Blood still rang shrilly in Brando's ears, though he doubted he could kill the young man. Maim him, maybe. But not kill him. He clenched his jaw to keep from laughing at the punk's fear.

"Smart kid. Now, stay in here till we're gone, and keep your mouth shut. If you start poisoning people against my daughter, I'll rip your testicles out."

He stormed out just in time to see Teri and Carmen embracing Carmen's parents, all four of them crying.

Miwa caught his eye and gestured for him to follow her out. All the Nakÿng had already exited. Once near the kamiono again, Miwa sighed.

"That's just scary, what she's able to do. I mean, making weapons shut down and transporting people through space in a snap is bad enough. But getting into people's heads? I don't know, Dad. That's a lot of power."

Unable to share his epiphany with Miwa or anyone else, Brando just nodded. "She swears it's all for the Nakÿng. I've decided to trust her."

"I wish she weren't being so tight-lipped about her plans, though. All she does is spout vague pronouncements. She's getting a little too, I don't know, *messianic* for me. But, hey," Miwa shrugged her armored shoulders, "if she can get the CPCC to exonerate me, she can *be* the Nakÿng's savior, as far as I'm concerned. Anyway, they need someone to pull them out of some of the messed-up stuff they do and teach the drones that they have souls."

Brando said nothing. Trying to explain his own beliefs about souls and the Path would be pointless at the moment. Father and daughter stood silently until Teri emerged.

"Is it true, then?" Miwa asked. "Are you and Carmen a couple?"

"We're not *bonded* yet," Teri said with a pointed smirk, "but yes, Minjo. I love her. Now, then. We're almost done. We're lacking the legislative building and the crisis depot. You guys head out that way once you get these soldiers into the rooms. Leave about ten drones here to guard them. You'll find that their suits have fallen off. Miwa might need to close her eyes, since some of them don't follow AF regulations about undergarments."

Miwa stuck her tongue out at her sister, and for a moment, it felt as if they were all in the ice cream parlor on Sunday after church, making jokes and having fun.

Incredible that they can be so resilient.

Then the humor was gone from Teri's face, and she went on.

"I'll go to the legislative building, then meet you as you're reaching the depot to give you a hand with the carpal sensors and all that."

"You can handle the soldiers there?" Miwa asked. "Are you sure?"

"Miwa, I could've done all of this by myself. I brought the Nakÿng and you two as a strategic thing. Did you see those people applauding us as we captured the soldiers? That's what will stay in their minds: the natives and the D'Angelos liberated Diadono. A powerful memory. A powerful tool."

Brando shook her head.

It's scary how much she thinks like Tenshi. And that's what I hoped for, the reason I raised her on this world.

"Take one away. Bring two back. Prepare them." The voice on his sea pilgrimage had been clear.

A leader. That's what Tenshi was meant to be, and that's what Teri has become. Despite all the other things I screwed up, I seem to have gotten this one right. Now let's pray she can undo all the tragedy.

Then the prisoners were in their rooms, and Brando, Miwa and thirty-one drones were on the move again, moving faster than before because there were no captives to watch or enemies to fight.

They rushed en masse toward the corpsmen being held hostage at the arms depot. Brando almost looked forward to the fight, and he guiltily wished it would last a long time. When this job was done, it would be time to face Rhea.

Compared to *that* confrontation, battling AF soldiers was easy.

INTERCHAPTER J

From: mifflint@shaka.gov.af

To: sorall@executive.cpcc.gov

Subject: Let's act now

Date: May 12, 2714 12:27:58 (SST)

Prime Minister,

I humble myself to ask for your understanding. I didn't contact you or respond to your messages adequately because I was on the horns of a dilemma. I was instructed by the Navarch, in violation of the chain of command (see the attached missive from him), not to act, to allow you to send in the XID and for them to clean up here. However, you are the leader of the bulk of human space, and I would be remiss in my duty to you if I did not tell you what has recently occurred on Terego. Following is a brief summary (full logs and reports are attached):

$\sum$ **Wednesday, 27:35 (local time)-**Large explosion at base of Kumora mountain, seeming to be local flivvers used by Captain D'Angelo for transport to that area

$\sum$ **Thursday, 00:15 (local time)-**Even larger explosion over last reported position of Captain D'Angelo's team. Intercepted transmissions from immediate minutes before the crash indicate that Miwa Miranda, clone of Tana D'Angelo, was responsible for both explosions.

$\sum$ **Thursday, 11:22 (local time)-** Communication between Phen Quat and Antonio D'Angelo intercepted. D'Angelo reports taking a native village, losing nineteen men, preparing to march south.

$\sum$ **Thursday, 11:49 (local time)-**Communication between Phen Quat and Dux Bulavas intercepted: Bulavas reports readiness to attack a native village, instructed to do so by Quat.

$\sum$ **Thursday, 17:03 (local time)-**The *Shaka* detects a quantum disturbance localized in the capital city.

$\sum$ **Thursday, 17:16 (local time)-**Frantic messages from Phen Quat to Dux Bulavas and Captain D'Angelo go unanswered by either man. Quat claims that Samanei Koroma entered the crisis ministry and somehow removed the executive council from the room they'd been detained in.

$\sum$ **Thursday, 17:20 (local time)-**Quat again tried to raise D'Angelo and Bulavas, amending his previous message to indicate that the intruder was not Samanei Koroma but Teri Miranda, and that she had whisked the Teregan leaders away using some sort of alien tech in the form of a glowing metal sphere.

∑ **Thursday, 18:00 (local time)-**The *Shaka* responds to a hail from the surface. Phen Quat asks my help in scanning for humans at the last known locations of the two teams. I agree, and discover D'Angelo's group intact at the same position, but Bulavas's men are located in a different place than their weapons and suits. I assume they have been taken prisoner.

∑ **Friday, 07:23 (local time)-**Quat begins to contact the Shaka with reports of a force of humans and natives entering the city. Soon local broadcasts confirm: Teri Miranda, Miwa Miranda and Brando D'Angelo head a force of native fighters, with executive council in tow in large troop transport full of unconscious grunts. Quat frantic, blockades building.

∑ **Friday 11:45 (local time)-**Despite minute-long break in transmission, local infotainment shows executive council entering crisis ministry and Quat being led away as a prisoner.

∑ **Friday, 14:32 (local time)-**The *Shaka* is contacted by Prime Minister Khumalo with the news that the Nakÿng (the official name of the natives) and the Tereganoj have signed a treaty. Both groups insist that the CPCC must immediately contact them and begin negotiating the release of the one hundred and twenty-three soldiers being held prisoner.

Moments before beginning this message, I was told by my first officer that scans of the forest detect a massing of Nakÿng some twenty kilometers to the south of Captain D'Angelo's position along with enormous quantum fluxes. It is unfortunate, but I have no means of contacting him. I request that we act now, that you give me the codes to unlock my fighters and order me to provide either backup for Antonio or to lay down fire for his retreat. I'm willing to go down and arrest him, if you want. I can't just sit here anymore, though. No matter what the Navarch says, you are my commander-in-chief.

Command me.

Tarka Mifflin

CHAPTER 62

BRANDO TOOK A QUICK SHOWER at the depot's locker room and slipped on a green one-piece used by maintenance personnel, the only one large enough to fit him. Word had come that he'd been released into Rhea's custody, and the native affairs czar would be around to pick him up in just minutes. Freeing the corpsmen at the depot had been easy, and now Teri had taken all but ten of the Nakÿng back with her to the forest, where she planned, as far as she let her father and sister understand her plans, to bring a force of drones against her "uncle" and his men.

Brando assumed that she needed the Nakÿng to knock out the AF soldiers and carry them to wherever she meant to hold them: she'd already shown she could disarm her enemies with the Urim, but Brando wasn't so sure that she could handle the actual apprehension of fifty-some grunts, despite her god-like powers.

Miwa, Shalura and the remaining Nakÿng were headed south to the flooded granite mine to secure the escape pods. Teri had explained that she didn't want any avenue of escape open to the AF on the planet, but the way her eyes glazed over when she talked about the vessels made Brando think that there was something else, some other reason for protecting the pods. Perhaps she wanted them, though Brando couldn't fathom why. For the Nakÿng?

His palms tingling with nervousness, Brando walked out to the gate. The kamioneto was already there, its silent engine idling. The window shot down, and Jakobo stuck his brown-topped head out to shout and wave joyfully.

"Daddy! Daddy!"

Brando sprinted over, his apprehension leaving him. His son, his precious little boy. Slender like his mother and just as talkative. *Yakkety-yak*, Miwa had always called him. Brando pulled open the passenger door.

"Slide over, boy. Giant adult coming through!"

Jakobo laughed and scrunched up between his mother and father, giving Brando a kiss on the cheek and grabbing a meaty, knotty-veined hand in his own. Brando glanced quickly at Rhea, who had the ghost of a smile pulling at her mouth and a hint of tears in her eyes.

"So, Dad, you fought those big monsters?"

As Rhea turned and started heading north, Brando nodded. "Yes, but, Son, like people, only some of them are monsters. The ones that are your sisters' friends are helping us out."

"Did you kill the bad ones, though?" Jakobo seemed a little too obsessed with the idea, Brando thought. Rhea frowned.

"That's enough, Jakobo. We're not to delight in the death of God's children, no matter what they've done."

Brando agreed with a somber nod. "Jakêjo, I had to kill some, yes, but it doesn't make me happy. I never wanted to kill anybody all my life."

Jakobo looked at him quizzically. "But you did, right? That's what everybody is saying, that you're a killer."

The tears that had been shining in Rhea's eyes began to dribble down her cheeks.

"It's kind of hard to explain, but sometimes life doesn't give you a lot of choices. Yes, I have killed people. But I was like a policeman, you see, and the men I killed were breaking the law and making other people, innocent people, die. In order to stop them, I had to do some things that people don't agree with."

"That's why you used a made-up name? Because they were looking for you?"

Brando heard Rhea's breath catch, but he didn't look at her. "Yeah. And I came here and met your mom. We made each other happy. Then you came along and made us even happier."

Jakobo smiled his big, goofy grin. "I made you happy?"

Brando nodded, gritting his teeth so as not to cry.

"I love you, Daddy. I missed you a whole bunch. I didn't have to go to school, though! That was good. I played a whole lot with Ken and Yuki, though. They have a pool inside their house, Dad!"

And with the resilience of the very young, Jakobo proceeded to animatedly explain all of the exciting activities he'd engaged in while his dad had been away. Brando laughed with him and nodded, asking just the right questions to let his boy find release from the fear that had no doubt been eating at him for most of the past month. The grizzled teacher had learned long ago that both his wife's and his son's tendency toward talkativeness was a release mechanism, one that he'd never needed but that he completely understood.

As Jakobo spoke, Brando stole glances at Rhea, who took her eyes from the guide strip from time to time to stare at him while the kamioneto was directed by its onboard computer. For a man who had killed nearly a hundred people in his life and now about a dozen Nakÿng, Brando felt small with those eyes on him, weak and defenseless.

The guide strip ended about a mile from the house, and Rhea steered the kamioneto over the gravel road that led to the narrow wooden bridge across the stream near their house. The nearly constant rain had slackened to a drizzle, and Jakobo unclicked his restraints in order to crane his head at the slow waters beneath the bridge.

"Oh, Dad, could we go fishing? Please, please, please? Come on, say that yes we can! Remember: the fish always bite more in the rainy time. You said, remember?"

"Well, sure, we can go if Mom says it's okay."

Rhea raised an eyebrow, as if to say *fine, good idea, but you're still going to get it from me later.*

"Of course it's okay, but just till the rain starts up again. Take the soccer ball for when you're waiting."

They pulled into the drive and Jakobo leapt from the vehicle, unlocking the door with an impatient palm and hurrying inside the house.

"He really has missed you, you know." Rhea looked back at Brando as they ascended the wooden steps to the porch. "So have I."

Inside, Brando changed into denim pants and a flannel shirt. Jakobo already had their slickers and gear waiting at the door, and the two of them trudged with galoshes through the mud to the rocky banks of the stream.

For the next four hours the two of them fished and laughed at silly primary-school jokes, and Brando tried to teach his son how to use head and knees when playing soccer. Several times during the outing, Brando imagined freezing the moment forever, the two of them eternally together, watching the water idle by, pulling large fresh water fish-analogs from the chilly ripples, doggedly trying to dribble on the uneven rocks and having to retrieve the ball from the greedy stream whenever their footwork failed.

But those yearnings were the last vestiges of Nano Miranda. Brando understood that the Path was already curving, leading him elsewhere. He was going to have to hurt the innocent all over again.

The rain began to quicken, and they stowed their gear and iced the fish they'd scaled and gutted. Back in the house, Brando and Jakobo showered together quickly while Rhea battered and fried the fish. Everything was infused with a somber hint of finality: lathering his son's hair, helping him rinse off, toweling him dry, Jakobo's insistence on dressing himself and trying to comb his unruly shock of gold-flecked brown hair. Brando fought back tears at the surety that this was the last time they'd do these things together.

At the table, Rhea had them sit as she set the plates and food before them. Then she joined them, looking at Brando with scowled expectation. He had always led their prayers: as head of a household on Terego it had been his duty and pleasure. But of course he couldn't do it anymore. The façade had dropped, and his lips simply would not form the empty words, no matter how much they meant to the other two people at the table. So Brando turned to Jakobo and smiled.

"Jakêjo, you're getting big. Time to participate more. You'll be a dad some day and it'll be your job. So why don't you say grace, okay?"

Jakobo nodded and clasped his parents' hands. With delicate caution, Brando took Rhea's other hand. It was cold, as her extremities always were, in need of warmth that he knew he could no longer provide.

"Dear Lord, thank you for the food that Mommy has made for us, and thank you for bringing Daddy back and for keeping Miwa and Teri safe. Keep us all together forever and ever. Oh, and bless the Nakungoj, too. Make them not kill any more Novasanktuloj. Amen."

"Amen," Brando muttered, letting Rhea's slender fingers slip from his gnarled hand. She nodded, as if to say *good recover* or *fine, no problem.*

As they ate, they listened to a radio rebroadcast of the events in Diadono. The legislature, despite having already signed the treaty with the Nakÿng, was still in session, discussing what course of action the planet should now take. The leaders of wards and stakes were uniting to prepare for the address that the Prophet had just announced he'd make to the whole planet on Sunday. All of Terego was abuzz, except for Kanaano, which simply kept broadcasting the feed off-world without any official comment from its local leaders.

After dinner, Brando put Jakobo to bed, reading him the story of Daniel in the lions' den, the boy's favorite. "That's what happened with you, right, Dad? God closed up their mouths so they couldn't bite you?"

"Something like that, Jakĉjo. Now go to sleep. Tomorrow is another busy day."

"Can we make a tent in the living room and play explorers?"

"Sounds good. Now, sleep." Brando kissed him on the forehead.

"Night-night, Dad."

Brando tousled his hair and slipped out.

Rhea was waiting on the sofa, drinking green tea, her legs curled up under her.

"Okay," Brando said with a sigh.

"Yes, okay. That's a good way to start. But it's not okay, you realize."

"I know."

"I mean, lying to me about who you were, about where our daughters came from, about the death and identity of your first wife, all of that was bad enough."

Brando put up a hand. "Look. I'm a Pathwalker, but your religion does matter to me. Our children are better off in a community of believers, so I thought it was a worthy sacrifice."

"Sacrifice? What, being with me?"

"No, Rhea. Pretending to believe. Pretending to be a Novasanktulo. Keeping my own faith a secret. It wasn't easy. But I did it, for them and for you."

Rhea was shaking her head. "You gave *classes*, Brando! People came to you for explanations. I saw you pray, saw you weep, caught up in the Spirit. How can that be faked?"

"It can't." His eyes closed for a second, saw Nakÿng dancing with wild abandon. "I was caught up in the Blue. Restitching my self around my spark. Building a soul."

Rhea smirked. "Sounds like your spirit was in communion with God. Is that so impossible?"

"Only one creature has ever called himself God," Brando groaned. "And he is blind to the truth of his own nature. That willful ignorance, that spiteful pride, it's what brought evil into the universe."

Rhea set her cup down and leaned forward. "Evil exists because men choose it."

He gesticulated sharply, his throat constricting as he rasped, "I didn't choose for them to be slaughtered, Rhea."

"No, but Santo did, Brando. How could you control that?"

Pacing back and forth, he responded at length. "I couldn't. No one could. That's how I know that the kind of God you believe in doesn't exist. Higher beings that allow evil to exist are either evil themselves or indifferent. Or broken and unable to interfere. Oh, I know what you want from me. Faith. Faith that your God has some mysterious plan, that I was supposed to lose Tenshi and Tana so I could clone them and bring them here and they would stop the AF and save the Nakÿng…"

His voice trailed off.

It's so close to the truth that the truth cleverly hides within that lovely fantasy.

Rhea's legs unfolded and dropped to the floor. "Sit down, Brando, you're driving me to distraction. If there's no God, what about our sealing? What are we to each other? I know what I *thought* we were: partners, sharing everything, supporting one another, making decisions as a team. So why don't you explain to me *how Jakobo was conceived.*"

Her voice sharpened in a way Brando wasn't used to as she pronounced these last words, making them slaps to his face. He dropped into the armchair facing her.

"No more lies."

"No more, Brando. That's the only way this will work, if it even can."

It can't. But I think you've already realized that fact, deep down.

Brando pressed his hands to his eyes, a prism of sparkling color and pain leaping to life. "It was right before your birthday, six years ago. Your biological clock was ticking down. We'd tried everything to get pregnant, even though it was clearly unpleasant for you. I felt you get up at night and go into the kitchen to cry. Imagine what that did to me, Rhea. You were raising the girls wonderfully, just like Tenshi would've wanted, but I could tell that you wanted a child that was yours, *ours.*

"When I first got to Terego, before I reported to the immigration authorities, I snuck around the sensors and landed my ship near Mount Kumora. I found a couple of caves that were the right size, and I stuck my equipment in them. The chirurgic I had with me, Kyr, I left in charge of all the scientific equipment. I reprogrammed him to be autonomous: I figured that with everything he'd been through, he deserved to be his own boss. The weapons I sealed in another cave along with a training program for the girls so that if anything ever happened to me, they could go there and defend themselves. Or whatever. I wasn't sure what would happen, but I wanted a sort of back door. Miwa found it recently.

"Anyway, I pestered you for a chance to get away for a while, and when you relented, I sped to the mountain. But I couldn't go north because of the forest, so I had to go through the pass to the east, then north along the volcanic plain and then west along the northern wastes till I came to Kumora. I convinced Kyr to help me, and we loaded up the equipment we needed and returned."

Rhea seemed ready to burst. "And that's when you opened me up, right? That's when you put me to sleep or whatever it was that you did."

"It wasn't like that! I never cut you: a little tube…"

"You stuck a tube up inside of me?" Rhea bit her lip. "Don't you understand what a violation that is? Why didn't you just *ask* me? Don't you think I would've wanted your help? Don't you think that I might've agreed?"

"In order to tell you, I would've had to reveal everything. How could I ask for your permission and still keep us safe?"

Rhea shook her head angrily. "We wouldn't have been in danger. There would've been a way to fix things, negotiate with the Consortium, something."

"No, Rhea. Once you dig a hole as deep for yourself as I have, you don't get out that easily."

"Who said anything about it being easy?" She stood up and walked across the carpet to stand in front of him. "When has anything been easy, Brando? Being righteous isn't easy. Being a husband and a father isn't easy. But you chose this road. You married me, you cloned those girls and gave me Jakobo, you beckoned to their little souls and drew them out of heaven to bond to these bodies your hands created. You are responsible for what happens now, Brando."

He reached out and took her hand. "I'm responsible for more than you can imagine. I made Kyr walk back to the mountain with the equipment. He wanted to stay, be part of our lives, but I ran him off. Told him to go back to the cave. I couldn't have him here, you see. I would've had to explain the lies."

Rhea knelt before him. "And he found the Nakÿng, didn't he? Found them and used them to hurt you."

Brando nodded, chest aching.

"And he has hurt you, hasn't he? Hurt you and hurt me and hurt us all."

"He's dead now. Miwa's friend destroyed him. But that doesn't ease my guilt. I should have known better. But I was so submerged in the persona I built that I couldn't see the danger. Forgot my purpose. Believed I truly loved you."

As if she'd been slapped, Rhea tumbled back onto the rug. "Are you saying you don't love me? After all that's happened?"

It's going to hurt, but you have to tell her the truth at last.

"No lies, remember? Rhea, you fell in love with Nando Miranda. I crafted him. He's a reflection in the social sphere of Terego of my rebuilt self. But he is not a part of my emergent soul."

Eyes red, chest heaving, Rhea managed to stutter fierce words. "You drugged Teri. Called her Tenshi. What are you hoping for, resurrection? Return? She's *dead*, Brando. I'm here, in front of you, still loving you after all this betrayal. What is WRONG with you?"

Brando stood, looking down at her. He hated himself, but he could see no other way.

"You and I were sealed in the temple. But that afterlife is a lie. That bond is an illusion. You have no soul, Rhea. Just a spark you've never seen. I don't think you'll ever choose to walk the Path, much less create a soul."

The choked gasp that hitched from Rhea's chest almost stopped him then.

But she needed to hear it all.

"Tenshi told me she would return. If this Grey Prison in which we suffer keeps her from me, I will be translated at the end of my life. I'll rejoin her in ra-Yindawo. Yes, Rhea. Even though I used you at first to be a mother for my girls, I came to love you. But Tenshi—I don't just love her. I walk the Path in her footsteps. She is my teacher. My angel. My goddess. I will tear down the universe to be with her again."

Rhea turned from him, crumpling into a ball, her heart breaking in shuddering sobs and muffled howls.

Brando didn't console her. He headed to their bedroom and took his travel bag from the closet. Turning to the dresser, he was surprised to find the datapad he'd loaded with Pathwalker texts.

And his wedding ring, glittering with impossible hints of blue.

Slipping it on his left hand, where it fit him to inexplicable perfection, Brando started pulling clothes from drawers and stuffing them into his bag.

"Where do you think you're going?" Rhea rasped amid sniffles from the door.

"Away."

"From Terego? How?"

"My ship. It's in the immigration warehouse, the big one."

With unexpected anger, Rhea hurried into the room and shoved at him.

"Brando, you will *not* escape the consequences of your actions, do you hear? You're not going anywhere! You've been released into my custody. I'm a government official now, Brando, and I'll probably be called as head of the Helpsocieto soon as well. I have a responsibility to this planet and to my church."

Brando clenched his fists. "So much for the love you profess to feel. Do you know what they'll do to me if they take me off this planet? Life, Rhea. Life on the military prison asteroid orbiting Yahweh in Mu Cassiopeiae. I have to be free for when the paradox unravels, damn it! Able to move where I'm needed, to protect the girls. To protect you and Jakobo, too Is your political ambition more important than this family?"

Rhea yanked the travel bag from his hands, her voice going cold. "You have no right to question my dedication to this family, Brando. Besides, they won't take you off this planet. Teri won't let them. Miwa said her sister was going to work out an immunity agreement for her. I'm sure she'll do the same for you."

She stepped through the door and started shutting it.

"What the fuck are you doing?" Brando demanded in Standard.

"Locking you the hell inside that room," she replied in the same language. "And activating the alarm. Don't look at me like that! I don't trust you. You've destroyed my trust in you. I swear, if you—"

She was cut off by the roar of aircraft rushing overhead, shuddering the walls and windows.

AF fighters, thought Brando as he pushed past Rhea and ran out into the chill night air.

"What is it?" Rhea demanded, hurrying after as the lights receded in the direction of the forest.

"The AF. I guess Mifflin decided to act, after all." The executive council had told him and his daughters about Mifflin's promise. "A little late, though. Looks like they're going toward Antonio."

"I should call Khumalo and check whether he knows about this yet."

Brando was about to agree when the sky above the forest to their north exploded in thousands of aching fragments of color.

CHAPTER 63

BY MID-EVENING, AFTER A GRUELING EIGHT HOURS of fenestration
that had left the Urim in need of down time, Teri had assembled her army
some twenty kilometers to the south of Dhureinghÿngigg village. The
logistics of her planned offensive were complex, but the Urim had convinced
her that using the Nakÿng was the best way. Teri held in her hands the
power to disarm the soldiers, to render their battle suits useless, but tracking
individuals down as they scattered through the forest was impossible, and
killing them all, besides being out of the question, would be difficult.

Since she couldn't afford to have a bunch of angry army personnel
running about the forest causing trouble, Teri had to first get the Nakÿng in
place, then lead them in, deactivate the weapons, and let the drones catch
the grunts. Twenty kilometers was as close as she wanted to risk fenestrating
them, as it took hours to bring them all through and Antonio likely had scouts

patrolling the area around the village.

The Nakÿng weren't accustomed to fighting in such large groups, but Teri, with the Urim's help, had imposed another level of structure on the new conglomeration of troops. Each troop leader was responsible to the *jerhùdaqih*, the general, as Teri liked to think of her. The drone in this position, picked by the Urim without a word of explanation, was Örhaexith, a seasoned warrior from one of the older villages closer to the sea whose prowess and feats were renowned throughout the forest. The other drones responded well to her leadership, and like the mythological Nakÿng armies spoken of in song and lore, the two-hundred strong group of natives moved as a single organism with hardly any drilling at all. The voices inside each one guided her to play her specific role with a precision and perspicacity that would have awed any human commander.

Teri was thankful for the general and the Urim, as—beyond her innate understanding of how to configure people in groups—she had no experience designing strategy, delegating authority or carrying out attacks. As much as it pained her to admit it, Miwa was probably better at battle. Tana's clone and Brando had always played war games on the computer, and while Teri had reluctantly learned all the martial arts that Brando had forced on her, she'd stayed far away from the other training. Now she wished she had paid more attention.

As the northward march began, Teri ran with the troops, her long, lithe legs carrying her toward their destination with little effort. Given her exhausted state after some five arduous days with negligible rest and the speed the army was moving at, she figured the otherwise quiescent Urim was still sustaining her. Running, Teri considered her next move: once she had all the AF troops under her control, she would contact Prime Minister Soral, perhaps using the same conference room that Brando's trial had been held in. From there she could negotiate a peace treaty that would ensure the Nakÿng's privacy during elevation and Miwa's freedom. Hopefully, the price for these items wouldn't be as high as she feared.

Without warning, she felt a sense of alarm wash over her.

«The third ship in orbit has just launched six vessels. They are armed. They've entered the atmosphere to the south. They are turning this way.»

Exhaustion and panic combined in her, and her mind shuddered with white noise.

Shit. Take me up.

She yelled at the general to continue, and a blue ball of energy rocketed her up through the trees and into the cascading rain falling from the pitch-black night sky. All that occurred to Teri was to stop the AF fighters, somehow, someway.

Head south. I want to cut them off before they're in a position to hurt the drones.

The rain blurred around her as the Urim hurled at ungodly speeds toward the southern edge of the forest, just kilometers north of the still semi-frozen lake. In her mind's eye she could see the fighters ripping through the clouds toward her position.

«They are close. They have detected the energy field about you. They are arming their weapons.»

Deflect them! Can't you make a shield or something?

A wall of indigo energy stretched down, up and to either side, plunging into the green depths that surrounded her bubble of bright calm. She was soon able to see the lights on the blunt noses of the fighters as they barreled toward her, swerving aside at the last moment, their missiles corkscrewing hungrily toward the warmth of the energy put out by the Urim. With numbing force, the twelve devices impacted against the wall of blue, one just meters from Teri's face, and exploded horrifyingly, nearly blinding her in a hellish conflagration that revealed seething verdigris heavens and impenetrable forest.

«They have gone higher and are passing over.»

Anger rising in her as her vision returned, Teri hurled a desperate, instinctive order.

Follow them. Catch them.

Reeling upward and toward the north, the Urim's bubble was soon racing between two of the fighters, deflecting sprays of energy that the AF pilots directed at her. Frustration and impotence blinded her to any alternatives. Her mind filled with a desire to destroy, but she couldn't afford any more deaths: her own conscience and the possible peace accords were too fragile to resist more bloodshed. She gritted her teeth savagely.

There's got to be a way to speed this up. Look, just do what I do; do you see what I mean? If I reach out to wrench a tree from the ground, do it. Don't wait for orders. Is that possible?

«Of course. However—»

Teri ignored the Urim's sense of warning and danger. Opening her mouth, she screamed, imagining her voice amplified loud enough to penetrate the cockpits of the fighters. It was.

"Get ready to bail out, because I'm going to rip your ships from the sky!"

Her arms shot out, and in her mind she saw her gigantic fingers wrap around the canopy of the two cockpits and peel them back. Blue energy hurtled out and did just that, adding to the drone of rain and engines the whining of twisting metal. The pilots and co-pilots immediately ejected. Teri curled her fingers around the fighters and slammed them together in her mind. In the air behind her, the vessels impacted with such force that the figures parachuting toward the canopy were lifted violently aloft and thrown southward, lambent flames nearly overtaking them.

Yes! The release that Teri felt at this show of power was incredible, intoxicating.

«We recommend not doing that again, Agent. You do not realize what energy is required to push that hard against gravity and moving mass. You will damage the Urim in your fury. It would be better to link to the navigational systems on the remaining vessels and fly them somewhere.»

Shaking free of the pleasure of power with a shamed shudder, Teri focused.

Okay. Fly them to the lake. Set them down on the southern edge and cripple their motors somehow.

Cables of blue energy snaked out, burrowed into the remaining fighters and then faded, though the Urim allowed Teri to see the flow of data that whizzed invisibly between them. In tandem, the ships and Teri's bubble turned and accelerated toward Lake Galileo. In scant minutes, the Urim was forcing the fighters' engines to shut down as it lowered them onto a large floe in the middle of the slushy early-second-spring waters.

Okay, now let's get back, fast!

Teri didn't think the drones had arrived at the village yet, but she wanted to hurry to rejoin them. The thought of AF soldiers opening fire on unarmored Nakÿng…

Take a look at the village.

«Weapons are being discharged along its perimeter.»

Shit, shit, shit! Don't fly: fenestrate us there! Now, damn you!

An explosion of chaotic light before she closed her eyes, a glimpse of a skein beyond human comprehension, and she was hanging above the smoking forest. She sank below the canopy and with Urim-enhanced eyes saw Antonio's men, perhaps warned of the Nakÿng's advance by scouts or Mifflin's fighters, blasting away at drones who flipped and hurdled out of the way of the volley. Despite their agility, dozens of them lay dead or wounded while their ineffective spears thudded against AF body armor.

Shut them down! Unseal their fucking suits!

Within seconds, the soldiers were staring at or pounding on dead weapons while clutching at pieces of their armor that began to fall to the ground. Teri acted quickly.

"Now, my drones! Attack, but do not kill! Save your grief and anger for another time! Today, no ingan dies, but none goes free!"

As the Nakÿng flung themselves at the dumbfounded soldiers, striking them brutally with the hafts of their spears, the Urim reached out to the fallen drones, trying to save the ones it could.

«Ten. Ten are salvageable. Forty-three dead, though.»

Forty-three? Oh, God.

She felt horrible despair clench her heart: after all the precautions she'd taken not to shed a drop of human blood, she'd ended up leading almost four dozen beautiful drones to their deaths. She did not want the guilt, refused the blame for their blood.

That third ship. Testing me. Wanting to see if I can handle the liberation of the village and an attack at the same time. You want to know my abilities, Captain Mifflin? Curious, are you, you son of a bitch?

«No. There is work to be done.»

They have more than six fighters, damn you. Do you want to face another energy-draining battle in the air? I don't.

«If the bubble loses integrity, you will die.»

Images of her body exploding.

You've managed to keep me safe so far. Let's get moving. Stop arguing!

A sensation of reluctant acquiescence.

«Such a display might enhance your leverage, Agent. But you must have a goal in mind. How will you demonstrate strength?»

Well, I'd love to just push that fool Mifflin out of orbit.

Approval.

«In space there is no resistance. It takes the Urim much less energy to move a vessel, even one as large as those in orbit.»

Perfect. Now, take me up.

As the tree limbs, rain, and gray-green clouds whipped past them, Teri kept seeing, superimposed on the blur, the destroyed forms of her adopted kinsfolk on the ground, limbs severed, bony chests ripped open. Indignant ire built in her until, an expression of wrathful determination carved into her face, she let go of the Urim and clenched her fists as if ready to strike out.

Then the cold blackness of space surrounded them, held at bay only by the thin bubble of energy, and the massive form of the AF galleon loomed before her eyes, eyes that narrowed as she thrust her fists forward, rose above the *Shaka*'s orbit and caused a flat plane of blue light to push down broadly across the length of the massive ship. The vessel shuddered under the impact and was bodily shoved toward the planet, maneuvering thrusters firing seconds afterward to try to lessen the speed of the caterwaul it had been sent into and reestablish an orbit before being drawn into the atmosphere.

Hook into their communications systems. I want them to hear me.

A tendril of light, then expectancy.

«Done. Speak.»

"If I were you, Captain Mifflin, I wouldn't try that again. Your mate Antonio just slaughtered forty-three natives, and I'm in a real pissy mood right now. So, just sit tight and let the big girls settle this one, what say? Tell Soral I want to talk to her as soon as possible to negotiate the release of about two hundred AF personnel and to reach some sort of peace agreement with the Consortium. I'm going to call on her tomorrow. Make sure I'm expected, *sir*." She spat the last word with sarcastic contempt.

Teri looked down then at the green expanse that filled the view beneath her feet. An abrupt sob shook her as she realized just how much that emerald orb below meant to her and how willing she'd be, even without the powers she now had, to fight to the death to keep Terego safe.

No price is too high.

The Urim said nothing for a while: it simply leaked the slightest sensation of dubiousness into her mind. Finally, the words formed.

«You will soon know for certain just how costly. The agent who came before you was unwilling to pay. Will you be different?»

Teri wanted to shout *yes*, wanted to berate the Urim for doubting her, but no words came to her. The dark frigidity of space stalked just beyond her bubble, mocking her masqueraded frailty.

We'll find out tomorrow, won't we?

They dropped back down through the thick shroud of mottled cumuli.

CHAPTER 64

WHEN THE WORD FINALLY CAME, Antonio was patiently nodding his head at the combined warnings of both the b-dux and the centurion, who were in agreement about wanting to move south before the XID showed up and found them waiting like fools for an enemy that had more sense than to return. It was bad enough that they couldn't raise Quat or anyone else, for that matter. Did they need to be humiliated by the intelligence team as well before being court-martialed?

Before he could respond with a withering estimation of their strategic acumen, one of his scouts came rushing into the tent.

"Captain," he said out of breath, "it's the clooties. There's a shite-load of them about five klicks from here, marching thisaway."

D'Angelo grinned. "Let's go meet them!"

As the three commanders emerged from the tent, the comtech shouted them over.

"Message from Captain Mifflin. Orders for us to pull us out. There are about two hundred grendels headed our way, and he says he's sending fighters to lay down suppressing fire while we retreat. Prime Minister Soral's orders, he says."

Antonio laughed. "Retreat? Tell him I said to bugger himself. We're about to nab that yakuza bitch, and they want me to retreat? Fuck that."

There was no argument from the other commanders. They all knew they'd come too far down this road to turn back now. They had to capture Samanei to save their careers.

Leaving behind the centurion and about ten soldiers, the dux and Antonio led the rest of the men southward until the natives' presence was made known by a hail of spears. One struck Captain D'Angelo full in the chest, but though he stumbled backward, the suit absorbed most of the impact.

Strong bitches, they can throw hard enough to stress a suit.

He'd have bruises in the morning; that much was for certain.

The men spread out and began firing at the natives, who sprang at the AF troops from every imaginable angle with a speed and ferocity that startled many into shock. But after a couple of the grendels had been disemboweled by rifle blasts, the grunts let go of their fear or channeled it. Antonio himself managed to down one of the shaggy beasts, punching a hole through its bony chest plate and sending it slamming against the ground, smoking and twitching.

"Anyone see humans?" he shouted into his cascom.

"Negative," came back several replies. The army personnel kept mowing down grendels, growling from time to time in pain at a blow from a spear or massive claw. Victory seemed clinched when suddenly a blue glow washed over all of them, fritzing their IR vision. Antonio continued fingering the firing stud of his rifle once the brilliance had subsided, but there was no response. Angrily, he jerked the weapon up toward his eyes. The readout indicated that his carpal sensor was unauthorized to use the rifle. A glance about him told Antonio that the silence was due to a failure of all the weapons held by the grunts. Without warning, Antonio's casque accordioned back into the suit's collar, and the armor itself began to fall to pieces, as if it had been suddenly unsealed. Grabbing at the rubbery gray sheets, the captain tried to reseal the seams.

From above him came a hideous, snarling voice barking in a rough alien language. Letting his weapon and suit pieces fall to the ground, Antonio, dressed only in his one-piece AF undergarment, leaned his head back. Descending through the green-hued darkness of the trees was a woman, dark and beautiful and obviously insane, enveloped in an aureole of brilliant blue.

It's her. Samanei.

But the satisfaction he had expected to feel at being face-to-face with her never came. Instead, a bizarre sadness began to flood him, until a sharp blow to the back of the next sent him tumbling into darkness.

SOMETIME LATER, ANTONIO AWAKENED. Inky blackness surrounded him. He started to voice the IR command, but he remembered that his suit had fallen apart. Limbs numb from the cold, he tried to stand. It was difficult, but he gained his feet and started to limp forward.

"If I were you, I would stop right there. You're just centimeters from the edge. Don't think you want to fall forty meters."

Antonio turned about. Though his eyes were becoming accustomed to the virtually non-existent ambient light, he could only make out bulky forms. A low blue glow started up to his right.

Samanei, holding a luminous metal orb in her hands.

"Ms. Koroma. You're under arrest."

She smiled grimly. "I don't know what's funnier: that you think I'm Samanei or that you think you can arrest me. You're Brando's little brother, no?"

Tony smirked, but didn't respond. Instead, he went on as if she had said nothing. "I don't see the point in denying who you are. As for me arresting you, you maybe caught me off guard with your alien weapon there, but Captain Mifflin is going to be along pretty soon, and we're going to see who captures who."

"First of all, I took care of Mifflin. He's just sitting nice and quiet, awaiting more orders. Second, this whole Samanei thing: you're a stubborn fool, Antonio. Do I really look that old look that old?" The light level increased, revealing her face more clearly than before. "I'm not Samanei, damn it. She'd look, what, forty years old? In stasis at twenty-five, then let out sixteen, seventeen years ago? Come on: I'm fifteen Standard."

Antonio understood in a flash. Tenshi's clone. "Teri?"

"Yes. Short for Çèrhingÿl, the Nakÿng's ambassador to humanity."

"The who?"

"The Nakÿng. The ones yall call grendels. The ones yall just slaughtered forty-three of. Their government has authorized me to apprehend you on their behalf for violating their territory without permission and using force against their citizens. In a few hours, when I talk with Prime Minister Soral, we're going to negotiate a treaty between the CPCC and the Nakÿng, and you and your men will find yourselves up on charges."

Fear that she might be right scrabbled like an animal inside of him, but he continued to push. "You really think there's going to be a treaty when your alien buddies are hiding wanted criminals? Come on, girl."

Teri sighed heavily. Antonio was unnerved by how beautiful she was and angered at his own instinctual reaction to her.

That bloody ball she has in her hands shut down our suits and weapons, made her float in the air. It's messing with me, making me feel drawn to her.

"Antonio, Samanei was never here. Brando left her on a planet that it's almost not even habitable around sixteen years ago. You don't believe me? Let me show you."

The brilliance grew till the whole habitation was brightly lit, and then it continued to intensify until it filled Tony's very thoughts. He was unable to focus: all that existed was that cobalt glow. Then he had the oddest sensation: *someone else was in his mind with him.*

You feel me?

"Yes. Get out. Please. Stop."

Don't speak. Think.

He remembered how helpless he had felt at five when he couldn't find his mother. They were in the central bubble, on a slidewalk, and a bunch of big people had gotten on and he got separated and couldn't find her and he screamed and screamed.

It's okay. You've got nothing to fear. I don't want to hurt you. Just look.

Unexpectedly, he was a chirurgic. Brando called him Kyr. He glanced at the holographic display above the navigation alcove's panel. The coordinates of the system glowed above a spinning image of the planet. They would be leaving her today. Tony/Kyr felt very angry, but Samanei had told him not to fight Brando's decision. She wanted to be stranded there.

A blue flash. Now Tony/Kyr spidered along a corridor in zero-g, carrying the Oracle in some of his arms. "It's okay, Kyr," she whispered. "I'm going to be fine. And going to come back for you. You have helped me so much. You and me, we're always going to be friends."

Another flash. Kyr/Tony stood with Brando, watching the escape pod enter the thin atmosphere of a forbidding planet. Brando sighed in relief.

Then the pace picked up, and fragments of Kyr's life over the last sixteen years leeched themselves onto Tony's mind in a fusillade of experience. He understood. Samanei had never been on Terego. She was probably already dead. Confusion and dismay, both at this understanding and at the strange feeling that he was now two people, seized him with violent spasms.

No. Calm yourself.

The men that had died because of his landing on this world. The terrified civilians. The dead natives. His career, cycled out over an edifice of suppositions and misunderstandings.

Stop. Antonio felt as if something were burrowing into him. *Stay away from the swirling black. Let me help you. Let me help you carry this weight.* Her presence filled him, and he remembered.

The revelation of his father's lies. His mother's nauseating fidelity to the man. Deceptions by friends. Understanding of the crookedness of politics. Favoritism in the academy. And finally, his beloved's body, dancing upon the hips of another man. The rending pain, the withdrawal. His body shuddered and trembled.

Antonio. I'm so sorry. Let me take some of your pain. Lean on me, take rest.

Such love filled him then, such compassion and understanding, that he thought he would come apart at the very seams. Antonio saw himself through her eyes, knew that his bitter search for justice had simply been his own way of dealing with the loneliness that had consumed him ever since he learned that the man he loved and admired was a fraud. She showed him how to push that feeling of betrayal into her mind. It was easy, really, for she was *in him*, Çèrhinghÿl was *in him*. He wasn't alone anymore.

"This is what the faithful mean. And to think that I mocked them like fools," he whispered. And for the first time in more than twenty years, Antonio wept, great heaving sobs of hurt and anguish and despair and hope. Hope.

Yes. This is communion. This is what we are capable of being.

Antonio realized that she was going to let him go, send him back to the AF to tell them Samanei's location and to bend his knee to the blind goddess. But she would be safe, and her cause would be advanced. He was not sad. Çèrhingÿl was justice personified, and he would obey.

And maybe, one day, when his sentence was finished…

Yes. I will always welcome you, Antonio. I am part of you now. I will be with you wherever you go. And when you come home, your new family will greet you with open arms.

Then her presence slipped with slow and ginger care from his mind, and he was left only with the sweet ache of remembrance.

CHAPTER 65

MIWA STARED AT THE WHITE OVALS dotting the plain around the quarry. Shalura had remarked that they looked like the abandoned eggs of a flock of the mythic birds called *Rhèxoggéingh*, waiting to hatch and unleash hungry fury on the world. Indeed, Miwa reflected, the eggs had burst open, and trouble had spilled out, but the amazing abilities of Teri and the strength of the Nakÿng were more than enough to handle the cocky soldiers. She and her dad had also proven valuable in the defense of the planet, for which she felt great pride. Despite the lies he'd told, Brando still understood duty and friendship, and though the Nakÿng made him nervous, he worked alongside them well.

The recent conversation between Miwa and her father had gone quite well. She was thrilled to see him again, walking among Shalura's people without attacking them. They had mainly caught each other up on what had happened during the last month, and Brando, though a little disturbed by it, accepted the initial revelation of a bond between Shalura and Miwa. Of course, she held off on the details.

One step at a time. No need to freak him totally out right now.

Seeing her mother again had also brought Miwa joy. Rhea was a government official now, realizing her dreams, able to impact the flow of political events on Terego. Miwa was happy for her. She was more nervous about her own future and that of Brando and Teri. Especially Teri.

Miwa didn't like the idea of her twin having as much power as she evidently did: Teri was a decent human being, but suddenly becoming a demigod had to be messing with her mind. In fact, the teen hardly resembled the old Teri, except in brief moments when the two of them were alone. Her voice and mannerisms had even changed. Miwa wondered whether that orb she carried with her might be controlling her mind.

But Terego needed Teri and her abilities now, and concerns about the repercussions would have to wait.

Glancing at Shalura, Miwa wondered for the hundredth time exactly what the two of them would do once the crisis was over. Shalura didn't want to live among her people anymore, and Miwa wasn't sure they'd fit into regular Teregano society well, either. It was a tough decision, and all Miwa knew at the moment was that she wanted to publish what she'd written about the Nakÿng. Maybe they'd go somewhere different, visit Earth. The birthplace of Joseph Smith was buried under glacial sheets, but there were still many other sites to visit on the mother world.

"How much longer must we sit and guard these flying eggs?" Shalura grumbled. "We have watched them all night, and no ingan has come to crawl back inside a shell. Can we not leave?"

Shalura had been tense ever since she discovered the identity of the Nakÿng's council leader, and Miwa was finding it more and more exasperating.

"Look, I am not liking the job much, neither, but that's what our tribe says for us to do. Stop complaining so much."

Shalura laid her ears back in embarrassment and said nothing. The air seemed to lighten, and Miwa looked up to see some breaks in the clouds that let in the early morning sunlight. Before she could relish the apparent end of the rainy period of second spring, her cascom chimed unexpectedly. Sealing the casque above her head, she answered.

"Hello? Miwa D'Angelo here."

"Miwa, this is Prime Minister Khumalo. Is everything all right at the quarry?"

"Yes, sir. There's not been any movement, or anything at all, really."

"Because I need your help. A ship defenestrated in-system a couple of hours ago. It just sent a shuttle toward the planet, and it should be arriving in an hour or so."

"Do you know who they are, sir?"

"XID. That's the intelligence division of the executive branch of the Consortium government. We've cleared their landing at the airport."

"So, you want me to go with the Nakÿng to help you deal with them?"

"As a precautionary measure. They say they have spoken with Captain Mifflin, who tried some sort of assault yesterday, you probably haven't been informed…"

"Against Teri?"

"Yes, but she rebuffed his attack. The XID want to talk with Teri, and we're trying to contact her, but in the meantime…"

Miwa nodded to no one. "We'll be there as soon as we can. Miwa out."

Shalura ducked her head sharply in an inquisitive gesture. "What is happening?"

"Your wish is coming true. We are leaving the eggs and going back to the big village to protect the leaders."

As they ran back to the depot, Miwa explained as best she could. A transport drove them into Diadono, to the airport, where a silvery shuttle was cooling on a tarmac and various Teregano functionaries and crisis corpsmen were escorting a dozen strangers into a nearby building that housed immigration and transportation checkpoints.

Stationing two drones near the shuttle and the rest at the entrance to the office complex, Miwa and Shalura followed the group inside. They had spread throughout the foyer, the largest room, and the XID field agents were coolly blending into the shadows with unobtrusive aplomb, their presence somehow capable of pushing one's attention away toward other objects in the room, Miwa noted as her own eyes flitted away from them.

Khumalo was talking to a gruff man dressed, like all the agents, in a steel-gray doublet and loose trousers piped in black and tucked into knee-high boots. The man turned his bush-hat-topped head as Miwa and Shalura entered, raising a casual gloved hand into which a small lazgat popped from nowhere.

"Who they are?" he inquired in cold tones that betrayed no fear or anger.

"Miwa D'Angelo, deputized by the crisis ministry to assist us, and Shalura, a representative of the Nakÿng military. This is Agent Minoungou, in charge of investigating our situation."

"Hey," Miwa said curtly.

"Miwa D'Angelo?" Minoungou looked at her carefully, his hand still pointing the barrel of the gun at her. "The one raised as Teri Miranda's sister?"

Miwa nodded. Shalura grunted. "If you want, I will disembowel the fool who is pointing that little gun at us."

Miwa tried to suppress a laugh. Minoungou eased his chin up at her inquisitively. "What did it say?"

"Not 'it': *she*. And she is really offended you're pointing a weapon at us. Her government might take it the wrong way."

Minoungou stared blankly at her, then lowered the lazgat with deliberate slowness, as if to show that he did so because he wanted to. "Ms. D'Angelo, we need to talk to your sister."

Khumalo smirked in exasperation. "I told you, Agent Minoungou, that she contacted us about fifteen minutes ago. We told her you were here, and she said that she'd arrive as soon as possible. She's been jailing the rest of the soldiers that invaded our planet, she said to tell you."

"Fine. We'll wait a bit longer, then. Prime Minister Soral is quite anxious to speak with this young lady that keeps defeating Army-trained men with such ease." The gleam in his eye as he said this suggested that their defeat gave him pleasure. "Afterward, though, I want to be given full access to the AF personnel under guard in Diadono. I'm sure you understand the urgency."

Khumalo nodded hesitantly. "Of course. We want to aid the investigation as much as we can, Agent Minoungou."

The door slid open, and the groups' eyes fell on the figure of Teri, who strode in with the orb resting dully in her hands. Her eyes seemed to burn with preternatural understanding as she stepped to Miwa's side, staring at the newcomers. Miwa could sense tension from the nearly invisible agents, and Teri frowned as she looked at them, closed her eyes, and then opened them again to stare at Minoungou.

"Yes, me too. And the best way to get the investigation moving is to asap a link between me and Soral."

Miwa could barely make out what happened next, but the hats of the other agents folded down around their faces, forming helmets, and the men seemed to meld with the shadows cast by the mid-morning sun through the lobby's high, rectangular windows. Before she could react, one of them glissaded rapidly behind her and attached something cold and metallic to her neck. She was instantly paralyzed. Another two cast some sort of energy net over Shalura, immobilizing the drone, as the remaining agents rushed Teri and tried to wrench the orb from her hands.

A wave of turquoise energy spiraled out from the teen's hands and hurled them against the walls of the foyer, pinning them there. Teri's eyes, which had closed during the seconds-long clash, opened narrowly at the head agent, who had not moved a centimeter from his spot beside Khumalo.

"Minoungou, your name is? Let's cut the rubbish. Initiate the faux-conference, yes? My patience with yall Consortium goons is wearing *really* thin."

With an exasperated cutting gesture, Teri caused the device to fall away from Miwa's neck, returning her mobility. Despite her reservations about her sister's mental state, Miwa felt like applauding.

Wow.

"Shalura," Teri said quietly, "when I free you, you are not to attack anyone here. Is that clear?"

Shalura grinned, and the netting fell away. The drone crouched in quiet readiness, but did nothing. Miwa stepped close to her to check whether the netting had harmed her in any way.

"I am fine, Lady, but if these gray ingan touch you again, I will slaughter them no matter what Çèrhingÿl orders."

Miwa knew she was serious.

Let's hope Teri's little conference works, or this is going to get very messy.

CHAPTER 66

WHY IS IT SO HARD TO SEE THEM?

«Close your eyes. They are using a type of light-bending technique. Their clothing is infested with molecular robots that can block multiple electromagnetic frequencies. In fact, due to their head coverings, they are probably immune to what your mind calls "forced faux-invasion." It would be a simple matter to tear those hats from them, however, if the need arises.»

With her eyes closed, Teri was able to plainly see the XID agents staked out against the walls, muscles tensing.

They are going to try something, aren't they?

«Yes.»

Opening her eyes, she stared at the head agent, whom Khumalo had just referred to as Minoungou and whose face was an unreadable chunk of stone.

"Yes, me too," she said, agreeing with the prime minister's desire for expediency. "And the best way to get the investigation moving is to asap a link between me and Soral."

«They strike.»

Teri shut her eyes as the agents' hats enveloped their heads and their nanobot-enhanced uniforms masked their movements. She saw them immobilize Miwa and Shalura as they rushed at her, and the Urim spun a burst of energy out that sent the men flying against the walls. Pulsing tendrils of light held them in place meters above the floor. Teri opened her eyes to glare at the head agent, who hadn't participated in the attack.

"Minoungou, your name is? Let's cut the rubbish. Initiate the faux-conference, yes? My patience with yall Consortium goons is wearing *really* thin."

The agent nodded nearly imperceptibly as she chopped at the air, commanding the Urim to free Miwa.

A sense of caution.

«The drone may attack them for attempting to hurt her bond-mate.»

Teri looked at Shalura. "Shalura, when I free you, you are not to attack anyone here. Is that clear?"

The drone signaled her compliance, and the Urim pulled the energy net from her enormous form. As Miwa hurried to the warrior's side, Minoungou addressed Teri.

"Let my men down, and we'll accompany you to the shuttle to use our faux-conferencing equipment. It bounces the signal off our ship in orbit, which tunnels the conference to Earth." Minoungou gestured languidly at the Urim. "I assume you'll not feel any concern for your safety with us. You understand, we had to try."

"Certainly. I never expected anything different."

Let them down.

The Urim eased the agents, befuddled but proudly stoic, to the tiled floor.

Teri gestured at Khumalo. "I need to talk to the prime minister of Terego for a moment. Is there a room we can go into?"

Terego's chief executive nodded and led her to a small office nearby while Minoungou conferred with his men. Inside, her eyes constantly flitting to the window to assure herself that Miwa's drone wasn't going berserk, Teri announced to Khumalo her need. He balked.

"A Consortium science post, Teri... Ambassador? On Novameriko?"

"Look, I know what you're thinking. Why should you allow this? Because there's no way they are going to leave this world without the Nakÿng's Urim unless I give them something equally valuable. Now that they know this technology exists, they won't rest till they have it. If I allow them access to something similar, they'll be appeased, as least until we have a better solution."

The prime minister rubbed his hand across his face.

"Access to what?"

"A ship. A highly advanced alien ship lying beneath layers of volcanic rock under the great marshes."

Khumalo's eyes went wide. "And you want to simply hand it over to them?"

"What else can we do, Brother? Would you have me instead turn the Nakÿng's only protection, their gift from God, over to the Consortium so its scientists can dissect it and learn new ways to kill? This ship has been buried for two thousand Teregano years. It likely doesn't even work, and it will take years for the CPCC to get anything out of it."

There was an ambivalent wave of doubt and consternation from the Urim.

"To be honest with you, Ambassador, the legislature and I had been considering offering the Consortium scientific and diplomatic access to the Native Teregans, before the crisis got out of control. But you're talking something more permanent and planetside. How long would we have to permit the station?"

"I'm not sure. A few years, so they can examine the region around the crash site, look for pieces of the ship that may have broken off, etc. Let's say three. I'm going to pull the main body of the ship from the ground myself to shorten their task, but they're going to want to be down there. What we *can* insist on, however, is that no military galleons be allowed to enter the system, only science vessels. You're going to have to face a difficult fact, however, Brother. Terego's isolation is over. The first non-human race we know of has been discovered here. You're going to have people coming to this world in droves, especially when the Nakÿng are ready to deal directly with humans in a few decades. My advice to you, one diplomat to another, is that you establish a long-range science exchange program with the CPCC's science ministry. Get on their good side while there's time."

The prime minister took a few moments to let this suggestion sink in, and then he sighed deeply. "I never imagined, Ambassador, that when I was elected to office I would have to grapple with these issues. My world seems to unravel before my very eyes. But I will do this. I will trust you. In exchange, though your work with the Nakÿng will no doubt take much of your time, I ask that you keep an eye on them. Help me protect the Tereganoj, all of them."

Taking both her hands from the Urim, which simply floated between them, Teri set her palms upon Khumalo's shoulders and looked into his eyes, which were on a level with hers. Here was an ally she could trust, a man who understood the weight of leadership.

"I swear it, Brother. I will give my life before I see even one of us harmed by them."

Teri released him then, her hands dropping as if by instinct back on to the globular comfort of the Urim, and reentered the foyer.

"Let's go," she said, not looking at anyone in particular, and without another word she turned and began walking out the door and toward the shuttle. Agents overtook her at a sprint and dashed up the disembarkation ramp. The two Nakÿng standing nearby grunted at her, and she waved their protective ire down as she started up the ramp, the remaining agents close on her heels.

"Everything's fine, warriors. Should I need you, I will call out."

They bared their teeth in understanding, and Teri slipped into the polished elegance of the shuttle's interior.

"Toward the back," came Minoungou's voice from behind her. She headed aft, where the two men who entered first were busying themselves near the irising entrance to a chamber.

I know these fools will try something while I'm under the pink lights, so please keep an eye on them.

Assent.

The metal whorl of the entrance gaped open as she approached. Minoungou entered behind her and gestured at a semi-circle of about seven white conference chairs, slightly tilted back, the connection equipment angling purposefully above each.

"She's expecting you. Just sit back, and you'll find yourself in the executive office. Ever been in a faux-connection before?"

Teri wanted to laugh. "No, but don't worry. Just hook me up, Agent, and keep away. Even with my mind in the ether, I can monitor yall."

Slipping into one of the seats, Teri closed her eyes and gripped the

Urim even more tightly.

Can't be any worse than connecting directly to another person's brain, can it?

Amusement.

«It will seem rudimentary to you.»

There was an odd click, and then she opened her eyes. She seemed to be sitting on a comfortable chair in a large, octagonal office. Before her, tucked behind a massive wooden desk framed by the Consortium and AF flags, in stark relief against the dark blue executive emblem that hung behind the desk, was Prime Minister Leyla Soral, her iron gray hair pulled painfully back from her lined and exhausted features. Cold green eyes stared out at Teri with deliberate frankness.

"I understand that you don't want to be called Teri Miranda," the older woman said abruptly. It was a good sign. No nonsense or attempts at ersatz niceties.

"Not Miranda, no. My name is now Çèrhingÿl. I am the ambassador of the Nakÿng, the native inhabitants of Terego, to humanity, specifically, to the Consortium. You may call me Ambassador Teri, if that's easier on your tongue."

Teri leaned forward. Her faux-body, her doppelganger, was a visual copy of her own self, and it wore the same fresh robe she'd donned in the morning after getting some much needed rest and a good cold bath. In her doppel's hands was a replica of the Urim.

"Fine, Ambassador. We seem to be facing a problem."

"Yes."

"The humans on Terego violated the terms of an important treaty with the CPCC by hiding the existence of the, uh, Nakÿng from us."

"I'm willing to take responsibility for that. Whatever their initial reasons were, I did also instruct them to give me more time, on my people's urging." Teri had decided to handle this much as Antonio would have; she could feel him in her, helping to form the words that a Consortium eyre would expect to hear. Even though she'd not completely joined with him, since she now realized the mental price such a union exacted, she still retained large chunks of Tony's personality, and the oddities of diplomatic speech were part of that fragmentary residue.

"Your people. The Nakÿng?"

"That is so."

"Let's not prolong this. I've got a couple of renegade captains on my hands, and a huge constituency of hawks behind them. I also have the images of AF soldiers marching in the streets of an independent world, without a resolution from the Diet or consultation with other independent planets. There's a whole other faction of people screaming for me to get the hell out of your system."

"Then you should."

"It isn't that simple, Ambassador Teri. You complicated things the minute you started using whatever that is in your hands."

Teri stared at the Urim a moment then lifted her eyes again to the prime minister.

"This is a tool for the Nakÿng, Prime Minister. Once we reach an agreement here, it will never be used against humans again."

Soral arched an eyebrow. "What assurances do I have of that?"

"It'll be easier if I explain what I envision."

The prime minister leaned back, smiled, and nodded. "Okay. Let's hear it."

Teri smirked at this condescension, but went on.

"All the Nakÿng want are two things: for the AF to withdraw from Terego and from the system itself and to be left alone for twenty years. In addition, I have a personal request: that you pardon Miwa D'Angelo for any crimes she may have committed while trying to defend herself and the Nakÿng from your 'renegade captains.' Hang on. Let me continue. In return, this is what we propose giving yall.

"First, to ease the concerns of those who agree with Antonio D'Angelo's mistaken theory that there are yakuza in the Nakÿng's forest, the AF will be permitted to make one intensive scan of the area. Yall will then see, as the captain himself can confirm, that the only human in there is me, once we hand over our prisoners. That's the second thing. Yall get the soldiers back, along with Captain D'Angelo, who knows what you really want to find out: Samanei Koroma's present location."

Soral narrowed her eyes in suspicion. That morning, over breakfast, Antonio had told Teri what he knew of the Centauri Rift and the possible connection between Yen Bandera, Domina Ditis, Samanei Koroma, and the being that had come through the rift. The information had surprised Teri, but the Urim had reacted with dizzying spirals of emotion. It had, as always, offered no explanation for its shock, though it did say it needed to access an AF computer.

"Prime Minister, I understand your fears about this technology I possess. You think it's somehow related to the Rift and the tragedies surrounding it. It's not, however. I can't expect you to just believe me and accept the fact that I have it and yall don't, however. So I'll offer you something that may even up the playing field. Buried on the northern continent of Terego's western hemisphere is a ship. An alien ship of a highly advanced technological level. I'm going to give it to you."

That got her attention, Teri thought as emotions flitted across the CPCC chief-of-state's face.

«The gray-suited ones just attempted to take the Urim. They were rebuffed. One of them was apparently injured by the drone you warned. Her mate was again threatened outside the vessel, and the drone attacked in response. All is under control, however.»

Frustrated at being stuck in limbo while people she cared about were in danger, she made an angry gesture with her free hand.

"You might want to tell your XID agents to stop undermining what we're doing here. If they keep it up, we may not be able to find a peaceable solution."

An irritated look in her eyes, Soral blanked out for a second, then her doppel resumed its livelier state.

"Dealt with. Tell me more about this ship. The sphere reached Terego aboard it?"

Teri decided to risk some truthfulness.

"Yes, though I don't actually know what for or where from. Like I said, the sphere is a tool. It has the location of the ship recorded along with some details about what happened to it later, but that's it. I already convinced Prime Minister Khumalo to allow a science post in the area, which is hundreds of kilometers away from the nearest human settlements. No AF scientists, just people from whatever ministry would be in charge of such discoveries."

"SÆT. Science and Technology Division."

"I'd pull the main bulk of the ship out of the rock it's encrusted in. Yall would just have to excavate the rest of the site."

Oh, she likes this idea. She's not even trying to mask it, is she?

After several seconds of consideration, Soral went cold and serious.

"Very tempting. Here's my problem: you want twenty years. Why?"

"The Nakÿng are stone-age people, Prime Minister. No match for humanity. I want to teach them, prepare them to be part of the realm of sentient beings."

The Consortium chief was shaking her head.

"We have protocols in place for such eventualities, Ambassador. We've spent centuries thinking about such an encounter. Species at their level of development should be left alone, guarded against interference."

«Fools. Arrogant fools.»

"What? That's foolish. Interference by what definition? Yall think that after thousands of years of wondering if we're alone, we should just *not talk* to the first species that we meet?"

"Ambassador, we don't believe in interfering with the natural development of species. Humanity developed in isolation, and other species should also get that opportunity."

The Urim flashed a vertiginous array of information it had already compiled from its study of the shuttle's computers into Teri's mind.

"Come, now, Prime Minister. The Lieske drive? Tunneling? These technologies aren't part of humanity's 'natural development.' They were reverse engineered from the CPCC's studies of the Centauri Conduit. And I don't think yall're going to turn down the ship that I'm offering yall because yall don't want human society interfered with. Who are we to dictate to the Nakÿng what they can learn and how long they must stay in the stone age? Besides, the CPCC says it's not going to interfere with them, but what about the demimundo, eh? The Nakÿng need to be ready."

"I'm willing to concede your point, and course all humanity would love to have a sister species. But what proof do I have that you're actually going to be teaching them and not, say, helping them create thousands of those spheres to take over the Consortium?"

The idea was so absurd that Teri had to struggle not to laugh in Soral's face.

Is there no way to share minds with her?

«No. The Urim's energy cannot reach across such distances without transition gates, and the equipment used for this connection is too primitive. She can be made to view images and feel sensations, however.»

Teri's mind was suddenly awash in technical information that exhausted her.

So "no."

Soral cleared her throat.

"Here's *my* demand, Ambassador. Are you listening?"

Opening her eyes, Teri nodded, her stomach tightening.

"Brando D'Angelo. I want you to hand him over. He's a wanted criminal under CPCC jurisdiction, and a material witness to crimes still being investigated."

Oh, God. Here it comes.

Cautionary whispers of worry.

«She is testing you.»

"I assure you any information you need from him is yours. He'll cooperate fully."

"No. You don't understand. I want *him*, in *our* custody."

Teri, her palms tingling, her mouth dry, clenched the Urim to her abdomen.

"I don't think *you* understand. Didn't Mifflin tell you what I did to his ship? This treaty is for *yall*. I could pull every AF ship yall send at me right out of the sky and fenestrate it into the sun. I could hang that over your head, Prime Minister, and force you to deal with me on my terms. But I'm going out of my way to avoid killing. I don't relish hurting anyone. I'm going to give yall a ship with technology beyond anything yall ever saw. Why do you demand this of me?"

«Stop, Agent. Why show her this? Why open yourself to her?»

Eyes bright with anger, Leyla Soral slapped her palms against the desktop.

"Threats? I don't really trust you, *Ambassador*. For all I know, you're being controlled by the same monster the USRN found in the Centauri Rift two centuries ago: maybe that damn sphere is his medium, like the Ditis boy was. Maybe you're being controlled. Or maybe you're just an arrogant teenager who thinks she can change the flow of events beyond her scope. In any case, you're misjudging your own strength. You think I'm afraid of warfare, of bloodshed? I have nothing to lose. Your planet has already ruined

my political career, Teri. If you want to go to war, see your planet invaded for

real, see your people die, just keep pushing me. That weapon of yours can't

keep working forever at all times. Everything has a limit. If I sent the flotilla

against you, thousands of AF ships, I've got a feeling I'd win. So I'll tell you

once more. Either you give me Brando or no deal, no matter how many ships

you offer up to me."

«Are you strong enough? You said you were.»

"But *why?*"

"To some extent, because he knows what and where Samanei is…"

"But I told you, so does Antonio! He can tell you the coordinates."

«With every word you give her more.»

"…but mainly because I need leverage against you. You say you're

simply going to teach the Nakÿng, but you don't want any surveillance, just

a single scan before we leave. I want to give you a reason to keep your

word. Brando, in a military prison, to be released when you can provide us

with proof positive that yall aren't a threat to us. I don't trust you, Ma'am. I

hope that's clear to you now?"

«Your tears have been stopped. She has devices for monitoring your

physical responses. Show her your strength, Agent. The Nakÿng depend on

such a demonstration. Give him to her. It is the only way.»

Her mind a razed and burning field despite the calm of her body,

Teri agreed.

"He's yours. Miwa's absolved, twenty years without interference."

Forgive me.

Soral smiled. "And the ship, Ambassador. This is how it's going to happen: today you'll turn Brando and Antonio over to the XID. Once they are onboard the *Sigil*, the *Diomedes* and the *George Washington* will leave orbit with the XID ship. Then you'll release the AF prisoners to Mifflin, who will send a couple of large transports to the surface. Once he's scanned the forest, he'll back away from the planet, but stay in-system until you dig up the ship and the SÆT team arrives. That's amenable to you?"

"Yes," Teri murmured from a maelstrom of sadness and guilt, and then several others joined them in the faux-office to help produce the actual treaty document that would certify their agreement.

Aside from its physical stabilizing of her vitals, the Urim offered no comfort to the agony Teri's decision was exacting from her soul.

In fact, it seemed too preoccupied with other concerns to even try to reassure her of the importance of the sacrifice.

She was alone in her betrayal.

CHAPTER 67

ON SATURDAY THE RAIN BROKE, the sun filtering warm and bright through tears in the dissolving clouds. Rhea watched from the porch as her son kicked a ball to his father, laughing when Brando failed to stop it from entering the makeshift goal they'd marked out with rocks.

With help from Teri, Rhea had finally convinced her husband—they were still married, no matter what awful things he had said and done to her—to forestall any attempts at leaving Terego in his mothballed spaceship.

"Until the AF leaves orbit," Teri had told him over the house com, "I won't even consider it. You know what I can do. I'll have the Urim incapacitate that ranfura of yours before it ever leaves the ground. Please, Brando. Just trust me. I'll find the best solution for all of us."

But husband and wife only exchanged the most perfunctory of communication now. Actual conversation felt untenable after the cruel revelations.

Now, for example, Brando lifted his muddy son onto his shoulders and tromped his way up the steps, kicking off his boots before ducking through the door.

Though Rhea looked up at him, trying to smile for Jakobo, Brando didn't meet her gaze or say a word beyond a grunted "bath time."

She was thankful that her personal communications device kept gurgling notifications: Teri had reached an agreement with the CPCC, and the local legislature was voting on a measure that would give the Consortium four years' access to an archeological site in the central marshland of Novameriko, an unexplored area in the shadow of heavily wooded, snow-crusted mountains. The region had never been mapped or visited because of its inaptness for human settlement. Rhea, though not altogether happy about the Consortium foothold on her world, was thankful the outsiders would be confined to such a remote, undesirable corner of Terego.

Her mood was further lightened by the good news that the month-long crisis was apparently at an end. With the AF soldiers being moved into a sporting arena near the outskirts of the capital in preparation for their withdrawal, Rhea imagined that the entire world was breathing a collective sigh of relief.

As if on cue, happy music floated from within the house. Brando and Jakobo were doing their own celebration, singing silly children's songs as her husband strummed the guitar he'd inherited years before from his own father.

Rhea opened the door and walked in, hoping to join them, hoping to bridge the chasm between the man she still loved and herself.

But then, solemnly, Brando began to intone *Volare* in Esperanto, Jakobo joining in on the chorus. Approaching her son's bedroom with quiet steps, Rhea saw her husband's eyes grow shellacked with moisture, and she understood that the song meant something deep for him, something she had never learned in the labyrinth of his lies.

Perhaps there will still be time, she thought, sad and wistful. *Time to discover all the hidden secrets of our hearts.*

She was standing out-of-sorts before the bathroom mirror when next her percom received a message. It was Miwa.

"Hey, Mom! Teri wants us to have a get-together this evening."

Rhea nearly clapped her hands for joy or perhaps relief.

"Wonderful! I'll make something special for supper. All of my babies, under one roof again."

"I'm, uh, bringing Shalura," Miwa added in tentative tones.

Rhea swallowed, but kept her prejudices down. She was, after all, the Czar of Native Affairs. The more contact she had with them, the better. "That's fine, Miwa."

"Great. See you at seven?"

"Sure, sweetie. Bye-bye."

Rhea nodded at herself in the mirror.

"I'll clean the house, then. That'll keep my mind blank. For a little while."

BY LATE AFTERNOON, JAKOBO FELL ASLEEP and Brando locked himself in his study after gruffly announcing he would attempt to mold Miwa's notes into a monograph. As Rhea was pulling a dish from the oven, the door started buzzing. She ran to answer.

The motley crew that entered had to be seen to be believed: Teri in her rough leather shift, her cornrows replaced by hundreds of small braids, the disturbing alien orb in her lithe fingers; Miwa in her battle armor, face smudged with grime, hair an unruly mop; and Shalura, ducking her massive head to clear the door jamb and trying not to knock the lamps over with her broad, flat tail.

The girls kissed Rhea on the cheek, and Miwa immediately asked to be excused.

"I've got to take a shower. I can't stand myself like this. I can show Shal our room."

The drone followed her uneasily down the hall while Teri sat at the dining room table, placing the Urim on the polished wood before her.

"Good to be home, Mom," she muttered, her voice distant, and though Rhea thrilled to hear the words, she knew that Teri's home was elsewhere now, deep in the dark green of the forest.

"It's good to hear you say that," Rhea replied, pouring a glass of lemon water. "I hear everything went well with Leyla Soral."

"More or less."

"I had to talk to her, too. A really tough woman."

"Not easy to negotiate with." There was an undertone to Teri's voice, a hint of sadness.

Does it pain her to have to say goodbye?

"Teri!" came a happy shout, and Brando walked in carrying a bleary-eyed Jakobo, who dropped from his father's arms and ran to hug his sister. "Wow, you look real different. Smell weird, too. Do they use leaves for soap in the forest?"

"Something like that," said Teri, kissing the top of his head.

"What a cool thing," Jakobo said as he pointed at the Urim. "Can I touch it?"

Rhea felt Teri hesitate and then relent. "Okay, but just for a second. It's not a toy."

Jakobo reached a shaking hand out and grazed the metal orb with the tips of his fingers. "It's all warm. What's it do?"

"It helps me talk to people and teach them."

"And blow stuff up, right?"

Brando gave a short, ironic laugh, and Teri glared at him. "Yeah, kid. It can blow things up, but only if they are trying to hurt me or the people I care about."

Jakobo seemed pleased at this news, and he sat to Teri's left, staring at the Urim as Brando tossed a salad in the kitchen.

"She's being strange," Rhea muttered as she passed behind him on the way to the sink.

"She's been through a lot. Using that thing has affected her, too."

It was more than he had said to her all day.

Teri raised her voice. "I could hear every word you were saying when I was Jako's age, guys. It's even more obvious now. Come out here and quit gossiping about me."

Sheepishly, Rhea took the casserole dish to the table. Brando followed with the salad bowl.

"Seriously, I'll be fine. This is my role, and I'm happy with it. You're still going to see me, Mom, so quit fretting. I'm their ambassador, and you're the Czar of Native Affairs. You're going to get sick of me."

Rhea smiled and wanted to feel relieved, but there was something in Teri's tired diction that hinted at hidden messages in every phrase. Rhea found herself examining her daughter's words as if Marlo Torres had spoken them.

"Oh, crap!"

Rhea whirled to see what Jakobo was exclaiming about. Shalura had just lumbered in, Miwa shaking her wet head behind the drone.

"Gee, Yakster, good to see mom's taught you so much vocabulary!" Miwa rushed to him and gave him a fusillade of kisses. "This is Shalura, my best buddy in the whole world, next to you, dork, of course."

"Wow, a real live Nakungo! He's scary!"

"Shalura's a she, Yakkety. She might look scary, but she's as sweet as pie."

Teri sighed and uttered a few alien words. Miwa replied in the same language, stuck her tongue out at her sister, and turned to tell Shalura something.

"Okay, Jakêjo, she's going to pick you up: are you ready? Don't be afraid. To her, since you're my brother, you're her brother, too."

Rhea started to put her hand out to stop them, but Brando cleared his throat.

"It has to start sometime."

Shalura bent and scooped the five-year-old into one of her arms, raising him to the level of her face. He reached out and touched her nose. "Hey, it's wet like a dog's!" he exclaimed, giggling. Shalura lifted her other massive claw and scratched lightly at his gold-flecked hair. Miwa murmured something, and the drone set the boy down.

"Wait till my class finds out I got a Nakungo sister! Talk about jealous!"

Everybody laughed, even Shalura, whose eerie yapping silenced them all.

"What's say we eat before the food gets cold?" Rhea suggested in the awkwardness that followed. They arrayed themselves around the table, the two girls at either end of the rectangle, Brando and Jakobo on one side, Rhea on the other, and Shalura crouching at a corner near Miwa, leaning back against her unusual tail as drones, Rhea had already learned, were wont to do.

It was Jakobo's turn to say grace, and he did so with the efficiency of a hungry child. Then everyone began to dive into the meal. Since Rhea was closest to Shalura, she had occasion to see how the native handled eating in a human setting. Despite the czar's expectations of bungling and confusion, Shalura took the salad bowl very gingerly in a hand and began picking out the vegetables with her claws, passing them into her mouth almost discreetly and with little noise.

Miwa noticed her mother studying Shalura. "Sound is key in the dark forest, Mom. They eat quietly and quickly so no one will hear them and so the sound of their own chewing won't disturb their ability to listen."

Brando grunted in approval. "Tell us more about this bond you two have."

Her expression somber, Miwa nodded. "You're not going to like it. You see... when she lost her tribe, I bonded her to me. Partly because she would've killed herself otherwise, but also because I care about her and want her with me."

"Bonded?" Rhea asked. "Like blood sisters?"

"No. Bonding like this is between highborn and drones. You know about the different groups, right?"

"Well, yes, but I'm not..."

Teri shook her head and interrupted. "They're married, Mom. Bonding is marriage. A highborn bonds a drone to her for life, to produce eggs for the household."

Rhea's fork fell from her fingers.

Married.

"You're such a jerk, Çèrhingÿl," Miwa growled. "I was going to explain it my way." The two started bickering in their adoptive tongue, its strange, discordant sound pushing Rhea further and further into shock.

"All you've been through," Brando interrupted as he saw Shalura stiffen at the exchange, "and you still act like a couple of whiny kids."

Miwa looked around pointedly. "Hrm, where's Carmen Allende, Ambassador? I mean, the whole family's here, so why didn't you bring your girlfriend?

Jakobo leaned toward Teri. "You have a girlfriend? But you're a girl."

Teri patted him on the head. "Girls can have girlfriends, too. And drone wives. Sorry, kid, but boys are overrated."

Rhea rubbed her temples. "I think I'm going to faint."

"Girls," Brando groaned. "Maybe ease your mother into your life choices."

"Father," Teri put in, "you really shouldn't bring up life choices. You've been lying for years about who you are and what you believe."

Brando narrowed his eyes. "I thought we'd gotten past that."

Miwa stood. "Look, I know it's hard for you to understand, but like Ambassador Moron here, I've picked a life for myself. I'm not going to fit in here. I'm a clone. I'm not mad about that or anything. I'm glad to be alive, glad that God made Dad do what he did. But I can't stay here, and I want Shalura with me wherever I decide to go."

Rhea managed to open her mouth long enough to whisper, "Do you love her?"

Miwa looked at her intently. "Yes, Mom. I do."

"And I love Carmen," Teri added.

They were never really mine, were they, Lord? I'll let them go, then, trusting that you'll watch over them.

With a shuddering sob, Rhea lowered her head. "Okay, then." She felt Brando stand as well, saw him signal for Miwa to follow him to his study.

"You okay, Mommy?" asked Jakobo. She picked up her head and looked into his deep brown eyes.

I still have you, little one. And maybe Brando. If Teri was able to convince them.

"Yes, baby. I'm fine."

"Married to a Nakungo. My nephews are going to be real funny-looking."

As Rhea began sobbing again, she heard Teri lead Jakobo out, perhaps taking him to his room.

A good move. He really is too young to understand what's happening here.

A soft noise made her lift her head from the table. Jakobo's plate was gone. The sphere had rolled directly in front of her and was glowing blue.

«A gift,» a soft chorus muttered in her mind. «She was going to wait until later, but now is better, we believe.»

Rhea shuddered as voices began shouting in harsh, guttural syllables in her mind. The sound crescendoed till it was almost painful and slowly eased to a quiet mutter. Then it died.

Something has changed.

"I will protect her with my life," Shalura said. Rhea could understand her. She felt disoriented, as if someone had secretly inverted the color spectrum. The sphere had given her the Native Teregans' language. She looked at the drone with new eyes, alien ideas filtering into her mind through the medium of words. Rhea tried to imagine how protected this hulking warrior had to make Miwa feel, tried to grasp how love could develop between beings so distinct.

"That you will," Rhea replied, her mind balking at the words that leapt to her lips, "or, despite your size, I will make you wish you had."

"She is my Lady. I will lay my life down for her."

"She is my child. Losing her hurts more than you can know."

Shalura's tail twitched against the floor. "You have not lost her. She yet lives, and she will bring much honor to the spirit of your tribe. I, however, have lost a child, and I understand completely the pain that such loss brings. I swear I will spare you this, Lady."

The sincerity in Shalura's words moved Rhea inexplicably. "Thank you. As difficult as it is for me now, I accept you, if that is what makes her happy."

Teri rushed back in, a bit startled. "The Urim? It acted alone?"

"Yes," said Rhea. "How can it do that?"

"I don't know." Her eyes closed a moment. "Because I wanted it done, I guess. I was going to wait until dessert, at least, though."

Rhea managed a small, humorless laugh. "I don't know whether to thank you or scold you. It felt horrible and invasive, you realize. Going into people's minds without their permission is not right, Çèrhingÿl. You're going to have to curb that desire. A diplomat uses her wiles, not advanced technology."

"Speaking of diplomats," Miwa said as she and Brando rejoined them, "what's the word? Do I have anything to worry about, Sis?"

Çèrhingÿl shook her head. "No. You've been absolved completely."

"What about Dad?"

Brando looked at Çèrhingÿl with sober expectation, but Rhea noticed that his daughter found it hard to match his gaze.

"That's a little more complicated. Brando, I know you just came out of there, but let's go into your study." She scooped up the sphere. "We need to talk."

Rhea bit her lip. She didn't want to cry again, but she felt a tide of despair rising in her as the two of them slipped out of the dining room.

"It's like a bus station in here," muttered Miwa to no one. "In and out and in and out. Where's Jakobo?"

"Eating in his room."

Pushing her quickly drying curls back behind her ears, Miwa eased into the chair beside Shalura. "I don't like this one bit, Mom. I'm not sure I trust her anymore."

"Çèrhingÿl gave Rhea the People's speech, Daenzhelo," Shalura announced.

Miwa raised an eyebrow. "Really? That is being great!"

Rhea understood immediately that her daughter's speech was very deficient. Nonetheless, her being able to speak the strange tongue at all was a miracle.

"You learned to speak by yourself in one month? That is incredible."

"Brando made me a language nut. And you used to complain that it was too much."

The memory brought a twinge of nostalgia.

"Yes. I was wrong about many things, dear."

"But right about most. That's the good thing. Let's eat, okay? I'm hungry, and we might as well enjoy this one last meal together, you and me and Shalura. I have a feeling we're not going to have much of an appetite in a few minutes."

They had barely taken a few bites, Shalura grimacing at the unusual flavor, when Brando's furious howl from the next room jerked all three of them to their feet.

INTERCHAPTER K

From: isabella@dangelo.per.oce

To: dangeloa@diomedes.gov.af

Subject: PLEASE READ!!!

Date: May 14, 2714 8:34:19 (SST)

Antonio, my one hope is that you read this letter. I never receive responses from you anymore, so I don't even know if you read what I send to you. But news of your arrest is all over the infotainment sphere, and I just needed to let you know that we're here for you. We understand that you did what you thought was right, and we'll never judge you.

Your father is really sick. Has been for years now. But despite his illness, he wakes up early each day to check the news and see how you are. He never stopped loving you, Tony. Even if you can't forgive him, he'll always accept you unconditionally. All he ever wanted was to make you happy.

Maybe luck will be on your side and you'll not go to prison. If I were religious, that's what I would pray for it. But if you do get sent to that detention asteroid, Sheol or whatever they call it, I hope you'll let us faux-visit you. It would mean so much to him.

I love you, Tony, my sweet.

Isabella Spinelli-D'Angelo

CHAPTER 68

"YIKES, MIWA," BRANDO SAID as he shut the study door, "You could've eased her into that a little better."

"Teri was no help. She's the one that made it sound totally different than it is."

Brando bobbed his head in reluctant agreement. "In any case, though I tried to prepare you for life's complications, you should consider consulting with adults before making these major decisions. I mean, you are still fifteen Standard years old."

Of course, she didn't seem fifteen anymore. She certainly *looked* like a woman, and though there was still a bit of petulant adolescence shining through her tough exterior here at home, Miwa more than acted like an adult. She was intelligent, big-hearted and strong, more than able to handle life on her own, just like her biological mother had at thirteen.

"Come on, Dad, that's ridiculous. The past month was more than enough proof that I can manage without supervision. What was the point of pushing me so hard if not for me to get an early start on the hard stuff? You know I'm just a year from graduation anyway; that's what, a year and a quarter standard? Let me publish the article you've been helping me with, and I can get into a university somewhere in the Consortium."

Miwa had always wanted fame, renown, attention. Brando knew that one of the reasons she had dedicated herself so fully to sports was the swell of applause and shouting that greeted her victories. She would never find what she needed on this world, and Terego's gentle but firm channeling of young ladies' energies into homemaking would inevitably clash with her own stubborn independence, not to mention with her decision to bond with a Nakÿng drone.

"Everywhere you go, people are going to focus on Shalura."

"I know."

"You're going to need to be on your guard always."

"Yeah."

Brando sighed. He had no desire to fight this. He'd given her what she required. It was time to let go. But first, there was something he needed from her.

"Here," he said, yanking a data storage device from his desk terminal. "I cleaned stuff up, turned it into a decent monograph. Take it or send it to Dr.

Luigi Serafini in Milan. We were students together. I gather he's now the department chair in linguistics. I've already messaged him, introducing you and all."

Beaming, Miwa threw her arms around him. The crown of her head fit just under his chin, and the smell of strawberry shampoo in her still-damp curls brought mist to his eyes.

"Thanks, Dad," she muttered happily. "I love you so much."

"Me, too, kiddo. Now here's the hard part. The immigration ministry has my ranfura tucked away in a warehouse. I check on it every six months, and I know it's in decent shape. It's programmed to unlock for your DNA. Yours and Teri's. The systems are automatic: you tell the somatoids where to go, and they do the rest. Manual in-system stuff you can more or less handle. I showed you the basics a thousand times on those simulators Teri used to hate."

Miwa laughed, remembering.

"The hypostasis pods are easy enough: you strip down, stow your clothes in a locker, and ease into the gel. The first time will scare you, because the ship inserts and attaches tubes here and there, if you get my meaning. But the faux-bridge is easy, and you went through the mountain training so you're familiar with the procedure."

"Yeah. I'm worried about Shalura, though."

"I'd say put her in stasis, not d-sleep. It's not probable that her brain is compatible with the neural-firing mechanisms of the faux-connection. She'd freak out, anyway. You can squeeze her into one of the larger pods. Your first priority after a short fenestration is to get a large animal transport pod."

As Miwa nodded, taking this information in, Brando took a deep breath and came to the final point. "In fact, you could do with some help. I've been thinking about leaving Terego myself."

"What about Mom and Jakobo?" Miwa asked, her brow furrowing.

"Oh, they'd come too," Brando said, not even flinching at the lie. "In the same way you don't think you fit in here any longer, I doubt we will, either."

Miwa pursed her lips in thought. "Let's see what Teri says about the criminal cases against us, yeah? I mean, if you have to leave, I'll help you, Dad. But the best option would be for you three to stay on Terego if possible."

Not wanting to push the issue further, Brando smiled and opened the door. "Sounds like a plan."

They walked back to the living room together. Rhea was insisting in her quiet but firm voice, "A diplomat uses her wiles, not advanced technology."

"Speaking of diplomats," Miwa said as she and Brando stepped through the archway, "what's the word? Do I have anything to worry about, Sis?"

Teri shook her head. "No. You've been absolved."

Brando felt a wave of relief.

"What about Dad?"

Brando looked at Teri, hoping beyond hope for good news, but understanding deep within him that this was impossible. The Consortium wasn't about to give him up. It was obvious that his daughter found it hard to look him directly in the eye: her gaze kept wandering to the wall behind him.

"That's a little more complicated. Brando, I know you just came out of there, but let's go into your study." Ominously, she gathered the Urim in her hands. "We need to talk."

Teri shut the door behind them once they'd entered the room. With a glance around at the huge wood bookcases that lined the walls, she wilted for the briefest of moments, then set her jaw with the sort of resolution that had made Tenshi so formidable.

"They want me to give you to them. It's one of their conditions for the treaty."

"But, come on, I'm insignificant in all of this. That doesn't make any sense."

"It's because of Samanei. They want her. According to Antonio, she has information they want, information about certain crime syndicates and the old Centauri Rift."

The rift. Samanei's last words, scored into Brando's innermost being by the fires of guilt and fear, came unbidden to his consciousness: *You've got no idea, Brando, who I am or what I see. I have been down to the deepest depths of Gumun Gereza, to the greyest of cells of this vast prison, and I saw Him, roaring orange in all his glory. Not Dresch, Doctor, but HIM. Domina's son. Sakra made flesh. He wants to meet you, Brando.*

Brando shook off the nauseating memory, tried to put Teri off that dangerous trail. "Oh, so now you trust Antonio."

Teri shrugged and looked pointedly at the Urim. Brando understood at once. She could get to the truth no matter what lies a person told.

"I won't tell them anything," Brando said. "Samanei, if she's not dead already, will die alone on that planet."

"I already know where she is. I got the coordinates from Kyr. You did a good job of hiding them, but there's no mental cranny that I can't get into it."

Brando's heart rate quickened. "You can't tell them, Teri! She'll get the upper hand, somehow. She's not even human anymore. I don't know how to explain it, but there's something evil in her."

Teri quirked an eyebrow, looking so much like Samanei that Brando took a startled step back. "What, Sakra? The Demiurge? That's who you think was inside the Rift, don't you? He's been sealed inside for a century."

Not asking how she knew, Brando ploughed on. He felt his veneer of sanity disintegrate as desperation built inside him.

"There's a crack," he moaned, "in his prison, Teri. He whispers through it. I've heard him. Samanei spent thirty years listening to his vile voice. Together, they will destroy us, baby. Please. Just leave her where she is."

"She deserves punishment. She killed Tenshi, didn't she?"

Brando's hands balled into fists that squeezed his knuckles white. "Punishment is what I'm giving her, damn it!"

Teri's face went slack. "Whatever. I'm done arguing with you about this. It's all your fault anyway. You're the reason everyone's life is fucked up."

Brando banged his fists against his thighs in rage and sorrow. "That's right, Teri, dehumanize me so your betrayal is easier."

For a moment it looked like she might use her sphere to rip him to shreds. "Dehumanize *you*? What about how you dehumanized me? I'm an illegal clone who's going to live her life out among aliens."

"As a virtual queen with your pretty girlfriend at your side," he shot back. "You're my wife's double, you arrogant little bitch. I know your hunger to rearrange lives and lord over them. Don't play the pathetic martyr with me."

Teri said nothing for a moment. Then, with a quiet and calm gesture, she pointed at a chronometer on the desk.

"Fifteen minutes, Brando. Then I escort you out of this house and into XID custody. I won't give up the security of this planet and the Nakÿng just so you can go free. You *did* commit crimes, you know."

Anger giving way to horror and despair, Brando pleaded. "Teri, yes, I did. But consider my motives. How could you fault me?"

"There's always another way, Brando, one that doesn't require death. You didn't even bother."

"You don't know what you're talking about. I spent years trying."

"I tried as well, and I succeeded. I found a way. Though it pains me, you're going with them. So go say your goodbyes, Brando, and let's walk out of here in the calmest, most casual of ways."

The inevitable loomed over him like a nightmare monster that had stepped under the lintel and passed into the waking world. Like a frightened animal, he wanted to bolt, to shove Teri out of the way and rush into the darkling air of evening. But there was that malicious orb, now glowing faintly, and Brando simply fell to his knees. He saw the lake before him, saw his fifteen-year-old face, tear-streaked, look up at him from the surface.

"Please," he begged in a choked whisper, "please let me run. Say I slipped by you, that you never saw me. I have to be free when the paradox unravels. Have to be able to act to protect you all."

"No, I can't. They'd never believe me. And no one needs your protection any longer. You're not the protagonist of this story, Brando."

"Don't do this to me. Don't do this to Jakobo. Think about him, growing up without me!"

Teri looked at him impassible, a tendril of faintest blue linking her temples to the sphere. "No. He'll be fine without you. We'll all be fine. It's time to pay the price, Brando. No more running."

In his despair, Brando remembered his sea pilgrimage on Jitsu, how the black spike had been thrust into his hands, how his ring had touched it, summoning Tenshi's voice.

Thrusting his left hand toward Teri, he seized the Urim.

And the world disappeared.

«WHAT DO YOU WANT? TELL US NOW.»

Brando could see nothing but swirling blue all around him. It glowed with the rhythm of the chorus that addressed him.

I think I understand what you are, what you're going to have to do. I want you to swear to me. Save her if you can.

«Teri? We will protect her from all harm.»

Not Teri. You know what I mean. Stop playing games. I tell you I know. Before you go, whenever that happens to be, protect Jakobo. I think he'll be in danger. Protect his mind.

«From whom?»

You're starting to piss me off.

«The one you call Sakra.»

Right. Are you listening? Save her. Protect my boy's mind. And...

«Yes?»

When he gets free, which I fucking guarantee he will, come get me. Wherever they put me. Do we have a deal?

Bemused silence. Then.

«Very well. Just keep that ring on your finger.»

CHAPTER 69

RHEA SHOVED THE DOOR OPEN and rushed in. Brando was kneeling on the floor, his hand on the Urim, his eyes closed. Teri kept trying to take it from him, but a sort of blue shield blocked her every attempt.

"Çèrhingÿl, you freak, what did you do to him?" Miwa demanded as she passed by Rhea into the study.

"I just told him he's got to give himself up. The CPCC won't withdraw from this planet unless he does. It's a sacrifice, but one that will save hundreds of lives, maybe thousands. He kept trying to weasel his way out. Then he grabbed *the Urim!*"

Rhea's heart plummeted.

Give himself up?

She hadn't expected this turn of events; she'd been depending too much on Teri's apparent omnipotence. Or had she? Already, her heart rate was slowing as she bent by Brando's side.

Didn't I accept this possibility weeks ago? Haven't I been secretly expecting it? Don't his lies almost make it the better way? Hasn't his cruelty and my distrust of him already started poisoning my love, turning it to hate?

Perhaps. Or perhaps she simply wanted to minimize her own pain by pushing him away now that there was no choice. In any event, she decided quickly that she would not fight Teri on this, would not oppose the CPCC. She'd researched the prison asteroid and knew that faux-conferences were permitted once a month.

Dear Lord, it will have to suffice, won't it? I will have to be enough for Jakobo, won't I?

Brando's hand slipped from the Urim. He opened his eyes.

"Ten minutes, Brando," Teri muttered, seizing the alien orb at last.

Shakily, he stood. "I'm ready."

Jakobo appeared in the doorway in that instant, beside Shalura. "What's wrong? Why did Daddy scream?"

Brando turned to him. "I was sad, son. Because I have to go away now. We'll still be able to see each other, I promise. But in order for the soldiers to leave us alone, I must accept punishment. You know that's never fun."

Tears glittered bright in Jakobo's eyes. "No. But it's what God wants, right, Daddy? We say 'sorry' and take our licks."

Reaching down to take the boy in his arms, Brando shuddered with regret. "Yes. And sometimes we take licks for others."

Rhea kissed Jakobo's head. "Like Jesus."

Teri grimaced and replied in Nakÿng, "He's a good man, but he's no divine savior."

Then she walked out of the study.

Rhea took Jakobo from Brando and passed him to Miwa. "Take him to the living room. We'll be right there.

Miwa, her lip trembling, complied somberly.

Shalura hesitated in the doorway a second.

"God's price is often more than we can bear. But we do bear it, somehow."

Rhea's arms prickled with gooseflesh. "Yes. That we do."

The couple was alone. Brando turned away, but his back was wracked by silent sobs that spasmed throughout his body. Rhea put her thin arms as best she could around him and waited.

After a couple of minutes, he stopped crying, and rubbed his eyes. His mien was altered completely when he turned to face her: cold, mechanical and distant.

"You didn't argue with her. You want me gone, don't you? I lied to you and used you and now you want me out of your life. But not on my terms, oh, no. The lawyer and politician has to play by the rules. So be it, then. You'll just have to live with the consequences, Rhea. Remember that."

He strode from the room, and she followed close on his heels. In the living room, Shalura was in a blue trance caused by the orb, and Miwa was muttered softly to Jakobo, whose cheeks were red and wet with tears. Rhea hurried to her son and daughter.

"She wanted to give me a gift," explained Miwa, "but I told her I didn't want anything from her, the traitor. Shalura really wants to understand human speech and culture, though, so she agreed."

Rhea didn't feel like arguing with Miwa about the rightness of Teri's choice. Her heart ached from so many emotional ups and downs, and all she wanted was to hold her son in her arms and for all of this to be over. She was tired, exhausted to the marrow of her being.

Teri's blue glow subsided, and she turned to Brando, who waited, his jaws muscles clinched tightly, by the door. "I have something for you, Brando."

"There's nothing you have that I want, Ambassador," he growled.

"Just two minutes left, Brando. Give them to me. I'm not sure what you got from the Urim, but I was always certain you'd agree to this deal. Tenshi knew you, Brando. I want everyone to see what she said about you in her last journal entry."

A blue-tinged holographic projection of Tenshi Koroma materialized before the orb. Rhea noted her beauty, her obvious strength, and the calm focus that rolled from her in waves. Tenshi was smiling slightly.

"I see the structure of people as well as things, Diary. I want to go beyond buildings, see? To build a new sort of society, one that works, that doesn't oppress its citizens, that won't fall apart from within nor be conquered from without.

"I think Brando understands, and in his quiet comprehension, I find peace. His heart is big enough to hold me and my people too, once I get him to share my vision. I've known many people in my life, and never did I meet one as compassionate. Tempered, he could be a leader. At the very least, he's going to be a wonderful father."

The image flickered into non-existence. Brando slumped a bit, and fresh tears made his eyes glisten.

"Okay," he said. "Time's up. I made a deal with the Urim. Let's go."

He went to the couch, kissed his daughter and his son briefly on the forehead as Jakobo's sobs grew into heart-rending wails, nodded at Shalura and Rhea, and then stepped through the doorway into the darkness of the Teregan night.

Teri followed, leaving the remnants of the family to mourn its own demise.

CHAPTER 70

I WONDER HOW THEY'RE TREATING BRANDO, Teri thought as the Urim dug deeper into the rock beneath the marsh. The aging linguist had said nothing to her while she'd escorted him to the XID agents waiting just a kilometer from the house, but when Minoungou had cuffed him, Brando had looked back at her.

"I hope it's worth it."

"It is, Brando. Forgive me. But there's a reason for the pain. Your love matters. Your sacrifice matters."

Taking a shaky, deep breath, he had nodded. "The day will come when you'll need to say those words to me again. Don't forget them. I need them in my heart."

Then they'd loaded him into the transport and driven away.

None of what she'd done had been easy, Teri reflected, but the price had to be paid. The independence and future of a planet, the elevation of a race of beings, the lives of countless humans and Nakÿng—of course these goals were worth Brando's freedom, especially when he'd forfeited that liberty by his own actions long ago.

Teri refused to feel guilty. She couldn't help feeling sad, however.

Luckily, the Urim gave her little time for sorrow.

«There. In a gas pocket formed by the lava striking the water of the lake. Preserved virtually as it was when it crashed.»

As the ancient ship, or the bulk of it, pulled free from the rock a hundred meters below ground level, the Urim allowed the marsh water to go gushing into the enormous bowl they'd carved out of the landscape to more easily extract the CPCC's new prize.

«They will have much difficulty finding the remaining fragments. It is best to leave them some mystery.»

Teri didn't reply. The Urim had baffled her more than usual over the past ten hours or so: giving Rhea the gift of Nakÿng speech before Teri had ordered it, making some deal with Brando it would not disclose, refusing to fenestrate to the crash site in west-central Novameriko because of some unspecified possible danger.

During the four-hour trip across the ocean and half a continent, the inscrutable alien tool had not conveyed a word or emotion, leaving Teri to nap and wonder at the remorse-tinged present and the hope-pregnant future in turns.

Now the Urim wanted to chat.

Just do whatever you wanted to do with the ship, and let's go.

Setting the ship on an island of volcanic rock it had fashioned from the rubble removed to reach its former home, the Urim asked Teri to enter. With tendrils of indigo force, the brassy orb brought the vessel partially to life, and the mummified remains of three other creatures similar to Teri's mental image of Zhehoha, her predecessor, were illuminated by a sickly yellow light.

«Strange. There should be four.»

A softer counterpoint whispered, «Where's his body? He ran from us, but his body should still be here.»

«Scans do not detect another corpse nearby. In any event, they cannot have access to our DNA. These bodies must be transported to the obelisk and immolated beside the bones of the other agent.»

An echo. «Zhehoha's bones.»

Another. «My bones.»

Wait. The "we" you always use. You're the crew!

«Were. Yes. Thousands of years comingled, we are now more one than four. But once we were Zhehoha. Mutlakhe. Ambleln. Echysmi. Elevation team Square Root of Helium Half Life.»

«And Selaha, wherever he has gone,» came the soft, plaintive undercurrent.

Where did you come from? Is your species alone, like humanity? No, that doesn't make sense given your mission. You're part of some enormous conglomeration of advanced species, right? Living in some distant corner of the universe?

The Urim answered Teri with images. A gorgeous region of space where galaxies were much more closely packed than was the case in the Milky Way's neighborhood. Teri caught glimpses of parsecs of stars networked together to generate massive amounts of energies for undertakings she couldn't begin to guess at.

«Elevation teams are equipped with the only most basic of technologies. Early disasters taught this lesson well. Should situations like the present agreement ever occur, illegal elevation cannot proceed to dangerous levels. Be glad. This system of governance your species has settled on is destructive. Private entities that accumulate wealth and power have become like governments. Governments have become like those profiteering companies. Corporate capitalism, your experts call it. Accelerated by ill-gotten advanced technology. Understand, Agent. That model has failed utterly in every corner of the universe it has arisen. After feeding off worlds and citizens, it always ends in self-destruction."

Teri balked. *I can't let that happen.*

«There's little that you, that *we,* can do. Thousands of years of negative cultural evolution. A vast hegemony of lucre and force. It cannot be easily undone.»

But some of us stand outside it. The Nakÿng certainly do. Can't we build an alternative?

The elevation team within the Urim were silent, pensive. Then:

«We see a path to one. But there is a horrible obstacle that must be dealt with first. Your help is needed. Now that we have more data, we are permitted to share certain details that will facilitate what must be done.»

Teri suppressed her frustration.

What 'must be done?' What's the horrible obstacle?

«Access to the ship's star charts and travel records is required. During this ship's fenestration, the conduit suffered a collapse, and the ship was sent randomly back into your spacetime. The Urim has spent two thousand jaroj without knowing the location of this world. There are no nearby communications outposts in higher dimensions. The Urim cannot choose courses of action on its own. Though our minds were translated into it at the moment of our deaths, we have limited control over it. The safeties built into the device mean it requires an external agent.»

Got it. I'm important. What did you find in the XID computers?

«Since the first fenestration you ordered, it has become obvious that something is wrong about this region of space. There is a conduit, an *imrizabu*, your species calls it, running through the star system, ancient like they all are, but it was abandoned soon after its creation millions of years ago, not used, maintained or monitored since. There is also an unsettling quality to the higher dimensions themselves.

«We were unsure why. Your mind yielded some information. Kyr and Antonio D'Angelo each had other pieces of the puzzle. Brando had more. The pieces are scattered, Agent, waiting to be discovered by one who can join them together.»

A shudder of horror from the Urim swept over her.

«It is as we first feared. Comparisons of the XID information and the records of this ship confirm it.

Confirm what? You've got me twisted in knots!

«Two hundred years ago your species found a tear in a closed imrizabu, one that had been sealed, its gateway into this spacetime destroyed millions of years ago. The tear was widened, and humans raced to reach this conduit for study or profit. Many were manipulated a force from higher dimensional space, the being Pathwalkers name the Demiurge or Sakra. It almost bent your species to its will, freeing it from its prison, but it was stopped.»

How?

The silence from the Urim felt muffled, as if one of the team wanted to speak but was being suppressed.

«Still unclear. But among those involved were individuals who founded Jitsu.»

Faces from her history books: Domina Ditis, Dédalo Mostrenco, and another person she'd never seen.

«This last one is Yen Bandera, later responsible for helping Samanei Koroma wreak havoc on Jitsu and the criminal organizations that found themselves embroiled in that conflict. Yet the sealing of the conduit once again left a tear, we believe.»

So Brando was right. The Demiurge has established contact with Samanei.

«Yes. He should have destroyed her when he had the opportunity. We must hope she is dead. Were it not for the repercussions, we would recommend blowing the XID vessel out of the sky now to prevent either Antonio or Brando from revealing her location.»

Teri's mind reeled.

What? How can you say such a thing? You know I would never agree to it! Why didn't you tell me this before? I would've never given up the information if I had known what was at stake!

«We regret the pieces were not all together when you gave Antonio the coordinates. What is done is done. Perhaps all will be fine. She must be locked well away, never given access to technology that would allow her to release the being that lies bound and quiescent beyond the edge of your spacetime.»

I'll make sure Soral understands the danger.

«There is more, however. You will have to elevate the Nakÿng now not only to prevent humanity's militarize corporate capitalism from abusing them, but also so they might help us. We must contact our species, either via a probe through physical space to request aid or by discovering the remains of the interdimensional umbilicus that once connected this galaxy to our own. The work could take centuries. With luck and Samanei's isolation or death, nothing should happen in the interim. The cell should hold its prisoner. With luck.»

Okay, now you're scaring the shit out of me. How can you be so sure based on this flimsy evidence that we're in so much danger?

«This is not the first time it has tried to reach into your lives and destroy your species. Hidden in the records of your people are clues, left by unlucky travelers who fell into this accursed region of space or came here because of misplaced feelings of charity. In your mind, for example, the Urim found the text of *The Book of Abraham*, one of your scriptures. Certain words seemed familiar, but not until now is it clear why. The book was written in English, but contains terms not in any language from your planet. *Enish-go-on-dosh, Kae-e-vanrash, Floeese, Kli-flos-is-es, Hah-ko-kau-beam.*»

No one is really sure what those words mean, the bishop told us.

«They have been distorted, but they are recognizably from the language of a race engaged in unauthorized elevation throughout the universe. The words form fragments of a message. *Xein Nizgo' Andoetsh*—this spacetime. *Qhaiei Vaengratsh*—the principal group in charge of elevation. *F'lueçeh*— damaged space. *Qh'lii F'lazis Xeç*—warning to all travelers. *Hax Qhokaw*

Mbii—the evil one awaits.»

A chill ran its way along Teri's limbs.

«As you would say, *fuck*. Scan complete. There is no doubt. The correlation of XID records and the charts on this ship confirm it. This galaxy sits in a region of the universe that has been shut off, condemned, sealed to the outside. Specifics cannot be revealed to you, but millions of years ago a terrible war was fought here. Trillions of beings were slaughtered and a great evil was locked away from the universe. It desperately wants out.

«Pray to your god that no one finds the key.»

CHAPTER 71

WHEN THEY HAD BROUGHT HIS BROTHER onto the shuttle, Antonio hadn't been able to see or speak to him as they were sealed in separate cabins. On board the *Sigil*, however, the two men were escorted to the gaol block and placed in adjacent cells. The only guard was stationed at the entranceway to the block, so Tony risked whispering, his face only centimeters from the energy mesh that held him inside.

"Brando. Can you hear me?"

A grunt.

"Good. All this time, and you and me without exchanging a single word. Strange. I came to Terego to bring you to justice, and here we go together. Who would have thought, eh?"

"Just leave me alone, Antonio," came Brando's hoarse voice.

The AF captain was not deterred. "I understand. You're not going to see your family for a long time. That has to be hard. But it's for a good cause, no? Teri has wonderful plans."

"Her plans? Ha. How did she turn you into a zombie? Did she get in your head, sing her siren song to you?"

Antonio's pulse quickened. "Brando, she's your daughter! You were ready to kill everybody to protect her. What changed? If you hate her so much, what are you doing here?"

"I don't have to explain myself to you."

Antonio pictured Brando's sullen features. He put an open palm against the wall.

So many years I hated you, Brother. How can I reach you now that I need you?

"No, of course you don't. But I think this is another of your extended phenotype Pathwalker con jobs. You actually *support* what Teri's doing, don't you?"

"Antonio, she took everything from me! I was stripped of my family once, and now she did it again. And with my head bent like some beaten dog, I let her! You want to rub it in? Go on. She knows my weaknesses, and she shut me down like an old, useless hulk of machinery. If you're foolish enough to swallow her messianic delusions, then just leave me the fuck out of it, understood?"

For the longest time, Antonio crouched on his heels, listening as the rhythm of his breathing, the humming of the energy net, and Brando's raspy, conflicted panting merged into a single sound. He understood how his changed outlook must seem to his brother, and to anyone else for that matter. Brainwashing, they would jeer.

But his mind was unaffected. He still reasoned and felt as he always had about nearly everything. The loss of his command and of the respect of his men pained him to the quick, as did the knowledge that much of his quixotic quest had been harmful to really good people. His sense of justice was intact, for sure.

All that had been added was the ability to forgive, the capacity to move on and give life a second chance. For Antonio this addition had been nearly instantaneous. Teri's presence in his mind, still thrumming wordlessly behind every thought formed there, had let him see how destructive his anger and resentment had been.

Brando, however, would require time.

"You never joined with Teri, right?"

There was no answer.

"I didn't think so. That's okay, though. You and me, we're going to be sent to the prison asteroid together. There will be time. Time for you to learn to trust me. You see, I need a family, Brando, and so do you. In prison, we're going to need each other even more. So if right now you hate me, if right now you blame me for going to Terego and stirring all of this up, that's okay. I just want you to know that I forgive you."

Brando's voice was harsh and full of hate as he spat. "You arrogant prick. *You* forgive *me*? What the *fuck* are you talking about?"

Swallowing heavily, Antonio muttered, "I forgive you for the weakness you can't forgive yourself for, Brother. On behalf of the two you can never bring back, not truly, no matter how hard you try. I forgive you for not being strong enough. Because they would have forgiven you, Brando. They would have wanted you to move on."

A muffled, ambiguous sound that might have been a growled curse or a strangled sob was his only answer as the *Sigil* continued moving implacably into the future, toward the world on which Brando had stranded Samanei and whatever fate awaited them there.

CHAPTER 72

THE NEW VOICE IN SHALURA'S HEAD, Çèrhingÿl's reedy whisper, told the drone that the building before them was a *warehouse* used for storing *space craft* belonging to immigrants to Terego. They had arrived in the *city* earlier that morning and spent several hours at the *Consortium Embassy*. Miwa wanted to gain entrance to the many nations that made up the union of humans that Shalura now thought of as the CPCC. But to do so, they first had to travel for many months to the independent world of Semanawak, where an *Intake Center* had been set up to prepare refugees and immigrants for entry into the Consortium.

So many strange new words and ideas. Everywhere Shalura looked as the pair made their way through Diadono, objects had sudden, if hazy significance.

A basic understanding of human culture, the Firstborn had said. *Knowledge of Baryogo and Standard. The rest you'll have to learn on your own.*

It was a generous gift, one that still glowed in her mind like muscles aching after a morning lope. Any rancor she'd felt toward the sister of Daenzhelo (*Miwa! Unpronounceable, but here in my head!*) because of the choice of council leader had been expelled by the unfathomable generosity.

A guard stood with his weapon at the entrance. He stiffened at the sight of Shalura's enormous frame and then relaxed with a nod of his head.

"Miwa D'Angelo, right? The prime minister himself called this morning. Yall're cleared. We have loaded yall's gear into the cargo compartment and everything."

Shalura noticed the downturn of Miwa's mouth, which the Firstborn's voice declared was a sign of unhappiness.

"Why are you using Standard?"

"I thought it would make you more comfortable. Figured since you're leaving the planet, you must want to be part of the rest of humanity. I envy you a little. I would love to see the galaxy."

Miwa nodded. "Well, like the teachers are always saying, *carpe diem*."

The corpsman raised an eyebrow, a gesture of disbelief or confusion.

"Nothing," Miwa said. "Can we go in?"

"Yes, ma'am. I'll open the far doors, and yall just use the runway that runs up to them. Good luck. God be with yall."

Shalura followed her mate as the guard waved them in with his *rifle* (*not reed*). They made their way among various large, bug-like ships till they reached the sleek, spear-shaped form of Brando's *ranfura*. Fast ships, Shalura understood. Little more than engines, those made-things that propelled the vessels, and sleeping rooms. The interior reminded Shalura of the cave where Brando's image had taught Miwa how to use weapons and *battle armor* (*not skins*). Shining metal and cool plastic, materials beyond Shalura's wildest imaginings, coated every surface.

"Go back to that room," Miwa told her in Standard, "the one at the end of this hall. You understand?"

Shalura nodded. "Yes. I cannot use the words, but I understand them."

"Good. Wait for me there. I'll program our course to Semanawak. It won't take long. Then I'll get you into the suspension pod. Remember, we talked about it. Like warm water, thick. Go on."

Shalura entered the chamber and stood staring at the five huge, clear pots (*pods!*) filled with pink gel. Her heart was filled with fear like she hadn't felt since the first time she'd been on the hunt, a fresh young drone with just her training.

Now as then she had an inkling of what was to come, but most of the future was shrouded as if in the heavy green clouds of Teregan rain. Shalura felt ill equipped for life among humans; her two main skills, hunting and fighting, seemed in limited demand, from what she understood of the culture of her new people. Miwa would be with her, however, and that was somehow enough.

Such devotion to and dependence on one individual went beyond all the lore and tradition of the Nakÿng, but Shalura no longer cared. Miwa had, weeks ago, tried to make Shalura understand this concept. Çèrhingÿl's voice now gave the drone its name: love. Shalura loved Miwa. That was the source of her hope. She had simply never had the word until now.

"Take off your harness and put it in a locker." Miwa instructed as she walked in and demonstrated how to open the irising compartments. As her drone complied, the human herself began to strip, and Shalura again regarded her mate's strange, *alien* form. She was not repulsed, however. What she loved about Miwa had little to do with her physical body. The human's spirit shone through brighter than the Unblinking Eye (*forgive my blasphemy*), purer than the cold waters that rushed down from the mist-shrouded mountains in verdant spring.

"Daenzhelo."

Miwa cycled the locker closed and turned to Shalura. "Yes?"

"Saran nimishaseru," ventured Shalura in Baryogo.

Tears in her eyes, Miwa took three steps forward and threw her arms about the drone's abdomen. "Oh, you silly drone, I love you, too. Now get into the gel before the ship takes off and slams our dumb butts all against the walls!"

Pressing her tail tightly against her legs, Shalura eased into the warm goo, so like the mucilage that had embraced her in the mouthpouch of her gestator twenty-eight years before. The fetal doubling up of her body reinforced this feeling and oddly comforted her. As she submerged her head, a breathing device gently pushed between her teeth just as Miwa had warned, and a slight prick to the base of her skull sent her mind flying, spinning toward a mythical dreamscape where, faced by a host of deadly foes, Shalura and her lovely mate fought valiantly, with hearty, fearless laughter ringing in both their throats.

CHAPTER 73

WHEN MIWA AND SHALURA LEFT SUNDAY MORNING, taxied away by a crisis ministry transport, Rhea had gone into the bathroom, opened wide the noisy faucets, and wept painfully, her body doubling up as she gripped the sink's edge and leaned her forehead against the mirror.

Gone, all of them.

Miwa had promised to visit soon, but Rhea understood loss. There was always the promise of reunion, whether in heaven or, though some miracle, in the physical world, but it was best not to obsess over this possibility. In fact, it became clear to her as the sobs subsided, letting go was the only way to achieve peace. So one by one she let them go.

Heavenly Father, I give you Brando. Help him to find his way to you, help him to release his pain and put it your hands. May he empty his heart of pride so that he receives a witness through the Holy Ghost of the only truth that can ever save him. I give you Teri. Guide her along the paths to righteousness. Let her be a beacon of hope for a race living in darkness. And I give you Miwa, sweet Miwa. Watch over her, Lord.

Rhea went on for a good ten minutes. Though the comfort she received from her prayer was hollow and would often disappear in the darkness of night, she was able to move forward, as she had ever done, even after the deaths of her loved ones. Life would not stop to allow her time to heal. Jakobo needed her. Terego needed her. She would survive, and the grief would simply have to be set aside.

She dressed Jakobo, trying her best to ignore his sullen silence. At the temple in Diadono, Prophet Disbergen was going to give his address, which would be broadcast to every cranny of Terego, even the continent of Kanaano, which seemed literally on the verge of rebellion. Rhea hoped his message would serve to placate and temper the agitated populace: the crisis, even as it wound down, was still sending shockwaves throughout Terego, and the world would likely never be the same again.

Nonetheless, a restoration of some semblance of its former unity was required, and the Prophet was the man chosen by God to ensure that solidarity, Rhea believed.

The temple, of course, was packed. Rhea and Jakobo sat near the front, in pews set aside specifically for members of the leadership of the stake. Judge Sanas joined them, his arm encircling Rhea's shoulders in the same paternal gesture that he'd used after every one of her losses. She leaned into him heavily, thanking God inwardly for the friends and brethren that the Church held for her. Without them she would never make it through a single day, she reflected.

The normal service was truncated, the songs and sacrament infused with an electrical tension. Finally, the Prophet emerged and stood behind the transparent lectern.

Rhea could tell immediately that Disbergen had been under considerable strain: his normally imperturbable, radiant mien had been replaced with a slight stoop, lined cheeks, hollow eyes. The Prophet still managed to smile at his flock, however, as he gripped the lectern with both hands and began to speak in his warm, fatherly voice.

"Like a few of you here, I remember arriving at this world, being awakened that morning after the month of scans and excursions by church leaders to the planet's surface. Looking out the viewports at that green-swathed ball of hope, I felt my heart surge and tears streamed from my eyes. I was old enough to understand the persecution we had been through on Earth, and the sight of our new home awakened in me a sense of freedom that even now I have difficulty expressing in words. The Lord had brought us here so that we could follow Him freely, so that our feet could walk the path of righteousness unfettered by political and social mores that conflicted with His will.

"When the Prophet, my predecessor, announced his vision, there was still some dissent, but for the most part, the Novasanktuloj embraced the idea that Joseph Smith himself ruled this world in his father's stead, much as Christ governs Earth. Of course, as the only begotten son, the one who died for our sins, Christ remains the door to eternal life with God. But the idea that we had been chosen to be the physical parents of the offspring of Smith as he took up the mantle of godhood, pulled across three centuries and a hundred light years to fulfill such a special role... well, it just swept us away.

"Perhaps it has made us too arrogant. This crisis has been hard, harder in some ways than the persecution the Novasanktuloj went through on Earth. And I am here to warn you: this trial is not over, Brethren. God has revealed to me that our pride is too great. Chosen by Him despite our faults, we have come to see ourselves as special *because of who we are* rather than because of His grace. Sometimes the Lord allows us to pass through tribulation precisely because we need to be shaped into better servants. In our eagerness to set ourselves apart, we have fallen prey to false pride and vain ambition. The Lord must prune such unworthy characteristics away so He can teach us discipleship.

"His all-seeing, unblinking eye is over us, however, ever watchful. The trials to come should not be cause for self-pity or shame, but reminders of who the captain of this boat is, He whose steady hand on the rudder guides us through all the storms of life. There are many things that we cannot change.

We all have difficulties and disappointments. But often these turn out to be opportunities. The Lord can measure how strong we are by how we handle these difficulties in our lives. As the Lord said to the Prophet Joseph Smith, 'Know thou, my son, that all these things shall give thee experience and shall be for thy good.'

"Only when His will becomes ours, only when we cease our useless striving, will the trials no longer affect us, not because they will cease, but because they will be irrelevant. This is the lesson the Lamanites and the Israelites struggled with for generations. Like all chosen peoples, we will have to learn it as well.

"Many of you have wanted to lash out at our unexpected neighbors, the Nakÿng. Many Novasanktuloj have died at their hands. But let us remember that the coming together of strangers is often traumatic at first. The strangeness of each group in the other's eyes breeds fear and hatred. But we have received the apology of the leaders of this planet's native race, we have been freed from occupation with their help, and now we must move on. In fifteen Standard years, their Council of Nations has agreed, they will allow missionaries to enter the forest and share the Good News. We must purge our hearts of resentment for them and prepare to make of them new brethren in God's family.

"Remember the scripture. Mosiah 26: 31 reminds us, 'And ye shall also forgive one another your trespasses; for verily I say unto you, he that forgives not his neighbor's trespasses when he says that he repents, the same

has brought himself under condemnation.' We condemn ourselves if we do

not move past this unfortunate first encounter. For human and Nakÿng both

share a similar bond on this world.

"Are we the children of Smith? I know that question is what many

of you are waiting to have answered. The Lord's response will surprise

many. I know it did me. Yes and no. Symbolically, as Smith has been given

stewardship over this world, we are his children. We are in his care. But all

of us, human and Nakÿng alike, have at our centers spirit bodies conceived

by the Father, as do all sentient beings in this universe."

Rhea felt the stir, but she didn't pay any attention to the hushed

mumbling. The Prophet went on, but she was no longer listening. Her mind

lingered on his message about tribulations; she seized on the hope his words

offered her.

There was a reason she suffered. There was a reason. A reason.

She gripped the Judge's hand tightly, and he brushed a strand of gray-

streaked brown hair from her cheek with an age-speckled hand. To her right,

Jakobo stared at the high-vaulted ceiling, expressionless.

Rhea supposed he was thinking of his own father and the parsecs of

black space that separated them. The thought that her own son was suffering,

too, because of his mother's pride tore at her heart. She swore that she would

humble herself, swore that she would find a way to ease the bereavement

Jakobo was suffering.

She couldn't hear the chant that echoed in her son's mind, blotting out everything except the bloom of spite that had taken root in the depths of his being.

I hate Teri, and I hate the grendels. I hate Teri, and I hate the grendels. I hate Teri, and I hate the grendels.

They had taken his father and his sister away from him, and the boy swore before God Himself in His holy temple that he would never forgive them.

Somewhere in the darkest recesses of his Grey Prison, peering through a crack in the universe, the Demiurge began to laugh.

EPIL⊙GUE

From: Minoungoua@sigil.xid.gov

To: sorall@executive.cpcc.gov

Subject: Findings

Date: June 1, 2714 23:17:52 (SST)

Decrypted: June 1, 2714 23:21:35 (SST)

Prime Minister Soral,

There's a mole in executive intelligence. When we arrived at the planet, we scanned for life at the coordinates D'Angelo gave us. There was nothing, so I sent down a team to investigate whether Koroma was dead. The team discovered, some five klicks from the original touchdown location of the escape pod, what appears to be an alien building of extreme age nearly completely buried in the sand. Energy readings from the site show the same quantum residue detected at the shrine on Jitsu. Inside the building it appeared that someone had ripped pieces of hardware from the walls at various locations throughout the structure, though much equipment was still in place.

We also found artifacts that seemed to show Samanei was living there recently. Analysis of charcoaled food and wood at her camp, plus human feces left in the area, indicates that someone was there up until about four days before our arrival. You see why I say there's a mole: someone leaked Koroma's location, and she was removed before we could get to her. Just XID knows about this, Prime Minister. I'm worried about the political consequences, but that's your area, and I'll leave you to it. You've got to protect the XID on this one, spin the situation so that we don't get investigated by the Diet. You need us, Prime Minister. Back us up.

Anyways, that's the bad news. It's obvious the good news is the discovery of the alien structure, which may be a scientific observation post. It looks like our science experts are going to be spending decades studying its technology. Initial analysis dates its age at ten thousand years, give or take. I'm assuming that access to its computers and the data they contain will tell us who built it and where those beings went. Maybe we'll find a map, some clue we can use to track down and contact them. Quite a better setup than what is being implemented at Terego now that SÆT found that ship's computers void of info. Makes you wonder if the clone knew, no? Let's hope the data here is intact.

I need a team asapped so the "Sigil" can take these two prisoners back to Consortium space and process them and so we can investigate more deeply. I suggest agents from a certain division, if you catch my meaning. Folks we can trust no matter what.

Here's the scary part. On one of the walls of a corridor of the building there were scrawled two words with Standard letters. We thought at first that some local plant had been used to create a pigment, but our science specialist tells me the substance is a mixture of excrement and blood. More Neog nonsense, more craziness from Samanei. The words, however, were a mystery to our field linguist-slash-anthropologist, so we shunted the words off to Agent Kanerva at Outpost Seven. He was able to give us an idea of what the words meant.

A couple of centuries ago, there was a huge project on Earth. Several quantum computers were linked and every human language ever recorded was fed into them, including the theoretical ancestors of those languages, like Indo-European, that were never written down. The task was to correlate every word and conjugation, etc. to try and extrapolate what the very first human language, or at least the ancestor of all human languages we know about, was like.

The results were weaker than hoped for. Only about three-dozen words and a rough idea of syntax could be produced, and the computer models showed a high probability of error. The findings were ignored, and linguists gave up ever peering a hundred thousand years into the past to find out how we once spoke. Well, Kanerva said that the words used were very similar to what the computer had produced, with slight variations from the model. In essence, he said, the words seem to be written in the most ancient human language ever thought to exist.

You're dying to know, right? They still weird me out, even as I'm writing.

The words were "Ngà' khé."

"I'm coming."

Albert Minoungou

Chief Operative

XID Field Junk Sigil

APPENDIX A: GLOSSARY

The origin of words not common in Standard is indicated by an abbreviation: B for Baryogo, K for Kaló, Sp for Spanish, E for Esperanto, N for Nakÿng.

Affer—Armed Forces (AF) personnel

Al-Muzzaml—private intelligence network run by Yen Bandera

Baryogo—a Belter creole spoken mainly by ethnic Aknawajin.

Casque—retractable helmet of flexsuits and other battle armor

Chirurgic—a now illegal AI medical robot (also *docbot*)

Chrome—projectile handgun whose nearly frictionless barrels and laser targeting give its bullets deadly supersonic speed and accuracy.

Conduit, the—discovered in 2523 by Dédalo Mostrenco near Alpha Centauri, the Conduit was a path through hyperspace which allowed Soltec and the military to dominate human expansion into space for close to a century, until Mostrenco killed himself in an explosion within the Conduit that closed it forever in 2619.

CPCC—the Consortium of Planets, Corporations and Colonies; the unified government of nearly all human habitats, founded in 2530 as a replacement for the dissolved United Solar Republics.

Çùthlÿngigg—(N) a Nakÿng tribe from the southern edge of the Great Seneka Forest.

D-sleep—the practical cessation of bodily function for the duration of a space flight to allow a body's encasement in suspensor gel. When accompanied by participation in a faux-life, d-sleep is referred to as hypostasis.

Defenestration—exiting higher dimensional space

Demimundo—(K) the underworld; the criminal underbelly of the CPCC

Dhureinghÿngigg—(N) "tree people," a Nakÿng tribe that captures Brando

Diadono—capital city of Terego, located on the continent of Zarahemla.

Diet—legislature of the CPCC, made up of three houses: the chamber of deputies, the citizens' assembly and the senate.

Doppel—a person's virtual avatar in a faux-life or faux-conference

Dropstick—a device used by military police to physically compel prisoners

Eight, the—(also called the *Ogdoad*) the eight-sided being, a quantum singularity believed by Pathwalkers to exist separately from our universe; two separated from the Eight, providing the basis for our universe. Every time a human reaches quantum enlightenment, a piece of the two is returned to the Eight.

Enlightenment—1) in Pathwalker theology, the gradual process of reaching *ra-Yindawo*, i.e., becoming a higher dimensional being (*quantum enlightenment*) 2) in underworld lingo, an assassination in which the body is left to be found, usually as a message.

Faux-com—technology that allows users to "exist" in virtual environments by means of direct neural stimulus.

Faux-confercrencing—use of virtual environments for communication.

Faux-life—a fantasy world generated by frames. During space flight, travelers typically log into a faux-life and mentally 'live' there in virtual bodies (*doppels*), interacting with *somatoids*, virtual personas that appear completely real, and surrounded by *keshiki*, interactive environments.

Fenestration—(also known as "holing") travel through higher dimensional space; a ship must accelerate to .6c in order to fenestrate, and upon defenestration, must travel a considerable distance from the defenestration point before holing again.

Gimmal—rotating chamber that creates gravity. Older ships without gravity sinks or gravity tiles have an outer hull around an inner gimmal that *purls*, or spins to create centrifugal gravity.

Great Seneka Forest—a dense forest covering thousands of square miles on the continent of Zarahembla

Grey Prison, the—Neo Gnostic term for the physical universe.

Hypostasis—the combined system of d-sleep and connection to faux-com or existence in a faux-life.

Ihéinghÿngigg—(N) "forest people," the Nakÿng tribe to which Shalura belongs.

Imrizabu—a tunnel through higher dimensional space

Ingan—(B) human (archaic)

Interstellar Net, the—information, communication, entertainment, education all depend upon this massive, Consortium-wide network that uses tunneled transmission beams to maintain its connections.

Jaro—(E) a Teregan year, 493 Earth days long (pl. *jaroj*)

Jitsu—(B, corruption of "Ditis") originally called Ares, Jitsu is the second planet of the binary star system Eta Cassiopeiae 2; claimed officially by Soltec in 2533, it was actually discovered by Domina Ditis twelve years previously when she was sucked through a spatial rift and stranded there with the abusive crew of her uncle's ship.

Kaló—an offshoot of Spanish spoken mainly by ethnic Simerianes

Kamioneto—a sort of small truck

Kanaano—a continent on Terego considered less pious and less urbane than Zarahemla.

Kaštoro—a dog-sized carnivorous beast with a triangular head and sharp teeth.

Kiyish—(B) a spike from the Urim carried on pilgrimages; dropped into the sea at particular coordinates dictated by the ramatini

Konk rifle—slang for *concussion rifle;* this weapon fires com energy waves and is typically used against large targets

Koptero—(E) helicopter (pl. *kopteroj*)

Kumora Mountain—where Brando D'Angelo has hidden his illegal technology.

Kyosu—(B) university professor

Lazgat—small energy pistol

Moku—(B) mild hallucinogen and depressant used in meditation, derived from the mohiyo plant

Nakÿng—(N) "one people," Native Teregans living on the continent of Zarahemla

Native Teregans—non-human sentient natives of the planet Terego, as in the *Nakÿng*

Narthex—airlock between sensitive systems on a ship; tubular interface between vessels.

Navarch—commander-in-chief of the Consortium Flotilla

Neo Gnosticism—*see* Path, the

Neog—(slightly derogative) Neo Gnostic, an adherent of Neo Gnosticism or pertaining to that religion. Preferred term: *Pathwalker*

Novameriko—(E) a mostly unexplored continent on Terego

Nova Mumbajo—(E) coastal city on the contintent of Zarahemla

Novasanktulo—(E) "New Saint," a term used for the human inhabitants of Terego (pl. *Novasanktuloj*)

Nuova Rinacenza—the New Roman Renaissance, a cultural movement that spawned the Nuova Pace Romana, a Wiccan Catholic Empire that lasted from

2305-2419. It was defeated in the Solar War (2410-2420) that gave birth to the USR.

Omedeyo—(B) a non-binary, intersex, two-spirit, or genderfluid person

Oni—(B) feathery haired, upright, meter-high monkey analogs

Oracle, the—Pathwalkers' direct connection to the Ogdoad. A sort of prophet, an Oracle appears once every century or so and is the only living being in constant communion not only with the Ogdoad, but also with the created souls that have been rejoined to it.

Osculate—to dock using a narthex

Path, the—religion begun by Alejandro Dresch on Earth in 21st century: very popular on Mars, Jitsu, the asteroid belt and some corporate platforms. Called Neo Gnosticism by many non-believers. Teaches the creation of souls through enlightenment.

Percom—a personal communications device

Pertran—small urban vehicle equipped with autopilot

Purl—(n) the spin of a gimmal; (v) to engage the gimmal

Quantum enlightenment—the final stage of enlightenment; the joining of the created soul to the Ogdoad.

Ramatini—Sage, an ancient title usually designating the closest companion of an Oracle.

Ra-Yindawo—(B) the nirvana-like plane that contains the Ogdoad

Sháinkhÿngigg— (N) "holy people," a Nakÿng tribe spreading the teachings of the Greenseer

Shell—illegal artificially intelligent mercenary robot

Sheol—CPCCAF Military Prison C-01, orbiting the star Yahweh in the Mu Cassiopeiae system

Sikarito—(K/B) lowest level in syndicate "army"; also a sort of cigarette

Slidewalk—common form of public transport for pedestrians.

Smitinfanoj—(E) "children of Smith," a term for human Teregans

Solpat—patois of Japanese, English, Spanish and other languages (similar to Baryogo)

Somatoids—computer generated pandemoniac personas within a faux-life. Can adapt and alter in personality, just as though they were actual people.

Squink—youngster (Martian slang, derived from K *eskuinkle*)

Standard—(also *Solar Standard*) derivative of English used as the lingua franca of the CPCC

Suspension pods—used for g-intensive spaceflight. One's body is cushioned and suspended in suspensor gel, simulating more normal gravity. As bodily functions must be slowed down to d-sleep for the duration of the trip, the pods are generally equipped with links to the Interstellar Net and a faux-life generating 'frame, allowing passengers to keep mentally active and crew to pilot the ship from a pseudo-bridge.

Suspensor gel—a high-impact colloid which cushions the body against the stresses of gravity-intensive space flight. Used in conjunction with suspension pods.

Teraplano—(E) hovercraft

Teregano—(E) inhabitant of Terego (pl. *Tereganoj*)

Umbini—(B) a dyad or dual being (normally used to describe any of four entities that make up the Ogdoad)

Unified Chinese—(Xīn Hànyǔ) unification of various dialects of Mandarin that was imposed on Unified China in the 23rd century.

Urdizih—(N) troop leader

Urim—1) a strange meteorite on the Southern Contient of Jitsu and 2) an alien device discovered by Teri Miranda on Terego.

Welkin—Solar slang for all space beyond the Solar System

Wende—(B) (also *awomi*) a psychological state in Pathwalker meditation, achieved typically through rapid, unthinking action. According to Dominian doctrine, *wende* occurs when the reconstructed self reaches out to the Ogdoad, yearning to become a soul and reunite with the source. Called the *Blue* in the original English version of the *Revised Bible*.

White Doom, the—the environmental and economic collapse brought about by mismanagement of Earth's resources by white hegemonic capitalism, leading to the present ice age.

Wiccan Catholicism—the faction of Catholicism that in 2305 joined forces with extreme leftist groups to exile the pope and dominate Earth, imposing brutal, Roman order on the deadly anarchy and destruction that had broken out after the beginning of the ice age. Through its Nuova Pace Romana, Wiccan Catholicism ruled Earth and parts of the Solar System for more than a century, till the Solar War broke up the empire and the United Solar Republics were founded.

Yaks—short for (J) *yakuza*: common term applied to underworld criminals

APPENDIX B: GLOSSARY

Allende, Carmen—a high school senior; Teri Miranda's girlfriend

Bandera, Yen—an ancient free-lance spy; head of the Al-Muzzaml network

Berdyaev, Nicholas—AF commodore, head of Outer Sector 1

Beserra, Konrau—kasike supremo or leader of the Brotherhood crime syndicate

Bos, Nestor—counselor to Konrau Beserra

Canales, Luisa—architect, protégé of Tenshi Koroma who runs the firm Izakiwo

Çèrhingÿl—a messianic figure the Nakÿng believe will return to rule them, the third reincarnation of the first highborn ever created by God.

Chuquipoma, Carlos—member of the Teregan Crisis Corps

Daenzhelo—the name Miwa Miranda uses among the Nakÿng

D'Angelo di Koroma, Tana—Brando and Tenshi's daughter

D'Angelo di Makomo, Brando—professor of linguistics from Earth

D'Angelo di Makomo, Edoardo—Brando's older brother

D'Angelo, Antonio—Brando's younger half-brother, captain of the *Diomedes*

D'Angelo, Giacobbe—Brando's and Antonio's father.

De Waal, Roberto—Terego's Minister of Crises

Disbergen, Zwelini—the Prophet, religious leader on Terego.

Ditis, Domina—first Oracle of the Path under the Third Dispensation. Her teachings inspired the founding of the Dominian sect.

Dixit, Sonali—a biologist

Dresch, Alejandro—author of *The Revised Bible*; founder of the Path

Eguzkitza, Andolin—science officer on board the *Diomedes*

Galardi, Elisha—a high school senior, one of Teri Miranda's friends

Greenseer, the—a mysterious prophet who warns the Nakÿng about humans.

Huaman, Ronaldo—young man from the continent of Kanaano doing his "missionary" work in and around Diadono

Khumalo, Zolile—Prime Minister of Terego

Koroma, Samanei—the third Oracle of Dominian Neo Gnosticism; twin of Tenshi Koroma

Koroma, Santo—uncle of Tenshi and Samanei Koroma

Koroma, Tenshi—architect and reformer leader, sister of the Oracle

Kumar-Miranda, Rhea—wife of Nando Miranda, mother of Jakobo and stepmother to Teri and Miwa. Later Czar of Native Affairs

Kyr—an AI medbot or chirurgic taken by Brando D'Angelo from Jitsu; interferes with the Nakÿng under the name Greenseer.

Lopes, Ambarina—captain of the *Velvet*, Tenshi's former lover.

Makomo-D'Angelo, Marie-Thérèse—Brando's mother; cleric in the Wiccan Catholic Church.

Mifflin, Tarka—captain of the *Shaka*

Minoungou, Albert—XID agent

Miranda, Miwa—clone of Tana D'Angelo

Miranda, Nando—alias used by *Brando D'Angelo* while living for fifteen years on the planet Terego

Miranda, Teri—clone of Tenshi Koroma

Mostrenco, Dédalo—former CEO of Soltec and founder of the Consortium

Mubarak, Ashar—commander, second officer on board the *Diomedes*

Mudumala, Josuo—young man from the continent of Kanaano doing his "missionary" work in and around Diadono

Mukerji, Buddhadev—Marshall of the CPCCAF

Muntso, Jetsu—prime minister of the CPCC from 2692 to 2698

Nishiguchi, Chiho—a friend of Rhea Kumar-Miranda who takes care of Jakobo

Oduyoye, Modupe—professor of comparative religion, friend of Brando D'Angelo.

Orbay, Enver—anthropologist on board the *Diomedes*

Piazetta, Dante—Navarch (chief admiral) of the CPCCAF Flotilla

Pishan, Meji—a religious leader on Jitsu

Quat, Phan—captain of the *George Washington*

Roshan, Vivek— psychologist and anthropologist from the Diadona Universitato.

Ru, Anyi—high school senior, best friend of Carmen Allende

Sainz, Juan—koptero pilot for the Crisis Corps

Sanas, Abhishek—a judge on Terego, Rhea Kumar-Miranda's mentor

Sekõtaldh—a highborn of the Sháinkhÿngigg tribe of Nakÿng

Shalurazhox—also *Shalura*. Leader of a group of drone warriors of the Ihéinghÿngigg tribe; companion of Miwa Miranda

Sitati, Elizaphan—Chief Corpsman in the Crisis Corps on Terego

Soral, Leyla—Prime Minister of the CPCC

Spinelli, Isabella—mother of Antonio D'Angelo; former lover of Tenshi Koroma

Spinelli, Ugo—maternal grandfather of Antonio D'Angelo; commodore in charge of Inner Sector 17

Tentisùxa—tracker for Shalurazhox's group of warriors

Torres, Marlo—Minister of Immigration for Terego; Rhea's former brother-in-law.

Ùshëshajirh—high priestess of the Sháinkhÿngigg tribe of Nakÿng

Wu, Ben—military officer, retired from the Consortium military and hired to lead an anti-terrorism squad on Jitsu

Xiggèr'enth—Shalura's bonded male, now deceased.
Zhehoha—an alien who crash-landed on Terego thousands of years ago

APPENDIX C: PLANETS
CPCC MEMBERS
ALPHA CENTAURI 3
Alpha Centauri A (Rigil Kentaurus)—4.4 ly from Earth.
- *Sihtu* (.5 AU or astronomical units from the star)—tidally locked world close to star. XID (the CPCC's Executive Intelligence Division) established its HQ on the dark side of Sihtu, in honeycombed caves beneath the surface, in 2530.
- *Sukra* (.95 AU)—rocky, hot world encircled by platforms and stations, heavily mined starting in 2540.
- *Dhara*—Settled in 2522 when it was marginally habitable. Terraformed completely by 2556. Home of CPCCAFHQ. Year is 1.34 Earth years. Two moons: Chandra and Marama. Principal city: La Caille.
- *Sani* (3 AU)—Gas giant with many moons and platforms.

Alpha Centauri B (Utu)—4.4 ly from Earth.
- *Ninsianna* (.75 AU)—Terraformed over a century, from 2530 to 2661.
- *Simuud* (1.2 AU)—cold hunk of rock; mining center, mainly.
- *Fetutea* (2.5 AU)—Smallish gas planet (a little smaller than Uranus) with ten moons, five inhabited (enclosed cities): New Nigeria, Kush, Nubia, Mali and Kerma.

Alpha Centauri C (Proxima)—4.2 ly from Earth. Site of one of the exit gates for the Centauri-Eta Cassiopeiae Imrizabu, dubbed The Conduit, which was destroyed in 2619.
- *Escher Wynde*—heavy comet shield/Oort cloud surrounding the triple system.

MU CASSIOPEIAE 2
Mu Cassiopeiae A (Yahweh)—24.6 ly from Earth.
- *The Firmament*—chaotic debris, asteroids and planetoids. Site of CPCCAF Military Prison C-01, also known as *Sheol*.

Mu Cassiopeiae B (Elohim)
- *Lilith* (.04 AU)—tidally locked. Claimed by Kozancorp in 2557.

BD+56 2966 (Nereus)—21.3 ly from Earth.
- *Thetis*—capital Ligyron
- *Peleus*—Major cities Neoptolemus, Hermione
- *The Myrmidons*—largish planetoids and asteroids in a belt
- *Achilles*—three moons: Briseis, Pyrrhus and Patroclus

Zeta Tucanae (Inti)—28 ly from Earth.
- *Atlantis* (1.14 AU)—settled in 2660 by Transcom (first new world settled since closing of Conduit). Year 1.25 Standard. Small island chains on mostly water-covered world. Avalon, Horaisan, Hy Breasail, Mag Mor, the Symplegades, Frisland.

CHI1 ORIONIS 2
Chi1 Orionis A (Gunana)—28.3 ly from Earth.
• *Yarsub*—settled in 2715
Chi1 Orionis B (Etugen)

BD+63 238 (Helios)—32.5 ly from Earth. Two settled planets:
• *Oceania* (.69 AU)—Discovered in 2650. Settled in 2673. Surface completely covered by water. Year: 212 Standard days.
• *New Mecca* (.55 AU)—Found in 2652. Settled in 2680. Barely habitable and quite hot.

Tau-Ceti—11.9 ly from Earth. Connected to Sirius 2 via an imrizabu.
• *New Beijing* (at .67 AU)—Settled in 2666. Year 225.6 Standard days.
• Lieske Scientific Complex—Established in 2680 on a planetoid at the fringes, near the imrizabu's exit point. Heavily guarded by the AF.

Sirius 2 (Dog and Pup)—8.6 ly from Earth. Restricted area dedicated to CPCC Ministry of Science and AF military science work. Scanned and mapped. Heavily guarded because of imrizabu between the system and both Tau-Ceti and HR 4523 AB.

Epsilon Eridani (Ran)—10.5 ly from Earth.
• *Podgoritsa* (0.51 AU)—Settled in 2665. Year 150 Standard days. Very few native organisms: bacteria and other single-celled creatures in the oceans.

Delta Pavonis (Mahajanaka)—19.9 ly from Earth.
• *Mani Mekhala* (1.09 AU)—settled in 2694. Year 395 Standard days. Capital city Phra Siamdevathiraj.
Gamma Pavonis (Phuong)—30.1 ly from Earth.
• *Cuoi*
• *Quy* (1.2 AU)—Home of the Dong-bao (that's what the first colonists of this world called themselves when they settled there in 2671). Capital city—*Dongson*. Two moons: Ong Trang and Ba Nguyet. Captain Quat is from this world. Seat of Octant Eight.
• *Ly*
• *Au Co*—gas giant. Its largest moon, Muong, is the seat of Outer Sector Eight.

---

61 Ursae Majoris (Musang)—31.1 light-years from Earth. Between Terego and Gaia. Site of Outer Sector One HQ.

HR 4523 AB
La—30.1 ly from Earth. One settled planet:
• *Nalupolu* (1.05 AU)

CONSORTIUM PROTECTORATES
ETA CASSIOPEIAE 2

Higante—19.4 ly from Earth. One settled planet, three others:

- *Waro* (.69 AU)—Originally named Archird.
- *Jitsu* (1.13 AU)—Found in December 2521, then rediscovered by Dédalo Mostrenco in January 2524, who named it Ares. Settled by Soltec starting in 2533. Independence won in 2621, under the name Jitsu. Year is 1.1 Earth years, or 401.4 Standard days (ten forty-day months plus an extra week every five years). Days are 23.8 Standard hours long.
- *Kurishto* (4.1 AU)—small gas planet with four moons (Maryam, Makdarena, Pejo, Sanchago)
- *Banken* (8 AU)—icy and barren

Kobito—19.4 ly from Earth.

- *Mimune* (.2 AU)
- *Chiye* (1.3)
- *Anjeliku* (3.2)—Originally named Tod.

Sigma Draconis (Kunti)—18.8 ly from Earth.

- *Bima* (.62 AU)—In 2589, the colony ship Bhatarayuda reaches Sigma Draconis, renaming the star Kunti and settling a world the colonists name Bima, which sits inside the orbital distance of Venus in the Solar System. It has an orbital period of only about 199 days, or over half an Earth year. One moon called Gatotkaca. Bima is the seat of the Kunti system's government. From 2589 to 2692, the system was a constitutional monarchy. In 2692, the last Maharajah sent an invasion force against Dhara in Rigil Kentaurus. From 2692 to 2695, the system was in chaos, caught between invading syndicates and CPCCAF peacekeeping forces. Finally, the system was occupied for fifteen years while the CPCC set up a democratic government. In 2710 most AF forces withdrew from the Independent Republic of Kunti (IRK), which remained a protectorate, ultimately under Consortium control.
- The Kunti system also contains five other planetary bodies: Karna, Harjuna, Yudistira, and the twin gas planets, Nakula and Sadewa.

Chara—27.3 ly from Earth.

- *Gaia* (at 1.1 AU)—colonized in 2666; discovered by CPCC in 2690; taken by syndicates (Wyjace Wilki and Servants of Shangó) by 2697; liberated in 2700.

---

41 ARAE 2—28.7 ly from Earth.

Amaterasu

- *Yamato* (0.64 AU)—taken from syndicate in 2707 (had been base of Machi-yokko Yakuza since 2658).

Haemosu

- *Nyubuyeo*

Gamma Leporis (Yi)—29.25 ly from Earth.
- *Fusang or Fusou*—Habitable world founded in 2661; controlled by Scarlet Chaos Triad; taken in 2706, made OS6HQ.

INDEPENDENT SYSTEMS
82 G. Eridani (Tawa)—19.8 ly from Earth.
- Puha (82 G. Eridani f, at .8 AU) and its moons
- *Semanawak*. Settled in 2605 by the natives of the generation ship Ilwikamina, which left Earth in 2218. Discovered by CPCC in 2698. Year 275 Earth days.
- *Tsoha*. Highly volcanic.

Beta Hydri (Ar-Rabba)—24.4 ly from Earth.
- *Hubal*—Centered around 1.9 AUs. Orbital period of about 2.5 Earth years. Settled in 2693.

61 Virginis (Al-Shams)—27.8 ly from Earth.
- *New Palestine* (.9 AU)—Settled in 2532 by Palestinian Arabs fleeing the devastation of the Second Middle Eastern War (2343)
- *Levant*—gas giant; 10 moons, one made of ice called *Jericho*

Rana—29.5 ly from Earth.
- *Clay* (1.7 AU)—Settled in 2693.

Beta Comae Berenices (Chrysomati)—29.9 ly from Earth.
- *Eudamonia* (.2 AU)—Settled in 2701. Found by CPCC in 2712

Alpha Mensae (Dagda)—33.1 ly from Earth.
- *Erin* (.91 AU)—Settled by Irish Travelers in 2529. Has a single moon, Manx.

44 (i) Boötis 3
44 (i) Boötis A (Rangi)—41.6 ly from Earth
- *Papa* (1.07 AU)—settled in 2668. CPCC finds in 2711.
  44 (i) Boötis B/C (Punga and Here)
- *Uenuku* (.74 AU)
- *Whatitiri* (1.02 AU)

47 Ursae Majoris (Chalawan / Suno)—45.9 ly from Earth.
- *Moroni* (at .75 AU)—rocky, barren world.
- *Terego*—Settled January 2656 (Day one of 1st month of Teregan year 1).
  —Teregan day: 28 hours 12 minutes (divides into 7-hour sleep period, 7 hour work and study period, 7 hour family period) 1692 minutes
  —Two moons: Luneto (called Xÿlqérho by the Native Teregans, God's swiftest drone) and Hyrum (very small, considered the spear of Xÿlqérho)

—Teregan year (jaro): 420.14 Teregan days (14 months of 30 days, every seven years there's an extra day) 710,786.88 minutes (about 493 Earth days, about a third more, so multiply/divide by 1.3)
—Diameter—4,470 km. Six continents: Zarahemla, Novameriko, Kanaano, Tevantepeko, Utaho, Misurio.
- *Taphao Thong / Enoš* (at 2.1 AU)—Massive gas planet that orbits once every three years. Very close to Terego. Many moons, including Nefi. Called Çìrhãná by the Native Teregans, God's foremost bonded male.
- *Taphao Kaew / Elija* (at 3.73 AU)—Massive gas giant with orbital period of nearly seven years.
- *Eter* (at 10 AU)—Gas giant whose orbit lasts 38 years and whose mass is 1.7 times that of Jupiter

---

70 Virginis (Odin)—50.1 ly from Earth.
- *Frigga* (.5 AU)—brown dwarf of some 27 Jupiters in mass. Orbited by several planets/moons (worlds):
- Valhalla—founded in 2697 by corporate-backed Kunti expatriates and separatists from within the CPCC who are disgusted at war. Found by CPCC in 2713. Conquered by Demimundan Alliance in 2722.
- Midgard—settled at the same time

Castor 6—51 ly from Earth. Samanei's world is in orbit around Castor Ca (YY Geminorum Aa). It lies at about .25 AU, has liquid water, but its life forms are not compatible with terrestrial ones and massive flares of x-rays bathe the world, making electronics virtually useless.

Iota Horologii (Aroji)—56.2 ly from Earth.
- Penjaga—massive gas giant, and its moon
  —Ra-Hamish, base for Al-Muzzaml

Beta Pictoris (El Webo)—62.9 ly from Earth. Surrounded by a circumstellar disk of dust and gas some 1,100 AUs wide. This disk is commonly called the Urakã Nebula and was first discovered in December 2521 by demimundan ships thrown there by entering the Centauri Rift. In June 2682, a Brotherhood schooner (El Pesau), preparing to fenestrate away from the 'nebula' after dropping supplies off to those readying Konrau Beserra's new HQ in a planetoid of that system, discovered an imrizabu which leads directly to the edges of the Nereus system. This information was kept secret for years, as those few privy to it were killed off in the fifteen-year Consortium war against the Demimundo (2697-2712).